AN·ECHO·OF·THE·ASHES

BOOK III

SONG

+ OF THE +

RAVEN

Cover by Damonza

Maps created by Charles Thompson @whitehawkcreekforge

Internal design by Book Burrow www.bookburrow.com.au

Printed in Australia

First Printing: November 2024

Paperback ISBN 978-0-6451842-2-8

eBook ISBN 978-0-6451842-5-9

A catalogue record for this
work is available from the
National Library of Australia

AN·ECHO·OF·THE·ASHES

BOOK III

SONG
· OF THE ·
RAVEN

· ANTHONY KEARLE ·

An Echo of the Ashes

-

Blood of the Eagle
Shadow of the Nightingale
Song of the Raven

Dedications

-

To Wayne.
Without whom these books would never have been published.

Acknowledgements

-

To the map maker, Charles Thompson,
who turned sketches into magic. Your work is unparalleled.

-

To the wordsmith, Anna of AtoB Editing
thank you for following me on this journey.
Your knowledge and skill show true dedication to your craft.

To Tarik and The Far North

Mithramir Sea

Larissa

Annora

To Berenithia,
Irene
and the
Westlands

Aureian Empire

Salvaar

Medea

Miera

Arisir

League of Trecento

The Valkir Isles

Sacasian Sea

Lupentine Sea

Gulf of Lamrei

Padsworth

Lorosa

Beyna

Sevillona

Loron-Lor

Annora

Twin Rush River

Laeoflaed

Kamlan-Lor

Caldonian River

Aethela

Medea

Arlona River

Caspin

Saragoza

Cretrian River

Eran River

Gialaga

Salazar

Arestia

Iham

Arzarlan

Valham

Bandor Forest

Valcia

Palen-Lor

Palen River

Wighthorn Forest

Bailon

Panala River

Aloys

Pergova

Balburgh

Foxford

Farren River

Odrysia

Ailgareth

Perena

Bandujar

Cacera

Valanza

Patchi

Valengos

Salvaar

Noyon

Aldor

Faolan

Oryn

Caelis

Arwan River

Argon River

Blaithin

Sacred Grove

Lake Thirlryda

Vadon

The Rift

Barona

Roricsford

Moonwatch

Chausae

Miera

Kinar River

Amalric

Phoenix River

Ruins of Israfil

Idrisir

Carlian

Warren River

Cardna

Loxford

Vanhair

Tribian Alps

Tallis

League of Trecento

Kiriador

Clara

The Dalkir Isles

Nesoi Island
Two Days Sail
From Lumis

Kamlan-Tor
Seven Days Sail

Daykis

Kattir

Lumis

Aihon

Pramier

Agartha

Elara
Seven Days Sail

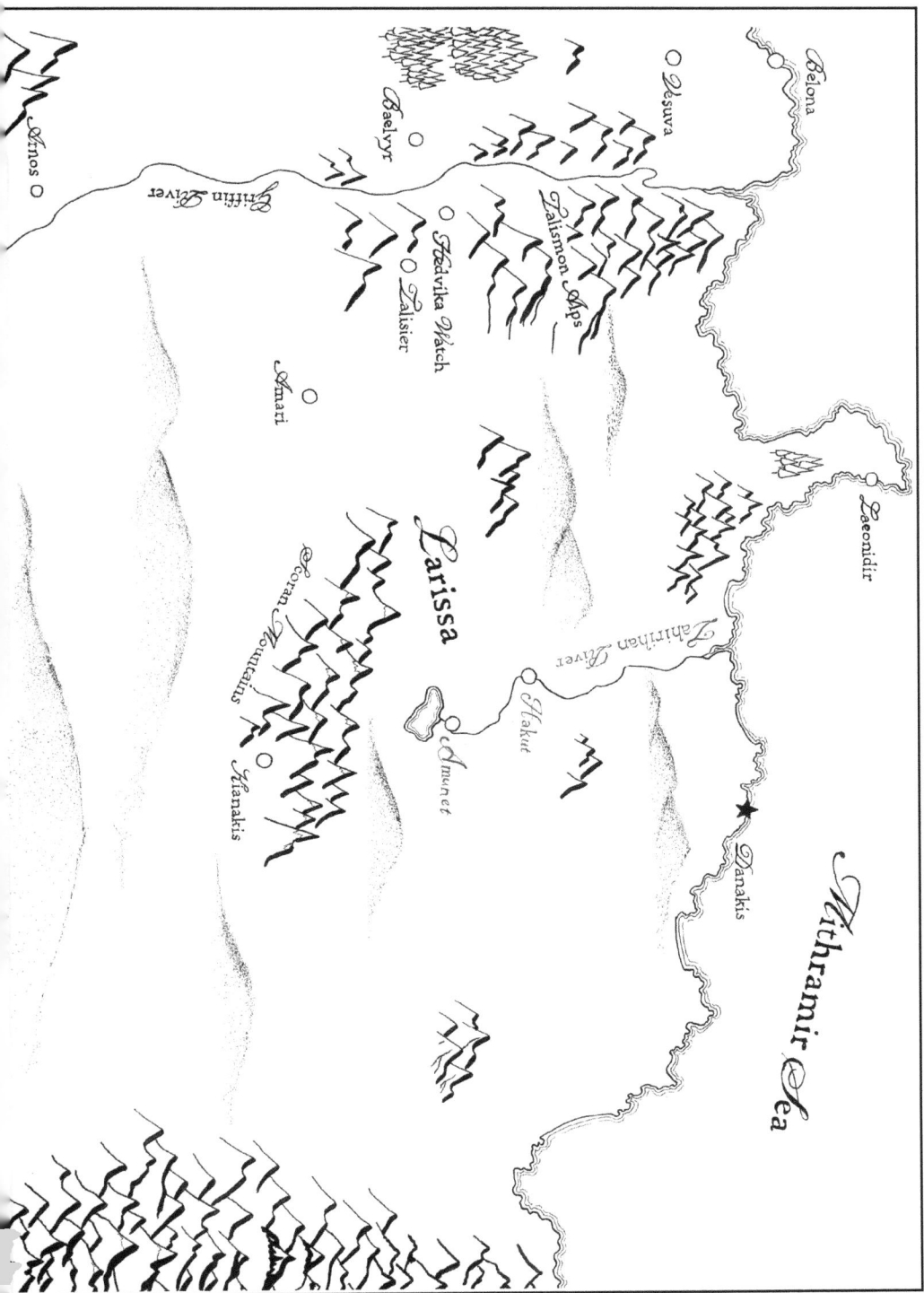

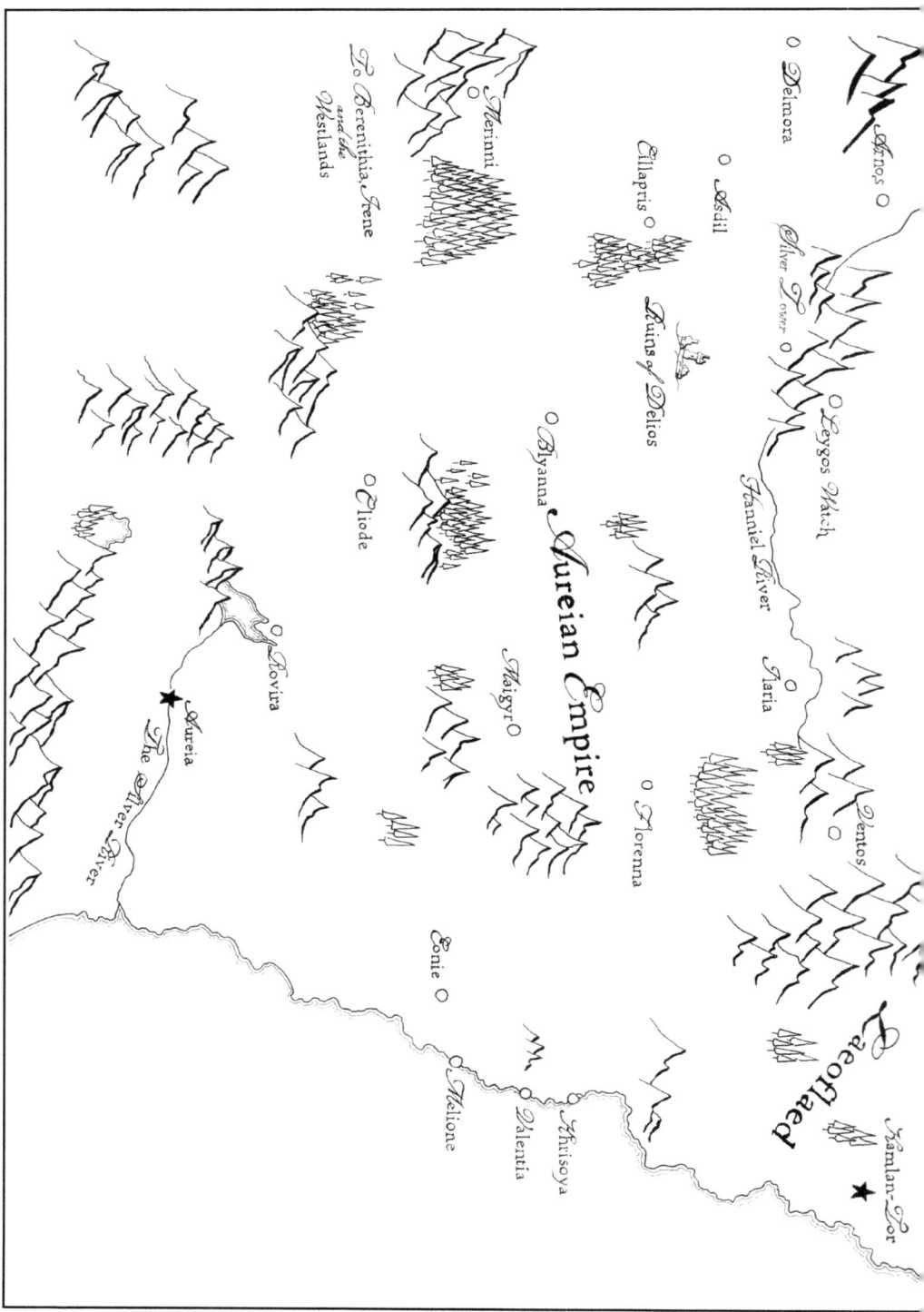

Arnos

Delmora

Silver Tower

Nerimni

To Berenithia, Irene
and the
Westlands

Ellapris

Asdil

Ruins of Delios

Leygos Watch

Hanniel River

Taria

Blyanna

Cliode

Aureian Empire

Lovira

Thaigyr

Aureia

The Silver River

Pentos

Torenna

Eonie

Melione

Valentia

Thisoya

Laoflaed

Tamlan-Zor

Lupentine Sea

Sacasian Sea

Gulf of Lanrei

Landonsport

Aaston

Androna

Lannier

Dacira

Yarreon

Ephileon

Laykos

Tykos

Ylarys

Lethys

Lanrei

Epona

Lira

Haevara

Lleara

Narvana

Deimos

Wedyn

Partharon

Nesston

Lasir

ONE

City of Elara, The League of Trecento

Elara was on fire. The bazaar had been pillaged and the arsenal had long since been breached. The streets were filled with rivers of blood as the gangs and pirates of the south took the city. The last of Elara's defenders had been driven back into the magister's palace. Soldiers rained down arrows from the keep's walls as the horde swarmed around it like water on rock.

"Tell me, Captain," Magister Imrohir said to the man at his side, "have you ever been sailing with your daughter?"

The stoic leader of the magister's guard was silent for a moment as the pair stared down from the balcony. Before them, their city was aflame and both men knew that it would not be long before the palace walls were breached.

"No, my lord," the captain at last replied. "This life has not afforded me that honour."

Imrohir nodded slowly as his hand tightened upon the hilt of his sword. "A shame," Imrohir told him. "I would have liked to have gone sailing with mine."

"There may still be a chance for you to escape, lord. You could still follow your wife and daughter. You could yet see them again."

"My family is safe." Imrohir allowed himself a small smile. "Elara is my city and by life or death I will defend it."

A roar came from beyond the palace walls as the gates were smashed open. A tide of gang men and Sacasian raiders surged forward with wicked cries upon their lips. Imrohir took a deep breath as he strapped his magnificent golden helmet over his head. He placed a hand upon the captain's shoulder.

"And now we meet our fate," the magister said.

Blood stained Imrohir's armour as the defenders backed down the long hallway. They fought for every inch and made their attackers pay in lives for every step taken. Imrohir blocked an axe with his shield before he countered. In two strikes, the unarmoured pirate was dead at the magister's feet. Two more leapt forward to replace their fallen comrade. Imrohir killed the first while one of his guards slew the other. His shield arm had long since grown weary and his breath had turned ragged. His body was battered and bruised, yet Imrohir would never bow down while his city was besieged. The last of their attackers fell to Imrohir's sword. The magister glanced around at his men. Only six of them remained. Only six of the six hundred that had reached the keep alive. If there were more Elaran soldiers scattered around the halls and corridors of the palace, then Imrohir did not know.

"Back!" the magister cried. "Back to the throne room!"

The seven men ran. They leapt over the bodies of friend and foe that filled the corridors. A pair of pirates appeared before the defenders. They held their ground before the great doors of the throne room. Imrohir raised his shield and barrelled into the first with a vicious war cry upon his lips. The pirate's spear glanced off Imrohir's shield and then the magister smashed into him. The pirate was tossed back. He slammed into the edge of the hard stone wall with a sickening thud. Imrohir finished him with a thrust to the heart. The second man was felled just as quickly by the captain of the guard. Imrohir led them into the throne room. His heart beat like a drum.

"Bar the doors," Imrohir commanded as he gestured towards them with his sword. He closed his eyes and took a long breath as the first door was closed.

Thud.

Imrohir's gaze flickered open. The soldier at the entrance fell to his knees as a sword was pulled from his throat. Blood pooled around the dying man's body. Imrohir looked to the doors and raised his shield. Their enemy had not yet revealed himself.

A silver ball was thrown through the entrance. It sang as it hit the stone. The canister exploded and then the room was filled with smoke. Fear crawled up Imrohir's spine as his sight was taken. He could see nothing but grey and could hear nothing but the pounding of his own heart. The first scream was muffled by the thick cloud. The cry was cut short. Armour rang as it met the floor. One by one, five screams joined the first. They came from every direction. He kept his shield up and his sword held at the ready, and yet he could not keep the tremble from his lip.

Silence.

The smoke began to dissipate. Imrohir saw the bodies of his fallen comrades as they appeared all around him. Then he saw the man emerge from the smoke like a demon. A knife dripping with blood was held in his hand, and a dark hood was pulled up over his head. A second figure joined the man. This one he recognised.

"Elise Delfeyre," he murmured as he looked to the Nightingale.

Her hood was lowered. Her mask and scarf hung at her neck. She had come to him as the woman and *not* as the fairy tale.

✦ ✦ ✦

Elise clenched her jaw as the man who had murdered her parents spoke her name. She said nothing and instead felt her hand tighten upon the hilt of her kukri knife. Elise's knuckles grew white as she glared at Imrohir. She met his eyes and her hatred for him grew stronger. Her mother and father, her aunt and uncle: all had been killed at his command.

"Your sword," Cleander ordered as he reached for his own.

Imrohir looked to the Annoran. "No," he said.

Elise watched as Cleander stepped forward. He tossed his bloody knife to the side and drew his longsword. Elise had seen him fight once before at her uncle's villa. Now, as then, it was like watching a demon fight a mortal man. Cleander was faster than Imrohir. He was stronger than Imrohir. Cleander blocked the magister's strike even as he danced to Imrohir's side. He countered as he moved and sliced his sword along Imrohir's arm, stepping back from the magister's hastily thrown reply. The tip of Imrohir's blade missed his chest by a hair's breadth. Cleander danced back in and carved a bloody furrow in the magister's leg. Imrohir screamed and lashed out with his shield. Cleander was too fast. The steel rim sped past and then Cleander smashed the hilt of his sword into his enemy's head. He tore the shield from Imrohir's hand and slid to the side as the magister lunged. Blocking the blade with his own, he slid his sword down into Imrohir's guard and locked steel against steel. His free hand latched around the blade of the magister's weapon. He angled his sword and flicked his wrists as he stepped to the side. With a savage wrench, he pulled the magister's blade from his grasp. Imrohir stumbled backwards as Cleander used his own weapon against him. The hilt smashed into the magister's helmet, the blow taking his balance. Cleander lashed out with his own sword and sliced it across Imrohir's thigh. Blood wet the air and then the magister fell with a scream.

Elise's heart began to race as Cleander stood over her fallen enemy. He tossed the magister's sword to the side. Imrohir knelt before him. Elise bared her teeth as her blood ran cold. She barely noticed that she had drawn her kukri. Everything seemed to slow as she walked towards her enemy. She was going to kill him. She was going to take a life for the first time. Elise pushed past Cleander and raised her knife. The ghosts of her parents filled her mind. With one hand she took hold of Imrohir's shoulder and with the other she placed the cold blade of her kukri against his neck. Elise could see her aunt and uncle as clear as day. Tears began to roll down her cheeks. The magister refused to meet her gaze.

"Look at me," Elise snarled. She snatched at his helmet and savagely forced his head up. Elise stared down into the darkness of his eyes. "All I ever wanted was a simple life and you took that from me. Everything that I am, everything that I have done is because of family," she growled, unable to keep the pain from her voice. "And now I *have* no family. My heart … that is what you have *taken* from me!"

Elise pressed her kukri into Imrohir's neck. He did not look away nor did he utter a word. A bead of blood rolled down his throat. Elise screamed as her emotion took control. Her weapon moved. Cleander's hand latched around her wrist and pulled her blade away from the beaten man.

"No!" Elise shouted as she struggled against Cleander. "Let me kill him! I need to kill him!"

Cleander ripped the kukri from her fingers and shoved her backward. Elise leapt forward, but it was too late. Cleander drove the kukri deep into Imrohir's neck. Elise froze as her enemy fell, his hands around his neck. Blood poured from his ruined throat. Imrohir gasped for air and clutched at his wound. Life fled his body and then he was still.

Elise was unable to tear her gaze from the lifeless corpse. After everything that had happened and everything that she had lost, another person had killed her monster. Her empty hands curled into fists as emotion warred within.

"What have you done?" Elise snarled. "His life was mine to take!"

"The tyrant is dead."

"You *stole* my revenge!"

"I will not apologise," Cleander replied as he turned to face her.

"You had no right!" Elise spat.

"I had the only right! I will *not* let you become like me."

Elise could see the flicker of pain in Cleander's eyes as he approached. He held her kukri by the blade and offered it to her. Elise grasped the knife's hilt, yet Cleander did not give it to her.

"Revenge is a choice, Elise. A choice that will whittle you down piece by piece," he said. "It is a path that once you step down it, there is no coming back. I will *not* allow the rage to consume you as it did me."

Elise's lip trembled as the man let her take the kukri. She wasn't sure what to think. She wasn't sure what to do. Elise stared down at the blade still awash with Imrohir's blood. Cleander gathered up the cloak of one of the fallen guards and began to clean the red stain from his sword.

Cheers echoed around the palace. Cries of victory.

"The palace is taken," Cleander muttered.

"What happens next?"

The cheers drew closer. Men were marching on the throne room.

"Some things you don't need to see," Cleander told her. He handed Elise the cloak and she turned it upon her knife.

"What things?"

"Human nature," the Annoran muttered. "We have to leave, Elise."

There was something new in his voice now. Something that Elise had never heard from him before. *Compassion.* She dropped the cloak and sheathed her kukri with a nod. The battle for Elara was over.

✦ ✦ ✦

Cillian Teague of the Oridassey walked through the streets of the arsenal as dawn's first light crept over the horizon. Smoke created a grey haze through the sky. It came from the burning buildings. It came from the pyres and mass graves. Teague had served with the imperial army long enough to know of the dangers created by thousands of bodies. He had seen both disease and plague before and knew that they must be avoided no matter the cost. Eventually, the people of Elara would begin to venture out into their city and the alliance had to be prepared to lead them. The ten men who walked with the captain were hard men. Like him, they were veterans of a thousand battles. Some had served at Teague's side in the Aureian fleet.

Teague glanced at the bloody body of a man. The corpse wore a faded blue sash around his waist. He was a pirate; one of the freemen of the Sacasian Sea. Teague knelt beside his fallen brother and gently closed the dead man's eyes.

"Rest easy now, brother," Teague said softly. "Drift deeper and deeper. The sirens are calling your name."

The crew watched on in solemn silence as their captain bid the dead man farewell. They all knew the risks that had come with the assault, yet their hands had been forced. When the Gulf of Lamrei had been set alight from west to east, their last safe hold had been destroyed.

"Captain Teague," a woman's voice called from further down the street.

Teague looked up to see a new group of pirates approaching. These ones wore sashes of green.

"Captain Marquez," Teague greeted her as he rose to his feet.

Luana Marquez, the Jade Queen and captain of the Emeralis, extended a hand towards her fellow captain. Teague clasped it firmly. Beside Luana was the ever-present Tariki warrior Calvillo. Teague gave the man a nod.

"The city is taken," Luana said simply.

"They were betrayed from within." Teague shrugged. "Never stood a chance."

"The world will begin anew, Teague," she told him.

The Aureian nodded. Those words did not belong to Luana Marquez. They were words from the sirens of thirty years ago.

"Everyone has landed," Calvillo said. "For now, our people will stay within the arsenal walls."

"What of Vanor Pasian?" Teague asked.

"We have taken the prisoner to the magister's palace," the Tariki answered.

The steel-barred door of the jail cell was forced open, allowing Teague and Marquez to enter into the darkness. Captain Vanor Pasian of the Red Fortune sat in the corner of the cell with his hands tightly bound by chains.

"Cillian Teague. To what do I owe this pleasure?" the prisoner grumbled.

"Your magister is dead," Teague told him.

"That changes nothing." Vanor rose to his feet and glared at his captors. "Over two months ago you took the Red Fortune. Over two months you've held me. In those two months, what have you accomplished?"

"Elara is ours," Luana said as she folded her arms.

Vanor looked her up and down. "And who are you? Mistress to the traitor of Aureia?"

Luana gave the prisoner a vicious grin. She chuckled as she pulled forth a knife embellished with emerald. Luana danced the dagger across her fingers – fingers bearing jewels as green as her sash, her sword and her bandana.

"Do you not know who I am?" Luana smirked.

Vanor's eyes darkened. "You are Luana Marquez. The Jade Queen. There are many who know your name."

The knife danced across her hand and then Luana snatched it. She stepped closer and placed the steel against Vanor's throat. "And do you fear it, *Captain* Pasian?"

"I do not fear your kind," Vanor growled.

Luana leaned in close, and her eyes never left those of the prisoner. She bared her teeth and then snatched her knife away from Vanor's skin.

"Captain Marquez has been absent much of the time you have been our guest," Cillian Teague told him. "While I plotted the course and prepared my people, it was her who convinced them to leave their homes. It was her who turned the gangs of Elara to our cause."

Luana spread her arms as she spoke. "And now we control *all* of this."

Vanor looked from pirate to pirate. His lips curled and then he chuckled drily. "You must know that you cannot hold this city," he said.

"Similar things were said by those who thought that I could not take Elara," Teague countered. "And yet I won her."

"Your people are not warriors," Vanor replied.

"One brave man fighting for his survival can be more powerful than three trained soldiers," Luana said.

"Your people are very brave, yes." Vanor snorted as he glared back at her. "But bravery can only get you so far. Look around you. Your people are carpenters, traders, merchantmen and sailors that have all fallen for your poisonous words and stories of grandeur. The gangs are little more than wild animals. They fight amongst themselves as often as they strike at the palace that they so despise. You have many men but few soldiers."

"Whatever storm comes for my people, we will weather it," Teague told him. "We will endure as we always have."

"I have fought your kind for over a decade. Perhaps you have fought well on the seas, yet behind these walls you are a long way from Lamrei. Your people are not disciplined. They are *no* army."

"What do you know of us?" Luana sneered back. "What do you know of our ways, you who has hunted and persecuted our kind for thirty years?"

"Enough to know that you cannot stop what is coming," Vanor said. "The fleet that you so avoided will come from the south. By now, birds will have arrived at Tallis and Kiriador. Our sister cities will send legions from the north. These walls that you have taken, these walls that now protect you have become the same thing that has trapped you. Here you are cloistered, yet here you cannot escape and there will be no mercy for you when the attack comes. You will be surrounded and wiped out. This battle is over."

Cillian Teague strode towards the prisoner. He glared down into Vanor's eyes. Stared deep into his soul. He had used his gaze to destroy lesser men in the past. Teague was so feared because of his name and reputation. He had killed countless men and had even slaughtered the crew of the Red Fortune before Vanor. Teague saw a flicker of fear cross Vanor's eyes. He let the Elaran see the rage in his gaze and smell the stench of his breath. Vanor looked away.

"This battle is over when I *say* it is over!" Teague snarled.

The cell door squealed as it shut behind the two pirates. They left Vanor Pasian alone with his fear.

"It is as I have foreseen," Teague told Luana as they walked through the magister's palace. "We're surrounded and do not have much time. Garrett Laven will return to us soon and the League's fleet will not be far behind. We have at most a month before the armies of the north and south descend upon Elara."

"Not enough time to consolidate with the gangs and Lord Stentor. Not enough time to stop the Elarans from rising against us," Luana added.

"Then you know what you must do?" Teague asked.

"I leave at dawn."

✦ ✦ ✦

TWO

King Dayne Raynor gazed around the bloody field. Death. It was all around him. Thousands of bodies, soldiers of the alliance and Salvaari alike. Wounded men cried out for help. Physicians and maija scurried around the battlefield in search of survivors. Ravens had begun to circle overhead. It would not be long now before they began to feast on the dead. When the Medeans and Knights of Kil'kara had joined Dayne's army and surrounded the pagans, it had been a slaughter. The king's strategy had worked and now the gateway into Salvaar was open. Despite the victory, Dayne felt nothing. His face was as cold as those of the men around him. Garrik Skarlit and a small contingent of the royal guard stood with the king. The guard opened a path to King Dayne as another man approached.

"The Salvaari will not soon venture from their forest," Tristayn Martyn said as he joined the king's side.

"Indeed," Dayne told his commander with a nod. "Tell me about the river."

"The construction of fortified camps has begun, my king. We control the western bank, though I fear it will take some time to make the crossing."

Dayne's hand tightened upon the eagle sword at his side as he stared towards the dark forest. Who knew what watched them from within those trees.

"You have given the Pale Horseman a mighty gift," Sir Garrik muttered.

Dayne's free hand rose to his amulet. He did not look away from the forest.

"It is a day that the Salvaari will not soon forget, I am sure," Dayne said. "How are the men?"

"Those who have been here before are wary of the woods, while those who haven't will have already spent half their spoils by nightfall." Garrik shrugged. "This was a great triumph."

"Aye." The king pursed his lips. "Yet this war is far from over. Sir Garrik, make sure the camps are complete and manned by sundown. If half the stories that I have heard are true, then we will all pay come the night if they are not."

"Yes, my king." The master at arms bowed before beginning to make his way towards Salvaar.

"Tristayn." Dayne turned towards the general. "That man you captured … Has he spoken yet?"

Tristayn shook his head as he replied, "No. We separated him from the rest of his people and now Duke Santiago watches over him."

The viper banners of House Caspin flew high in the breeze. Soldiers clad in green cloaks filled the campsite. Some sat around fires while others hoisted tents up. Some sharpened blades or patched wounds. Dayne paid them no heed as he walked through the Caspin camp with Tristayn and his guard. They marched through the camp until a huge tent arose before them. Three men stood within a perimeter encircled by Caspin house guards.

"King Dayne," a strong Medean voice called out in greeting.

Dayne glanced towards the voice and recognised the man who bore it. Santiago Caspin, head of the Caspin family, gestured for his guards to let the Annorans through. His emerald cloak was trimmed with gold and his armour was of the highest quality.

A snake was etched upon his breastplate and a thin silver band ran across his brow. Santiago's face was scarred and lined, yet he was anything but frail. The duke stood with two other men: his brother, Aquale Caspin, and his commander, Rodrigo Santana. Like Santiago, both men were clad head to toe in the finest armour of chain and plate.

"Duke Santiago." The king addressed his father-in-law as he made his way towards the men. Dayne took Santiago's outstretched hand before turning to greet the other two men.

"Aquale." Dayne addressed Santiago's brother.

"King Dayne."

"Rodrigo."

"Lord king."

Dayne clasped his hands. "Your soldiers fought well," he said.

"Your strategy worked. Gave us this great victory," Santiago replied with a smile.

"Much is possible when the sons of Annora stand shoulder to shoulder with the sons of Medea," Dayne returned. "The gods were with us."

"And all glory goes to them," Santiago agreed.

He resisted showing the bitterness that he felt when he looked at Santiago. Behind the smile and silver tongue was a man much akin to the snake symbol of his house. His words were as poisonous as his actions in the dark. Dayne knew of Santiago's hand in the murder of his father, Dorian. Dayne knew of the duke's sins.

"Take me to the prisoner."

Santiago Caspin led the Annoran company through the maze of Medean tents. The captives were kept in a makeshift prison. It was more of a pen than a jail. Salvaari of every tribe and painted with varying colours were bound by chains tied to a long wooden rail. There they sat under the stern gaze of armed Medean soldiers. The Salvaari were both men and women and each was as strong as the last. They watched their captors with hate-filled, wild eyes and bared teeth. They had been hard to capture and harder still to bind. Dayne felt some pity for the pagans, yet he did not show it. He showed nothing. Instead, the king walked past the prisoners towards a wooden cage. A bear of a man with a bushy beard and long shaggy hair sat within. His face was marked with blue woad. The Salvaari's back was pressed up against a wooden post to which he was bound. At a gesture from Dayne, one of the Medean guards opened the cage door. The king entered the cell and crouched before the captive.

"You're the one who rallied your people in a final stand."

"You're the one who invaded my land," the Salvaari growled.

Dayne met those dark eyes and saw the rage within. He was a strong man and not just in body. It went beyond the torc that hung around the Salvaari's neck. Dayne knew him to be a chief of the Aedei. Yet there was something else about him, something familiar.

"You ... I know you," Dayne stated. "We have met before."

"In another life, in another time, king," the Salvaari replied with a sneer. "When last we met, it was within the walls of Palen-Tor."

"You're the man who crossed Miera to reforge the alliance of old," Dayne murmured. "You're Cailean of the Aedei."

"Indeed."

"Then you were but a warrior, yet now you wear the torc of a chief."

"And now you stand as king," Cailean replied.

"Much has changed," Dayne told him. "Once our fathers were allies. Now we are foes."

"That was not my doing," the Salvaari growled bitterly. "It was not the Aedei who gathered their armies to slaughter and conquer."

The king did not look away from Cailean's eyes. "No, it was not," he replied. "But your people have crossed the Arwan year after year for a century. You raid and pillage along the Medean border and for what? To turn the entire west against you?"

Cailean snorted and bared his teeth. "Just as they do to us," the Aedei snarled.

"Tell me. Had your druids commanded you to cross the border at the whim of your spirits, would you have done it? Would you have marched into Medea and taken town after town? Would you have crossed the Eretrian and laid waste to Annora?"

"You are very clever, king." Cailean chuckled drily. "Yet it was your kind who started this war a long time ago."

"A comfort to all the innocents in Bandujar that you have killed," Dayne countered.

Cailean leaned towards the king. "Would you like to know who led the raid?" he said.

Dayne stilled, careful to keep his face impassive. With his cold blue eyes locked on the chief's face, he knew the name before it left Cailean's mouth.

"Your brother Lukas," Cailean told him.

"He lives then," Dayne murmured.

"The last of the Raynor clan with honour," the Aedei said.

"What have you done to him?"

Cailean's lips curled back into a sneer. "His heart has never flown with Annora, with your ways and with your gods," Cailean told him. "You know this. His eyes have merely opened to the truth."

"And what truth would that be?" Dayne asked.

"The truth of Salvaar."

"Is that why he burnt a temple and slaughtered unarmed priests?" Dayne stated.

Cailean said nothing, yet his brow twitched into a frown.

"You did not hear about Valham?" the king continued.

"No."

"You see, we found his sword amidst the ruins covered in ash and dust. It was a message. My brother has spurned his family and heritage for what? For whom? The Káli he rides with?"

"Maevin," Cailean muttered.

"Is that her name?" Dayne asked. "The witch?"

For the first time, Cailean looked away. "I warned him," the Aedei said through bared teeth.

"Who is she?"

"She who serves the Lord of the Veil. She who lives for Tanris. She is a priestess of the Dark One."

King Dayne nodded slowly as he listened to Cailean. "And what? My brother has been cheated by her spell?" he said.

"Yes."

"And you believe that some kind of magic is the sole reason that my brother sundered a temple?"

"I know that you do not believe, king," Cailean said as he met Dayne's eyes. "Maevin, like the rest of her kind, uses her beauty, her guile and her words to corrupt and seduce even the strongest of wills. She will speak of riddles and prophecies; she will make you strong … yet her words are poison. She *is* poison."

"And now she has ensnared Lukas," Dayne murmured as he ran a hand across his sun and moon amulet. "Superstition, Cailean. She will have poisoned him with words, not magic or enchantments."

"Words once spoken by your brother," Cailean muttered. "Listen to me, king. You are a warrior the same as I. Dark stories, illusion, trickery: that is all beyond us. But do not let that cloud your judgement."

"If you are right, then I should have killed her when I had the chance."

"You cannot change the past, nor can you run from it," the Aedei told him.

"No, you cannot," Dayne agreed as he rose to his feet. "Yet you can use it to manipulate what happens next."

The king made his way to the cage door before he turned back and looked to the prisoner.

"I have arranged for you and your people to be moved to

Kilgareth until the war is over," Dayne told him. "You will not be harmed."

✦ ✦ ✦

Hadwin Weles of Torosa, mercenary under Bellec, brought his sword to bear. While his master was in the east, Hadwin served Lukas the One-Eye. His armour and helmet bore the black markings of the Káli. Hadwin deflected a spear thrust with his shield, stepped forward and then buried the edge of his sword in the Medean's neck. The spearman topped over in a spray of blood and was dead before he hit the ground. Hadwin moved on instinct as another Medean charged him. Hadwin thrust his shield skyward and caught the Medean's sword in the air. Hadwin lunged forward and drove his blade up under the man's chin. He savagely wrenched his blade free and slammed his shield into the Medean's chest. Hadwin glanced around as the Medean fell. His mercenary companion Layan fought by his side, as did three Káli warriors. The Arwan River flowed past them and the thick trees of Salvaar rose all around. Rodion of the Káli cut down another Medean, yet more were coming. The men of House Aloys flooded the trees all around them. There were too many.

"Run!" roared Layan as he slew one of the Medeans.

Without hesitation, the five men charged back into the forest. Trees flashed by and the earth sprayed underfoot. The snapping of branches and heavy footfalls came from behind. Shouts rang from Medean mouths as they closed in on the fleeing band of Káli and mercenaries. The Medeans advanced from the north, south and west. There were many and they were gaining.

A spear flew from the side. Hadwin barely avoided the bladed tip as he danced around it. He had no time to stop, no time to angle his blade. Instead, Hadwin slammed the crossguard of his sword into the Medean's jaw. Hadwin did not turn to see his attacker fall.

"Run!" he cried.

The soldiers of Aloys came at them in a great tide. Hadwin bared his teeth and ran for all he was worth.

"Hadwin!" One-Eye's voice filled the woods.

Lukas and a dozen Káli materialised before the fleeing men. Hadwin threw himself to the side. His companions leapt for cover. Bows sang and arrows were sent forth. Each one found its target. The honed tips pierced chainmail, gambeson and flesh. Within moments, the Medeans and their blood littered the ground.

✦ ✦ ✦

Lukas' grip tightened on his crutch as he limped across the earth. He gazed around at the fallen Medeans. Over two dozen had been killed this day. His plan had worked as he knew that it would. Rodion and one of his people had gathered up the only living Medean. An arrow was embedded in the wounded man's stomach. A savage grin played across Lukas' lips when he saw the bloody tinge splashed across the white lion symbol. The Káli held the man tight as they brought him to Lukas. The Medean was in agony and no man could have hidden the pained grimace that he bore. The Medean barely had the strength to look up into Lukas' eye.

"Do you know who I am?" Lukas asked with a smirk.

The Medean was silent as he saw the crutch, the brace upon Lukas' knee and the cloth covering his empty eye socket.

"You are Lukas, son of Dorian," the Medean said quietly. "The Black Eagle. There are many that fear you."

"And do you?" Lukas asked. One-Eye reached down and took hold of the arrow that protruded from the Medean. The man winced. "Do you fear me?" Lukas asked again.

Before the Medean could reply, One-Eye twisted the arrow. The man screamed like a wild animal. His face contorted in agony. "Yes," he managed.

"I want you to deliver a message to my brother," Lukas told him as he continued to turn the arrow.

The Medean cried out as the pain flared. His stomach was on fire.

"Can you do that?" One-Eye asked.

"Yes," the Medean stammered. "Yes …" He screamed again.

Lukas began to tug on the arrow as he twisted it. "You will cross the river. You will run back to your people. You will go to your lord, Duke Alejandro. Tell him who sent you, and tell him that beyond the Arwan, the forest belongs to the Salvaari."

Lukas viciously pulled on the arrow and ripped it from the Medean's stomach. The soldier's feet gave out and only the Káli holding him kept him from falling. Lukas glanced at Rodion and then gestured west towards the river. The two Káli dragged the Medean back a step and then threw him into the ground.

"Run," Lukas commanded.

Without another word, the soldier staggered to his feet. He gasped as he clutched at his bloody stomach. The Káli watched with burning eyes as the Medean stumbled past his fallen companions and then began to make his way towards the river.

"They're getting bolder," Hadwin said. "They know that they need to cross soon. Every moment that they delay gives us more time to prepare."

"Do not fear, mercenary," Maevin said as she approached. "The spirits are with us."

"I for one would prefer to have an army of sellswords join us than rely on the goodwill of your spirits," Layan replied.

Hadwin chuckled.

"In time, you will see," Maevin told them.

"This one still breathes," Rodion interrupted as he crouched over a fallen soldier.

The man he spoke of had two arrows driven into his body. One was planted in his side, while the other had found a home in his shoulder.

"Bind his wounds and tie him to a horse," Lukas commanded. "He's coming with us."

"Yes, lord."

"What shall we do with the dead?" Layan asked, glancing at Lukas.

One-Eye said nothing for a moment. He ran his hand up the shaft of the bloody arrow that he had pulled from the man he sent as his messenger. He brushed the steel tip and then tossed it to one of the Káli bowmen.

"Salvaar is strongest when it is feared," Lukas said slowly. "We are too few to keep them at bay, yet we have shown them vulnerable. We showed them that at Bandujar and Valham. We showed them at Palen-Tor. They know better now than to think that we will meekly submit."

Lukas hobbled into the field of bodies as he spoke. He planted his crutch in the earth and rested his hands atop it, gazing down at one of the slain Medeans. A pair of arrows were driven deep into his chest and his blood had become a gift for forest floor.

"String them up."

✦ ✦ ✦

THREE

"We gather here today to discuss the threat of Aureia," Erik Farrin said as he glanced around at the assembled warriors, jarls and earls.

They stood within Erik's longhall. The home of his father. The home of his sister. A great banner bearing the mark of the raven hung from one of the walls. Painted shields, wicked axes and long spears lined the others.

"A threat of your making," Earl Einri of Kattir muttered.

"I slaughtered the ambassador Valan Azure Aldrich and his men, Earl Einri," Erik growled, "and I will not apologise for that. Yet it was not I who started this war. The ambassador told us so himself. In less than a month, an imperial fleet will set sail from the south to bring about the doom of Miera."

"The empire wants to take the steppe while all eyes are turned elsewhere," Jorun Thorkel spoke up.

"They wanted us to aid them in this endeavour," Erik continued. "In one move, they would have crushed one enemy and weakened another. Weakened us. We would have returned from war tired and weary, yet within a day we would have seen the griffin upon the horizon. This war is about more than just Salvaar, my brothers. It always was."

"They did the same with Delios, did they not?" Torben the bloodsworn began. "After the great King Nykalous Gaedhela passed, his sons turned their swords upon each other. All of them wished to inherit the Chimera's empire. In the chaos that ensued, when the children of Gaedhela spilled their own blood, it was Aureia who watched. They waited and they prepared until only two of the princes remained. The great philosopher Khrysaor and Conlaed, the oldest of the sons. Only then did the griffin make its move. Only when Delios was so weakened. Only after Nykalous the Chimera was dead. When the princes learnt of Aureia's plans, they joined together once again but it was too late. They were slain one by one. When Conlaed fell, the path to Delios was made open. Aureia marched through the lands of her ruined enemy. They took town after town until Emperor Hanniel and his legions arrived at the city of Delios itself. The Chimera's once great city burned, and his daughter was slain upon the very steps of his throne room."

"And so fell the greatest empire of its time," Earl Imelda said.

"After the fall of Delios, Berenithia followed. Irene followed," Erik told them. "The Inquisition tore Medea from its people. When Reshada of Larissa dies, it will be Aureia that inherits her land. We know this. I ask you now, each of you, once Salvaar falls –and it will fall – do you think that whoever takes the silver throne in Darius' stead will stop with the forests of the north and the plains of Miera?"

"We would be surrounded," Jorun muttered. "It would have been only a matter of time before they came for us."

Erik looked to Earl Einri and met the older man's eyes for a moment.

"I know that many of you did not want this," Erik said. "I know that many of you would have preferred to live the rest of your lives raiding and sailing. I would have preferred that. No … my heart longs for that. My dreams lie in the south. My dreams now share a spirit with those of Astrid. If she cannot explore the south, then I will. I did not want this any more than any of you, yet it is done. It is done. This war that we now find ourselves in will test us, but if we succeed – and we *will* succeed – then we will have peace. Not just for us, but for our children and their children. For the first time in our history, we can accomplish what so many of our people have sought. Freedom. The great warrior Freydis tried. The explorer Iren Brightblade tried. Astrid tried. None have been so close to it as we are right now, right in this moment."

"Our people have always lived in darkness," Einri said. "We have always thought ourselves as free, but that is anything but the truth. We have lived … we have survived because men of privilege and wealth allow us to."

"In one battle, we could change that," Erik told him. "The empire knows that to fight us now would be to overreach. Valan taught me that. Why else would he have been sent to recruit Arndyr and his people for their war? Why else would the ambassador have resorted to threats when confronted? The empire's attention is not fully on us, and they are spread thin."

"This Aureian fleet, wherever it is, will not idly sail by our isles anymore," Jarl Ulfric added. "It cannot afford to."

"No, it cannot," Erik replied.

The former bloodsworn could see the looks in the eyes of his people. All of them were with him. It was only Einri that he was unsure about. Only Einri whom he had to convince.

"You avenged Astrid, you brought us together," Einri said and met Erik's gaze. "You killed Valan and broke the peace … But what I want to know, Erik, is will you finish what you started? I want to know if you are more than just a warrior trying to play at war."

Erik knew his words before he spoke them. Flames surged through his blood. Flames waiting to be unleashed. The wound on his arm itched. It had been only days since Erik had carved a bloody furrow through the serpent mark. It had been only days since he had sealed it with fire.

"Family, honour and my word. Those are the principles that I serve, the tenants that I live by," Erik told him. "My family is dead.

All of them. When I took up my blade and severed the serpent's mark, I knew what I was sacrificing. My word. My honour. Yet in that moment, I knew with a clear certainty that for this fight to be won, I needed to walk away from who I once was. This war means *everything* to me. I promise you now that I will stand with you to whatever end."

Einri met his stare. He let the earl search his eyes and search his heart. He showed Einri everything. His pain and his anger, his rage and his fear. His will. Erik would not fail. He could not fail.

"To whatever end," Einri growled and gave Erik a solemn nod.

Erik returned the gesture. "We have to find the fleet," he said. "Find where it harbours. Find where it makes berth. If we do not defeat it before it arrives upon our shores, then it may already be too late. And I for one would rather die than see my home destroyed and my people in chains."

"What do you suggest?" Ulfric asked. "Between us we can summon a fleet of fifty ships. A fleet more powerful than any that we have ever assembled before and yet there are some Aureian ports that we could not stand against even with such numbers."

Erik clasped his hands behind his back and walked out into the middle of the hall. The question had plagued him for days. Where did they begin? How did they find the answers that they sought?

"We do not know when the empire will attack and we do not know if the ambassador was telling the truth," Erik said. "The fleet could well be on its way here in this moment. We cannot leave the isles undefended, and for that reason many of us will have to remain here to prepare our defences and defend our families. Those few who set out to raid will have to divide. We can use our knowledge of the Lupentine and our seamanship to evade Aureian patrols. We will need to strike the silver coast from Valentia in the north to the cities of the far south. Ports, harbours, even fishing villages. We raid them all. There will be shipmasters, merchants and magisters in the larger towns. Someone will know the truth. Someone will know the location of this fleet."

"And our people?" Jorun spoke up. "Everything that you have spoken of has been about our warriors, our jarls and shieldmaidens. What of those who cannot fight?"

"They may have to," Earl Einri replied. "From today we must proceed with the notion that until all of us are safe, none of us are. Every man, every woman, every child who is old enough to swing an axe or wield a bow must be taught to. We must be ready for whomever comes to our shores. We must be ready to fight."

"Even the children?" Ulfric shook his head.

"They may not have a choice," Einri told him. "We have no harbours that we can fall back to, no safe havens in which we may weather this storm. If we cannot find this fleet and the empire arrives on our shores, they will be met with a most unpleasant welcome."

Erik folded his arms as he looked from man to man. The rumbles of discontent amongst the men were to amount to nothing more: Einri was right.

"Do you disagree, Ulfric?" Erik asked.

"No."

"It's settled then," Erik told the gathering. "Each isle is to send a crew to Nesoi. From there they will stage their raids into the empire and attempt to unshroud this fleet. The rest of us will remain and prepare. Blacksmiths are to work day and night. Hunters and foragers are to be sent into the mountains while farmers must prepare to harvest. The food stores must be full. When the griffin comes, our defences *have* to hold. They *will* hold."

"Then let it be done." Earl Imelda dipped her head to Erik. "My hunters shall sail for Nesoi by nightfall. You have my word."

"And mine," Einri chorused.

One by one, the other earls voiced their agreement. One by

one, they pledged their ships. The fate of the Valkir rested in the balance.

Erik glanced towards Jorun Thorkel. The man that they called Bloodaxe was one of the greatest bloodsworn to have ever sailed for Agartha. A fierce warrior and steadfast jarl with one of the strongest crews in all of the isles. Vicious in battle and ruthless in victory, the warriors of Bloodaxe fought like their ship's namesake. The Harpy. The winged demon that was part eagle and part woman was a creature from hellish nightmare. A figurehead of the monster adorned the prow of Bloodaxe's ship.

"Jorun," Erik called to his friend and former shieldbrother. "Prepare to sail. I need you in the west."

"My crew is ready," Jorun replied. "They hunger for blood and battle."

"Then they shall have it," Erik said as the pair clasped arms. "Our hopes and dreams sail with you."

"I will not fail you," Jorun vowed.

"You never have." Erik clapped Jorun on the shoulder. "May the Sea-Father sail with you, scâldir," he told his friend.

Jorun joined the jarls and earls as they began to make for the doors of the hall.

"A moment, my brothers," Ulfric called after them.

All eyes went to the grey-haired jarl who now approached Erik. "We should talk, you and I," he said.

Erik looked to the old warrior who had once fought side by side with his own father. "If something is on your mind, speak," Erik told him.

Ulfric glanced first at Einri and then to Imelda and the other earls. One by one, they nodded as if agreeing to some unspoken word.

"I once came to you in Scaeva's hall. I pressed you to lead. I implored you to search your soul and answer the question that I posed you."

"In every man's life, there comes a time when he must choose between who he is and who he wants to be," Erik replied. "I remember."

"It would appear that you may have found the answer," Ulfric replied.

"When I cut the serpent mark, I freed myself of the tenants that bound me to the bloodsworn's creed," Erik said. "I knew in that moment that if I did not sever my bindings, I would not just be running from my people, but I would have been running from myself."

Ulfric looked him in the eye. His hair might have been grey, but the old jarl's gaze was filled with the intensity of a storm. "Perhaps then it is time to put aside the bloodsworn and put aside the jarl," Ulfric said. "Become who you were *meant* to be."

Ulfric reached under his cloak and pulled forth a triple necklace. The three leather cords were covered in an assortment of rings, shells and carved metal. It was a sailor's necklace. It was a warrior's necklace. Each ornament or jewel had been added by one of the long line of earls that had borne the triple band. Each relic had meaning. Each relic had strength.

"The earl's jewel," Erik murmured as Ulfric held the necklace out.

"This belongs to you," the jarl told him. "It is time that you took your rightful place as king."

Erik froze. His blood chilled and his eyes widened. "King?"

Ulfric gestured to the earls as he spoke. "After Vay'kis. After Scaeva and Valan, we talked and we decided. There is only one who can bring us together. Only one who can unite us in common cause. Only one to lead us against the empire. That is you. The son of the great Lief Farrin. Brother to Astrid the Raven Jarl."

"We do not need another jarl or an earl," Imelda said. "What we need is a king."

"A Raven King," Einri finished. "A man who all of us choose. A man we can all call brother."

Erik did not hesitate or question. There was no choice at all. This was the fate that he had long since been set upon. This is where he belonged. Erik took the triple band and tied it around his neck. The necklaces hung alongside his raven head amulet.

"King Erik Farrin," Ulfric roared. The jarl took a knee and bowed his head.

"King Erik," Torben echoed as he knelt.

The cry filled the longhall as it was taken up by warrior, jarl and earl alike. All knelt before Erik. All did so willingly. What Erik felt he wasn't sure. Was it pride and elation? Was it fear? Never in the history of its people had the Valkir Isles crowned a king. Never had they united behind a single leader. He had started down this path to avenge his sister. His purpose had changed like the tides, yet it had never been so clear. When his journey had run its course and all was said and done, Erik wanted nothing more than to know he had honoured Astrid's memory.

Erik gazed across the bay from the hills beside his hall. The sun had begun to set, and the waves were painted in brilliant shades of orange and red. Ships sailed from Agartha and out into the Lupentine. Jorun's ship was already long gone. He would be upon the shores of Nesoi within a matter of days. The newly crowned king ran a thumb across the surface of his raven head amulet. Even now he could feel Astrid's strength residing within it. He could feel his mother and father. His hand lingered for a moment before his fingers brushed the triple band. Erik knew that he had made the right decision and yet it plagued him. Astrid had been a natural leader yet had *hated* the idea of assuming command. She had not even wished to be jarl. Erik had only ever wanted to fight side by side with his people. He had wished to lead them into battle. Now he stood as king. Erik had been granted the title that had so rightfully been Astrid's. He could only hope that some of her wisdom had stayed in the wooden amulet that he now wore.

"Erik."

The king turned to see five figures approaching. Torben led them and in his wake walked the brothers Nenrir and Laerke, the helmsman Fargrim and Mayrun, the carpenter's daughter. All five served about the Ravenheart. All five he held to heart.

"We have something for you," Fargrim said.

The four men stood aside and allowed Mayrun to walk before them. A shield was slung across her back. Erik frowned as the woman unslung the shield and revealed it to Erik. It was painted blood red and bore the image of a flying raven. The bird was of deep black yet bore scarlet eyes. A rounded boss adorned the centre of the shield, and a steel rim wrapped around its edge. Erik took the shield. He felt its strength and felt its weight. He slid his arm through the straps.

"This is a good shield," he said.

"It's layered linen wood," Mayrun explained. "It will not easily break or splinter."

"A king deserves a king's shield," Torben said.

"Thank you," Erik told them sincerely. "All of you."

"Your family have led us this far and never led us astray," Laerke said. "We believe in you."

"We will stand with you, brother," added Nenrir.

"Always," finished Fargrim.

✦ ✦ ✦

FOUR

City of Belona, Aureian Empire

Zahiir Alsahra stood sentinel on top of the safe house that he had procured. He had given his word to Bellec that he would make haste to Belona and secure a hideaway for the mercenary company. The house that he had found was almost a villa. It stood three floors high and was filled with dozens of rooms. Zahiir had brought a dozen men with him to Belona, men who now stood at every entrance and watched every horizon. Zahiir had honoured his promise to Bellec and now he gazed out from the third floor with his eyes fixed upon the south. He saw the dark speck against the sky before he heard the bird's cry. Zahiir gave a long and sharp whistle. Within moments, the speck grew into a hawk as it dived towards the safe house. He raised an arm aloft as the dark-feathered bird descended and then landed upon it.

"Sabra," Zahiir murmured as he stroked the hawk. "Where you been, eh? Where you been?"

✦ ✦ ✦

Kitara stared out from the depths of her wide hood as the party rode towards the walls of Belona. The thick cloak was pulled tight around her body to shield her armour from sight. If anyone saw the thick golden braids or the embossed cuirass, they would be discovered.

Kitara held Aeryn close. The moonseer sat before her on their horse and directed the mount after the men who led the company. Sakkar and Senya rode at the front of the column with Bellec at their side. Galadayne, Jaimye, Kompton and the other mercenaries surrounded Aeryn and Kitara's horse. The mercenaries kept keen eyes over Kitara, ready to strike at anything that turned her way. Bellec brought the column to a halt as they reached the open gates.

"What business brings you to Belona so armed?" one of the gate guards said as he stepped forward.

The Aureian's face was lined and weathered. A scar was visible beneath his helmet and his armour shone in the sun. Three fellow soldiers made their way to their leader's side.

"My companions and I were summoned to Belona by our master," Bellec told the man.

"Mercenaries?"

"Aye," Bellec replied.

The soldier gazed among the ranks of riders. He searched face after face. Kitara looked away, half burying her face in Aeryn's back. A hawk's shrill screech came from above.

"And who is your master?" the gate guard asked.

"That would be me." Zahiir's voice came from behind the man.

The Aureian's turned to see Zahiir and two of his men sitting astride dark-skinned horses.

"Lord Zahiir." The gate guard nodded towards him. "I did not know that you were bringing guests."

"And yet it is so."

The gate guard bit his lip. "Right you are, then," he said and gestured for his fellow soldiers to stand aside.

Zahiir led the company through the straight streets of the Aureian city. The roads were filled with people, but all gave way as the horsemen rode through their midst. After what seemed like an age, they arrived at the large gates of a walled house. The gates were flung open and a pair of Larissan soldiers ushered them inside. They followed Zahiir into a courtyard of stone. Before them stood the three-floored safe house. Kitara swung her leg over her horse's flank and lowered herself to the ground. Her ankle still hurt from the fight in Vesuva although she could now put some weight on it. Kitara pulled her hood back and let her braids fall free. Aeryn dropped down beside her and gave Kitara a smile.

"My brother." Sakkar grinned and embraced Zahiir. "How did you come by a place like this?"

"This is not my first time in Belona. I have traded with these people," he explained. "I know the magister."

"Good," Bellec cut in as he approached the pair. "We cannot stay here. I need you to help me find a ship to take us east."

"Of course," Zahiir agreed. "Whatever you need."

Bellec turned to his men. "Galadayne, Kompton, go to the market and find Kitara some clothes. Only a fool would not recognise her by the armour she wears. I am sure that men from Vesuva will not be far behind us."

"Boss." Kompton nodded.

"Jaimye, you're in charge while I am gone," Bellec continued. "No one leaves and no one enters."

"Of course."

"And tend to your wound."

Galadayne clicked his tongue and pulled on his reins. Then he and Kompton were gone, riding back through the gates from whence they had come. Bellec led his horse towards his daughter. Kitara wasn't sure what to feel when she looked at the man. For so long, she had been sure that he had abandoned her and her mother all those years ago. She had been sure that he had abandoned her when Sir Rowan and his men had captured her in Salvaar. Now it seemed that she had been wrong.

Bellec reached out and placed a hand gently upon her shoulder. "I will be back soon," he told her sincerely. "We can talk then."

"We will," Kitara replied.

With that, Bellec heaved himself up into his saddle once more. He gestured to Zahiir and the pair rode from the courtyard. The gates closed behind them and a bolt was driven home.

The bathhouse was warm. Kitara had filled the wooden tub with water, for her body was worn and travel stained. Dirt from the streets of Vesuva mingled with drops of dried blood upon her skin – her own blood and that of her enemies. She held back a sigh as she reached for the clasp of her cloak. She untied the band and let the garment fall to the floor. Kitara pulled free her greaves and boots. Her bracers followed. She unbuckled her sword and placed it to the side. The door opened and closed. Kitara glanced over her shoulder and saw Aeryn. She saw those big silver eyes and the slight curl tugging at the corner of Aeryn's lips. She smelt the scent of wildflowers blooming in spring. Kitara smiled as the moonseer approached. Aeryn reached out and tugged on the red sash that was bound around Kitara's waist. She pulled it free and then ran her hands across the armour to the lacings of the cuirass.

"How do you feel?" Aeryn asked.

Kitara was silent for a moment as she thought. "For so long I was living in darkness as a prisoner and slave ... Now I feel life in me again," Kitara told her. "I feel free."

Aeryn untied the last of the lacings and then eased the cuirass from Kitara's body. Kitara rolled her shoulders as she felt some of the tension leave her back. She took Aeryn's hand.

"I have thought of you often," Kitara murmured as she ran a thumb across the back of Aeryn's hand. "But I did not think that I would see you again."

Aeryn gently pressed her brow into Kitara's. "Do you remember what I once told you? What I once swore to you?" Aeryn said softy. "I will stay by your side for a day, a month, a year ... forever."

"But you are moonseer ... I know of the pledge that you once made."

"I made a vow to my people that I would do my duty as moonseer before all else," Aeryn replied fiercely. "In coming for you, I broke that vow. I would rather break my oath and see you again than I would spend my entire lifetime alone with the honour of my vow."

Kitara bit her lip. A deaf man could have heard the truth in Aeryn's words. Kitara gently placed a hand on Aeryn's soft cheek. She stared deep into those eyes of blazing silver. Their lips brushed. Kitara felt her heart race as she pulled the other woman closer. She breathed in Aeryn's scent and felt her warmth. Kitara kissed Aeryn as if she wanted to write poetry on her soul. Where first there had been soft lips and gentle touch, they now grabbed at each other with hungry hands and kisses filled with passion. Aeryn's sleeveless gambeson was unbuckled, and her shirt was pulled free. Kitara's tunic joined them on the wooden floor. Aeryn's arms, covered in the hard muscle of an archer, enveloped Kitara. Her fingers traced Kitara's spine and the canvas of scars that covered her back. No kiss was deep enough; their entangled bodies were not close enough. All Kitara felt was Aeryn.

✦ ✦ ✦

Zahiir led Bellec to the Belona docks. Dozens of ships were moored in the bay. Some were the massive vessels used by merchant traders, while others were armed for war. Weathered sailors, armoured soldiers and traders going about their business filled the harbour. The pair rode past them all without a second glance. The great walls of the Belona arsenal rose before them. Violet banners marked with the silver griffin hung to either side of the massive gates and steel-clad soldiers watched from the battlements. Bellec followed Zahiir through the open doors and into the depths of the fortress. Bellec took everything in, from the walls to the warriors who manned them. He committed it all to memory. Hope for the best yet prepare for the worst. Those words had been instilled in him from boyhood. If anything went wrong, then they may have to fight their way free of the arsenal. They dismounted in a courtyard of stone before a towering keep.

"We're here to see Master Vangelis," Zahiir told the soldiers that approached.

"Right this way, Lord Zahiir," came the reply.

Master Vangelis' office was small. Bookcases lined the walls and tables were laden with scrolls and logbooks. The two men waited for the ship master to arrive. Bellec scanned the room, his eyes flicking from the maps that lined the walls to the books that filled the shelves. His gaze stopped at the spine of a leather-clad book. It was a simple design and no different to most of the other books in the room; however, this one wasn't a log. The name Vesperan was printed upon its side. It was a name that every child of the empire had been taught since birth, a name that had power in even the far reaches of Medea. Bellec pursed his lips as he reached for the book. He pulled it from the shelf and flicked it open.

"Gentlemen," an Aureian voice called as the office door opened. "I apologise for being late. I did not realise that I was to entertain today."

"The fault lies with us for not sending word." Zahiir extended a hand. "Lord Vangelis."

"Lord Zahiir," the Aureian replied as he took it.

Bellec glanced up at the man who had entered. His face was clean shaven and his clothing neat. His arm was strong, and he had the weathered face of a lifetime of sailing. As was the tradition, Vangelis had proven himself by rising through the ranks as opposed to being chosen by his name or class.

"The great Vesperan's journal," Vangelis said as he gestured to the book in Bellec's hands.

"His life was quite the story," Bellec replied as he closed the journal and placed it back upon the shelf. "The man who took Delios and defeated Prince Drystan Gaedhela in single combat."

"Indeed," Vangelis said. "You are a learned man."

The mercenary nodded. "I'm Bellec, Lord Vangelis," he told the Aureian.

The pair clasped hands. Vangelis gestured to the seats that surrounded his large desk. The three men sat.

"How can I be of service?" Vangelis asked them.

"We need ships," Zahiir said.

"I have two questions. What is the cargo and where are you going?"

"Twenty-three men and equal their number of horses," Bellec replied.

Vangelis' brow furrowed ever so slightly. He leaned forward on the desk and his eyes did not leave Bellec. "You're a mercenary then?"

"Mercenary, sellsword, soldier of fortune – call me what you like," Bellec told him.

"I see," Vangelis said. "And where do you wish to go?"

"Valengos."

"Medea? What takes you so far east?"

"Unfortunately, the war," Bellec said. "We have business to attend to."

"And such is the life of a blood merchant," Lord Vangelis replied. "I will be honest with you. Most of the ships that you saw in the harbour are now under the employ of the imperial court. A lot of coin and a lot of blood has been tied up in this crusade to the east. With the emperor's death, there is a lot of uncertainty within the imperial halls."

"These are uncertain times, my friend," Zahiir said. "Perhaps we can help each other. Find the ships that my companion here requires and in return you will be well paid for any … uncertainty."

Vangelis stroked his jaw. "You would need two ships," he told them. "One for man and one for beast. The cost of procuring them would be great."

"Then allow me–" Zahiir started.

"I can pay you two hundred crowns," Bellec interrupted. "A further five hundred upon docking at Valengos." Bellec wanted to leave Aureia far behind and return to a place where they were not being hunted.

Zahiir stared at him. The man could have *bought* his own ships with that kind of gold. The ship master kept his face still, yet his eyes shone. Everyone had their price, and it had been found.

"The ships will be ready to leave at dawn," Vangelis told them.

"No." Bellec shook his head. "We leave *today*."

✦ ✦ ✦

The water was cool on Kitara's skin. She sat in the large tub almost fully submerged. The last of the dust from the road had long since been pulled from her body. She leaned back with closed eyes and let her braided hair fall beyond the bath. Aeryn sat outside the tub and slowly began to work Kitara's hair free of the tight braids. Kitara's hand moved to her upper arm. Her fingers caressed the small cut that had begun to heal over.

"How did you get that one?" Aeryn asked.

"It was a parting gift from the house of Nilor," Kitara replied.

A gift given by the glass of the window through which she had jumped.

"It will leave a scar, I am sure," Kitara continued. "My face, my back, my arms; my body is a canvas of scars. They tell a story. They remind me of all the times that life tried to break me and failed."

Aeryn paused for a moment. "They show that you survived," she said. "That you were stronger than whatever tried to hurt you."

"There are times when it doesn't feel like that," Kitara murmured.

Aeryn gently caressed her cheek. Kitara nuzzled into the moonseer's hand.

"The past can hurt," Aeryn told her. "But you can either run from it or you can learn from it."

"Someone once told me that the strongest of hearts have the most scars," Kitara said.

"Who said that?"

Kitara eased her back against the edge of the tub. "Luana, her name is," she told Aeryn.

"And this Luana … Did she have many scars?"

Kitara did not have to turn to see the humour dance across Aeryn's face nor did she have to look to see the ever-present smirk curl her lips.

Kitara grinned. "Yes."

Aeryn continued to free the braids one by one.

"Tell me about the changing," the moonseer said. "Has it happened since Salvaar?"

She meant when Kitara's gaze shifted from green to purple; she meant when Kitara could see and feel everything.

"Twice. Once on the slave ship and the other in Nilor's house. The first time it came, it awoke me from my sleep. I could feel the waves beneath and the birds in the sky above. It hurt, threatened to break me … and then I remembered your words." Kitara glanced over her should at Aeryn as she spoke. She spoke her next words in Salvaari. "Remember the sea … Remember her voice."

"Did they work?"

"Yes. The pain faded and I felt strong. I could see everything, I could feel everything, I *was* everything. When it happened again in Nilor's house, it was I who called upon this sight. It was I who used it to escape."

"Then at last this nightmare has become a gift," Aeryn said. "Though from where it came from, I do not know. The spirits gave me my eyes. They have given me this gift to see through darkness and I will use it. Yet to be so blessed with sight … with *true* sight … that is something that I have never heard of before."

"Not even in Salvaar?" Kitara asked.

"Not even in Salvaar," Aeryn echoed. "It is a curious thing."

"How so?"

"In some ways it reminds me of a story I heard as a girl," Aeryn told her.

"Tell me."

"When Tanris freed himself from slavery, when he escaped the Dark Ones, he was trapped in shadow. He couldn't see, let alone navigate through the bowels of the earth. Tanris used his power to cross into the Veil and there he sacrificed an eye to Sylvaine to acquire sight. When he returned to the mortal world, he could feel the earthen tunnels and walls. He could feel rock and stone. With this gift, he escaped his prison."

"That is quite some story," Kitara said.

"Perhaps when we return to Salvaar, we should seek out the druids," Aeryn suggested. "If anyone can give you the answers you seek, it is them."

"Are you sure?"

"They chose *you* to look upon Sylvaine for a reason. I am certain of it."

"Maybe you're right," Kitara said thoughtfully.

Aeryn freed the last of Kitara's hair from the final braid. "There," the moonseer told her.

Kitara reached up and ran her fingers through her golden hair. With that, the last trace of Alessandra was gone.

"Can I ask you something?"

"Anything," Aeryn replied.

Kitara held her left arm out and showed the moonseer the collection of rings that adorned it. Her own arm ring sat alongside the ones belonging to the fallen Káli.

"I was not the only one who made it to Vesuva alive," Kitara told

Aeryn. "There were others … Sereia, Morlag. They're all gone now. I avenged their passing and took these from the one who wore them as trophies. I want to honour their memory but do not know of any Salvaari tradition."

"You want to honour them?" Aeryn said as she rose to her feet. "Keep them. Wear them. Bring them home. Then we can bury them beneath the trees under the golden sun."

✦ ✦ ✦

Bellec returned and the company gathered in the courtyard once more. They had been granted a pair of ships and could finally be on their way to Salvaar. Sabra circled high above while the companions made ready.

"Brother," Sakkar called as he approached Zahiir.

"You're going with them, aren't you?" Zahiir replied.

"I am. For many months I rode with Kitara and then Bellec. They ride to war now against Annora, against Prince Lukas," Sakkar said. "To have come so far and to have seen so much … If I can help them, then I must."

"What about your family?"

"I am going too," Senya cut in as she stepped to her husband's side. "We will not be parted again." She led a pair of horses by their bridles. One was her own, while the other she handed to Sakkar.

"Please be my brother now and do not try to dissuade me," Sakkar added and clapped a hand on Zahiir's arm.

Zahiir took his brother's shoulders with his hands. "If this is your wish, then may Amkut protect you both."

Sakkar pulled his brother into an embrace. "One day we will return home," Sakkar vowed.

"See that you do."

Senya and Zahiir hugged.

"Take care of him," Zahiir said to her.

"Always," Senya vowed.

"He may never look for trouble, but it always finds him."

"I have a knack for it," Sakkar told him with a grin as he heaved himself up into his saddle. "Farewell, brother."

"Safe travels," Zahiir replied and pressed a hand to his heart.

Sakkar returned the gesture. The company rode out from the villa gates.

✦ ✦ ✦

FIVE

The knights rode in silence as they took the road north. Alarik set the pace, and they pushed their horses hard. They had to get to Tallis, and they had to get there with haste. Not a word had been spoken between Kyler and his mentor since they had begun their ride. Kyler's mind was plagued with thoughts, memories of Elena and memories of the day before. The fight in the tunnels beneath Elara, Olivera and the death of Elena. Alarik's last words before they had left that hill. It had been he who had murdered Amaris Delodrysia. Kyler's hand wandered to his throat as the horses slowed to a canter. Instead of reaching for the sun and moon amulet, his fingers went to the silver necklace. Elena's necklace. The jewel he had given her when she left Adrestia years ago. A jewel that she kept and finally returned to him upon her death.

"We will rest here tonight." Alarik's stern voice broke the silence.

Kyler nodded and followed the battlemaster as he rode towards a small grove of trees off the main road. Alarik dismounted and untethered Arntair's horse from his own mount's saddle. The Elaran merchant had given the knights one of his horses to pull the wagon with which they had fled the city. The wagon that they had since abandoned to grant them speed.

Kyler swung a leg over Asena's flank and dropped to the ground. He bit back a wince as a wave of pain hit him. His body was battered and bruised and his armour still covered in blood and filth from the tunnels. It clung to his chainmail and soaked through to his gambeson. Kyler pulled off one of his gloves and ran his hand down Asena's neck. He looked into the horse's big eye. With the deaths of his parents and Elena, Asena was the last thing he had to remind him of home. The horse nudged Kyler's shoulder. The knight stroked the side of the mare's face.

"They're all gone, girl," Kyler murmured. "It's just us now. Just us."

Alarik piled up small branches and twigs. He pulled out his flint, and within moments a fire was sparked to life. Kyler unslung his shield from his back and pulled his helmet from his head. He pushed back his coif and unbuckled his swordbelt before sitting by the blaze. After digging around in a pouch, he procured his whetstone. Moonlight danced along the blade of his longsword as he pulled it free. Without a word, Kyler slowly began to grind out the imperfections that had appeared along his sword. The fight in the tunnels had left its mark upon both man and blade.

"Pisspot," Alarik called from across the fire. His voice was solemn, and his eyes never left the flames.

"Sir?"

"You know the truth. You know what I did," Alarik continued. "Before we return to Kilgareth and the war that the Order is now embroiled in, we should have a few moments of honesty."

Kyler looked towards his mentor. "You killed the grand master," he said.

"I did," Alarik replied.

"Why?" Kyler asked.

"For the same reason that I joined the legions. For the same reason that I swore my vows to the sun and moon. Duty."

"Duty?" Kyler shook his head in disbelief. "What *duty* commands a man to murder a friend ... a brother?"

"Do not believe that I have taken any joy from it," Alarik told him.

"Then why? Why betray the vows that you swore?"

"My duty comes first to the gods and *then* to my brothers. Do you remember the oath, the words that were instilled in you? We stand as Durandail's sword: a mighty instrument to bring justice to his people and strike down their enemies. We stand as Azaria's shield: to serve all in need and to protect those who cannot protect themselves. Amaris broke these tenets." Alarik ran a hand across the silver of his amulet. "I have served for years in the Order of Kil'kara. I have known Amaris for over a decade, long before he became Delodrysia and took on the mantel of grand master. As the years went by, as the sandglass of time turned, it became readily apparent to me that something was changing Amaris. He saw the Salvaari raids into Medea and he knew of the ruins left when they crossed the river. Unprovoked incursions into the land of our brothers went unpunished. I saw the faces of the slain left in the wake of Salvaar. I saw the ashes that remained of villages. And do you know what Amaris spoke of in quiet moments? *Peace*. The people do not want peace, I told him. They want justice. Often, we had this debate. Sometimes when we were alone, sometimes in the chambers of the Circle. Always it was the same. I did not know what had happened to make him believe that the Salvaari would leave Medea in peace. It is not in their nature."

"I know of the raids," Kyler said. "I was raised hearing the stories about the attacks into the lands of Bailon and Aloys. All that death … all that slaughter."

"The Order of Kil'kara was created to protect pilgrims upon the road to Rovira. From the day that those eight knights founded our creed, we have been warriors. We are knights, we are warriors; we are *supposed* to fight for those in need, regardless of their beliefs. I pleaded with Amaris to let me ride north with the Order and defeat our enemies. I begged him, but he refused. He did not wish to risk the lives of his brothers. He did not wish to spill more blood … our blood. But it was our duty. Our sacred duty. We could not stand idle and leave the Medeans to be butchered."

Kyler frowned. The whetstone stopped its work.

"Why would Amaris not want to help his own people?" Kyler asked. "He who was the blood of Duran Cormac."

"I don't know," Alarik said quietly. "To this day, I do not know. I met Arntair many months ago when we needed to find a new supplier for the maija. I travelled to Elara and sought the merchant out. It was from him that I acquired petals of the bludvier plant. It was from him that I learnt its secrets. It started with small doses sprinkled in Amaris' drink. When we left to find the Spear, it gave me the perfect opportunity to increase the dosage. A chance to kill Amaris and be free of the suspicion that would follow. It worked. At least for a time. I will not ask how you came by information that led you to discover me. You were only doing your duty the same as I."

Kyler pursed his lips. He cursed his loose tongue.

"And so you killed Amaris."

"And so I killed my brother."

"What happens next?" Kyler asked. He kept his hand near his sword. Now that Alarik had revealed his deed in full, he may well turn his blade on his pupil.

"That depends on you, Pisspot," Alarik told him. "You did your duty and that led you to me. What you do with this knowledge … that is up to you. In a few weeks, we will be riding through the gates of Kilgareth. You will have a choice to make. You can report what you have uncovered to the Circle. You can tell them about what I have done. Or you can say nothing. Where does your allegiance lie? Where does your duty lie? That is something that you must decide for yourself."

They rose before the sun. Kyler splashed water across his weary face. He had barely slept, for the nightmares would not leave him in peace. When he was awake, his mind would not be silent.

"Knight!" Alarik called from across the campsite. "Break. Battle."

Kyler looked up to see a training sword flying towards him. He snatched it from the air and stepped back just in time to raise his guard. Alarik's blade came down. Wood sang as the staunches collided.

The knights rode as dawn's light crept over the horizon. Tallis awaited. Kilgareth awaited. Kyler could only pray that he would make his choice before they reached the great fortress. The thought consumed him. If he told the Circle, then Alarik would be excommunicated from the Order and executed. His mentor and friend would die. If he did not, then the killer of his grand master would escape justice.

✦ ✦ ✦

The tunnels beneath Elara echoed with sound, though for the first time, the ruckus was caused by the events unfurling on the streets above. Bhaltair's men, Stentor soldiers and the pirates roamed the streets. No longer did they have to live in the shadows.

After the death of Imrohir, Cleander had escorted Elise from the palace and now led her towards the safety of the chambers underground. Elise felt the sting in her leg grow as they reached the hideaway of Bhaltair's gang. It was only after they were allowed inside that she started to limp. Elise winced as she glanced down at her aching calf. Dry blood tightened skin. She remembered the spear that had grazed her leg when she had taken the belltower.

"You're wounded." Cleander's voice held a tinge of worry.

"A spear in the belltower," Elise replied. "I'm fine."

"Let me see."

"I said I'm fine."

"Let me see," Cleander growled again.

There was no room for compromise. With a sigh, Elise hobbled over to one of the nearby tables and sat upon an empty chair. She pulled her boot from her foot and rolled her pant leg to her knee. A layer of blood ran across the hard muscle of her calf. A thin wound was carved through her skin. It was long but had not cut deep.

"See. It's just a scratch," Elise told him.

Cleander gathered up a water skin and handed it to her. "Tend to the wound," he said.

Elise uncorked the skin and poured the water across her cut. It stung but she had endured far worse pain in recent days. Elise wiped the water and blood from her leg with a scrap of cloth. Cleander knelt before her with a small vial.

"Here," he said. "Hold still." He gently smeared a few drops of ointment upon the cut. "What do you intend?" Cleander asked her.

"Pardon me?"

"As you may recall, I once told you that you had become a symbol to the people," he said as he procured a makeshift bandage.

"I do not want it," Elise shot back. "I will not listen to this again."

"Yes, you will," Cleander snapped. "The days of you slipping back into the shadows may have come to an end. The people know your name now, Elise. There will come a time when they seek you out."

"And as *you* may recall, I am good at hiding my tracks," Elise told him.

Cleander wrapped the bandage around Elise's leg and pulled it tight. "Yes, you are," he replied. "But that was before you escaped your own execution. That was before you took the belltower. That was before we dealt with the magister. You're quickly becoming a legend." Cleander gestured to the Nightingale mask that lay on the bench. "Perhaps even more so than your namesake."

Elise met Cleander's eyes as he stepped back from her. She

pursed her lips and glanced at the mask. "For so long, I have known nothing but darkness. I took up the mask to find answers and instead I found only questions," Elise started. "In the last two years, I have lost my entire family, Cleander. I did not even get to bury my aunt and uncle. From the day that I decided to follow the path that I chose, from the day that I became the Nightingale, I swore to myself that I would not let it change me. That my parents' deaths would not change me. For so long, it didn't. All of the pain, all of the rage – I channelled it into uncovering the man who murdered my mother and father. For a *long* time, I was able to. Until tonight. Until I tried to kill Imrohir. I fear that if I ever put that mask on again, it will consume me. I can feel it in here." Elise placed a hand over her heart. "I cannot put that mask on, Cleander. The Nightingale is dead. Buried."

Cleander did not look away as she spoke. He did not interrupt nor question. "For a long time, I wanted you to step into the role that had created itself. The role that, when it was all said and done, would help the people rebuild Elara. It was a burden that you should never have had to bear but one that you were suited to. There are many among the gangs who would wish to see you as their symbol. I was one of them until tonight," Cleander said. "The dark road that you started on is hard to survive and once you take one step too many, you cannot leave it. I feared that if you killed Imrohir there would have been no turning back. That Elise Delfeyre would have died, her light extinguished. I do not want the darkness to consume you as it has me. And so now I will help you evade those who would use your name for their own desires."

Elise's breath hitched in her throat. She could barely believe it. "What?" she murmured. "You're going to help me?"

"Aye, lady, that I will."

"Thank you," Elise told him sincerely. For so long, she had toiled alone. To have someone offer to stand beside her ... Elise had almost forgotten what that felt like.

The door boomed open.

"Show me where she is," shouted a deeply accented voice.

It was strong. It was loud. It was Berenithian. A pair of gang men tried to hold back the huge dark-skinned man as he pushed his way into the chamber.

"Tariq!" Elise cried and leapt to her feet. She raced across the chamber as Tariq shoved the two men aside. Elise jumped into his arms and was enveloped in a bear hug.

"I'm sorry I left you," she murmured.

"It's alright, Elise, it's alright."

Elise stepped back from her friend and at last saw the second man with him. Unlike Tariq, he wore the steel garb of a soldier, a sidesword swinging at his hip.

"Lady Elise." Captain Marshall gave her a bow.

"It's good to see you, captain," she told him.

"Forgive me, my lady, but I am sworn to protect House Delfeyre," Marshall said. "How can I protect you if I know not where you go?"

"I am sorry, Marshall, but I had something to take care of," Elise replied.

"So I have heard. I must tell you that I do not believe it to be wise," Marshall told her. "Taking down the belltower ... infiltrating the palace. You could have been killed. I swore an oath to your uncle that I would never abandon you and I won't."

"I know you mean well, captain." Elise sighed. "But I am sorry. I did not ask for your oath or your counsel. I had to do what I thought was right, no matter the consequences."

"I have heard those words before but not from you," Tariq said.

"They were my father's," Elise replied sadly. "Once ... a long time ago, he sat me down and told me about the history of our name. It was then that he spoke those words to me."

"Imriel always knew the power of words and a name," Tariq said. "He said that they could give a man strength when there was none."

"That is true now more than ever," Cleander told them as he approached. "Elara has changed hands over night. Lord Stentor is meeting with Bhaltair and the pirate Cillian Teague to decide what Elara's fate shall be."

"What is your intention?" Marshall asked him.

"I don't yet know," Cleander replied honestly. "Once, I had thought to remain in Elara. Now I am not so sure. My fate was never tied to Bhaltair or the gangs. Perhaps it is time to forge my own path. However, I shall wait to hear what the council has decided. The city is caught between three forces who will wish to see us removed. Eventually they will come. We will see sails to the south and armies to the north. We cannot stay here; that much is certain."

"Then we leave," Tariq said.

"Aye," Elise spoke up. "But where to? The other free cities would be all too happy to stretch our necks one by one. If we tried to take a ship, we'd never make it out of the harbour. We will wait for now at least. Underground, we can disappear. Underground, we are free."

✦ ✦ ✦

SIX

Káli Lands, Forest of Salvaar

A rider appeared before them, materialising from the trees like a ghost. Lukas brought his horse to a stop and the column of Káli at his back halted. One-Eye recognised the black paint that the rider wore on his face. He recognised the silver eyes and the powerful warbow that the rider held. Had Lukas and his people been anyone else, they would have become pincushions for arrows a long time ago.

"Well met, Myrdren," Lukas greeted the moonseer in the language of Salvaar.

While with the Salvaari, One-Eye had long since ceased using the common tongue of the west. He used the language of his people only when conversing with the mercenaries who rode with him and when he was forced to talk with his enemies. He clicked his tongue, and his horse began to walk towards the moonseer.

"Lord," Myrdren replied as he angled his mount beside that of Lukas. "How was your hunt?"

"Two dozen more Medeans sent to the afterlife," Lukas told him. "We caught them trying to make the crossing half a day west of here."

"A mistake that they will not soon forget," Maevin added.

"You have a prisoner," Myrdren said as he gestured to the man tied to the back of Hadwin's horse.

"For now," Lukas told him.

"What is your intention?"

"I will meet with Etain tonight," One-Eye replied. "I have questions for this man, and I would assume that she does too."

The first of the tents appeared through the trees. Warriors marked in war paint filled the Salvaari camp. They sharpened steel and fletched arrows. Some tended to horses while others prayed to their spirits. Men and women both. They were all wild. They were all strong. They were all Káli, their clothes as dark as their painted faces. Two hundred warriors in all and they were all pledged to Lukas. One-Eye glanced back at his second.

"Rodion, tell them to break camp," he said. "We ride south."

In times of war, the Salvaari acted as nomads, and as such, they were making their way south within the hour. They moved at speed and with purpose. Myrdren and the other two moonseer had ridden out to watch for the enemy, while Lukas had sent Rodion to warn Etain of their approach. It did not take long before birdsong greeted Lukas' ears. Only it wasn't birdsong. Lukas pursed his lips as he had been taught and whistled. His reply sounded identical to the sound he had echoed. Within moments, green-painted Icari emerged from the trees alongside Rodion. The highland warriors wore thick sashes from shoulder to hip and carried an assortment of vicious weapons. Their faces were calm, yet their eyes were full of danger. The Icari tribe was small, but it had given birth to the greatest warriors among all the Salvaari. They trained in the mountains and used the terrain to grant them endurance over their strongest enemies.

Lukas looked towards the man who rode at Rodion's side and, without a word, unstrapped his helmet. He pushed back his coif and met the Icari's eyes. The rider wore a shirt of chainmail beneath his green and red sash. His thick, orange beard was adorned with braids and a small helmet covered his fiery hair. A shield was slung across the rider's back and he grasped a spear firmly in his hand. The Icari returned Lukas' gesture and pulled his helm from his head. Long, flaming hair fell down the rider's back like a waterfall of fire. Lukas walked his horse over to the Icari and the pair clasped arms.

"Your name precedes you, One-Eye," the Icari told him.

"Then you have me at a disadvantage, brother," Lukas replied.

"I'm Ardor, lord. Chief Etain's second," Ardor said.

"Then take me to her."

They reached the Icari camp as the sun was beginning to fall. Orange rays of light caressed Etain's encampment. There were hundreds of green-painted warriors. All of them watched with curious eyes as the smaller Káli force began to dismount and set up their own camp alongside the Icari. Ardor took Lukas, Hadwin and their prisoner to meet with his chief. Some of the Icari stared at the pair of Annorans as they rode through their midst. The story of One-Eye had travelled far and wide in recent days, yet to see another westerner who had joined the Salvaari cause was strange. They were so used to the idea that it was them against the world that many did not know how to react to the sight of the Annorans.

They found Etain outside her great tent. The chief stood alone, and her emerald eyes were fixed upon the dancing flames of the fire that burned before her. She clasped her hands behind her back. A sword was buckled over her armour of mail and furs. An evergreen cloak hung from her strong shoulders and her muscled arms were bare.

"Lukas the One-Eye is here, my chief," Ardor called out.

"Thank you, Ardor, you may go," Etain said as she turned to face them.

Her second bowed his head and rode away.

"I have a gift, chief," Lukas told her as he dismounted.

He pulled his crutch from his saddle and used it to take the weight from his injured knee. Lukas gestured to his companion who cut the Medean from his saddle and let him crash to the ground. No longer were their arrows in him but the pain remained. The prisoner cried out as he hit the earth.

"You." Lukas indicated the prisoner. "Up."

Hadwin grabbed the man by his arm and heaved him to his feet. Hadwin was on him in an instant. He stepped close to the man's back, drew his knife and swiftly placed it against the Medean's throat.

"Who is this?" Etain asked as she approached.

"A soldier who marches under the banner of Alejandro Aloys," Lukas explained as he placed both hands upon his crutch. "We found him and his people trying to cross the Arwan."

Etain stepped before the prisoner and extended a hand. She tilted his chin up and met his eyes.

"What is your name?"

He said nothing. Hadwin drew the knife closer and let the steel kiss the Medean's skin.

"Your name," One-Eye growled.

"Vincente." The prisoner grimaced.

"Vincente," Etain echoed. "I have a question for you, and you will do your best to answer it."

"Why would I do that, heathen?" the Medean snarled.

"If you wish to see your home again, then you will answer me," Etain said as she glared at the man.

Vincente said nothing. Lukas watched him slump ever so slightly. He was resigned.

"Days ago, when your people joined the battle, were you with the riders?" Etain asked.

"Yes," Vincente said through bared teeth.

"Did you pursue us into the forest?"

"Yes."

"A man stood against you. He was Aedei marked in the blue

woad of his people," Etain explained. "He rallied some of my people to hold back yours. He wore a golden torc."

"Yes, I remember."

"What happened to those who stood against you?"

"We cut them down," Vincente replied. "Some we captured."

"And the man?" Lukas asked. "The one with the golden torc."

"Santiago Caspin has him."

"You're sure?" Etain said.

"I saw him dragged away in chains," Vincente told them.

"What happened to him?" One-Eye watched him closely.

"I don't know."

"What happened?" Lukas repeated.

"That's all I know," came the growled response.

Lukas could see the truth in Vincente's face. He could hear it in his voice. The Medean was not lying. He was just a soldier and would not be privy to the conversations and decisions of his betters. Lukas looked to Etain and caught her gaze. "There is no lie in his eyes," he said in Salvaari.

Etain did not acknowledge his words and instead turned to Hadwin.

"Take him away," she told the mercenary.

Hadwin gave her a bow before shoving Vincente back whence they had come. He sheathed his knife and drew his sword. Hadwin pressed the cold steel into Vincente's back as he gathered up his horse's reins. He walked a few steps behind the prisoner as he directed Vincente towards the Káli camp.

"So Cailean is alive," Etain said at last.

"They will keep him in chains," Lukas replied. "He will be kept as a hostage, though he will not be used to bargain."

"How do you know this?" Etain asked. "They have not come to take our land and burn our homes. They have come for us. For my people. Why would they keep him alive if all they want is our death?"

"Because my brother leads them," Lukas explained. "If it were anyone else … If Darius was still alive, then Cailean would never have lived to see the sun rise again. But Dayne is different. He is not one to so lightly throw away an advantage. The prisoners will be moved to Kilgareth where they will be beyond reach. Of that I am most certain."

Etain crossed her arms. Her brow furrowed slightly as she thought.

"Then we wait," Etain said. "We bide our time. We stand against our enemy and when the time is right, when opportunity presents itself, we will go for Cailean."

"What of Henghis?" Lukas asked.

"My cousin has spread our forces along the river. The Coventina has ridden out to reinforce the Belcar and Niavenn. Henghis is strong and his will unbreakable. If anyone can stand against the west … if anyone can defeat them, it is him."

"I hope that you're right," Lukas replied.

"We do not know what the spirits will, Lukas," Etain said. "Only that they will not abandon us. Not now. Have faith. Have faith in them. Have faith in us."

One-Eye ran a hand across the arm ring that Vaylin had given him. For the first time, he had someone to believe in. He had *something* to believe in.

"I do," he said.

"Vaylin chose well," Etain told him. "When she gave you that ring. When she gave you her people to command. She chose well."

"In time, I pray that I will have the chance to earn the trust that she has given me," Lukas replied.

"I have no doubt."

"Come morning, my people will break camp," One-Eye told the chief. "We will make our leave."

"Where will you go?" the chief asked.

"I plan to head further south. We may be able to slip through their lines and raid along the frontier. If there is a chance to get my brother to have one eye fixed upon us, then perhaps there will be a chance for Henghis to achieve victory in battle."

"Then may Sylvaine watch over you," Etain said and held out her arm.

Lukas took it. "I promise you. If there is a chance that I can free Cailean, then I will. No matter the cost."

✦ ✦ ✦

"King Erik," Jarl Ulfric called as he pushed his way through the doors of the king's longhall.

All eyes turned to the old jarl. Erik could see the look upon Ulfric's face. He could see it in his eyes. Fear.

"What is it, Ulfric? What have you seen?" Erik asked.

"Sails on the horizon," Ulfric shouted.

"The empire?" Erik said as he strode towards the man.

They were already here. All his plans had been for nothing. They had no time to leave and had received barely a few days to prepare their defences.

"Not the empire." Ulfric shook his head.

"Then what is it? Who is it?" Erik asked as confusion furrowed his brow.

"One ship," the jarl said. "It comes from the east. It bears green sails."

Erik looked from face to face of all those gathered within the hall. They all looked as confused as their companions.

"Green sails?" Torben asked.

"That is no imperial ship nor is it from the colonies," Fargrim added.

Erik turned back to his chair and snatched up his axe belt. He strapped it on.

"Sound the alarm," he commanded. "Get ships in the water and assemble warriors at the bay. If they have come for a fight, then they will get one."

Erik stared out over the bay as the ship angled towards a pier. Four Valkir ships crawling with raiders watched it warily as if they were daring it to attack. Erik was clad head to toe in his scaled lamellar armour. A great helm covered his head, and his red raven shield was slung across his back. His right hand rested dangerously upon the pommel of his sword. The king's eyes did not leave the ship with emerald sails. The vessel bore the figurehead of a winged dragon. Erik could see figures scurrying through the rigging while others stared back towards him from the prow. The ship was triple-masted, yet Erik had not seen its likeness before.

The ship made port and was swiftly tied off. The sails were furled, and two figures descended from the deck. One was male. His body was strong and his eyes eaglelike. He wore a brigandine over a loose white shirt and dark trousers. A long Dao sword hung from his hip. He was foreign, that much was certain. A brilliant emerald sash adorned his waist. It was the only similarity that he shared with the woman at his side. A small green pin sat upon the black tricorn atop her head. The hat shrouded her features in shadow. A wave of dark brown hair tumbled down her shoulders and back. An ebony shoulder cape trimmed in emerald was tied over her left side, while an equally black vest all but hid the chainmail beneath. Rings of silver, jade and emerald covered her hands, and her shirt was the colour of moss. She wore black bracers and thick black leather boots. The wide belt that was buckled around her sash held a broad-bladed sidesword over her left hip and a dagger over her right. The knife's pommel was imbued with jade. Had she borne no weapons, Erik could have told from her poise that she was a warrior. She carried herself with pride and great strength.

"Who are you to arrive unannounced?" Erik called out.

"I am Luana Marquez," the woman replied. Her voice was accented and bore a resemblance to the graceful tones of Medea. "Captain of the Emeralis. This is Calvillo of Tarik."

"I will ask you again," Erik answered. "Who are you?"

"We are from Lamrei, although we sailed from Elara, if that is what you mean," Luana replied smoothly.

"If you made port in Elara, then you are *with* the empire," Erik growled. His hand tightened upon his sword.

"We *took* Elara," Luana told Erik. The captain pulled her tricorn from her head, revealing the dark green bandana that wrapped around her hair. Beads were tied through her locks and her eyes shone green like grass brought back to life after winter. There were rings in her ears and a slight curl tugged upon the corner of her lips.

"You took Elara?" Torben growled in disbelief.

"Aye," Luana replied. "I sailed at the head of a great pirate fleet with Cillian Teague and together we ripped the city from the hands of its magister. Imrohir is dead."

Erik unstrapped his helmet and handed it to Torben. "Then you are most welcome," he said. "I am Erik Farrin."

"And I take it that you are the earl?"

"No," Jarl Ulfric said. "He is king now. King Erik Farrin. The first king of the Valkir."

If Luana Marquez was surprised, then she did not show it. She met Erik's eyes. "Well then, King Erik, I bring word from Captain Cillian Teague. There are things that we should discuss."

Erik watched her eyes closely. There was a shadow in Luana's gaze. A shadow that the captain had tried to hide yet could not fully shroud.

"Your people have had a long voyage, Captain Marquez. The hospitality of Agartha is theirs," Erik told her. He gestured to Ulfric as he continued, "Jarl Ulfric will see to it."

Luana nodded her thanks.

"Walk with me," Erik told her. "We can talk further in my hall."

✦ ✦ ✦

SEVEN

Coast of Aureia, The Mithramir Sea

Beneath the light of the sun, a pair of ships sliced through the calm waters of the Mithramir. Both had three masts filled with massive sails. Both were merchant ships that once carried great loads of silks, furs, jewels and other trade goods. Now the Tanith carried horses, while the Despoina had a cargo of mercenaries. Kitara watched from the bowsprit as gentle waves kissed the hull of the Despoina. The wind raced through her hair that tumbled down her shoulders in a golden wave. A pair of small braids hung over her left ear. Instead of the cuirass, armour and soiled tunic that she had once worn in the arena, Kitara was now clad in a midnight blue shirt with elbow-length sleeves. Her trousers were black and her swordbelt was tightly bound around her waist. She closed her eyes to the lullaby of the ocean and breathed in its salty breath.

"The captain says that we should pass into Larissan waters by nightfall," Aeryn said as she approached.

Kitara did not look from the water. "I've missed this," she said as she watched the waves. "The sea breeze upon my skin, the taste of the ocean, the caress of the wind through my hair ... all of it."

"How long has it been?" Aeryn asked as she leaned on the railing beside Kitara.

"Six summers," Kitara told her. "I was eighteen when last I sailed aboard the Emeralis. This, here, now ... it's a taste of a past life."

"The taste of home."

"Yes," Kitara said quietly, "and no. Part of me will always belong to the sea, yet now my heart longs for forests and rivers, for mountains and the song of my people."

"Salvaar calls to you just as it does me," Aeryn replied. "It is in your blood. Your mother's blood."

"I never knew her," Kitara said as she stroked her mother's sapphire ring. "I never heard her voice or saw her face. Yet sometimes I think of her. I imagine what she looked like, what she sounded like. Is that strange? I do not even know her name."

"Speak to Bellec," Aeryn told her. "His words will paint a picture of your mother."

"I do not know." Kitara pursed her lips. She was torn about him just as she always had been. Since before they had met in that tavern in Miera. So much had changed and yet nothing was different.

"Your father is a good man," Aeryn said. "He loves you dearly. He always has."

Kitara gritted her teeth. She was afraid of no one. She was afraid of nothing. But the thought of a conversation with Bellec terrified her.

"Talk to him," Aeryn said and gestured towards the mercenary captain.

At last, Kitara nodded. She bit back a grimace as she clapped Aeryn on the shoulder and turned towards Bellec. Kitara took a breath as she crossed the deck towards where her father sat with Galadayne. Memories filled her mind as emotions churned within. She buried them all. The two mercenaries looked up as she made her approach. Words died on their lips. Kitara looked at Bellec. She stared into his dark eyes. "We should talk," she said.

"Of course," Bellec replied.

The mercenary captain glanced at his companion and that was enough. Galadayne rose from the barrel upon which he was seated and strode away.

"How are you?" Bellec asked as Kitara sat beside him.

"Cuts and scrapes. Nothing that won't heal," she replied. "I did not expect to see you again."

"I would *never* abandon you," he told her.

Kitara snorted. "You did once before," she said.

"That is not true."

"I grew up lost and alone. I grew up in a den of thieves and liars. I had no one. *No one.*"

"I tried to find you," Bellec told her desperately. "I tried."

"Then help me to understand," Kitara pleaded.

Bellec brushed a ring that adorned his left hand. A ring embellished with a small sapphire. "I met your mother many years ago," he began. "At the time, I served as a captain in the Aethelan royal guard. I worked closely with King Dorian and his brother, Lord Eldred. A year into the war, Dorian wanted to sue for peace. He sent me as his ambassador. I stayed with the Aedei for some time. Learnt their culture, learnt their customs and learnt their tongue. I was with them for the great festival of Sylvaine."

"It is a beautiful thing when the heavens are painted with violet light," Kitara murmured as she remembered. "The druids; they came to me."

"You were chosen the same as I once was," Bellec continued. "When first we met, it was a few days before the druids came to me. A few days before the changing."

"What was she like?" Kitara asked.

"She was the sun," Bellec murmured. "She had golden hair. I ... I could see the fire in her eyes and hear the songs in her voice. She was as pure as dawn's first light yet as wild and strong as a winter storm. She came to me one night when the sky was Sylvaine's canvas. It was the first time we met. We walked through the woods until I was lost. We told each other stories, we sang and danced beneath the light of the moon ... We loved. We were kindred spirits, she and I."

"What was her name?"

"Her name was Oriana, but when I first met her, she was called Sylvaine."

Kitara's eyes widened as she heard the name. "What did you say?" she breathed. Sylvaine, the First Woman, Great Queen of the spirits had chosen Bellec.

"She was Sylvaine," Bellec repeated quietly. "For five long years, she served as a vessel for the Great Queen. For five years, she had carried a great burden. The night that we met she did not come to me as Oriana ... she had not *been* Oriana. It was as the Great Queen. When a Belcar girl took the mantle from her, it was I who stayed by Oriana's side. It was I who helped her, I who tended to her, I who healed her. Being the vessel takes a toll, and for so long it had consumed her. Oriana was kind. She was wild and free. She was brave. We fell in love. Oriana started to accompany me on my diplomatic missions between Annora and the tribes. With her knowledge of the Salvaari and with the regard in which they held her, we began to make some headway. After she became pregnant, we were married in secret. Only a few of the Aedei knew of the ceremony for it was too much of a risk to tell my own people. We began to make plans for when the war was over. We would make a house and raise our child ... raise you. And then our world was shattered. Prince Eldred and a company of his men rode to meet with Chief Raywold of the Aedei. They talked and made peace. Eldred took a secret route back to the Aethelan camp. A route that few among us knew. On his return, the riders were ambushed. An enemy, whoever it was, found them. To this day I do not know how. Raywold sent a man to warn me. Through him I learnt that one of Eldred's men had survived long enough to reach King Balinor's camp. Through him I learnt that the ambush and its blame had fallen upon me. They said that I was its architect, that I had sent Lord Eldred to his death. King Dorian sent riders for me. I was named an outlaw and a traitor. I was banished from my country and marked for death. We had no choice but to flee. In the escape, I was wounded."

"Where did you go?" Kitara asked her father.

"Medea for a time," Bellec told her. "We found refuge with a healer in Sevillona. Her name was Belladona. She would not let us leave until my injuries had healed. I grew strong. I learnt her trade, and for some time it appeared as though we had escaped the clutches of Dorian. But we were betrayed, and the king's dogs found us. One day, Oriana went to gather plants from the nearby hills. She never returned. Then they came for me. I killed them … all but one. He told me that they had taken Oriana, that they had taken the woman that I loved. Dorian ordered her to be taken to the coast and sold into slavery. More soldiers came and I had no time to fight. Belladona sacrificed herself to give me the chance to escape … She gave her life so that I lived to find Oriana. I tracked them to the coast, but it was too late. Oriana and the ship that carried her was gone. The men who had captured her did not know of the ship's destination, so in my anger, I slaughtered them. I killed the harbour master and many others. When at last more of Dorian's dogs found me, I was enraged. I was fighting in a battle that I could not win. I was wounded, outnumbered and without hope.

"And then Galadayne found me. With him were a dozen of the royal guardsmen. They joined my side, and we won our way free. I left the name Theron Malley behind, and I took the name Bellec in honour of the woman who had given her life for mine. We searched for Oriana and my child for fifteen years … fifteen years. We followed every whisper of a story no matter how impossible it was. We crossed the breadth of the empire and used the spy network in Eonie. We scoured the mountains of Berenithia and the desert sands of Larissa. We spent time with the Valkir and rode with the horsemen Miera. In time, we returned to Medea with nothing. We had found not a trace of Oriana or the child that she had carried. We began to deal in the only trade that we knew: that of blood. We earned honour, reputation and a great deal of gold … yet none of it would ever fill the void. Over two decades had passed when we heard a tale of the golden-haired woman in Miera. A woman who used a sword and had Salvaari blood in her veins. It was a faint hope, a fool's hope, but still we rode out. It was then that our paths crossed in Chausac. I knew who you were from the moment I saw your face. You look just like her … just like your mother."

Kitara stared down at her mother's ring. The sun kissed the blue and danced across its surface like sapphire fire. She wasn't sure what to feel. Her mind was blank, but it wasn't a peaceful emptiness. "Why did you not tell me?" she murmured.

"You did not trust even those men whom you rode with. If I had approached you with tales of the past, tales of your mother … had I said who I was, what would you have done?" Bellec met her eyes as he spoke.

"I don't know," Kitara replied honestly.

"Judging by your reaction when Prince Lukas told you who I was, I would suggest that the news would not have been well received," Bellec continued. "I intended to win your trust and in time tell you my real name. To tell you why I stepped between you and the Mierans. To tell you why I took your cause as my own. And then you were taken. I would never have abandoned you, Kitara, never."

"I was wrong about you," Kitara told him. The words were strained; they caught in her throat. "About everything."

"You weren't to know."

"I don't trust … I can't trust and that has kept me alive," Kitara said. "I cannot give you that, Theron. Not yet."

"I understand," Bellec replied. There was a hint of sadness in his voice, but he would not press it. Bellec nodded towards Aeryn as he spoke. "You trust her, don't you?"

"She might be the only person in the world whom I trust. The only one who knows where I come from, who knows what I have suffered. Do … do you know what it is like aboard a ship in the heart of winter? Now imagine it behind bars on deck. No shelter from the ice and snow. That is where this lifetime of horrors began."

"How did you survive?" Bellec asked.

"I learnt the sword, I learnt to lie, I learnt to watch my back, yet there was something else," Kitara began. "Something that kept me moving forward when everything was lost. You know, there were times that I thought about leaving. Times when I dreamt about finding a boat and sailing away. I dreamt about tracking the man who had abandoned my mother and I, the man who had set us upon our fate. I dreamt about finding the man who had no face or voice. I dreamt about putting my blade to his throat … Dreamt about telling him how much I had lost, about how much I *hated* him. I dreamt about killing him. About killing *you*. It was that dream that kept me alive; it was that dream that allowed me to survive. That hatred."

"I'm sorry," Bellec said softly. "I know that it will never be enough, but I am sorry."

Kitara could see the sorrow in his eyes. The pain. Every word that he had told her had been true. It was an honesty that she had only ever experienced with one person before: Aeryn. Now it came from her father as well. A man whom for so long she had hardened her heart against. A man whom she had blamed for everything. Bellec hesitantly extended a hand and reached for hers. Kitara flinched back as if she had been struck, an instinct that she had developed so long ago. Kitara glanced at her father's hand and then took it. His skin was like her own: calloused and hard from a lifetime of fighting. She could feel Bellec's story on the back of his hand. His truth. His torment. Kitara stared into his eyes for a moment. She prayed that he could not see how torn she was, prayed that he could not see the war that was being fought within her heart. Then

Kitara left. She released his hand as she walked away. She had no words. She had nothing.

Kitara pulled her hair away from her face and tied it all back save for her twin braids. She unbuckled her swordbelt and drew her blade. Flickering lamp light caressed the steel as she freed it from her scabbard. She stood alone in the hold of the Despoina; alone save for her sword. She needed time to herself, time to clear her thoughts after what Bellec had told her. Kitara placed her belt to the side and closed her eyes. She took a long breath and let her emotions leave as she breathed out. Kitara's body knew the positions and moves before she had even thought of them. She moved slowly at first. Her feet slid atop the wooden flooring. The steel came up and then it began to dance. Kitara was slow and her form perfect. Each position had been practised thousands of times. Each position was natural. Kitara started to move faster. Her sword sang as it carved a path through the air. She spun and twirled with the grace and skill of a dancer. Her feet were light upon the ground. It had been so long since she had danced with her sword and yet it was if they had never been parted.

✦ ✦ ✦

Earth and dust filled the air as the rider sped across the plains. After nearly a week in the saddle, the Mieran capital Carlian arose before Silas Barangir. Great stone walls cocooned the city, while phoenix banners flew above. Silas rode through Carlian's gates and made haste towards the palace. Soldiers took his horse as he was escorted into the labyrinth of stone.

Silas paid no attention to the bare walls and chambers of the palace as he was led through them. Zoran and all the kings that had come before were warriors first and foremost. They cared not for embellishment or decoration. The clash of steel greeted Silas as the doors to the throne room were opened for him. Nobles stood in a wide square. To outsiders, they would have appeared as no more than warriors. They carried swords at their sides and wore fierce expressions. To a man, they were clad in armour with faded red cloaks hanging from their shoulders. The only decorations that they bore were the rings in their left ears.

Swords sang as two men fought for advantage in the centre of the square. They were both shirtless and covered in strong muscle. Both men carried longswords and round shields. The taller man had a large beard to match his long hair. He stood as a great bear. The smaller man had a shorter beard and fierce eyes. Though his left ear was adorned with golden rings, a single ruby-inlaid band hung from his right. He appeared as a wolf.

Silas said nothing as he watched the contest. The two men danced back and forth as they exchanged blows. How long the fight had been going, Silas did not know. Both men were masters of their craft. They moved fast and every blow was swung with precision and intent. The smaller man deflected his opponent's sword with his shield even as he leapt forward. His blade came up and then darted forward over the taller man's shield. The sword tasted blood as it sliced its victim's cheek. The nobles roared. Then it was over. The duel had been to first blood. The wolflike man glanced at his wounded foe.

"Three thousand riders are to make for the northern border at once," he commanded.

"Yes, my king," one of the nobles answered and strode from the room.

Silas allowed a smirk as he watched King Zoran turn to the defeated man.

"Well fought, brother," the king told the man.

"I nearly had you."

Zoran grinned as he handed his sword to one of the nobles and unstrapped his shield. "Nearly."

"Silas Barangir is here from the north, my king," Silas' escort called out.

"Azrial Dathmir sent me with tidings, my king," Silas spoke up.

King Zoran nodded as he took his sword back. "This way," the king said as he turned towards the back of the chamber.

Silas followed Zoran from the throne room and into a smaller chamber beyond. The king placed his sword upon a round table and turned to Silas.

"Lord Acrasia wished for those riders to remain in Carlian. He believes that a storm is gathering all around us and that we must be prepared to send soldiers to whatever border requires them the most when it breaks," Zoran told him. "I disagreed. The north has always been the heart of Miera. I have this feeling in my bones that the storm is about to break in the north, and so it was my wish to send them there. We settled it in the way that all true disagreements should be settled. Traditions are important, are they not?"

"They remind us of those who came before," Silas agreed. "Our heritage is all important."

"You bring word from Azrial."

"Yes, my king," Silas told him. "As you know, some time ago we learnt that the kingdoms of the west had marshalled their armies and were descending upon Salvaar. They met upon the fields of Bandujar. There was a great battle. The tribesmen were defeated and now King Dayne and his people prepare to march into the forest."

"I had a feeling that such a fight was brewing," King Zoran said as he pulled on a shirt. "I received word that a company of griffin bearers had ridden into the Rift and were raiding the Salvaari border. This war ... it draws near."

"The Aureian horsemen engaged the Belcar and Niavenn and prevented them from joining the great battle," Silas said. "Thousands fell on that field. The full might of Annora has joined forces with the duchies of Medea and the imperial legions. The

Order of Kil'kara has mobilised and lotus bearers of Larissa ride with Aureia along the Rift, burning as they go. This is no mere army. This is an invasion."

Zoran glanced at a stand at the back of the chamber. It was adorned with the king's armour. Chainmail and plate covered the stand. A phoenix was carved upon the chest piece and a mane of fiery hair created the helmet.

"When one city, one nation, falls to the empire, more follow. This has always been the way," Zoran muttered. "Our people will prepare. They will be ready to fight and bleed and die if called upon. Tell your father to sharpen his blade and await my call. This council may be in need of Zandir's voice once again."

✦ ✦ ✦

EIGHT

City of Bandujar, Duchy of Aloys, Medea

Sir Hugh Karter slowly moved through the sword dance. His form was neat and precise, and his movements flowed like water. He wore nothing more than his blue gambeson and loose trousers. It had been months since the Sword of Kil'kara and acting grand master Sir Corvo Alaine had taken him under his wing. Every waking moment that the acting master had to spare was spent turning an already gifted warrior into a true swordsman. His training had been a trial by fire. As an initiate, he had sparred solely with other recruits. As Sir Corvo's apprentice, he had fought against veteran knights with sword, shield and spear. He trained on both horse and foot. He learnt fighting techniques from Larissa, Berenithia and Aureia. He learnt styles of fighting from the Valkir Isles and forms from Tarik. If there was a way to fight, then Corvo knew it and readily passed it on to his apprentice. It had been hard, especially at first, but Hugh had revelled in the challenge. These new skills had served him well upon the fields of Bandujar. Many of the heathen Salvaari had been slain by his hand, and when at last the bloodshed had concluded, Hugh had known in his heart that the sword was his destiny.

"Faster," Sir Corvo ordered.

Hugh obeyed on instinct. His longsword whistled as it cut through the air. He lunged forward, moving across the grassy field.

His feet grazed the earth and then he pivoted. His hips moved and his wrists flicked. Hugh's blade came around as he turned. Steel sped around and then came down.

"What is the purpose of the Tariki sword dance?" Corvo asked.

"It serves a dual purpose, master," Hugh replied as he moved. "It refines technique. Moulds it. Perfects it. It also teaches one to move like water. To flow from one form into the next without thought, so that in the fire of battle, one has command over both mind and body."

"Precisely," Corvo said as he walked in slow circles around his apprentice. "To be water is the Tariki way. When you pour water into a bowl, it becomes a bowl. Adapt to everything. Flow like a gentle river and then crash upon your enemy with the fury of a mighty wave. Be calm. Fight without emotion. Don't rush. Don't hesitate. Use your instincts. Learn to think ahead. Anticipate your opponent's move and surprise him."

"Yes, master," Hugh said. He flowed as his mentor spoke and effortlessly glided from pose to pose.

"Set your foundation strong and you will not be toppled."

"Yes, master."

"Where were you first prepared to serve the order?" Corvo growled.

"In my heart," Hugh answered as he brought his sword around.

"Where was your heart tested?"

"Upon the fields of Bandujar."

"And where does your path now lead?"

"Victory."

"Say it louder," Corvo snarled.

"Victory!"

"*Mean it!*"

"VICTORY!"

Hugh thrust out his sword. Sunlight danced along steel. A bead of sweat rolled down his brow. He held his form and composed his breath.

"Good," Corvo told him. The acting master clamped a hand on his apprentice's shoulder and met his eyes. "You proved yourself worthy in battle, Hugh. You revealed your soul to the gods and they in turn saw fit to guide you," he said. "Never forget that."

"I won't, master," Hugh replied.

When Corvo had first told him that he was to become his apprentice, Hugh had never been so proud. He had been elated. For the first time in his life, he was able to walk a path that he had chosen. A path far from the reach of his father, the same man who had banished him from his home.

"Pack your things," Corvo commanded. "We are to break camp."

Hugh sheathed his sword and gave his mentor and inquisitive glance. "Where do we ride?" he asked.

"Verena. The northern outpost of our order will serve as a staging ground for this war. While the men of Bailon, Aloys and Salazar remain here to entrench themselves along the border, we shall gather our strength along with House Reyna. King Dayne has a strategy, I am sure."

"The gods are with him," Hugh replied. "With us."

"Prepare yourself," Corvo said. "Join your brothers and meet Grand Master Bavarian at the south of the camp. I will find you then."

"Yes, master."

✦ ✦ ✦

It took the better part of a week for the walls of Tallis to appear before the knights. They pushed their horses hard and did not stop for respite, only for sleep. By the time they reached the city, both man and beast were weary, yet neither of the two men complained.

"We do not have time to rest here tonight," Alarik said as they approached the city gates. "We will charter a ship to Annora and from there it is a straight ride north to Kilgareth."

"Why not travel through Miera as we once did?" Kyler asked.

"When we rode through the steppe, the horsemen were ignorant of the storm that was about to break," the battlemaster explained. "Miera under the threat of war is an entirely different animal altogether. If we attempt the crossing now, I fear the horsemen may not be so willing to let us pass, even with the brand of their king."

It made sense. The Mierans were not known for their forgiving nature or their willingness to accept outsiders. In times of peace, making the crossing without aid was almost certainly a death wish. In times of war, it was impossible. Two men could not fight an army.

"To the port then," Kyler said.

Alarik shook his head. "Not yet," the battlemaster replied as he angled his horse towards the centre of the city. "Follow me."

Kyler could not help but stare as they travelled through the streets of Tallis. Soldiers filled the streets. Not just men of Tallis but mercenaries from all corners of the empire and beyond. Some were mounted whereas others walked on foot. All made haste towards their destinations with purpose. Tallis was preparing for war.

"The people are frightened," Kyler murmured as he watched the commoners scurry through the town.

"Can you blame them?" Alarik replied. "Tallis and Kiriador are strong, but Elara was always the heart of the League. Refugees will have arrived and brought fear with them. These are desperate people."

A thunder of hooves cleared the street and a dozen riders galloped past. They were clad in armour of mail and plate with shields slung across their backs and long spears in their hands.

"Soldiers, mercenaries … When last we travelled through Tallis, there were not so many," Kyler stated.

"Aye," Alarik said. "Judging by their number, Magister Calaval must have received word some days ago about the attack on Elara. Imrohir must have sent messengers before the fall."

"If Tallis is preparing then Kiriador will be as well," Kyler said. "There will be no shortage of volunteers from the free cities. When one goes to war, they *all* go to war. Before the next moon, Elara will be back in the hands of the people, where it belongs."

The knights followed the busy streets for a time and then passed beneath the gate of the arsenal. Soldiers carrying halberds and shields bearing the triple moon of Tallis watched all comers warily. Massive warships filled the arsenal docks, while the buildings that filled the inner sanctum were blacksmiths, stables, armouries and barracks.

Sir Alarik led the way through the paved roads to the stone walls that surrounded the towering city palace. The soldiers that manned the gate stared at the riders as they approached. Men atop the gatehouse watched with cold eyes as they held vicious crossbows at the ready. No doubt the men before them appeared as little more than a pair of mercenaries.

"Hold there," called one of the gate guards as the riders approached.

Alarik reached into one of his saddlebags and withdrew a small scroll. He extended it towards the soldier. "Sir Alarik, battlemaster of the Order of Kil'kara," he told the guard. "My companion is Sir Kyler Landrey. We seek an audience with your master, Magister Calaval."

The guard squinted as he read the contents of the scroll. "You do not bear the colours of your order," he said.

"Our path did not permit it," Alarik explained.

The guard handed the scroll back. "Right you are, sir knight," he replied and gestured for the riders to pass through the gates.

"Light of the gods be with you, brother," Kyler said as they continued on their way.

"And with you, sirs." The guard offered a curt nod.

The knights rode into a courtyard of stone. The statue of

a mounted rider stood in the centre of the square. He wore magnificent armour, and his cloak was so well carved that it appeared as cloth. His right hand held aloft a silver griffin standard, while his left bore a scroll.

"General Tallion of Aureia," Alarik explained as Kyler stared at the statue. "It was he who led the expedition east and founded the colonies. Tallion served as the first magister of this city."

The knights dismounted and stableboys came to take their horses. They were met at the stairs to the palace by a company of the magister's soldiers.

"My lords," the first soldier said as he nodded to them. "Your weapons."

Alarik shared a glance with his companion. Kyler could see some amusement in his mentor's eyes. He unslung his shield before handing it to one of the soldiers. His swordbelt came next.

"Careful with that," Kyler told the guard with a smirk as he extended his sheathed blade.

"My men tell me that you are Knights of Kil'kara," Magister Calaval addressed the companions.

The man before them was strong, proud and clean shaven. Like all men of his rank, Calaval had been required to serve in the legions for ten years before taking up his mantle. The habits that had been instilled in the Aureian military often remained with the magisters, and as such, Calaval, like many of his brethren, still trained with sword and shield.

"That we are, lord," Alarik replied and placed a fist over his heart in salute. "Sir Alarik Sindra. I serve the Twins as Kilgareth's battlemaster."

"Sir Kyler Landrey," Kyler said and gave a salute.

"My father raised me on the great stories of heroism of your order," Calaval told them as he returned the gesture. "You are welcome in my city and hearth for as long as you require."

"You have our gratitude," Alarik replied.

"Forgive me, Sir Alarik, but your armour … It does not bear the mark of your creed."

"I apologise for the deception, lord, but we did not travel with our colours."

"Tell me. What brings the knights of the sun and moon this far east?" Calaval asked.

"We had important business to settle on our order's behalf," Alarik said. He met the magister's stare. Alarik was not to be pressed on the matter.

"I see," Calaval said after a moment. "What can I do for you?"

"Our business took us to Elara. We were there when it fell," the battlemaster replied.

"You were there at the end?"

"Yes, my lord," Kyler said. "We fought against the invaders in the tunnels beneath Elara. When we returned to the surface, the arsenal had been breached."

"Our road leads back to our order, yet we have information that may prove an asset for you," Alarik said.

"Magister Imrohir sent birds when his palace was under siege," Calaval replied. "The writing said that a great army had appeared from below as a dread fleet of pirates arrived from the south."

Alarik clasped his hands behind his back. "The army that he spoke of was comprised of soldiers under the employ of rebellious nobles, namely Priamos Stentor, along with pirates and the gangmen that led them through the underground," the battlemaster said. "Imrohir was taken by surprise. It was a slaughter."

"He was betrayed by the very city that he led," Kyler added bitterly.

"They took the gates and lower city first," Alarik said. "They attacked the walls of the arsenal and laid siege to the heart of the city. A diversion. A second force slipped inside and took the belltower unnoticed. By the time that the magister's men saw the fleet, it was too late. The ships were already in the harbour. The pirates cut off the retreat to the palace while the arsenal gates were breached. Few made it back to the keep."

"That was the last we heard," Kyler finished.

Calaval turned and glanced towards his throne. Behind it hung the three banners of the three cities. The centre one bore the triple moon of Tallis. The banner to the left displayed the eclipsed sun emblazoned upon a sea of ebony belonging to Kiriador. The third flag to which Calaval looked held the image of a fragmented silver star over a field of black and gold. Elara's symbol.

"Tell me everything," Calaval growled.

"Priamos Stentor is the man who stands at the forefront of the attack. He was on the council, and from there the alliance gained a leader with knowledge and an insight into the corridors of power," Alarik told him. "Yet Stentor is only one of the heads belonging to this beast. I do not know who leads the gangs, who united them in common cause, only that his reach is long. Whoever that man is, he is fed information by inns, spies and whores. There is one who may interest you. Her name is Mellisanthi."

"Mellisanthi?" Calaval did not turn from the banners.

"Her establishment has close ties to the gangs," Kyler told him. "She works with them. Uses her girls to gather information and then passes it on to a man named Cleander."

"Yet there is one name above all else," Alarik said. "One name that you should concern yourself with. A name whose owner was the architect of this attack. Cillian Teague."

"Teague?" Calaval murmured. "A madman turned traitor. No more than a common pirate."

"A pirate, yes, but he is no common man," Alarik replied. "I was a young man when I joined the silver legions. It had been barely three years since Teague had turned his back on the empire. Barely three years since he had returned from the south. The stories that he had spoken of upon his return were too mad to be true, yet even at his young age, his reputation from before … that cannot be ignored. He knows the empire, my lord. Knows its ways, knows its secrets. Do not underestimate the man who brought Elara to its knees."

"You served in the legion?" Calaval asked as he turned to face the battlemaster.

"For over a decade, lord," Alarik replied.

"Now you stand as one of Durandail's executioners."

"By his will, yes."

"And all those years of bloodshed, have they honed your mind, priest?" Calaval inquired.

Kyler glanced at his mentor. Upon being granted knighthood, the men of Kil'kara also attained the position of priest, though that title was rarely used.

"Being tested in the theatre of war has given me perspective."

"Then what would you do, sir knight, if you were in my place?" Calaval asked.

Alarik pursed his lips. "You do not stand alone in this fight," he said. "You have your armies, you have the men of Kiriador and you have the Elaran fleet at your disposal. You have the position to muster an army more deadly than any that the free cities have ever seen. You can take the city and kill the men who have claimed her. Nobles such as Stentor lose power when they are defeated upon the field. People such as Mellisanthi can be discredited. Elara will be yours again and those who took her slain. Yet you *cannot* win this war until you cut off the head of the snake. Until you kill Cillian Teague and his equal within the gangs. Do that and they will go back to fighting amongst themselves. Do that and you will have victory."

Calaval looked at the knight thoughtfully. Kyler could see the man's mind at work as he mulled the words over.

"I thank you for your counsel," Calaval said. "When Imrohir sent word, he did not just write to me but to Magister Vander of

Kiriador and to Commander Javais. Our plan is already in motion. We will reclaim Elara and see an end to those who tore her from the League. Gods willing, the city will be restored by the next full moon."

"The free cities must stand together. They must be strong. Now more than always," Alarik replied.

"When Tallis was born, Elara and Kiriador soon followed," Calaval told them. "They were united not just by their people but by a common cause. Nothing of that magnitude had been done before. Three great cities forged from nothing but the hands of the people who live there. Can you imagine anything more magnificent? Tallion and his fellow magisters swore a vow that if one of the cities goes to war, then they *all* go to war. I will honour this pledge. I will honour my predecessor's word."

"I expected nothing less, lord," Alarik said.

"The world is changing, is it not? This war in the north. I received word from the cardinal some months ago informing me that that Spear of Durandail had been found." Calaval looked from man to man. "Is this true?"

"As true as you or I," Kyler said, unable to keep a hint of awe from his voice. "I have seen the Spear. I have felt its power."

"Then I pray that it guides us to victory." Calaval glanced at one of his guards. "Forgive me, noble knights, but I have much work to attend to and a war to fight. If you require anything, then my city will see it done."

"Thank you, lord," Kyler told him.

"Know that the prayers of Tallis go with you on your journey north. May the warrior grant you victory and may Azaria's light be ever at your side."

"Grace of the gods be with you, my lord," Alarik replied as he dipped his head.

Kyler followed his mentor's lead. They turned as one and strode for the doors.

The companions retrieved their weapons and then sought out some much-needed food and drink. They resupplied and made their way to the harbour. It did not take the knights long to locate a merchant captain who planned to make port in Annora, a captain who was easily persuaded to stop off at Loxford. They boarded the vessel and were underway by nightfall.

✦ ✦ ✦

Lysandra of the maija gazed at the patron goddess of her sect. Azaria's face was of the purest marble. Somehow the sculptors had created such a fine image that the silver lady radiated with compassion and wisdom both. The arc'maija did not reach for her amulet. Instead, her hands were gently clasped behind her back. Lysandra did not look to the likeness of Durandail nor the silver spear that the gods held between them. She did not take her curious gaze from the goddess.

"Did you come seeking solace, my lady?" a kind voice called behind her.

Lysandra glanced back with a smile and gave the cardinal a polite bow. "Actually, your magnificence, I did not come here for solace, nor even to pray," Lysandra replied honestly. "In truth, I came here for peace."

"Then I shall leave you in the same."

"No, it's alright," Lysandra said.

Cardinal Aleksander moved to her side and together they turned their eyes towards the gods.

"What is on your mind?" the cardinal asked.

"Many things. Swirling and writing as if in a storm," Lysandra said. "You see, father, my mind is adrift."

"You worry for the future?"

"Yes," she replied. "And no."

"You have a good heart, my lady, and a gentle soul," Aleksander said. "Do not burden yourself with dark thoughts. What is done is done and what will come to pass will come to pass. The gods guide us all. They have a plan."

The cardinal approached the twin statues and removed the Spear of Durandail from its place. He held it out towards her with a smile. "Trust them as you always have. Let them guide you."

Lysandra tentatively reached out. Her fingers halted inches from the silver lance. Light danced along the Spear. She placed her hand upon it. Lysandra shuddered.

Shadows crawling through a forest. Arrows driven into the earth. Ravens crying. Unintelligible whispers coming from the mist. Two figures shrouded in darkness. The first, a woman on her knees. A woman of white hair and blazing blue eyes. The second figure, further away, almost hidden by the dark. His eyes of crimson fire and a black eagle perched upon his shoulder.

Lysandra gasped as the visions faded. Her hand flew from the Spear. Her breathing was ragged and her heartbeat fast.

"What did you see?" Aleksander asked. "What did Durandail show you?"

"Shadows. Nightmares. Dreams," Lysandra replied. "There will be a great battle. Azaria's moon illuminated the skies."

"The victory that we seek will be ours in time."

✦ ✦ ✦

NINE

City of Verena, Valley of Odrysia

"What is your strategy?" Santiago Caspin asked as he shifted one of his latrunculii pieces across the white board.

"The Salvaari hold the eastern bank," Dayne said as he moved one of his own. "They know the forest far better than we ever could. Rather than charge head on into whatever they have prepared, I thought it best to plan attacks along the frontier. They only delay the inevitable."

"To what end?"

"I am a patient man."

Santiago glanced at his opponent as he thought about his next play. Dayne watched him with clasped hands and without emotion.

"Patience? What time do you think we have?" Santiago inquired as he made his next move.

Dayne's piece was in position before the Medean duke had finished speaking. "Time enough to do what must be done."

"Forgive me, my son, but I must ask: What time do you think *you* have?"

The two men locked eyes. Santiago made his move. Dayne took one of the duke's pieces.

"My health comes and goes like the tides, Duke Santiago," the king told him, "yet my resolve has never been stronger."

"I ask only for my daughter. For my unborn grandchild,"

Santiago said as he watched the board and continued to play. "Should you fall in battle or to this sickness, what then?"

"Plans have been put in motion. You can be assured of that."

"Sofia is my *only* child," Santiago pressed. "My only wish is that she remains safe."

"Sofia is my wife," Dayne countered. "She is the queen of all Annora. Do not forget, Father, that she bears my name now."

"Of course."

"A strange thing … family," Dayne said as he shifted one of his pieces. "You can fight. Betray one another. Yet there is nothing that you would not do for your own blood. Wouldn't you agree?"

"Indeed." Santiago met the king's stare as he replied. "No matter the cost. No matter the struggle. Family is family. There is no greater bond than blood, no greater power than love. The love for one's family. The love for one's children. It can drive men to unimaginable deeds."

The slight smirk that graced Dayne's lips vanished. He did not look away from his father-in-law as he countered the duke's move.

"What was it like to lose them?" the king asked.

"When the plague came … when it claimed the lives of my children, of my pregnant wife … it nearly broke me," Santiago told him. "To lose everything that you had worked for. To lose more. To lose your *name*. That is to know true torment. My brother has only daughters and all my sons are dead. We are the last of noble House of Caspin. All that can be done now is ensure the survival of my family."

"Then perhaps we are not so very different, you and I."

"In what way?" Santiago asked as he took one of Dayne's pieces.

"With the death of my father, the world has shifted underfoot," the king replied. "My brother has spurned our name, and in time Kassandra shall lose hers. I am young, and yet time moves against me. If Sofia does not bear a son, then the House of Raynor will crumble and fall."

"We can only pray," the duke told him.

"In times of struggle, it is easy to turn to the gods for salvation," Dayne said. "However, I must say that I am glad that my father never helped me. He taught me to find a way."

"It is a pity that he is gone."

"A pity, yes," Dayne replied as he positioned one of his chips. "All that can be done now is honour him."

Santiago made his move. "And how do you plan on doing that exactly?"

"The way that all soldiers are honoured," the king told him. "With blood and the death of his enemies."

Dayne reached out and shifted the final piece into position. He surrounded Santiago's king. Dayne did not look away and did not acknowledge that he had won the game. He could see something in Santiago's eye. Fear. The duke did not know whether or not Dayne knew of his involvement in the death of Dorian Raynor. For now, it was enough that he feared the possibility of discovery.

"A game well played, King Dayne," Santiago said. "A game well played."

"I have only just begun."

The door opened and in walked Sir Garrik Skarlit. "My king," the master at arms began, "they have arrived."

"Thank you, Sir Garrik," Dayne replied.

"They, my king?" Santiago asked with a furrowed brow.

Dayne rose to his feet and glanced back at Santiago Caspin. "My apologies, Duke Santiago," he said with a curt nod. "I sent word to Kilgareth. My household arrives now. My wife among them."

Dayne walked through the corridors of Verena. He had seen the truth in Santiago's face. The eyes gave a glimpse into the duke's heart, and they did not lie. He knew that Santiago was the one responsible for the murder of his father, yet he had no proof. Who would believe the ramblings of a woman who spoke under duress?

Who would take those words as truth over those of Santiago? Dayne did not know who the duke's allies were. Was Sofia one of them? Did she have a hand in Dorian's death? And then there was the murder of Darius. Dayne brushed the thoughts from his mind as he opened the doors to his newly acquired chamber.

There she was. Sofia. The queen glanced up as she saw her husband enter. A smile curled her lips as she looked towards him. Dayne felt a slight flutter in his chest as he saw her. Long hair the colour of the midnight sky fell down her back and across her left shoulder. Her graceful features radiated all the joys of the sun, while her eyes burned with hazel fire. Her sleeveless dress of yellow, orange and crimson appeared as a summer flame. Gods, he had missed her.

"My love," she called as Dayne closed the door to the room.

They were alone. The king crossed the room in moments and placed a kiss upon his queen's lips.

"Sofia." He murmured her name.

She kissed him a second time and then took his hands. He looked her in the eyes and saw the love and compassion harboured within. There was a slight furrow in her brow. Sofia pursed her lips.

"I heard about the attack," she said with worry lacing her voice.

"It's nothing," Dayne told her.

"No, it isn't." Sofia squeezed his hands.

"It did not prevent me from riding into battle alongside my men," Dayne replied.

Sofia snorted and humour danced in her eyes. "I am still trying to decide," she said.

"Decide on what?"

"Whether my husband is brave or a fool."

"One part brave, two parts fool," Dayne chuckled.

"Ever the fool then," Sofia replied with a grin.

The pain came on as quickly as rain in winter. Dayne grimaced in agony and clutched at his body. His insides were on *fire*. He staggered back a step as he fought to keep composure.

"Dayne!"

"No." The king held up a hand to halt her.

He took his other hand away from his searing stomach and then slowly clenched it into a tight fist. Dayne steadied his breath as his knuckles whitened. He took a long draught of air and closed his eyes. Then it was over. The pain receded.

"It is getting worse, isn't it?" Sofia said softly as she placed a comforting hand on his arm.

Dayne nodded slowly. "The ache has become an ever-constant companion." His voice was calm. "I made a promise, Sofia, a promise. I will not let this weakness destroy me. Not while I have strength left. Not while there is so much work to be done. The gods have given me this burden to test me, and I will not fail. I will not."

"You are destined for great things." Sofia placed a hand over his heart. "This war will test us all as the shadows draw near. Yet you will be the one to lead us back into the light. That was why the gods chose you. You are their chosen king. Believe in that."

"There are those outside these walls who think my illness is a weakness. For a time, I believed them. Yet I was wrong. The gods gave me my mind. What is in here is a gift." Dayne tapped his brow and then his stomach in turn. "And what is in here is a gift. It has given me a strength that even I did not know that I had. While those men who play their games in the corridors of power circle like vultures, I do not want to forget why I am truly here."

"And what reason is that?"

"I can never forgive them for sundering my family and murdering my father," Dayne replied with a slight growl in his voice.

"What have you heard, Dayne?" Sofia asked. "What secrets have you uncovered?"

The king could hear concern when she spoke. Genuine concern. He looked at her. His wife. His queen. Could he trust her when her own family was against him?

"That is the very reason why I called you here," Dayne told her. "On the eve that we departed Palen-Tor, your friend and confidant Lady Eveline vanished. She left word that she had taken up with a soldier and had joined the follower's camp. This is far from the truth."

"What do you mean?" Sofia murmured. "Dayne, where is she?"

"In a cell, being watched day and night," he replied.

"And why is that?"

Dayne reached into a pouch and withdrew a small knifelike hairpin. He held it up so that Sofia could see.

"Eveline killed my father."

"What?" Sofia's eyes widened as she took the pin. "No … she couldn't …"

Dayne clasped his hands together. "We found a strand of her dress in Dorian's chamber on the night that he died. When brought for questioning, she denied it for a time, but when we found this pin, her resolve shattered. She has since admitted to the murder," the king explained, "though she will not say her reasoning."

"And what do you think?"

"If Eveline killed Dorian, then your father gave the order," Dayne said. "I am sorry."

"No," Sofia shot back with a break in her voice. "How can you even say that?"

"From the day that you arrived at Palen-Tor, Lady Eveline positioned herself closely to my father. She earned his trust and earned his confidence. In time, she shared his bed. I see everything … I hear everything. It was not long after you came to me and told me about our child that my father met his fate."

"And you believe that they are connected?"

"Something is out of place," Dayne said. "My brother is gone. My sister cannot inherit the crown. Riona holds little sway over the court and now my father is dead. I believe that Santiago has his eye on the throne. If the child is a boy, if you give birth to a son, then there is to be a new male heir in line to the crown. An heir with Caspin blood."

"What are you saying, Dayne?"

"I am saying that Santiago killed my father to challenge me for the throne. I am saying that if we have a son, he will no doubt seek to finish what he started. If he gets the chance, he will cut my throat and no doubt he has already made plans."

"I don't believe this," Sofia said quietly. "I can't."

"I am truly sorry, Sofia."

"And do you think he killed Darius as well?"

"No, I don't," Dayne replied.

Tears threatened as Sofia looked towards her husband. "I didn't know … How could I have known?" she implored. "Dayne, whatever my father has done, you cannot believe that I had a hand in it."

"I don't," he said sincerely. "Sofia, when I left my home, I left knowing that my brother was an outlaw while my father and friend were murdered. I have no one that I can call upon. No one that I can trust, and the only things that I have to explain the deaths is a single strand and a pin. Sofia, I need your help."

Her face paled. The news had devastated her, and if Dayne had not seen the truth in her eyes or heard it in her voice, then that would have been enough. She knew *nothing* of Dorian's murder.

"What do you want me to do?" she breathed.

"Find your father. Ask him about all of this."

"You want me to discover his truth," Sofia said quietly.

King Dayne nodded. "Yes. He will tell you what he knows," he said.

"And then what?"

"The only evidence that I have is that of a hairpin, a strand of silk and the ramblings of a woman spoken in duress," Dayne told her. "I need something more. I need something as strong as stone. I need the truth from his own mouth."

"You're going to kill him, aren't you?" Sofia asked. Her voice spoke of the heartbreak that was reflected in her brown eyes.

"He has become a very real threat to my family," Dayne said as he turned away. "But in truth, I do not know. This alliance balances upon a knife's edge. One word and it could all be undone. I know what I am asking of you. I know that it would mean betraying your family."

Dayne felt Sofia take his hand. He felt the softness of her skin and the warmth held within.

"You *are* my family," she told him. "More. You are my husband, my greatest love and my king. I will do what it is that you ask."

"But your father–"

"If what you say is true, then he has betrayed everything. He has turned his back on our people, he has turned his back on the gods, and he has turned his back on me," Sofia said. "I am no longer just Sofia of House Caspin. I am Sofia Raynor. I am of two peoples."

"Then it falls to us," Dayne replied, "to stand side by side at a time when our families could not be further apart."

It was late when King Dayne returned to his office. It was a large room. A room that had served as a study for the maija who resided within. It held everything he needed: histories, books on culture and art. Candlelight filled the room. Maps and writings covered the large desk, and a worn leather-clad book rested in the hands of Kassandra.

"Father's journal," Dayne said as he gestured at the book.

"For a man not prone to reading, he wrote a lot of words," Kassandra replied as she put the book aside.

"Indeed. A strange thing that something so small could have helped our cause so greatly," Dayne told her.

"Ah yes, the *fearsome* Salvaari," Kassandra said as she rolled her eyes. "Did you know that their most sacred festival is an entire month of singing and dancing and *peace*. They do not fight. They do not so much as draw blades."

"No, I did not," Dayne murmured.

His father's journal spoke only of their ways and how they fought. Dayne had learnt from his father's victories and failures. He knew how to fight the Salvaari. He knew how to kill them. He knew how to defeat them.

"A shame," the princess told him.

"How was the journey?"

"I am an accomplished rider," Kassandra replied. "Mother was with me. Marian and Sofia as well. When I grew tired of their company, I would talk to the men."

"The soldiers?"

"Of course. I am a princess of Annora. I should know my people," she said with a shrug.

Dayne looked at her with some amusement as he approached the desk. His half-sister was a rarity indeed. Many of the other noblewomen, had they been in Kassandra's shoes, would have stayed within the comfort of their carriage. They saw the soldiers as no more than servants. Dayne gestured to the jug.

"Drink?"

"A little inappropriate, don't you think?" Kassandra chuckled.

Dayne snorted and poured two glasses. "You have been sneaking wine since you were knee high," he replied. "If there is one thing that I have learnt in the last year it is that you are not a child and should not be treated as such."

A surprised look flashed across Kassandra's face, but she remained silent. She took the glass and allowed herself a sip.

"I take it that by you being here you wanted to talk about something?" Dayne asked.

"I have a question."

Dayne gestured for his sister continue.

"Do elves exist?" Kassandra asked.

The king froze on the inside. Had she discovered something? Had she discovered the creature that Cardinal Aleksander had caged, the elf that had been imprisoned for one hundred years? The last of its kind.

"Elves?"

Kassandra nodded. Dayne hoped that she had not seen him hesitate.

"Elves, if they ever existed, died out with the ruskalan," he told her.

"I know that they haven't been seen in a hundred years," Kassandra said. "I know that many still believe them to be nothing but fantasy. But what if they aren't gone?"

"If they existed and if any survived Duran Cormac, then they will have fallen long ago," Dayne told his sister. "Where is this coming from, Kassandra?"

"I read about them in the maija's library in Kilgareth," she explained. "Great stories and tales, myths and legends, all written down in old books. Stories so magical that they could not possibly be real. They say that elves have hair whiter than winter snow and eyes bluer than the Mithramir Sea. They say that elves can live until the end of time, so long as they are not slain by blade or spear."

Dayne sighed and sat upon one of the chairs. "What I have heard about elves comes from the stories told by the soldiers that fought them. They said that elves were fire to the ruskalan's ice. That elves would fight and kill for pleasure. That though few in number, they were a mighty opponent. They practiced sorcery and learnt steel from our kind. Learnt its ways and secrets. And then turned it upon man. While the ruskalan spread their web of shadows through Medea, it was the elves who served as soldiers."

Kassandra pursed her lips as he spoke. "Do you believe them?" she asked.

"The word of man is easily corrupted," Dayne said. "If elves were real, then no doubt the stories have changed throughout the years. History is written by the victors. By the men who forged it."

"So what do you believe?"

Dayne thought for a moment. A thousand answers he could have given and if a hundred people had asked him the same question, all would have heard different. Yet Kassandra was his sister. He would not lie to her nor distort his truth.

"I believe that a hundred years ago Duran Cormac and his knights rode into Medea at the head of a great army. I believe that they saved Medea from terrible fate. Whether or not elves, ruskalan or other creatures of darkness existed, I am yet to decide. But I believe that it makes no difference. That fight was a long time ago and the past cannot dictate the future. And that is the end of it."

Kassandra took another sip from her glass. She gave her brother a smile and he could see her thinking. His sister had independent thoughts and would not follow anyone or anything blindly.

"I believe," Kassandra said. "I could tell you that something changed when I was in Salvaar. That that something caused me to believe the stories true. Yet it would be a lie not to say that in my heart a part of me has always believed."

Dayne stared into the distance as he took a drink. Beliefs, values: they were what drove people to unimaginable deeds.

"My belief is reserved for what my eyes allow me to see," he told her.

"Even the gods?" Kassandra raised her eyebrows.

For the first time Dayne grinned. He thumbed his amulet. "You're confusing stories that I believe with my actual beliefs. My values," Dayne said. "In that instance I believe first and foremost in my gods. I believe in my people. I believe in my family."

"All of us?" Kassandra asked.

"Of course." Dayne leaned across the table towards her. "Before he died, Father told me that there is *nothing* more important than family. That is a value that I share. I would do anything for you, your mother and for Lukas."

Kassandra's eyes brightened at the mention of their brother. "You believe that there is hope for him?"

Dayne extended a hand and placed it on his sister's.

"There is always hope."

✦ ✦ ✦

TEN

City of Elara, League of Trecento

"What do you think they are planning up there?" Mellisanthi asked as she stared out the window of her office. Her eyes were drawn to the towering structure of the magister's palace. The fortress was a distance away, yet from the vantage of the third floor, its peak could be seen from the brothel.

"Our survival," Cleander said from his chair.

"Really?"

"If we continue on our present course, then we may find that it leads only to the gallows," Cleander told her. "What Bhaltair, Teague and Lord Stentor all have in common is their will to survive. That same strength now dictates that they must work together to achieve an outcome that is equally good for us all."

Mellisanthi turned from the window and looked to Cleander. "You know something, don't you?" She raised her eyebrows.

"I know the clay from which they now craft their plans," Cleander said.

"And that is?"

Cleander sighed and gave his friend an amused look.

"The Emeralis set sail over a week ago alone," Mellisanthi continued. "I hear that the Jade Queen was chartering a course to the west. From there I can only speculate as to where she sails."

"And how far have you speculated?"

"Far enough to assume that her course and whatever is happening up there," Mellisanthi said as she gestured towards the palace, "are one and the same."

"So, what do you think?"

"Come now, we *both* know that I will have that information and more by dawn," Mellisanthi told him as a smirk tugged on her lips.

"You're probably right," Cleander conceded.

"So, tell me then. What do they plan?"

"Right now, they are discussing ways to convince the gangs and their families, Stentor's soldiers and their families and the whole of our following within the city to abandon their homes here," Cleander murmured. "Right now, they are preparing to send out word that the city must empty. They are searching for the words that will convince thousands to do what must be done."

"And Marquez?"

"She sails for the Valkir Isles with the intent to rally them to our cause," Cleander explained. "With their ships, we could break free of the blockade and open the gates to the Lupentine."

"Then as was foreseen, we are surrounded," Mellisanthi said.

"This may be our only way out," Cleander agreed. "We cannot stay here. None of us. The gangs, the Sacasians, those lords who allied with us. All the families. When the city is retaken, and it *will* be retaken, then all those with ties to this rebellion will be put to the sword."

"And all the steel in this city cannot hold back that storm," Mellisanthi replied. "Among us we have no shortage of courage and daring. We have willing hearts, yet we have no army. I know this. Against the might of the league, we would crumble."

"And so it is in the Valkir that we must place our fate," Cleander told her.

"You seem certain."

"I am."

"What makes you so certain?" Mellisanthi asked.

"I have faith," Cleander said.

"You speak of the gods," she replied slowly. "Yet for so long you have fought against those men who serve them."

"I fight against man, *not* the gods," Cleander told her. "This path that I have been set upon has cost me my home, my brothers and my life. It is a path that I refuse to let anyone else take."

"Is that why you help the Delfeyre girl?"

"Yes," he replied. "This burden that I carry … I carry so that no one else will. That the gods have set me upon my path."

"How do you know?"

"All you have to do is close your eyes and place yourself in their hands," Cleander said quietly as he met his friend's eyes. "Despite everything, I have never stopped believing."

"Tell me."

Cleander took a breath. He closed his eyes and he remembered. "After the fall of the Silver Tower, I was thrown into the river that swept far below. I couldn't breathe. I couldn't move. All I saw was darkness. Hundreds died … My brothers had done this. They took everything from me. My sword. My amulet. My faith. When I had nothing left to live for, I prayed for death. I begged the gods to end my suffering. But they didn't. Instead, they sent Lysandra. To this day I believe that there is a reason that they spared my life."

"And now they guide you to leave this city."

"I cannot stay here," Cleander replied.

"Where will you go?"

"I can never forget where I come from. I can never forgive. There is much that the Order of Kil'kara must atone for."

"I see," Mellisanthi murmured as she sat opposite her companion. "Do you really hate them so much?"

For a moment, Cleander searched his mind. He had hunted these men for years. He had killed countless of those he had once called brother. The fight he had with them tore at his soul and yet the answer was an easy one to give.

"Do I hate them? No. I feel nothing."

"You were a knight once."

"To betray one's brothers is a hard thing," Cleander said. "Yet to stand idle while their quest for these artefacts destroys everything was harder still. I tried to reason with them, but they would not hear me."

"And so now you hunt them from the shadows."

"With their arrival here, I can only assume that they now know who I am. That they now know my name. My true name. This life in the shadows served its purpose and it served it well. It hid a ghost from the past. Now the dead have arisen. In the chaos, the world has turned upside down and we are adrift. We are in the end times. In this chaos, there are monsters. This man that I have become … this man who is capable of so much darkness is yet to truly reveal himself."

"And this man, is he angel or devil?"

"Cleander was born from tragedy and those born from such dark things can only be harbingers of great tragedy. I know who I am. I know what I am. And only when we have admitted what we are can we do what needs to be done."

"Then your mind is made," Mellisanthi said.

"It always has been," he replied honestly.

"I will stay in Elara."

Cleander's eyes flicked towards her. "You can't stay here," he growled.

"And why is that?"

"Those men you helped lure to the tunnels were knights. Sir Alarik Sindra and Sir Kyler Landrey," Cleander told her. "They serve the Order of Kil'kara."

"What is that to me?"

"Olivera never returned and so I went looking for him. There was a fight. Beneath the city, I found a field of bodies. It would appear that my people and the pirates turned upon each other. I searched everywhere for the knights, yet of them I found no trace. They escaped."

Mellisanthi's face paled. "If they got away, then they may have made it out of the city," she whispered. "And if they made it out of the city, then they will have reached Tallis or Kiriador by now. Knights of Kil'kara would not return to their Citadel without first speaking to the magister. They will know my name. They will find me."

"Not if you leave." Cleander tried to keep the desperation from his voice. "Not if you come with me."

Mellisanthi raised a hand to her brow. She closed her eyes. "I'm sorry ... Elara is my *home*," Mellisanthi told him sadly.

"I know," Cleander said.

"For all its curses, this place gave my family so much. We were slaves once. Slaves who lived under the boot of Aureia. When the practice was deemed illegal by the council, it gave my family hope. We shed our chains and rose from the squalor. My father became a courier to one of the prominent families. It was he who taught me that knowledge was far greater than any army. It was my mother who showed me that even the lowest among us can rise to the heavens. They inspired me to take control of my own destiny. Now I control an empire of knowledge hidden in the shadows. We came from nothing ... From nothing to something to everything. Elara gave me that opportunity."

"You accomplished all of that when you had nothing more than your wit," Cleander told her. "The things that you have created, the things that you have done since then – you are a queen upon a throne of wisdom. You have wealth and you have position. You have followers and you have an undeniable will. Now you could accomplish far more."

Mellisanthi sighed and gave a sad smile. "The Valkir prize a strong arm and a sharp blade above any amount of information," she said. "Yet perhaps I could change that."

"Without a doubt," Cleander replied.

Mellisanthi rose to her feet and looked towards her friend. "Well then, I suppose that I should put my house in order and prepare everything for travel," she said. "There is much to be done."

"Of course," Cleander replied as he stood. "I will make my leave."

The former knight took her hand a placed a kiss upon it. He made for the door.

"And one last thing, Markus, before you go."

Cleander turned back and raised his eyebrows.

"You have not spoken to Emberly since before the council hall," she told him. "I am not judging you, but she has stood by you always. Unconditionally. Talk to her. Whether you see a future with her or not, she deserves that much."

"She has a pure heart, Mellisanthi. What I have done in recent days will be unforgivable to her. I could not lead her down such a dark road."

"Talk to her."

Tresses of long dark hair, smooth olive skin and the back of a deep blue dress gave Cleander pause as he opened the door. The woman turned. Eyes as deep and timeless as the ocean washed over him like waves. She froze. Her full lips quivered.

"Emberly," he called her name.

"You didn't return," she said.

"I couldn't."

"I thought you were dead," Emberly said. "I thought that all of the violence that plagued the gangs … the violence that spilled into the city streets had at last taken you."

"I had no choice," Cleander replied. "I was called upon."

Emberly shook her head and gave him a sorrowful look. "You did not even say goodbye."

"The time had come for dark men to do dark things," Cleander said. "I did not want to involve you. You deserve better than that. You always did."

"I would have followed you." Her eyes implored him to believe her. She may as well have been on her knees, pleading.

"All I wanted was for–"

"What I wanted was you," Emberly interrupted. "I couldn't bear the thought of what could have happened to you after you left."

"I could not endanger you," he told her.

"Cleander … why have you come?"

Cleander moved towards her and did not tear his eyes from her gaze. "This city stands in the eye of a storm. The magister's fall and the battle for Elara were just the beginning. We have but a few moments peace before the storm breaks once again. I needed to see you. I needed to hear your voice."

"So, at this late hour, you come?"

"There was a plot. Rumours about an important event."

"There are always plots," Emberly murmured. For the first time, there was a hint of amusement in her voice.

"I came to this city as a warrior, yet now I find myself embroiled in conspiracies and plots. It is a curse."

Emberly reached her hands out and Cleander took them. He could not help the smile that tugged at the corner of his lips. He had never spoken the words and had never admitted it to anyone, but when he looked at Emberly, he felt something stir in his heart. For the first time, he had something to hold on to that was neither god nor steel.

"Then perhaps we must find a priest to put an end to this curse," Emberly said with a smile.

She moved closer and wrapped her arms around his neck. Cleander could see the fire in her eyes. He could smell Emberly's scent and could almost feel the joy that radiated from her.

"Perhaps we must," Cleander chuckled.

He kissed her once. He kissed her again, but this one was deeper.

It was an apology and a thank you. Cleander had missed the taste of her lips.

✦ ✦ ✦

Elise rolled her shoulders back. She took a long breath and closed her eyes for a moment. She felt the breeze as it caressed her cheeks and swam through her hair. Her brown locks were braided back into a bun to keep the strands from her eyes. She wore neither dress nor her Nightingale garment. Instead, her garb was that of a shirt, loose trousers and boots. Elise stood in an abandoned part of the arsenal. The magister's soldiers that had once patrolled the arsenal were dead or imprisoned in one of the city's vast warehouses. Now the streets were quiet.

Elise began to run. She pushed herself into a sprint. She marvelled at the feeling of freedom that came with the speed. The stone wall rushed towards her. Without stopping her stride or hesitating, Elise planted her lead foot on the stone and pushed up. She flew up and her left leg rose with her. Driving her foot into the wall and launching herself backwards, she turned in the air. Arms outstretched, she grasped the small ledge of a building. Her feet met the wall. She heaved up with her arms and kicked off with her feet. She flew back towards the great stone wall. Her hands found the lip of the wall and she pulled herself up in a single fluid motion. She accelerated along the stone before launching herself into a roll, aiming for the edge of the wall. Her feet met stone and with her arm she pushed herself into the air.

Elise fell. Her boots found purchase on the roof of a small alcove and her hands met the tiles. She swung her legs between them and launched herself from the roof. Once more, she was airborne. The wind whipped her face. Her heart raced. She hit the ground with a roll and accelerated towards the side of a building. She took three steps up the wall and then sprung into a backflip. The air rushed around her as she spun through it. Exhilaration, elation, joy, passion, love. She felt it all as she touched down. A grin spread across her lips as she began to walk back through the courtyard in which she found herself. Her fingers brushed along the side of a building.

"You'll have Captain Marshall in a fit if you keep wandering off alone," Tariq called as he saw her.

Elise rolled her eyes. "I know he means well, but I spent months atop the roofs at night."

"Elise–"

"*Alone*," she said with a sigh. "A few moments of peace. That is all I ask for."

"A rare commodity in these times," Tariq replied. "I fear that the days of you going unnoticed may be at an end. Cleander was right about one thing. The men in the palace – Lord Stentor, Bhaltair, even that pirate Cillian Teague – they will all try to use you. To ally your name with their own. If they haven't come yet, then they soon will."

Elise looked to her friend. She saw something pass through his eyes. There was something that he wasn't telling her, but she could read him like a book.

"Someone sent you, didn't they?" Elise pressed.

Tariq nodded. "Bhaltair sent a man for you. I told that man that you were out and that you would not be back for some hours."

"All the more reason that I should make the most of the time I have to be alone," Elise replied. "Can they not leave me in peace?"

"I fear that we may have to leave if only to escape their black games," Tariq said.

"We were going to anyway," Elise told him with a shrug. "We have the money to do so. A simple life, Tariq. The dream that you once had. I trust that you still have mind to it."

The Berenithian smiled. "The world has changed; my dreams have not," he said. "This life that we have built here … it doesn't feel like living. But I have hope. I have faith in the gods. Do you?"

"The gods? No." Elise chuckled and shook her head. "For me, spirituality is something that you find with time. What I have … it is not a god-related spirituality. The gods are something that you feel in your heart. They are not tangible. You cannot touch it with your hands or feel it in your grasp. When I fly across the rooftops, when I leap up walls, when I feel the wind in my hair and the fire in my blood … that is the greatest connection with nature. That is where my spirituality lies. With it, you can transform the environment from something that looks like nothing into something extraordinary. With it, there is possibility. With it, there is creativity. With it, there is freedom. No, Tariq. When we leave this city, it will be on our own terms. We create our own fate. Not Bhaltair. Not Cleander. Not even the gods."

✦ ✦ ✦

ELEVEN

Isle of Agartha, The Valkir Isles

"When last I heard, a dread fleet had sailed from the free cities with the intention of destroying what was left of your kind," Erik told Luana Marquez once they were alone. "Now Elara belongs to the Sacasian raiders. Tell me a story. Tell me how this came to pass."

The pirate captain glanced around the longhall curiously. Erik doubted that she had ever seen the home of a Valkir leader before.

"May I?" Luana said as she nodded towards a chair by the king's table.

Erik shrugged and gestured for her to take it. Luana unbuckled her sword belt and placed it on the table beside her tricorn. She glanced at the jug of ale and, without a word, poured herself a cup. Cup in hand, she swung her boots up onto the table. Erik watched her with a bemused look as she took a long gulp of ale. Where other men and women of rank showed all manner of decorum, Luana showed none.

"To tell a story," Luana said as she looked to the king, "it may be best to go back to the beginning.

"It started thirty years ago. It started with a single purpose. Liberation. When Cillian Teague returned from the south, he did so with more than just stories of wonder. He returned a changed man who refused to be a slave to the empire's will any longer. He believed in the rights of all men from slave to emperor. A dangerous notion.

"Teague left the empire. A man of great reputation just vanished and that appeared to be that. Yet he was not idle. In his exile, he made allies. He was forgotten right up until he returned a few years later and liberated a slave market in Valentia. With six ships, they sailed to Ephelion and from there began to carve themselves a new home. A new life. They turned an uninhabited island into town and from there it grew into something more. In time, they began to hit fat merchant ships in the Sacasian Sea. They took the plunder and the prize, yet, most unique of all the pirates of Lamrei, offered the crew a chance to join them. Most accepted. Within a few years, six ships became sixteen. Within a few years, Ephelion wasn't enough and more islands in the gulf were claimed. Deals were struck with Landonsport and the harbour town of Lamrei. The pirates became strong. Ten years after the attack on Valentia, Cillian struck at a ship bound for the empire from Elara. The last slave ship that the League would ever send west.

"That's when he found me. I was twelve summers. My father, gods rest him, had tried to sell me to a whorehouse. Teague saved me from that life and granted me a new one. A life of freedom. A life without care or worry. I learnt to fight. I learnt to sail. I learnt to lead. For twenty-five years, I have sailed with my brethren. Those years granted me wealth and reputation. In time, our network grew. We established colonies upon all of the islands in Lamrei, but our actions did not go unnoticed. It began with the sacking of Sacira. We were unprepared for an attack and when it came, it came with fire. The League dispatched a fleet of unprecedented strength. Famier and Androna were next. Landonsport betrayed us. The Old Guard who had given birth to our nation were hunted down and killed. All save one. All save Cillian Teague. We evacuated our islands and left nothing for the League. We burnt everything that we could not carry."

"How did you survive?" Erik asked.

"This is how we survived. While my people fled into the seas, we used deception to keep the League at bay. While Commander Javais was led on a dance around the gulf and the Sacasian, I slipped north unnoticed. I met with the gangs and from there we forged an alliance. My people arrived soon after. While the gangs showed us how to navigate the tunnels beneath the city, an attack was launched in the streets. We caught them by surprise. While Imrohir's eye was fixed upon those within his walls, our own fleet arrived from the south. We snatched the heart of the League in one night."

Erik watched Luana curiously as she trailed off. She was a most unique woman indeed. A freedom fighter who had come from nothing and now commanded a ship and an infamous crew.

"I am not entirely sure what impresses me more, Captain Marquez," Erik told her. "The story of how you took Elara or the skill with which you told it."

"Never underestimate the power of a good story or the strength of a song," Luana said.

"A girl who came from humble beginnings yet now commands a great pirate fleet and who cities fall before," Erik replied. "That would make for a grand tale."

"Perhaps one day you shall hear it," Luana said as she met his eye.

Erik nodded and allowed a smirk to tug at his lips. "Alright, you have my interest," he told her. "It seems as if your problem is neatly resolved, but here you are having sailed to my shores and bring nothing save stories of freedom and grandeur. What is it that you want, Luana Marquez?"

Erik let her name roll from his lips slowly. He wanted to see her reaction. If the pirate captain cared, then she showed not a sign. Instead, she pulled her feet from the table and leaned towards him.

"I have a ship. I have a crew. I sail at the head of a fleet and have thousands of willing souls within Elara to aid them. What I do not have, *Erik*, is a way to protect my people."

Despite her words, there was no tremble in her lip or desperation in her voice. Her words were strong and filled with hope.

"How do you mean?" Erik asked with a frown.

"Magister Imrohir was my enemy, but he was no fool. Before the palace fell, he would have sent word to the free cities. Birds will have flown, and by now the magisters of Tallis and Kiriador will have begun to assemble their armies in the north. Commander Javais and his fleet will have been told of Elara's fall and no doubt will have begun to set up a blockade around the city. Within a few weeks, maybe a month, my people will fall. Elara will be retaken."

The king wished that Astrid was with him. He wished that he had her mind and her voice. He wished that he had her thoughts. He did not. Instead, Erik tried to think as she would have thought. Information was worth far more than any amount of coin.

"You know the inner workings of Elara," Erik said. "If they herald victory over you, what comes next?"

"After the fall, they will turn their swords on Miera. Not so very long ago they voted to sunder the Accords. With the three cities united and with the backing of the newfound alliance of Annora, Medea and the empire, they will crush the horsemen. Salvaar will follow if it hasn't already fallen and then ... then you remain the *last* free kingdom."

The pirate slowly extended a hand towards one of the candles upon the table. Luana's fingers brushed the tiny bead of fire.

"You know of the empire's greed. Of the league's greed," Luana murmured as she ran her hand through the flame and then snuffed it. "Your world shall fall. Like all the others."

"I know of the empire's thirst for blood," Erik said quietly.

"The empire's greed is insatiable," Luana told him. "Like a demon, it sucks the life out of everything and everyone around it."

"Their temple, their faith, had my sister executed," Erik growled. "She was not a warrior nor a chief upon a throne of blood. She wanted peace. She wanted nothing more than to sail to uncharted lands and endless seas. She fell to the knife of a betrayer who served the sun and moon. When the empire sent ambassadors seeking to enlist us in their crusade, I killed them. It will not be long before the griffin begins to wonder where its emissary was waylaid. I was once nothing more than a warrior. When I killed the empire's man, I became an outlaw like you."

"Then we find ourselves linked by destiny."

"Destiny or a curse," Erik replied.

"Regardless, our fates are entwined," Luana said.

"More closely than you know," he replied. "There is a second fleet gathering like a storm to the west. A fleet that intended to land upon the Mieran coast. A fleet that I fear will instead turn towards us."

"The League will strike from the east. The empire will strike from the west," the captain said. "They will defeat us one by one. Alone we are divided. Alone we are weak."

"What do you propose, Luana Marquez?"

Luana pulled a slender knife from her boot and let it dance around her fingers. While the blade moved, she did not take her eyes from Erik.

"My purpose in coming here was to seek your aid in our war. A war not of your making but one of vital importance to all," Luana said. "Instead of finding your people at peace, I found them preparing for their own war. What I propose, King Erik, is that we help one another."

"You want me to sail east. You want me to help defeat the fleet that stalks your people."

"My people have nothing. The gangs have nothing. The displaced families have nothing. I know that even together we do not have the strength to defeat the armies of both Tallis and Kiriador, so instead, I ask that when the blockade is broken, we can make a home here for a time."

"I see." Erik gave her a thoughtful look and gestured for her to continue. "And what do we get in return?"

Luana gave him a deadly grin and the knife stopped spinning in her hand. "My people are few, but we Sacasians are formidable upon the sea. Help save us and in return I swear that we will turn our steel upon the silver fleet. Save us and we will give you victory."

"Victory," Erik said softly. "A true victory."

"Not just for us. But for our children. And their children."

"Your people. How many are you?" Erik asked.

"Twenty ships. Two thousand people. The greater sum can and will fight," Luana told him. "Of the gangs and Lord Stentor's men, they number perhaps double my own."

"Six thousand," Erik murmured. "And in the harbour are there more ships?"

"Some."

"Some … so I would have to hold the full might of the League at bay while at the same time dividing my force so that my ships may help to carry your allies."

"I did not say that it would be easy."

"My warriors are strong. They are fierce and they are angry," Erik said. "But I cannot leave my own shores undefended and so the league's fleet shall outnumber mine greatly."

"No, they won't," Luana promised.

"What do you mean?"

"Because I brought a mighty weapon. I brought the greatest weapon that the west has ever seen. I brought the very weapon that forged the Aureian Empire."

"What weapon?"

Luana Marquez led Erik aboard the Emeralis. The crew watched Erik with wary eyes as the towering Valkir warrior walked among them. Erik barely gave them a second glance yet did not let his hands wander too close to the sword, axe and knife that hung at his belt. Only the Tariki warrior Calvillo gave him pause. Even this far south from Tarik, the title was well known. They were swift and silent poets of the kill.

"Here," Luana said as they reached the centre of the deck.

Erik's eyes wandered to the small wooden cages. Within them, he saw grey feathers and tiny beaks.

"Pigeons," Erik exclaimed.

"Yes," Luana replied. "With them, we can send word to Cillian Teague. With them, we can warn my people inside the city of our approach. We can summon them from Elara. We can pincer Javais and his blockade between my people and yours. We can sow fear and panic into their ranks. While they are lost in this nightmare, those within the city can escape. We can defeat them, and we will."

It was a sound plan, Erik knew it. Yet there was something that Luana Marquez had not mentioned. There was something that even Erik did not understand.

"And are you prepared to so easily give up the city that you fought for, the ground that your people bled and died for?"

"We did not want this war," Calvillo spoke up. "We did not want to be forced into a life of blood. The League gave us no choice. We had no choice to take their city for there was no other way to gain passage to the Lupentine. We showed them what it felt like to lose what they loved. We showed them what it felt like to lose their home. Now we just want our own. A measure of peace … that is what we all seek."

Erik looked to the Tariki and gestured to the man's sword. "And could you who has spent your entire life fighting set aside your sword? Could any of you?"

Calvillo swept his gaze around the deck of the ship and took in the faces of the crew. Erik could see the sunken eyes and tired faces. These were not true soldiers or warriors. They were sailors.

"We were prepared to do that a long time ago," Calvillo told him.

"My people are tired of bloodshed," Luana said. "We have strength enough for one last fight."

Late was the hour when Erik left the Jade Queen and made his way to the home of his oldest friend. He told him Luana's story.

"What are you thinking?" Torben asked.

Erik looked to his friend. The grey that had once merely streaked through the bloodsworn's hair and beard had at long last begun to take the place of his dark locks. Torben had been a champion among the Valkir. He had been Erik's father's closest friend and had been a mentor to him since the time he was a child. In time, Torben had become a second father to Erik.

"I am thinking about what comes next. I am thinking about the future that Astrid wanted for herself and for her people. I am thinking about how that future can be achieved."

"What does your heart tell you?"

"For our people, peace has always been harder than war," Erik told him. "If that is true, then should we not try to achieve the more difficult outcome?"

"Yet to find this peace, we would have to go to war," Torben said.

"Yes. Ironic, isn't it?" Erik allowed a small smile as he spoke.

"And this choice that you are making. What of that?"

"Ships have sailed. Jorun and the other jarls now hunt a most elusive prey. The chances of uncovering that which does not want to be found are slim. Even if Jorun heralds a miracle and discovers the location of the fleet, we do not know if we have the strength to defeat them. And if we do, what of the cost? What if some of the ships slip past us and reach the Isles? If we fail, then our world burns. I have antagonised the beast and now I can feel it stirring."

"And now a pirate captain sails to our shores seeking our help," Torben said. "If we aid in her endeavour, there is no telling if this silver fleet will appear *before* we return. There is no telling how many of our peoples' lives will be lost in breaking the blockade."

"And there lies the nightmare that plagues my mind," Erik told him. "The rewards for entering such an alliance with these people could be great, but in doing so, I risk weakening my people to attack at a most perilous time. However, just as we could be the salvation for the Sacasians, then so too could they be ours. With them, we would have a very real chance of defeating any who come to claim our Isles. With them, this peace that my sister so longed for could become a reality. This dream of hers, Torben, is now my dream. The Sea-Father guided Cillian Teague in sending Luana Marquez to our shores. He has offered me this chance to save my people. If I am forced to choose between the very real possibility of losing this fight and risking everything so that we may triumph over our enemy, then there is no choice at all."

"You are decided then," Torben stated.

"I am committed," Erik told him. In his heart, he knew it to be the right choice. "Messengers need to be upon the water at once. We will take thirty ships east. The earls are to meet me five miles offshore in two days. From there, we must sail to Elara."

✦ ✦ ✦

TWELVE

Coast of Larissa, The Mithramir Sea

Gulls soared high above. The salty spray of the sea filled the air. Kitara could taste it upon her lips. The gentle rocking of the ship beneath her feet was no stranger to her. After years upon the sea, Kitara felt as stable on a ship as if she were on solid ground.

Sunlight glinted on the sword as it descended towards her. Kitara deflected the blade as she stepped to the side. Gliding atop the deck, she circled the man bearing the sword and buckler shield. She would have finished it then had the fight been more than just sparring. The sailor matched her movement as he watched her intently. One of the crew's mercenaries had seen her going through the motions of her sword dance this morning and had challenged her to spar with him. Kitara had been all too happy to oblige him. The sailors had said that he was the best among them. Now crew and passenger alike watched as the pair faced off.

Kitara's eyes were glued to his centre, for it was that which told her everything. The eyes could lie but the body could not. The sailor came at her. She slid back, blocked once, twice. She danced to her right and thrust her sword forth. It snapped the sailor's buckler back. Changing her angle, she brought her sword around and attacked low to the left. The sailor caught the blow with his blade and punched out with his shield, but Kitara was already gone. The buckler found nothing but air. Kitara danced back from the counter. She gave the sailor a toothy grin and allowed a laugh to escape her lips. Usually when she fought, she did so without emotion, but they were sparring, and she *knew* that there was nothing that the sailor could do to hurt her.

Kitara pressed forward. She deflected the sailor's lunge, sliding aside from his shield as he followed through. She countered with a diagonal stroke followed by a horizontal one. Her footwork took her behind the sailor. With a flick of her wrist, she smacked the flat of her sword across his rear. The assembled crowed roared with laughter as Kitara twirled away with a grin. She pivoted to face the sailor. Her sword came up to block the counter just as she had been trained. The blow never came. Cheers filled the air. Those who watched clapped and stamped their feet. Not a man or woman among them wasn't smiling or laughing. The sailor shook his head with a grin and lowered his weapons. Kitara twirled her blade and admired its beauty as the sun kissed the steel.

"Damn your Tariki tricks," the sailor called.

"Call me a magician if it will make you feel better." Sarcasm laced her voice.

"I preferred it when you didn't jest." The sailor chuckled as he approached.

"Improve then," Kitara said with a roll of her eyes.

The song of a lute filled the air and then Kompton's voice followed.

"The sailor thought that with steel he fought
the girl would crumble before him!
He stabbed and he thrust,
he countered and lunged!
Yet the girl was his match this morning!
She danced and she moved,
twirled her sword with a leer,
and stuck the sailor hard on the rear!"

All eyes went to the bard. Kompton's grin covered his face, and his eyes ignited with the laughter that came from his soul. The crew howled and guffawed heartily at the song. Their laughs were long and loud and filled with joy. The sailor waved his hand disdainfully at the bard, though a snigger broke his lips. Some of his comrades gave the mercenary band dark looks as they handed over purses of coin. Many had wagered bets on the match. Kitara passed her sword to her left hand and extended her arm to the man. The sailor gathered up his sword with his shield hand and took Kitara's arm.

"Well fought," Kitara told him.

"When next we meet, I shall give you proper contest," he replied.

"You can try."

"I will succeed," the sailor said in good humour.

Kitara snorted as she retrieved her swordbelt. "Then my sword shall find your arse once again," Kitara said as she sheathed her blade.

"Pah!" He chortled incredulously.

With a grin, the Aureian swaggered away. Kitara buckled her sword around her waist and gathered up her waterskin before heading to the side of the ship. She leaned over the railing and gazed out into the ocean. Uncorking her waterskin, she took a long draught.

"It is a thing of beauty when you dance with your blade," Aeryn said as she approached.

"Dedication and time are the masters of all things," Kitara told her.

Aeryn leaned on the railing beside her and followed Kitara's gaze across the gentle waves. "I once told you that forests of home were wild, untamed … beautiful. You said that that was just like the sea," Aeryn said softly.

"You remembered?"

"Of course," Aeryn replied. "Now that I am here, now that I

can see the ocean, now that I can *feel* it, I understand what it is that you meant. My sister Vanya would have loved to see such beauty."

"We will have to show her one day," Kitara told Aeryn as she handed over her waterskin.

"You would like her, and she would like you," Aeryn said.

"What of the rest of your family?" Kitara asked. "Tell me about them."

A smile crossed the moonseer's lips. "I grew up in Faolan. It is a small village. Quiet … peaceful. The people live simply. It is there that you will find my family. My father Eivor raises horses. Had I not been born with silver eyes, there is no doubt in my heart that my path would have followed his. He would tell you that there is nothing as alive and beautiful as a horse in the spring."

"And your mother?"

"Corre," Aeryn told her. "She is a healer. A kind and gentle soul with no inclination nor want for fighting."

Kitara could hear the happiness in Aeryn's words. She had a family. A real family.

"A peaceful life," she said. "That doesn't sound so bad."

"No, no it doesn't," Aeryn agreed.

"I should like to meet them all," Kitara told her sincerely.

"I would like that. Very much."

Kitara glanced from the horizon and then to Aeryn. "There will come a time when there is no fighting, no bloodshed, no war," she said.

The corner of Aeryn's lip curled. "And what would my woman do without a fight?" Aeryn replied with a chuckle.

Kitara sniggered. "Grow old. Build a home. Raise horses."

The moonseer's eyed widened. The waterskin stopped halfway to her mouth. "Are those just words or a promise?"

"A promise," Kitara vowed.

Aeryn grinned and then took a sip from the skin. She lowered the bottle in surprise as she swallowed the drink. "This is just water," she said simply.

Kitara nodded as she heard the question in Aeryn's voice. "I'll never drink again," Kitara replied. "No more wine. No more ale. No more … I can't."

Aeryn gave her a compassionate look and Kitara knew that the moonseer understood. Kitara stared back across the blueness of the Mithramir as she gathered her thoughts.

"My whole life I have used drink to drown my demons," she said. "I used it to escape the torment that came to me every night in my dreams … every *day*. When I first arrived in Salvaar, when I told you their names, I was finally able to shake them free. But when I was taken, I heard them whispering my name once again. The fear returned and it brought the anger with it. I started to drink again, and I did it until the demons stopped calling my name. I felt a great weight upon my shoulders – it was suffocating. The demons took their toll. The drink took its toll. And when you found me in that street, I had given up. For the first time in my entire life, I was helpless. You saved me when I could not save myself. The drink nearly broke me … and I know in my heart, in my soul, that if I drink again, there may be no turning back."

"And these demons. Do they still stalk you day and night?"

Kitara bit her lip. "I can feel their presence. Yet each day it lessens. I find myself at last being able to look back. I can go back to the beginning in here." Kitara placed a finger on her brow as she spoke. "I can see the ghosts that haunt me. I can say their names. I can at last move forward from what happened to me. I think that I can finally close the pages of that book. A new chapter of my life has begun."

✦ ✦ ✦

"What's in your head?" Galadayne asked as he approached Bellec.

The mercenary leader glanced back at his friend as he joined him below deck. "The journey that we now find ourselves upon," Bellec replied as Galadayne sat beside him.

"What are you thinking?"

"This road is built upon possibilities. In a few days' time, we will make port and from there ride into Salvaar," Bellec said. "From there, we are entering a theatre of the unknown. What awaits us within those trees, who awaits us … These questions repeat themselves over and over in my mind. There is a shadow that I can't seem to shake. As if something draws near."

Galadayne snorted. "When did you become so superstitious?" he said wryly.

Bellec chuckled darkly. "Since we are travelling into a landscape of which we do not know the lay. When we left Salvaar, the people were hopelessly outnumbered by those who stood against them. We do not know if Cailean or Henghis still live. We do not know if they have yet to meet the west upon the fields or if they have already been defeated. We are now travelling into the dark without first illuminating it. No matter who lies beyond the trees, be they friend or foe, we will be met with unforeseen consequences."

"We will meet them together as we always have," Galadayne replied. "What can happen and what will happen are very different entirely. The Salvaari yet live. I am sure of it. All we need to do now is illuminate the shadows and uncover what lies within. We have done it before, and we will do so again."

"Aye," Bellec said. "We will fight and survive as we always do. The men that you chose to sail aboard the Tanith, are they true to their purpose?"

"They stand ready," Galadayne told him. "When the signal is given, they will act."

"Good … good. There is something else," Bellec said after a moment. "Something that we have not yet talked about, but it is something that we should discuss."

The two men locked eyes.

"Dorian's death," Galadayne muttered.

"You know me well."

"The days of me not knowing your thoughts are long behind us, my friend."

Bellec could only nod. They had been as brothers when they had served the Aethelan throne. That had been over twenty-five years ago. The bond that they now shared went beyond words.

"Whatever happens in the coming months, whether Salvaar rises in victory or suffers defeat, we will have a choice to make."

"You believe that after so many years, we will finally be able to return home without the fear of the hangman's noose?"

Bellec shrugged. "Whatever Dorian's disagreement with us, I doubt that Prince Lukas feels the same," he replied. "Not after Miera. Not after Salvaar."

"Home." Galadayne chuckled. "I can scarcely remember what it looks like."

"It has been nearly three decades since I last saw Palen-Tor," Bellec said as he remembered. "I wonder ... will she welcome us? Will we be met by those we once knew, or will we be greeted by nothing more than the whispering of the wind?"

"Will she recognise us?" Galadayne murmured. "No ... it is strange. Strange that even after being forced to run and hide, after being forced to flee my own land and live as an outlaw for so long, I had hardened my heart to the idea of ever returning to Annora. Yet now that the gateway has again been opened ... I can feel its call. A call that for so long had been silent."

"Times have changed," Bellec said simply. "We are different men now. The sins of the past have evaporated like smoke. We have been granted a second chance. We live in a new time, with a new king."

"A king who is untested."

"A king that has more cunning than any three of his predecessors,"

Bellec countered. "You have heard the stories same as I. Dayne *Raynor*. The Eagle's son. He has never fought a battle that he could not win, never laid siege to a town that he could not take. Ruthless. Uncompromising. As skilled in politics as he is upon the field."

"Clearly he will make a fine king."

"And now we stand on opposing sides in the same war. A war that he now commands."

"Fighting against the very man who could pardon us." Galadayne grimaced.

Bellec bared his teeth. He felt the rage that he had kept in check for so long begin to stir. It threatened to consume him. He felt its flames as fiercely as he had on the day that Oriana had been taken from him. It was a blaze that knew his heart better than anyone, and when asked, his heart had but one answer. It just wanted to see the world burn.

"Even if the king offers us pardons, the price is surrender," he growled. "To beg forgiveness from the thing that took my home from me? Took my brothers from me? Took my woman? I can walk back home if I sign my name and swear an oath to never again stand against Annora. No. The eagle has taken everything from me. If the king offers pardons for crimes that we did not commit, then I say that offer is the mark of a coward. Do you want to surrender to a coward? To apologise for crimes that you had no hand in? Apologise to those men who took your land, your name, your family?"

"You would so easily give up your freedom?"

"I am a free man!" Bellec snarled. "I am not prepared to get down on my knees and beg forgiveness. Are you?"

"Whatever I feel, my path took me from Annora long ago. The king could offer us our pardons. He could offer us freedom. But what of Ander? What of Hakon and Raylor? What of the others? Our brothers that followed us from Annora? Brothers made outlaw by the same crown that would pardon them. The crown that would seek to make them free men. But they're already free. They're dead. Am I prepared to beg forgiveness? No. None of us are."

✦ ✦ ✦

Kitara rotated her wrists as she slowly spun through the ship's hold. Candlelight flickered along the naked blade of her sword as it turned in her grasp. She brought the blade up slow and with precision. She moved with purpose. The swordsong took over. They were not singular. They were as one.

"Tell me about tarkaras," Aeryn said as she watched Kitara move with her sword.

With a flick of her wrist, Kitara rotated the hilt of her blade so that she held it in a reverse grip behind her back.

"The swordsong is the soul of those who practice it. The soul happens only when the singer has disappeared into the song. They are no longer separate. Some unknown force has done it through them," Kitara replied. "Tarkaras is a song of the heart. A song of the soul. It shows the truth. It *is* the truth."

"There is something calming about it," Aeryn said. "As if it can possess your mind in such a way that drives all else from concern."

"It helps me to see clearly," Kitara told her. A thought struck her. Her eyes shone as a smirk crossed her lips. "Come here," Kitara said and beckoned for the moonseer to approach.

Aeryn frowned and then did as she was bid.

"Give me your hand," Kitara continued.

"Am I to dance?" Aeryn grinned as she raised her hand.

Kitara took it with a smile. She placed her sword in Aeryn's hand and then curled her fingers around the moonseer's to wrap them around the hilt.

"Take it," Kitara said as Aeryn gripped the sword. "The song that I practice is slow and precise. Everything is done with purpose. It is more for fighting. Yet the song that I want to teach you is more of a dance. A union between blade and body."

Aeryn said nothing and watched Kitara with curious eyes.

"Lower your centre," Kitara directed. "Hold the sword with one hand ... Good."

With each direction, Kitara helped Aeryn adjust her form. Gentle touches upon hip, wrist, hand, arm and back.

"Bring your left arm up like so. Your grip must not be too loose or too tight. Relaxed yet firm. Strong yet moveable," Kitara instructed. "Now ..." She turned Aeryn's hand, moving the sword in a circle. "Keep your wrists crossed. Let the hilt pass between your hands as it spins," Kitara said as she helped Aeryn turn the sword.

The sword spun in slow circles as it sliced through the air. Kitara stepped back and watched Aeryn turn the steel. Her brow was furrowed slightly in concentration and her silver eyes shone. Kitara couldn't help the smile that danced across her lips.

"Now move your feet. Turn your hips. Turn your body. Let the sword sing."

✦ ✦ ✦

THIRTEEN

Coast of Miera, The Lupentine Sea

The voyage from Tallis began as smoothly as it went. The ship did not stray far from the Mieran coast. The horsemen did not have any vessels bigger than small fishing ships, because, as the captain said, the Valkir were ever dangerous, and he did not want to risk a fight. The merchant captain had employed a crew of skilled sailors and mercenary warriors. One could never be too careful in the treacherous seas.

"Captain says that if we have a fair wind then we should make landfall by morning," Alarik told Kyler.

The Medean glanced at his mentor as he approached. "The packs are ready," Kyler replied. "A week's worth of provisions will see us to Kilgareth."

"Gods willing, the road will speed us on our way and grant us more time to shower them in heathen blood."

"I will prove myself worthy in honour of the glory of Durandail," Kyler told him.

"You already have, Pisspot," Alarik said. "In all the hellholes from Kilgareth to the Vault to Elara and back."

"Then I shall do so again," Kyler said. "As long as I breathe, I trust the sun and moon. I will kill many Salvaari. I will send them to meet our gods atop blood-drenched stone."

"If it weren't for them and their ungodly ways, then the

Inquisition would never have happened and this war in which we now find ourselves would not exist," Alarik replied. "Yet they have killed untold thousands of our people. Medean, Aureian, Annoran. That cannot – that *will* not go unpunished."

"The gods have given us a chance to correct the past," Kyler murmured.

One of the older sailors made his way towards them. His beard was grey and his face weathered. "You two heading north?" he asked. His accent was Annoran.

"Aye, sir," Kyler answered.

"You are Knights of Kil'kara then?"

"That we are, friend."

"Then my prayers have been answered," the old sailor told them. "You ride as Durandail's wrath. You ride as Azaria's judgement. Bring those heathens who destroyed the temple of Saint Daleka and murdered my brother to justice."

The knights exchanged a look. Kyler knew of the temple. It was the most sacred site in all of Annora. Saint Daleka had been the first man to bring the religion of the Twins to Annora. To the north of Aethela was Valham, the city that played host to the temple. Kyler had never had the chance to visit the sacred site, but as with all within his order, he knew the name well.

"The heathens attacked Valham?" Alarik said with a frown. "What happened to the temple?"

Pain filled the Annoran's eyes. Something inside him had been broken.

"Salvaari came. They killed everything and everyone within the temple. My own brother who was a priest … None could stand against them and live. They started a blaze, and by dawn nothing remained of the temple but ash and scorched earth," the sailor told them. "I implore you. Please do not let their deaths go unavenged."

"What kind of men burn temples?" Kyler growled.

He glanced from the sailor to Alarik. His heart had frozen.

He could scarcely believe that even the vilest of the pagans could commit such an unspeakable act. To kill warriors was one thing; to slaughter unarmed priests and burn their place of worship was another thing entirely. It made Kyler enraged.

"Those pagans are *not* men," the sailor snarled. "They're monsters. They string the dead from trees, carve symbols in their flesh and leave them for the crows."

"Your brother. What name did he carry?" Alarik asked.

"Tybalt, sir."

The battlemaster placed a hand on the old sailor's shoulder. "Then I give you this promise," Alarik said. "Tybalt will not go unremembered. We will bring all those who have wronged Valham to justice."

Kyler's hand rose to his amulet. "Hear my prayer," he said fervently. "Let the wrath of Durandail fall upon these heathens who desecrate the holy places of our land. Let the gods' holy warriors arm themselves against these worshipers of the devil. Let them fall to our holy steel. Father of all fathers, do not let the vile murders of your children go unpunished. Let us be your instruments of justice. Know that we shall bring these pagans to heel."

"You came back, followed me to Elara, knowing it could mean your life," Kyler murmured to the one who lay beside him.

"Kyler, I choose you. I chose you in Adrestia, I chose you in the cave," Elena told him. *"I will keep choosing you until the end of time. The fight that once was between your people and mine … we will overcome it. Together."*

"You truly believe that?"

"I have to," she replied. *"I have to believe that there is still some good in this world, some good that comes after everything that has happened. A dawn after the darkest night."*

"Then this dawn you speak of, I will give it to you."

Darkness gathered. There was a scream. Kyler now stood in the

*tunnels of Elara clad in bloody armour with his sword stained red.
He turned to the scream. He saw the pirate drive his sword deep into
Elena's body. Kyler watched her stagger. Blood ran down from her lips.
Elena fell.*

"ELENA!" he roared.

Kyler awoke with a gasp. His heart was racing and his skin hot.
Sweat soaked his clothes. His breathing was rugged. As he sat up in
his hammock, he gathered his thoughts. He could still see her face.
He could still see her death. Hands trembling, he reached for the
silver necklace. The jewel that he had once given Elena. He closed
his eyes and felt his wet eyelashes caress his skin. He gritted his
teeth and dropped from the hammock. Glancing around the hold,
he buckled on his swordbelt. Alarik and the ship's crew slumbered
without a care. Without releasing Elena's necklace, Kyler made his
way through the darkness and up onto deck.

The silver light of the moon caressed the vessel. At the prow of
the ship, he stared out into the black. He took a long breath and at
last composed himself. Every night was the same. Every night he
saw ghosts. Those of Elena. Those of his parents. Those of Torin, Sir
Matias and all the other knights that had fallen in the Vault. Kyler
winced as if struck. The constant ache that had started in his head
more than a week ago remained. He felt pain surge through his
mind. Like a great wave of fire that sought to consume him. Sweat
rolled freely from the knight's brow as his breathing grew laboured.
He could hardly think. He could hardly see. He hammered his fist
into the railing of the ship, hoping for some relief. Nothing. His
hand flew to his amulet. Kyler's eyes slammed shut as he fought the
surging tide of pain. Alarik's words resounded within him: *When
there is nothing else to hold on to, hold on to your faith.*

"Azaria's strength flows through me. Azaria's shroud protects me.
Azaria's love heals me," Kyler growled through gritted teeth. "Take
me up into your silver light. Surround me with it. Free me."

His fingers unfurled. His breathing slowed. The trembles that racked him ceased. Kyler took a long breath as the pain receded. He ran a hand across his sweat-laden brow.

"Thank you," he murmured.

They arrived at Loxford at dawn. The small Annoran border town greeted the merchant ship enthusiastically. It had been a long time since the town had played host to a merchant vessel of this size, and for the people who lived in Loxford, the possibilities were endless.

"Pisspot," Alarik called as he approached his fellow knight.

Kyler glanced at his mentor. He saw Alarik's face contort with a worried frown.

"You look tired," the battlemaster stated.

"Sleep evades me." Kyler shrugged wearily. "No matter."

Alarik clapped a hand on Kyler's shoulder. "Take the horses ashore," he said. "I need to have a word with the captain."

"Sir."

Kyler gathered up their mounts and led them by the reins from the deck, across the wide gangplanks and then down into Loxford's harbour. Kyler could not help but feel relieved. For the first time in a week, his feet touched dry land. He exchanged greetings with the locals as he walked through the bustling harbour. He tied the reins to a post and gently ran his hand along his horse's side, smiling as he stroked the black pelted mare. Slowly, he made his way across her back and along her strong neck. He caressed her jaw.

"Peace, Asena," Kyler whispered. "We're on dry land again, girl. We'll be home soon, ey? We'll be home."

"Beautiful horse," a voice called out. "Medean stock?"

Kyler turned towards the Annoran who approached. "Northern blood, aye," Kyler told him. "Born and raised in the Adrestian highlands."

"Good land," the man replied. "Name's Filip."

"Kyler."

"What brings you to Loxford?"

"We're returning home after a long absence," the knight replied.

Something in Kyler clicked. He grimaced and shook his head. The pain had returned, yet this time it brought more. It grew worse. He felt anger. He felt rage. He felt suffering. Kyler became them. He felt a great hunger. A hunger to hurt the man who had approached.

✦ ✦ ✦

Filip saw the Medean freeze. The Annoran frowned as he stared at the man. He could hear the Medeans' rugged breathing. He was in pain, that much was certain. Blood drained from the Medean's face. He looked more than just tired. He looked exhausted. He looked like a dead man walking.

"Everything alright?" Filip asked.

The Medean did not reply.

"Sir?"

Filip extended a hand and placed it on the man's shoulder. The Medean swivelled around at the touch. Filip flinched back and then a fist cracked heavily into his face. His nose shattered as he fell back with a cry. The Medean jumped on top of him and started raining down blows. Filip fought back with a snarl. He tasted blood – his own blood.

✦ ✦ ✦

Kyler awoke.

"Pisspot," Alarik's snarl greeted his ears.

The battlemaster's arms wrapped around Kyler's waist and threw him from Filip.

"PISSPOT! What have you done?"

Kyler did not reply. He could only stare in horror. The blood of Filip's broken nose and split lip covered his hands. The anger was gone; only confusion remained. He remembered attacking the man. He had been present in the fight. But he did not know *why* he had attacked Filip.

Annorans started to gather around. Kyler rose to his feet. Filip rose to his feet. Alarik shoved Kyler backward.

"What is going on?" one of the Annorans called angrily. "You alright, Filip?"

Filip spat a glob of blood to the side and glared at the knights.

"I don't–" Kyler started.

"Shut your mouth!" Alarik snarled as he turned his livid eyes on Filip who had started to approach. Alarik extended a hand as he roared, "STAY THERE!"

Unease ran through the Annoran contingent. They were about to turn.

"He attacked without cause," Filip growled and did not avert his furious gaze from Kyler.

"STAY THERE!" Alarik repeated.

Hands balled into fists as the crowd stirred. Angry words were spoken.

"He attacked one of our own," an Annoran said. "Do not come between us."

For the first time, Kyler was glad that he did not wear the blue and silver armour of the order.

Alarik snatched a purse from his saddle bag and tossed it to Filip. "For your injuries," Alarik said, knowing that the sum far outweighed the wounds. "I will deal with my companion. You have my word."

"I want justice," Filip snapped back.

The battlemaster didn't look back at Kyler, but the Medean could tell what the battlemaster was thinking. The Annorans had surrounded them. They were impassioned. The flame was about to spark.

"Get on your horse," Alarik commanded.

The knights made for their mounts and untethered them. Insults came from every direction.

"Oi!" Filip shouted. "Stop!"

Alarik turned on instinct as the Annoran reached for his shoulder. The battlemaster half drew his sword. "Do not test me," he growled.

If the sight of steel scared Filip, then he did not show it. The Annoran merely spread his arms and stepped back. Kyler heaved himself up onto Asena's back. He was still in shock. Alarik mounted beside him. The crowd closed in. There was no time to delay. Alarik kicked his heels in. Kyler followed suit and the pair were racing through the town, leaving behind nothing but the shouts that followed.

"STOP!"

"BRING HIM BACK!"

The knights did not stop.

They rode for miles and had barely dismounted when Alarik shoved Kyler with a thunderous look. The rough leather of the battlemaster's glove slammed into Kyler's cheek as Alarik came at him. He shoved the Medean back into a tree and wrapped his fingers around the front of Kyler's gorget.

"The fuck was that about?" Alarik snarled. "Speak quickly!"

"I don't know!"

"Don't lie to me! Tell me or I swear I will take you back and hand you to those men."

"Alarik, I swear that I didn't mean to hurt him."

"Make your choice, boy!"

"I don't know what happened," Kyler exclaimed. "What started as pain in my mind has grown into something else. I feel like a puppet. Unable to think. Unable to control what I do."

"And something out there," Alarik said incredulously as he gestured towards nothing, "told you to do that? You're mad!"

"It's not a lie!" Kyler growled. "My body swung the blows, but I did not command it to act. I swear to you. By the gods, I swear it."

"Kyler … Soldiers fight. Soldiers brawl. Soldiers act on emotion. But we are not soldiers. We are Knights of Kil'kara. We are better than this. *You* are better than this." Alarik did not look away from Kyler's eyes as he placed his fist over the Medean's heart. "I know you're hurting. Your parents. Elena. I know. You are tired. You *need* rest. Do not let that pain destroy everything that you have built."

"I won't," Kyler swore.

Alarik grimaced and then released Kyler. "When we return to the north, there will be much blood to be shed."

"And until then?"

"Rest. Recover your strength. Praise the gods that I found you in time."

✦ ✦ ✦

Hugh Karter took a steady breath as he adjusted his grip on his sword. He stood armoured in his midnight blue gambeson and mail shirt. A steel gorget and pauldrons protected his lower neck and shoulders, while greaves and bracers adorned his legs and arms. A crestless helm was atop Hugh's head, and he carried his longsword and shield in hand. The shield, like his garb, did not bear the mark of Kil'kara. That honour was reserved for the knights, dozens of which now formed a wide circle around him. They stood side-on with their own shields bearing the sun of Durandail facing him. They were linked in an unbreakable wall. His mentor, Sir Corvo Alaine, stood among their number, as did the warden Sir William Peyene. Hugh paid them no heed.

Steel flashed towards his face as his opponent moved. He deflected the sword and lashed out with his own. The knight took it upon his shield. Hugh circled and then engaged. He was fast and his instincts honed by Corvo had grown sharp. Feinting, he unleashed a flurry of blows. He found angles for his attacks and then created more. He overwhelmed the knight and drove the crossguard of his sword into the man's helmet. He struck once, twice and then, as the knight fell back, sliced the blade of his sword into the knight's helm. Hugh ducked a wild blow and sent his sword into the knight's armoured shin. The man's balance was taken, and he crashed down heavily into the mud. Raising his shield, Hugh rested his sword upon its lip, turning left and then right. His eyes never left the ring of faces surrounding him.

Hearing a new opponent moving behind him, Hugh pivoted and raised his shield in time to catch the downwards strike, lunging as he skipped to the right. His sword caught the knight's shield as he changed angles. Feinting right and then cutting left, he punched his shield into the knight's thrust, slicing his sword along the knight's bracer. Steel kissed steel. A shift of footwork took Hugh behind his opponent. He danced to the side as he lashed out. His change of angle took the knight by surprise, allowing Hugh to slam his sword into the knight's back. The knight barely grunted as his armour took the blow. The knight swivelled back and sent the rim of his shield towards Hugh's face. Hugh slid to the right, avoided the blow and then drove his own shield into the knight's side. The knight fell back, but Hugh stayed on him. He battered the knight with sword and shield until the knight fell to a knee. Hugh's final blow came from his crossguard. He slammed it into the knight's armoured cheek and put him down.

Hugh heard the whistle of steel and turned. His shield came up. Just in time. The sword slammed down hard. The shield caught some of the blow, but his pauldron took the brunt. His armour rang and his shoulder ached. The force drove Hugh to a knee. Gritting his teeth and driving forward, he leapt into a lunge. The knight blocked, but the blow was not meant to harm.

It gave Hugh space and momentum enough to leap to his feet. He charged into the fire that was the knight. Sword and shield were his weapons. Weaving in and out as he fought, angling one way and then attacking another, Hugh deflected the knight's sword and leapt forward. Hugh raised his shield high and came down over the knight, catching the man hard in the helmet. The knight stumbled. Hugh rushed in. Dropping to a knee, he wrapped his arms around the knight's torso and drove himself forward. Both men crashed to the ground. Hugh leapt on top. With a savage cry, he slammed the pommel of his sword into the knight's helmet three times. Hugh cast aside his blade, tore his knife free and pressed it to the knight's chin. The knights surrounding the pair began to beat their fists upon their shields, slowly at first, but with each pound the speed grew. They said not a word. Hugh glared down at the man beneath him as he pressed the dagger close. The knight released his sword. It was over. The song of fist upon shield grew into a roar. Exhilaration flooded Hugh as he rose to his feet. Pride, joy, triumph. Hugh tossed his dagger aside and punched his fist into his heart. He beat his breast as the knights beat their shields. He let out a long bellow of victory.

The acting grand master Sir Corvo stepped into the circle of knights. "Initiate Karter, you have passed the final trial to gain entrance into the Order of Kil'kara," the acting master said. "Kneel."

Hugh did so. He bowed as Sir Corvo drew his mighty sword.

"Those who are soldiers of our church are soldiers of the gods. Will you stand with us?"

"I will."

"We stand as Durandail's sword, a mighty instrument to bring justice to his people and strike down their enemies. We stand as Azaria's shield, to serve all in need and to protect those who cannot protect themselves. Will you take up arms for your faith?"

"Honour, valour, justice, truth, compassion, allegiance: these are the tenants that guide my blade, and in the gods' name, I shall bear it."

The sword touched Hugh's right shoulder.

"By the will of the father of all fathers," Sir Corvo began.

The sword met his left shoulder.

"And by that of the silver lady, I knight thee, Sir Hugh Karter. Arise now as one of Durandail's chosen. Arise, a Knight of Kil'kara."

✦ ✦ ✦

FOURTEEN

Sofia Raynor walked slowly through the evergreen gardens alone. The sun shone brightly high above and its rays were warm upon her skin. Songbirds flew overhead and flowers bloomed all around her. Were it another time, she would have revelled in the beauty of the day, but her mind was taken. The news of her father's potential involvement in the murder of King Dorian chilled her. Sofia was the queen of Annora, yet she was a *foreign* queen. For the beloved king to have been slain by not only one of her people but by her own father threatened both Sofia's position and her life. A game was being played between Santiago and Dayne. One that would have great consequences regardless of who triumphed.

Sofia found her father sitting before a small wooden table in the heart of the gardens. A quill was in Santiago's hand and a piece of parchment was neatly laid out before him. A simply clad servant stood next to the table awaiting instruction. Beside them was Aquale Caspin, Santiago's younger brother and Sofia's uncle. Aquale saw Sofia first and made his way towards her.

"Your grace," Aquale said softly and offered her a bow.

"Please, uncle, there is no need for such formality between us," Sofia replied with a grin.

The pair embraced.

"You look radiant, Sofia," Aquale told her with a kind smile.

The queen glanced past her uncle towards Santiago. His eyes did not leave the parchment that he was now filling with words. His brow was furrowed in concentration. He probably did not even realise that she was here.

"My father?"

"Important matters of state," Aquale replied. "Or so he tells me."

"So I see."

Santiago finished whatever he was writing, placed his quill to the side and then rolled up the parchment. He sealed it with his ring and handed the letter to his servant.

"Take this to Saragoza," Santiago commanded. "Ride hard. Don't look back."

"Yes, my lord," the servant said, placing the letter within his satchel.

With a bow, the servant scurried from the gardens to do his duke's bidding. Aquale gestured towards his brother. Sofia stepped forward.

"Sofia, my dove." Santiago took her hands and placed a kiss on each of her cheeks.

"Hello, Father."

"I apologise that I have not been able to see you of late."

"There is nothing to forgive," Sofia said, and she gestured into the gardens. "Perhaps you might be tempted to spare a few moments away from this war of yours."

"Go on, brother," Aquale added. "I can handle business for a while."

"I never could refuse you anything." Santiago chuckled as Sofia wound her arm through his.

"Saragoza?" Sofia asked.

"Lord Garcia took an arrow upon the fields of Bandujar," her father grimaced. Sofia's eyes widened. Garcia had been with her family since the days of her grandfather. He was a close friend and confidant, her father's sworn sword despite his age.

"Is he?"

"No," Santiago replied.

"Thank the gods. I have given command for he to return to Saragoza. To rest. To take charge."

She led her father along the sandy paths through the gardens. Some of the maija tended to the plants and flowers that grew, but for the most part, the gardens were empty.

"Azaria has blessed us this day," Sofia said. "Her sun is light and warms the skin. The gardens are filled with life. It is beautiful. Beautiful enough that one almost forgets the chaos of these times."

"Indeed, it is," Santiago replied. "When you were a child, we went to the lotus gardens in Danakis. Do you remember?"

"A little."

"You would have been around six summers." Santiago smiled. "Knee high to a grasshopper you were. Now look at you."

Sofia grinned and let her free hand wander through the flowers beside the track. "We were all there that day. You and I. Pederico, Javier, Armaund and mother."

"Esperensa," Santiago said fondly. "She loved those gardens. The cool, clear waters and warm, Larissan sun. The flowers that bore every colour of the rainbow. Their soft petals and sweet scent. Your mother would have loved it here."

"I wish I could have known her better," Sofia replied. "It is one thing to know her as a child, but to know her as a woman – that would have been something truly special."

"From the moment you were born, she loved you fiercely. There was nothing she would not do to protect her cub. She doted upon you."

"Just as you do." Sofia chuckled.

"There is so much of Esperensa in you," Santiago said. "Not just your shared love of poetry and books. You have her eyes. You have her grace and her wit. You have her strength. She would be so very proud of you, Sofia. Just as I am."

"My childhood with her is something that I will always cherish," Sofia told him.

A sad look crossed Santiago' face. "After your brothers were taken most cruelly and my Esperensa lay on her death bed, she made me promise to *always* protect you. If by my life or death I can, then I will," he told her. "I have always and I will always do so. Everything that I do, whether on the field or in politics, is to keep you from harm."

"Father, what are you talking about?" Sofia pressed.

The duke halted and stared out into the gardens. "I have done things, Sofia. Terrible things. I have …"

Sofia stepped in front of her father and looked deep into his eyes. "Killed?" she murmured.

"Yes."

"Tell me, Father," Sofia said softly.

"I killed the king," Santiago told her.

Sofia felt the blood drain from her face. Dayne had been right. Her husband was a brilliant man, but until her father said those words and admitted his guilt, she had harboured doubts.

"What are you saying?"

"I took his life to deliver you into something better," her father said.

"But why? Help me to understand, Father," Sofia pleaded.

"You are queen now and in time your child will inherit it all. Annora … my lands. It will all be for you."

Sofia frowned. "For me? I cannot inherit land or title."

"I know," he replied. "And I will not see you cast aside as all queens are."

"Then Dayne," Sofia whispered as she at last understood.

"If your child is born a son, then the king will be dealt with. He is weak, Sofia. The gods have cursed him, and it will not be long before the Pale Horseman rides to meet him. What then? I will not have my daughter set adrift, forgotten by the people she served."

"And you would kill two kings?" Sofia said. She was barely able to hide her horror.

"I am resolved," Santiago said. "I would do anything for you. Anything to honour your mother."

"You miss her so much?"

"Every day."

✦ ✦ ✦

Dayne deflected Sir Garrik's wooden staunch with his own. He slid aside from Garrik's follow-through before countering with a thrust. The king sent three lightning-fast blows towards his sparring partner, blows that would have toppled common men. Garrik Skarlit was not common. He was commander of the royal guard and the master at arms of Palen-Tor. He blocked the first two, parried the third and then replied. Dayne caught the counter with his high guard, shifted his feet and made to attack. The pain came from nowhere. Boiling, searing pain. Dayne gasped and clutched at his stomach. His staunch hit the ground.

"Your majesty!"

Dayne's legs went out from under him. His vision flickered white. All he could feel, all he could see, was pain. The king crashed to his knees as he fought against the agony. He raked a hand through the earth and balled it into a fist. He tasted blood. Yet still Dayne fought. He held up his other hand to halt Garrik's approach.

"No!" Dayne growled.

The master at arms froze at the direct order from his king. Dayne grimaced. His body shook. He closed his eyes and bared his bloody teeth. His fist tightened. Snarling and striking the ground, he spat to the side, blood splashing to the earth. He opened his eyes and took a long breath. He slowly rose to his feet and let his hands unfurl. It was getting worse. Dayne could see the fear in the eyes of his companion. Garrik was scared for his friend and could sense the pity that came from the older man's gaze. The king gathered up a handkerchief and wiped the traces of blood away from his mouth. Garrik at last approached and held out his waterskin. Dayne nodded his thanks as he took it. The water washed away the taste of blood.

"Sir Garrik, if you would please gather the council," Dayne told his friend. "I wish to speak with them at sundown."

"Yes, my king."

"Only the Annoran contingent."

The guardsman frowned but gave a nod.

"Oh, and Sir Garrik," the king continued. "Best not to tell anyone about this. Not our own nobles, not the guard, not the maija and certainly not our allies."

"It will be done."

Dayne kept his composure as he walked through the castle. No good would come of the attack and only the worst would come if anyone learnt of it. Many among the nobility were circling like vultures. None more so than Duke Caspin. For Santiago to have mentioned the affliction days ago meant only one thing: that the duke's fear of Dayne was lessening. He was growing bolder. Dayne opened the door to his chamber. He was greeted by the light of candles and his wife sitting before his desk.

"A poem?" Dayne asked as he entered.

Sofia glanced up from the page before her and gave him a sad smile. She spoke the words that she had written.

> "Leaves fall from a single oak,
> adrift, discarded,
> cast aside by a single stroke.
> The tree is a rot,
> and its blood decayed.
> This darkness gathered,

because from the path it strayed.
Oak crumbles to ruin,
shattered and desolate.
What was once strong
betrayed by its root."

Dayne stared at his wife as her voice trailed off. The poem was haunting, filled with sorrow.

"As beautiful as it is sad," Dayne murmured as he approached his queen.

"The words have haunted me for some time, but until today I did not have a proper ending," Sofia said.

Dayne walked behind where she sat. He placed a hand on each of her shoulders and planted a gentle kiss upon the top of her head. Sofia reached up and placed her hand on top of Dayne's. She leaned back into his chest and closed her eyes.

"And now you have found it," Dayne said.

"As you will have found the meaning held within my words."

"I have," Dayne told her. "Sofia … I can only imagine how hard this must be for you. Whatever happens, you will remain my dearest love."

"Just as you are mine," she replied as a tear rolled down her cheek. "I am a Raynor now. I am your queen. What kind of queen would I be if I did not protect my own people?"

"Sofia, I need you to do something for me. I need you to find Kassandra and her mother and return to Kilgareth. Verena has become too dangerous," Dayne said. "What I am about to do will change everything."

Sofia rose from her chair and turned to face her husband. She did not let go of his hand. "You're going to kill him, aren't you?"

"I don't know. If Santiago dies, then this alliance that hangs by a thread may snap, and I will not let that come to pass. In this world, few things are certain. What will happen in the coming months, we can only guess. Santiago will be dealt with and this war between families will end."

"Our marriage may be the only thing that holds our alliance together," Sofia said. "At the same time, it is our marriage that others wish to exploit for their own profit. I look into their eyes each day and I see the thrones that they long for within."

"We are the centrepiece of this game that is waged in the corridors of power while a defining war is being fought upon the field," Dayne replied. "I swear to you that I will not let the enemy win this war nor destroy everything we have built from within."

"It is us or them."

"I know," Dayne admitted.

"I promise you, my dearest love, that my faith will always remain strong," Sofia vowed fervently. "I will do what it is that you ask."

"Tomorrow then, you must leave. Take my family. Above all else, you must be kept safe."

King Dayne clasped his hands as the last of his council assembled. The royal guard captain Garrik Skarlit and General Tristayn Martyn watched with emotionless faces. The lords Harold Robare and Edmund Hornwood stood in their fine armour. Galan the high lord of Torosa stood alongside Balderik, his counterpart from Laeoflaed. They had all come.

"My lords," King Dayne started. "We are now facing an enemy of unprecedented nature. An enemy that has already struck at the very heart of our nation. At the heart of the palace itself."

"Do you speak of King Dorian?" Lord Galan asked.

Dayne nodded to the Torosi leader. "Indeed. My father's death was only the beginning," the king replied. "I have uncovered a thread. A thread that, once pulled, threatens to unravel our kingdom."

"If you have uncovered the murderer of King Dayne," Edmund growled, "then tell me. I would love to kill him for you. Nothing would please me more."

"That is the very reason why I have called you all here, Lord Hornwood," Dayne said. "For the killer is one trusted above all else. One whom I hold as family. A man who has betrayed us all. The architect of my father's death bears the name Caspin."

Eyes flew to King Dayne's face.

"Then they have betrayed us all," Tristayn snarled. "My king, give me leave to take a company of the guard into their camp. I will bring them before you in chains."

"What of your wife?" Balderik asked. "Is she responsible?"

"No," Dayne snapped. "Sofia had no part in this, and she is not to be harmed. Do you understand?"

"Yes, your majesty."

"Now, we will not strike at the heart of those who have wronged us," Dayne replied. "We cannot risk all that we have built. I know that Santiago Caspin killed my father, yet what I do not have is a confession. A confession from a member of his family involved would see their house crumble. Their allies would turn. There would be no war. Only justice."

"So, this confession. How do we come about it?" Garrik asked.

Dayne glanced at the captain of his guard. He had pondered the question for days. Eveline's confession would mean nothing. The word of a lady in waiting would never be taken over that of a duke. Dayne needed something else, something stronger that could take Santiago down. He had the knife, he had the killer – now he just needed an unquestionable confession.

"We can't take Santiago. Not yet, at least. That would start the very thing that I wish to avoid. Without the head of the snake, the rest would attack without question. No … Santiago must remain so that he can take charge of his people," Dayne said. "There is only one man whom we can reach. Only one man who can tell us what we need to know. General Tristayn. Tomorrow night you are to send men to arrest Aquale Caspin and bring him to me."

"It will be done, my king."

✦ ✦ ✦

The cooing of pigeons filled the aviary in Kilgareth. Dozens of the small birds filled the great chamber atop the maija's library. Arc'maija Lysandra held one of the pigeons close as she gently placed a small roll of paper in a tiny ring that was tied to the bird's slender leg. She gently handed the pigeon to her younger companion. Like her, the girl wore the robes of the maija.

"It takes many months to ride from Kilgareth to Rovira. In urgent times, much could have changed before such a messenger had ridden from north to south," Lysandra explained. "With pigeons, a message can pass between my hands and those of Arc'maija Hellio in a matter of days."

The younger maija carried the bird to one of the huge balconies that ringed the aviary. With a nod from Lysandra, the girl launched the pigeon into the sky.

"How do they do it?" the girl asked.

Lysandra gave her a smile. "To this day, no one truly knows," she said. "Though perhaps one day, Kaira, you will be the one to unshroud this mystery."

"I truly hope so," Kaira replied with a grin.

The two maija gazed out from the balcony. A dark speck appeared on the horizon. Kaira pulled out her spyglass and turned it towards the dot. The tiny form of a pigeon could be seen through the glass. It grew larger by the moment.

"A message from the north," Kaira said.

"Verena, most likely," Lysandra replied.

The pigeon arrived shortly after. Lysandra extended her arm and let the bird come to perch on her wrist. She unbound the small message from the pigeon's leg and the bird fluttered into the aviary.

"What does it say, my lady?" Kaira asked.

"Here." Lysandra held the note out. "You read it."

"It is in old Aureian," Kaira told her. "Duræn ĕya su'ren váyle tælyr cerey su'murn."

"And that means?" the arc'maija pressed.

"The sun rises to the north while the eagle cries to the south."

"Just so," Lysandra said with a smile. "And what meaning does it carry?"

"The Order is the sun and the eagle King Dayne," the young maija replied. "The army is about to march again. Bavarian has led our brothers in the wake of the Medeans while Annora plans to begin his attack from further south."

"Thank you, Kaira," Lysandra told her as she took the message back. "If you will please pass this news on to Sir Mortimier."

"Of course, my lady."

✦ ✦ ✦

FIFTEEN

Káli Lands, Forest of Salvaar

Several days had passed before Lukas and his companions reached the southern border of Salvaar. Though still within the lands beholden to Vaylin, they were camped barely a stone's throw from territory that belonged to the Catuvantuli. Night was fast approaching when Lukas and his band of two hundred Káli warriors set up their camp. From here, they could sneak along the border and raid with near impunity. Perhaps they could even pass behind enemy lines.

Scouts and moonseer were sent in every direction to watch for their foe. Orange light cast by the horizon seeped between the trees when the Káli formed a circle. Some among the inner row carried flaming torches. Hadwin and Layan stood to either side of Lukas at the very front. One-Eye stared at the lone figure within the circle. Raven black hair and blazing emerald eyes. Her clothing was dark and left much of her skin bare. Winding tattoos marked her flesh, while an amulet in the likeness of a snake hung at her throat. The black paint that covered her skin and white grease that pushed back her hair only added to her ferocious look. Dark and alluring, she was like a wild tempest. Her presence was more powerful than all the western kings. Lukas could not tear his gaze from the she-wolf. The dark priestess. The one who served Tanris. Maevin. In her hands clasped at her waist was a long silver knife.

A single opening broke the circle, a pathway that a pair of torchbearers stood alongside. Three figures appeared at the end of the corridor through the black-painted Káli. Two were Salvaari. One was a man, the other a woman. Both were marked with war paint. Both were warriors. Like the rest of their people, they appeared primal, scantly garbed in black, tattooed, and with small bones and relics woven through their hair and clothing. The man was Rodion and the woman, a moonseer, Aelida. Their hands were tightly locked around the arms of the third person. Vincente. The prisoner that they had taken at the Arwan days ago. The soldier had been stripped down to his tunic and trousers. His hands were tightly bound behind his back and his mouth was roughly gagged. Vincente's muffled screams began when he was led into the open ground within the circle. Maevin turned to face him. Vincente saw the knife. He struggled but the Káli held him tight. Rodion and Aelida forced the captive to his knees. The Káli began to chant. They did not speak words. Instead, they created a more primeval sound. A savage sound. Maevin spread her arms and then spoke in the tongue of Salvaar.

"Tanris, gatekeeper of the Veil. Lord of the Dead. Dark One. We, your faithful servants, will bless those who would challenge you with a searing kiss. You will bask in their song! A song of lamentations and the screams of the damned. May the agony of the enemy echo beyond the Veil for eternity. Curse them, lord! Drench them in fires and plagues just as we will drench you in their blood!"

Maevin bared her teeth as she spoke. Her eyes were wild and her voice passionate. Those who watched her bore the same expressions. Fervent expressions. The fires of their souls blazed in their eyes. Their chants grew louder. Lukas felt a shiver roll down his spine. It did not chill him; his blood ran hot as if a blaze had awoken within. A thin smirk contorted his lips. Vincente was frozen. His face was a painting of fear. He could not move. He could not scream or struggle.

"Master of blood and bone," Maevin roared as she drove her silver blade skyward. "Accept our sacrifice this day. May this man's life serve as harbinger to the fate that we shall inflict upon your enemy! May our gift, like your foe, bleed!"

The chants grew into a crescendo. They became howls. Then they stopped. All grew still. Maevin grasped Vincente's hair and tipped his head back. She stared deeply into his eyes and basked in the fear that she saw looking back. She placed her knife against the side of prisoner's neck. Lukas caught his breath. The priestess savagely bared her teeth as she stabbed the blade deep into Vincente's neck. She watched the light fade from his eyes as he struggled to breathe. Maevin adjusted her grip upon the bone hilt and then spun backward. The knife tore apart the prisoner's throat as its bearer carved it through. Blood spewed forth in the blade's wake.

The Káli roared as Maevin held the bloody knife aloft. Vincente's lifeless body crashed into the ground. The priestess cast the knife aside and knelt beside the corpse. She dipped her hands in Vincente's blood and splashed it over her face.

Lukas trembled. He had not noticed that his hands had grown white around the handle of his crutch. He knew so little of the Salvaari culture, yet the more he discovered, the more it called to him. It was of the heart. It was wild and free.

Maevin howled as she turned away from the corpse. She stared towards Lukas. With her lips drawn back into a vicious grin, her face wore a mask of blood. Lukas met her eyes. He saw the passion within. The hunger. He felt *alive*.

The Káli began to disperse. Rodion and Aelida gathered up the dead man's body. Lukas remained where the circle had once been, and his eye flicked to the Káli who started to drag Vincente's bloody corpse away.

"By your leave, lord," Layan said.

Lukas glanced at his Annoran companions. They had both seen death before, but this was something else entirely. Human sacrifice. There was darkness in the eyes of the mercenaries. Lukas nodded and waved them away. Layan and Hadwin dipped their heads before making for their tent. Only then did Maevin beckon him. He followed the priestess into the woods. Maevin's fire burned brightly. Her touch and lips were as hungry as her eyes. She pulled Lukas towards her as she backed into a tree. One-Eye felt the warm blood on her face. He tasted it. He did not pull away.

Lukas sat upon the trunk of a fallen tree. His crutch leaned beside him, and in his hand was a cup of the witch's brew that took away his pain. The drink that tasted of strawberries. The strip of white cloth that was tied around his head to cover his eyeless socket had long since faded to light brown. His hair had grown long enough to bear a thin Salvaari braid, while a short beard now covered his jaw. Lukas wore stripes of black paint down across his right eye. Most haunting of all were the small droplets of Vincente's blood that clung to his beard. He could still taste its warmth. Even without his garb of mail and Salvaari furs, Lukas doubted that anyone he had known growing up would recognise him anymore.

A gust of wind breezed through the woods. It disturbed the fallen leaves and threw them up into the air. Lukas' gaze was drawn to them. His gaze was drawn *past* them. Out in the blackness there stood a man. He was barely visible, yet even Lukas' one eye could recognise him. The air grew cool to the touch as Lukas stared towards the figure. A pair of scarlet eyes stared back. He gathered up his crutch and slowly began to make his way into the forest, towards the man he knew as Harkan. Lukas left the camp far behind as he made his way to the ruskalan. He swivelled his head to search the surroundings – this time it was clear that the dark-clad Harkan was alone. Pale skin, pointed ears and a beardless chin revealed the ruskalan. Dark runes covered his skin and long raven hair hung down his back. A white scar ran its course down the left side of Harkan's face.

"Lukas the One-Eye," Harkan said with his melodic voice. "When last we met, you were but the shadow of a broken man. Now you bear the favour of Tanris. You are his messenger."

"Avenging the bloodmoon was only the beginning," Lukas replied.

"The sandglass of time pours, broken man," Harkan told him. "One stage of your journey is over. Another begins. There is a task now to be done. You must be swift, broken man, for your prey has a head start."

Lukas frowned curiously. "My prey?"

"The princess who married an eagle."

Lukas' mind darkened. Only one man bore the symbol of the great bird.

"Sofia Caspin," Lukas said.

"This day will pass and then she will ride. She travels by carriage," Harkan told him. "She will be slow. Protected by only a dozen knights."

"How did you come by this?" Lukas asked.

The ruskalan bared his fanged maw. "I hear all, broken man, I see all," he said. "The road she travels will take her from Verena to the citadel."

"Kilgareth," Lukas breathed. "If this is true, then it would take a number of thousands to storm the valley. Numbers that we do not have."

Harkan began to circle One-Eye as if the Annoran was his prey. "No army could take the eagle's queen," the ruskalan said. "You must ride out and meet her. Once more, you will be the wind."

Lukas watched the ruskalan and turned to follow his movement. "To gain the valley we would have to pass the mountains. Even if we left now, there is no way that we could cross them before they reach Kilgareth," Lukas replied.

"There is another path," Harkan said with a dark smile. "A hidden path. I will tell you how to find it."

Lukas pursed his lips as he thought. Somehow, someway, Harkan had received word from inside the lair of the enemy. Somehow, he had gained information that could almost certainly condemn much of the western armies to ruin.

"Then Sofia Caspin will see their alliance fall," Lukas said. "With her we can keep my brother from the field and therefore deprive them of their greatest warrior. We can divide them and then crush them one by one."

"What do you foresee, broken man?"

"I see the death of our enemies," Lukas replied. "We don't divide these people through force. We do it with whispers. Whispers to my brother shall lure him away. Whispers to Santiago Caspin, the commander of the legions and the other forces in the south, shall keep them fixed in place. Whispers to those men in the north shall bring them to their doom."

"Good," Harkan said as his eyes blazed crimson. "Then let's begin."

"If I take the queen, then we can keep my brother from the field. Once I have her as my prisoner, word shall be sent to the king. I will summon him to Thirlryda and draw him and his men away from the battle. He will expect a trap, yet he will come anyway. He will have no choice. I will meet with him and fill his ears with silver words. Duke Santiago will have no path to take but to remain in Verena with his army while most of our foe will be scattered in the north. There will never be a better chance for Henghis to exact his revenge."

Harkan grinned. "The spirits flow through you," he called. "I can see them. I can hear their call. My blood runs in the north. I can send word with but a whisper in the wind. The great chief will be ready for war."

Lukas' lips curled into a smirk as he watched the ruskalan. "I leave tonight."

"Once more, the leaves shall fall," Harkan murmured. "Though this time it shall be my people who decide their fate."

Sylvaine's silver moon was at its peak when Lukas commanded his people to break camp. Fifteen of their best warriors would accompany Lukas, Maevin and the Annoran mercenaries as they made for the mountain pass. The rest would follow Rodion to Lake Thirlryda.

✦ ✦ ✦

"Word has reached my ear that King Dayne and his Annorans will soon be marching further east," Henghis told the assembled chieftains. "With the Caspin duke left to watch over Verena, there will never be a better chance to defeat those who remain in the north."

"The invaders yet outnumber us," Balor of the Sagailean said.

"But they do not outmatch us," the great chief pressed. "If we can draw them into battle, then we can defeat them."

Vaylin stroked her jaw. "What do you propose?" she asked.

Henghis strode into the circle of Salvaari chiefs.

"As of this moment, the invaders have been unable to cross the river," Henghis said. "I say that we let them cross. Let them build their camps. Let them believe that they have beaten us. Let them think that they are safe, that no force can challenge them. Our people can lure them into battle … and then when the night comes, they will be greeted by death."

"A trick?" Etain inquired.

"A diversion," Henghis replied. "For their scouts will tell them that we have pulled back. Many of you will have, at least. I shall remain with a few of my warriors, and we will pick them off one by one, until they decide to face us in the field. We will lure them further and further into Salvaar, away from their camps. Close enough that their horseman will grant them no advantage. Close enough for the axe. Your tribes and your warriors will fall upon them from every side. We will cut them off from their camps. Encircle them. With small war bands we can divide them from their army and scatter them. Lead them away from the battle. By the time that the enemy have realised, the moon will have risen."

Balor took a step towards Henghis. Passion flowed from the Sagailean leader – his face was set, his shoulders square.

"They will cling to each other in the darkness, praying for salvation, but there will be none," Balor growled. "The darkness is the moonseer home. The silver eyes shall pierce the shadows with steel."

"We will push them back to the river and paint it red with blood. We will drown them in it and purge them from our lands," Henghis continued fervently. "For those of them who live to see the dawn sun, they will know that Salvaar will never be enslaved!"

Henghis gazed around at his fellow chiefs. His blood ran hot though it was not from the fire beside which he found himself. His faith and his passion had been reignited.

"Friends, the spirits are with us," Henghis told them.

"What Henghis says is true," Vaylin's cool voice added as she slid into the circle beside him. "I watch the stars, for they are my peoples to watch. The eyes of Tanris draw near, the Whisperer has begun his song and now the Veil has been opened."

"What meaning does that carry?" Etain asked.

"Our ancestors gaze upon us even as the spirits show us the way. As Henghis shows us the way," Vaylin explained. "Our ancestors await those of us who will join them in the coming days. They *long* to bask in the tales of triumph that will rise with the dead."

"My wolves long to hunt," Balor growled through bared teeth. "The screams of our enemies shall lull them to sleep."

"Then we are all agreed," Etain said before she turned to one of their number who went unspoken – the man who bore the blue markings of the Aedei. "What say you, Eilith?" Etain called to him.

"The world mourns for the loss of your chief," Henghis told him.

The Aedei glanced from leader to leader as a dark looked crossed his eyes.

"My people weep for their chief," Eilith told them. "Yet their hearts have not become empty vessels. Their hearts have become *filled* with hate. My heart has become filled. We long to avenge Cailean. To avenge what happened upon those fields. Let us fight. Let us pass these tears to our enemies. Instead of water, they shall weep tears of blood."

Henghis gave the Aedei a solemn nod.

"Then we will stand side by side, my brother," Henghis vowed.

✦ ✦ ✦

The moon had reached its peak when Dayne found himself gazing at the stone likenesses of Durandail and Azaria within Verena's temple. His hand was clasped tightly around his medallion though he said not a word. The king's mind was taken. Sofia, Kassandra and Riona had left mere hours before. It had become too dangerous for them to have stayed in the city. With what he had ordered, the world was about to shift, and he would not have them caught in the political battlefield that the city was about to become. The thought of them safely on the way to Kilgareth gave the king some comfort. Now he had but to win a war, find a rogue assassin and defeat a most dangerous political rival, all the while keeping the alliance strong.

The temple doors boomed open and Dayne's peace was broken. Loud footsteps came towards him across the tiled floor. He knew that they were Sir Tristayn's footsteps, as the general was walking towards him with haste. Something was wrong.

"Your majesty," Tristayn called. "You had better come quickly."

Dayne turned towards his friend and saw the worried look upon his face. "What is it, General?"

"It's Aquale Caspin. He's dead."

Dayne froze. He had commanded Caspin's arrest, not his death. The king wiped emotion from his face and for the first time felt comforted by the presence of his sword. He did not lower his hand to its pommel nor reach for steel. He would show Tristayn nothing and he certainly would not show anything to anyone beyond the temple, Annoran or Medean. He was a king.

"Take me to him," Dayne commanded.

Tristayn led his king through the castle of Verena. The corridors seemed to be colder and longer now. The air seemed more still. It was quiet. A company of royal guardsmen led by Sir Garrik surrounded King Dayne and the general as they made for the Caspin quarters. The first thing that Dayne saw was the pair of green-clad soldiers at Aquale's door. The Caspin household guard. Lights flickered within as a maija rushed inside. Two of the guard accompanied Dayne inside the room. The lavishly furnished room was little different to his own save for one thing. The blood. It was everywhere. A pair of red-clad Annoran soldiers lay on the floor as stiff as wood. They were dead. The weapon that had claimed their lives was a sidesword that lay beside the third body. The sword's pommel was just beyond the reach of Aquale Caspin's unmoving hand. The duke's brother lay in a pool of his own blood. An Annoran dagger was buried in his heart. Aquale Caspin had been murdered. The culprits were the very same men who had been sent to take him prisoner.

Dayne shared a glance with Tristayn. The fraying thread that had held Caspin and Raynor together had been severed. Its death throes came in the form of Santiago's screams as he saw his dead brother.

✦ ✦ ✦

SIXTEEN

City of Elara, League of Trecento

Elise Delfeyre sighed as she pulled on her leather jerkin. Most of her clothing had long since been packed, though the awful dresses that had become all too common in recent months were to be left behind. Like her mother before her, Elise did not care for the lavish gowns and frocks that the women of Elara wore. She preferred something more practical. Now that she was leaving the city, she saw no need to take anything more than her shirts, boots and baggy trousers. Tariq had procured her the jerkin, and after a few adjustments made by Elise herself, it fit perfectly. Elise buckled her kukri to her side and placed an empty satchel over her shoulder. Next came her green cloak.

A fist pounded upon the door to her room. It was time. Elise took a breath and then headed to the door. Striding out into the passage that led to the network of tunnels, she could see Tariq and Marshall patiently awaiting her, flaming torches in hand. Both wore dark cloaks and empty satchels. Marshall was clad in his armour: a long-sleeved gambeson covered by a shirt of mail, chestplate, greaves, bracers and helm of embellished steel. A round shield was slung across his back and a sidesword hung at his hip. The guardsman had come prepared for a fight.

Tariq, on the other hand, looked no more than a rogue from the pits, wearing a roughly cut tunic over trousers and boots that matched. The war hammer that he had procured on the night of Elise's hanging was shoved through his belt, while thick gloves covered his hands. But they weren't just gloves. Steel plates covered the brawler's knuckles and vicious points adorned them. Unlike Marshall, he wore the wide hood of his cloak up.

"The way is clear," Marshall told her as he extended his second torch.

Elise pulled her hood up and took the burning brand.

"We should be able to slip in and out unnoticed," Tariq added.

"Shall we?" Elise said and gestured down the passage.

The three companions followed the network of sewers and tunnels. Miles upon miles of stone labyrinth stretched out in every direction, chambers, passages and corridors all. There was no light save for the torches that the three carried. The stench that they had long since become accustomed to barely gave them pause – once, it had made them recoil. They saw few enough people within the network and for that Elise was eternally grateful. She did not trust any of the pirates or gangmen as far as she could throw them. The bodies that had once filled the tunnels had all been removed in the weeks after the attack, but traces of the fight remained. Splashes of blood appeared on stone. Tarnished remnants of clothing, weapons and armour could be found if you looked closely enough. The stench of death still filled some of the caverns.

After a time, they passed beneath the river that divided Elara. They continued through the tunnels until at last Tariq began to lead them up. The Berenithian glanced back at Elise and Marshall, who brought up the rear, and then tossed his torch into the murky waters of the sewer. The flame hissed angrily as it fizzled out. Elise and Marshall followed suit and the three were enveloped in darkness. They climbed higher and higher until they reached a wooden ladder. Tariq gestured to the ladder. No words needed to be spoken. Elise pulled forth a small dagger and gripped its handle between her teeth. Then she began to climb. Tariq went next and Marshall watched from the base of the ladder with his hand upon his sword. The guard looked back from whence they had come, his eyes keenly peeled and searching for any who may have followed them. Elise reached the top of the ladder. A closed, wooden door rested in the stonework above. She pressed it with her hands, but the door was locked. Elise nearly smirked as she took out her small knife and drove it into the gap between stone and wood. She made not a sound as she worked. The single arm that gripped the ladder was easily able to take her weight. Her brow furrowed in concentration ... and then the door jolted. Easy. Sheathing her knife, she once more tried the door. It slowly eased up. Elise's touch was gentle, and she used little force. She peered out the small crack that she had created. Nothing moved. Elise opened the door fully, grabbed a ledge to the left and right and then heaved herself up. Her boots lightly touched down on the floorboards as she took it all in. Thin slivers of moonlight came through the windows and cracks in the wooden walls. Rows upon rows of shelves filled the massive room. They were lined with jars and crates, silks and steel. A merchant's warehouse, just as Cleander had told them. Tariq and Marshall followed Elise up into the massive shed and closed the wooden door behind them. The three left the warehouse and snuck into the abandoned street. They rounded corners and kept to back alleys. Elise felt her blood begin to chill with each step. It appeared before them just as magnificent as it had been the first time she had seen it. Her uncle's home. The Delfeyre villa.

The air was cold. Elise's breath had turned into a white mist. Marshall's hand did not stray from his sword as they walked through the villa. Elise could see it all clear as day. Her aunt humming as she sewed atop one of the balconies. Her uncle laughing in the courtyard. Her eyes moved to the pool and her breath caught. Blood stained the floor before it. The blood of Raphael and Claudia. The blood of her family. She could still see their bodies as if they had not been removed. Elise's eyes grew wet.

"Elise," Tariq said quietly as he placed a comforting hand on her shoulder. "Elise."

She gritted her teeth and bit back the sobs that threatened. She gulped in air through bared teeth and blinked back the tears.

"This is for them," Tariq told her with a smile.

Elise nodded her head. "I know," she replied softly.

With that, they made their way up the stairs towards Elise's chamber. The shutters were still closed, for she had last been in these rooms the night that she had sought out the healer Casimir Dusan, the man who had poisoned her mother at Magister Imrohir's request. It was quiet. The only sound came from the footfalls of the soldier and the brawler. Elise glanced around the room and her eyes were drawn to the far corner. A canvas sat upon a stool of wood. The image of a dark-eyed woman was painted upon it. She wore an outfit of blue and white and held a silver mask mere inches from those brown eyes. Catinya Delfeyre.

"You painted this?" Tariq asked as they made their way through the room.

Elise glanced back at him and nodded.

"She's exactly like I remember," Tariq told her.

"I wish we could take her," Elise said.

"And who says we can't?"

Elise rolled her eyes, eyes that matched those upon the painting.

"I don't suppose that there will be much room where we're going," she replied.

"Maybe not for the painting, my lady," Marshall said. "Though her mask … I have seen its likeness before. I believe it to be in this house."

"You do?"

"Yes, lady," the guard told her. "By right it belongs to you. I shall find it." Without another word, Marshall marched from the chamber and made his way deeper into the villa.

Elise ran a finger down the edge of the canvas and gave the painted woman a final glance. She didn't say a word as she stared at the image of her mother. Then she left the stool and walked further into the room. She walked with purpose. Elise gathered up a candle holder and sparked the candle to life. Tariq followed Elise to the edge of the room where she knelt by the wall. She brushed her hand along the wooden boards and felt for the loose one. Placing her candle to the side and drawing her knife, she dug into the crevasse and pried the boards apart. The sight of a chest greeted her. Elise reached into the wall and pulled the box forth. Dragging it out, and with a self-satisfied smile, she tipped the lid back. Gold, silver, jewellery and gemstones filled the chest.

Tariq whistled as he saw the contents. "You have been busy," was all he said.

"All in a few months," Elise replied as she opened her satchel. "Here."

Together they started to fill their bags with the fortune that Elise had stolen from the nobility. Footsteps. Marshall returned. In his hands he held a small ivory box. He extended it towards Elise as she rose to meet him.

"It's yours now," he told her.

Inside was a finely embellished silver mask. It would cover the face from nose to brow, shielding everything except the eyes of its wearer.

"Mother's mask," Elise whispered as she glanced from the box to Marshall. "Thank you."

She closed the lid, flipped the lock shut and then lowered it gently into her satchel. It would be safe there. The song of bells filled the city. Elise met Tariq's gaze.

"We have to get to the harbour," he said.

✦ ✦ ✦

Erik Farrin stared out at a black horizon. The gentle Sacasian waves lapped at the prow of the Ravenheart. All was silent aboard the ship. The warriors and shield-maidens who crewed the mighty vessel watched from the deck as they sailed further east. Like Erik, they were fully kitted for battle in their armour. Shields bearing monsters and symbols were slung across their backs and weapons were held in hand or hung from their belts. Like their king, they all wore white ochre upon their faces. Erik did not look to Torben, who stood to his side. He did not look back to Fargrim at the helm of the ship. His eyes were drawn to the faint, flickering lights that shone ahead.

Two days ago, Erik had ordered his vast armada to sail through the night without using candles or any kind of light. He had ordered total silence in the darkness. Erik would not give their position away to anyone who sailed in the dark seas. The League's fleet under the command of Javais was under no such obligation. Who would attack such a mighty fleet, let alone in the night? They had no enemies save those poor souls trapped in the city. It was towards these lights that Erik and his thirty ships now sailed. Sea-Father had blessed them with a cloudy night. The moon would not give them away yet.

Erik tightened his grip upon his helmet. Ringing echoed across the water: the sound of bells. He shared a glance with Torben. Luana's birds had gotten past the blockade. Those fleeing the city would be gathering in the harbour while a fleet of pirate ships was assembling to come to the Valkir's aid. More than that, the song of the bells would draw the attention of Javais and his men. Erik could not see those aboard the League's ships, yet he knew that right now all eyes would be turning towards the tolling of the Elaran bells. The raven king placed his helmet over his head and pulled the strap tight. He slid his crimson shield onto his arm and pulled forth his axe. The lights of the enemy's ships grew closer. Without a word, Erik held his weapon aloft. The Valkir donned helmets and drew steel. The bells song grew louder and louder. Erik could make out the first of the League's ships. Fargrim slightly changed the angle of the Ravenheart's vicious ram and turned it towards the very centre of the ship opposite. Erik stepped back from the railing and a rank of archers took his place. The king's eyes went to the deck of the opposing ship. He could see tiny shadows dancing around as sailors ran by candles. A shout came from across the waves. An Elaran voice. The Ravenheart had been sighted. Warning bells began to sound aboard the Elaran vessel.

"RELEASE!" Erik roared.

Arrows sped through the darkness. Dozens of soldiers fell. Volley after volley followed the first. Steel ripped through canvas, splintered wood and pierced flesh. The Elaran ship tried to turn. Too late. The archers moved back. Erik, Torben and other heavily armed warriors took their place. Erik braced himself against the rail, staring across the abyss. Soldiers began to swarm up from the lower deck. Few wore their armour; none had expected a fight. Cries of fear and panic ran through the Elaran ranks.

The world shook and Erik was thrown into the rail. The Ravenheart's ram bit in deep to the side of the enemy vessel. The height of the bow gave them the high ground. Archers began to take aim. With a vicious war cry, Erik vaulted over the rail and dropped down onto the Elaran deck. His boots touched down and then his axe tasted blood. Erik caught a second man's blade with his shield and caved in his chest. Torben and Laerke dropped to Erik's side and together they formed an unbreakable shield wall. Three men became five. Five men became a dozen. Erik led the charge as they fought for control. The deck became awash with blood as the Valkir slaughtered their foe. Erik brought his axe down hard on the shoulder of a sailor. The man collapsed to his knees. With a roar, Erik punched his shield out and sent the dying man down. His axe tasted blood again as a mercenary soldier came at him with a hammer. He caught the blow high with his shield and cracked its steel rim into the Elaran's jaw. His axe followed closely behind. The dead soldier had not yet hit the deck when Erik saw another man raise a spear. The Elaran was going to hurl it towards Laerke. Erik shot his axe arm forward and launched the weapon into the air. It spun, head over end, even as Erik broke rank. The vicious head sliced into the Elaran's shoulder. The man fell with a scream and dropped the spear. Erik drew his sword as he darted towards the fallen man. He buried steel in the spearman's throat. With the formations breaking and the Elaran's morale shattering, Erik swung his shield back across his shoulder and snatched up his axe. He made for the helm with a weapon in both hands. Three men stood in his way, turning at his fearsome roar. Erik felled one, felled two, felled three. No man could stand against his blades. No man could stand against him. Erik took the steps two at a time as he barrelled towards the finely clad captain and his guard. He battered aside the first man's shield with his axe and drove his sword through the guard's neck. The captain backed away as his last guard engaged the king. Erik blocked the incoming sword with his own and countered with his axe. It found nothing but shield. Erik changed angles and lunged. The guard caught it with his shield but stumbled back at the force of the blow. Surging forward, Erik brought his sword around. Again, the guard blocked it. Sliding his axe beneath the guard's cover, Erik carved through his thigh. The Elaran fell with a scream. Erik's sword found a home in his shoulder and then his axe silenced those screams.

Erik stared towards the captain. His lips were drawn back into a wordless snarl. Blood covered his blades and armour. The Elaran captain held a sword of steel, his nerves made of anything but. Erik could almost taste the fear.

He saw the lunge coming before the man moved. Swinging his axe around, he deflected the sword. Steel met flesh as Erik drove his sword deep under the man's chin, tearing through the back of the captain's neck. Erik buried his blade to the hilt. The king saw the life flee the captain's eyes. Blood covered his skin and his fine clothes. It covered Erik's sword. Erik turned as he viciously tore his sword free and sent the captain's body down onto the deck.

The crew of the Ravenheart stood victorious. Not a man was left alive aboard their prize. Finally allowing himself to breathe, Erik took a long look up and down the line of ships. His people had all but devastated the first group of the League's vessels. But more were coming. Dozens more.

"THE SACASIANS!" Fargrim roared from the Ravenheart. "THE SACASIANS ARE COMING!"

The crew gave a mighty cheer as their allies were sighted surging forth from Elara. The League's fleet was surrounded.

"BACK TO THE RAVENHEART!" Erik bellowed.

✦ ✦ ✦

The Emeralis sped through a gap that had opened in the blockade. Luana's grip tightened upon the wheel. She had seen the Ravenheart engage its foe – her signal to advance. Ten Valkir ships sailed with Luana. Some bore skeleton crews, while the others were overflowing with armoured warriors. Luana was to lead the near-empty ships into the bay and give those stranded townspeople a way out. Luana spared a glance down the line to see a great blaze erupt. One of the Valkir ships had used flaming arrows to set the sails and rigging of an Elaran ship alight. The vessel's wood was thick and strong so it would take a miracle to burn unless left unattended. The crew hurried around the ship fetching buckets of water to save the incapacitated vessel. In one move, it had been removed from the battle.

"Captain," Calvillo called out. "Chasers."

Luana followed the Tariki's gaze to where a pair of the League's ships had angled towards her formation. Shouts came from the Valkir warships and then two peeled off to face the newcomers. That would buy her landing party time. The flames from the burning ship lit the Sacasian and gave Luana a view of the battlefield. Most of the Valkir ships were engaged in melees. Some danced around the perimeter and launched volleys of arrows. Others would board ships that were already being taken to help their comrades. If the League had brought a smaller fleet, then the pirate and Valkir alliance may already have won. But the League's wealth was vast. Dozens of ships were cutting through the flame-lit waters towards the fight. Luana saw the Ravenheart engage a ship from Tallis. A second League vessel came from behind and boarding hooks and gangplanks were sent across. The king's flagship was under attack from both sides. Luana could only pray that Erik was strong enough to overcome the odds stacked against him.

She turned her thoughts away from the king and looked to the bow. There they were, emerging from the Elaran bay before them. The Oridassey swam at the head of a great pirate armada. The Aglaeca, the fearsome warship of Garrett Laven, sailed beside Teague's mighty vessel. The final two Valkir warships left the convoy to intercept other League vessels that targeted Luana's fleet. The Oridassey and the Aglaeca parted and the ships behind them followed suit, creating a tunnel for Luana and the rescue ships to sail. Luana aimed for the gap.

✦ ✦ ✦

Erik fought for every step of the Ravenheart. His crew had formed up along the deck of their ship and had since been broken into smaller shield walls. What began as the simple task of taking a simple ship had changed most dangerously when a second vessel had arrived from their unprotected portside. Even then the Ravenheart crew had been taking ground. And then a third ship had come. It had attached itself to one of the other League vessels, its soldiers swarming from ship to ship to reach Erik's position.

They were outnumbered three to one and no longer had surprise on their side.

"HOLD THE LINE!" Erik bellowed. "HOLD THE LINE!"

With overlapped shields, they fought their vast opponent. Nenrir had long since run out of arrows and stood sword in hand beside his king in the wall. To Erik's right were Torben and Fargrim. To his left Nenrir, Laerke and Mayrun, side by side as they always had been. Erik shoved his shield into the path of an axe. He followed through low with his sword and was rewarded by a scream. Erik stabbed again and painted the deck with his opponent's blood. One of the Valkir fell. Then another. The shield wall grew smaller. More enemies came on. A spear glanced along the side of Erik's helm. A sword grazed his arm.

"HELM!" Fargrim cried.

Erik glanced towards the quarterdeck of the Ravenheart and saw Elaran archers take aim. "SHIELDS!" Erik bellowed.

He threw his arm up. Bows sang. Shafts rained down, two thudding into his shield. One of the Valkir cried out. If they stayed still, they were all dead. Erik leapt to his feet and charged the Elaran ranks. His roared as loud as he was able. He felled men left and right. In the chaos, he lost his shield. The king fought like a demon with blade and axe as he moved towards the helm. He killed a man. An arrow struck his left shoulder, its steel tip driving deep into his pauldron and kissing the muscle beneath. Pain flared to life. Erik snarled as he fought. He caught a sword with his own and then killed its bearer with his axe. An archer raised his bow, but Erik launched his sword at the man, the flying length of steel hitting the bowman. Torben sped past his king and engaged the enemy. Erik snatched at the arrow embedded in his shoulder. Roaring, he tore it free, skin ripping and blood spurting. A blade slid across the steel of his armour and spun Erik around. The force of the blow dropped Erik to a knee as he fell back. His axe flew from his fingers. The Elaran charged, bringing his sword down. Erik raised his bracers and caught the blade on steel. He leapt to his feet, tackling the man back, heaving with all his might and clutching at his enemy's wrist. He slammed him back into the bottom of the quarterdeck. Erik struck the man's arm hard against the wall once, twice. The sword fell from his fingers. The Elaran thrust his head forward, his helmet connecting heavily with Erik's. Erik staggered back. The soldier's armoured fist struck his head. Erik roared through bloody teeth and drove his full weight forward. He threw the man back into the wall and reached for his belt. The soldier came at Erik. He didn't see the knife. Erik slid aside from the punch and drove the short blade up beneath the Elaran's arm. The soldier gasped as the knife cut straight through to his heart. Blood erupted from the wound. His eyes went dim. The Elaran fell.

Erik's hand clenched around the hilt of his bloody blade as he turned back to the deck. His body ached. His breathing was ragged. He froze. He could not tell how many of his crew were still living. Fighting raged below deck while those few left alive above were pushed to the bow. They were surrounded and cut off. Five Elaran soldiers stood before Erik. All were armed. Two held spears. The king had only his dagger. Erik bared his teeth into a bloody grin. He raised his knife. The Elarans made to charge.

Pirates, wearing sashes of navy blue, swarmed across the railings from every side. They carved into the League's soldiers like slicing a cake. The Valkir fought back and rose in numbers from below. Two of the men opposite Erik were cut down. The king charged the third and caught him by surprise. Erik drove his knife up under the man's chin. As the body fell, Erik snatched up his fallen axe and engaged the next. The soldier fell in a heart's beat with Erik's axe embedded in his neck.

The third and final man was slain from behind. The wicked blade of a sidesword ripped free of his chest. The Elaran's spear fell from nerveless fingers as his life fled. The killer cast the body aside. And so fell the last of the League that had come aboard the Ravenheart.

Torben limped to Erik's side. A gash was cut in old warrior's leg though he would offer no complaint. They looked to Erik's saviour, the man who had come to his aid. Scars adorned the pirate's weathered face. Dark hair and a darker beard covered his head, and his powerful form was clad in a long coat of midnight blue. He grinned and extended a bloody hand. Erik passed both weapons to his left hand and then clasped the pirate's arm. Blood dripped from their fingers and wrists. The blood of their enemies.

"Cillian Teague." The pirate introduced himself.

"Erik Farrin."

✦ ✦ ✦

SEVENTEEN

Fortress of Kilgareth, Valley of Odrysia

More than a week had passed since Kyler and Alarik had left Loxford. The towering mountains of the Valley of Odrysia rose around them. An all but impassable wall of earth surrounded the mighty city and fortress within. Odrysia appeared first. Tall spires appeared over the huge stone walls that encircled the magnificent city. Odrysian banners flew high and armoured guardsmen patrolled the walls and streets. The knights turned from the city as they galloped across the plains. They crossed the stone bridge that ran astride the Odrysian River and suddenly Alarik brought them to a halt with an upraised fist.

"What is it?" Kyler called as he looked to his mentor.

"Look," Alarik said as he pointed above the fortress of Kilgareth with one hand and clasped his medallion with the other.

Kyler followed his gaze. His eyes widened as he saw it. He could not tear his gaze away. Like Alarik, he took hold of his amulet. Above the fortress, a great pyre burned. The great flame had been lit for the first time in the northern garrison's history. The last time Rovira's flame had been set alight had been as Duran Cormac led his men against the heathens. That had been a century ago.

"When the fires of the Citadel burn, the Knights of Kil'kara shall ride again," Kyler murmured.

"The Order has ridden to war," Alarik said fervently. "We're in the silence now and the storm is upon the horizon. Have you made your decision yet? Will you tell any of them of my sins?"

The question took Kyler by surprise. More than that, the battlemaster's tone revealed that he almost did not care for the response.

"Would you believe me if I said that I don't yet know?" Kyler replied.

"To betray a brother regardless of what they have done is a hard thing. I understand that best of all," Alarik said before nudging his mount into a walk. "Come. We must hurry."

From there began their ascent up the mountain. Trees passed on either side as they followed the road. The woods thinned out and then there it was, standing atop the great mountain. A long causeway led to shining gates of bronze and impenetrable walls of solid stone. Blue standards bearing the silver sun and moon waved in the midday breeze. Heavily armoured knights stood sentinel above the walls and gates. Beyond the vast defences, Kyler could just make out the pinnacles of the Citadel and the maija's library.

They crossed the causeway as the gates opened and rode into the courtyard. Cobblestones rang under the hooves of their steeds. Kyler glanced around the streets and took in the crowds of people. Kilgareth was as bustling as it had been upon his departure, although now it seemed quieter. The families of the knights and maija who called Kilgareth home would have been missing their husbands and wives, fathers and mothers, brothers and sisters; knights of the sun and maija of the moon who had ridden into battle, perhaps to their death.

"Welcome back, brothers," called one of the approaching gate guards.

"Sir Hanniel." Alarik greeted the knight.

"Master," Hanniel said as he dipped his head to acknowledge rank. "Sir Kyler."

"Gods be with you, brother," Kyler told him.

"It is good to have you back," Hanniel continued.

"Master Corvo has marched to war," Alarik stated.

"Yes, sir. The Order rode out a month ago with Grand Master Bavarian and King Dayne. They met the heathen in battle upon the fields of Bandujar and won a decisive victory."

Alarik nodded as he took it in. "Our brothers bring honour to themselves and to the gods," he replied. "Who commands Kilgareth in the grand master's absence?"

"With the masters Corvo and Sir William Peyene gone, command of the garrison has fallen to Sir Mortimier, sir," Hanniel said. "Lady Lysandra is in charge of the fortress. Cardinal Aleksander has taken residence within the Citadel as well."

Kyler hid his surprise. He had heard nothing of the cardinal leaving Rovira.

"The cardinal is in Kilgareth?" he asked.

"Aye. That he is."

The knights rode through the city and made their way behind the walls of the Citadel. So few of the holy warriors remained within Kilgareth, no more than two or three hundred at the most. Kyler and Alarik dismounted before the statue of Durandail that sat within the fortress yard.

"Pisspot," Alarik called. "Clean yourself up. Gather your armour and get some rest. We ride north at dawn. I'm going to speak to Mortimier."

Kyler could only nod. After he had seen the burning pyre, he had expected as much. At last, he would be re-joining his brothers.

"Dawn it is then," Kyler said.

Alarik clapped him on the shoulder, and they parted ways. Kyler led Asena straight to the Citadel stables. He penned her, removed her saddle and brushed her coat.

"We're home, Asena," he murmured as he ran the brush along the horse's neck. "Perhaps just for a night, but we're home."

Kyler grinned as Asena nuzzled his arm. He stroked her jaw and then fetched the mare food and water. From there, the knight took his bags to his lodging in the Citadel. Before long, he stumbled into the bathhouse. The heated building was one of the finer Aureian inventions to have travelled north with Duran Cormac a century ago. He pulled off his travel-stained armour with a sigh. His body relaxed. He had only taken the chainmail, plate and gambeson off a handful of times since he had ridden out from Kilgareth *months* ago. Kyler stretched his aching back and shoulders and gently lowered himself into the warm water. Slowly, the dust and dried sweat that clung to his body began to slide away, revealing the skin and muscle beneath.

And then he saw it, just beneath the shoulder of his left arm: a thick line of mottle bruising. Kyler frowned. He could remember taking the wound in the tunnels. A warhammer had struck him when he had moved to save Elena. At the time, adrenaline had taken the pain away. Afterwards, he had expected the ruskalan blood to have healed the wound as it had for all the others. His brow furrowed further. The wound he had taken from the crossbow bolt in Durandail's vault had left not a scratch, just as the leg wound he sustained in Elara during the riots had left no mark. Yet the small cuts he had taken in the tunnels had left marks. A small scratch was visible just above his knee and there were others. Why had he not healed? Kyler ran a hand across the wounds and then cast them from his mind. He leaned back. Sleep took him.

✦ ✦ ✦

"Alarik."

"Mortimier."

The two knights grinned and embraced. They stood in the great hall of Kilgareth, a room that usually played host to the grand master yet now served Sir Mortimier. The garrison commander was around

Alarik's age, with dark hair streaked with silver and broad shoulders to match his companion. They had served together for many years.

"It is good to have you back," Mortimier told the battlemaster.

"It's good to be back." Alarik chuckled. "Tell me what has happened in my absence."

Mortimier grunted. "It began as expected," he said. "The legions assembled in the south alongside Grand Master Bavarian. Together with the cardinal and his guard, they made the journey north with the intention of assembling at Palen-Tor with the Annorans. There was some trouble on the road."

"I did hear something about the murders," Alarik told him.

"Imagine losing both Emperor Darius and King Dorian on the very eve of war."

"I trust that those who committed the vile acts have been dealt with."

"No," Mortimier said with a shake of his head. "The men who did it were like ghosts. Vanishing into the night and leaving no trace. The Annoran prince started investigating but the war forced him to march."

"I see," Alarik murmured.

When he had first heard of the deaths, he had barely believed it. Yet for the killers to have escaped … for justice to not have been dealt – that was inexcusable.

"The army arrived at Kilgareth with Prince Dayne," Mortimier continued. "And then Cardinal Aleksander placed a crown atop his head. He is king now. More. It is Dayne who *leads* our great army. It is he who crushed the heathens upon the northern fields. General Ilaros stands with him. The houses of Medea as well. Together with our order, Alarik … can you imagine such a sight?"

"A great sea of men and steel." Alarik gave his friend a smile. "When I last marched with the legions, such a host was assembled that the earth shook beneath. Where is the Order now?"

"Far to the north," Mortimier explained. "Beyond Bandujar.

Word came days ago that Bavarian and Corvo ride to join the Houses and cross the river. With the legions attacking from Bandujar while Annora and Santiago Caspin strike from further south … Salvaar will fall."

The battlemaster felt his heart race. The pagans of the forest were no different to the monsters that he had faced in Irene. He could still remember those nightmares despite the years that had passed. He still bore those scars. He felt his anger rise at the thought of those demons who had for so long preyed upon the weaker Medean settlements.

"That is glorious news, brother," Alarik said. "In the morning, I will ride out to meet the grand master."

"Pray that you reach the battle before it is won," Mortimier replied with a grin.

"Tell me, my friend. You spoke of General Ilaros yet there was another Aureian who made the journey."

"Commander Velis?" Mortimier asked.

Alarik nodded. "I served with him in Irene."

"I am told that he arrived at Palen-Tor but took a different path to King Dayne. He and his riders made for the Rift with the intention of dividing the pagans," the garrison commander said. "A good strategy. From what I hear, it worked. There were tribes not at Bandujar."

"Always was a clever bastard." Alarik smiled.

"I have never met the man. Tell me about him."

"Velis Demir is one of the strongest commanders that Aureia has known," Alarik told him. "And the finest horseman that the world has ever seen. He is a keen intellect and a feared warrior, renowned throughout the empire. He is a simple man who seeks neither fame nor glory. That is why Emperor Darius chose him above all to serve him in the Larissan court."

✦ ✦ ✦

He may have been asleep for minutes or hours, Kyler couldn't be sure. When he awoke, he awoke to the sound of Elena's voice.

"Lysandra will help us."

The words echoed in his head for a moment. His fingers reached for the silver and pearl necklace on instinct. He took a breath, splashed water over his face and then heaved himself from the water. He shaved the short beard that was beginning to grow and tied his hair back. It had grown longer in the months he had been gone. Kyler pulled on a fresh tunic, trousers and boots. He strapped on his sword and made for the maija's quarters. Through the corridors and up winding staircases he went until he came to the library. Kyler greeted Rene Aristo, who directed him towards Lysandra's office. Within moments of Kyler rapping his knuckles on the wood, the door eased open and there she stood, clad in the faded purple and blue garb of the arc'maija.

"Kyler Landrey." The women's lips curled into a joyous smile.

"Lady Lysandra." Kyler dipped his head.

"Come in."

She closed the door behind him and pulled him into a warm hug. The knight embraced her. He knew that she had always been close to Elena. Lysandra was kind. She had a gentle heart.

The arc'maija stepped back allowing Kyler to examine the room. Just as in the library, books lined the shelves of Lysandra's office. Scrolls filled shelves and maps covered walls. Quills of ink adorned her desk. She was a scholar through and through.

"I heard about Elara. About the riots and then about its fall," she told him sadly. "I was worried for you."

"What I remember about the city, about its final days, is chaos," Kyler told her. "All that death. All that slaughter. It reminded me of why we fight and about the evil that we fight against."

"There is darkness all around us. It seeks to corrupt and destroy.

Darkness has many names and many faces. Yet if you look close enough, you can always find a light. A light that we can take up to illuminate the darkness."

"I found the merchant. I found Arntair," Kyler blurted. Finding the words hurt. Speaking them was worse. Yet he would not lie. He could not.

"What is it?" Lysandra asked as she took in his expression. "I can see that the answer you found pains you."

"You were right. You were right the whole time. It was poison. Arntair supplied one of our brothers and he in turn used the bludvier to poison Amaris and rob him of life," Kyler muttered. "The merchant spoke of a soldier. An Aureian. In time, I learnt the truth."

Lysandra pursed her lips. "It was Alarik," she murmured. "Wasn't it?"

Kyler nodded sadly. He knew that she could read the answer in his eyes. "When confronted, he told me that Amaris was weak. That he was making *us* weak."

"I had my suspicions about Alarik … I can see that it troubles you so say no more," Lysandra told him softly. "You have found the answer to my question and for that I am grateful. Let me handle it from here."

For a moment, Kyler felt nothing but hate. Hate for himself. He had betrayed Alarik.

"I wish it had never come to this," he said sorrowfully. "Betraying a mentor. A friend. A brother."

"We do what we must and what you have done is no easy thing. It may feel wrong, but Alarik has betrayed us all."

"What will happen to him?"

"In time, he will be dealt with," Lysandra replied. "Though for now, we are at war and men such as Alarik could prove vital in the days to come. All we can do is trust in the gods, trust in the purpose for which they have set us."

"I hope you're right." Kyler clasped his hands to still his nerves. It was all out of place. The world was out of place.

"Did you find the man for which you searched?" Lysandra asked after a moment.

Kyler shook his head. "Wa'rith ... We searched everywhere for the man yet found nothing but whispers and his name," he told her. "A former knight of Kil'kara. Markus Harvarder. Alarik told me everything."

"I remember him," Lysandra replied, her voice heavy and thick with memory.

"You knew him well?"

"Well enough to mourn him," she replied.

"He works with the gangs now," Kyler said. "Leads men. That man who attacked us in Odrysia last year, the one who shot Hugh and murdered my parents, he was there. His name is Olivera. He worked for Harvarder."

"He was once with the bandits, was he not?"

"He's dead now," Kyler replied quietly. "I ... I killed him."

Lysandra placed a comforting hand on his arm. "Your eyes speak of a great sadness," she murmured. "What happened in Elara?"

Kyler let out a long breath and composed himself.

"We were lured into the tunnels by Harvarder on the night of the fall," Kyler said. "It was a trick. We were attacked. The men who came for us ... they killed her. They killed Elena."

Lysandra's eyes widened. She stepped in close and hugged him tightly. She said no words.

"After fleeing Durandail's Vault, she followed me to Elara. She sought me out and explained everything. Who she was, why she followed me. All of it. When we went after Harvarder, when we entered into that hell beneath, Elena followed. And then I held her in my arms as she died."

"Kyler, I am so sorry," Lysandra said softly.

Tears stung the knight's eyes. He refused to cry. He refused to fall apart.

"I'm sorry too," he said. "I know she was like a daughter to you."

Lysandra stepped back and gently placed a hand over Kyler's heart. "We lose the ones we love, and we cannot change that," she told him. "Yet they will live forever in here. In memory."

"I think about her every day."

His words were soft, barely more than a whisper. Kyler felt the pain in his heart as he spoke, but he quietly vowed to remain strong. He would be strong for her.

"You loved her, and she loved you," Lysandra replied. "You wear her jewel."

Kyler touched the necklace. "Once, a long time ago, I gave her this. In Adrestia. Before our lives changed. She wore it until the day she died. With her last breath, she returned it to me. It is the only thing I have of hers. The only thing to remind me of her. I will wear it always."

"Take comfort in it. Know that she will be with you … always."

Kyler blinked away his tears and composed himself. Elena had told him to trust Lysandra. It had been Lysandra that she had told him to speak to. It had been Lysandra that she would entrust with the secret of her blood.

"Lysandra, it's true," Kyler began. "What they were saying. She had ruskalan blood. Elena told me so."

The arc'maija paused for a moment. She gave away nothing. Lysandra *knew*.

"I know, Kyler," she told him. "I have always known."

What? Kyler froze as he stared at her.

"I can see that you are surprised," Lysandra continued. "Trust me when I tell you that I alone know."

"How did you come by it?"

"Three years ago, when Elena first came to study here, I heard that her mother was of ailing health."

"Yes, I remember," Kyler replied. "Rohanna was always sick. She did not even go outside. I never got to meet her."

"I went to visit one day," Lysandra explained. "And when I found Rohanna, I discovered why she never left the house, why no one ever saw her. You see, Kyler, she wasn't sick. Far from it. She was of ruskalan blood."

Kyler felt as if he had been struck. "No … you're wrong," he stammered.

"It's true," Lysandra told him. "Though she appeared as human as you or I, she was far from a common woman. You know the tales. The ruskalan are pale of skin and black of blood. They have fangs and pointed ears. Eyes of raging fire. The stories say that once bloodlines are joined, the gifts of the ruskalan can pass down through generations. Perhaps an ancestor from before the Inquisition gave Rohanna her power. But Rohanna … she had long since lost control over her unique gifts. At any moment, her eyes could change to red. At any moment, she could appear as ruskalan."

There was no lie in her words. No one in Adrestia had ever seen Rohanna. Elena needed family to pass on the ruskalan blood. If her father was not the source, then Rohanna had to be.

"To have gone so long without seeing the sun," Kyler murmured. "I cannot imagine."

"What do you think would have happened had Rohanna ventured out in Adrestia, in Odrysia? What would have happened if she had lost control, revealing herself to be more than just human?" Lysandra said. "She spent her life inside rather than let her family be destroyed by who she was. By what she was."

"There is something that I do not understand," Kyler said. "You are the arc'maija. You serve the gods, same as I. There is not a man or woman within these walls who do not hate the ruskalan for what they once did. You knew that Rohanna had ruskalan blood. You knew that Elena had ruskalan blood. Yet you did not tell the Order."

"No, I didn't. And would you like to know why?" Lysandra replied. "I do not believe that a person's blood defines who they are. I swore an oath, a sacred vow, to help all those in need, regardless of their allegiance. Perhaps there is more to the stories of old than the tales we have been told, Kyler. Perhaps the ruskalan, perhaps the elves, weren't as evil as we supposed. By what right do we judge those whom we have never met guilty of crimes that we did not see? By what right do we condemn those who lived generations ago? By what right …"

Kyler met her eyes as she trailed off. Her face rippled as she seemed to hold back tears. Her shoulders seemed to sag under the weight of her compassion. Above all else, he knew that she was right.

"Had you said that before the Vault then I would have called you a blasphemer," Kyler told her truthfully. "Now … I love the gods as I always have. I will serve them. I will fight and die for them. Yet the ruskalan were condemned by man, *not* the gods."

"Precisely," Lysandra agreed. "At last, you may now understand."

"I knew Elena better than I know myself, but now it is as if I did not know her at all," Kyler said after a moment.

"And how does that make you feel?" the arc'maija asked.

Kyler bit his lip as he thought. He felt torn. He felt confused.

"Knowing that there was so much that went unsaid between us, knowing that there was so much that she wanted to tell me but ran out of time before she could … *hurts*."

"Elena wanted to protect you."

"I know," Kyler said quietly. "She saved my life. In the Vault. It was her blood that saved me. By the look in your eyes, I can see that you knew that too."

"I am sorry, Kyler. I truly am," she replied. "But I feared what would happen if what I knew became well known. If you had told someone … if you turned against me, I would be dead. I did not trust you."

Her admission shocked him for but a moment. He knew if their places had been exchanged, he would have done the same.

"And now you do?"

"Now I do," she told him. "Tell me about it. Tell me every detail."

"The first thing I remember was awaking from a dream. I could remember the crossbow. I could remember falling … dying. Yet when I awoke, there was no mark, not even the shadow of a scar. For a long time after that, nothing changed. Days went by. Weeks. When we arrived in Elara, nothing had changed. And then in the riots, I was wounded. A sword opened my leg. I survived, made it to the arsenal. The wound was bound … but that night it came for the first time. A great pain, as if I was being ripped apart from within," Kyler said with a grimace. "Everything *burned*. My blood turned to black and then I collapsed. When I came to, the pain was gone and the wound along with it. All that remained was a dull ache in my head, an ache that to this day has never left. It has been hard to think and hard to focus ever since."

"And these changes. Have they happened since?"

"Twice," Kyler told her as he remembered. "One was the same as the first. I collapsed. Nothing had changed."

Lysandra frowned. "And the second?" she pressed.

Kyler closed his eyes. He remembered Olivera. He remembered the tunnels.

"After Elena died," he murmured. "To survive, we fought side by side with Olivera. In the end, few of us remained. I alone with he and two of his men. That's when it happened. I had never felt so much pain. So much *rage*. When I came to, they were dead. I stood above them with my sword awash with their blood. Only they weren't just dead. They had been butchered. In that moment, I did not control my hand. There was another force at play. Some kind of puppet master."

"Do you remember the attack?" Lysandra asked him.

"No," Kyler replied. "All I remember is waking up. And there is more." The knight reached up and pulled his tunic away from his shoulder to reveal the dark bruising. "The wounds that I received in the tunnels have not yet faded," he said. "Whatever once healed me is failing."

Lysandra gave him a worried look. "Then it has begun."

"What has?"

"Kyler, Elena, like her mother, only bore ruskalan blood. She was more human than not. If what I have read is true, then beings like Elena and Rohanna can only tap into their power in moments of great distress, when their emotion is out of balance. Unlike pure-blooded ruskalan, they could not use their gifts whenever they chose."

"In the tunnels Elena held our enemy at bay with her eyes for a moment," Kyler said. "She controlled him to save our lives yet could not call upon this gift when the attack came."

"There is much that she did not know about her people. There are two ways to create half-bloods among the ruskalan. Children sired by human and ruskalan will appear as human but bear the gifts of the other. These gifts pass on through generations even if no other ruskalan joins with them. That is how Elena's family received their ability. Perhaps a distant ancestor of hers was ruskalan. We may never know."

"And the second?"

"A more dangerous joining," Lysandra replied. "That of mixing blood. You see, Kyler, in her haste to save you, that is what Elena did. She believed that her healing blood would be enough and in some regard it was. Had she not been interrupted, then you may well have become a half-blood. But she was stopped before she could complete what needed to be done, and in so doing she has tainted your blood. Human blood is incompatible with that of the ruskalan; their blood is stronger. When two bloods are mixed unnaturally like they were with you, for a time there is harmony.

This could be days. Weeks. Months. But then the ruskalan blood starts to tear away at the human blood. In time, the healing properties will cease, and the pain will begin. Answer me true: is it getting worse?"

"Yes," Kyler admitted. "There is no respite. Not anymore. Each day it grows stronger."

"I thought as much. I can see how tired you look, how drawn," she said quietly. "That is the ruskalan blood. And the blood takes its toll."

Kyler let out a long breath. So, his blood was tainted. Elena had not known. How could she have known?

"What are you saying?"

"In time, you will start to lose control over your actions even when the blood does not call to you. It may have already begun."

"I think it has," Kyler muttered. "In Loxford, there was a man. I attacked him … I do not know why. I was there … but I could not stop it."

"Then we may not have much time."

"What happens next?" Kyler pleaded.

He could see the concern on Lysandra's face. He almost knew the answer before she spoke.

"Two bloods cannot coincide. Not with an unnatural union," she told him. "The ruskalan blood will destroy its host from within. One condemned to such a fate will become a shell, barely able to recognise themselves let alone control what they do. The red blood of a human will be gone. The torment within will change the bearer both in the mind and body. Once the last of the human blood is gone, the host will die."

Horror filled Kyler. The pain had been bad. The changing had been bad. But what Lysandra spoke of was torture. Torture from within. He glanced at his hands and saw a tremble shake them.

"How do we stop it?" He barely kept the sound of begging from his voice.

"I don't know," Lysandra whispered.

Blood drained from Kyler's face. He had been afraid before. But this was something else. This was pure fear.

"We're leaving tomorrow," Kyler told her. "Alarik and me. We're riding north to rejoin our brothers."

Lysandra took his hand and squeezed it. "Kyler, I *swear* to you that I will find a way to fix this."

He shook his head and tried to clear his warring mind. "I have to go," he muttered as doubt took control. "Goodbye." He stepped back and made for the door. He was lost in confusion.

"Kyler!" Lysandra called. "I made you a promise. Trust in me. Trust in Elena."

Kyler nearly ran to the temple. He fell onto his knees before the marble statue of Azaria and reached for his amulet. Tears spilled down his cheeks.

"Oh, merciful lady, I am in such need of your mercy now. My mother. My father. My blood. Alarik a traitor and Elena gone," he whispered. "Everything is just slipping through my fingers."

Kyler slept like a baby, but when he awoke, he was still exhausted. He rose before the sun in doubt and confusion. Kyler gathered up his armour, his *real* armour. The armour of a knight. His hands slowly ceased to shake as he pulled on mail and plate. The thick, sleeveless coat with the white sun came next. His swordbelt, sapphire cloak, shield and helm followed. There he stood in his full glory, a knight of Kil'kara. Kyler saddled Asena and then met Alarik at the gate. Together, the knights galloped north. They galloped into war. Yet all Kyler could think about was his fear. His tainted blood.

✦ ✦ ✦

Sir Hugh Karter held his spear high as the mounted knights surged into the waters of the Arwan. There were over a hundred of them brilliantly clad in armour of silver and blue; the sun of Durandail emblazoned hot on their chests. Hugh gazed out from under his helmet as they reached the halfway point in the river. He searched the opposite bank expecting to see shadows moving. He expected to see arrows flying towards them. *Nothing* came. Master Corvo reached the opposing bank and led the knights free of the water's embrace. At dawn, hundreds of knights had been gathered into half a dozen groups and commanded to take the eastern bank. They were to find the enemy and engage them. They were to buy time for the Medeans to cross and establish a foothold beneath the trees of Salvaar. Master Corvo led one group, while the warden Sir William Peyene led another. The others were commanded by Grand Master Bavarian and his Circle. Hugh kicked his heels in as his mount raced up the bank in the wake of his mentor. Though now a knight, he still served as Corvo's apprentice.

"It's quiet," Hugh murmured as he mode to his master's side.

"They're there," Corvo replied with a stoic expression.

Corvo slid his shield onto his arm and the rest of the knights followed suit. They held their spears tightly and watched the trees with wary eyes as the last of their comrades crossed the river. Corvo clicked his tongue and slowly the knights began to move out. They rode through Salvaar at a steady canter yet prepared to accelerate into a gallop or charge at any moment. Some of the knights murmured prayers. There was a sense of anticipation through the ranks of holy warriors. They were waiting for their enemy to show themselves and attack. There was a light mist in the forest and even without it they *knew* that the enemy could be hidden all around them. Hugh had never been nervous before a fight. Never. Yet with each step they had taken towards Salvaar, for each stride through the Arwan, something burned. They closer they had come to the forest, the more confident he had grown. Now that he was here beneath these trees, he felt invincible. Hugh wondered if his master felt the same. If Corvo did, then he did not show it in his face. He showed nothing. It was then they saw the bodies.

"Heathens," one of the knights snarled.

"Devil ghosts," growled another.

Hugh looked left and right. Through the mists hanging from trees all around were a dozen Medean bodies. The dukes had sent men to try and cross yesterday. None had returned. Now they hung lifeless from branches. They had been stripped of their armour and shirts and bloody symbols had been carved into their naked chests. Sacrifices to their evil spirits. The sight did not make the knights scared or nervous. It enraged them. Hugh ground his teeth as he looked from body to body.

"What kind of man could do such a thing?" he muttered.

"These are not men," the knight beside him replied angrily. "They're monsters."

"RIDER!" A warning was bellowed from the south.

Hugh wrenched on his reins and spun his horse towards the shout. Shields came up and spears were levelled. They awaited Corvo's command. A single rider wreathed in mist appeared. He came closer and closer. The knights swept their gaze in every direction as they formed a circle. They were Knights of Kil'kara and would *not* be taken by surprise. Hugh saw the spear and the crest as the rider drew closer.

"It's one of ours," Hugh called down the line.

The last of the mist slid away from the rider, revealing his garb. Hugh's brothers lowered their weapons yet did not take their weary eyes from the woods.

"Master Corvo!" the newcomer called.

Corvo clicked his tongue and made for the rider. Hugh and a number of other knights followed.

"What is it, brother?" the master asked.

"Grand Master Bavarian sent me, sir," the knight said. "You had best come quickly."

The company followed the Aureian knight for miles through the forest. They saw not a soul. Not a trace of their enemy. There were no more bodies in the trees. There was nothing save the wind and the cries of ravens.

The knight led them into the remains of a vast campsite. Nothing had been left behind save the ashes from fires. Hundreds of knights from the other companies had already arrived. They gathered in groups and formed a perimeter around the camp. Hugh stared at the blackened remains and followed his master and their guide towards a congregation of dismounted knights. Hugh slung his shield across his back as they rode. Like many of his brothers, he was confused. Had the Salvaari given up the very ground they fought for?

Hugh and his mentor handed their spears to other knights and dismounted. He saw Bavarian within the small circle along with his own commanders. William Peyene was there as well. William pulled off a glove and knelt by the remains of a fire as Corvo and Hugh joined them. He ran his hand through the ashes.

"Still warm," William muttered.

"The Salvaari have moved on," Bavarian told them.

"The tracks suggest that they left some time in the night," William Peyene said. "They lead east."

"Could be a ruse," Corvo muttered.

Bavarian nodded and fingered the hilt of his sword.

"I have sent outriders to watch for any hint of a trick," the grand master replied, "but for now, we are alone."

✦ ✦ ✦

EIGHTEEN

Coast of Medea, The Mithramir Sea

Sakkar gazed out across the Mithramir towards the sister ship of the Despoina, a consort to the vessel upon which he travelled. The Tanith, which carried their horses, was a larger ship, a merchant trader. Its crew was under the employ of the Despoina's captain, Tybura Valloma. Formally a privateer who served under the imperial crown of Aureia, Tybura had put aside his sword and taken up the more lucrative merchant's trade.

Sakkar glanced up towards a hawk's song. Sabra dove down from the heavens and soared between the Despoina's masts. He grinned as he watched the bird fly. The hawk soared through the air and angled back towards him. She soared over his head and, with a flap of her light brown wings, perched atop an outflung arm. Senya's arm.

"You like the sea breeze, eh, Sabra," Senya said with a grin as she stroked the bird's feathers. "The skies are clear, the sun shines and the waters are beautiful. It lifts the spirits."

Senya extended her free hand as she approached. Sakkar took her hand and gave it a squeeze before gently running a finger down Sabra's neck.

"When last I saw the ocean, I was but a boy," Sakkar said, smiling as he remembered. "My father took me to Danakis when King Serephin still ruled. I had never seen such a thing, Senya.

Water from horizon to horizon. He took me down to the beach. We swam and sang and danced all day and all night. He sat me down and told me that our stories are just like the sea. You cannot stop the tides, he said, be they great or small. But if you're brave enough, you can flow with them."

"A wise man," Senya said as she slowly stroked the hawk.

"When I was a boy, I swam in the sea. As a man I sail across it," Sakkar replied. "I should very much like to return one day, to feel the ocean upon my skin and taste its breath. Perhaps even with a child of my own. Our child."

Senya glanced up at him. Her eyes sparked with joy and her lips curled into a smile.

"There is nothing in this world that I want more," she told him. "Nothing."

"Then we had best survive to see that day," Sakkar replied.

"Oh, we will." Senya chuckled. "Nothing could take you from my arms. Not steel, nor even death itself. Now that you have promised me a child, if you even think about dying, Sakkar Alsahra, I'll kill you myself."

Sakkar laughed and wrapped an arm around her waist tenderly. They stood side by side watching the waves, looking to the horizon.

"Captain says we'll make landfall tomorrow," Sakkar said.

"Bellec has left instruction. It happens tonight. At dusk we should dance, you and I."

The ocean turned into a sea of orange as the sun began to lower. The men and women aboard the Despoina basked in the glorious light as they filled the decks. A large circle was formed. Someone had found Kompton a drum and he slowly began to play. Sakkar rolled his bare shoulders back as he took up his staff. He stood naked aside from the baggy trousers that covered his legs and waist. Beside him was Senya. Like him, she carried a long wooden staff. Her scant clothing revealed her muscled arms and stomach. A small skirt hung to her upper thighs to allow her free movement. They exchanged a glance as Kompton's drum began to sing. It had been *years* since they had last danced together. Far too long. They emerged from the hold and were greeted only by the beat of the drum. Those watching did so in silence. Sakkar and Senya barely saw them. A torch burned brightly and Sakkar used it to light both ends of his staff. Flames erupted as the material caught aflame. He approached Senya and they placed their staffs together. They met each other's eyes as the fire from his staff ignited hers. They moved slowly. They moved in unison. Their wrists twirled and their feet glided across the deck. The staves spun faster and faster. Their pace quickened. Their muscles glistened as the light of the flames caressed their skin. The drumbeat grew faster. They pirouetted and danced through the ring of flames that drew a web around them. They moved as one. They became one. They were the fire's masters. Their movements followed the rhythm of the drum, rising and falling as the melody dictated. Sweat swam across their bodies as their muscles flowed. They came together, the fire dancing around them. Sakkar felt the intensity in Senya's amber eyes; he felt her passion, her strength, and she felt his. They slid apart. Their feet floated and their bodies moved. The drum reached its crescendo. They stood back to back. The drum ceased. They slammed their staffs into the deck. Silence.

Sakkar felt alive. Sweat covered his warm body. His chest rose and fell rapidly as his breath slowly returned. His eyes reflected the flames of the burning staff.

The cheers of the crew and the mercenaries echoed across the sea. Only then did he look to Senya, the jewel of his life. Her hair hung wildly across her back and shoulder. Her lips were drawn back into the hungry smile of a hyena who had found its prey.

✦ ✦ ✦

The moon had long since risen in the sky, but Kitara and Aeryn had remained on deck. They had found some cargo to lounge on and had stayed up to watch the stars on this cloudless night.

"At night, when Sylvaine is at her strongest, she opens a doorway to the Veil," Aeryn murmured quietly. "Each silver star represents one of those who came before. The ones who made us who we are. Our ancestors. Yours and mine. At night they look down upon us."

Kitara smiled at the thought. "You believe that?"

"Of course."

"Where I grew up, the people who raised me used the stars to navigate the seas at night," Kitara told her. "There were those who mapped them so that they would never be lost."

"Their ancestors showed them the way," Aeryn replied. "They will always guide us home."

A thought came to Kitara. She tried to repress it, but curiosity got the better of her.

"My mother is up there?" she asked.

"Of course." Aeryn looked over at Kitara. "Kitara, what you told me about your mother, about who she was. In all of our history, that has never happened before. Sylvaine has never loved a mortal man."

"It was not Sylvaine who left Salvaar with Bellec," Kitara replied. "It was Oriana."

"Maybe not in body, but a part of the Great Queen will always remain," Aeryn said. "Without consulting the druids, I can only assume that it was Sylvaine's love that granted you your gift."

Kitara let out a breath and bit her lip. "Perhaps …" She trailed off as she heard footsteps approaching.

Kitara and Aeryn turned as Bellec walked up beside the cargo.

"You're true to your task?" Bellec asked.

"We're ready," Kitara told him.

The mercenary nodded. "Good," he said. "Before this begins, come with me. Both of you."

They followed Bellec down into the hold of the Despoina. They walked by the sailors sleeping in their hammocks and made their way further into the ship. Bellec led them into a smaller room, a room that held most of the spare items the mercenaries had brought along. Bellec pulled forth a rectangular wooden chest. Kitara cocked her head to the side and watched with curiosity as Bellec placed the chest between them and unlocked it. He pulled the lid back and reached within. Steel glinted within. A pile of chainmail lay beside folded gambesons. Bellec pulled out a shirt of mail and held it up.

"We're riding into battle," he told them. "Seemed only fitting that you dressed the part."

Bellec handed the steel garb to Kitara as he reached for a second chest. Kitara ran her gaze over the steel. It had short sleeves that would hang to her elbows. The chainmail was strong and sturdy and would easily turn aside sword and knife. Even one not trained in the blacksmith's art could see it, and Kitara had been around armour her whole life. It was not the brigandine that she had lost in Aureia, but it would serve its purpose well. The garment would not slow her down in battle when she needed her movement the most.

Bellec opened the second chest and revealed another set of armour.

"It's beautiful," Kitara told her father.

"May it serve you well and watch over you whenever I cannot."

Bellec left them; nothing else needed to be spoken.

Kitara placed the chainmail shirt aside and unbuckled her sword. She reached for the gambeson. It was of faded sage green. Unlike the chainmail shirt, it had long sleeves. Kitara pulled the garment on, followed by the mail. She rolled her shoulders back and twisted side to side. She felt its weight, felt its strength. It was perfect. Next came steel bracers and greaves of steel to grace her arms and legs. Thin fingerless leather gloves covered her hands. A helmet sat in the wooden chest and so she pulled it out and held it in the light. The steel was beautifully made, with simple embellishments carved across its surface. Just like the rest of her armour, the helmet seemed *made* for her. It would not obstruct her vision. Kitara placed the helm to the side and then strapped on her sword. She would not need the extra protection. Not yet.

Kitara turned towards Aeryn and ran her eyes up and down the moonseer. She allowed herself a smirk. She had never seen Aeryn in such armour, and it suited her well. Like Kitara, Aeryn wore a faded gambeson that hung to her thighs. A chainmail vest was pulled over it and fingerless gloves adorned her hands. A bracer was strapped to her right arm, while her legs were clad in greaves. She spread her arms and spun slowly in a small circle.

"Well?" Aeryn asked in Salvaari.

"Like one of Lycan's hunters," Kitara replied in the same tongue.

Aeryn grinned like a wolf and looked out into the hold. Something had drawn her gaze. Thin strands of light were starting to flow from above deck down into the ship.

"The sun rises," she said.

Kitara nodded and reached into the racking that surrounded them. Her hands found Aeryn's bow, quiver and axe belt. She handed them out. Aeryn met her eyes as she took the weapons. The moonseer slung her quiver across her shoulder and strapped on her belt. Her hand-axe and knife hung at her right hip. Aeryn strung her bow, and it joined her quiver across her back. Sharing a knowing look, the pair made their way back up on deck. Sailors were beginning to emerge from below. Most of the mercenaries were on deck, gathered in small groups. They wore their armour. Kitara and Aeryn made their way to the bottom of the steps that led to the helm. It was not long before Bellec and Galadayne strode past. Kitara leaned back on the ship's railing and watched them approach Captain Tybura.

"The wind is fair," Tybura called. "We should reach Valengos within the hour."

Bellec shook his head. "We won't be going to Valengos today," he said.

Tybura frowned. "My orders were to–"

"Take us to the easternmost port of Medea. We know." Galadayne cut him off. "But we are now changing those orders."

"You will signal the Tanith to follow," Bellec continued. "And then you will take us further east. To the border of Salvaar."

Tybura shook his head in disbelief. "Absolutely not," he snapped. "I am captain, and this is my ship. I will not sail into those heathen-infested waters at the whim of a–"

In less than a heartbeat, Bellec's sword was at his throat. Sailors and their own mercenary guards hurried towards the helm. They reached for weapons and shouted as they saw their captain attacked. Kitara hopped off the rail as four burly men made for the helm with steel in their hands and anger in their eyes. She moved between them and the steps to the helm. Sunlight glinted upon the blade as she drew her sword. The men stopped in their tracks as surprise contorted their expressions. Kitara levelled her sword and angled her body. Aeryn's bow came up. The lead soldier glared dangerously towards Kitara as he adjusted his grip upon his sword.

"Steady there, friend," Aeryn warned him.

All around the ship, Bellec's men had drawn steel. They forced both sailor and soldier alike back against the railing. Though they may have been outnumbered by the crew, the mercenaries that Bellec led were veterans of a hundred battles. They feared nothing and no one. They easily outmatched those who manned the merchant ship, and Tybura's men knew it. Tybura's eyes flickered shut and he sighed. In that moment, he had lost.

"Captain, what do we do?" one of the sailors called.

"What can we do?" Tybura replied.

"You may be the captain, but I am in command," Bellec growled as he withdrew his sword. "Now signal the Tanith. Salvaar awaits."

✦ ✦ ✦

Princess Kassandra's hair flew behind her like a chestnut waterfall as she rode down the small column. A group of mounted Annoran royal guardsmen surrounded the beautiful carriage drawn by four horses. The knights were clad in shining scale armour and brilliant scarlet cloaks. Shields were slung across their backs and swords hung from their sides. Most of them carried leaf-bladed spears. One held the Raynor banner aloft allowing the great red eagle to soar through the wind. The company had left Verena in the morning and were now well on their way to Kilgareth. The mountains that ringed the valley rose to every side and the sun shone gloriously high above. There were tall trees and wildflowers growing all about them.

Kassandra flicked her wrists and brought her snow-white horse alongside one of the knights. The mare, which she had dubbed Ely, had been with Kassandra for years, ever since she had first begun to disobey her father and stay out late with the horses as a girl. Ely had been a gift from Lukas.

"A fine day for a ride, my lady," the knight called as she approached.

"Every day is, Sir Landon," Kassie replied with a grin.

Landon Montbard chuckled. "Aye, my lady."

Kassie gave the knight a sidewards glance. Landon was cousin to the slain Sir Elion Montbard; one of Dayne's closest friends from his first day up until his last in Oryn. Sir Landon had accompanied Sir Garrik and Kassandra to Salvaar in pursuit of Lukas many months ago.

"Sir Landon, we once travelled together for many weeks," she told him. "We rode into Salvaar … into untold dangers. We shared the same food, drank the same drink and slept on the same hard earth without comfort for weeks. Yet still you treat me with the utmost decorum."

"It is only right, my lady," Landon replied seriously.

"We are friends, are we not?" Kassie said.

It was more statement than question, but all the same Sir Landon met her eyes as he replied. "That we are," he told her.

"Then enough of this 'my lady' nonsense," Kassie replied with a laugh. "Kassandra is enough."

Sir Landon returned the laugh. "I would like nothing more, my lady," he said. "Yet out of respect, I must decline."

"Out of respect?"

"Yes, my lady. Respect for *you*," Landon said.

Kassie shook her head and grinned. "I could order you," she joked.

"I would refuse."

"That would make you a traitor."

"If you say so, my lady."

Kassandra rode with Sir Landon for a time. She'd taken up the habit of riding along the column and talking to the soldiers when she'd first left Palen-Tor to follow Dayne east. She enquired about their lives back home, their families. Kassandra made the effort to talk to warrior, squire, servant and knight alike. She enjoyed it – what better way to get to know her own people? In Kilgareth and Verena, she had done the same and now knew many by name.

Eventually, Kassandra returned to the carriage and joined her mother and Sofia.

"You ride well." Sofia gave Kassandra a smile as the princess sat opposite her. "As if you were born to do it."

"I have been riding since I was this tall," Kassie said as she stretched out her arm and lowered her hand.

"Truly?"

"Since she was six or seven summers," Riona told her proudly.

"So young," Sofia said with raised eyebrows.

"Yes, Father was mortified." Kassie gave her half-sister a grin.

"As were the priests," Riona added.

"Well," Sofia replied as she leaned towards the princess, "I would say that it is very brave. Who taught you?"

"My brother," Kassie said.

Sofia raised her eyebrows in surprise. "Dayne?" she asked.

Kassandra shook her head and gave Sofia a sad smile. "No."

"I see." Sofia gave Kassie a knowing look. "Perhaps when we have returned home, you can teach me to ride even half as well as you."

Kassie's lips twitched up as she looked into her new sister's mischievous eyes. "I would like that," she said.

A shout came from outside. More cries joined them and then came the unmistakable sound of steel being drawn.

"What is going on?" Riona muttered and then reached for the carriage door.

Something hard struck the wood and Riona leapt back. The tip of an arrow broke through.

"ON ME!" Landon's voice boomed. "PROTECT THE CARRIAGE!"

"We're under attack," Riona said.

A chill ran down Kassandra's spine as she looked from her mother to Sofia. Shouts and screams echoed outside the carriage. Horses cried out. Bows sang. Landon's voice could be heard bellowing commands, though it was almost drowned out by savage war cries. Then came the clash of steel and the shrill braying of horses. Sofia's hand went to her amulet, and she uttered a silent prayer. Riona followed suit as the screams of the dead and dying came from all sides. Kassandra reached for the edge of a curtain that covered the small windows. She pulled it back long enough to glimpse a mass of men and horses, Annoran and Salvaari both. Something heavy slammed into the carriage and Kassandra fell back with a yelp. It was a royal guardsman. Kassie heard him roar and then engage the one who had thrown him. The princess' breath quickened. She recognised the black war paint of the Káli. How had they gotten past Verena? How had they found their way so deep into the safety of the valley? Instead of reaching for her medallion, Kassandra delved into the depths of her dress and pulled out a slender knife.

The shouting stopped. The song of steel came to an end. Kassie could hear men talking outside in the tongue of Salvaar. She could hear horses moving, and in that moment, she knew that the Annorans had been defeated. The princess felt fear threaten to overwhelm her. She had never been this scared before. She would *not* let it destroy her now.

The door rattled. Kassandra moved across the carriage to her mother and Sofia. She extended her knife as the door was pulled back. Her heart raced as a hand emerged through the opening. A Káli warrior leapt inside. His hair and beard were long and shaggy. Black paint covered his face and bare arms. He stared at the women as they stared back. He seemed surprised, almost as if he had not expected there to be three of them. Kassandra looked from his eyes to the axe at his belt and then back. The warrior smirked as he saw the dagger. Another man entered the carriage. His hair hung to his shoulders. A short beard graced his jaw, and a helmet sat atop his head. He wore a shirt of mail beneath Salvaari skins. Kassandra gasped. She saw the cloth covering an eye. She saw the knee brace.

"Lukas…" she breathed.

Lukas' eye widened as he saw his sister. The Káli warrior glanced at Lukas, and in that moment, Kassie knew that her brother was the leader. The warrior muttered something in Salvaari. Lukas frowned but did not take his eyes from Kassandra. The warrior reached out a hand towards the princess. Lukas moved faster than a man with one leg should have been able to. He grabbed the Káli's wrist with one hand and slammed him against the carriage wall with the other. Before the Káli could react or cry out, Lukas had covered his mouth and driven a knife deep into his heart. Lukas clamped his hand down to stop the screams. He drove his knife deeper into the warrior. The Káli struggled for a moment and then he was still.

Lukas slowly lowered the lifeless body and cleaned his knife on the man's cloak. He said not a word as he sheathed the blade and turned back to his family. None of them said anything. Kassandra could not find words. Her brother had just killed a man in cold blood, a man who was his ally. She saw no emotion on his face. She watched as her brother held a single finger over his lips. He did not want them to speak. Something in his eye warned them against it. Lukas turned to Sofia and held out an open hand.

"It will be better if you come without struggle," he said.

After a moment, Sofia nodded and rose from her seat. She squeezed Kassie's hand and left the carriage at a gesture from Lukas. Kassie could not take her eyes from her brother. She had heard about the massacre at Valham. She had heard about Bandujar and all the other horrors that her brother had been party to. He looked Salvaari now, but he was still there. Beneath the paint and armour, under the furs and skins, he was still Lukas. He gave them a final look before leaving the carriage in silence. Kassandra did not look away from the closed door. Words were spoken outside in Salvaari. Horses were mounted, followed by the thunder of galloping hooves. Then there was nothing.

Riona was the first to move. She peeled back the canvas curtains and stared out from the carriage. "They're gone," she said quietly before turning back to her daughter.

Kassie's hand trembled and the knife fell from her fingers. "Sofia's gone," she murmured.

Riona wrapped her arms around her daughter. Kassie held her tightly and pressed her cheek into her mother's. She could feel cold tears against her cheek.

"Why did Lukas kill that man?" Riona muttered.

"I don't think they expected us to be here," Kassie replied. "He was surprised. You could see it in his eye. Perhaps my brother wanted us to remain secret."

"Perhaps," Riona said.

Kassandra gathered up her knife, just in case any of the Káli remained. They clambered down out of the carriage. Bodies lay strewn around the wagon, Annoran and Salvaari alike. There was blood everywhere. Tears ran down Kassandra's cheeks as she stared around at the slaughter. Arrows riddled the bodies of the Annorans.

"How could the gods have allowed this?" Riona murmured.

"The gods had nothing to do with this," Kassandra said.

One of the bodies stirred. A groan came from a fallen Annoran's lips. Kassie ran over to the man and fell to her knees beside him.

"My lady," he managed with a wince.

No arrows had pierced him; he had been felled in close combat then. Kassie reached for the straps of his helmet and pulled it from his head.

"Steady, Landon," she told him. "Lie still."

The knight groaned again. "I'm sorry," he said.

"No … You fought bravely."

Sir Landon gritted his teeth and met her eyes. "I should be dead," he said. "When I was fighting one man, another felled me from behind. It was him … He was here, my lady. Your brother."

"Lukas did this to you?"

Landon nodded.

"He saved us," Riona told him as she crouched beside the pair. "The man who first came into the carriage was surprised. Clearly, they knew of Sofia's presence, yet they had not been told of ours. When the warrior tried to take us, it was Lukas who intervened. He killed his own companion to keep us safe … though where he took the queen, we do not know."

The knight pushed himself up and took a long breath. Every

part of his face spoke of pain, but Landon did not utter a sound or complaint.

"The prince was trained with a sword from birth. He must have known that I was not dead," Landon said. "That the blow he struck me down with was not mortal. Why would he have spared my life?"

"And before he laid eyes upon us," Riona continued.

Kassandra glanced around the plain and then froze. Her eyes locked on Ely. "My horse," she murmured.

"Your highness?"

"A long time ago, Lukas gave me my horse. We used to ride together every day," Kassie said. "If anyone knew Ely from a look, it would be him."

"If that is true … if he did come to that conclusion before he unhorsed me, then perhaps he wanted me to watch over you. See you home safe."

"We can't go home. Not now." Kassie glanced at her mother as she spoke. "We have to warn Dayne."

"The three of us will return north," Riona added. "The king was intending on riding for Salvaar and by now he will be miles from Verena. It is there that we must go."

"No!" Landon growled as he rose to his feet. "As a member of your guard, I *cannot* allow you to ride into battle."

"Dayne must be warned," Kassandra said sharply.

"He will be, your highness," Landon replied. "We are half a day at most from Kilgareth. It is a three-day ride to Verena, and it would take far longer to reach his army. No, my ladies, we *must* return to Kilgareth. You will be safe there, and we can get word to the king faster. We can send birds … birds that can fly faster and longer than any man or horse can run."

Kassandra and her mother exchanged a look. Kassie nodded after a moment. It was a better idea.

"Then that is what we will do," Riona said at last.

The knight found his fallen sword and returned it to its sheath. He whistled and his mount cantered over. Kassandra and Riona found their horses and the three riders galloped south.

✦ ✦ ✦

NINETEEN

The line of Salvaari prisoners wound from near the gates of Kilgareth to the valley below like a great serpent. Aedei, Catuvantuli, Icari, Káli ... they were all there. Their wrists were bound by rope so tight that it cut through the flesh of the Salvaari. The westerners were taking no chances with the small army of tribesmen. The march from the forest had been long and yet none of the Salvaari had offered so much as a complaint. They were saving their strength. Hundreds of mounted soldiers encircled the tribesmen and watched on with hateful eyes and eager spears.

All of this and more, Cailean had taken in. He had made note of every hill and grove of trees, every river and bluff. If the chance for escape came, the chief would be ready. Cailean pressed his shoulder into the man trudging at his side. He held the man's arm in an attempt to keep him upright. Like Cailean, Scada was covered in the blue woad of the Aedei. Like Cailean, he was a warrior. Where the chief's face was battered and bruised, Scada wore a blood-soaked bandage wrapped tight around his thigh. All of the Salvaari had fought ferociously, even in the face of defeat. Not a man or woman among them had been captured without slaying many of their enemies. Not a man or woman had been taken without their skin or bodies being broken by the swords and spears of the west.

The great fortress of Kilgareth arose before the column. Massive towers and walls of stone soared into the sky, dwarfing any that Cailean had seen before. The gates were clad in shining bronze and atop the walls were knights in silver. Banners of the sun and moon flew in the wind. A mighty fire burned constant atop the largest tower of all, one that arose within the heart of Kilgareth. Horror spilled through the Salvaari ranks. What could their people do against the strength of such a vision? What could they do against those who had built it?

The bronze-clad doors opened as the song of a horn echoed down from the walls. A company of Knights of Kil'kara rode out to meet them. Blue cloaks, surcoats and plumes glistened, while the white sun upon their chests blazed. The knights greeted the prisoners' escort before turning their mounts and leading the way into the heart of Kilgareth. The tribesmen stared as they were corralled inside. The streets had been cleared of the townspeople. They were met by rank upon rank of armoured knights – guards left behind while the Order was fighting in the north.

Scada staggered as they entered a great courtyard of stone. He fell; his wounded leg gave out. Cailean's arm shot out, but the ropes cut him short. Scada hit the ground hard. The chief dropped to his knees beside his fallen friend. Knights noticed the commotion and were beginning to close in on the pair.

"Get up," Cailean growled in Salvaari as he took hold of the man's arm. "Scada, get up!"

Scada groaned and heaved on the proffered arm. He met Cailean's eyes as he struggled to a knee. "Chief," he managed.

"Back in formation!" a voice called out in the common tongue.

Scada fell again.

"Come on. Get up!" Cailean snarled in his own language. "This is no place to die!"

The end of a gnarled cane was shoved into Cailean's chest as the chief rose to his feet. He took a single step back and turned his glare upon the knight who wielded the rod.

"Tell him to get up," the knight barked.

"He is wounded," Cailean shot back. "He can't walk without help."

"Then he is of no use to us."

"Let me help him."

The knight scoffed and glanced from Scada to Cailean. "And how do you propose that exactly?"

"Untie me," Cailean said and extended his bound hands. "I will take his weight."

"Untie you?" The knight laughed. "Do you take me for a fool?"

"Let me help him walk," Cailean growled, menace cutting its way into his voice.

The knight met the chief's stare. "Back in formation or you will share his fate."

Cailean stepped forward and bared his teeth. The cane pressed into his chest. Other Salvaari were beginning to notice the confrontation. Their hands were bound and they were wounded, yet they stood behind the chief of the Aedei. Eyes hardened into glares. Hands balled into fists. They would fight. Knights and soldiers began to circle.

"Stand back," the knight told him.

"No."

Silence filled the courtyard. The ringing of a cane upon the stones broke it. The hiss of steel followed and, before the song of wood upon stone had ended, the blade of a sword was pressed to Cailean's neck.

"I said back in formation!"

The chief's eyes burned with the same passion that flowed through his veins. He shrugged a shoulder and forced the sword to edge into his skin. He was not afraid. He felt a trickle of blood run down the side of his neck.

"Go on," the chief of the Aedei dared the knight. He grinned savagely and did not look away. "What are you waiting for?" Cailean spat.

Hooves echoed upon the road from behind. A horse whinnied as it was brought to a halt.

"What are you doing?" a woman's voice called.

Shoes hit the stonework. Knight and Salvaari alike turned towards the open gates. Cailean's eyes widened. Three horses, two riders and a third person, the one who had dismounted, on foot. One of the riders wore the garb of the Annoran royal guard. The other was *Queen* Riona Raynor.

"Step away from him," the girl on foot cried as she strode forward.

It was Kassandra Raynor. Her hair was wild and her dress travel-stained, but her voice was a strong and fierce as her face.

"Princess Kassandra, this man–" the knight began.

"Is a man, *not* a monster, and you shall treat him as such," the princess barked.

The knight grimaced before lowering his sword. Cailean felt a wicked smile tug at his lips as the man spoke.

"By your order, princess."

Kassandra met Cailean's eyes, and the tribesman knew that she recognised him. She said not a word to the Aedei chief and instead straightened her back. She turned her thunderous gaze upon the gathered soldiers.

"These people are *not* animals," Kassandra said loudly. "You will show them respect." The princess glanced down at Scada and gestured towards him. "Can't you see that man is hurt? Help him!"

Knights hurried over to Scada and hauled the tribesman to his feet. Within moments, the column was on its way again, marching deeper into Kilgareth. Cailean locked eyes with the Annoran princess and gave her a single nod before he rejoined his people.

✦ ✦ ✦

Velis Demir stared towards the forest with a steady eye. The horse beneath him barely moved or shifted. The stallion had been with Velis for many years and the pair had forged an unbreakable bond, a bond forged in the fires of battle. They stood almost a mile away from the vast forest that sprawled from horizon to horizon. Four thousand heavily armed horsemen rode at Velis' back. Two thousand were knights of Aureia and veterans of the bloody fields of Irene. Equal in their number were Larissan riders sent by Queen Reshada. Velis paid them no heed as he gazed across the barren land of the Rift, his eyes drawn deep into the woods. He held his spear loosely with his calloused hand.

Return with your spear or do not return at all.

That had been Queen Reshada's last command. Her last words to him. He had fought against the Salvaari for weeks yet had not been felled by spear or axe. Would today be the day?

"No sign of Jasir," the Larissan beside him murmured.

"It will be soon," Velis replied without looking at the man.

Chiher was the man who Reshada had sent at the head of her horsemen. He was a skilled warrior and a shrewd commander. Chiher was a man whom Velis could rely on in the heat of battle and he could ask no more than that. Jasir, the man who served as Velis' second, had taken two thousand of the Aureian riders into Salvaar to hunt those who called the woods home. He was to draw them into battle in order to lure them from the woodland. Silver flickered in the trees.

"There," Velis said.

The first of the Aureian riders emerged and began streaming towards them. Velis strapped his griffin-embossed shield onto his arm and raised his spear. He said not a word, yet the first of Jasir's men had barely cleared the forest when Velis and his army were racing towards them. Dozens of fleeing Aureian riders turned into hundreds. They charged straight for Velis, straight for their kinsmen. Velis showed no emotion under his helmet, yet he knew that he had timed the charge perfectly. The slight hill and the retreating backs of Jasir and his men would completely conceal Velis' riders. He could not hear the screams of the Salvaari over the thunder of horses' hooves, but he knew it was there. Velis relaxed in his saddle. His place was by no warm hearth or in a comfortable home. It was not in kingdom or empire. It was on horseback.

Jasir and his riders drew ever closer. Three horn blasts echoed across the Rift. Jasir's men split down the centre. One group angled to Velis' right flank, the other to his left. As the gap widened, screaming Salvaari warriors appeared. Some were mounted and some were on foot. All were covered in war paint. The Belcar and Niavenn tribes. Velis had no time to see the surprise light up their faces before his cavalry smashed into their splintered formation. He felled a rider with his spear as he charged through the Salvaari ranks. Velis' blade tasted blood again as he slew a man on foot. The Aureians and Larissans tore through the Salvaari. The massed ranks halted the charge, but the damage had been done. Chaos spread along the battlefield. Jasir's twin columns continued their gallop and slowly came around, circling to the east and west as Velis engaged the enemy. They charged now from both sides and hit the Salvaari hard. Velis spun in his saddle and plunged his spear into a warrior's chest. Tribal horns sang and the Salvaari began to scatter back towards the forest. Velis led his army after them. Spears tasted blood as the Aureians carved into their routing foe.

"Commander!" Jasir's voice broke through the din of battle. "Commander!"

Velis locked eyes on his second. Jasir's armour was stained red. He thrust his spear to the west. Velis followed the gesture and saw a line of horsemen appear through the trees. Their faces were awash with white paint. A new tribe had come. Velis turned to his horn bearer.

"Tell the men to break off and form on me," he commanded.

Three long blasts filled the air. Within moments, the Aureian and Larissan riders peeled off from their pursuit and galloped towards their commander. A gap grew between the silver horsemen and the fleeing Salvaari. Velis watched the mounted tribesmen surge forward. They were angling to cut his men off from their fleeing kin.

"If they turn to us, we take them head on," Velis said.

The line of Aureian and Larissan riders grew. The last of the pursuers had regained their senses and galloped towards their countrymen. Still Velis did not turn from the white-painted warriors.

"Reform the line!" he ordered and waved his spear. "Reform the line!"

Jasir and the other captains shouted orders and horns blew. The soldiers made ready. Horses pawed the ground. Velis adjusted his grip on his spear. The attack never came. The newcomers only sought to shield the retreat of the routing tribesmen. Where other men would have ground their teeth or cursed at the sight of their enemy escaping, Velis merely watched them. The last of the white-painted riders disappeared into the forest, vanishing like ghosts.

"Velis," Chiher called as they rode back through the Rift.

Velis glanced at the Larissan and then followed Chiher's nod to the south. Atop a ridge to the south there were two riders. They were far off, no larger than an outstretched hand.

"Mierans," Velis replied simply. "They have been watching us for days."

"Do you think they will move against us?" the Larissan asked.

Velis shook his head. "Why step in when your enemies are spilling their own blood?" he replied. "No, Chiher, those riders revealing themselves such as they have is a different challenge entirely. They want to see if we are afraid of them."

With that, Velis kicked his heels in and broke from the column. He galloped to the south alone as Jasir took command of the army. Once atop the small hill, he brought his mount to a halt. He did not reach for steel or ride closer to the Mierans. Instead, he stared towards them, unflinchingly. The riders gazed back at him for a few moments, staring at the lone horseman as his army continued west. After a few moments, the Mierans vanished from the ridge. Only then did Velis re-join his men.

Campfires crackled as the cavalry made camp. The soldiers unfurled bedrolls beside their horses so that if the horns were sounded and the enemy sighted, they could be ready to fight within moments. Velis sat with Chiher and Jasir, though he sat in silence. The light of the fire illuminated the pages of the book in his hands.

"What is that dusty, old thing?" Chiher asked after a while.

Velis glanced up from the book. "A journal written by an Annoran knight," he replied. "It comes from their days fighting the Salvaari."

"What use do you have for it?"

Velis at last closed the book and set it aside. "To know my enemy," he said. "Action is useless without knowledge, just as knowledge is useless without action. The white-painted warriors that we saw today were Coventina. The Niavenn and Belcar do not stand alone any longer. I did not know my enemy and as such did not want to venture into their hell."

"What does the journal say?" Jasir asked.

"Unlike the other tribes, the Coventina come from the far north of Salvaar. Theirs is a horse tribe. Their children learn to ride from birth. There are plains beyond the forest that the white-painted warriors ride. Apparently, the Coventina are horsemen of some renown, skilled both in the woodland and across barren fields. They held their own against the heavy cavalry of Annora … or so the journal says."

"And now they are here," Chiher muttered.

Velis brushed the golden chimera ring that adorned his finger. He felt its curves and points. The ring of the great Nykalous Gaedhela.

The ring given to him by Gaedhela's last descendant Reshada. The last Delion. The queen of Larissa. His queen.

"Nothing has changed," Velis told his companions. "I intend to follow out Emperor Darius' last command. I will crush them all."

✦ ✦ ✦

Cailean leaned back against the cold stone wall of his cell. Dozens of Salvaari filled the prison in Kilgareth. Men and women from every tribe, warriors all. Chains bound their wrists to the walls against which they sat. They had nothing more than their clothes and arm rings to keep the cold at bay. A constant guard stood outside the cells. The Knights of Kil'kara watched them with wary eyes despite the steel bars, stone walls and tight chains that trapped the prisoners.

Cailean glanced at the man beside him. The older warrior with grey hair sat with his eyes closed. Like Cailean, he wore the blue woad of the Aedei. His face was weathered with age and a bloodstained bandage was wrapped around the warrior's thigh.

"Never thought that I would see a place so far underground," he muttered. "So far from the sun."

Cailean looked up and stared at the cold, grey ceiling. "It is up there, Scada," Cailean replied. "The sun still rises. It will rise on us again."

"Aye, chief, that it will," Scada said. "If I am to die here, then I would ask a favour."

"Anything."

"Burn me," Scada told him. "Gather my ashes, and if you cannot return me home, scatter them in a strong eastern wind. Somewhere beneath the sun. Somewhere free. I would like to see my home one last time."

Cailean frowned as he heard how strained Scada's words were. "You will not die here, my friend," he said.

Scada did not reply. Cailean turned to the older warrior. Scada's eyes were still closed and his head still tipped back. He wasn't moving.

"Scada?" Cailean murmured and then shook the older warrior. "Scada?"

Nothing. The chief reached out and tugged on the bloody cloth that bound Scada's leg. It was soaked through. Blood and discolouration covered Scada's ruined skin. The wound was infected. If it was not tended to, then Scada would almost certainly die.

"Knight!" Cailean called out in the common tongue.

The holy warrior glanced through the cell bars.

"This man needs help," Cailean told him. "His wound–"

The knight turned away as if he had heard nothing.

"The wound is infected!" Cailean snarled.

"Quiet down back there," came the reply.

"He is going to die."

"A blessing then," the knight growled back. "Justice for all the innocent lives that he has stolen. Death is the best place for him."

Cailean bared his teeth as the knight moved away. There was nothing he could do. Cailean looked to his companion and placed a comforting hand on Scada's knee.

"You will not die here," he muttered in Salvaari. "Do you hear me? You will not die here."

A lock creaked and then the cell door opened. In came a pair of knights brandishing swords. Cailean rose to his feet. His lips were curled back into a snarl and his hands balled into fists. The other Salvaari followed suit. If the knights had come looking for a fight, then they would get one. Not *one* of the Salvaari was going to be touched. Not one. They were chained and bound but would fight even against men with armour and swords. A third figure walked into the cell. A maija clad in blue and purple as opposed to the browns and greys of the other healers.

"Please," the maija said as she tipped back her hood and revealed her face. "I mean you no harm."

She had a kind face and compassionate eyes. Despite everything, Cailean felt the urge to trust her. He did not know why. None of the Salvaari backed down.

"This is a waste of time, my lady," one of the knights muttered. "Why do you try to help them?"

"They are no less man than you or I. If our places were exchanged, then I would hope that I would be treated with equal compassion," the maija replied before looking to Cailean. "Please, your friend. He is hurt."

Cailean at last tore his eyes from the knights and gave her a simple nod. The tribesmen stepped back but kept their gazes on the soldiers.

"Thank you," the woman said sincerely as she approached and knelt before Scada. "My name is Lysandra. I am here to help."

✦ ✦ ✦

TWENTY

The Lupentine Sea

"Hold a moment," a voice called. Its owner held an arm out to stop Elise from passing.

Elise pursed her lips as she gave the man a once over. A thick cloak was draped across one shoulder and a wicked sidesword adorned his belt. His face was rugged and his hair, short and greying, matched his beard. Rings adorned his ears and there was a dangerous glint in his eyes. Elise's eyes hardened as she looked into his gaze. She knew who the man was despite the fact that they had never spoken. The man was Bhaltair. The same man who had been tracking Elise for weeks in search of her assistance.

"Yes?" Elise asked.

"You're the one who–"

"I assure you we've never met." Elise cut him off.

"You're the Nightingale," came the reply.

Elise could hear a flicker of irritation in his voice. It wasn't much, yet she could not resist.

"Delfeyre. Elise Delfeyre," Elise told him. "And let me guess. You would be Bhaltair."

"Charmed." Bhaltair gave her a short bow. "I have a proposition."

"I'm not interested." Elise rolled her eyes and made to pass.

Bhaltair clamped his hand on her shoulder. "A moment is all I ask, Lady Delfeyre," he said.

Elise gritted her teeth, cocked her head slightly and then glared at Bhaltair. He was going to ask her to help him lead what remained of the Elaran gangs. To be their *symbol*.

"Go on," she said.

"These are dangerous times," Bhaltair said. "Four thousand of our people have given all that they own to find a new life. A better life. They did not choose to leave their home; they did so because they had no choice. Many of those who sail with us, Elaran and raider alike, have nothing … not even hope. It has been taken from them."

Elise crossed her arms. "You say that they had no choice in the matter, yet it was *you* who forced their hand," she replied sharply. "It was you who riled the magister up. It was you who started the violence. It was you—"

"We all had our roles to play." Bhaltair cut her off. "Yours, whether deliberate or not, was to inspire the people. Mine was to liberate the city from a tyrant. And I did."

"Oh, you did, did you?" Elise said sarcastically.

"Yes, and I would do it again. I gave much to see Imrohir removed from his throne, and I would have given far more if I had been asked," Bhaltair told her. "My lady, the task at hand is vital if our people are to survive – no, more – if they are to *flourish*. Along with Lord Stentor, I can help guide them, yet there are hundreds of men like us. What we need is someone who can play the role of a sculptor. Someone who can cultivate the people's trust. Someone who they can rally behind. Someone who can give them hope and sculpt them into something more. I would ask your help in solving this problem."

Elise thought back to Elara. She thought back to the gangs. She remembered the explosion that had begun the war in the streets. The war that had claimed the lives of her aunt and uncle.

"You want my help?" Elise asked incredulously. "I wonder, Bhaltair, is that because you have learnt that not every problem can be solved by blowing things sky high?"

"We all have our sins, Lady Delfeyre, and we must live with them," Bhaltair replied. "I have not always done good, but in order to save my people, the old had to be replaced with the new. From the ashes we will rise. Help me create a better future for our people."

He spoke well, but Elise had grown up with a circus. Bhaltair had a performer's tongue. Perhaps it would have been enough to persuade someone else.

"That sounds absolutely ridiculous," Elise told him. "My answer is no."

Bhaltair frowned as if he was surprised. "Lady Delfeyre, I am not sure that you understand the gravity of the situation."

"Oh, I understand perfectly," Elise growled. "You wish to ally my name to your own. You wish to use the Nightingale's name to raise you above all else and there enable you to cast Lord Stentor and the others aside. I am not a leader. I am not a politician. I am not whatever it is that you think I am."

"You are the Nightingale."

"The Nightingale was never real. Just a means to an end and it worked well. That end has been accomplished. The Nightingale came from nothing and now to nothing the Nightingale will return. It will fade away and vanish just like that." Elise snapped her fingers.

"Then what are you?"

"I am Elise Delfeyre," she said. "Nothing more and nothing less."

"And what are you doing?"

"I am protecting my household."

"So you're taking over where your uncle left off?" Bhaltair replied bitterly. He could not hide the irritation anymore. Elise was not a child who could be so easily manipulated. Not anymore.

"Someone has to," Elise said.

"Lady Delfeyre, I beg you to reconsider–"

"I said that I'm not interested," Elise interrupted in exasperation. "Did you not listen the first two times?"

With a roll of her eyes, Elise shoved past Bhaltair and continued on her way across the deck. She could feel the gang leader's glare boring into her back –she did not care. She had *never* cared about the kind of authority that he was offering her. Elise wanted nothing more than for her name to vanish from the mouths of all those of rank and position. She crossed the deck towards Tariq and Marshall.

"Did that man bother you, my lady?" Marshall asked with a nod towards Bhaltair.

Elise glanced back at the gang leader and saw that he was walking towards the helm. Cleander and Captain Marquez were there. Elise held up a hand and revealed the small coin purse that she had snatched from Bhaltair when she had passed him.

"Nothing that I could not handle," Elise replied as she tossed the guardsman the purse.

"There is a devil in you, Elise," Marshall said with raised eyebrows.

Elise gave them a grin. "You're right about that."

She made her way to the railing and gazed out across the gentle waters of the Lupentine. She turned her eyes to the east, towards where they had come from. Somewhere well beyond the horizon was Elara.

"Have you ever left home before?" Elise asked her companions.

"Yes, my lady. A decade spent upon the sea will take you across the known world," Marshall replied with a fond smile. "Aureia, Annora, Idrisir. I have been fortunate enough to see them all. I have seen the halls of Tallis and journeyed to the Erebian Alps. I have served the magister of Kiriador and trained men upon those sandy proving grounds."

"That is quite the journey," Elise said as she glanced at the soldier. "Do you ever miss it? The freedom to move from place to place, to come and go as you please?"

"There are some days I do," Marshall told her honestly. "Yet when I was employed by your uncle, I was given a chance to lay down my troubles and walk away from the sea. Lord Delfeyre gave me peace. At least for a time."

"And do you regret it now?" she asked.

Marshall shook his head. "No, my lady. It is hard to regret not knowing one possibility when the one I chose gave me so much. After all that I have been given by your family, my fate has been forever tied with your own."

Elise nodded and glanced at the Berenithian. "And what of you, Tariq?"

"Once," Tariq replied. "Many years ago, my family left Berenithia in search of a better life. I was only a child then and the lands from which I hail are but a distant memory. I do not remember much of the voyage except the waves and the sickness that came with them. Berenithia, home – it is not so clear in my mind."

"Do you know something? I am not sure that Elara is my home anymore," Elise said. "I thought I would feel something when we left. Some kind of sadness. Instead, I don't feel really anything."

"In all of my travels," Marshall began, "I have learnt that home is not Elara nor some distant land. It is in us."

✦ ✦ ✦

"Miera," Torben said as he approached Erik.

The king glanced at his friend before looking back to the north. The coast stretched from horizon to horizon. The Steppe of Miera, land of the horsemen.

"I have seen the great grass sea before. The hills and rolling plains as far as the eye can see," Erik replied. "Though it has been years since I was this close."

"Three summers," Torben said with a nod. "I remember."

"A simpler time," Erik told him.

"As I recall, that was the first time that your father let Astrid chart our course."

"Aye, it was," Erik murmured. "We had many tales to tell …"

He was unable to take his eyes from the Mieran coast. Something about it called to him. Erik narrowed his gaze as it washed across the great plain.

"What is it, Erik?" Torben asked as he followed his friend's stare. "What draws your gaze?"

"Miera … the war in the north. To those who fight for freedom the same as us. To those to whom the empire has turned steel upon."

"Salvaar? With such a host assembled against them, none will survive," Torben replied as his brow furrowed.

"And if what Luana has told me is true, then once Salvaar has been dealt with, Miera shall follow."

Torben merely shrugged. "What are their quarrels to us?" he said. "These foreign wars mean nothing to our people."

"Until they do." Erik at last turned from the coast and looked to his companion.

"Erik, I–"

The king clapped a hand upon his friend's shoulder.

"Blow the horns. Signal the captains Teague and Marquez to our ship."

The song of Valkir horns echoed across the Lupentine, and before long, the Emeralis and the Oridassey had made their way alongside the Ravenheart. Gangplanks were extended and then parties from both ships came across. Luana Marquez, Cillian Teague, Calvillo, Bhaltair, Lord Priamos Stentor and Cleander joined Erik and Torben in the captain's cabin.

"No doubt you are wondering why I called you here," Erik began.

"If you have something to say," Lord Stentor said as he gestured for the king to continue, "then speak."

"All of us here have been chosen to represent our people. Our alliance was one born out of necessity, yet I believe that we can turn it into something better," Erik told them.

"What do you propose?" Teague asked.

"My sister's last words were of peace. She believed in a better world. One where her people – where *all* people – could have a say in their own destiny. Astrid did not want to spend her years raiding and fighting. She *hated* it. She wanted nothing more than to take a ship south. To sail and explore every corner of the wide, wide world. That future was stolen from her. But I tell you now that her dreams of peace and freedom are stronger than ever, for they are now *my* dreams. To accomplish them, I will have to fight. I fought against the League to help your people, and you in turn will stand beside me when the empire comes."

"Between us, we have enough ships to even the odds." Bhaltair spoke up. "We have warriors to crew them and sailors to sail them. Yet something tells me that you do not merely speak of fighting this great fleet."

"You're talking about what comes next. Aren't you?" Luana stated.

"All of us came together in common cause to create a better future for our people," Erik said as he glanced from face to face. "My friends, that future is closer than ever. I tell you now that if we continue down our present course, we will *never* find it."

"My people did not cross two oceans and suffer such loss only to be told that they will never know peace," Teague growled. "Speak plainly."

Erik looked to the captain. "We beat the League," he said. "Maybe we beat the Aureans. Let's say that we defeat them. Let's say that we win the day. It would only be a matter of time before they try again. They would send fleets and armies in a cycle of blood. This is what it would be time and time and time again without end. We hold them off once. Twice. Perhaps even a third time. Eventually we will lose. Eventually all of us will be dead. And then what? Our ghosts will not be able to save our people."

Outraged cries erupted. Shouts filled the cabin.

"You are wrong to despair," Lord Stentor snarled. "We can – we *will* win. I refuse to lose."

"He's right." Bhaltair's voice rose above the din. "The king is right! In some way we have *all* fought against the empire, be it the navy or their colonies. The empire is tenacious. If it wants to kill, it kills. If it wants to take, it takes. They will never stop hunting us."

The last of the cries died down. They all knew it to be true.

"It will start with the fall of Salvaar," Erik told them quietly. "Once the northerners are dealt with, the empire will turn its attention to Miera. We know this. The Accords have been broken. It may take months, even years, but before long, we will be the *last* free people. The last free of their ways and their religion. Then they will come for us … and there will be no stopping them."

"Then what do you suggest?" Lord Stentor asked.

Erik took a breath. It had been on his mind for a long time, but until today he had been unsure of how to proceed. Now it came to him.

"For years we have all been divided. We have been rushing around taking what we wished and sating our own desires. We did not give a tinker's curse for those we hurt, and so when we looked around, when the sun was setting upon our people, we had no one standing beside us. That same fate is befalling Salvaar right now, right in this moment. The war in the north shall determine the fate of us all. If the northerners fail, then we *all* fall to ruin. I suggest that we help them."

"How?" Teague asked. "We have no mighty army and those we do have are needed here."

"There is one army that could swing the balance," Erik replied. "One that could turn the tide. That of Miera."

"Miera?" Torben was aghast. "You would call upon them to

fight, they who despise all beyond their realm and care nothing for the troubles of others?"

"Were we so different?" Erik asked as he turned to his friend.

"This is madness," the bloodsworn replied incredulously.

"Is it, really?" Luana Marquez said. "We would need the support of King Zoran. Only he could marshal his people."

"My only question would be how do we gain an audience from a man who would happily see us dead?" Teague asked.

"We tell them of the League's treachery," Erik started. His hands danced through the air as he spoke. "We tell them of the broken Accords – that will gain us Zoran's ear. But to get his help ... For Zoran to turn his sword north against the empire, it would take more. As you once said, Captain Marquez: never underestimate the power of a good story or the strength of a song. This story will be that of the Raven Jarl. That of Astrid. A tale of freedom ... of victory."

"Such a thing is possible. The Mierans may easily turn upon those who seek their help, yet we *all* know that King Erik is right," Luana said. "If we do not do this, then in time, we will all die. The empire will have won. For this task I will offer my ship and my life."

"Are you sure?" Teague asked her. "We need you here."

"No, you don't. You have Captain Laven," Luana told him. "And I insist that I go along. For this task to succeed, someone will need to accompany me. Someone who *knew* Astrid. Someone who can add life to this tale."

Erik nodded and turned to Torben. He knew that Luana spoke true. She had never met Astrid.

"Forgive me, my friend, for asking this of you," Erik said. "But I *need* you to go with her. Only you knew Astrid as well as I. Only you could convince the Mierans of her truth."

Torben met the king's eyes. "If you ask this of me, then I will go," Torben told him. "I will bring honour to you both, and I pray that my words can move them."

Erik clapped a hand on Torben's shoulder.

"You will need me," a new voice said.

All eyes turned to the hooded man as he stepped out of the shadows. It was an Annoran voice.

"You … I don't know you," Erik said.

"Cleander," the man replied.

"He is one of the finest swordsmen to have ever lived," Bhaltair added. "Take him with you and you will not regret it."

"The more the merrier," Luana told him. "He may be useful on the road."

"Captain." Cleander dipped his head to her.

"Then we are decided," Erik said. "Captain Marquez, send any passengers that you have across, and I will see them to safety. Then you must sail."

✦ ✦ ✦

The Oridassey broke off from the Ravenheart and word was spread through the Emeralis that all who weren't crew had to board King Erik's ship.

"I'm leaving," Cleander told Elise.

Elise frowned. "You're travelling to Miera."

"Captain Marquez is taking a most dangerous road, and my sword could be all that stands between her and death," Cleander explained. "We have been given a chance to defeat our enemy, and I will take it."

"You have hope then?"

"Only a fool's hope," Cleander replied.

"Your friend, Bhaltair. He came to see me," Elise told him. "He wanted to use my name. I said no. You have never lied to me, Cleander, so I pray that you do not now. Will he keep trying?"

Cleander pursed his lips. "I have known the man for many years, Elise," he said. "Bhaltair is a man of deadly passion. When he wants something, he will not rest until he has it. Your name ... your reputation will not shield you from him, even as he tries to join them to his own cause. I will not lie and say that this will not put you at cross-purposes with him. The very thing that made Bhaltair the man to lead the gangs from the darkness is the thing that will make him a most dangerous enemy. His will. His conviction."

"So even if we win ... even if we triumph over the empire, he will not stop?"

"No," Cleander replied. "The Nightingale is too much of a threat to his position and his fight against the magister has made him most suspicious. If push comes to shove, he will not hesitate to kill you."

"I never wanted to fight," Elise said sadly. "I donned the black to bring justice to my family. I fled Elara to escape the cycle of violence. Now I find myself still caught up in it."

Cleander looked at her thoughtfully for a moment. "You could come with me," he said.

"What?"

"Come with me to Miera," Cleander continued. "Bring your friends. You will be out of Bhaltair's sight and reach. I can protect you from him. I know those who can give you a new start. A new beginning. A place where the Nightingale is not known. A place where the name of Bhaltair has no meaning. A place that you can live. Truly live."

Elise bit her lip as she looked at Cleander. "You would do that?" she murmured.

"You have given enough," Cleander replied. "I would not see someone that I have grown fond of come to harm."

Elise gave him a grateful smile. She felt as if a burden had been removed from her shoulders. Cleander was offering her a life free of politics and backstabbing, a life free of the violence that had plagued it of late.

"Then I will come to Miera," she told him.

"I pray that you're doing this for the right reasons," Mellisanthi said as she appeared before her friend. "Even though I know that you're not."

Cleander glanced up from the pack that he was preparing. "The future of our world is at stake," he replied. "What happens in the north will decide the futures of all."

"This isn't just about convincing the horsemen to join our cause and you know it," Mellisanthi told him. "This is about so much more, even if you will not admit it. I saw you talking to the girl. Right now, she is convincing her companions to follow her with you. I almost wish that does not sway them."

"And why is that?"

"You are fond of her. That much is painfully clear, Markus," Mellisanthi said. "Yet something warns me that you asking Elise to follow you goes beyond that. I am forced to wonder if this is not merely a ruse for you to get closer to the Citadel. That this is some part of a game that will allow you to continue your vendetta against the order. Tell me that it isn't."

Cleander met her eyes and held her gaze a moment. He slung his pack over his shoulder. "It is not."

"Markus," Mellisanthi sadly replied. Her voice was quiet. "I have known you long enough to know when you are lying."

"Mellisanthi, I *cannot* let those men pursue the artefacts," he said forcefully. "I have seen what they can do, and I cannot let them keep the Spear. No one should wield that kind of power."

"Then the girl is not involved?"

"I will make you this promise that she will be kept safe," Cleander vowed. "By my life I swear it."

"Then fortune be with you, Markus Harvarder," Mellisanthi said. "May you find whatever it is that you seek."

Cleander pulled her into an embrace. "There are no words for all that you have done," he told her. "I do not deserve your friendship."

"No, you don't," Mellisanthi said with a smile.

Cleander made to walk away. Something stopped him at the door. He turned back to face her.

"Mellisanthi, if I never see you again, know that it was you who saved me. It was you who believed when no one else would." Cleander reached out and took her hand. He placed a kiss upon it before he continued. "Knowing you has been my greatest honour, and I will always hold you to heart."

"As I will always hold you."

Cleander looked deep into Mellisanthi's eyes. He knew that she could see into the depths of his soul. She knew his heart and she knew his truth. Cleander reached up and pulled his sun and moon amulet from his neck. He handed it to Mellisanthi.

"For Emberly," he told her.

"Is there a message?"

"None that need be spoken."

Cleander could see the first hint of tears in his friend's eyes as he spoke. He knew that she could see the fate that he was committed to. In his heart, Cleander knew that the quest could claim his life and Mellisanthi saw that.

"Farewell, Markus."

"Farewell, Mellisanthi."

✦ ✦ ✦

TWENTY-ONE

The border of Salvaar, Duchy of Aloys

The Annoran and Medean army had left Verena two days ago. In their company travelled a group of maija to serve as advisors, healers and messengers. With the maija came pigeons to maintain contact with their brothers to the north in Verena and Kilgareth.

King Dayne set up camp half a mile from the edge of the forest. Mounted scouts patrolled the border of the woodland, while those encamped were on high alert at all times. Many of the Annorans were veterans from the last war with Salvaar and knew all too well the horrors that the pagans could inflict if caught unawares. Soldiers sat around fires in their full kit talking and laughing – but at the same time, they were prepared for the worst. Despite the alliance, despite the close ties between the Raynor and Caspin families, there was a deep-rooted tension between the two forces. The death of Aquale Caspin had brought it to life almost overnight. Annoran and Caspin soldiers sat apart and gave each other nothing but dark looks and tempered words.

Tristayn Martyn, knight of the realm and general of the Annoran army, strode through the camp. Like the rest of the soldiers, he was clad in his armour and wore a sword at his side. The general carried his scarlet-crested helmet under his arm. High lord Galan of Torosa and a pair of Torosi knights walked with Tristayn as he did his rounds. Like him, the three men of the western province watched their surroundings with wary eyes. The distinguishable path on which they walked cut between the Caspin and Annoran camps.

"I've given order for the remnants of the follower's camp to return to Kilgareth." Galan's voice was dark. "The situation here is growing too volatile. The death of Aquale Caspin has caused stir enough among the men and I would not have those who follow the army descend into chaos."

"There are wolves among the followers. Veracious wolves," Tristayn replied. "The further they are from here the better."

Lord Galan glanced at his companion. "Your niece is not with them anymore is she, General?" he said.

"Marian?" Tristayn replied with a shake of his head. "No, lord. I made sure that she did not venture further than Kilgareth. The princess even forbade her from accompanying her to Verena and for that I am eternally grateful. War is no place for a child. Especially now when we cannot know who our enemies are."

"Things were simpler twenty years ago, were they not?" Galan said. "When men stood before us, sword in hand, and declared themselves our foe. They did not fill your ears with silver words and then stab a knife into your back."

"Your daughter remained in Torosa, did she not?"

"Iesha is as far from here as possible," Galan told him. "She stayed in Toron-Tor to watch over my lands and estate."

"A fine choice, lord."

"Upon my return, I will have to find a suitable union for her," Galan replied. "She has been unmarried for too long, General. She was supposed to have been married to my former ward this summer. Iesha had grown quite fond of the prince during his time in my house."

"Nasty business with Prince Lukas," Tristayn said with a grimace. "We can only hope that…"

The general trailed off as shouts filled the camp. He exchanged a look with the high lord and the pair hastened towards the roar that had arisen. They came across a thick circle of soldiers, and in that moment, Tristayn knew what had caused the commotion. He shoved his way through the red-cloaked ranks of Annoran soldiers until he reached the centre of the circle. Green-cloaked Caspin soldiers stood opposite. Four men exchanged blows as they fought. Two were Annoran and the others Caspin. Tristayn shoved his helmet into the hands of an Annoran soldier and waded into the fight.

"STOP THIS MADNESS IN THE NAME OF THE KING!" the general roared as he threw one of the Annorans back.

He stepped between the combatants and then Galan was beside him. The two sides glared daggers at each other. Blood spilled from wounds and bruising was beginning to form. None had gone for steel – not yet. Two of the fighters did not heed the general's command and still wrestled upon the ground. Galan heaved the Medean to his feet and drove his fist hard into the man's stomach. The soldier groaned and fell back. Galan then turned upon the Annoran and slapped him hard across his face.

"You were given an order," he snarled before turning his wrath upon those who watched. "Now back, all of you!"

Those who did not know the faces of the general or high lord recognised their fine cloaks and armour. Tristayn looked from Annoran to Medean and back.

"Which one of you started the fight?" he growled.

"I threw the first punch, General," one of the Annorans admitted.

"And why did you do that?"

"He slandered the king's name, sir. Called us all godless traitors."

Tristayn turned his glare upon the Medean soldier who had been accused. "Is this true?"

"Aye."

Tristayn crossed the ground between them and shoved his face to within inches of the soldier's. The general's eyes hardened as he stared *through* the Medean.

"Aye, *what*?"

"Aye, sir."

"Let me remind you, *soldier*, that we – all of us – are on the same side. King Dayne defeated the Salvaari. Have you forgotten? He stood shoulder to shoulder with you. He did not hide behind his army. He was crowned by the cardinal, the most holy leader of our faith. His queen is the daughter of your duke. We are brothers, you and I. *Brothers*. I promise you that King Dayne had *nothing* to do with Aquale Caspin's death. I promise you that right now the king is hunting the murderer. And I also promise you that the next man who slanders name or throws a punch against his brothers will be sent to the stocks. Annoran and Medean *both*. Am I understood?"

"Yes, sir," the Annorans who fought echoed.

Tristayn glared at the Medeans. "Am I understood?"

"Yes, sir," they replied.

"Good," Tristayn growled before snatching his helmet back.

"All of you back to your places now," Lord Galan commanded.

The crowd dispersed quickly and soon enough only the general, the high lord and the two knights remained.

"It's getting worse," Galan muttered.

Tristayn could only nod. He knew that it would soon reach boiling point. Something had to change before it was too late.

"Lord Galan, General Tristayn," a man's voice called.

The two men glanced up as a maija approached. Like the rest of his creed that had ridden out from Kilgareth, the maija wore a shirt of mail beneath his robes. The short sleeves of the shining steel emerged from the depths of the man's robes and hung to his elbows.

"Maija Gawen," Galan greeted the man.

"Word has come from the Citadel," Gawen told them. "The king has called council."

By the time that Tristayn and Galan arrived at the king's tent, the council had all assembled. Santiago Caspin stood with his commander Rodrigo Santana. Duke Anejo Reyna was there along with his captains. The king stood with Sir Garrik, Edmund Hornwood and High Lord Balderik of Laeoflaed.

"I hear that you wish to command my men," Santiago Caspin growled as he saw Tristayn enter.

"There was a fight, Duke Santiago," the general replied calmly. "Men needed to be disciplined. Had you been there I am sure that you would have done the same."

"Soldiers fight and soldiers play," Santiago said. "It is only natural. What was the cause?"

"My man threw the first punch though it was yours who slandered the king's name."

"The king, yes." A dangerous glint burned in Santiago's eye as he spoke. "I hear that the Valkir have united behind their own now. Annora, Salvaar, Miera, the Valkir … four kings. With each new crown the power of the kings lessens, and before this war is over, there may be no crowns left. I *pray* that this *tragedy* does not occur."

"Thank you, Duke Santiago," King Dayne cut in calmly. "Your *compassion* is a boon in this troubled time."

"If only my brother had been shown the same."

The council grew silent. Eyes widened and all looked to Duke Santiago and the king. The duke's face burned with anger. The king showed no emotion.

"Aquale's murder weighs on us all, duke." Dayne's tone was measured. "The loss of a brother is a blow keenly felt. Take comfort in the fact that he will be with the gods now. In death as in life he was given the honour he deserved."

"He was given the honour of Annoran steel," Santiago countered.

"We do not know what led to his death," Dayne told him. "I sent those men to summon him to me. I wished to speak to my uncle; you know this. I told you before we burned his body. I wish that he was not dead. I wish that he stood with us now against Salvaar. But we cannot change what happened. I did not kill your brother, and I do not want the pain of his death to spill through the ranks."

A grey-haired noble stepped forward. He wore fine, golden armour with a tiger etched upon his breastplate. An Aureian-style shoulder cloak covered his left arm, partially hiding the shortsword beneath.

"Your man said that news had come from Kilgareth," the Medean lord said before Santiago Caspin could continue. "Troubling news."

Tristayn breathed a sigh of relief as Duke Anejo Reyna spoke up. Santiago was a tenacious man who would not so easily give up a fight, even a verbal one. The Reyna family had been close with Annora ever since the mercenary Bellec had saved them from rebellion years ago.

"Indeed, Duke Anejo," Dayne told him as he held up a letter.

He handed the letter to Tristayn who in turn gave the king a confused look as he saw the symbol on the broken seal.

"This bears the eagle's seal," Tristayn said.

"Princess Kassandra?" Garrik asked.

For the first time, a brief flicker of pain crossed King Dayne's eyes and Tristayn doubted that it was from the illness.

"They were attacked on the road," Dayne told the council. "Somehow, someway, the pagans found a way to cross the mountains. They killed the guard and took Queen Sofia."

Tristayn stared at his king. His pulse quickened. If Sofia had been taken, then their position had changed. If she had been taken, then Salvaar almost controlled Annora and Caspin.

"They took my daughter?" Santiago said in disbelief.

Dayne nodded. "Princess Kassandra, her mother and one of the guardsmen alone escaped," he said. "As of this moment, we do not know what the Salvaari want, though we should expect a messenger from them within the next couple of days."

"How could this have happened?" Rodrigo Santana asked.

"From what the maija have told me, there are hidden passages through the mountains," Dayne replied. "Somehow they have become known to the enemy."

"Then once again, I have lost family at the hands of Annora," Santiago snarled as he strode towards the king. "You had best hope that she is returned alive."

"Was that a threat, Duke Santiago?" Sir Garrik replied.

"No, it is a promise."

Anejo Reyna stepped forward and placed a hand on Santiago's shoulder. "Calm yourself, my friend," he said. "We are all on the same side."

"Are we?" Santiago spat.

King Dayne held his stance before the Caspin duke. "You have lost a daughter; I have lost a wife. We cannot let this loss come between us and destroy the friendship that we have built." Dayne extended a hand. "We can deal with our grievances when Sofia is returned to us. Until then, we must set aside the past."

Santiago gritted his teeth and, after a moment, took Dayne's hand.

The noon sun was high in sky the next day when shouts filled the camp. They started in the south. Horns were blown and soldiers gathered up weapons and armour. A lone rider marked with black paint rode through their midst. He carried an olive branch of peace. The Salvaari warrior did not turn his head or acknowledge the jeers and curses that came his way; he was too dignified for that. Word had quickly spread, and by the time the rider had reached Dayne's tent, the rest of the council were there. The Salvaari did not dismount. Instead, he gave the king an arrogant smirk as he tossed a ring onto the ground. Dayne picked the jewel up from the earth and ran his eyes across it. It belonged to Sofia.

"Is she alive?" Dayne asked the Salvaari.

"For now," came the reply. The rider spoke louder as he continued so that all could hear. "I have a message for King Dayne of Annora from Lukas the One-Eye."

"Speak, then," Dayne growled at the mention of his brother's name.

"To my brother the king. Your wife is in my possession. In four days, I will be at the edge of the forest north of Lake Thirlryda. If you wish to see your wife again, you will come. If you wish to see your wife again, you will not send men to attempt rescue. If you wish to see your wife again, you will honour the rule of parlay. Break this sacred trust and she dies. If my messenger does not return unharmed or of his own volition, she dies. If any man who does not bear the title of Annoran rides with you, then she dies. Her fate is in your hands."

Dayne clasped his hands to stop them from balling into fists. He was enraged, but he would not give the Salvaari the satisfaction of seeing him show such emotion.

"You," Dayne said to the messenger. "Ride back to your master. Tell him that I will be there as he has asked. Tell him that if any harm befalls Sofia, if so much as a strand of hair plucked, then no man, no steel, no spirit will be able to save him. That is my word."

The army began to disperse before the Káli warrior had ridden from the camp. It was agreed that Santiago Caspin and Anejo Reyna would hold their positions and keep the Salvaari blockaded to the north and south of the Medean border. General Tristayn along with the high lords Galan and Balderik and their forces would stay with the Medean contingent. King Dayne mustered what remained of his army and within an hour they were marching east towards Thirlryda. Towards Sofia. Towards Lukas.

✦ ✦ ✦

Lukas One-Eye led his column through the first line of trees and into the forest. His company had been removed from Salvaar for many days and now finally they could find some form of safety within the woodland. Aelida met them as they crossed the Arwan River and then she led the column to the Káli camp. They had left Vaylin's lands days ago and now had made Henghis' territory their home. The tents of the two-hundred-strong army stretched deep into the forest. Scouts patrolled the trees and plains beyond Salvaar. Aelida rode at Lukas' left hand while at his right were Hadwin and Layan. Of the twenty that had ridden out, eighteen had returned. One had fallen in battle and the other Lukas had killed himself. The rain of arrows that his people had unleashed had saved many lives.

One-Eye swung his leg over his horse's back and slid from his saddle. He pulled his helmet from his head and shook his hair free. He took his crutch from his saddle and turned to see Rodion and Maevin approaching.

"Lord," Rodion greeted Lukas.

"Rodion." Lukas grinned and took his friend's arm.

No words were exchanged between Lukas and Maevin. Instead, they clasped arms and pressed their foreheads together in greeting. Maevin's eyes flicked over Lukas' shoulder.

"*This* is the eagle's queen?"

Lukas glanced back to where the dark-haired beauty rode. She sat before Hadwin on his horse for but a moment before the mercenary dismounted and pulled her from the stallion. A strip of cloth was roughly tied around her mouth to gag her and her hands were tightly bound. Sofia showed no fear.

"Sofia Caspin, aye," Lukas replied before gesturing from Aelida to the queen. "Aelida, cage the prisoner."

"Yes, lord."

Aelida glared at the Medean woman. Her people, both Medean and Annoran, had been responsible for the deaths of so many Salvaari. Aelida bared her teeth savagely and shoved Sofia further into the camp. A small cage was built against a thick tree, fashioned with branches and rope. Aelida forced Sofia inside and shoved her back against the tree. The Káli cut Sofia's bindings. A wooden stake was driven deep into the earth beside the queen and the chains that hung from it were locked around her wrists. Sofia did not offer so much as a grunt. She did not complain. Instead, Sofia just stared at Aelida.

"Your people should not have crossed the river," Aelida snarled in the common tongue. "They should not have slaughtered my people and burned their villages."

The gag prevented Sofia from speaking so she just looked into the Káli woman's eyes.

"Aelida," Lukas called as he entered the cage. He nodded towards the makeshift door.

Aelida gave Sofia a final venomous glare before striding from the enclosure. Lukas gave Sofia a glance before hobbling over and pulling the gag from her mouth.

"I apologise for the unpleasantries," he told Sofia. "But you understand."

"Actually, no I don't, Lukas," Sofia replied. "You killed Emilian Aloys. You burned Valham to the ground and slaughtered the priests. You sacked Bandujar, and if that wasn't enough, you turned against your family. You betrayed us all. And for what?"

"One day, if we both survive, I will tell you," Lukas said.

"Come now. We are brother and sister, are we not?" Sofia pressed. "And more likely than not, I will not be walking out of this forest alive."

"I do not bear you ill will, nor will I harm you. So long as the king does not attempt anything foolish, you will not be touched," Lukas told her. "You will return to your home and family alive. You have my word."

"The man you killed, the one that came for us in the carriage. Why did you take his life?"

Lukas took a step closer to the Medean woman. He could see no fear in her eyes and there was not even a slight tremor in her voice. If she felt any kind of fear, then she hid it well.

"You were supposed to be alone in that carriage," he told her.

"So you were given bad information. That explains nothing."

"Kassandra's horse."

"Pardon me?"

"I saw her outside your carriage," Lukas said after a moment. "I knew in that moment that I had to be the one to capture you. Kassandra did not need to see any of this. I would not turn her into a piece in this game played between brothers. Whatever has happened, whatever has come between us, I would not see any harm befall her. Had my man left the carriage and taken my sister or her mother, then they would have been captured or worse. I did not want that to be her fate."

"Then Dayne is right." Sofia reached out and lightly touched Lukas' hand. "There is still some of the prince in you. He can see it. Your sister can see it. I can see it. You need to see it."

"No," Lukas said with a shake of his head. "There is no turning back now."

"There is always a way back," Sofia told him.

"I do *not* want to go back," Lukas replied.

"So you don't go back then," the queen continued. "But going *forward* isn't necessarily an ending."

Lukas brushed her hand with his thumb before pulling away and meeting her eyes.

"No. The spirits have decreed that I be here now. This is my fate. All of my life has come to this point; there is nowhere else to be but here. There is nothing else to do but stand against my brother. To be here now is the only thing that matters."

✦ ✦ ✦

TWENTY-TWO

Road to Bandujar, Duchy of Aloys, Medea

They ate and drank in the saddle, stopping only for sleep. They would rise before the sun and Alarik would push Kyler through a gruelling sparring session. By night it was the same. When at last they stopped, they would spark a fire to life and train in its light. Each day Kyler felt himself getting better. They had done the same when they had set out in search of the Spear and then again on the passage to and from Elara. Kyler had begun to not only learn how to fight but how his mentor fought. The bruising that he had once suffered at Alarik's hand grew less and less with every passing night and he was also starting to inflict his own in return. Sword, shield and knife had become as much a part of Kyler as his own arms.

Thud. The wooden staunches that they used for training met heavily.

"That's enough for one night," Alarik said as he stepped back and lowered his makeshift blade.

Kyler nodded and tossed his staunch to the side. The layer of sweat that covered his body and rolled down his face had drenched his hair. He wore his full kit save for his cloak. He had only worn his armour a few times before they had left for Elara, and now they were riding into battle. He needed to learn how to move and fight in it. Kyler placed his shield against the base of a tree before unstrapping his helmet and pushing back his coif. He placed the helm beside his shield and pulled off his thick gloves. Alarik took a long gulp from his water skin.

"Pisspot," he called out before tossing the skin.

Kyler caught it and took a draught, relishing the cool liquid as it rolled down his throat. "I'll take first watch," Kyler told his mentor.

Alarik clapped him on the cheek as he walked past with a smirk. "As you wish," he replied.

Alarik lay down on his bedding and was asleep within moments. Kyler gathered up his swordbelt and sat against a thick tree. He placed his sheathed blade upon his lap and stared out into the blackness. They had taken turns sitting watch since they had left for Elara, but this was different. Despite his exhaustion, Kyler could not sleep. His conversation with Lysandra had only added to his worries. If she did not find a way to cure him of the cursed blood, then he was dead. Each day it became harder to focus and harder to think. Kyler could barely remember what it was like to know peace.

Eventually, Kyler traded watch with Alarik. He lay awake watching the moon for what seemed like an eternity before a semblance of sleep finally came.

"Pisspot," Alarik said as he shook Kyler awake. "Time to move."

Kyler groaned and heaved his exhausted body up. He snatched up his waterskin and splashed some of the cool liquid across his face. Only then did he notice the sliver of light upon the horizon.

"The sun is rising," Kyler said with a frown. "We should have left by now. Why did you not wake me?"

"You've not been sleeping," Alarik stated simply. "Not since Elara. When you do, it is always restless."

"I'm fine," Kyler shot back.

"Look at you." Alarik ran his gaze over the boy. "You're exhausted. I did not wake you sooner because you need to rest."

"No," Kyler replied and shook his head in irritation. "We need to keep moving."

"Do not take me for a fool, boy," Alarik growled. "Your concentration is slipping. You're slower and your gaze is distant. You need rest."

"There will be time enough for that once the war is won," Kyler muttered.

"You're adrift and you have been for some time. Whatever it is that has made you so, I suggest that you get it under control."

"The burden is *mine* to carry," Kyler said as he pulled on his cloak.

"Do not let it kill you," Alarik replied as he handed the Medean his sword.

"I don't die easily." Kyler buckled on the weapon.

The knights strapped on their helmets, gathered up their shields and mounted their horses.

"We're half a day's ride from Bandujar," Alarik said. "We will meet outriders there and be with our brothers by nightfall."

They were met just south of Bandujar by riders bearing the white lion of Aloys. The knights were directed across the plains where a great battle had been fought. The bodies had long since been burnt, but the signs remained. Small glints of silver could be seen. Broken links of mail, shattered arrows and fragments of cloth were scattered amongst the earth and grass. The ground was still churned, and the stench of death remained. This was where the king and his army had crushed the Salvaari in battle.

"The Pale Horseman had his say here," Alarik murmured as they rode through the field.

"And so he will again in the battles to come," Kyler replied as he stared around at the tarnished fields. "I can only pray that before he speaks his last I will have a chance to prove myself worthy in his eyes."

"We are mere moments away from the greatest prize of all," Alarik replied.

"And what is that?"

"Areut talc cuun'ect."

Blood or immortality. That was their way. The words had been branded into Kyler's heart and mind long ago.

"The Fiodine says that the precipice between life and death is when one is most alive," Kyler said as he thought to the holy text of his faith. "That in that place, one is closest to the gods."

"In the hellish forests of Irene, when I stood side by side with brothers as our enemy closed in around us, when we were outnumbered and outflanked, I could hear them singing. I could *hear* the gods. I knew in that moment that they would not abandon us. I knew that if by my life or death we could herald victory, then I would. The gods are with us, Kyler. Always. All you have to do is close your eyes and place yourself in their hands."

"I always knew what the price of standing as a defender of our faith could be. It is a price I am willing to pay. It is time to honour the vows that I swore as an initiate," Kyler said. "I shall give all glory to the gods, and whenever they deem it, as a loyal servant, I will surrender my life for this oath."

"Oaths made, oaths kept," Alarik told him. "The gods do not forget those who honour them."

They rode through the battlefield and into the deep dark of the forest. From the edge of the woods, hundreds of Medeans were at work cutting down trees. A rough track had been established that led into Salvaar. Trees fifty feet either side of the path were cut down to their roots, granting all travellers a clear line of sight in every direction. The logs were transported east upon carts and wagons and there they were used to create a pair of large walled camps either side of the Arwan. Soldiers bearing the griffin of Aureia manned the battlements, while within the defences huge worksites had been created. Men were cutting up the fallen trees to add to the camps' walls and the watch towers that stretched down the track.

The lessons hard learned by the Annorans many years before had become tools for the newly crowned king. Thanks to the many writings left behind by those who had fought in the bloody war, along with the teachings of Aurea, Dayne had moulded them to win this fight. Once a foothold was forged in the forest, it would be all but impossible to lose.

Deep ditches had been carved into the earth surrounding the wooden fortresses to break any Salvaari charge. Because of the cleared trees, the bowmen atop the walls would be able to shower the pagans with steel without fear of reprisal. The Aureian-designed marching camps were incredibly difficult to attack and overcome, yet the ones that straddled the river were different. These ones were not single-walled marching camps; these had a second higher wall behind the first. These had been built to stay. They were all but impregnable. Forges had been set up within the camps. Bowyers, siege engineers and other craftsmen had come. Soldiers drilled in practice yards. Mounted riders patrolled the forest in groups.

Yet more impressive than the forts was another structure, one that Kyler and Alarik only saw when they were well within the first camp. A great bridge had been built across the Arwan. It was wide and strong enough to allow an army to cross without getting so much as a foot wet. This is what war looked like and Aureian's were masters of it.

Kyler and his mentor crossed the bridge and rode through the second fort before continuing down the man-forged path. The smoke from fires reached them long before the camps came into sight. After a word with one of the scouting parties, they were directed to one of the marching forts. Instead of the griffin, the eagle or the symbol of any Medean house, this one bore the sun and moon of their order.

The gates opened and the knights made their way inside. A sea of tents filled the fort, and horses were tethered along log fences. A huge wooden tower arose in the heart of the camp that soared over the tallest trees. Four knights stood on its raised platform, a small pyre between them. Kyler and Alarik greeted knights and maija, many by name, as they rode through the camp. They dismounted before the shimmering white command tent and tethered their horses. The knights unstrapped their helmets and flicked back their mail coifs.

"Alarik, you old boar." Corvo's voice came from behind.

They turned to see the acting master – he was not alone. Hugh Karter stood at his side, clad in the armour of a knight.

"Light of the gods be with you, brother," Alarik replied with a grin as he took his friend's outstretched arm and pulled him into an embrace.

"It's been too long, brother," Hugh told Kyler as they shared the same greeting.

"Hugh Karter," Kyler said as he clapped his friend on the back before running his eyes over the Annoran's new armour. "You're a knight now?"

"Aye … You look terrible."

Both men laughed, yet Kyler knew that it was only half a joke. Hugh could see his sunken eyes and pale face.

"Did you find him?" Corvo asked.

"Yes, master," Alarik replied. "Wa'rith *is* Markus Harvarder. He is living in Elara under the guise of Cleander. He is the traitor who betrayed our order. Not only that, but we found the one they call Olivera as well."

"Olivera?"

"He worked for Harvarder, master," Kyler told him. "Olivera was the man who led the raids in the valley and attacked Hugh and I in Odrysia."

"Then the man who sought the artefacts and the bandits were connected," Corvo muttered. "There is something out of place, though I am not sure what. When word of Elara's fall reached us, I feared that you had been lost. I assume that Harvarder was in some way responsible for its fall."

"The gangs stirred up the people, and then when an alliance with the Sacasians presented itself, they jumped at the chance to take the city," Alarik told him. "Upon our return, we met with Magister Calaval of Tallis. I can only imagine that his army has laid siege to Elara and will soon retake her."

"Then you haven't heard?" Hugh spoke up.

"Heard what?" Kyler asked.

"Those dark men have already abandoned the city," Corvo said. "Soon after you left, Commander Jarvais and his fleet blockaded the city, though not before a ship slipped through their midst. This ship somehow got word to the Valkir and from there returned with an armada of unprecedented strength. Together, the Valkir and Sacasian raiders broke the blockade and fled towards the Lupentine. The gangs and their allies are gone."

"A Valkir fleet?" Alarik said with raised eyebrows. "They have not come together in such numbers in their entire history even *once*. Why would they come together and sail to the aid of those who would never have done the same?"

"Things have changed," Corvo replied. "An emissary by the name of Valan Azure Aldrich was sent to the court of Earl Arndyr Scaeva. He did not return. I have heard that Arndyr was responsible for the death of one of their jarls. Valkir revenge is swift, and no doubt Arndyr was killed for the murder. Vay'kis and its earls have always been friends and allies to the empire. If Valan arrived in Lumis to find his ally killed, he would have attempted to make peace with the invaders. We both know how the other isles view the empire and if an imperial ally murdered a jarl, then those resentments would have been inflamed. There is no doubt in my mind that Valan was killed."

"In murdering an ambassador, they show their true colours.

Breaking the laws of parlay … They have *no* honour," Alarik growled.

"A survivor from the battle claims that the Valkir have united behind a king. The brother of the murdered jarl," Corvo told them. "It would appear that whoever this man is, he has found a cause to bring his people together. What this cause is, only the gods know. But now a fleet of Valkir and pirates will harbour in the Lupentine."

"That is some story," Alarik replied. "But what is done is done. Tell me about what happened here."

"There is not much to tell," Corvo said honestly. "We defeated the heathen in battle and slew thousands of them. We pursued them into the forest and from there they were saved by some kind of godless mist. As you can see, we have established a foothold. There are seven camps each with a beacon." The acting master gestured towards the huge tower that sat within the heart of the marching fort.

"What purpose do they serve, master?" Kyler asked.

"From atop the tower you can see for miles and miles in every direction. The forest may shield any Salvaari approach, yet as you can see, the towers rise above the trees. If one is lit, then the other camps can see the blaze."

"And from there the sentinels can see the fire and direct the armies towards the sole flame," Kyler said as he realised.

"Precisely," Corvo replied. "Within hours, our entire strength can come together. One of King Dayne's ingenious ideas."

"I hear that the cardinal himself crowned him," Alarik said. "Is it true what they say about him?"

The acting master nodded. "He is the gods' king."

✦ ✦ ✦

Kassandra Raynor flitted through the maija's library, as she had done for days. With much of the Order in the north, there were few who had remained and as such the maze of shelves and tables was all but empty. Only a few maija and townspeople could be found roaming the massive building. She had read every book, text or scroll about the Inquisition that she could get her hands on, but so far, her search yielded no fruits. She found nothing about elves, ruskalan, other races, ancient religions or magic. She found little that suggested that the old powers even existed, and those few that did condemned them. Kassie's fingers brushed the spin of a book. *The Last Days of the Inquisition* by the maija Calandra. She pulled it from the shelf and flicked through the old pages with care.

"You won't find what you're looking for in there, Princess," a woman's voice called.

Kassie glanced up from the book to see Lysandra approaching. "Arc'maija." She gave the woman a smile.

"I hear that you have been studying the old ways," Lysandra said. "Or at least have been trying to."

"I have read every book, text and scroll on the Inquisition and the time before Duran," Kassie replied with a sigh. "And yet I have found nothing that suggests that the elves and other races even existed."

"Then you believe?"

"Of course," Kassie told her. "Behind every tale is a hint of truth. I find it hard to believe that the ruskalan and elves were only superstition and fantasy. I saw things in Salvaar … such things that have made me question what I have been told."

"I see," Lysandra replied. "Would you like to know a secret? I believe as well."

"Truly?"

"Truly," the arc'maija replied matter-of-factly. "There is much here hidden in this library that can teach you more about the old ways than texts written on the basis of myth that condemn what they do not properly understand. I can show you, but you would have to promise me that you will not tell a soul."

Kassie felt a tingle of excitement run down her spine. "I promise," she swore.

"Then come with me."

Kassandra followed Lysandra through the library. The arc'maija opened a door and led her inside a smaller room. The walls were lined with shelves and bookcases filled with scrolls, texts and books. Maps adorned what remained of the covered walls and a large desk sat within the room. Lysandra walked over to one of the cases and pulled forth a large leather-bound book. The arc'maija held it out to the princess.

"*Sapphire Snow*," Kassandra read as she took the book.

"By the maija Avyanna," Lysandra said. "Everything known about the elves is here in this text. Avyanna defied the Order by writing this and so now only a few know of its existence. There are more tomes in this room that can teach you about the time before, about Medea before the Inquisition. About the ruskalan and the old ways. You are free to read what you wish. I must warn you that *nothing* can leave this room. You see, the reason that the elves and ruskalan, that stories of the old days, have vanished into myth is because the great knight, Duran Cormac, ordered all such histories destroyed and burned from the pages of history. Only one book remains beyond the walls of this room … Those within were saved by the arc'maija Stefanos."

Kassandra recognised the weight within Lysandra's eyes. There was a flicker of fear in there as well. Did anyone know of her collection?

"Of course," Kassandra told her.

"Then you can stay as long as you wish and come whenever you choose. I implore you to always come alone. This is my private study," Lysandra said. "And I should like it to remain as such."

"Thank you for your trust," Kassie replied.

"It is not every day that someone shows interest in this subject that most interests me," Lysandra said with a smile. "If you have any questions, you can always ask."

✦ ✦ ✦

TWENTY-THREE

Vanhair, Steppe of Miera

Water rippled as the heavy iron anchor sank deep into the depths of the Lupentine. The bladed hooks raked into the seabed until they found a home. The Emeralis held fast a quarter of a mile from the coast. The warning song of a town bell echoed across the water from the Mieran village. A small boat was lowered into the sea and a dozen of the crew clambered down into it. Torben spared his companions a glance as he took up one of the oars. Among them were Luana Marquez, Calvillo, Cleander, Tariq, Marshall and Elise Delfeyre. The rest he had been assured were all skilled warriors. Forty remained aboard the Emeralis, but in the harbour it would stay. If the company could not convince the headsman to allow them passage north, then they may well be running for their lives.

As he rowed, Torben could not help but feel his gaze be drawn to Cleander, who sat further down the boat. Of all the company, it was only Cleander he knew nothing about. He had some sort of bond with the woman Mellisanthi and worked with the gangs, yet he had kept to himself for much of the voyage. Torben could only hope that Bhaltair's boast that Cleander was one of the finest swordsmen alive was true.

Their destination sat upon the coast. The fishing village of Vanhair. He had been here before … He had *raided* here before with Jarl Lief Farrin.

"They come," Luana called from the prow. "When we reach the shore, no one is to so much as think about touching a weapon or I'll kill you myself. These men are no more savage than you or I. If we treat them as such, they will do the same."

Torben could not see what lay before them, but there was no doubt in his mind at what awaited. Luana spoke of warriors. How many, he did not know, yet they would be enough to wipe out the companions without shedding so much as a drop of sweat in return.

As the boat closed in on the docks, the sounds of hooves and horses carried to Torben's ears. He could hear commands being called and whistles sounding as the Mierans organised their ranks. Torben could remember those shrieking whistles well. It was the eerie song of the horsemen as they manoeuvred without speaking.

"Oars," Luana ordered as they closed in on the beach.

The six poles rose out from the water and were stowed within the boat as it kissed the sand. Torben followed the captain's lead as she leapt from the boat. Water splashed over his boots and rose to his knees. The rest of the small crew disembarked and together they heaved the small boat up onto the sandy shore. Only then did Torben see the horsemen descending upon them. They were armoured from head to toe in mail and steel. Many of the horses wore armour over their faces. Leaf-bladed spears and sturdy shields were held tightly in the grasp of their riders. Some of the Mierans carried bows with readily nocked arrows. There were dozens of them, and they were ready for war.

"Steady," Torben growled as the Mierans barrelled towards them.

"Show your hands," Luana ordered as she held hers up and open.

One by one, the companions followed suit. They backed into a tight circle as the Mierans surrounded them. Sand sprayed up under the horses' hooves. The air grew hot. Spears were lowered towards them and bows raised. The riders showered them with hateful glares while their mounts pawed the ground.

"I am Torben of Agartha, and these are my companions," the bloodsworn called to the riders. "We come here in friendship."

"And what would a Valkir know of friendship?" one of the Mierans countered as his horse butted Torben's shoulder.

The bloodsworn gritted his teeth in irritation as the Mieran tried to push him back with his mount. "Enough to know that there is trust between friends," he replied.

"Trust is not given. It is earned."

"That is why I am here today."

"And what would a man such as yourself know of earning *our* trust? A man whose people have raided our shores for generations without cause. I wonder, have you spilled the blood of my kin?" the Mieran growled as he angled his spear towards the bloodsworn. "Speak if you must and pray that I do not find your words wanting."

Torben gestured to Luana. "We must speak to the headsman," he told the rider. "I bring word from Elara."

"You are in no position to make demands."

"Word about the Accords." Luana spoke up.

The Mierans grew silent and Torben could see their leader grimace. The air settled. In that moment he knew that they would not be killed. The Accords. Those two small words had saved them.

"Free their weapons," the Mieran commanded. "Bind their hands."

Riders leapt down from their horses and roughly *liberated* the weapons from the foreigners. Like his companions, Torben kept his hands up as the Mierans moved among them. They pulled his shield from his back and snatched his sword and axe from his belt. Torben's broad knife followed, and his hands were tightly bound with rope. Once every trace of steel had been taken, the Mierans still on foot shoved their prisoners towards the village. Some of the riders stayed with the boat and kept wary eyes on the Emeralis. The others formed a ring around their newly acquired captives as they led them through the town. Torben caught glimpses of the villagers through the guard of their captors. Women in dresses shared the same expressions as the men with golden rings in their ears. That of loathing. These people had seen more bloodshed than the rest of the kingdoms and provinces combined. The Valkir had played their part in the ever-growing distrust that the Mierans had for foreigners.

A simple wooden lodge rose before them. It had two floors and a large, slanted roof of tiles. Like the Mieran people themselves, the lodge bore no embellishment or unneeded decoration; to them it was just a house. The Mieran who had spoken to Torben dismounted and led the captives inside the headman's lodge. Like the rest of the building, the hall was simple. A fire crackled hungrily in its centre and its walls bore no more decoration than a few hung shields and weapons.

Three men surrounded the fire. They were all armed and armoured as warriors. They had scars upon their weathered faces and their untamed hair hung behind their backs. Two would have been in their forties and bore five golden rings in their ears. The third man was older. His hair was as grey as his beard. His face was grizzled, and his eyes were those of a man half his years. If that had been all Torben had seen, it would have been enough to know that this man was not to be trifled with. Yet it wasn't all. It wasn't the longsword at the man's side that drew his eye, nor was it the brigandine and chainmail. The man wore six golden rings in his ear, but they were not alone. A seventh silver band joined them. Torben knew enough about the Mierans to know that the silver ring was only granted to the headman.

Torben and his companions were shoved into a line before the Mieran leader. The headman strode towards the captives and swept his gaze across their faces. His hand did not leave his sword.

"My name is Jaigir, son of Adonis," he growled. "What business do a Valkir and a warship have in my harbour?"

"We have come with news," Torben replied. "News that you must hear."

The headsman stepped before him and glared deep into his eyes. "When last I looked, it was the Valkir who sent messages in the form of blood and ash," the headsman said. "It was the Valkir who appeared from the depths of the sea to burn our villages and slaughter our people. Now you come seeking friendship?"

"This isn't about friendship," Luana cut in. "It's about survival."

The headsman turned towards the captain and made his way towards her. "What is your name?"

"Luana Marquez." She met his hard stare with her own. "Captain of the Emeralis."

The headsman wasn't the only Mieran who chuckled at that. "A woman?" he said with a smirk.

"Aye," Luana told him and stepped closer. "I stood shoulder to shoulder with Cillian Teague as we fought against the League. It was I who sailed into Elara. It was I who convinced the people to join us. I was there when Elara fell. I was there when this man *killed* the magister." She gestured to Cleander as she spoke. "I was there when a fleet of Valkir and pirates broke the League's blockade."

"That is some tale, yet it does not explain why you are here," the headsman said.

"What this is about is the enemy that is out there," Luana said as she gestured towards the doors of the lodge.

"We know of the great army, and if you think that we fear it, then you are gravely mistaken."

"And what do you know of the League?" Cleander asked him. "What do you know of their sins?"

"We have been at peace for many years."

"Yes. For now," Cleander countered. "Like you, I thought the battle between Miera and the League was over. That is until a few months ago when the Elaran council voted to rescind the Accords."

Growls filled the hall as surprise broke through the Mieran ranks.

"Then they have betrayed us all," snarled the Mieran who had captured them.

"Peace, Danavir." Jaigir held up a hand to silence the warrior. "Why would they break the peace that has prevented bloodshed for decades?"

"Because we are all the same to them," Luana said. "Valkir, Sacasian, Salvaari, Mieran. We're all just heathen. Godless. This army in the north has emboldened the League. A deal was struck with the empire. Once the Salvaari are defeated, the invaders will turn south to your lands. While your people turn their eyes to this new threat, the League shall cross the Alps and burn their way north."

"If this is true and they come, then we will defeat them," Jaigir replied.

"Say that you can hold them at bay for a time," Torben began. "Say that somehow you defeat one of the armies. There is a third. When King Dayne attacks, when the League crosses the Alps, another will land at the coast. A fleet of unprecedented strength. A hidden fleet. One that will only appear when it makes its move."

"How did you come by this?"

"Because not all that long ago my people were asked to join it," Torben replied.

"By you being here with them I take it that you refused?" Jaigir stated.

"The empire killed my king's sister without cause," Torben said. "That cannot be forgotten. That cannot be forgiven."

"Yet now you come to us, to men you have been killing for generations."

"It is King Erik's deepest wish to change that," Torben replied. "He sent us before you knowing the risk that you would not hear us. Now that you have, I would ask that you allow us to travel north to your king."

"Your people killed my father and my brothers," Jaigir growled. "You speak of not forgetting – we Mierans have long memories. The last time ambassadors came to our lands seeking to meet with the king, Israfil burned. Its ruins serve as a constant reminder of the dishonour that plagues the land outside our borders."

"Do not forget Israfil," Torben replied. "Do not forget your family that my people took from you. I'll *never* forget the family that yours took from me. But this goes beyond that. Grant us passage north. Grant us an audience with your king and I swear to you that my people will *never* raid your coast again. Those days are done."

Jaigir locked eyes with Torben. Neither man backed down.

"Tell the people that remain on your ship to come ashore," Jaigir said without looking away from the bloodsworn. "Until you return, they will be my *guests*. Know that if you break my trust, their blood will be on your hands. Danavir Calin, gather your men and find these people horses. Escort them to Carlian. Take my seal and let them stand before King Zoran."

"It will be done," Danavir replied.

"And you," Jaigir said to Torben. "You have done us a great service, but do not think that my king will be swayed by whatever message that you have for him. We know what promises are worth. We know how easily they are broken."

Their weapons were returned shortly after Danavir led them from the lodge. Horses were found and a company of thirty Mieran riders began to assemble. Luana called her crew to land. Jaigir had called them guests, but in truth they all knew that they were no more than hostages.

Torben slung his shield across his back and pulled himself up into the saddle. The Mierans took up position around them. Danavir gave the order, and they rode north towards Carlian. They rode north towards King Zoran. Torben had only days to think of a story to convince the king to join their cause.

✦ ✦ ✦

The plains that ran alongside the coast of Medea slowly began to morph into woodland as the Tanith and Despoina sailed east. Bellec waited until they had passed the Arwan before he finally gave the order. It was near dark when they chose a place to land. Captain Tybura reluctantly signalled the Tanith, and the two ships made for the thin strip of beach that lay between them and the forest.

Kitara breathed a sigh of relief when they made landfall. The hulls of the ships ran too deep, so the horses had been forced to swim ashore under the guidance of the Tanith's crew. Kitara and her companions took longboats to the beach. For days, they had been forced to watch the crew of the ship in case they betrayed them. Kitara felt that tension all but evaporate when she leapt over the side of the boat. Salty water splashed over her boots and armour as she made her way up onto the sand. She breathed in a long breath, relishing the clean Salvaari air. True to his word, Bellec handed over what remained of the agreed sum to Captain Tybura. Kitara pulled herself up onto her horse and gazed towards the green trees.

"Home," Aeryn murmured in Salvaari from her side.

The companions crossed the tree line and rode into the forest and the safety of the woods. They made camp once the last of the sun had slipped beyond the horizon. Aeryn gathered up thick bark and created a makeshift bowl before she vanished into the forest.

"Do you want to go out?" Sakkar said to Sabra as he stroked her feathers. He raised his arm and sent her skyward. "Go on."

The hawk soared into the sky and then was gone. Aeryn soon returned and filled the bowl with ingredients before setting to work pounding it with a thick stick.

"So, what's the plan?" Galadayne asked when they had gathered.

"We follow the river until we find someone, be they friend or enemy," Bellec replied. "We have to know what has happened here and find the Salvaari."

"Sabra will find them," Sakkar said.

Aeryn unbound her hair and slicked it back with white grease to keep it from her eyes. Kitara held still as the moonseer ran the sticky glue through her blonde locks. Then came the black paint and blue woad that Aeryn had mixed together. Aeryn gently smeared the ebony pigment around Kitara's eyes.

"Why the black?" Aeryn said in Salvaari.

"To fend off the dark ones," Kitara replied in the same.

They changed roles and Kitara lightly brushed the paint around Aeryn's eyes.

"And the woad?"

"For the spirits."

Aeryn covered half of Kitara's face with the blue paint and in return Kitara drew lines across Aeryn's. With each touch and each stroke of blue, Kitara felt the lifeblood of the forest call to her. She felt the strength of the Salvaari fill her. Aeryn took the woad bowl to their companions and handed it to Sakkar.

"You will need this," she said simply.

The Larissan dipped a finger into the paint and then raised it towards his face.

"No," Aeryn said. "Only Salvaari may wear the woad upon their skin. It is sacred. Put it on your clothes, on your armour, on your horses even. I would not have my people mistake friend from foe."

One by one, Sakkar and the others did as they were bid. As they painted what they could get their hands on, Aeryn walked to the edge of the campsite. Her silver eyes were drawn deep into the forest. Kitara made her way through the trees and stood beside her. She followed the moonseer's gaze.

"Do you feel it?" Aeryn asked.

"I feel it in the earth. I feel it in the air and trees," Kitara replied solemnly. "The lifeblood of the forest. The call of home."

"There is something at work here," Aeryn said. "The trees are as old as time itself. They speak to each other. They speak to us. Listen close enough and you can hear them."

Kitara closed her eyes and relaxed her breathing. She listened. Though no sound greeted her, she felt something cold run through her blood.

"I feel something. Some kind of coldness."

"The forest is sad," Aeryn replied. "A great evil has happened. A bloodmoon. Many were lost."

"That does not mean that it is over," Kitara told her.

"Bellec is right," Aeryn said. "We need to know what lies ahead. I will ride out tonight and return when I have found our people."

When the company rose in the morning, Aeryn was waiting for them.

"There is a village just south of here," she told them.

They gathered their things, mounted up and then set out behind Aeryn. The company rode for a few miles beneath the trees of Salvaar before they came to the small river village. The people who inhabited it, from child to elder, all wore the black of the Káli. They turned from whatever task they were doing and gazed at the mercenaries. They all wore suspicious expressions and watched the riders warily. Had it not been for the blue woad, the Káli may well have attacked them. With every face that she saw, Kitara's curiosity grew.

"Children and old folk. Where is everyone else?" she asked Aeryn.

"I'm not sure."

Aeryn led them towards the large chieftain's hall that sat at the centre of the village. An old woman emerged from behind the wooden doors and walked out towards the mercenaries. Her clothes were as black as the paint that she wore, though her hair was as white as winter snow. Her face was wrinkled and weathered by age, and she stood proud and tall.

Aeryn dismounted and made her way to the woman. She offered a bow to the elder and then they spoke in Salvaari.

"What do you think?" Bellec asked Kitara.

"There is no fear in their eyes," she replied after a moment. "Whatever has happened, these are people who are far from defeated. There is something else … something unspoken. It is almost like they are anticipating something that has not yet come to pass."

Bellec nodded. "Aye, I thought as much," he said. "In times of war, the warriors are called upon to leave the villages but *always* the younger men would remain to protect the village. Yet they are not here."

"Mmm."

"You have kept the arm rings," Bellec stated as he indicated the silver bands that ran down Kitara's arm.

Though they had returned to Salvaar, Kitara had not yet buried the arm rings. They were all she had left of Sereia, Morlag and the others. Aeryn had promised to show her how to honour them upon their arrival in the forest, yet fate had decreed that they had not been granted the time.

"When I have the chance, I will honour their memory," Kitara told him. "Until then, they stay with me."

Aeryn offered the old woman a short bow again and returned to the company.

"She is mother to the chief and leads in his absence," Aeryn explained. "There was a great battle weeks ago upon the plains of Medea. My people were defeated and forced back across the river. But now the winds have changed. All men and women, child to elder, have been called to gather in the south."

"Why?" Bellec asked.

"She does not know," Aeryn replied. "None of them do. But if everyone has been called, then that can mean only one thing: Henghis is about to make his move. Something draws near."

"Henghis is there?" Bellec asked.

"Yes," Aeryn replied as she pulled herself up into her saddle. "We will ride to meet him."

They spent the days travelling from before dawn until after dusk. Aeryn spoke to every Salvaari that they met in the forest and every leader in every village that they passed. The story was always the same: the warriors had been called by Henghis. The time for revenge for the fields of Bandujar was upon them. By day they rode, while at night they spent the small hours resting and gathering their strength. Even on the nights that they rested in Salvaari villages, they took turns at watch. Who knew when the enemy could appear? When they slept in the forest, they lit no fires. Kitara curled up with Aeryn in the darkness. There she found peace. There she found home.

Kitara turned to face Aeryn. She reached out with her fingers and caressed Aeryn's cheek. The moonseer smiled. She took Kitara's hand.

"A war has come here," Kitara murmured. "To your people, your tribe, your family. Are you afraid?"

Aeryn kissed Kitara's hand. "Come with me," she whispered in reply before she rose to her feet and led Kitara into the forest.

They walked together until the camp was beyond sight and hearing. Only the sound of the forest was with them. The birds and the wind. Aeryn unslung her bow from her shoulder.

"Can you shoot?" she asked simply.

Kitara shook her head with a frown. "I have never had the chance to learn," she replied.

"Here," Aeryn said as she handed her bow to Kitara. An arrow followed in its wake. "Let me help you." Aeryn stepped in close to Kitara. She used her hands and hips to gently move Kitara into position. Her left hand wrapped around Kitara's as she raised the bow and her right followed suit with the arrow. Without words, she used her body to teach. They were so close that they could feel each other's every move. Kitara felt Aeryn's breath upon her cheek, felt the warmth of her body. Aeryn's right hand moved from the arrow to Kitara's waist.

"Go on," she whispered.

The bow sang and the arrow sliced through the air. There was a thud as the steel-bladed tip bit deeply into the trunk of a tree. Kitara smiled. She hadn't missed. Aeryn still held her. She kissed the side of Kitara's neck.

"You asked me if I am afraid," she said. "I am. But I learnt a long time ago that thinking about something you cannot control is a good way to drive yourself mad. There is no war here in this moment. There are only the trees, and the stars, and us."

✦ ✦ ✦

TWENTY-FOUR

Catuvantuli Lands, Forest of Salvaar

"Do you think he will come, lord?" Hadwin asked.

Lukas turned his eye to the mercenary. "Oh, he will," he replied. "My brother has no choice. If he does not, then his alliance with the Medeans shall splinter. And so he is forced to divide his army rather than watch it destroy itself. That is my strategy."

"How many men do you think he will bring?" Layan chimed in.

"Fifty men, ten thousand, it would make no difference. There is not going to be a battle today. My brother is not foolish enough to attack us; he does not know how many warriors we have." Lukas' lips curled into a savage grin. "And besides, his men fear the *evil spirits* that haunt the forest."

The mercenaries chuckled.

"Right you are, lord," Hadwin said with a smirk.

"You both served my father, did you not?" Lukas stated as curiosity at last got the better of him.

"We did," Layan told him.

"What was it that made you choose Bellec over the man you were sworn to?"

Layan pursed his lips. "When Balinor sent word of Prince Eldred's death, we feared that the peace we had fought for would be undone. That the murder came at Bellec's hands only made it all the worse," he said. "And yet Bellec had saved my life in battle many times. The guard was a brotherhood. We shared things that you could not imagine. When King Dorian accused our captain of the deed and banished him, many among us questioned it. We knew of the ever-growing rift between Aethela and Laeoflaed. Perhaps it had all been some scheme of Balinor. We tried to speak to the king … He was enraged. He turned us away. Dorian sent men to kill Bellec without question. When they failed, it was to the guard the king turned, to the men who knew Bellec as well as they knew themselves. When we found our captain, our brother, our friend, he was broken. The king's men had captured his wife and unborn child and sold them into a life of slavery and death. Bellec confirmed what we already knew in our hearts: that he had played no part in Eldred's death. And so we were forced to choose between our oath to our lord and king and our loyalty to our friend, a man who had saved our lives times beyond count. A man who had committed no crime save loving a woman. We had seen the darkness in King Dorian, and we *knew* that his lust for revenge would not end until Bellec's head was brought before him. In that moment, we broke our oath."

"When the king heard about what happened, he banished us from our lands and families. He would not listen to reason," Layan told Lukas. "We may be oath breakers, but our loyalty to our brothers is absolute."

"You are men with no lands, no families, no home," Lukas muttered. "Tell me: When this fight is done, what will you do?"

Layan glanced at his companion. "Perhaps I'll stay," he replied. "Marry a beautiful Salvaari woman."

"And what, be chief of your own village?" Hadwin said with a grin.

"Has a nice sound to it, aye. You will be my royal arse kisser, won't you, Hadwin?"

The three men laughed.

"What about you, lord?" Layan asked. "What do you intend when all is said and done?"

Lukas took a breath as he thought.

"I was once a prince. When I killed the boy Emilian, I lost my home, my lands and my title. I could no longer call myself Lukas of Annora. That life is lost. I no longer feel shackled. Here I am, free to choose my own path. I have a woman." Lukas glanced through the small camp towards Maevin. "I have people here. Brothers. My fate is tied to Salvaar. Of that I am certain."

With that, he clapped Hadwin on the shoulder and heaved himself to his feet. Lukas gathered up his crutch and hobbled through the camp. The pain in both his knee and head were almost gone, but he still relished in the drink that Maevin concocted. He drank it three times a day and sometimes more than that. Its taste and the feeling that came with it were intoxicating. He made his way to the tree line and gazed out across the fields. Lake Thirlryda spread across the land while the river flowed deep into the forest.

"You see the past," Maevin said as she appeared at his side.

"Memories of another life," Lukas replied. "I remember the waters lapping at knees as we made the crossing. I remember the storm. I remember the red warriors charging from every side. I remember Oryn."

"The spirits brought us together that day," Maevin replied. "Do you know what they whispered to me that night?"

"What did they say?"

"That we were bound, you and I," Maevin told him. "That we would always be together."

"Our fates are entwined," Lukas agreed. "I hear them now. In the blowing of the trees and the echo of the cold earth, in the whispering winds and howling storms. When the sun rises, I see Yorath and feel his fire burn. In the silver moonlight, I see Sylvaine. I hear her voice."

"What does she say?"

"This path we now tread is the only path that matters," he said.

"Shadows of the past fill my dreams. The echo of a time before. I can see it."

"In time, the past always repeats itself," Maevin replied. "Things have changed. I can feel it in my blood, and I know you can too. Fates are never truly set, and as this one unfolds, it will change the fortune of all. One hundred years ago, my people fought against the west, and they failed. We will not. Our time has come again."

A flicker of movement appeared across the river. A dark shadow that grew closer and closer every passing moment.

"Rider," Lukas murmured.

The horseman galloped across the plains and splashed into the river. Water lapped at his legs as his horse surged forward through the current. At last, the rider charged up onto the bank and urged his mount into a gallop towards the trees. Lukas and the Káli had gathered up their weapons by the time he arrived. Like them, he wore black paint across his body.

"They come?" Lukas called as he approached the man.

The Káli horseman slid from his saddle. "Yes, lord." He gestured across the river. "Half a mile downstream."

"And their army? How big is their army?"

"Thousands."

The Annoran army set up across the river. Banners bearing the scarlet eagle flew high as rank upon rank of men and horses faced Salvaar. Lukas had given order for his own people to stay behind the tree line. When the Annorans saw nothing but two roughly hewn chairs, One-Eye and six of his warriors in the open ground, they would be confused.

Lukas sat in his wooden throne. At his back were Maevin, Rodion, Aelida, the warrior Adair and the mercenaries Hadwin and Layan. Like Lukas the four Káli wore their black war paint across their skin. The sellswords wore black cloaks and sported the paint upon their armour. All were armed. At Lukas' side was his hammer and Salvaari daggers adorned his belt. His crutch leaned against the side of his chair. One-Eye flicked his hand towards the Annorans and sent Rodion across the river with his terms. It did not take long before seven steel-clad Annorans broke off from the army. They rode massive chargers and ruby cloaks fluttered at their backs. Rodion returned to his position at Lukas' back before the Annorans arrived.

The seven armoured men dismounted and approached the chairs. Dayne came first. The king wore his eagle sword at his hip. Dayne pulled his crested helmet from his head and placed it on the ground as he sat on the empty chair. The six followed in the wake of their commander and unstrapped their helmets. They held them tightly under their arms.

Lukas looked from face to face. He recognised Sir Garrik and the other royal guardsmen. Neither Tristayn nor the high lords were here, and so Lukas knew that they had remained with the rest of the Annoran army in Medea. Lukas looked to his brother. Like him, Dayne had taken in those at his brother's back.

"Where is my wife?" Dayne called.

"She is safe," Lukas replied with a smirk.

Dayne's eyes were cool. "Where is my wife?" he repeated louder.

"Safe," Lukas told him. "Are you scared?"

"Should I be?" Dayne replied. "We are brothers, are we not?"

"Even now?"

"You are a Raynor," Dayne told him. "You and I will always be family."

"No." Lukas held up a hand. "I ceased to be a Raynor when I lay in a pool of my own blood."

"It is true that I left you in Oryn. It is true that I have fought to maintain relations with Aloys even after what Emilian did. It is true that I had you banished. But if you can forgive me, Lukas, let us make an accord."

"An accord?"

"Let us put aside our differences for the sake of our family."

"Why would I want to do that?" Lukas replied.

"A war between us can only bring tragedy and weaken our family," Dayne told him calmly. "Is that truly what you want?"

Lukas leaned forward in his chair and met his brother's cold, blue eyes. "My dear brother, have you not considered that I would *never* join with those men who seek to exterminate the Salvaari because they are *pagan*?" he replied incredulously. "Villages were burned, homes destroyed, thousands killed. Your religion did that."

"Is that why you destroyed the temple, slaughtered the people of Bandujar and hung bodies from trees?" Dayne countered. "Lukas, I did not come here to dig up the past. I came for you. I came for the sake of our father. I came for the sake of our mother. I came for Kassandra. It would be a terrible thing to destroy our family."

"Our family was broken a long time ago."

Dayne turned his eyes from Lukas to Maevin. "Is that what *she* tells you?" he asked. "That our family is broken?"

"I may have only one eye," Lukas replied, "but I can still see."

"She has been lying to you."

Lukas snorted. "Actually, brother, it is she who has never lied," he said. "She has never treated me like a well-heeled dog as Father did. She never tried to command my destiny. Nor did she trade her own blood to forge an alliance with a murderer. If that is what the crown of Annora does, then I am glad to have no part in it."

"And so you have adopted their ways, their traditions, their spirits?"

"I have."

A crack appeared in Dayne's composure; a small spark of anger flickered across his face.

"You spit upon every value we hold dear," the king growled.

"I do not think so."

Dayne ground his teeth and composed himself. "You will have heard, of course, that our father is dead. Killed by vipers."

"Vipers?"

"It was Santiago Caspin."

"Caspin did this?"

Dayne nodded. "The ones we love the most are the ones most likely to betray us."

"Why would he do that?" Lukas asked.

"Sofia carries my child," the king explained.

"Then Santiago has his eye on the throne. Why not kill him?"

"I think about it," Dayne admitted. "But I cannot. For the first time in our history, all of our faith is united. I would not tear apart everything we have built."

"If you have a traitor in your court, then he must be dealt with."

"In time," Dayne replied as he leaned towards his brother. "I find myself unable to trust even my own people. The eagle is entangled with the viper at a time when they need to be together. Come home, brother. Come home to your family. Help me save it."

"My family is here now," Lukas told him.

"Then this is a waste of time."

"No," Lukas said with a smirk. "You can surrender to me now. You keep talking about saving family, about saving your people. Leave Salvaar. Go away. Return home. Do not gamble their lives."

"I will never surrender to you," Dayne growled.

"Consider the best option," Lukas told him with a shrug. "Let your people live in peace."

"Return my wife," Dayne said loudly as if giving an order.

Lukas bared his teeth and grinned.

"You gave me your word," the king continued.

Lukas bit back a chuckle before he held up a hand. "Hadwin, bring the queen."

"Yes, lord," the mercenary replied.

Dayne's eyes widened as they went to the warrior. "Wait," he called. "You're Annoran?"

"When it suits me," Hadwin replied.

The mercenary mounted his horse and made for the trees. Dayne rose from his chair as he watched the rider vanish into the woods. They waited. Nothing happened. Nothing emerged from the forest. Lukas rose to his feet and rested both hands upon his crutch.

"Brother, if you have harmed her–"

"What will you do?" Maevin gave him a dangerous look.

"If your *witch* has harmed her …" The king trailed off as a pair of horses broke the tree line.

The first was Hadwin, the other Sofia. Annoran and Salvaari grew silent as the riders approached. They reached the gathering and dismounted. Sofia strode through the Káli contingent and made straight for her husband.

"Are you hurt?" Dayne asked as he ran his eyes over Sofia.

"No," she told him. "They treated me with respect."

"A pity that respect was not shown at Oryn," Aelida snarled from behind Lukas. "An eye for an eye. We should kill her now."

She spat to the side in contempt. Lukas snorted as if it were a joke. The Annorans did not take it as such. Garrik was the first to draw his blade. Steel rang as Annoran and Salvaari alike pulled their weapons free.

"If you threaten my queen again–" Garrik snarled.

"Threaten?" Aelida growled contemptuously as she stepped forward, her hands clutched at her axe.

Lukas held out an arm and stopped the Káli in her tracks. "No," he commanded.

Dayne looked from Aelida to Maevin and then to Lukas. "I don't recognise you anymore," he muttered.

Lukas shrugged. "There won't be a battle today, brother," he said. "Not here. Your friends in the north are dead already."

✦ ✦ ✦

When the scouts returned, Tristayn suspected a trap. They

reported that the Salvaari village that they found had been completely abandoned. After speaking with lords Galan and Balderik along with the dukes Santiago Caspin and Anejo Reyna, he proceeded with caution. Dayne had entrusted the greater sum of the Annoran army to him and he would not fail the king. The scouts swept the surrounds and then at last the army began to filter through the pagan village. Tristayn's eyes flicked left and right as he rode through the streets, searching for any kind of trap or ambush.

"Where is everybody?" Anejo Reyna muttered from his side.

"Check every house!" Tristayn bellowed to his men.

Soldiers rushed from hovel to hovel, searching as they went. No stone was left unturned, not one inch of the village left unchecked. Tristayn watched from atop his horse as they worked. High Lord Galan rode towards the general.

"My men have swept the outskirts," he said. "There is nothing. No food, no livestock, no sign of life."

"What is going on?" Anejo murmured.

"I don't know, Duke Anejo," Tristayn replied. "But I think it's time we find out."

With that, the general dismounted and made for the closest house. His hand never left the hilt of his sword as he entered the hovel. Like the rest of the Salvaari dwellings, it was a simple home, little more than four wooden walls and a thatched roof. He wondered how they lived this way as he ran his eyes around the house. He frowned as he saw the crude table in the centre of the dwelling. Upon it was a doll made of carved wood. Tristayn made his way over and picked up the children's toy.

"The village is empty," Lord Balderik said as he entered the house.

"The people have left and have taken all their food, yet they intend to return." Tristayn showed the lord the doll.

"Lords." Duke Santiago greeted them. "My finest scouts found another village two miles north of here. It's empty. No one but ghosts haunt it."

"Very strange," Tristayn said softly as he placed the doll back on the table. "We will have to be on our guard. Have the men begin work on the camp. I want to be behind walls by nightfall."

✦ ✦ ✦

Harkan of the ruskalan felt the breeze grow cool long before he heard the song of ravens. The crows flew through the trees overhead, filling the wind with the sound of their wings and their piercing cries. Harkan had a moment to glance at his kinsmen. The other five. The pure blooded. The *last* ruskalan.

She appeared before them, hair like flames, eyes of violet fire.

"Can you hear them?" Sylvaine said. "The sound of a million forgotten souls? Their screams in the wind, the cries of the victims, the dearly departed. The enemy draws near."

Harkan looked to the Great Queen and bowed low.

"Our voices shall echo while we are hidden in the shadows," he replied. "Justice shall follow, and they will pay for the bloodshed."

Sylvaine looked to each ruskalan in turn. "The pierced night is upon us," she cried. "The eyes of Tanris have returned. The fates have been written. All that remains is balance that must be returned. You are the blood of Tanris, and it is you who must return it."

"Things are in motion, Great Queen," Harkan told her. "My kin grows strong with the enemy's walls. Alliances are being forged. Soon she will have enough strength to free the she-elf. Balance will be restored."

"This is a black game that you play with the fates," Sylvaine growled as she circled him. "Who is it that you serve?"

"Tanris is my master. It was he who made me his hand. He showed me that there is a flame still burning in this world. It flickers in the wind, yet it survives. It is my task to find it."

"Are you sure that you're ready, blood of the Firstborn?" Sylvaine asked as she circled Harkan. "Ready for what you will find?"

"We will see."

"The Veil is restless. The dead are singing your name." The Great Queen reached out a hand and ran her fingers across the dark runes on the ruskalan's skin as she spoke. "Your story is marked upon your skin."

"What does it say?"

"You will see," Sylvaine replied.

The First Woman stepped back from Harkan and stood in the centre of the six ruskalan. She looked high above. Her eyes closed but her gaze pierced the Veil. She could see Tanris in his pale robes.

"The time has come, my son," Sylvaine spoke. "Make your play."

✦ ✦ ✦

TWENTY-FIVE

Fortress of Kilgareth, Valley of Odrysia

Princess Kassandra made her way through the streets of the huge city. Be it here, in Palen-Tor or in some army camp – it was always the same for her. Kassie could not sit still and wait for news that would eventually find her regardless. She enjoyed visiting the people and talking to them. If in some way she could help them, then she would. Today was market day and Kassie saw no reason why she could not visit. Her friend, confidante and maid, Marian Martyn, was with her. Behind them, watching the crowds like a hawk, was Landon Montbard. Ever since the carriage attack, he had been her shadow. If somehow the Salvaari had crossed the mountains, perhaps they had found a way to secrete themselves within the walls of Kilgareth. At least so was Sir Landon's suspicion. Kassie could only smile as she looked around at all the people in the bustling streets. She greeted many and they in turn greeted her back.

"Look at them all, my lady," Marian said happily.

These days, more than just the knights, maija and their families called the fortress city home.

"With the arrival of the followers camp, the streets are filled with life again," Kassie replied as she took in the colours of a dozen lands. "Annorans, Medeans, people from every nation. It lifts the heart to see."

"They're happy. Market day reminds them of a time before," Marian said. "For a few moments, they can forget the war."

"Ah, the sounds, the smells." Kassandra took a long breath in as they walked. "They remind me of home."

Food, silks, precious stones and oddments from every corner of the empire filled exotic stands. The princess gave a storeowner a grin and exchanged a coin for an apple.

"Thank you, my princess." The man's eyes widened as he saw the gold. "But I cannot accept this much."

"I insist and I'll hear no argument," Kassie told him with a smile.

"Thank you," was all he managed before the three continued on their way.

Further into the market a minstrel had set up with a lute and his song echoed through the streets. A small crowd gathered to listen. Kassandra and her companions joined them as the Annoran musician played and sang. His voice was light as air, and he moved through the notes of the song like a boat moving down a slow-flowing river on a warm summer evening. He held the audience captive. When at the last of his words faded and the final stroke of the lute rang, the crowd roared and clapped. Kassie added to the applause and for a moment found herself laughing. As the crowd began to disperse, the princess made her way towards the man as he collected all of the coins that had been tossed his way. Kassie reached into her purse and handed the minstrel five.

"You are most kind, princess." The musician bowed as he accepted the coins. "Word of your generosity and beauty reached me some time ago. I see now that those stories do not do you justice."

"You flatter," Kassie told him with a grin.

"No, my princess. I but appreciate."

"What is your name, minstrel?" she asked.

"Rikard Emory," he replied, bowing theatrically. "From the lands of Torosa do I hail. I am a minstrel, a troubadour, a songsmith, if you will. I sing for my supper."

"And what brings you so far east?" Marian asked.

"I am in search of inspiration, my lady," Rikard told her. "New ideas, new stories, new songs. The deeds of great knights and heroes. Perhaps you could help, princess."

"Help you?" Kassie said curiously.

"Indeed." Rikard grinned as he spoke. "Through my travels across the land, I have heard tell of how a young princess rode into the devilish lands of Salvaar at the chance of saving her brother."

"What sort of princess would I be if I did not defend my own people?" Kassie told him.

"Even though it meant going astray from the traditions and expectations of your people?"

"As a princess of Annora it was forbidden, but as a daughter of Dorian I was only doing my duty."

"Yes, of course." Rikard spoke as if taken by an idea. "But what if this adventure had plunged you into the chaos of battle?"

"It would have had the same outcome as if I were asked to ride to war today," she replied. "If I must fight, then I will. Before all is said and done, if I am forced to ride into battle, then I will."

"You would knowingly ride into a fight, princess? That is forbidden."

"If I must, I will. I am devoted to Annora."

"Just as your people are devoted to you." Rikard grinned once more. "I thank you for your time, my princess."

"And I thank you for your song, Rikard Emory," Kassie replied as the minstrel bowed low. "It was beautiful."

Shouts interrupted them. Screams followed. Without a second thought, Kassandra charged into the crowd towards the ruckus. The sound of punches landing reached her ears before she saw the fight. It had started with two men, but more were joining by the moment. Some wore the soft flowing tunics of Medea; the others wore the rough shirts and trousers of Annora.

"Our kin and Medean." Marian gasped as the fight unfolded.

"We should leave, my lady," Sir Landon growled to Kassandra as he watched the cheers and cries come from the crowd. "Before it spreads. The knights will put a stop to it."

"No, Sir Landon," Kassandra commanded. "We must remind them what it means to be Annoran."

With that she strode into the fire.

"Listen to me!" the princess cried as she walked between the fighters. "LISTEN! LISTEN!"

Some of the cheers started to die down. Sir Landon waded into the brawl. He grabbed men by their limbs and by their clothing. He hurled them apart.

"LISTEN!" Princess Kassandra shouted.

More eyes turned to her. The last of the fighters stepped back as they saw the armoured knight place his hand upon his sword. One of the Medeans spat at an Annoran's feet. Before even Sir Landon could react, Kassandra stepped between Annoran and Medean. She strode up to the man who had spat and halted mere inches from him. She glared up into his eyes. Blood leaked from his nose and dribbled down his chin. He met her gaze, but Kassandra was unrelenting. She dared him without words. She challenged him. At last, the Medean stepped back and offered a curt bow.

"Listen to me!" Kassandra cried again to silence the crowd as she looked from Medean to Annoran alike. "You're cut from the same cloth, you and he. Annora. Medea. I came here to stand between you both, yet over the past days I have seen how readily our two nations stand together. You do not want this fight and you never wanted it. We are two nations, but we are one faith. We are one people. Let this be the last day of blood between us. Let it be the beginning of the longest age of friendship between Annora and Medea. Together we can reach heights that we cannot even imagine. Together we can forge a path that goes beyond Annora and Medea. One people. One path. One destiny!"

The song of steel broke the silence as Sir Landon thrust his sword sky high.

"The Lady of Annora!" he roared.

The crowd cheered. Medean and Annoran cheered.

✦ ✦ ✦

The midday bells rang through Kilgareth. Lysandra had been in the infirmary for some hours tending to the wounded alongside many of the other maija.

"Here," she called softly as she approached a man sitting on one of the beds. Lysandra gave him a smile as she continued. "Your hand. Let me take a look at it."

The man extended his hand and revealed the true extent of his injury. All his fingers were badly twisted and crooked as if they had been a deformity.

"Nasty," Lysandra commented. "What was the cause?"

"I was riding," the man grunted. "I fell and tried to brace myself."

"May I?" Lysandra gestured to the hand.

The man nodded and the lightly took hold of it.

"Your fingers are badly dislocated," she told him. "If I don't set them now, you may never use them again."

"Go on. Do your duty."

Lysandra smiled and met the man's eyes. "Wild creatures, horses," she said. "Never know when they're going to do something unruly. I have fallen from them myself many a time."

The man returned her grin. "Truly, my lady?"

"Truly. Not long after my arrival here I had to learn to ride. I had never seen a horse so close before, let alone ridden one."

Click. Lysandra did not look away from the man's eyes nor did she stop talking as she popped the first bone back into place.

"I was young then. No older than sixteen or seventeen."

Click.

"I pulled myself up into the saddle, started to walk."

Click.

"I had barely made it from the stables when I fell."

Click.

"Right in front of the arc'maija."

Lysandra chuckled as she remembered. She reached for a thin strip of cloth and set about tying it tightly around the man's fingers.

"I had never been so embarrassed," Lysandra told him as she fastened the cloth. "Done."

"Thank you, lady."

"Be gentle with them for a few days," Lysandra commanded. "If they worsen or you hurt them again – I know what you men are like – come back immediately."

"Yes, lady." The man gave her a thankful smile as he hopped off the bed.

Lysandra tidied her things, arranging bandages, salves and ointments. She glanced around the infirmary and saw that all of the patients were being tended to.

"Eight more today," the maija Kaira told her as she approached. "Dislocations, breaks, gashes. Two will need to stay here for some time."

"Soldiers and camp followers." Lysandra shook her head with an amused chuckle. "Always injuring themselves in one way or another. That reminds me: the wounded Salvaari is in need of new dressings."

"Shall I come with you?"

"No, thank you, Kaira," Lysandra replied. "You do good work here. Call for me if you need anything."

"Of course."

With that, Lysandra filled her satchel with the required items and left the infirmary. She made her way out into the corridor.

"Lady Lysandra," a voice called to her.

She turned to see the white garb and kind face that she knew all too well. "Your holiness." Lysandra greeted the cardinal and gave him a short bow.

"How are the patients?"

"They are well looked after, I promise you."

"That is good." He smiled as he spoke. "By your leave I should like to visit them."

"Of course," Lysandra told him. "It will do them good to see you."

"I have only been here a matter of weeks, yet one thing has become abundantly clear," Cardinal Aleksander started. "This city sings your praises from dawn until dusk."

"I do not seek it," Lysandra said.

"No, my child, but you have earned it," Aleksander said. "In all of my years, in all of my travels, I have never known someone to have become so skilled at the healing arts. Great healers do not cure by chance but by exact knowledge. What was it that made you answer the maija's call?"

"I grew up around soldiers," Lysandra replied. "I saw so much violence … The world needs more healers. To wound others comes so easily, yet to be a healer is far more rare. I wanted to help people, and if I can, then I will – no matter who they were born as or where they come from. This world needs more light, your holiness."

"You may not hear it often, my lady, but know that you are a light in the darkness," Aleksander told her before dipping his head in respect. "I bid you good day."

Lysandra wound her way through the passages and corridors of the Citadel before taking the winding stairs down into the heart of the mountain fortress. She arrived at the prison and, with a word to one of the guards, slid inside the wounded man's cell. The Salvaari stepped back as soon as they saw her enter their midst. Her work with their comrade had earned their respect at least.

"How is he?" Lysandra asked as she crouched beside the wounded man.

"His strength is returning," the Salvaari called Cailean told her.

Lysandra set about changing the dressing. "I have told the guard to summon me if his condition worsens," she said with a glance at Cailean.

The Salvaari gave her a grateful look. "Why are you helping us when all others have turned away?" he asked. "Are we not your enemy?"

Lysandra met Cailean's eyes as she finished changing his companion's dressing. "You are not my enemy, Cailean of the Aedei," Lysandra whispered in Salvaari. "You never were."

The chief's eyes widened. "How do you know our tongue?" he replied in the same.

Lysandra stared into his eyes. "I am of the old blood," she told him.

✦ ✦ ✦

Kyler stood atop the wall of the marching camp. He stared out across the open field into woods. One hundred paces from the wall, the short stumps of cut trees merged into the forest. The darkness of the woods beckoned.

"Sir Kyler, come to keep us company?" Hugh Karter asked as he approached along the wall.

"It's not my watch," Kyler replied with a shrug. "I'm just wondering what is out there."

Hugh stood by Kyler's side and followed his gaze. "The Salvaari … they're there," he said. "Hiding in the shadows like animals."

"You fought them on the fields at Bandujar," Kyler stated.

"I did."

"What were they like?"

Hugh thought for a moment before replying. "They dye their skin with paint and puncture their bodies with ink. Tattoos cover their bodies beneath cloth and armour. They scream to make themselves appear horrifying before charging into battle." Hugh glanced at his companion. "What were they like? Fearless."

"It's quiet here," Kyler muttered.

"We tricked them upon the field. Lured them into a battle that they could not win, yet here is different. The Salvaari chief Henghis is cunning. He will not be drawn into an open battle. Instead, he raids along the frontier, picking us off one by one. That was why it took so long to cross the river. Now we have a foothold, and he will not so easily risk his people."

"We've come a long way since that brawl," Kyler told him with a grin.

"Aye," Hugh said, laughing. "You found a mentor in Sir Alarik and I in Sir Corvo."

"The Sword of Kil'kara," Kyler replied. "I spent most of my time in the practice yard or on horseback and have barely exchanged words with the man."

"My master is a great man," Hugh told him. "The kind of man that people would sing songs about … write poems about. And yet he goes unsung. He seeks no glory or praise. Sir Corvo is a philosopher and not just a blood poet."

"Now you are his apprentice."

"And for that I am eternally grateful."

Horns blared along the walls.

"The warning." Hugh cursed as both men turned towards the eerie song.

They ran along the walls as cries filled the air. Captains shouted orders and the knights were called to arms. Rank upon silver rank filled the grounds. Horses were mounted and helms buckled. Kyler and Hugh at last reached Alarik and Corvo who watched the forest with wary eyes. A shadow broke the tree line. A single horse and rider. It galloped towards the fort like hell itself was chasing. Ice cold hands clutched at Kyler's heart as he saw that the rider lay face down across his horse's back.

"Open the gates!" Grand Master Bavarian's command echoed down from the walls.

Kyler followed Alarik, Hugh and Corvo as they descended down from their post and made for the entrance. The gates were pulled back, and the horse made its way inside. Arrows pierced the knight's body.

"PHYSICIAN!" Alarik shouted as he took hold of the rider and gently lowered him to the ground. "PHYSICIAN!"

The battlemaster unstrapped the knight's helmet and pulled it from his head. His breathing was laboured, and his expression pained.

"They're here," the knight managed.

"How many?" Sir Corvo asked him.

"Hundreds of them."

"And their tribes?"

"A sea of red warriors."

"Catuvantuli," Bavarian muttered. "Henghis."

"What of the patrol?" Alarik asked.

"They took them …" The knight trailed off as his last breath fled his body.

Alarik closed the dead knight's eyes as he held him. "Cuun'etca hĕy'læn," he said softly. "Be at peace, brother."

The gathered knights were silent for a moment.

"The Salvaari are here," Sir William Peyene murmured.

"Henghis' army draws near, master," Corvo said as he turned to Bavarian. "What are your orders?"

"They have captured our brothers," the grand master replied loud enough for all to here. "A dozen knights held captive. We have all seen what the heathen do to the dead. They carve symbols onto their flesh and hang them from trees as offerings to their spirits. They wish to make us fear them. I will not. I will not abandon my brothers to torment and death. The Catuvantuli are alone, and the gods have given us this chance to defeat them once and for all.

They have given us this chance to cut off this snake's head and cure the poison that it casts across the land. Sir Rysand, gather your men and mount up. Lead the way as outriders. Find the enemy. We will be behind you."

"Yes, master." Rysand nodded before calling to his brothers.

The knights leapt into their saddles and galloped through the open gates.

"It could be a trap," Alarik said after a moment.

"Then we will trap them," Bavarian told him. "Light the flame. Our army will assemble, and we will surround them. Henghis will rue this day. Prepare to march. In honour's name. In duty's name. For Durandail, the Father of all Fathers!"

The camp erupted into movement. The tolling of bells filled the cool air. Knights gathered up the last of their kit and mounted their great steeds. Standards bearing the sun and moon were clasped tightly in hand. The pyre high above on the tower was lit. Its flames danced and the call was sent. The great army would assemble once more. Henghis and his barbarian hordes would fall.

✦ ✦ ✦

TWENTY-SIX

Káli Lands, Forest of Salvaar

There was a slight fog in the air as the line of silver-clad knights rode beneath the trees. They were covered head to toe in plate and mail. Their horses wore armoured masks. They formed an impenetrable wall of steel. Kyler held his spear close, while his shield was tightly secured to his left arm. He had lost track of how far the knights had ridden from the camp. A few miles, maybe more. Kyler rode by his mentor's side. The stoic veteran's presence was calming to the men about to enter battle. The first thing that they saw were the bodies hanging high from the trees, blowing in the breeze. Blood dripped down from the furrows carved into their flesh.

"The patrol," Alarik muttered.

Horses pawed at the earth while their riders stared at their dead brothers. Beneath the hanging corpses lay more bodies, man and horse alike – armoured knights and their mounts. Arrows riddled their lifeless bodies. The scouts.

"Sir Rysand," cursed the knight to Kyler's left as he recognised the bodies.

Savage screams came from beyond the mist.

"Salvaar comes," the battlemaster growled.

"IT'S A TRAP!" roared Bavarian from down the line.

Ravens cried all around. The chanting screams grew louder. In that moment, Kyler saw a flicker of light break through the canopy. A single stream of the sun's glorious rays. Kyler felt a warm presence envelop him.

"Durandail," he murmured, driving his spear towards the light. "Look, brothers! The light of the sun! The Father of all Fathers is here. He has taken that shape to show us that he is with us!"

"KEEP RANKS!" Sir Corvo's voice rang. "HOLD THE LINE! WE WILL TAKE THEM HEAD ON!"

"The Lord is here to give us the strength to drive the heathens back into the shadows from whence they come!" Kyler continued as his companions looked to him. "I can feel his presence. Durandail will not abandon us on this day!"

Shadows began to emerge as a line of Catuvantuli horsemen materialised from the fog.

"Fight for your brothers!" Kyler cried. "Fight for your gods!"

Bavarian drove his spear into the heavens as a great roar erupted from his lips. "TO BATTLE! FOR AZARIA! FOR DURAINDAIL! AREUT TALC CUUN'ECT!"

"AREUT TALC CUUN'ECT!" the knights cried.

The line of steel and horses accelerated forward. Everything slowed. The screams of the enemy grew louder. Thunderous hooves shook the ground. Sharpened spears lowered. The line of silver and blue surged towards men and horses covered in red. Kyler's lips curled back into a snarl. The beast of war woke within him.

"KIL'KARA!" the war cry rose from the throats of a thousand knights.

Man and beast came together in a great crash. Warriors were thrown from saddles. Horses screamed. Men fell. The steel-clad knights drove like a lance through the ranks of the Salvaari. Kyler's spear turned crimson as he thrust it through a red warrior's chest. He ripped it free, swivelled in his saddle and then plunged it into the throat of a second. Kyler kicked his heels in to Asena's side, arrows flying all around as some of the Salvaari riders unleashed hell with their war bows. He lifted his shield and a pair of steel-tipped shafts tore into the defence. The knight beside him fell, arrows sprouting from his chest. A scream filled the air as a rider charged towards Kyler. Kyler rode to meet him. He drove his shield into the path of the Catuvantuli's axe. Steel hit layered wood and then Kyler pushed his spear forward. The Catuvantuli fell with a shout as the spear tore through his ribs and plunged deep into his heart. The momentum of the charge faltered against the ranks of the enemy. The chaos of battle filled the forest. A great war cry went up and lines of Catuvantuli appeared on foot, surging towards the battle in a wave of steel and flesh. They fell upon the knights with spears and axes. Like the horsemen, they wore the red paint of the Catuvantuli. Like the horsemen, they were hungry for blood. Kyler felled one with a thrust and smote a second with a slash. A spearman drove his spear towards Kyler. The knight kicked his heels in. Asena reared away from the spear. As Kyler raised his arm to thrust, a Catuvantuli rider charged his horse straight into Asena. Kyler fell. His horse fell. The spear left his fingers as he crashed to the ground. Rolling free of Asena as she struggled to her feet, Kyler deflected the spearman's blow with his shield and punched it into the warrior's face. The Catuvantuli stumbled back, and Kyler tore his sword free. Cutting through the chaos, another footman barrelled towards him. Kyler blocked his axe and countered, driving his sword through the man's unprotected throat. He spun back, parried a spearman's thrust and opened his neck in reply. Men and horses churned the earth all around, though of Asena Kyler could see no sign. He slogged his way through the battlefield and joined with an ever-growing band of knights that had been unhorsed. They stood shoulder to shoulder, linked in a shield wall. Some carried longswords, others spears. Together they crested a small ridge and fought against the horde of Catuvantuli. Time passed as the battle raged all around. The heat grew stifling. Kyler's arms grew weary. Aches had begun to grow as axes, spears and swords found their way past the shields and glanced off his armour. The shouts of knight captains could be heard above the din. Horns blared. Medean horns.

"MEDEA!" cried one of the knights. "MEDEA IS HERE!"

The stag of Salazar, the bear of Bailon and the white lion of Aloys appeared on standards and surcoats. Horsemen and infantry charged into the battle. Arrows and spears greeted them before they crashed into the Salvaari ranks. The pockets of unhorsed knights formed a line of shields and swords and surged towards the Catuvantuli. More horns sounded. Lines of silver and violet appeared through the mist. Aureia had come. Cheers filled the allied ranks as the imperial soldiers joined the fray.

"FIGHT ON!" Alarik's voice could be heard. "FIGHT FOR THE WEST! FIGHT FOR THE GODS!"

The three armies joined and step by step began to push the Salvaari back. Moment by moment, they took more ground. Salvaari bodies began to pass beneath Kyler's feet. They pushed forward, relentlessly and without mercy. Kyler's sword tasted blood again and again. The pain of his aches faded as new energy filled him. They were pushing the Salvaari back. They were winning. Salvaari riders raced up and down the flanks of the army. They shot volleys of arrows before retreating as allied horsemen saw them off. Yet the Salvaari kept picking at the scab. More heathen cries echoed through the trees. The Catuvantuli warrior in front of Kyler fell to his sword and then another took his place. Then he saw it. The new warrior did not wear the red of the Catuvantuli. He wore the green of the Icari.

"ALARIK!" Kyler roared as he saw his mentor's helmet. "THE TRIBES! THEY'RE ALL HERE!"

"HOLD THE LINE!" came the shouted reply. "WE BREAK THEM HERE!"

Slowly, a line of shields appeared before them as the highland tribe took the place of Henghis' people. The two shield walls came together, but this new tribe did nothing to stem the momentum of the allied army. They drove them back step by step. More tribes appeared. The Aedei, the Káli, the Sagailean, more. All those not at the Rift had come. Some on horseback, others on foot. The swelling Salvaari ranks slowed the advance, but they could not hold it. Kyler roared and launched himself at his enemy.

✦ ✦ ✦

Kitara and her companions had been riding for days through the forest and had seen little more than empty villages and few tribesmen beneath the trees. Aeryn rode out ahead of the column to scout the lay of the land before them. The moonseer told the company that she believed they drew near to Henghis and his army. Suddenly, Bellec held up a hand and brought the company to a halt.

"What is it?" Kitara called.

"Shhhh," he whispered. "Listen."

Kitara frowned as they all grew silent. Horses pulled at the reins and shook their heads. Kitara's eyes widened as a faint sound reached her ears. A roar and the clash of steel. Kitara stroked her mount's neck to comfort the horse.

"Battle," Bellec called.

The companions exchanged glances. Sound played tricks and the battle may not be close, but the song was unmistakable. Sabra screeched high above and then circled down to land on Sakkar's outstretched arm.

"It's getting dark," he said.

"Nightfall is nearly upon us," Senya said.

A bird's cry echoed through the forest. All turned as riders materialised through the mist. Hands went to weapons.

"It's alright," Galadayne called. "It's Aeryn!"

Relief flooded Kitara's body as the horsemen approached. Though she would never have admitted it, she had been worried for Aeryn. Kitara ran her gaze over the riders as they drew closer. There were over a dozen of them all painted with blue woad. They all carried bows. They all had silver eyes.

"The tribes fight the west a few miles south of here," Aeryn told them. "Henghis has drawn them into battle and lured them far from behind their walls."

"Every moonseer from every corner of Salvaar has come," another of the Aedei said. "This night we avenge the dead beneath Sylvaine's moon."

"We will join you," Kitara told them as she rode to meet Aeryn.

"No," Aeryn replied. "The moonseer must ride alone."

"Then we will help your people," Bellec said.

Aeryn gave him a nod before turning to Kitara. The mercenaries began to ready themselves. Helmets were strapped on, and cloaks stowed in saddle bags. Aeryn reached out a hand and Kitara took it.

"May the spirits watch over you," she whispered in Salvaari.

Kitara cupped Aeryn's cheek and kissed her hard on the lips. They pressed their foreheads together.

"Come back to me," Kitara told her.

"Nothing will keep me from your arms," Aeryn swore.

Then they parted. The moonseer vanished into the mist as darkness began to fall. Kitara pulled her coif up and strapped her helmet on.

"Whatever happens, stay together," Bellec called. "We ride to victory, or we ride to defeat. Yet we ride."

Prayers were uttered and quiet words exchanged. Sabra took to the sky. They turned their horses towards the sound of battle.

✦ ✦ ✦

The night came and it came fast. The last shred of light vanished beyond the canopy of the trees. Darkness crept into the forest.

Kyler struck down a Salvaari and took a breath. With each passing moment, it was becoming harder to see. No longer was the leer upon his enemy's face easy to make out. No longer did the war paint come in many types. All colours faded and blurred. The screams of the wounded and dying echoed through the forest. The stench of blood and sweat filled the senses. The earth had turned into a slurry. Kyler adjusted his grip upon his sword. In the distance, Salvaari horns sounded. Shouts in the pagan tongue spread through their ranks. The Salvaari began to pull back. They disengaged the shield wall and began to scatter.

"REFORM THE LINE!" Bavarian commanded. "REFORM THE LINE!"

The army began to shift as the Salvaari broke off. Shields were brought to bear and overlapped once more. Kyler squinted as he watched the Salvaari disappear. They vanished like ghosts. Soon none remained. The allies were left alone with the dead. They watched the trees warily. What were the Salvaari playing at?

"Damn the dark," Kyler cursed.

"Torches!" The order passed through the allied ranks.

Kyler looked this way and that as flames slowly came to life. He walked back through the rows of knights until he found Alarik. The battlemaster stared into the forest.

"What is it?" Kyler asked.

"We're not alone," Alarik told him. "The trees watch us."

"The Salvaari are still out there."

Alarik nodded. "They're there," he replied. "We are a long way from our walls. With me."

Kyler followed his mentor through the ranks of knights. With each step, their pace quickened.

"Master," Alarik called as they caught sight of Corvo.

The acting master stood with Hugh and Sir William Peyene.

"How far do you think we have come?" Corvo asked Alarik.

"Five miles. Perhaps more."

Corvo nodded slowly. "We need to get out of here," he said before turning to Hugh. "Find the grand master."

"Master." Hugh saluted and heaved himself up into his saddle.

The light of torches sparked amongst the allied lines, an orange glow emanating around them. The light did little to quell the nameless fear that was beginning to gnaw at Kyler. The chants began. Slowly at first, yet more savage than the most vile of beasts. It grew faster and louder. It came from every direction.

"What kind of hell is this?" Kyler murmured as he shared a look with Alarik.

"HOLD THE LINE!" Corvo roared as he leapt up into his saddle.

Arrows rained down. Screams filled the forest. Despite the blackness of night, despite the mist, the arrows *always* found their mark. Man and horse fell beneath the steel. Kyler raised his shield overhead. The acting master galloped over to a company of mounted knights, leaving Alarik in charge of those on foot. Horns blared.

"Bavarian has sounded the retreat," Kyler growled.

"STEADY!" Alarik bellowed. "WE MARCH AS ONE!"

They took a slow pace and kept the shield wall. The steady stream of arrows grew into a rain, flashing in the darkness. Shadows flickered here and there. Kyler caught a glimpse of horse and rider. Men fell with screams upon their lips. The torch bearer closest crashed to the ground with a shaft through his neck. Another was slain further down the line. Another. The Salvaari were targeting the bearers.

"PROTECT THE TORCHES!" Alarik shouted.

✦ ✦ ✦

Aeryn guided her horse with her knees as she rode through the shattering ranks of western soldiers. Mount and moonseer moved in unison as they galloped across the earth. Aeryn swivelled in her saddle and let an arrow soar behind her. The moonseer did not watch to see if her aim was true and instead turned her attention to new targets. The arrow flew as she knew it would and struck a knight through the throat. Aeryn did not need to see his fall to know that his body lay lifeless upon the ground. She steered her horse between man and steed and never slowed from a gallop. Hundreds of silver-eyed moonseer charged through the battlefield. Some worked alone, others in small groups. All used their bows with deadly skill. None could stand before them as they worked to sow chaos through the western army. They targeted the torchbearers to hinder the enemy's sight. They targeted captains yelling orders and bodies of men trying to hold formation. The moonseer were agents of chaos. They commanded chaos. They revelled in chaos. One by one, the last of the torch flames were extinguished. Darkness blanketed the forest. The Salvaari chants grew louder as the western formations crumbled before them. As the silver-eyes killed at will, those not moonseer began to charge in numbers at fragmenting ranks. The first of the westerners began to break off and flee as the fear spread.

✦ ✦ ✦

Kyler watched in horror as a line of horses appeared from the blackness and crashed into the Medean ranks. They hacked and slashed for mere moments before fleeing back into the forest, leaving only the dead in their wake. The arrows continued to rain. Medeans, Aureians and knights fell in droves beneath the storm. The horsemen continued to harass their position.

"BAILON!" a Medean cried before leading his cavalry into the darkness after their retreating foe.

They were never seen again. Only their screams returned. Fear spread through the allied ranks like wildfire. Slowly the three armies began to splinter. The barrage of arrows slowed pockets of men while the Salvaari horsemen cut them off from their comrades. Soldiers began to break off from the formation and run. Captains tried to restore order – the Salvaari were relentless. Shouts and screams came from all around. Tribesmen on foot and horse streamed forward. They crashed into the shattering ranks of the western armies. They fell left and right. The once solid line disintegrated. Kyler and Alarik were cut off with no more than fifty of their brothers. The knights fought for every step and paid in blood. They did not flee. They did not run. Instead, they slowly started the march west and held formation. Arrows felled a dozen of them and then the tide of Salvaari surged into their shield wall. They came from every direction. Kyler threw himself into the front line and engaged the enemy. He skewered a tribesman and took the head of a second. A spear glanced off his armoured shoulder and he slew the man in reply. A line of horsemen appeared. Armoured horsemen. These were *not* tribesmen. For a moment, Kyler felt relief until he saw the blue woad covering steel. The riders charged.

✦ ✦ ✦

Kitara held her sword high as they charged through the disintegrating ranks of western soldiers. Few tried to stand their ground and those who did soon fell to Salvaari steel. They fled back from whence they had come in groups. Some tried to hold formation and marched as units. Others ran without thought. The moonseer galloped beneath the trees killing indiscriminately. If a shield was held too low, the bearer died. If a soldier tried to rally fleeing men, he died. If someone went for a torch, he died.

Kitara's sword found the neck of a retreating Medean. She pulled hard on her reins, spun her horse around and felled a second soldier. Through the blackness, she saw the robed druids. They held wicked curved swords covered in runes and with that steel sated their blood thirst upon the invaders. Those men who were captured by the druids were executed as offerings upon altars of stone. What little resolve the westerners still had began to falter.

Kitara saw Henghis riding through the chaos with his scarlet shield and longsword. Her eyes flicked across the battlefield. The moonseer sowed fear and chaos through the allied ranks as they killed with impunity. The rest of the tribal warriors picked off the weak and those who fled while doing all in their power to force breaks in the enemy lines. The moonseer widened the holes with their arrows and drove the splintering formations apart. This was not a fight. It was a massacre.

"With me!" Bellec cried as he angled his horse towards a circle of knights.

They were being assaulted by the Salvaari. Wave after wave of arrows drove towards the westerners. Many of the knights fell and the unrelenting wave of Salvaari crashed into their shields. Kitara urged her horse towards Bellec. He raised his arm and with a cry led them towards the formation of knights.

"BRACE!" a man within the silver ranks cried.

Sakkar opened a hole in the shield wall as he sent an arrow into the throat of one of the knights. The man fell backwards, and the company crashed into the ranks of knights.

✦ ✦ ✦

"BRACE!"

Alarik's roar still echoed when the riders charged into their formation. Man and beast fell as the knights were driven back.

"HOLD THE CIRCLE!" Alarik bellowed.

Kyler cut a Salvaari down and caught a glance of the riders cutting into his brothers. They were not Salvaari, yet they fought against the west. Traitors. Kyler charged at one of the mounted men. He lunged and drove steel towards his foe. The warrior blocked the blow with his shield. Kyler ducked the counter as he closed the distance. The rider blocked once again, but Kyler's attack was a diversion. He released the handle of his shield and caught the edge of the rider's. He gave a savage tug while slamming the blade of his sword into the armoured back of his foe. The mail stopped the blade, but it was enough to take his balance. Kyler pulled him from his horse. The warrior hit the ground with a shout, only managing to get his shield up in time to save his life. Kyler's sword glanced off the steel rim and then the warrior was on his feet. They exchanged blow for blow. Kyler feinted high and angled low. His sword sliced through the warrior's unprotected thigh. As the warrior staggered, Kyler lashed out. The warrior barely got his shield up in time. Kyler battered the shield with his sword and then slammed it into the warrior's helmet. The warrior fell. His shield fell. Before long, he rolled to his feet again and raised his sword. The warrior blocked once. Kyler's sword found his arm. Blood flowed and the warrior roared. Kyler's shield swatted the warrior's sword aside. Kyler lunged, ripping steel through the warrior's throat. He saw a flicker of fear cross the man's eyes before he smashed him backwards with his shield and wrenched his sword free. The warrior fell.

"KOMPTON!" one of the other riders screamed.

Kyler did not react nor hesitate. He stepped back into the shield wall.

"HOLD THE CIRCLE!" Alarik cried again.

Shouts in the heathen tongue filled the air. The Salvaari began to scatter. The riders broke free. The earth thundered and a line of silver and blue crashed into the rear of the Salvaari ranks. Mounted Knights of Kil'kara. They drove through the fleeing tribesmen like a blade through the air. Those who did not run were drowned by the wave of steel. Kyler saw Hugh through the chaos.

"BACK TO THE CAMP!" Sir Corvo shouted.

The knights held formation as they made their retreat across the blood-soaked ground. Men screamed. The dying screamed. The

Pale Horseman rode among them. The Salvaari chanting did not cease. Thousands fell to the onslaught of Salvaar. The west had entered their hell.

✦ ✦ ✦

Ten knights were all that remained of Bavarian's company as they ran through the forest. They had no horses nor means of calling to their allies. All they could hear were screams. All they could smell was death. They kept together. They kept moving. Bavarian held his bloody sword in one hand and a banner of their order in the other. Salvaari cries drew near. Dirt was thrown up by hooves. Riders flashed by on both sides. Knights fell as arrows rained down. Only five remained. The Salvaari charged them. Bavarian and his knights held their ground. He killed one, killed two. The knights fought their way up onto a small ridge. A knight fell to a spear, and another was dragged down beneath the tide of tribesmen. An arrow drove deep into Bavarian's shoulder. Another found his stomach. He would not fall. He *refused* to fall. Only he remained. Water splashed under foot as he staggered into the river. Tribesmen streamed all around him. He fought through the waters until he reached a small island. He drove the end of the standard into the earth and held his ground to defend it.

"KIL'KARA!" he screamed as the Salvaari charged.

His sword tasted blood again and again. An axe drove him to a knee, yet he slew his attacker with a thrust to the heart. Blows bent his armour and opened wounds. He was the grand master; he would not fall. Bavarian created a field of death. He could feel the Pale Horseman's presence. Bavarian turned aside a spear and opened a Salvaari's chest. He trembled and staggered, barely able to keep his footing. Salvaari surrounded him. They did not move.

"COME ON!" he screamed. "DO YOU FEAR ME?"

Bavarian met their hate-filled glares. He turned this way and that, never lowering his sword. His breathing was ragged, and his body broken. He would not fall.

The Salvaari began to back away. He could only watch in silence as they vanished into the night and left him alone with the wind. Bavarian bared his teeth. He heard ravens calling to each other. The song of their wings echoed through the trees. The air grew still. Through the blackness he saw burning red eyes. Bavarian froze. They came from every side. Six of them. Dark clothing, dark hair. Pale skin covered in black runes. Pointed ears and white fangs. They were nightmares. They were demons. They were ruskalan. They were supposed to be extinct. A very real shiver ran down Bavarian's spine. One began to walk through the water towards him. Bavarian levelled his sword. He would not, he *could* not, let these creatures take the standard.

"DEVIL!" Bavarian bellowed as he met the ruskalan's blazing eyes.

The twin fires burned ever bright. They called to him, drew him close. Bavarian's body froze as he stared deep into the pits of hell. In them he saw true darkness. He saw rage. He saw pain. He saw fury. His sword fell from his fingers. Then he saw darkness.

✦ ✦ ✦

TWENTY-SEVEN

Lumis, Isle of Vay'kis, The Valkir Isles

The song of welcoming horns echoed across the waters of the Lupentine as the fleet began to sail into the bay. The warships of jarls and earls alike returned to their homes while King Erik led the vessels transporting the Elarans along with the pirate armada to Lumis. One by one, the ships began to dock. Those that could not enter the bay anchored just off the coast and ferried their passengers to land aboard their longboats. The townspeople left their homes to watch curiously as thousands of men, women and children began to disembark. The streets filled from the harbour to the steps leading to the hall of Auraeva.

Erik left the Ravenheart and led the leaders of the alliance through the packed streets of Lumis. They made their way up the massive hill and into the hall. It was more of palace than any jarl's or earl's dwelling. A stone wall surrounded it and huge pillars ringed the hall. Its roof was red tiled instead of the wood and thatch used by the Valkir craftsmen. It was Aureian from its pinnacle to the ground beneath. Bhaltair, Priamos Stentor, Mellisanthi and the pirates Cillian Teague and Garret Laven followed him into the hall. Braziers burned brightly in the marble palace and light streamed in through the windows. Where once the banners of the drake and griffin had hung, now there was nothing but bare walls.

"This hall is Aureian," Teague stated as he looked around the great chamber.

"Its previous owners had close ties to the imperial throne," Erik explained.

"Where are they now?" Priamos asked.

"I killed them," Erik replied. "As you can see, there are no banners here."

"Why bring us to Lumis?" Bhaltair inquired.

"With the earl and his brother dead, Vay'kis is in need of new leadership," Erik said as he looked to his companions. "I thought that between yourselves *you* might be able to govern this isle."

"Should not the leadership of a Valkir isle fall to the Valkir?" Mellisanthi spoke up. "Are you sure that you want the five of us to be the leaders *together*?"

"Why not?" Erik said with a shrug. "Your people need a place and Vay'kis is the largest of the isles. This place needs strong leadership, and the people here are different. As you can see, they are as much Aureian as they are Valkir. Many of you know the imperials better than I ever will. If you can come to some kind of agreement on how best to govern this place, we can make it prosper once again."

"It is a fine idea," Bhaltair said as he crossed his arms. "But I worry. I have spent *years* fighting for my brothers and sisters. From the slums of Elara to the steps of the throne room, I have seen it all. I know what people are like. I know what they can do. So I ask you now: If we were to carve a place for ourselves here, would the people who inhabit this isle let us live peacefully?"

"You are right to ask," Erik told him. "There is a deep history between Vay'kis and its sister isles. Many here think the eastern isles are too primitive. Many of the eastern isles think the people here too aloof … too civilised. Yet one thing that unites all Valkir is honour. Their earl, through his treacherous actions, brought war to them. They may dislike me for killing their people. Perhaps they hate me. However, in their hearts they all know who is responsible and that man they will all despise until their last day. If your people live in peace, then they will do the same. It will take time to earn their trust, but when you do you will have their love as well. I can assure you of that."

Garrett Laven looked to Teague. "It could be done," he said. "We've done it before. There is good land here. We could rebuild what we lost."

"It's yours," Erik told them. "All of yours. So long as you promise to fight beside us when the real war comes."

Teague stepped forward into the midst. It was he who Erik knew so little. The pirate captain was more than just a warrior, he was a visionary. Erik had heard of Teague before – his name was spoken in whispers by the people of Vay'kis. He knew that the man had forged the settlements in the gulf of Lamrei himself and that he had liberated many slaves.

"Once, a long time ago, I was warned of this fight," Teague told them. "Warned that the silver empire would wash across the world like a great wave, crushing everything in its path. Warned that they would come to take it all. That was why I broke from the empire, why I stood against the League. Now, as then, the empire is on the move. If you had not offered us a new home, that would have been enough. But you have and I will not forget that. I will stand with you, King Erik. My ships are yours; my warriors are yours."

"You are most welcome, my brother," Erik said, clasping the pirate's arm.

"My men are not sailors, but they are good fighters," Priamos Stentor spoke up. "Let them stand alongside your people on Valkir ships and they will not fail you."

"The same for my people," Bhaltair added. "They're not much for manners but they are good in a fight."

"I hold no title like Lord Stentor nor am I a warrior like the rest of you," Mellisanthi said. "I have never seen battle, nor have I held steel. I cannot help you fight this war, but I *can* help you in other ways. I know the people and more importantly I know their hearts, their dreams and their desires. I understand information and the power that comes with it. I know how to use them. I may not be able to fight, but I can help build us something better here."

"It's true," Bhaltair said as he walked to her side. "Mellisanthi used her position to help both the gangs and the city people. She has standing with every Elaran in this island and has experience leading."

"Have you governed before?" Garrett Laven asked.

"Information is the key," Mellisanthi replied. "I have people everywhere. I know everything. Once you learn to listen to the people, you can lead them."

"Forgive me, my lady," Priamos Stentor said as his brow twitched into a frown. "But while we are absent from these isles, while King Erik is absent, why would the Valkir listen to you? You're a foreign woman who knows little about the culture."

"She won't be alone," Erik replied and gestured to another of the Valkir.

The man stepped forward. His clothing was a mixture of rough Valkir cloth and fine Aureian craftsmanship. Like the men of Vay'kis, his dark hair was cropped and his beard short. A thick headband was wrapped around his brow and a thick fur cloak was draped over his shoulders.

"I am Harald Vrandyr," he told them.

"In our absence, the people of Vay'kis chose Harald to stand as steward until such a time as a new earl rises," Erik explained. "Together you will be able to help both peoples."

"It seems then that our problem is neatly resolved," Mellisanthi said.

"One, yes," Erik said wryly before turning to Harald. "In the weeks that we have been gone, what has changed? What word from Jorun and the other jarls?"

"A large base has been established on Nesoi," Harald began.

"While ships and men are prepared, Jorun and four of the other jarls have crossed the Lupentine. Word has reached us here that they have begun their attacks. Merchantmen and traders that they have come across in the sea know nothing."

"Then there are survivors?" Priamos Stentor asked.

"No, lord," Harald replied. "We cannot risk the empire knowing about what we seek. Men cannot be spared to sail the prizes, so the ships are fired and the bodies dumped overboard."

Hundreds, if not thousands, had been slaughtered and returned to the deep. Erik knew it, but he could not turn or run from it. The survival of his people depended on it.

"Our people should arrive at the Aureian coast any day now," Erik added. "Today is a day that your people find land to settle. Under Mellisanthi's guidance, preparations can begin. But tomorrow we must sail for Nesoi."

Harald gathered some of his people to show the newcomers a place further along the coast. There was good land for farming and plentiful game in the forest that led into the mountains. The beach was long and the ground hard enough to build a harbour. By nightfall, a huge, sprawling camp had been assembled. Pirates, Elarans and Valkir all came together. They drank, danced and sung around fires. For the first time in many years, the Elarans and pirates knew peace.

Erik sat on the beach with Fargrim, Laerke, Nenrir and Mayrun. They laughed together and made merry. Darkness and blood had been their dreams of late, and if the Sea-Father granted them only one night, then they would make the most of it. So they drank and remembered happier times.

Erik downed a draught from his cup before glancing up from the fire. Dozens of fires had been lit along the beach, each and all surrounded by men and women. He saw her by one of the blazes. Golden hair hung in waves down the side of her face. Her eyes of copper fire sparkled as she laughed. If the shadows had hidden her face the woman could have been Héra. It was like staring into a dream. Her shirt was white, while her boots and pants dark. A thick, blue sash was bound around her waist. She was a pirate. The woman caught his gaze and smirked. She glanced at her own fire and then back at Erik. The smile remained. The shine in her gaze remained. Erik downed the last of his drink and crossed the beach towards her. She rose to meet him. There was a hunger in her gaze, a hunger that was reflected in his own eyes. They found their way to a tent, and she led him inside by the hand. The copper pools of her eyes washed over Erik as they came together. Her golden hair spilled across his arm like a waterfall of silk. Her warm breath forced its way through the memories that swam within Erik's mind. She was intoxicating and he drank her in. He felt the coarseness of her hands as they entwined, coarseness from a lifetime at sea.

"What is your name?" he breathed.

"Halitreia," her voice was soft, like early morning birdsong.

Erik's fingers ran through her hair. He pulled her close and then tasted her lips.

The fleet left by noon the next day, pirate vessels and Valkir ships both. While the thousands of non-combatants stayed on with Mellisanthi and Harald, all those who could bear arms took to the ships. Lord Priamos Stentor and his soldiers joined crews. Bhaltair and his ruffians gathered their arms and added their strength to whichever ship would take them. The Ravenheart sailed alongside the Oridassey at the head of a great and terrible armada. Ships beyond count followed in their wake. Every jarl and every earl from every isle was there. Every pirate, every raider, every gang man sailed west. For that was their fate. They sailed into war before the war could find them.

✦ ✦ ✦

The Harpy gently rocked in the waves just off the Aureian coast. The vicious figurehead that adorned the Valkir ship gazed to the south across the ocean. An anchor held the Harpy in place, and little more than a skeleton crew remained aboard. The longboats had all been launched before dawn at Jorun Thorkel's command. Now Bloodaxe and forty of his finest made their way across the beach, through hills and under trees towards the Aureian town of Khrisoya. The woodland enabled the Valkir to get close to the village long before they could have been spotted. Archers eliminated the watch on the small wall and Jorun led his men at a sprint across the open field towards Khrisoya. Four makeshift ladders created a way up, and by the time the warning bell sounded, it was already too late. Townspeople screamed as the roughly clad raiders appeared atop the walls. Jorun shouted a warning and gestured further down the wall. Soldiers began to stream towards them in a silver tide. The Valkir bowmen unleashed hell and sent the Aureians to meet their gods. Jorun tore his axe free and swung his shield onto his arm. Embellished with the image of a winged harpy, the shield only added to the aura of fear that Jorun gave as he unleashed a blood-curdling scream. He charged down the ramparts with his warriors and drove into the broken ranks of Aureians. His axe tasted blood as he drove through them. Jorun interlocked his shield with the warrior to his right and left and then they surged forward. The silver-clad soldiers did the same and then shield wall met shield wall. The Aureians were well trained, but they were only city watch; they weren't the men of the legions. Jorun and his crew had been hardened by more than a decade of seafaring and battle. They were strong. They were fierce. They were relentless. Step by step, they pushed the enemy back. Shouts and the clash of steel came from below as warriors of the Harpy leapt down from the wall and made their way into the town streets. Jorun cut his axe down over the shield of an Aureian. Steel kissed the soldier's neck, and he fell with a scream. Jorun risked a glance down at the street below and saw his men preparing to make their play.

"NOW!" the jarl cried out.

Arrows flew from the bows of his men towards the tightly packed Aureians upon the wall. They could not move to avoid the shafts. Steel ripped through flesh as the formation melted under the storm. The Aureian ranks broke. Those not claimed by the arrows became easy targets for Jorun's axe. The last defenders upon the wall fell within moments. The jarl dropped down from the battlements and led his crew as they dealt with the soldiers that stood against them. Jorun beat his way past an Aureian's shield and knocked his spear to the side. With a roar, he brought the blade of his axe down viciously upon the man's neck. Blood washed over Jorun's helmet and face like a mask and the soldier crumpled before the jarl. Hooves thundered upon cobblestones as a line of horsemen charged down the street towards the Valkir. Lances were lowered as they galloped towards their foe. Jorun thrust his arm forth and sent his axe spinning through the air. It turned end over end and then steel struck one of the riders in the face. Before the man had fallen from his saddle, Jorun snatched up a dead man's spear and braced himself. The line of Valkir held strong. Three more riders fell to a hail of arrows and then the Aureians hit the shield wall. Man and beast fell with screams. Riders broke through the lines of Valkir only to be greeted by the swords, spears and axes of the Harpy's crew.

Jorun caught a thrust with his shield and then countered. His spear ripped through the Aureian's throat. The jarl tore his weapon free, and the rider crashed to the ground before him. Within moments, the crew overwhelmed the Aureians. The fight was over in mere minutes. The foot soldiers and riders who escaped axe and arrow fled back through the city streets. Jorun cast the spear aside and strode towards the body that held his axe. Blood dripped from steel as he tugged it free. He beat his axe upon his shield as his crew gathered all around him. They made for the centre of Khrisoya. Those townspeople too slow to flee fell before the weapons of the Valkir; those who cowered within their houses were ignored by Jorun and his people.

In the heart of Khrisoya lay the magister's villa. It did not take long for the Valkir to smash in the thick doors. None could stand against them as they fought to the villa's courtyard. Though fear of the dreaded Valkir alone kept most of the household cowering in terror, there were some who resisted. It seemed almost a waste to kill the poorly armed servants that came to fight for their master. Slowly, Jorun's warriors corralled what remained of the household into the tiled courtyard. Like all great Aureian houses, a small pool decorated its interior. It was barely a foot deep, and its waters splashed across the tiles as the Valkir shoved noble and servant alike within. A man stepped forward and released a woman's hand as he did so. He was dressed more finely than the rest. His robes were of the purest white with a purple sash wrapped around his body from shoulder to hip. He was old though he showed no fear. He tore a golden ring from his finger and tossed it at Jorun's feet.

"Take what you wish, Valkir," he said. "Gold, jewels, coin. Then leave us in peace."

"You are the master of this house?" Jorun asked.

"I am Magister Kassair Ambrose," the Aureian replied.

Jorun gestured towards the man with his axe. Without a word, two of the Valkir strode into the pool and clamped their arms around the magister before dragging him from the pool. The household cried out and screamed, but the steel of the Valkir soon stopped them. The warriors forced Kassair to his knees and held him tight. Jorun squatted before the magister.

"I would like to leave you in peace," he said. "Yet before my companions and I leave your shores, we need an answer to a question, an answer that you yourself may know."

Kassair Ambrose glared at Jorun as he spoke. "Speak then."

"Word has crossed the waves that tells of a great Aureian fleet marshalling against we Valkir," Jorun told him. "Tell me where."

The magister said nothing.

"Tell me *where*," Jorun repeated.

"I do not know of what you speak."

"Very well," Jorun said. He rose to his feet and gestured once more towards the household. This time it was a woman pulled from their ranks. The woman whose hand had once tightly clutched Kassair's.

"There is no need for that," Kassair growled.

"Your wife?" Jorun asked.

"She is *innocent*."

"None of us are innocent," Jorun growled before gathering up the magister's fallen ring. "Gold purchased with blood."

"You say that as if you are more than a thief."

"We steal to survive, not for pleasure. You call us thieves." Jorun chuckled drily. "Yet we are not the ones who deal in lives. We do not take slaves and condemn those we defeat to a lifetime in chains. We do not burn cities and wipe out entire cultures because our god demands it. Where is the fleet?"

"Your words ring with the sound of desperation."

"An ambassador from these very shores came to the isles not so long ago. He threatened my people with slavery and death. They brought this war to us, and it would be foolish not to admit that the empire can summon a force far greater than any the isles have ever seen. I have become *very* desperate, magister." Jorun waved to the man who held the magister's wife.

In turn, the warrior placed the edge of his sword against her neck.

"You will tell us what you know," Jorun commanded.

Kassair gritted his teeth. "Some months ago, I heard whispers that a great war chest was being compiled to the south. Since then, I have heard *nothing*. Perhaps the chest could lead you to the fleet."

"Tell me where the fleet is."

"That's all I know."

A hand clamped down on Jorun's shoulder. The jarl glanced back as one of his warrior's leaned in.

"A man was seen riding south towards Valentia," the Valkir whispered. "He will call for reinforcements. We haven't much time."

Jorun nodded before turning back to the magister.

"Then it would seem, Magister Kassair, that you are no more use to me," the jarl told him. "In other circumstances, we would take what gold we could find and leave you in peace. However, you are now aware of what we seek and that is something that I cannot abide. We cannot afford for word to spread that we know of this fleet."

Faces paled and cries of horror echoed through the villa. The Valkir silenced the screams with steel.

✦ ✦ ✦

TWENTY-EIGHT

Road to Carlian, Steppe of Miera

Danavir Calin set a mile-eating pace from the moment the company left Vanhair. They crossed rushing rivers and passed over hills. They rode through canyons and evergreen forests. Those were all that broke up the great sea of grass and rolling plains that swam from horizon to horizon. The Steppe of Miera was vast and untamed. Massive herds of wild horses galloped across the open fields and birds cried high above. They passed simple villages and larger, sprawling towns. Greetings were always exchanged between the countrymen. At first, Elise had thought it strange when she had seen the Mierans trade for supplies rather than use coin, but it made sense. The people of Miera cared not for possessions and wealth; even the headsmen lived simple lives. They ate, drank and slept no differently from those who toiled in the fields. Here, everyone was equal. Some nights the company slept in inns, whereas others would lay beneath the sea of stars. Though they spared none of the foreigners from snide jokes about their horsemanship, the ever-suspicious Mierans watched the foreigners warily. By the third day, Elise couldn't help but groan when she slid from her horse. She had rarely ridden before Miera, and her body ached from saddle soreness.

Danavir grinned as he saw her wince. "It gets easier," he told her with a chuckle.

"Does it?" Elise grimaced as she stretched.

"In time."

One of the Mierans took out a tinderbox and used a flint to spark a flame to life. The fire rose as the orange light of the setting sun washed across the land. The flames danced angrily in the northern wind. Elise rolled her shoulders back and stretched her arms skyward. Slowly, her muscles began to relax and ease. Steel grated as Danavir began to run a whetstone down the length of his longsword.

"Elise," Tariq called.

Elise glanced at her friend just in time to catch the palm-sized rock that he threw. She snatched it out of the air without so much as a blink. Tariq gave her a wink and tossed another. Elise grinned as she caught it, knowing full well that a third was on its way. She flicked her wrist and tossed one of the stones before grabbing the third out of the air. She moved on instinct as, one by one, she sent the stones to dance in the air. Her eyes flicked this way and that as she juggled them. The grin never left her face and the Mierans began to take notice. She relaxed into the art. Her breathing was steady, her movement lithe and her mind still. Without a word, she sent them back one after the other to Tariq. Her friend caught the stones and exchanged a grin with her. Elise saw the glint in his eyes and knew that they shared the same thought. In a single graceful movement, Elise pulled a pair of knives from her boots and a third from her belt. One after the other, she sent them skyward. The light of the flames caressed the steel as they sliced through the air. Elise danced and turned as she juggled the blades. Always moving; that was what she had been taught. One needed to capture the crowd.

"Tariq," Elise called to her friend as she juggled.

He rose to his feet and moved to stand opposite, a trio of knives in his hand. He began to match his movements to Elise's and let his blades float through the sky. Their movements and that of the spinning knives became synchronised. An unspoken agreement passed between them. The knives followed. The silver of the blades flickered in the light of the setting sun as they flew between the pair. Elise and Tariq moved in perfect unison. They had been together since the day Elise had been born and shared a greater bond than fellow performers. They were family. It was here in this trance that Elise felt most alive. Circus and carnival were as much a part of her as her own flesh and blood. They were her true loves. As one, Elise and Tariq stopped sending the blades across the space between. As one, they began to work alone. As one, they caught their first two knives with a single hand. As one, they spun and caught the third. They bowed low. They bowed theatrically. Elise grinned as she rose; it had been far too long since she had danced with knives. The small audience applauded. Even the horsemen of the steppe broke their Mieran reserve and showed their appreciation.

"Do you not fear the knives?" Luana asked as Elise returned to the company.

"No." Elise shook her head as she replied. "You sense them … You know where they will be and then you catch them. There is no room for fear."

"Where did you learn that?"

Elise sat by the fire. "My parents taught me long ago." A knife danced through her fingers. "I was born and raised into a life of circus and carnival. Tariq was my father's closest friend and part of our troupe."

Danavir glanced up from his sword with a slight frown upon his brow. "What is a circus?" the Mieran asked.

"You don't know?" Elise countered incredulously.

Danavir shrugged. "I am Mieran," he said simply. "I know how to ride and fight, how to bind wounds and how to keep clean so I don't get sick. I know how to make horseshoes and repair armour. That is to be Mieran. We do not throw knives like that."

"Juggle," Elise corrected him.

"Juggle," Danavir agreed slowly as if were the first time that he had said the word. He probably hadn't heard of it before either.

"A circus is ..." Elise paused as she looked for the right words. "Imagine a crowd watching on as performers act before them. Colourful masks and costumes, knives and horses, dancing and clowning, acrobatics, even illusion and tricks. Every skill is used to draw the eye, every tool used in a way to captivate the crowd. The cheers, the roars ... the silence. I can see it all now."

"For a few moments, you are more than just you," Tariq added. "It truly is glorious."

The Mierans exchanged humorous glances and chuckles as if it were all some kind of joke.

"You outlanders and your games," Danavir said with a smirk. "You amuse me."

"Yes," Elise replied with a hint of sarcasm. "That is the point."

Another of the Mierans nodded to a lone figure not far from the camp. It was the Tariki Calvillo swinging his sword around like a dancer.

"Your friend," the Mieran said. "Every night it is the same. What does he do?"

"It's called tarkaras." Cleander glanced towards Calvillo. "The sword song. A Tariki tradition used for the purpose of turning steel into an extension of the body."

"You know of tarkaras?" Luana asked him.

"I've seen it before," Cleander told her.

"You know it, don't you?" Tariq asked. "And not just the dance. I saw the way you fight ... the way that you move. Like a rhythm; like a song."

"Perhaps I do."

"Then if Calvillo's dance is as useful as you claim, why do you not do it?" Luana inquired.

"I do not draw steel often," Cleander said quietly. "When I do, it is with the intention of using it. When I fight a man, it is always to the death. I will do all in my power to take his life and grant him every chance to deny me. Though I know it, I do not practise the sword song because when I fight a man, I do not want him to know what I can do."

✦ ✦ ✦

Torben stood alone as nightfall blanketed Miera in darkness. He looked to the north towards Carlian. He had only a few days to think of something that would convince King Zoran to raise his army, to convince a man who *hated* all outsiders to join them.

"What is it?" Luana's voice called as she approached.

"It's out there," Torben replied as she joined him. "Carlian. Three days away, and yet now I find that I do not have any time."

"What do you seek?"

"I seek words," Torben said. "Words that will convince a king about all of this."

Luana followed his gaze across the rolling plain.

"When Cillian Teague returned from the south, he did so with stories. Stories so incredible, so outlandish, that they could not possibly be true," Luana said. "A white mist that blanketed the air and sea like snow. Songs washed across the deck like waves, voices so beautiful that they could possess a man's soul so that he would be willing to die for them. They called to the sailors, spoke their names, and the sailors leapt into the icy waters to their doom. When the ship at last ran aground on an island, those voices spoke in the wind. They called to Teague, summoned him. Enchanted, he pursued the melody into a cave, a rare chasm that ran deep into the rocky ground. The maze was long and dark, yet Teague would not be turned away. Find the voices he did — and the bearers of them. A cavern stretched long beneath the earth filled with waters as clear as a summer sky. And then he saw them."

"Saw what?" Torben asked.

"The sirens that sung his name. Creatures so beautiful, so wild, that they claimed the sailor's soul. A great destiny, they told him, a destiny that even in that moment was unfurling before him. They spoke of victory. They spoke of greatness. It was this story, this tale, that Teague used to convince men to follow him. The siren's promise of freedom drove people to his cause."

"And is it true?" Torben looked to Luana.

"What difference does it make?" she replied. "All of us are here for a reason. Some want peace, others liberty. Some want to repel all outsiders. If it is the sirens that brought us together, then I bless them. There is truth to the tale; of that, I am sure. All the best stories have an element of truth and memory. For what is a man but the sum of his memories? The stories and tales that we live and tell ourselves. The sirens and their song have become a symbol of freedom. And so I am decided that the sirens can have me so long as they don't stop singing."

"Memories, aye," Torben murmured. "They weave together like a story, like the fates."

"You believe in your god, yes?"

"Aye."

"Then tell me this: What is a god if not a symbol?"

"The Sea-Father spins a great web of destiny," Torben replied with a frown. "He is—"

"A symbol to your people. A name … a story that you tell yourselves," Luana interrupted. "I do not mean to offend, merely explain. When one can learn to understand the meaning of a name or symbol, *that* is power."

"The Jade Queen," Torben said.

"Yes," came the reply. "Luana Marquez is a Medean name. Luana Marquez does *not* command respect or fear. A woman's name spoken to old seafarers and veteran warriors will be greeted with nothing but mockery and scorn. I had plans above my station and so I forged this name for myself. Where Luana Marquez was forced to fight for every morsel, every scrap and every prize, the Jade Queen could take a ship without so much as drawing a sword. Do you know why? Because I cultivated the name. I built it through blood and with each passing day added to the story. The Emeralis is feared through the entire breadth of the Sacasian Sea. Men flee before my sails and kings fear them. *That* is greatness. That is the power of a name, of a symbol. If you are to succeed in this undertaking, then that is what you must do now."

"I do not know where to start."

"Then go back. Back to the beginning," Luana said. "Find a symbol. Find your own siren. Find something to unite those of different creeds and cultures behind a single banner. The Mierans are not like us; they are not beholden to great tales of heroism and courage. Don't tell them of ships and fantastical adventures. Tell them a simple story with a simple symbol. Astrid – what was her image?"

"A raven."

Luana placed a hand on Torben's shoulder and met his eyes. "Sing them the song of the raven."

✦ ✦ ✦

Tristayn Martyn stared out from the ramparts of the marching fort, his eyes sweeping the trees that wrapped the camp in a tight embrace. The air was still, and the blackness of night shrouded all within its arms. The Annoran army, together with Anejo Reyna and Santiago Caspin, had crossed the border into Salvaar days ago. With every village, every farm, every shack that they found, it was the same story. No people, no food, nothing. It was as if the Salvaari had vanished into the trees like ghosts.

"Where do you think they are?" Lord Balderik asked as he joined Tristayn on the rampart.

"Their scouts will have warned of our approach, I am sure,"

Tristayn replied. "They will have slipped away into the interior rather than stand and fight. Home and farms can be rebuilt; lives cannot be replaced so easily. They will be out there somewhere in the darkness. But behind these walls, they cannot touch us."

"Devil ghosts," Balderik growled. "They flee to the east rather than facing us in the field. They know that they cannot defeat our army in open battle and so they retreat before us. Day by day, we drive deeper into Salvaar. Further from the border. Further from our country. I do not like this."

"Nor do I, lord," Tristayn replied. "But here they have the advantage. The Salvaari can outlast us if we do not lure them into battle. We have no choice if we are to win this war."

"I pray that the king returns soon," Balderik said.

Tristayn could only agree. Before Dayne's departure, relations between the Annoran and Caspin camps had been bad. Now they were at breaking point. Not a day went by where harsh words didn't turn into violent actions. Fights often broke out between both nations and Santiago did little to quell the growing anger. The two camps were forced to remain separate by their officers to slow the burn. So it was left to Tristayn, Balderik and Lord Galan to ease tensions and prevent bloodshed. Thus far, it had worked, yet only the gods knew how long the fragile peace would hold. If King Dayne returned with Queen Sofia, then perhaps they could put an end to the fighting.

The wooden rampart echoed as a soldier ran towards the commanders.

"Lord Balderik, General Tristayn." The soldier offered a bow. His face was pale and he chewed the inside of his lip.

"What is it, soldier?" he asked.

"It's Lord Galan, sir," came the reply. "He was attacked."

Tristayn and Balderik followed the soldier down into the camp and made haste towards the Lord of Torosa's tent. Annoran soldiers gathered in the rows between the neat columns of tents. They all wore sorrowful expressions. With each passing step, Tristayn felt the horror in his heart grow. After Dayne, it was Balderik and Galan who ruled Annora. It was the high lords who helped hold the nation together. Galan of Torosa had always been like a brother to the Raynor family; his own daughter had once been pledged to Prince Lukas. Tristayn shoved his way through the ranks of soldiers and pushed his way past the Torosi guard. He pushed back the tent flap and walked inside. Balderik was a mere half step behind Tristayn and nearly crashed into him when the general stopped abruptly. The large bedroll and thick blankets lay undisturbed. Lord Galan lay within. The pillows beneath his head were blood soaked – his throat had been torn open. His eyes stared emptily towards the sky. His chest was still. Blood covered his shirt and blankets, and a dagger was driven so deep into his heart that only its hilt was visible. Tristayn approached the bed and knelt beside Galan's body. He closed the lord's eyes with a gentle hand.

"They cut his throat to stop his shout and then stilled his life with a blow to the heart," Tristayn muttered.

"Murder," Balderik cursed.

"Whoever it was, they knew what they were doing," the general replied. "The guards saw no one and the killer made not a sound. Each blow was precise."

"They left the weapon."

"Perhaps the killer got spooked," Tristayn said as he reached for the dagger. He gently pulled it free before continuing. "Medean make. The message is clear. An eye for an eye. Galan's life is payment for Aquale's."

Balderik closed his eyes and let out a long breath. "We can't stop this now," he said.

A contingent of Annoran knights gathered around Tristayn as he strode through the camp once more. His sorrow had been replaced by a burning anger. His people had not been responsible for the death of Aquale Caspin and yet the Medeans had seen fit to murder Galan in his sleep. Tristayn crossed into the Caspin encampment and made straight for Santiago's command tent. Green-clad soldiers stopped and stared as the Annorans marched through their midst. Tristayn ignored every call that came his way, his hand tightly clutching the bloody knife that had taken Galan's life. The bloody *Medean* knife. Alerted by the disturbance, Rodrigo Santana and a number of Caspin guards appeared between Tristayn and Santiago's tent. Caspin shields formed a wall before them. Tristayn tried to shove his way through, but the soldiers blocked him with their shields.

The general met Rodrigo's eyes. "Let us through," he commanded. "You know who I am."

"I know who you are," Rodrigo shot back.

Tristayn's glare hardened as he stepped closer to the Caspin general. "I want to speak to your duke. Now, get out of the way," the Annoran growled before gently placing his hand upon the hilt of his sword. "If you do not move, then I will water the ground with your blood."

Rodrigo glared back, silent. Tristayn sneered and shook his head before he pushed through. He came face to face with Santiago Caspin.

"General," Santiago greeted the man coldly.

"This belongs to you." Tristayn cast the bloody knife before the duke's feet. "We found it in Lord Galan's heart. This eye for an eye ends now. Make amends, Duke Santiago. Make amends *before* King Dayne returns. You have been warned."

With that, Tristayn turned and pushed his way back through the Caspin soldiers. He could feel Santiago's eyes on his back and knew in his heart that Galan's death would not be the last.

✦ ✦ ✦

TWENTY-NINE

The fort gates were opened during the night to allow the steady stream of fleeing soldiers to reach safety. The garrison that had remained lined the ramparts with bows and crossbows and watched the trees with wary eyes and bated breath. They heard the screams of their comrades as the Salvaari routed them in the woods. Sir William Peyene gathered two hundred of the knights and formed a guard not far into the tree line. The men of the Order formed a wall of steel with archers standing behind them, ready to unleash hell. Kyler and Alarik joined them upon their return. Blood covered their swords and armour, their bodies were battered and weary, yet still they joined the wall. They repelled countless Salvaari attacks through the night and held their ground to protect the stragglers of their once-great army. Corvo Alaine gathered up a company of mounted knights and swept through the forest to find and save whoever they could. It was only when the sun began to rise that the men of the shield wall marched back to the fort. They let their guard down only when the sturdy gates closed behind them.

Kyler strode angrily back through the rows of neat tents. His shoulder ached though he could not remember being struck. His rage forced back the exhaustion that he felt. He tossed his bloody sword to the ground with a snarl and tore at the straps of his shield.

He cast it aside before he pulled his helmet from his head. Steel rang as it hit the earth. Kyler held his head in his hands as he fought back flashes of what happened. Fury boiled within him.

They had lost. Thousands of western soldiers lay dead beneath the trees. His head seared with pain and as Kyler reached for his temples he staggered into a tethering post. He gritted his teeth and with a groan rolled his aching shoulder back and clamped his hand down on the injury. His head screamed. With a roar, Kyler drove his armoured fist into a wooden post. The wood rang and pain lanced through his closed fist.

"Pisspot," Alarik called as he approached.

Kyler glanced up as his mentor approached. He fought to compose himself, yet the anger burned bright.

"You fought well today," Alarik continued.

"I fought well?" Kyler growled back. "We were defeated!"

"We live to fight another day."

"Thousands of our brothers are dead."

"And thousands more escaped," Alarik countered. "Because of the grand master's reaction, most of our army is still intact. We still have strength, strength enough to defeat our enemies. The Fiodine tells us that we must show no mercy to those heathens and non-believers. The gods have a purpose for all. Every victory, every defeat. The gods work in mysterious ways. Ask yourself: Do you know their ways?"

"No," Kyler admitted.

"Then have faith," Alarik replied. "We will revenge ourselves on the heathen for this defeat. This is not the end, Pisspot."

"I … I *saw* Durandail's light before we met them in battle," Kyler muttered. "I thought that it was a sign that we would not lose."

"Perhaps it was a sign that he worked through you," Alarik suggested. "You killed a great many warriors. I have fought many wars, Pisspot. I have known victory and I have known defeat.

There will be more battles to come in which we may honour the gods. This war is far from over."

"I swear to you that we will not lose," Kyler vowed.

"Good. Now see yourself to the maija."

"The maija?"

Alarik frowned. "Your face, Pisspot," he said. "You're wounded."

Instead of going to the hospital Kyler made for his own tent. He had not taken a blow to the head during the battle. With each step, his haste grew. What wound? Kyler pushed through the tent flaps and strode inside. He rummaged through his bags and withdrew a small mirror. Kyler examined his face, horror freezing him. It wasn't the sunken cheeks or the bags under his eyes that drove fear into his heart. Patches of skin around his right eye were torn open. It was as if his skin had been ripped apart. Sticky redness formed a brutal ring around his eye that stretched from his nose to his ear. Punches from a gauntlet of plate could have wounded him so and yet he had never been struck, nor was there any bruising. An unnatural union, those had been Lysandra's words.

"Ruskalan blood will destroy its host …" Kyler said quietly as he realised.

He felt his rage and his sorrow grow. Pain. It ripped through his body. He glanced back at the polished glass and saw his eyes shift to crimson red. The mirror dropped from his hand and shattered as it hit the hard earth. He staggered and as he caught himself, his eyes went to the entrance to his tent. He saw the robes of maija. Her back was to him. Long, dark hair spilled down her shoulders and back. She turned. Kyler fell to his knees. He saw her face.

"Elena," he breathed.

Then he saw black.

✦ ✦ ✦

A small pyre had been constructed by the men of Bellec's mercenary company. Annorans and Medeans alike gathered branches and sticks. Kitara, Aeryn, Sakkar and Senya all did their part to help the sellswords. They were all quiet despite the aftermath of the battle. Victory had come at a cost and one of their number lay dead. None of the company had spared a moment to clean themselves of blood and dirt. Their loyalty to their friend came first. Galadayne wrapped Kompton in a cloak and with the aid of his brothers placed the body upon the pyre. Jaimye retrieved the bard's lute from his horse and placed it on Kompton's chest. Kitara watched on sadly as they gathered around the pyre. They said little and shed no tears, but the sorrow for their fallen brother was etched upon every mercenary's face. Kitara had seen Kompton fall. She had seen the knight that had dealt him the mortal blow. It had been a quick and clean death and for that she was grateful. Bellec brought a torch to life and joined the ring of comrades. They stood with their heads bowed and their hands clasped at their waists.

"Kompton of Annora." Bellec said the fallen man's name one last time.

"Kompton of Annora," the mercenaries echoed.

The torch came down and then flames danced. The sellswords stood in silence as the fire burned.

Salvaari of every tribe gathered their own dead and with fire sent them to the Veil. Each clan had their own customs. Some worked in silence, others sang or told stories. All grieved. Henghis and the other chieftains moved through the forest. They spoke to their people and shared in their sorrow. Horsemen had been sent to watch the walled camps of the western armies. For a time at least, they were safe. Kitara used her waterskin to clean her hands and face of dried blood, sweat and dirt.

"It's time," Aeryn murmured from her side.

Kitara glanced up at the moonseer. "For what?"

Aeryn gently touched the arm rings on Kitara's wrist. "To say goodbye."

"Here?"

"Here. This is Káli land. This is a field of victory and Yorath's sun is burning high above," she replied. "There is no better place but here, no better time but now."

Kitara followed Aeryn through the trees until they were alone. Together they dug a hole deep into the earth. One by one, Kitara pulled the rings from her arm and lowered them within. Morlag's ring. Sereia's ring. Kitara remembered the girl's face. She remembered her smile and the light that Sereia brought to the world.

"If you have words," Aeryn said quietly, "now is the time."

A tear rolled down Kitara's cheek as she spoke. This would truly be goodbye.

"Rest easy now, my friends. My brothers. My sisters. Drift deeper and deeper. The sirens are calling your name."

"We release those who have left this plain into your hands, Tanris," Aeryn softly murmured in Salvaari. "Guide them through the Veil and let them walk into the blessed gardens of the ancestral plain. Let them be free. Let their silver light shine through the sky."

Together they buried the arm rings and stood silently. Kitara blinked back tears. In all the years since she had been forced from Lamrei, she had never let anyone in. She had not trusted nor held anyone to heart. Aeryn had been the first to find a crack in her walls. Sereia had been the second. Aeryn gently linked her fingers through Kitara's and pulled her into a hug. They held each other close and tight. For a moment, there was nothing outside of the embrace.

Time passed and funeral fires burned. Kitara was grinding out chinks in her sword with a whetstone when they appeared. There were four of them, each clad in the same dark, gnarled robes. Black eyes peered out from within their deep hoods and runes and scars covered their skin. The druids had come. Kitara had seen them in the battle, chanting as they stalked through the chaos. Their wicked blades had slain many westerners, some in battle, some as sacrifices.

Kitara and Aeryn rose as the druids approached.

"The spirits have spoken to us your name," one of the spirit callers said to Kitara in a hushed voice. "And so now you must come with us."

Kitara sheathed her blade. "Alright," she told them.

"I'm coming too," Aeryn said.

"It was not your name spoken, daughter of the moon," the druid replied.

Aeryn stepped towards them with a retort upon her lips, but Kitara stopped her by wrapping her hand around Aeryn's wrist.

"They can tell me about my mother," Kitara told her. "I have to do this myself."

Aeryn grimaced and, with a nod, stepped back.

"Come." The druid beckoned to Kitara.

Kitara did as she was bid and followed the druids through the forest. They led her to a place where the sun did not breach the canopy, a place where the only sounds were the whispering of the wind and the song of ravens. There were dozens of druids gathered in a circle. A chill ran down Kitara's spine as she was led into the centre of the gathering. Her hand rested lightly upon the hilt of her sword and her gaze flicked from face to face. Runes were carved upon the earth.

"What do you want with me?" Kitara asked them.

"The spirits have heard your call, outcast," one of them spoke.

"What call?"

"They hear all," another druid said. "They see all."

"You wish to know who you are," called a third.

"Yes," Kitara replied.

"Good," said the druid who had led her. "Then let us begin."

"Tell me about my mother."

"Never before has the Great Queen chosen a mortal man to father her child. It was not Oriana who chose him, for she was but a vessel. It was the First Woman, the Great Queen, the moon, the mother. A great prophecy was written that night, one that is carved across the stars."

"One that only the spirits can read," another druid continued. "One that they speak to us in the blackest night."

"The eyes of Tanris have opened," called another.

"The eyes of Tanris have opened," said another.

"The eyes of Tanris have opened," echoed another.

"The revenge will be upon us on the day that the eyes of Tanris slay the cursed blood."

"What does that have to do with me?" Kitara asked them as she turned from voice to voice.

"Ask yourself this, outcast: What do you know of Tanris?" one of the druid's replied.

"He is the Dark One, second child to Sylvaine and Lord of the Veil," Kitara answered.

"What do you know of his history?"

Kitara thought back to what Aeryn had told her, about what she had overheard from other Salvaari.

"I know that he was once taken by the Dark Ones. That he was tortured and enslaved," she told the druids. "That he gave an eye to acquire the power to free himself. The power of sight."

"Yes, good," a druid called. "Tanris gave his left eye. In return, the vision of the Veil became his. He escaped his black prison and slaughtered those who had so condemned him."

"Yes, I have heard that before," Kitara told them.

"Your story is one of many thousands, one of great tragedy, yet it is not the first time that it has been sung. Time repeats itself and your song is one that has echoed through eternity," a druid called.

"What are you saying?" Kitara said.

"Look to your eye, outcast, look to the mark bestowed upon you."

Hesitantly, Kitara raised her hand. Her fingers ran along her smooth skin before crossing the thick scar that was carved through the left side of her face. A mark that ran from brow to cheek, broken only by her eye. Her *left* eye.

"There has to be some other explanation," Kitara growled. "Until recently, I did not even believe in the spirits. Now you tell me what exactly? That somehow, someway, I am linked to Tanris?"

"Even when you were across the sea you were an outcast. You were betrayed and captured, enslaved, marked and tortured. Your story, your song, your life was wreathed in darkness. A darkness not of your making, but one that made you strong."

"Like the Dark One, you are a child to Sylvaine," cried another druid. "And like he, there is power flowing through your veins."

"The sight," Kitara murmured.

"Exactly," came the reply. "Why do you think you were chosen many months ago to witness the changing ritual? Why do you think that the Great Queen spoke those words to you alone? Do you remember them?"

Kitara thought back to the time she had witnessed Sylvaine changing hosts. "Yes, I remember," she said softly.

I am sorry my child. Those had been Sylvaine's words.

"You are a child of fate," a druid continued. "A child of prophecy. Your destiny has been written, yet like the sea, it can flow anywhere. Your choices, your decisions, can change it. Sylvaine has granted you that gift."

"Know this, outcast," called one of the spirit callers. "You are Sylvaine's daughter, just as you are the eyes of Tanris, the Dark One's gaze, death's visage. The spirits favour you. However, that favour can be taken away at any moment."

A cold wind howled, and ravens cried out. There was a fluttering of wings and a storm of black feathers. The song of the wind vanished. The druids did not move. There was silence. Kitara felt a presence behind her. She turned to see a flame-haired Icari woman. A woman who held a gnarled staff. A woman with violet eyes.

"Sylvaine," Kitara murmured.

The Great Queen slammed the butt of her staff into the ground. Her eyes blazed with light. Shadows swam around the pair. The druids vanished and the forest changed. Kitara's gaze shifted to purple. They were alone. Kitara looked all around. The forest was dark and wreathed in an aura of power. Tall stones covered in runes surrounded them.

"Where are we?" Kitara asked.

"The Veil," Sylvaine replied.

Kitara looked her up and down. She took her mother in. Sylvaine looked just like any other woman. She did not appear as an immortal spirit. Kitara felt her emotions stir. Grief for a life she did not have. Confusion on what to think. Doubt. Even fear.

"Mother," Kitara said softy as she fought to compose herself. "I never thought I would ever get to say that word."

"You are much more than my daughter," Sylvaine replied.

"I know that I am the eyes of Tanris."

"No," the Great Queen said. "You are Kitara and that is the end of it."

"I wish that you had told me who you were that day in the grove."

"I could not," Sylvaine replied. "I am sorry that you were alone. I was not there for you."

Kitara gritted her teeth. Anger, rage, pain, sorrow, joy. They all flowed through her like a river. For years she had hated her father and blamed her parents for leaving her alone. Now she learnt that her father was alive, that her *mother* was alive.

"I was angry at first. At you, at Father, at the world. Angry for being abandoned. A part of me still is and a part of me always will be," Kitara admitted. "And yet I am glad that you were never there to help me. I learnt to pick myself back up. I learnt to become strong."

"We haven't much time," Sylvaine told Kitara as she stepped forward and placed two fingers on her daughter's face next to her eye. "Your eyes are a gift. Use them; do not fear them. You believe your path to be a terrible one, but know this, my daughter: there is more than one path to the top of the mountain. It is a road less travelled, a road that will not always take you where you wish to go. You are strong and wise, led by your head and not your heart. Look inside yourself. There is a source of strength that will always spring forth if you but look. Fate does not lie in the stars; it lies within you. Whichever way your story goes, know that I stand with you."

Ravens cried all around them. Sylvaine stepped back.

"If we never meet again, know that I love you."

"Mother, I–"

Shadows flickered, the Great Queen's eyes blazed and then Kitara was standing back in the forest. The druids were gone. The purple of Kitara's eyes changed back to emerald green. Her heart raced and her breath was shaking. They had barely exchanged a handful of words and yet they had meant everything to Kitara. Perhaps she was not as alone as she had once thought. Kitara took a long breath and stilled her racing heart. She began to walk back towards the Salvaari. Towards her people.

✦ ✦ ✦

THIRTY

Your friends in the north are dead already.

Those were Lukas' words, the last he had spoken. It had been a trap, just as Dayne had thought it to be, and yet he had been given no choice but to ride straight into it. Whatever form that trap took, it had been for the armies in the north. It had taken a great deal of restraint for King Dayne not to ride ahead with his heavy cavalry and charge into whatever hell awaited the Annorans. He did not know how many men Lukas had with him; there was a chance that if he left his infantry, then they would be dead by sundown. They marched westward along the Arwan River for a day before crossing into the forest. This time, Dayne did not send Sofia away. If the Salvaari had captured her once, then they could do so again. He was blind to the resentment that the pagans held for her. If they captured her, then there was no way of knowing if this time they would spare her. She rode at Dayne's side surrounded by a company of scarlet-clad royal guardsmen. A rider broke through the ring of guardsmen and made for Dayne.

"My lord king," the knight bowed.

"What is it?"

"The village is empty."

Dayne frowned and looked to one of the guardsmen. "Captain Bronimir, stay with the queen," he commanded.

"Yes, my king," the guard replied.

Dayne kicked his heels in and left the circle of royal guard. Half of the protectors remained with Sofia, the rest rode after their king. Dayne lowered his visor as they closed in on the Salvaari village. Annoran soldiers on foot and horseback flooded the streets of the pagan town. They made their way through houses and hovels as they searched for any sign of life. There was none. Dayne pushed his visor back up and dismounted. His hand rested gently upon his eagle sword. Without a word, the guard joined him on foot. He scanned the surrounds. There was no sign of food or livestock nor trace of any warriors. His eyes were drawn to a trough of water. Dayne stared at the liquid gently lapping at the edges of the trough. He could not help but feel that the air they breathed was as deadly as any pagan spear or arrow.

"Tell the men to not touch anything," Dayne commanded. "We are in the land of the Káli now. Treat everything as poison."

"My king." One of the guards saluted before hurrying off to give the order.

"A village of ghosts," murmured another of the soldiers.

"They will have fled to the interior," Dayne replied. "The Salvaari are spread thin and had no way of protecting all their towns and villages."

"Lord king," a rider called out as he and a company of knights approached. "We found this planted in the earth before the chieftain's hall."

The knight extended a standard. The banner was ivory white with a great red eagle flying upon the silk. Dayne took the flag from the knight.

"Tristayn was here," he told his people. "We are not far behind them. Sir Medina, take a company of riders north and find the general."

"Yes, my king."

"We need to find them before they walk into whatever hell

awaits," Dayne continued. "We have a few hours of sunlight left and we must use them. The sooner we find our people, the sooner we can win the war."

✦ ✦ ✦

Bavarian Delrovira awoke. His body was cold and his breath was mist. The chains that bound his wrists dug deep into his flesh. His arms hung from above, for they were tied to the very top of the stake against which he sat. The hard earth beneath offered no comfort and he had been stripped of his armour. The thin tunic and trousers offered no protection against the biting chill of the wind. Bavarian was alone, surrounded by nothing but trees and darkness. His amulet had been torn from his throat.

"Azaria, Silver Lady. Durandail, Father of all Fathers, hear me now. Protect me onwards through the night. I do not pray for strength, for you have shown me the strength within." Bavarian saw shadows flicker in the woods but he did not stop speaking. "I do not pray for courage, for I followed you willingly into battle." He heard a rustle upon the ground from behind. Bavarian's skin crawled. "If the pale rider and his steed of pure white summon me this night, then I am ready. I will leave this life gladly, knowing that death rides for the last of the devil incarnate. Deliver me, lords, from mine enemy."

"Your gods can't hear you, human." The smooth ruskalan voice sliced the air like steel.

"They can hear us all. They are a part of us all."

"You are misguided."

"Who are you?"

"I am the demon that stalks you day and night," the dark-clad ruskalan replied as he walked before the chained grand master. "I am the blood of Tanris. I am ruskalan."

"How is this possible?" Bavarian growled. "Nothing remained of the ruskalan but ghosts."

"The ruskalan are not dead," came the reply through bared fangs. "I am still here. Harkan the Firstborn. Son of the Dark One. First of the ruskalan. An echo of the ashes."

"After the last war, it was believed that you fell along with the rest of your wretched kind."

"That purge nearly destroyed us all," Harkan snarled as his eyes flashed. "All of the elves, all of the ruskalan. I was there when they burned. I can still feel the heat of the fire on my face even now. Fortunately, there were some who survived your cruelty."

Bavarian snorted. "*Our cruelty*?" he shot back. "It was your cruelty, your malice and your lust for power that started that war and plunged Medea into chaos. It was the machinations of the ruskalan that led to sundered villages, rivers of blood and fields of raging fire. Corruption, deceit, murder ... Your *people* did that."

Harkan crouched before Bavarian and watched him coldly. "You've been lied to," he said.

"No." Bavarian shook his head but did not tear his gaze from those red eyes. "My lord Durandail knows who you are. What you are. He is the god of my salvation, the lord of truth. He sent us his Spear for a reason. He chose us to end your savage kind. The Spear shows the truth, and you are anything but."

Harkan looked amused. "Brave words spoken from a heretic," the ruskalan replied.

"Heretic?" Bavarian said with a mirthless chuckle.

"You have seen the Spear of Yorath and felt its power," Harkan told him. "You believe the blade to be your own, yet hundreds of years ago heretics stole *our* weapons. They claimed that those same artefacts were gifts for *their* gods. No. I was there when they were made."

"Your words are poison."

"No more than the lies you've been told, human. You call us

pagan, yet it is you who worships false idols. You pray to the sun, to the moon, to death – the triple gods of your faith, but they were never your own. Your kind just claimed them as your own. You say that Durandail is a great warrior, the father of truth and justice. Tell me this, human: What makes him so very different from Yorath the warlord?"

"Durandail is true. He is the sun. He is the light," Bavarian countered.

"Just as Yorath is," Harkan told him. "You worship the one you call Azaria. She is wisdom, she is knowledge, she is a healer, she is the moon. A wretched, deformed lie. No more than an illusion of the truth. A lie created by your ancestors when they cast the Great Queen Sylvaine aside."

"I see through your lies and manipulations," Bavarian growled savagely. "Every word you speak, every tale you tell, bears no more truth than a dawn without the sun. You are a curse upon this land."

"Death. Your Pale Horseman. What makes him so different from Tanris? What makes you so sure that your god is real?"

"Yes, we worship the triple gods. We worship the true gods. Yet do not mistake them for those dark spectres that you conjure. You have many spirits, but I have faith."

"It is true that there is a great pantheon of spirits that live in all things. The fates unfurl as they so deem. Deny the truth if you will, human. Deny Sylvaine, Yorath and Tanris. Deny that your forefathers came from these very woods. Deny that they stole not only our weapons but our faith as well. Your whole life, the lives of your brothers and sisters, the lives of all your people have been spent worshipping those very same things that you hate. If I am pagan, if I am heathen, what does that make you?"

"You cannot corrupt my faith with your lies. I am not afraid to die for the gods in whom I trust. I am a knight, and I will die a knight. If my time has come, then I am ready. The gods, the order, the Spear ... They will be your undoing."

Harkan spread his arms wide. "Why should I fear the artefact that I commanded you to find?"

"My master Evalio Delrovira–"

"Was no more than my puppet upon his deathbed," Harkan snarled. "The right poison given at the right time. Words delivered by the right person and one can pull the strings of even the strongest of minds. Your Order found the Spear, yet they found only what I wanted to be found. Your people stole it centuries ago and we want it back."

"It was you, wasn't it?" Bavarian asked. "You sent the one they call Wa'rith to try and claim it."

"Yes!" Harkan exclaimed. "Very good, human. It was I who sent the fallen knight to reclaim what was ours, although he did not know for whom he did his bidding. He believed that his journey was one solely of his own making. No. I have eyes everywhere. I manipulated the events surrounding him so that he could track your knights to that cave. He did not know that it was I who fed him information."

"Unfortunate then that he failed," Bavarian replied with a smirk.

"Unfortunate, yes," Harkan told him. "However, all things change like the wind. This is a plan long in the making, human. Nothing has changed."

"What do you mean?"

"For a hundred years, we prepared," Harkan said darkly as he began to circle the post. "While you rested in your citadels, we grew stronger. While you believed that you were protected, we sired children with the humans and trained them. We filled their hearts with hate for your kind, and when they were ready, we sent them out into the west. They secreted themselves in every court and palace – even within the walls of Rovira itself. They earned your trust, yet you were deceived. In time, they sired children of their own who, like them, appear as human as you. They bear our blood and carry the same hatred in their veins. They continued what their sires began time and time again for a hundred years. The half-bloods created a web in the shadows with strands reaching so far that none who they command know of the masters that they serve. Everything that you see around you, everything that has happened since before your master died, bears the mark of Harkan. I sent you upon your quest for Yorath's Spear. Wicked men plagued your valley, and you thought them no more than that, but they were my messengers tasked with spreading anger and disloyalty to your order. When the silver amulet was torn from the throat of one and sent to my blood within the walls of Kilgareth, it was a message. Our time had come."

"There is a traitor then."

"The blood of my blood controls your citadel. You know of whom I speak. She is first among scholars and wears the robe of a healer."

"Lysandra," Bavarian murmured with growing horror. "If Lysandra is with you, then you know everything that we think, everything that we have thought."

"It is through her that I learnt of the queen's journey from Kilgareth to Verena. It is through her that I was able to gain the knowledge that would separate Annora from her allies by such a distance that reinforcement would be impossible. It is she who communes with Wa'rith. It is she who informed me of your progress locating the Spear."

"Lysandra was not part of that company," Bavarian replied.

"No," Harkan countered. "But there was another."

"You were not there."

"No. I was here among the sacred trees. I belong in the undying forest. Here I can hear all. Here I can see all. Humans pass word along my web, and when it reaches my kind, they commune through their blood," Harkan told him with a growl. "I used a wanderer and his tricks to start a war among the tribes. With his death and in the chaos that followed, I united the scattered Salvaari behind their greatest leader. I marshalled *your* armies and sent them east. It was I who toppled your emperor and set you upon your fate."

Bavarian felt icy dread seep into his heart. He had been taught long ago about the lies and manipulations of the ruskalan. They were said to be the schemers of the old world, while the elves were the warriors. It was the ruskalan that had started the war then, and if Harkan now spoke the truth, so it was again.

"You killed King Dorian."

"We did not kill Dorian Raynor, nor did we play any role in his death," Harkan replied. "If Darius alone had been murdered inside the walls of Palen-Tor then the alliance would have fallen that day. The griffin would have been at the eagle's throat. No, human, the death of the eagle came at the hands of the viper. While the Medean lord seeks Annora's crown, it is one caught within my web who even now works to destroy that fragile peace. The word of man is easily broken. Soon the eagle and the viper shall fall. It had already begun. When King Dayne was lured from the great army, it was by my will."

"You have ensnared Lukas Raynor."

"Yes."

"Durandail shall guide him back into the light."

"No." Harkan continued to circle. "He is my messenger. He is the wind. He is the Whisperer. I turned brother against brother to sunder a kingdom."

"If any of what you say is true, it does not matter," Bavarian told him. "The armies of faith will not be broken. The gods guide them. They will find you. This time they will not fail. They will defeat you and drive your savage kind back into the darkness from whence they came."

"Perhaps you mistake my intent," Harkan called. "The ghosts of those slain in the last war cry out for justice. Everything that I do, everything that I *am*, is to avenge them. This goes beyond

Salvaar. Beyond Medea and the silver empire. Your heresy, your faith, your gods: that is what I will destroy. This war in the north is merely one part of this game. The shadows grow with each passing day, and I command them. I am their master. I killed the Valkir raven for wanting peace and directed her people's fury towards the empire. I placed a warrior upon the throne, a warrior whose soul has become an empty vessel that only Aureian blood can fill. There will be peace in the sea but only after the tides run red with blood. It was I who sent the great Cillian Teague south to discover his fate. It was I who set him upon his path. It was I who gathered the right people around him at the right time. His war with the League was begun by my hands. I stoked the fires in Elara. I am the one who burned it. In time, they shall sail east and crush the dread fleet that has assembled.

"But that is not all. The horsemen shall muster. They will ride out to meet you. The walls of your citadels shall fall. Your banners will burn. The world will never know that your order existed at all. I will erase the memory of your gods from the histories. Every priest, every book, every scrap of parchment shall burn. Your armies will bleed, and your nations will sunder. We will reclaim the land that you stole from us, and your people will beg for death before the end. I can hear the screams of the dead in the wind. All those souls lost at the hands of your order. Those you drove from Medea, those whom you purged. The Salvaari. The elves. *My* people. I will avenge them. This is your reckoning. This is your judgement. You were deceived and now your order shall fall."

Bavarian leaned back to look Harkan in the eye. As he met the red gaze of the demon, a chill trickled down the back of his neck. Fear froze his blood, chilled his heart, threatened to consume him.

"Everything that I fought for, everything that I believed, all of it was a lie," Bavarian murmured.

"And now you have been destroyed by it."

Bavarian Delrovira, grand master of the southern order of Kil'kara, glared into the red pits of Harkan's eyes.

"You can break my body. You can take my life. But you *cannot* corrupt my faith," he snarled with all the pride that he could manage. "You brought us here, you did not, what does it matter? My people, my brothers, will fight. They will fight and keep on fighting. Durandail watches over us. Azaria watches over us. Paradise awaits us. Are we afraid of death? Not me. Not any of us. Before our time is done, the Pale Horseman will have his say."

"Tanris already has spoken," Harkan replied. "You can hear his voice in the wind, in the earth, in the water. The Dark One basks in the death cries of ten thousand western souls. Now he comes to me. He whispers your name."

Harkan reached into the depths of his sleeve and withdrew a long knife. From the tip of the blade to the end of its pommel the dagger shone silver. Runes were carved into the metal. The weapon appeared as a sister to the Spear of Durandail. But Bavarian had faith.

"Cuun'etca hěy'læn," he whispered.

Immortality in paradise.

He closed his eyes as the prayer left his lips. His faith was unshakable. Bavarian had felt the warm rays of Durandail's sun. He had known the peace of Azaria's silver moon. They gave him strength and purpose far greater than any fear that he felt. Bavarian felt the terror wash away even as the demon before him moved closer. No matter what Harkan said, he believed in the gods. He believed up until the moment the blade sliced his throat. The grand master was at peace long before his blood watered the earth.

✦ ✦ ✦

THIRTY-ONE

Catuvantuli Lands, Forest of Salvaar

Lukas and his band of Káli moved swiftly through Salvaar. They rode all day, slept on furs at night and then rose before dawn to continue on their way. Scouts had been sent out in every direction, yet none were as important as those who tracked Dayne's army along the border. The Annorans had crossed into Salvaar some time ago and had found the first of the abandoned villages. The orange rays of the setting sun had begun to break through the canopy when Aelida galloped towards the company. Lukas brought his horse to a halt as she approached.

"Lord," Aelida called as she reached him.

"What have you seen?"

"The Eagle's army has just passed Bláithín," the moonseer told him. "The second village that they have found on their way north."

"So my brother is marching to join the rest of his army," Lukas replied with a nod.

"Yes," Aelida said. "They will be no more than a day behind now."

Lukas shared a glance with Rodion who rode at his side.

"If we were to change course and ride north directly, then could we not overtake them and find Henghis?" he asked.

"We could," Rodion said. "The Annorans would join before we reached the chief, but it could be done."

"Then that is what we will do," Lukas decided. "We will rest here tonight. Tomorrow, we ride north."

Rodion clicked his tongue and rode back down the column to give the orders that they were to make camp.

"What of the villages?" Lukas asked Aelida.

"The invaders do not touch anything," the moonseer replied disdainfully and gave a dangerous smirk. "They fear our poison too much for that. Instead, they make camp outside of the villages."

"Dayne will expect a trap," Lukas muttered.

"Yet his men see nothing." Aelida's eyes flashed with amusement.

"Then that is how it shall remain," Lukas replied. "Follow them. Report back to me if anything changes."

"Lord." Aelida bowed her head and placed a fist over her heart before riding back into the forest.

The Káli warband spread out beneath the tall trees and found places to rest in the undergrowth. Scouts were sent to keep watch and no fires were lit. Lukas gritted his teeth as he slid from his saddle. Pain lanced through his knee as it struggled to take his weight. He retrieved his crutch from his saddle and planted it firmly upon the ground to remove much of the tension. He winced as he began to hobble through the woods. His breath came through bared teeth and every step was agony.

"Are you alright, lord?" Hadwin called as he heard Lukas grunt in pain.

"I'm fine," Lukas snapped back as he reached the trunk of a thick tree.

Slowly, he lowered himself and leaned his back on the trunk. Lukas closed his eyes and took a long breath. His hand unconsciously moved to his knee and gently rubbed it. The brace was the only thing that kept the injury from crippling him. He glanced up to see Maevin approaching.

"It's been over two months to the day since Oryn," Lukas murmured as she reached him. "I can still feel the hammer."

"Give it time," Maevin said as she knelt before him.

"It will never fully heal." Lukas looked into her eyes. "Will it?"

"Only the spirits know." She handed over her cup. "Yesterday is a myth. Tomorrow is a prophecy. Today is life. That is Salvaari."

"Yes." Lukas gave her a smile. "Yes, it is."

He reached out a hand and stroked her cheek gently. Maevin stared into Lukas' eyes as she cupped his cheek. She pushed her forehead into his. Lukas smelt Maevin's sweet scent and felt her power. He saw it in her emerald-green gaze. Then she was gone. Lukas raised the cup to his lips and closed his eyes as he drank a mouthful of the brew.

"What's that then?" Layan asked as the mercenaries made their way over.

Lukas frowned as he looked to the Annorans.

"The drink," Layan continued as he motioned to the cup. "When first we met in Miera, there was nothing of the kind, yet now as far back as when you returned from Palen-Tor, you've been drinking it."

"It was not so long ago when that boy Emilian Aloys gave me this," Lukas said as he tapped the brace strapped to his knee. "I thought I'd never walk again … and then Maevin saved me. This brew that she makes takes away the pain."

"It does?" Hadwin asked.

"Look at me," Lukas told him. "What do you see?"

"The man who pays us."

"I am a cripple. A broken man. A reject. As a cripple, I was given pity, but do you know what was worse? Everyone wanting to help me. No. I will not be helpless. I will not be pitied or treated less than a man. This affliction will not destroy me. I will not let it. With the drink I can ride again, I can lead men into battle, I can fight, I can *think*. So I have one eye, so only one leg works: it does not matter. Nothing has changed from when I had both. I do not know if I will ever be able to walk again, yet I am at peace with that. When you find peace, you open yourself up to many possibilities. I will not be weak. I *refuse* to be weak."

✦ ✦ ✦

The walls of the marching fort rose around Dayne's army as the sun began to set. Each day it was the same. The army would rise in the morning to tear down the walls and towers of the small fortress so that the Salvaari could not use it. After that the army would march all day until a few hours before sundown, then they would down their packs and gather up axes and picks. A new camp would arise. Soldiers manned the walls while teams of scouts patrolled the woods around. Sentries, scouts and the soldiers within their tents all felt the same unease. They *all* knew what was out there beyond their walls. Many of them had served in the last war against Salvaar. Many had buried friends in the forest.

King Dayne placed his helmet upon the small table within his tent. His face was beginning to pale. When he looked at the hand that had put his helm aside it was shaking. He could feel his body growing weaker day by day. He closed his eyes and took a breath. His hand curled into a fist as he fought against the trembles.

"Dayne?" Sofia asked as she entered the tent to see him frozen.

The king could hear the worry in his wife's voice. "It will pass," Dayne said calmly.

He felt the congestion rise in the back of his throat. The iron taste of blood filled his mouth. He snatched a handkerchief from the table and lifted it to his lips. The shakes contorted his body, and he doubled over. Dayne could not stop the coughs. Each was more agonising than the last. They came without mercy. It felt as if the dull blade of a rusty knife was being driven through his gut. The only thing keeping him up was his hand planted firmly upon the table. Sofia took his arm and helped brace him.

"Imagine that you're in a field of evergreen," she murmured, holding him tight. "The sky is blue as sapphires and clear as polished glass. The sun shines high above as the morning breeze kisses your skin. You close your eyes and reach out a hand. Someone takes it. Who is it?"

As she spoke, Dayne began to gain control over his body once more. The shakes began to fade, and the pain started to ease. He lowered the handkerchief stained with his blood. He took a breath.

"It's you," Dayne replied.

"Always."

With a grimace, the king extended a hand and placed the handkerchief upon the table. Each move was agony.

"How bad?" Sofia asked.

"Pain is irrelevant," Dayne said.

"There are potions and medicines," she replied. "Things that could help with the pain. You know this, yet you let yourself suffer."

"Those treatments dull the mind. Better it is to suffer than to lose judgement," the king said, turning to face her. "The mind is master of the body, and I am the master of my mind. No sickness will ever change that."

"How do you do it?" Sofia asked after a moment. "Bear so much pain while at the same time fight a battle on two fronts? The Salvaari and within our own camp."

"The illness is a test. Of that I am most certain," Dayne said. "It is a burden that only I can bear, a burden that rests upon my shoulders rather than those of my people. I know pain; I know how to fight it, and I know how to beat it. My people do not know that it was Santiago who killed my father. They do not know that right now dark forces are plotting against them. It is a burden that they should never have to bear. So I am resolved; I will bear it so that they do not have to."

"You don't tell them to save them from what would come if you did?"

"Yes. I do it to save their souls," Dayne replied quietly. "My people and yours are different in so many ways, yet we have come together. We are united by our one faith. We can learn from one another … We can deliver them into something better if this alliance holds. To make the truth known would only bring chaos, calamity and death. The knowledge that Santiago murdered my father would turn words of anger into actions. Nothing could stop that tide once it begins."

"The alliance was already splintering in Verena. When a lord is murdered by the hands of an ally, everything begins to collapse," Sofia said. "Though your people did not kill Lord Aquale, it started us down this new path. This new present in which we find ourselves is held together by only one thing."

"Our marriage," Dayne replied with a chuckle.

Sofia smiled as she poured wine into a pair of cups and handed one to her husband. Dayne took it gratefully and raised it to his lips. The wine temporarily washed away the bloody taste that had become a constant companion.

"In the days to come, we will join with Tristayn and my father," Sofia said. "We have no way of knowing what is waiting for us."

Dayne paused for a moment as he lowered the cup. He met his wife's dark eyes.

"You are surrounded by a pack of wolves. What do you do?" he asked. "Don't run, for you will look like prey and wolves are *hunters*. Don't stare them down, for this will appear as a challenge and a threat. Don't turn your back. Don't show fear and do not fall for those will encourage attack."

"Then what do you do?"

"You must earn their respect," Dayne told her. "Show them strength. Appear as two men, three men, ten. Show them that you are not afraid. Show them that you are the hunter and not the prey. If given the chance to climb, do it. Get beyond their reach and bide your time. Wait out the storm and then act. That is how you survive."

"That is what you are doing now, isn't it?"

Dayne gave her half a smile. He was letting his enemies make their moves, letting them play their hands while he watched. When the storm had passed, it would be his time to act.

"I have something to show you," he said.

The king led his queen to a tent not so far from his own. Sir Garrik's tent. The master of arms and commander of the royal guard was seated by a fire that burned before the tent. With a nod from his king, Garrik rose and led them inside. The prisoner sat on the hard earth with her back pressed tight against a solitary wooden stake. The captive's hands were bound by rope as thick and strong as that which tied her to the post. A gag prevented any sound. The prisoner's clothes were those of an Annoran soldier. Rough boots, trousers, a thick gambeson and a woollen cloak. Dayne pushed the hood back from the captive's face to reveal what lay beneath. Smooth skin, rich dark eyes and raven black hair.

"Eveline?" Sofia murmured as she saw her former friend.

"Yes, I keep her here," Dayne said as he looked down at his father's killer. "Close to my side where I can keep both eyes on her."

"Why not leave her in Verena?" Sofia asked.

"I did not want to risk her escaping," Dayne replied. "She would have friends in Verena, no doubt. The city borders onto your father's lands. Within a day she would be out of reach. If by some miracle she escapes here, she would be dead by daybreak. I trust Sir Garrik to keep her hidden and secured. I did not trust those men who lived so close to Medea."

Sofia glanced from the prisoner to her husband. "Why keep her alive?" she questioned. "She did not give up my father when you asked. She will not do it before a court."

Dayne looked into the prisoner's defiant eyes. "I was hoping that she may change her mind."

Eveline growled beneath her gag. Barely a sound came from her mouth, yet her face was alight with fury.

"She won't," Sofia told him.

"Forgive me, my queen, but how can you be sure?" Sir Garrik asked.

"I have known Eveline for most of my life." Sofia looked down sadly at the bound woman. "She was raised in the same corridors of nobility as I was. She knows how to lie, and she knows how to hold her tongue. Eveline believes in my father. That belief is unwavering. If my father chose her above all others to kill a king, then he did so knowing that if she were caught, she would not speak."

"Then what do you suggest?" Dayne asked.

"We cannot risk her escaping and getting back to my father, nor can we risk her being discovered," Sofia replied. "The fact that she has remained with the camp so long and not been found is a miracle. Miracles don't last."

"The queen is right," Garrik murmured. "She's too big a risk."

Dayne did not take his eyes off the captive. "I know," he said before turning to Sofia. "She's your friend."

The queen bit her lip. Dayne could see the sadness behind her eyes. Sofia squared her jaw. She was strong. She was a *queen*.

"Not since the day she planned to bury a knife in your father's chest," Sofia told them.

Steel rasped as Garrik drew a knife.

"By your order, my king," he said as he looked to Dayne.

The king gave a single nod. Fear flashed across Eveline's eyes as the soldier took a step towards her. She saw no emotion staring back. She had killed Garrik's lord. His brother in arms. His friend. His king. There was no mercy in his heart. Garrik extended the knife.

"Wait," Sofia commanded.

Both men turned to face her. The queen stepped towards Garrik and held out a hand.

"I brought her into your house. Had I not then King Dorian would still be alive. I will do what I must."

"As you wish." Garrik handed her the knife.

Sofia did not look at the steel blade as she crossed the tent towards Eveline. Her eyes were fixed upon the woman who had once been her confidante. A tear ran down Eveline's cheek as the queen knelt before her.

"You betrayed my family, you betrayed your people and you betrayed me," Sofia said.

Eveline recoiled as the cold blade kissed her skin. The queen felt the taste of death when steel met flesh. She remembered the sickness that had killed so many of her people when she had been a child. Sofia was no stranger to death. Eveline struggled at the ropes. She tried to shout and scream, but the gag gave up little more than a croak. Sofia gripped the knife tightly. She did not look away from Eveline's eyes. She would not cower from her duty. The queen took a breath. Sofia carved a line of red across her friend's throat.

✦ ✦ ✦

THIRTY-TWO

Road to Carlian, Steppe of Miera

Hooves thundered upon the ground as the small column of horses galloped north. Manes and tails flew behind like waterfalls of black, brown and ivory. The powerful muscles of the Mieran horses carried them at great speed across the rolling hills and plains of the steppe. The sound of hooves kissing the earth was the sacred heartbeat of Miera. The neighing of horses was the land's lifeblood. The riders were its soul. The fiery orange light of the falling sun shone across the land as day began to turn to night.

"We will reach the city of kings by nightfall tomorrow," Danavir Calin told his companions as he slipped from his saddle. "The information that you brought us is the only reason that you still draw breath. It has gotten you this far, though I suggest that you prepare yourselves. We do not take kindly to outlanders in Miera."

"We will earn your trust yet, horse lord," Torben told him.

The Mieran snorted in disdain and led his steed away. The companions dismounted and brought fires to life. The Mieran horses did not need to be tethered for they would not wander. They stood as still and silent as stone by their masters. When Elise dismounted, she took only her satchel with her. The vast wealth within would see her to a new life and a new beginning. Tariq and Marshall both did the same and kept their bags close to hand. If they were betrayed by the riders, they would lose their horses but not their future.

"One more day in the saddle and then we're at Carlian," Tariq said as he sat beside Elise.

Elise grimaced and glanced at her friend. "Never thought I'd miss walking," she told him.

"Saddle sore?"

"All of me is sore."

"Don't tell me that you have gotten soft," Tariq replied with a grin.

Elise returned the grin. "Never," she said.

"Are you still glad that we came?"

"The choice was removed from my hands." Elise shrugged. "I know that you did not want us to follow Cleander, yet you know what would have happened if we had stayed."

"You say that you had no choice in the matter, but you made a choice."

"I did. I would not have been safe in Vay'kis. I would not have been safe while Bhaltair and men like him exist. I do not care for my own safety. I care for yours. I care for Marshall's. My being in Vay'kis would have put you both in harm's way and that is something that I could not abide. This path leads to a new future. A future far from the shadow of death."

Tariq looked towards Cleander who sat apart from the group. "I don't trust him."

"I know," Elise replied. "And I don't either. I don't trust anyone who isn't us. I am not asking you to trust him. I am asking you to trust me."

"Always."

Elise took his hand and gave it a squeeze. "You and I will always be family," she told him. "Soon it will be just you and me and Marshall. Just as it should be. We will have a home … be able to start anew."

Tariq squeezed her hand back and gave her a sad smile. "You deserve nothing less," he said. "Whatever the cost, I will see you to this future, this promise. Whatever it takes."

"All we have to do is follow Cleander for a few more days."

"And this future into which he leads us," Tariq began, "has he told you what it is? Where it is?"

"Not yet," Elise admitted. "But I think it's probably time that I find out."

Elise rose from her spot and slowly made her way over to the Annoran. Cleander glanced up as she approached yet said nothing.

"Who are you?" Elise asked as she sat beside the man.

"Pardon me?"

"The man who hides his name seeking to be someone he is not. I have lived in Elara my entire life. I grew up in the slums and lower district. I know the pits. I saw men of the gangs every day of my childhood, yet you do not carry yourself as they do. You are an Annoran in hiding who knows how to fight as most know how to breathe. You know the Tariki swordsong and you are a skilled apothecary. Who are you?"

"I'm no one," Cleander said simply.

"I first thought that you may have been of noble birth, yet now I am not so sure," she replied. "A knight, perhaps?"

"A lifetime ago," Cleander told her quietly.

"So you were seeking a new beginning much like I am now," Elise said.

"In a manner of speaking, yes."

"When you spoke of this future into which you now lead us, you did not say where that future was."

"And now you wish to know?"

Elise nodded. "We will go no further with you than Carlian if you do not tell me."

"Very well," Cleander replied with a shrug. "When we are given the chance, we will begin to journey west. There is a place far from here that could shelter all of you. A place where you would all be safe. A place where a pair of Elarans and a Berenithian would cause no questions. Valentia."

"In the empire?" Elise said with raised eyebrows.

"Precisely," Cleander replied. "You know Elara, you know how it works. Valentia is the same. A city of trade and prosperity yet one without the plots and schemes of men such as Imrohir. There you could live out your days in peace."

"You've been there?"

"I have," Cleander answered. "The waters are calm and gentle; the people are happy. Children play along the beach. The magister is both kind and fair. Beloved by his people. It is as good a place as any to start a new chapter of your life."

"Well." Elise smiled. "That doesn't sound so bad."

"No. No, it doesn't."

✦ ✦ ✦

They rose before dawn, stowed their packs and then mounted their horses. Danavir gave a long piercing whistle and then the company began to ride north. They passed forest and town yet never did they stop. Rivers, mountains and gullies filled the plains with life.

To Torben, it all went unseen. He wore his armour and bore his shield across his back; things that would usually give him comfort, but now his mind was absent. For many days, he had been thinking of words and he could only pray that they were the right ones. Torben glanced at Luana Marquez who rode at his side. It had been she who had put the idea of a story in Erik's head and through that deed had conjured this present. Perhaps this whole journey was her idea. Torben buried the thought as he mulled over the words again and again.

The sun danced across the sky and in the light of its evening rays Carlian arose before the riders. Riders patrolled the plains and river surrounding the capital, some clutching phoenix banners in their hand. More of the standards flew atop the thick stone walls that encompassed the sprawling city. There was nothing glamorous or beautiful about Carlian. There was nothing graceful for the poets to sing about. It was a city built by warriors. Every stone, every brick, every thatched house was crafted by calloused hands forged by sword and spear. Carlian had been born at the first king of Miera's command. It had been hundreds of years since King Zavian had taken the throne, yet in all that time the city had never known defeat.

Torben's gaze drifted from Carlian as he noticed movement upon the plains. A company of riders had taken note of their approach and made to head the column off. Torben followed Danavir's lead and slowed his mount into a walk as the band of spear-wielding Mierans drew near. There were eight of them all armoured in chainmail. They wore helms of steel and had shields slung across their broad backs. All of them wore the same dangerous look as they swept their eyes across the company of outlanders. All of them save their grey-haired leader. The captain removed his helmet and let his long hair cascade past his shoulders. A short beard bristled along his jaw and scars covered his weathered face. His eyes were pale and ten golden rings adorned his ear. Torben knew what that meant. The man was a veteran among veterans. A man who had fought countless battles. A great warrior.

"Lord Zandir." Danavir offered a short nod to the captain.

"Danavir Carlin, it's been a long time." Zandir extended an arm.

The two men clasped hands. The Mieran lord's eyes flickered across the faces of those at Danavir's back.

"I see you've brought guests," the gruff voice continued.

The Mierans surrounding the company chuckled. They watched the foreigners like they were prey. Not one of them backed down from the horsemen.

"Yes, lord," Danavir said. "They travelled across the sea and brought word of Elara's treachery with them."

"Treachery?"

"The Accords have been rescinded. The League has broken its word."

"I see," Zandir replied before walking his horse closer to the outlanders. "I am Zandir Barangir. I see Valkir, I see Elara and Berenithia, I see Annora, and by your garb, I would assume you are Sacasian. A great evil has brought you together, of that I am certain, but coming here has placed you in the lion's den. Why are you here?"

"My name is Torben. I am bloodsworn and shield-brother to King Erik," Torben said. "My companions and I came to Miera with word from Elara. Out there, beyond your land, the world is changing. We have to meet with your king."

"You have to, do you?" Zandir's lip curled.

"If we do not, then we will all be dead within a year," Luana called. "This will have been in vain. Please. We must speak to King Zoran."

Zandir Barangir glanced at Danavir. "If you brought them this far, then Jaigir gave the order."

"He did, lord," Danavir replied.

"Very well." Zandir looked to Torben and strapped his helmet back on. "This way."

The people of Carlian stopped and stared as the foreigners were led through their midst by Zandir Barangir. Warriors rested hands on weapons, while women and children held their ground just the same. They watched with anger, disdain, contempt and curiosity. Few enough had seen those from other nations let alone such a gathering of races. Blood divided them yet they were united in cause. Torben kept his gaze forward. Most had never seen a Valkir before and he would show them strength. He wore no expression on his face save for a dangerous glint in his eyes to show that he was above it all. The sounds that greeted Torben's ears were those of blacksmiths, those of orders shouted and commands given, hooves upon cobblestone and the shrill cries of horses. Zandir led them through the streets and under the gateway of the inner wall. Soldiers lined the walkways and phoenix banners flew high in the breeze. They dismounted in a courtyard of stone, Zandir vanishing into the palace beyond.

"What does your heart tell you?" Luana Marquez asked as she slid from her saddle beside Torben.

"That we will succeed," he replied, willing himself to believe the words as they left his lips. "We have to."

Mieran soldiers came to take their horses and weapons and soon enough they were left with nothing save the disdainful glares of the horsemen. There was a flicker across the gaze of each of the Mierans. They would not strike the first blow, but Torben knew that that look was to dare the companions to make a move. The Mierans wanted to fight. It was all that they knew. Soon enough, Zandir returned.

"The king will see you now," he said.

Torben exchanged a look with Luana before they followed Zandir up the stairs and into the palace.

"I am told that you are to thank for bringing us knowledge of the League's treachery," the man with the ruby-inlaid earring called.

"We are, King Zoran," Torben replied as he took the man in.

The Mieran leader wore armour no finer than that of his men. The sword that leaned against the side of his simple wooden chair had no more ceremonial value than the seat. The only embellishment that the king saw fit to carry was the small ruby within the ring that hung from his right ear. Mieran soldiers filled the hall. All of them kept their hands tightly bound to their blades.

"My lord King Erik sends his regards," Torben continued.

"Another king?" Zoran gave a mirthless chuckle. "How many kings there are these days? I've lost count."

"As you say."

"Tell me." Zoran leapt to his feet. "How did such a company of outlanders find their way into the heart of my kingdom?"

"We came seeking an audience."

"I see," Zoran replied as he walked in front of the line of companions. "The Valkir have raided the Annoran coast for generations, yet here you are united. The Sacasians have been at war with the League for thirty years, yet here you are. Then there is Berenithia." Zoran glanced from Tariq to Elise and Marshall. "Either you arrived in Elara as a slave or your parents did. But you ride with them."

"We are united in common cause," Tariq told him.

"And what cause would that be?" Zoran asked.

"We come seeking an alliance." Torben watched the Mieran king.

The hall echoed as the Mierans filled it with laughter.

"An alliance?" Zoran scoffed.

"All of us" – Torben gestured to his companions – "and all of you have been hurt by the empire and her allies in some way. Loss. That is what brought us together. They lost friends, homes, families. I lost a daughter … No more. A future for our people was snuffed out like a candle all because of the empire's contempt for pagans. Make no mistake, King Zoran, Aureia does not see us as different. We're all the same to them. Uncivilised. Barbarian. Heathen. The westerners have united against Salvaar. All of them. Aureia has already declared against my people. Their colonies seek to wipe out every last trace of the Sacasians. One by one, they will turn on us all. One by one, they will fight us all. One by one, they will defeat us all. Against the power of Aureia there can be no victory."

"We do not fear the griffin," Zoran countered. "We do not fear death."

Torben met the king's eye. "You do not fear for yourself, but do you fear for your people? Your children? They won't have children of their own if we don't band together."

"Miera will fight. That is how we win and that is how we die. That is the Mieran way. In victory or defeat."

"Then you choose death before friendship?"

"When I look at all the people before me, I see the faces of those who have invaded my land," Zoran growled. "I see the faces of those who have killed my people. I see the faces of those who, in times of peace, have betrayed us. Yet you come here and ask me to trust you?"

"No." Torben shook his head. "Trust must be earned. What I ask for, king, is the chance to earn it. Our message about the Accords is only the beginning. If you give us this chance, you will not regret it."

Zoran stepped back towards his throne and clasped his hands.

"I will give you a chance to speak if that is what you wish," he told Torben. "You have earned that much."

Torben gave him a single nod in thanks. "I travelled across the sea with a story," he said.

"Then sing me a song, storyteller, and pray that it's a good one."

Torben looked from the Mieran king to Luana and then closed his eyes. He searched his heart and reached into his soul. Torben found the words. His eyes flickered open. He began.

"It begins with a raven. The gentlest breeze caresses the bird's black feathers. Fire dances through its intelligent eyes. The woman's hands are steady, their grip on the blade perfect. Eyes as blue as the sea do not leave the raven. The bird's song is met only by the echo of a blade through wood. The woman moves cold steel along the block as gentle as a lover's caress. That touch is a word, a promise. The wood begins to take shape. A raven's skull is born from the woman's hands. With a string she binds the amulet around her throat. A symbol of wisdom. A symbol of adaptability.

The woman, a mother, returns home before the coming night. A kind heart, a bright flame, a fearsome lioness. Yet the world is cruel. A sickness blows across the ocean from the west and, in its fury, claims the woman's life. The raven survives and passes to a new bearer. It comes to the woman's mate, the great seafarer Lief Farrin. Its wisdom grants the sailor reputation and power over the ocean.

"Yet things stir in the dark. While the sea breeze kisses the sailor's cheek, a wolf begins to circle. Fangs of silver steel, a coat black as ash, eyes the colour of death. It stalks the seafarer through the blackness of night. The cold wind howls and dances through the seafarer's hair. The wisdom of the raven flows through his veins, but the wolf is ever hungry. Beneath the crimson of a betrayer's moon, the beast's fangs claim the raven's bearer. Another comes. She finds his blood upon the cold iron earth, for she is the daughter of the lioness and the seafarer. She feels the cold air in her lungs, the seaborne breeze on her cheek. Her breath is steady. A promise carries through the wind. A solemn vow. A wind of vengeance. The raven cries and flies to an altogether new bearer. The navigator. Chased from her home by the wolf, the navigator flees into the sea. Yet she is not guided by the raven. She *is* the raven. She is all knowledge. She is all wisdom. The navigator's mind, like the raven, is deceptive. And so the woman given up for lost returns home. Fear does not grip her as she faces the wolf. Her hands do not tremble as the great beast lunges. A raven's song carries across the waves. The navigator emerges from darkest night, the black pelt of a wolf cast across her back. She returns from the dead. She returns to her people. She returns as the raven. She returns, our jarl, Astrid!"

The Mierans cried out as Torben roared the last words. They stared at him with hungry eyes as he held up his hands to halt the ruckus.

"It comes to her at night. A whisper. A dream. A fate worthy of the Raven Jarl. Astrid, like the raven, longs to explore. The passage south is long since closed, yet the navigator ascends to Ra'Haven and convinces the Sea-Father to open it. Unchartered waters and mystic lands become the dream of every Valkir. This promise ushers in an age of discovery. An age of freedom! An age without blood and turmoil. Peace comes with it and that is the raven's dream. It comes from the blackness bearing the guise of lover. Yet beneath the silver words and golden laurels is a grotesque breed of dragon and griffin. The cold wind greets the raven like a tender kiss. Her blood is warm, her mind shrouded by the smoke of a dream. Her eyes are as fire. The dagger is as winter ice. The beast moves swiftly, called by the sun and moon. He is precise. The raven falls. At last, she feels the winter cold. At last, it chills her blood. She hears the death throes of the beast as it falls in service to its masters. Her last breath fills the wind. The words 'Remember why' become its message.

"And so she dies. The dream dies. The age of freedom hangs by a thread. But under the bloodstained moon hope is born, for another bearer comes. The warrior, brother to the navigator. He takes the raven for his own, his hands clasped around the last thread of the dream. With his left hand he shields it while with his right he strikes at the beast's lair. Word from the enemy's master reaches his ear. Word carried across an ocean. Word bearing the mark of Aureia."

Cries of anger filled the palace hall.

"*Remember why*. Words as simple as can be spoken. Words I have long since pondered. A cryptic message that only the chosen can find answer. The warrior cannot and so he becomes something more. After slaying the beast, he rises a Raven King. For many nights, he searches for this answer. Find it he does. *Remember why*. Those were no mere words spoken without cause. They were spoken in the hope that all would remember why Astrid fought. That they would remember the dream to which she gave her life. An age of freedom. An age of peace. That was her hope.

"I come to you now at the behest of the Raven King to tell you that none of us are safe. A woman who wanted peace was slain for no cause. One by one, they will come for us all; they have already begun. Now, as before, a new beast has come. A mighty griffin. Its shadow covers all the land and its call echoes across the death cries of thousands. The griffin's treachery seeks to turn us against one another. It seeks to destroy us. It started in the north. The people of Salvaar face obliteration and we will soon follow. Alone, we cannot stop them. Only together. Only together can we breathe life into the raven's dream. We can usher in a future brighter than anything we can imagine. It has been over ten years since the gentle breeze and the raven's promise. Across the years it has passed, yet the song of the raven is still sung. You can hear it in the breath of the wind, in the shrill cries of birds high above. And so I ask you now: Can you hear it?"

✦ ✦ ✦

THIRTY-THREE

The westernmost island within Valkir territory was filled with activity, far more than it had ever seen. Nesoi had only ever been used as a staging ground for raids into the empire. There was a small but constant garrison of warriors that called the island home, but now Nesoi played host to dozens of ships and thousands of warriors. The forges burned day and night, bowyers added to the ever-growing pile of arrows, while jarls oversaw any last maintenance that their ships required. Some were refitted while others were pulled ashore to have their hulls cleaned so that they may travel at greater speeds.

King Erik knelt with his arms outstretched as the salty sea breeze kissed the bare skin of his back. He had kept this pose for hours now as the great Rusikora Bannik worked. The skilled artisan was the finest tattooist that the isles had ever seen. It has he who had spent years adding to the serpent that snaked down Erik's shoulder and arm – the mark of a bloodsworn. The black snake now bore a long scar through it thanks to his own knife a month before. Now Rusikora worked on the finest piece that he had ever created. With his needle upon the canvas of Erik's shoulders and back, he forged a pair of massive raven wings, a great tribute to the king's heritage. Sailors, warriors, leaders; it was time that Erik embraced it all. Rusikora had started his work under the light of the dawn sun, and it was many hours before he at last stepped back from Erik and downed his tools.

"Done," Rusikora said.

Erik rolled his shoulders back to ease some of the tension before he slowly rose to his feet. Small tendrils of pain lanced through his lower back and shoulders – to Erik it was nothing.

"Thank you, my friend," Erik replied sincerely as he pulled on his raven amulet.

Rusikora's work always came at great expense, yet every prick of the needle showed the great artist's skill.

"Mind yourself for fourteen days," the tattooist told him. "Do nothing to irritate the ink."

The king gave him a nod.

"Erik!" Mayrun made her way towards the pair.

"What is it?" Erik asked as he looked towards her.

"It's Teague. Says he's thought of something."

"Where is he now?"

"The hall."

Erik glanced at Rusikora and clasped the tattooist's arm before following Mayrun back up the hill towards Nesoi's great hall. He did not pull his shirt over his head for the tattoo needed time to breathe. Erik felt every caress of the wind as it brushed against his raw skin.

A great city of tents had emerged across Nesoi over the last few days. The hall and few houses had been filled within moments, leaving thousands without shelter. From the beach to the woodland to the hill upon which the hall was built, tents belonging to Valkir, Sacasian and Elaran covered the ground. Erik and Mayrun reached Nesoi's hall and made for the entrance. A pair of Earl Wulf's grizzled warriors stood guard. They let the king and his companion in without a word. A few of the other earls stood with Cillian Teague and Garrett Laven in the centre of the hall.

"Has Jorun sent word?" Erik asked as he approached.

"We've heard nothing," Earl Wulf replied. "Not even a whisper. He has men of Vay'kis aboard, men who know how to use the pigeons. If he finds anything, we will know."

The pigeons had been one of Teague's ideas. If the raiders took a number of the birds west, they could easily get word to their fleet far faster than any ship ever could. If Jorun found anything at all, they would know within a matter of days.

"Then what is this about?" Erik said as he looked to Teague.

"Sending your people west in search of information was a good plan," the pirate replied. "However, it relies upon the fact that someone knows of this imperial fleet. I served the empire for many years, and when it came to delicate information it was only shared with those who needed to know. There may not be a magister outside of the capital who has heard about it."

Erik crossed his arms. "There was nothing else to do but send raiders," he said. "We are seafarers, we are warriors. We have no other means of tracking this fleet aside what has already been done. If you have another option now, then speak it."

All eyes went to Cillian Teague.

"As far as I can tell, there may be one place outside of the imperial palace that can give us the answers that we seek. There is a place barely a few days inland that could give us everything that we need."

"What is this place?" Earl Wulf asked.

"Eonie," Teague replied.

Erik shrugged. He had never heard of it.

"I have never heard that name," Earl Imelda started as she glanced at the man to her side. "Einri?"

"No," Earl Einri added.

"Eonie is a great fortress rich in both wealth and history, yet it is home to something of far greater interest. The Tower of Whispers," Teague told them. "You see, Eonie is a city of couriers. The founders of the city were the first to use pigeons as messengers and the first to establish a network of couriers that reaches every corner of the empire. Every word penned, every whisper murmured, every last detail mentioned always reaches that city. They keep records of every conversation and every deal. If anyone knows about this fleet, it is Eonie."

"You mentioned that it is a fortress," Erik said curiously. "How many soldiers?"

"Two legions. Ten thousand men."

"We barely have that many warriors combined," Bhaltair of Elara said. "Even if we could cross the empire to reach the city, we could not take it. We would be wiped out at the city gates."

"You misunderstand me, my friend," Teague continued. "I do not want to attack Eonie. I want to infiltrate it. Two men can go where an army can't."

"And how do you propose that we do that exactly?" Erik asked. "I have no doubt that if any Valkir were to appear at Eonie's gates, they will be killed or worse."

"You see, there is always a way in," Teague replied. "What we need is someone who could secrete one of us past the guards and into the Tower. I know just the man."

"Who?" Priamos Stentor asked.

"A man who once served the imperial court as a messenger. Janis Tethis is his name."

"You would trust an imperial agent to get us into the city?" Erik scoffed. "As soon as those doors shut, he would slit his companion's throat."

"Not if we have leverage," Teague explained. "Leverage that we can get, but we need to act. Each day brings the end times closer. Jorun will not find the information that he seeks, of that I am certain. This could be our last chance – our *only* chance."

"The decision is yours," Priamos told Erik. "Whatever you choose, my men and I will follow."

Erik glanced from face to face. "If we don't find this fleet and defeat it, then we will be fighting for the rest of our lives," he said.

"We are Valkir," Wulf replied. "Fighting is who we are. Fighting is what we are. That is how we live. That is how we survive. If we do not defeat our enemy in battle, then that is what we shall do."

"That is true, Earl Wulf," Erik agreed. "There is not a man or woman among our people who has not fought for everything that they possess. We fight and we kill and we survive. For generations, all of us, every isle, have acted as if war is easier than peace. For a long time, I believed that. Now I realise that true strength lies in achieving the more difficult goal. For that I say we *must* achieve peace. Whatever the cost."

"Then you agree with Captain Teague?" Earl Einri asked.

Erik looked to the pirate captain. His mind had been made up and for better or worse he would not stray from the path he had chosen.

"I do," he said. "However, I will not stand by and let another fight my battles for me. I would never ask any of you to do something that I would not do myself. I will accompany Captain Teague into Aureia."

Shouts filled the hall as the Valkir cursed the idea of their king taking the risk.

"King Erik, you cannot seriously be considering following him into the *heart* of the empire," Earl Imelda called.

"I am not considering it," Erik growled back. "I am doing it."

"King Erik–" Wulf began.

Erik held up a hand to silence the earl. "Everything is in motion," the king told them all. "The ships are being prepared and the warriors with them. There is nothing to do here now but wait and listen. I will not ask any of you to burden yourself with this risk. I will do it myself. This is not a debate." Erik turned to Teague. "When can we leave?"

"I will have my ship make ready. We can leave by sundown," the captain replied.

"Then that is what we will do."

Garrett Laven stepped forward. "If I may," he said with a glance at Erik.

The king gestured for him to continue.

"All we've been discussing are ways to find this secret fleet," Garrett continued. "But what about what comes next? We have put so little thought into how we are to fight it. We may have assembled one of the greatest fleets in history, but we will be fighting a mighty opponent. This is no mere fleet of the League, of the Valkir, of Landonsport or even Annora. This is the imperial fleet. Their ships are fast and their crews strong. However big our own force is, theirs will be far greater in number. Those ships will not just have sailors aboard, they will have soldiers of the legions. Men who have spent their lives training and fighting. They have discipline, they have will and they have experience. There won't just be a few, there will be a hundred aboard each ship. This is a foe that we may not be able to defeat through strength of arm. Valkir steel and Sacasian ships will only get us so far."

"We will take them head on as we always do," Erik replied. "Who has more experience upon the Lupentine than us? Who knows more about fighting at sea than us? They may spend their lives training for this, but it is in our blood."

"Forgive me, King Erik, but that is not a plan," Garrett told him. "I have ideas, ways in which we could even the odds."

"Go on."

Garrett turned to Bhaltair and Priamos Stentor. "With you came more than just soldiers," he said. "There were alchemists, scholars, craftsmen, physicians and men who trade in rarities. Those who practice medicine and chemistry."

"Of course," Priamos replied. "We brought our people, not just our warriors."

"I have studied Delion history. Tariki history. There are some things that I have learnt that may be able to help us now," Garrett told them.

"What things?" Wulf asked.

"Weapons. Powerful weapons."

"What is it that you need?" Bhaltair asked.

"I need you to send for those men," Garrett said. "Bring them here. Their inspired minds may yet save us all."

"It will be done," Priamos said. "We can have them here within a couple of days."

Thousands gathered on the sands of the beach to watch the sails unfurl on the two warships. The Oridassey led the way out into the open ocean while the Ravenheart followed close behind. The risk was high and those men and women on the beach knew that they may never see the pirate lord or their king again, yet they would not give up hope. The setting sun painted the ocean waves orange and red as the ships carved their way through. Erik stood at the helm beside Fargrim as the helmsmen steered the ship west. He wore a loose shirt over his fresh tattoo instead of his armour. There would be a time for his lamellar of steel and leather, but it was not now. Until the Ravenheart landed upon enemy shores, he would allow his back to heal.

"You're sure about this?" Fargrim asked from his side.

"I have to be," Erik told him.

The cool night air gusted through the deck of the Ravenheart when Erik made his way down from the helm. A skeleton crew tended to the rigging while most of the others rested down below. They would take turns doing all that they could to keep the ship stable and able to travel at speed. Erik found Mayrun sitting above deck atop a small barrel. She wore a fresh kit of lamellar armour and her dark hair was pulled back into a single long braid. A shield rested at her side and she ran a whetstone down the length of her axe blade. Erik approached his friend and extended a hand. Mayrun paused what she was doing and handed her weapon over. Erik felt the weapon's strength even as he held it. The king gave the axe a twirl.

"Yah!" He grinned and handed it back. "This is a fine axe."

"It was Raol's," Mayrun replied.

"You honour him by wielding it," Erik told her as he sat opposite.

"Just as you honour your family," she replied.

Erik ran a thumb down his raven amulet. "Always," he said.

"I did not mean with your amulet," Mayrun said. "I meant with your deeds. What you're doing now … fighting for a better future. That is what Astrid wanted. It is what she fought for. Your father brought us together. Not just our crew, but all of Agartha. Your sister wanted to deliver us into something better. I wonder, Erik, could you be the one to do both? Not just for Agartha, but maybe even all of our people."

Erik met her eyes. "I've done a lot of things in my life, yet this may be the only thing that matters."

"If we do this, if we defeat this enemy and all that we hope for comes true, then you have a chance to go down as the greatest contradiction in history. The warrior who brought peace. Whatever anyone tells you, you are a peacemaker, my friend."

"We still have a long road to travel before it comes to that," Erik replied.

"And I know that you will succeed."

"Because if I fail, we will almost certainly die."

"No." Mayrun shook her head. "Because I know more than just what it is you are fighting for. I know *why* you are fighting, Erik."

"And why is that?"

"I think that you first took this cause upon your shoulders to honour Astrid, and while that is noble, I believe things have changed," Mayrun said. "I think that you have changed. This cause that was once your sister's is now one that you fully believe in. You have set your heart upon it and when you do that, anything is possible. That is why you will not lose."

Erik stared at her for a moment. Somehow, she was right. He had never spoken those words to anyone, yet it was Mayrun who seemed to understand him best of all.

"And how did you come by this?"

"Because your wish to honour Astrid is the same honour that I wish to show Raol," she replied sincerely. "Perhaps I understand that more than anyone."

"Aye," Erik murmured. "Perhaps you do."

Mayrun reached out and placed a hand on Erik's. "They would be proud of what you have accomplished. Your mother, Lief, Astrid, Hélla, me … all of us on this ship. Your family. Your scâldir."

"Then I pray that when I meet the fallen in Ra'Haven that I have not failed them."

"You won't."

Erik rose to his feet and clapped Mayrun on the shoulder. "Get some rest," he said. "You'll need your strength for the battles to come."

✦ ✦ ✦

THIRTY-FOUR

Kilgareth, Valley of Odrysia

The aviary echoed with the song of hundreds of pigeons, none more important than the one held in Lysandra's hands. Lysandra gently removed the small message from the tube tied to the tiny bird's leg before handing the pigeon to another of the maija. There was a small marking drawn upon the roll of parchment. A griffin.

"This is from the imperial palace," Lysandra told her companions.

"The senate has decided then?" Kaira asked as she approached her mentor.

Lysandra nodded. "Empress Sienna and a small council are to serve in the emperor's stead until Darius' son, Eladis, comes of age," she said. "Aureia will then be led by an altogether new emperor. May the gods and his new mentors lead him into the light."

"Long may he reign," Kaira replied.

"Long may he reign," Lysandra agreed.

"Lady Lysandra," another of the maija called as he approached.

Lysandra glanced from the man to the note that he held. "What is it, Inari?" she asked.

"Word from Duke Caspin."

Lysandra took the parchment marked with the snake symbol and held it up into the light.

"We crossed into the forest some days ago and have found nothing but the haunting shadows that have made a home in abandoned villages. We continue the march north in pursuit of our foe. Will we find a host of Salvaari or nothing but the cold and lonely whispering of the wind?" Lysandra glanced up as she read.

"This must have been sent before the attack," Kaira murmured.

"Perhaps they were far enough south to escape the massacre," Inari suggested.

"If Santiago and his men did not reach the grand master in time, then they will almost certainly be safe," Lysandra told them. "The duke's words speak of the same migration that we heard about from both Bavarian and King Dayne."

"The Salvaari gave up ground to lure them close enough for the sword," Inari cursed.

"Perhaps," Lysandra replied with a shrug. "Or perhaps they did not want to put their elders, their children, their families in harm's way. And who could blame them?"

Kaira walked across to the huge map that hung along one of the aviary walls. She looked to Salvaar and ran her gaze along the great sea of trees.

"The main army attacks from the west, King Dayne and Duke Santiago from the south, and Velis from the east," she said. "When the circle at last closes there will be no escape for the Salvaari."

"I pray that we find a swift victory, yet my heart tells me that this war is far from over," Lysandra said as she looked to her companion.

"The gods have a purpose for everything," Inari said. "I am sure that the path will be revealed in time."

"That it will," Lysandra told him. "There is work to be done. Send for me if word comes from Salvaar."

"Yes, my lady," Inari replied.

Lysandra wound her way down the long staircase and then made her way through Kilgareth to her office. She locked the door before sparking a candle to life. From her sleeve she pulled the parchment that she had secreted away. The letter from Santiago Caspin.

Lysandra held the parchment close to the flame. The heat of the small fire conjured words to life across the back of the letter. This was word from her agent in Santiago's camp. A human assassin under her employ. Lysandra cast her eyes across the parchment.

I continue to pick at the scab left by Dorian's death and now it begins to bleed. The woman who sought to kill a king was found and I believe has been killed. As you know, the Eagle's death was Santiago's doing, and as you have commanded, the work continues. This army will splinter long before Salvaar comes for it.

That was where the letter ended. Lysandra's name was not mentioned, nor the assassin's. It was far too dangerous for that. When Lysandra had first approached her agent, it had been with the intention of solely killing Darius, yet this had changed and the plan had long since adapted. For a handful more coins, the assassin had secreted himself amongst the camp of Santiago and Dayne and now turned brother against brother. The agent knew nothing about Lysandra, nor had they even met. They knew nothing about the ruskalan. The only thing that was certain was that the agent knew they worked for someone who wanted Salvaar to win – that was enough. Lysandra held the note up to the candle though this time she let the flames lick the parchment. She watched the letter burn before her eyes and only when it had been consumed by the fire did she turn away. A knock came from the door and not a moment too soon. Lysandra made her way over and drew the bolt back.

✦ ✦ ✦

"Princess Kassandra?" Lysandra's lips curled into a smile as she spoke. "How can I help?"

"I'm sorry for disturbing you, but I have questions," Kassie told her.

Lysandra beckoned her into the office.

"Thank you," the princess told her as the door closed behind her.

Her eyes instantly went to the shelves of books, books in which she had immersed herself in past days. Kassandra ran a finger across the spines of a few of them before turning to Lysandra.

"Some … *many* of these have ideas and notions in them so dangerous that speaking them could get you imprisoned or worse," Kassie said. "A different truth to what we are taught. Heresy in every sense of the word. Yet you keep them knowing what could happen if they were ever found."

"The truth should be fought for and preserved regardless of how it offends," Lysandra replied after a moment. "History is history. It cannot be destroyed or forgotten lest we make the same mistakes again. Things that our ancestors did, horrific things, in the name of country or glory or love, whatever the cause, should not be used to define, only to *learn*. We are not to blame for the sins of our fathers or their fathers before them."

Kassandra slowly nodded. "In that we both agree," she said. "I am glad that you kept these books and grateful to have read them. Now a thousand, thousand questions swim through my mind."

"Speak them" – Lysandra gestured for her to continue – "and I will do my best to help you find the answers."

"The books that I have read span centuries and longer. They tell different stories and illuminate what was once dark, yet they *all* speak of one thing. Balance. That the world is a better place when everything is aligned."

"Balance is the key to everything," Lysandra replied. "It is the essence that binds us all together. We are not put here to fight the world; we are put here to listen to it. If you open your mind, then you will find balance … then you will find peace. When balance is disrupted, everything changes. Sometimes I ask myself what it all means. Why do the gods allow such terrible things to happen? All of the slaughter, all of the death and ruin. You see, Kassandra, that is what my predecessors wrote about. When balance falls, the harmony that binds us frays and darkness is allowed to slip back into the world."

Kassandra frowned thoughtfully. "If this is true, then how do we restore balance?"

"There are those who believe that it comes from the sun and moon – the idea that there cannot be light without darkness. The idea that within every light there is shadow, just as within every shadow you can find light." Lysandra gathered up a book. "However, there is an even more dangerous idea that I have stumbled upon. That balance does not stem from the sun and moon at all but from the ruskalan and the elves."

"How?" Kassie frowned.

"The ruskalan are creatures of the mind. They are not beholden to acting on impulse or emotion. They are great thinkers and have more patience than time itself. Elves on the other hand are creatures born of the heart. They act first and are prone to letting their emotion lead them. These acts are what made them such ferocious warriors, yet they are also what got them killed. You see, Kassandra, the elves and the ruskalan are two sides of the same coin, two sides of our nature entangled in the dark."

Kassandra thought back to the she-elf that she had seen. She thought of the cold, white hair and the eyes of dancing sapphire flame.

"But they're gone," Kassandra said. "Aren't they?"

"One cannot exist without the other," Lysandra told her. "At least so was the superstition. Whether they are gone or hiding, we may never know."

"And because of this, balance has been destroyed."

"That is the belief." Lysandra handed over the book. "Take this. Read it. Decide for yourself what you believe to be true."

Kassandra ran her fingers across the bare leather-bound book. It bore no words or images across either side of its cover, yet Kassie knew that it was of far greater value than any other within this room.

"Thank you," Kassandra said sincerely.

"You're most welcome," Lysandra said. "I enjoy our conversations."

Kassandra gave her a smile. "My lady, if I may, there was something else."

"What is it?"

Kassie thought back to when she had seen Cailean and the other captives being taken into the fortress.

"In the grand master's absence, you watch over Kilgareth. Upon my return, I arrived when the Salvaari prisoners were being escorted though the gates. One of them I met during my time in Salvaar. He travelled with Lukas many months ago. He is a friend."

"And you would like to see him?"

"Yes," Kassie said. "Perhaps he knows something about my brother."

Lysandra gave her a nod. "I will see to it," she told the princess. "Until then know that I have made sure that they are being cared for."

✦ ✦ ✦

The light of a burning fire illuminated the dark of the forest as Henghis made his way towards those assembled. There were eight others, each clothed and painted different from the next. One of their number did not stand as a chief of his tribe: Eilith of the Aedei. Together with Henghis, they made up nine of the leaders of the newfound coalition. Only Dáire of the Coventina, Morrigana of the Belcar and Eira of the Niavenn weren't with them. Henghis' hand brushed the hilt of his sword as he made his way into the midst of his companions.

"Brothers, sisters," the great chief began. "We stand upon a field of victory drenched with the blood of our enemy. For every insult, for every home burned, for every hair plucked from an innocent child's head we made them pay with their lives. They have fallen back to lick their wounds, but they are not defeated. They outnumber us. They will return. I say this: if you have to fight a monster, you should go to its lair before it comes to your village."

"You want to go after them?" Etain asked.

"There will be no better time than now," Henghis replied. "They have been defeated. They have lost thousands of men. They are *divided*."

"My scouts have seen the fires of war camps to the south," Vaylin added. "Annora was not upon the field. They were not here. Lukas' diversion worked."

"Daire, Morrigan and Eira have put a halt to the Aureian incursions along the Rift," Balor of the Sagailean said.

"That leaves but a few for us to contend with," Henghis continued.

"It is true that we know the land," Etain said. "And my people have sheltered all those who cannot fight in the highlands. We can move where the enemy cannot and strike them where they least expect it. Where are Lukas and his two hundred now?"

Vaylin stepped forward. "Riding north to join us as we speak," she replied. "They will be with us in a matter of days."

Etain glanced from Vaylin to Henghis. "If anyone knows weaknesses in the walls and towers of their camps, it will be Lukas," she told the chieftains. "With his knowledge it will still be difficult, but it can be done."

"No." Henghis waved his hand. "You have all seen the camps that they have constructed along the river. I will not send my people over walls into the embrace of such a mighty opponent. They have more men. They have trained for that kind of fight. If we fight that way, we will lose. We are *not* fighting it that way."

"Then what do you suggest?" Eilith of the Aedei asked.

"We beat them in the field because we changed how we fought.

We lured them from their camps into battle and then drew them even further away. That will not work again and so we will adapt. We will march south," Henghis told them.

"You want to go after the other forces while they march?" Vaylin asked.

"Yes," Henghis replied. "We can defeat them one by one. We have found victory in a single battle, but the war is not won. We have shown them that they are not invincible, but that is not enough. We must show the world that they are not. We must *break* this army here."

"We *will* break it," Eilith growled. "We will cast them from our lands and show them such fear that they will *never* return."

Henghis clapped a hand upon the Aedei's shoulder. "Your tribe has chosen you to lead them, yet you do not wear the torc of its chief," Henghis stated.

"Chief Cailean was not slain in battle. He was taken as a prisoner," Eilith replied. "Perhaps he is dead. Perhaps he is not. Until we know, I will not take his place."

"You are a great warrior," Henghis told him. "But a more honourable man, there is none."

The Aedei gave his leader a nod as Henghis moved past him.

"I will have my people bring word of the enemy," Vaylin said. "We will watch from the shadows as we prepare to attack."

"What of our people fighting along the Rift?" Etain asked.

"They will be needed here," Henghis said. "For the first time in our history, the tribes shall fight as one. We will be united."

Etain's lips curled. "The griffin has come and now the world will burn," she spat.

"They have come here to Salvaar to bring their ways and destroy ours," Henghis said. "They need to learn that beneath these trees there is *only* Salvaar. Will we let them subjugate us or will we fight?"

"We will stand together," Balor growled.

Henghis pulled forth his knife and drew it across the palm of his hand. Blood flowed and he curled his fingers into a fist. He stared up towards the moon, towards Sylvaine and the Veil.

"Sylvaine, Great Queen, give me courage and strength," he whispered.

The flames of passion evoked something within Henghis. In that moment, he knew that Sylvaine had answered. His lips curled back and he bared his teeth. Henghis pounded his chest with a fist as he walked among his people.

"We Salvaari are born of blood and honour; we are descended from mighty warriors!" Henghis cried. "When we fight, we fight with one soul! Whatever we fight for we pay in blood! But I am not fighting for my kingdom and glory now. I am fighting as an ordinary person. For my enslaved brothers and sisters, for my home, for my family, for the liberty that those men wish to steal, that *they* have stolen. Consider how many of you are fighting and why! Then you will win this battle or perish. That is what I, a free man, shall do!"

"We will follow you," Etain vowed as she stepped towards her cousin. "We will all follow you."

✦ ✦ ✦

THIRTY-FIVE

Salvaari encampment, Káli Lands, Forest of Salvaar

Sabra soared high above the green trees. She soared in the wind as her eyes peered down below. From here, the only signs of the great army below were the thin tendrils of smoke that broke through the canopy. Wind caressed the hawk's feathers as she dived down towards the trees. Sabra's piercing cry echoed through Salvaar as she broke through the canopy. Only then did the thousands of marked warriors become visible: men and women from the nine tribes that had risked all to fight against the west. The hawk glided beneath trees and between branches. Tribesmen stopped and stared as the desert hawk flew among them. The cool breeze was not felt by Sabra as she flapped her wings and dropped down onto Sakkar's waiting arm. The Larissan stood sat with his wife. A hum echoed from Senya's lips as she watched the bird land.

"They've been looking at you every time you do that," Galadayne said from his place across the fire.

"You interest them," Senya added as she glanced from her husband to the Salvaari watching.

"They can't take their eyes off me," Sakkar replied with a grin as he stroked Sabra's feathers.

"We've noticed," Bellec growled.

"Always the centre of attention." Galadayne chuckled.

Sakkar gave three short whistles and Sabra launched herself

skyward. He smiled as the Salvaari watched the hawk vanish through the canopy.

"Careful now," Jaimye said. "They will think you're connected to their spirits. They might even decide that you're some kind of god."

"Perhaps I am." Sakkar laughed as he joined them by the fire.

"They wouldn't agree, you daft bastard." Galadayne chortled.

"They might if I told them so," Sakkar returned.

"Half of them wouldn't understand you, you fool," Bellec told him.

"But as for the others," Sakkar said as his eyes flashed.

"I wouldn't do that." Jaimye's lips curled as he spoke.

"You be careful," Galadayne added.

"I think they'd tell you the Salvaari word for *fuck off*." Senya grinned and shook her head.

The companions roared with laughter.

"Aye, they might." Sakkar snickered.

"Conceit," Bellec said. "A *virtuous* quality. Often possessed by those wishing for an early grave."

"So they say." Sakkar smirked.

Bellec tossed the Larissan a wineskin. Sakkar took a long draught of wine and relished the alcohol as it ran down his throat. He passed the skin to Senya who in turn took a gulp before handing it to the next mercenary.

"Yes." Senya grinned as she looked to her husband. "You would know a lot about conceit."

Sakkar wrapped an arm around his wife's shoulders as they laughed again.

"Must be love," Galadayne said cheerfully as he watched them.

"Must be." Senya smirked as she interwove her fingers with Sakkar's.

The band drifted off into silence for a moment as they passed around the wineskin.

"Is it strange?" Senya asked as she looked to Bellec. "Being back here?"

The mercenary captain pursed his lips. "Sakkar told you?"

Senya nodded.

Bellec sighed. He glanced around at his men, many of whom had served in the war that had cost them everything. A war that had begun here in Salvaar.

"Is it strange?" Bellec began. "No. It feels almost like fate to be back in Salvaar fighting against those who have come to destroy it. It feels right. For the first time in a long time, I am fighting for a cause that I believe in."

There was some grumbled agreement from the mercenaries, grumbles that ended when a small band of black-painted Káli made their approach.

"The hawk-bearer returns to Salvaar," their leader called.

Sakkar paused for a moment as he recognised the warrior. He was a man whom Chief Vaylin had trusted to lead a great warband. One who had helped free Oryn from the clutches of the Catuvantuli.

"Eirian." Sakkar greeted the man. "It's been a long time."

"Indeed, it has." Eirian looked around the foreign faces. "Henghis has ordered us to break camp come morning. We march to battle."

"West?" Bellec asked.

"South."

The mercenary leader nodded slowly. They had all heard of the western forces scattered along the border. Which one would fall next?

"Months ago, I sent two of mine into Salvaar to warn of the gathering storm," Bellec said. "They were supposed to stay at Cailean of the Aedei's side. Hadwin Weles of Torosa and Layan Asgeir of Aethela."

"The chief was taken by the enemy upon the fields of Bandujar," Eirian replied darkly.

"Captured?"

"Yes," the Káli said with a nod. "Fortunately, your people were not with him. They fought by One-Eye's side and now they ride south with him to draw our enemy away."

"That's why the eagles weren't here." Galadayne let out a surprised laugh.

Many of the mercenaries exchanged glances. None had seen the red eagle banners of Raynor here. None had seen Annoran soldiers or steel. Now they knew why.

"Who is One-Eye?" Sakkar asked with a frown.

"Your friend," Eirian told him. "Lukas of the Káli."

✦ ✦ ✦

"So Sylvaine is your mother?" Aeryn asked.

"I was conceived before she changed hosts." Kitara spun a knife around her hand absentmindedly. "Once more, Oriana was nothing more than a vessel."

"That's incredible." Aeryn was awestruck. "And no one knew apart from she and the druids."

Kitara watched the dagger as it danced between her fingers. "Bellec had an inkling, but I do not believe that he fully understood," she said.

"How could he?" Aeryn replied with a shrug. "Such a thing may have never happened before. You are a child of Sylvaine much like Tanris. It explains your gift."

Kitara paused and the knife came to a stop. "We cannot tell them who I am," she said.

Aeryn stared at her for moment before nodding. "This is a miracle, and my people would believe that you were sent by the spirits to protect this world," the moonseer told her. "They would come for you again and again and again … You would never know peace."

Kitara twirled the blade a final time before sheathing the steel. She gazed out into the trees and saw more than just the woods. She saw the smoke of the campfires. She saw the Salvaari joking and dancing around them. She saw freedom, true freedom.

"This land gives me hope," Kitara said, "and I will fight to defend it. I do not fear those men who march from the west nor any others who would harm us. That is *my* choice. It is not that of the spirits, of Sylvaine. It is my choice."

"You are the chief of your destiny," Aeryn replied. "You are the guide of your fate. You can fashion a course for your life and death, and no one can take that from you."

"For once, I would like to live a normal life," Kitara said. "To know peace. This gift … my mother … that changes everything."

"Does it really?" Aeryn replied. "Your mother is Sylvaine and so what? That does not mean that you in turn will be heralded as a spirit. Where we begin does not define who we will become."

Kitara's lips twitched into a smile as she looked towards Aeryn. "Nothing ever dampens your spirits, does it?"

"No." Aeryn chuckled. "Life goes on and you must live it with each breath."

Kitara's hand went to the sapphire ring that hung from her throat. "What of Bellec?" she asked. "Should he be told?"

"Of everyone in this world, he has the only right," Aeryn replied before leaning towards Kitara. "Your father loves you, Kitara. He was prepared to sacrifice everything so that you may live. He would have followed you to the ends of the earth."

"You truly think so?"

"I *know* so." Aeryn was sincere. "I know his story as well as you. What happened to your father was a terrible crime. His soul shattered a long time ago. Yet he is still your father."

Kitara took a long breath. Bellec had followed her from Salvaar to Aureia without so much as a question. He had risked everything, his life and those of his men, on the muddy streets of Vesuva. He trusted her with his story … Perhaps it was time for her to trust him.

"Then I will tell him," Kitara murmured. "When the time is right."

"I know that must be hard."

Kitara could only nod. Only she seemed to understand. Only she who she trusted most of all.

Aeryn rose to her feet and with a grin extended her hand. "Come," she said. "That is enough heavy thoughts for one night."

Life with every breath.

Kitara smiled and took Aeryn's hand. They both laughed as Aeryn twirled Kitara into her arms. Kitara leaned back into Aeryn for a moment. She felt the strength of her arms and tasted the sweetness of her scent. Aeryn's hair tickled her neck and her breath caressed Kitara's ear. Kitara's feet glided upon the ground as she spun. Their hands squeezed each other as they came face to face. Their eyes locked. Kitara's gaze melted in those pools of silver fire. It was as if Kitara could see into her heart, see the joy that radiated within. She felt the warmth of Aeryn's lips as they kissed. Kitara could not stop the grin that pulled at her own. Aeryn took her hand and together they began to make their way back towards the camp.

They found the mercenaries by the fire. Kitara frowned as she saw Eirian of the Káli rise from beside Bellec. Five other black-marked Káli were with him. Eirian gave Kitara and Aeryn a nod as he saw them approaching. He remembered them from Oryn. He remembered how they had helped save his people. Kitara returned the gesture and Eirian vanished into the trees with his people.

"You heard him, lads," Galadayne said as he rose to his feet. "Get some rest."

Grumbles rolled around the campfire as the order was given. With the speed that only veterans could muster, the warriors gathered up their kits and began to disperse. Kitara exchanged a look with Aeryn before making straight for her father and Galadayne.

"What is it?" Kitara asked.

"Henghis has given orders," Bellec explained. "We march at first light."

"Wants to strike those armies encroaching from the south while those in the west lick their wounds," Galadayne added.

"A bold move," Kitara said.

"The last one they'll expect," Bellec agreed. "Scouts have already been sent. It has begun."

Hooves thundered upon the ground. The mercenaries all turned towards the four riders who charged towards them. The four Salvaari were marked with the blue of the Aedei. Even their horses bore the woad paint. The leader leapt from his horse long before it came to a halt.

"Get out of my way," he growled as he shoved through a group of mercenaries. "Get out of my way!"

His face was weathered and scarred and his hair was black and wild. His frame was strong and his eyes of dark blue. Aeryn's eyes widened.

"Father," she murmured in Salvaari.

The words had barely left her mouth when the black-haired man enveloped her in great hug. They held each other tightly.

"Eivor." Bellec greeted the man.

The Aedei released his daughter and clasped Bellec's arm. Kitara looked from man to man. They had met in Faolan when the mercenaries had begun their journey to Aureia.

"Father, this is Kitara." Aeryn gestured to her.

Eivor turned his gaze to Kitara. "You're the one for whom my daughter crossed mountain and ocean for," he said in the common tongue.

"You're the one who blessed her to do so," Kitara replied in Salvaari.

Eivor's lips broke into a toothy grin. "You speak my language." He laughed.

"As you speak mine," Kitara countered, again in Salvaari.

Eivor extended his arm and Kitara took it gladly. Without hesitation, Aeryn's father pulled her into a one-armed embrace. For a reason that Kitara could not name, the itch to reach for a blade never arose.

"I am glad you made it back," Eivor told her before pulling away.

There was a warmth in his eyes that was kindred to that in Aeryn's. There was true kindness in them. Aeryn gathered up the reins of her father's mount and gently stroked the horse's powerful neck. Aeryn had once told Kitara that her family bred horses and that was how she mastered her skill with them. The moonseer murmured something into the mare's ear with a smile before looking to her father.

"Mother and Vanya?"

"Safe in the highlands," Eivor replied. "Along with many of our kin."

"We rode from the north," Bellec said. "Saw villages that all the warriors had left. Others still that were empty."

"To the south, they will all be empty," Eivor told him. "Everyone who cannot fight is making for the mountains beholden to the Icari. There they are far from the threat of war and death. There they are safe. Every man and woman from every tribe who has held axe, spear or bow is here. Salvaar is united."

"When we left, peace had returned to the tribes, but they were scattered," Galadayne said. "When we returned, we find that they have united behind Henghis. Eirian of the Káli told us that this is the first time in a century."

"A common enemy unites even the oldest of foes," Aeryn told him.

"My daughter speaks true," Eivor added. "Had we not banded together, then we may well be dead already."

"What happened?" Kitara asked.

"A massacre at Oryn," Eivor said through bared teeth. Rage burned hot in his words as he spoke. "Not long after you left,

Dayne of Annora and the boy Emilian Aloys attacked. They slaughtered everyone."

Kitara stared at him in disbelief. "What?" she muttered. "Why would Annora sack the very town they once had a hand in saving?"

Eivor snorted. "From what they told One-Eye, the attack was a mistake. They had no knowledge that the Káli had become our ally, nor that peace had ended the war," he said.

Sorrow hit Kitara as Eivor spoke. She remembered Oryn and she remembered it well. They had celebrated long into the night after they had liberated it from the enemy. She remembered being happy. Even now, Kitara could see the wars in the eyes and faces of her companions. They were hurting.

"It did *not* end with Oryn," Eivor continued. "To the north lies Aildor, a village that bore a shrine to the great sun spirit Yorath. They sundered the town and the shrine along with it. None survived. It was there in the ash that Henghis called a conclave. All the tribes were there. They gathered in those ruins, in a place of fire and blood and dust. It was there that the great chiefs pledged their lives and blood to Henghis. They believe that he is the only one who can deliver us from this darkness."

"And what do you believe?" Bellec asked.

Eivor frowned. "Before all of this happened … all this death, all this slaughter, I would not have followed a king," he replied. "My heart beats for the Aedei. My soul breathes for my tribe. Before this, Henghis was respected and admired by all, even those who fought against him. He is a great warrior and a greater leader. He brought us peace and I believe that he will do so again. In the past days, he has proven that that belief is well placed."

"Did Henghis not kill both Malakai and Cyneric?" Galadayne asked.

"Yes." Eivor turned to the mercenary. "He killed both chiefs. I have not forgotten. None of us has forgotten. I also have not forgotten that, if our roles had been reversed, I would have done the exact same thing. Cailean swore an oath to him even after Henghis slew both of his brothers, and would you like to know why? This is not about friendship. It is about survival. Cailean will never forget his dead, but he knew. He *knew* that Henghis was the only man who could have united us all. He knew that Henghis was the only one who could turn enemies into trusted friends. He knew that only Henghis could win this war. That is why."

"And now he brings you victory," Bellec growled.

"Yes. We Salvaari have long memories. We fight and kill for generations until we have forgotten why we were fighting in the first place. Henghis ended that. Blood feuds have come to an end upon his command. He walks among the people, shares stories with them, breaks bread with them. He mourns the dead and makes the living believe in the promise of better days. He is no longer marked with the red of the Catuvantuli. He wears the colours of every tribe. He rose above loyalty to one tribe. He rose above the Catuvantuli. He has risen above the idea of tribes. We are all the same. One tribe. One people. That is why we follow him."

"Then he shows us the way," Aeryn whispered.

"Make no mistake," Eivor added. "When we win this war, it will be because of Henghis."

The first hint of sunlight broke through the canopy when the Salvaari began their march. Eivor and the Aedei warriors of Faolan rode with the mercenary company. Thousands upon thousands of Salvaari on foot and on horse began the march. There were no horns or shouted commands. Moonseer of every tribe had been sent forth to eliminate any western scouts. This was an ambush, and the enemy would never know about the hell heading their way until it was upon them. Henghis had made his will known. The spirits were with him.

✦ ✦ ✦

THIRTY-SIX

Annoran and Medean encampment, Káli Lands, Forest of Salvaar

Hooves churned the soft earth as hundreds of steel-clad riders rode through the forest. Many were knights in mail armour. Many were royal guardsmen in their garb of plated scale armour. All wore the red of Annora. Eagle banners flew overhead as they followed in the wake of King Dayne. Outriders had returned not so long before bringing word that the camp of Tristayn and Santiago Caspin was not far ahead. What they were riding into, Dayne dreaded to guess. If Santiago was committed to playing this game in the shadows with Dayne, then the king was resolved not to lose. The duke had his eyes on Dayne's throne, that much was certain. The future of his family, the future of Annora and the future of this war against Salvaar could rest solely on how Dayne navigated the game. Sir Garrik, ever the constant companion, rode at his king's side at the head of the column. Queen Sofia was safely surrounded by a ring of Annoran steel in the heart of the army. They did not have the men to arrange a safe escort to Verena or Kilgareth, not now that they knew the passage was compromised. For the time being, the safest place for the queen was with the king.

Tristayn's scouts met Dayne in the woods and led the way north. It wasn't long before the song of axe upon wood greeted Dayne's company. The trees began to thin as teams of axemen appeared. Dayne's orders had been explicit: *every* army was to end the day's march early so that they might camp behind walls. A large manmade clearing emerged, a clearing in which the beginnings of a camp were about to arise. Men with shovels stood in ditches three feet deep that ran around the wooden foundation. The walls were already taller than any horse and the towers had appeared. Every soldier not building stood armed and in formation at the very edge of the clearing. They were taking no chances. They did not know who could be watching. As Dayne rode into the construction site, the tensions were apparent. The Annorans stood as far away from the Medeans as they could. The banners were divided. Both sides watched each other warily. Something had happened. Even the men of House Reyna had found their own place away from the viper and the eagle.

"Sir Garrik," the king said as he brought the column to a halt.

"It has gotten worse," the guardsman replied as his eyes swept the camp.

"Place a guard on the queen and then come with me," Dayne commanded. "Sir Edward, sweep the woods. The rest of the men are to help with the construction. I want all of us within those walls by nightfall."

"Lord king." Garrik rode back down the column to give the orders.

"Lord king," Edward echoed and then called forth a company of the guard.

Dayne looked towards the Caspin camp as his army began to disperse. Dark looks came his way from the men wearing the green of Santiago. When he had left to meet with Lukas, those looks had been of irritation and anger; now they were unbridled hate. Whatever had caused the rift between the two peoples must have been grave.

Dayne swung his leg over his horse's back and dropped down to the ground. He unstrapped his helmet and pulled it from his head before pushing back his coif. Sweat greased his hair back.

"Your majesty," a familiar voice called.

"Tristayn." The king greeted his general as he watched him approach.

"My king," Lord Balderik of Laeoflaed said from Tristayn's side.

"Lord Balderik."

Dayne clasped their arms in turn.

"I see that you found the queen." Tristayn looked over Dayne's shoulder.

The king glanced back to see his wife dismount. "Safe and in high spirits though prepared for the worst," Dayne replied.

"What of Prince Lukas?" Balderik asked. "Is it true what they say?"

Dayne held back a grimace. That was the most disturbing news of all.

"My brother's path is no longer with Annora." Dayne kept his emotion in check. "His fate is no longer in our hands. He is no prince. The banishment stands."

"Then all the stories …" Balderik trailed off.

"They're true. All of it is true," Dayne said. "Valham. Bandujar … It was he who led the slaughter in the north."

"Then he has betrayed us all," Tristayn muttered.

"And that betrayal will make us stronger," Dayne replied. "In time, Lukas will be dealt with. You have my word." The king paused and looked from man to man. "Something has happened. Something has changed."

"Lord Galan is dead," Balderik growled. "At Caspin's hand."

Dayne's hand tightened upon his eagle sword. He had expected Santiago to move against him in his absence, but to kill a high lord … that was madness.

"Then Santiago Caspin courts war with us."

A ring of royal guardsmen surrounded the king's tent. Their hands never left their swords, while their wary eyes were ever watchful.

Within the shielded walls were six of them. All felt the same anger, all showed it differently. Blazing eyes or curled fists. Tensed jaws or hands tightly wrapped around weapons. Only Dayne kept his reserve. Only he stood relaxed. His hands were lightly clasped at his stomach. Sofia stood at his side while Sir Garrik, Tristayn, Lord Balderik and another nobleman completed the six. They stood around a bare table atop fine pelts.

Tristayn gestured to the noble from Laeoflaed. "The soldiers of Laeoflaed have chosen Lord Asteryn to lead them," he said. "It is likely that he will succeed Lord Galan when the council chooses."

Dayne let his eyes wash over the lord. He was young, a year or two younger than Dayne himself. The king knew of Asteryn and knew of his capabilities.

"What say you, Asteryn?" Dayne said. "Are you the one to succeed Galan?"

"When we return home, the lords will gather and choose," Asteryn replied. "But yes, I believe it so. If they ask it of me, I will gladly lead Laeoflaed."

"Young for a high lord," Dayne told him, "and yet stranger things have happened. You proved yourself a dozen times at Bandujar. I have no doubt you will continue to do the same in the days to come."

"Thank you, my king."

"Tell me about your men." Dayne motioned towards him. "What are they saying?"

"They speak of vengeance," Asteryn growled. "They speak of *justice*. They know who killed their lord and their anger is rising. I keep them in check as best I can, but retaliations have already begun."

Dayne frowned. "Retaliations?"

"Last night, three Caspin men died," Asteryn explained. "My people know that they cannot reach Santiago, so they strike lower. None have come forward to answer the allegations, yet we know it was them."

Dayne looked from Asteryn to Tristayn. He needed to know what pieces lay upon the board on which he was about to play.

"Seven days I have been gone and a high lord is dead," he said calmly. "Tell me everything."

"Not long after you left, the fights began anew," Balderik said. "Santiago believed you responsible for the queen's capture. He did not hold his tongue."

"No, I can't imagine he did."

"The fights began soon after," Balderik continued. "We tried to stop them, but the men are passionate. Stop one and another rises in its place."

"We believe that Lord Galan's death was the price of Aquale's," Tristayn added.

"And yet I did not kill Aquale Caspin," Dayne replied.

"All that matters is that they think you did," Asteryn said. "Words are no use here."

"I went before Santiago Caspin with a knife covered in the tears of Galan's blood." Tristayn folded his arms. "His guard would not let me pass. When the duke at last saw me, I begged for him to make amends. To make them *before* you returned, my king. He did not. Instead, people are dying on both sides."

"What about Anejo Reyna?" Sofia asked. "I saw the tiger banners. Does he stand idle while the snake and eagle tear each other apart?"

"The duke keeps well out of it," Tristayn told her. "He knows not who is innocent and who is guilty. He will not risk his men in a battle not of his making. His hands are tied."

"Then he is a coward," Garrik cursed. "After what Annora did for him—"

"That was another time." Dayne cut him off. "With another king. It was the mercenary Bellec who ended the rebellion long before our troops could cross the border. Anejo owes us nothing."

"I fear that he will be drawn into this fight," Tristayn said.

"House Reyna is allied to Annora, yet they are Medean same as Caspin. Unless we can prove that we did not kill Aquale, we may need to stand and fight rather than be torn apart from two fronts."

"Let's hope it doesn't come to that," Dayne said as his lips twitched into something of a smile. "With the safe return of Sofia, they may see reason."

"I doubt it," Garrik muttered. "They killed a high lord in his tent. There is no walking away from that."

"I will talk to Santiago," Dayne told them. "Things will be made right."

"He will not see you," Balderik said. "He will not see any of us. Whether he fears reprisal or something else, we cannot get close. Not since the general went to meet him days ago."

"Then I will go." Sofia's voice was steely. "I will see my father. At the least I can convince him to meet with you."

"Forgive me, my queen," Asteryn replied, "but you were born Medean and a Caspin."

"What are you implying?" Sofia stared at the lord.

"It would not look good for you to cross into *your* father's lines when the hour is late," he said. "Not after what we are discussing."

Sofia met his hard stare. "Do you fear that I will betray you, Lord Asteryn?" she asked as she looked from face to face. "Do the rest of you?"

"My queen—"

Sofia held up a hand to silence the young lord. "I am here in this tent," she told him. "I am helping you against my father. It was I who brought the king a confession from my father about his own father's death. I was born Caspin, but that is no longer my name. I am a Raynor. I am of Annora. Sofia Raynor of Annora – that is my name. I love my father, but what he is doing is *wrong*. What he failed to consider was that I have a new family now. A new people. I will not side with a family that murders another. That is a thing that I cannot abide. I swore allegiance to Annora on the day that

I received its crown. Being here now is my duty. To my family. To my husband. To my people. If this fight comes to bloodshed, then so be it. At least I had a say in my choice, and I *choose* Annora."

"Spoken like a queen." Garrik gave her a small bow.

"If anyone questions my loyalty, then say so now," Sofia continued.

None spoke. Humour flashed through Dayne's pale eyes. She was good at this.

"Good," Sofia said after a moment. "Then it's decided. Men are dying and I cannot sit idly by. I will speak to my father."

✦ ✦ ✦

Sofia approached the line of Caspin soldiers alone. They wore shirts of mail and their silver plates were trimmed in gold. Their long, green cloaks brushed the earth, while the viper was emblazoned upon their round shields. Their weathered hands were wrapped tightly around the shafts of tall spears. Helmets shielded their faces, and their plumes were the same emerald as their cloaks. These were the veteran mercenary soldiers that made up her father's private guard. Brave, skilled and loyal without fault. They saw the duke's daughter approaching, and for the first time, they hesitated. She was a Caspin, yet she was also a Raynor. Sofia said nothing. Instead, she tilted her head slightly and glared deep into the guard captain's eyes.

"Make way for the queen," the captain commanded.

As one, the guard stood aside. Sofia did not spare them a second glance as she made her way into her father's camp. She ignored the looks she was given as she walked through the maze of tents and soldiers. Sofia was the daughter of their duke and as such was above them.

She found Santiago talking in confidence with Rodrigo Santana and his other commanders. The Medeans looked up as Sofia appeared before them. All talk was silenced.

"Leave us," Santiago ordered.

His companions vanished within moments. Santiago's eyes softened and a smile crept across his lips.

"The gods smile upon us at last," the duke said and stepped towards his daughter.

Sofia returned the smile and embraced her father. There was a coldness in his gaze that had not been there when she had left Verena. His face was drawn.

"You look tired," she told him.

"It's nothing," Santiago replied and shook his head. He tried to look away, but Sofia moved and refused to break eye contact.

"It's true, isn't it? What they're saying?" she asked. "Men are dying."

"Soldiers die in war," Santiago replied. "That's what war is."

"I do not mean the Salvaari, and you know it," Sofia countered. "I can hear it in the walls of this camp. It's in the air. This is the sound of war. War between you and my husband."

"I am sorry to put you in this position, my daughter," Santiago told her as blazing fires came to life in his burning gaze. "But they killed Aquale."

"And in return you killed Lord Galan," Sofia said. "The cycle of killing continues. What if they did not kill your brother?"

"They did and to deny it would be to turn away blindly," Santiago growled. "Do not let your marriage to their king enslave you to them."

"I am no one's slave," Sofia snarled. "This fight must end and it must end now. I know about the defeat in the north. I know about how Salvaar triumphed. Is it really wise to continue this petty squabble while the real enemy is out there beyond these walls?"

"Then what would you have me do? Ignore the murder of my brother? Forget it?"

"No, I would have you live!" Sofia shot back. "Do not let your pride see to not only your death but the death of our faith, for that is what will happen if you continue down this path. I am not asking you to forget Aquale. I will never forget him. I am asking you to think of the future and so I beg you: meet with Dayne. Reason with him. Put this behind you until such a time as we can leave this forest forever."

✦ ✦ ✦

Kassandra Raynor followed a knight down into the depths of the Citadel. The warrior held a flaming torch with one hand, while his other rested atop the hilt of his longsword. Beneath Kilgareth there was a labyrinth of caves and tunnels that stretched for miles and miles. Beneath the keep's beating heart was the prison. Dozens of chambers filled with carved earth and stone mingled with thick steel bars lay before them. The knight led her up a small flight of steps and into one of the stone paved chambers. Braziers lit the room and a pair of armoured knights stood sentinel. A nod from Kassie's guide got them past the watch and into the room. The princess' eyes swept around the room. Behind the bars and hidden in the shadows were dozens of chained Salvaari. Some sat against the cavern walls; others leaned against the steel bars. Some of them stared at those outside of their cells with unbridled anger. Others lay in exhausted piles. They were wounded, tired and hungry. A part of Kassie's heart broke looking at them.

"Careful, your grace," the knight said as they made their approach. "These people would gladly see everyone in this mountain dead."

"Yet they are still people," Kassie replied before turning to her guide. "Please wait by the entrance."

"As you wish." The knight gave her a curt bow before backing away.

Kassie took a breath as she took the prisoners in. She felt a flutter of fear in her chest, but she repressed it. These people were not monsters. She had eaten with them. She had danced and sang with them. The Salvaari stared as the seventeen-year-old girl approached the steel bars alone. Her eyes searched the dark cell.

"Princess?" A low growl reached her ears.

There was a rattle and then the sound of chains scraping along stone. A man rose and slowly edged towards her.

"Cailean?" Kassie whispered as she recognised the man. "It's good to see you."

The chief placed his hands upon the cell bars. "If only not here," he replied.

Kassie stared at the big Salvaari. His blue woad was worn, and his hair matted. There was some dried blood still on his body. His face was weary, yet the fire in his eyes still burned.

"I'm sorry," Kassie said quietly. "I did not want this to happen to you."

"This was not of your making."

"I wish I could go back," she told him. "Make things different. Make things right."

"You cannot change the past," Cailean said. "You can only move forward. Only forward."

Kassie nodded and glanced back at the knights guarding the chamber. They were watching intently.

"We haven't much time," Kassie whispered. "Are they feeding you?"

"As well as you would expect," Cailean replied. "The maija Lysandra visits. She helps the wounded. She is keeping us alive. If not for her …" The chief chuckled bitterly and glanced at the guards. "And if not for you. What you did at the gates for me, for Scada, I will not forget."

That must have been the wounded man who Cailean had protected. The one that he had nearly been killed for when he stood up to the knights.

"How is he?" Kassie asked.

"He lives."

"I'm glad." She chanced a small, warm smile.

Cailean met her gaze. "Tell me," he said. "My people beyond these walls. Do they live?"

"Yes. There was a battle and … your people were victorious."

"Then the spirits have blessed me," Cailean said with a relieved smile. "What of you?"

"What of me?"

"A brother on each side. That must be hard."

"It is," Kassie replied. "Lukas fights alongside the Káli, yet he also saved me from them."

"What do you mean?" Cailean frowned.

"Princess," one of the knights called. Her guide. "We have to leave this place."

Kassie did not react. Instead, she placed her hands gently on the chief's.

"Keep faith." She did not let her gaze waver from his. "Have hope. I cannot help beyond these walls, but I can make sure that your people here are cared for. I promise you."

"Princess," the knight called again.

Kassie squeezed Cailean's hands before turning and making her way towards her guide. She spared the Salvaari prisoners a final glance as she left the chamber. Kassandra would not give up on them.

✦ ✦ ✦

THIRTY-SEVEN

Carlian, Steppe of Miera

"And so I ask you now: Can you hear it?"

Torben's last words echoed around the Mieran court. No one spoke. No one moved. He had never been more than a warrior, but even Torben could see the cold fires sparking in Mieran eyes. He could see the anger in the clenching of fists and squaring of jaws. The words that he had spoken questioned everything that the horsemen believed. For good reason, Miera had remained isolated from the outside world for centuries. Hate, distrust and suspicion were the only thoughts they had for outsiders. *Outlanders*, they called them; people who had invaded them time and time again without mercy. Torben had asked them to forget their fears, fears that had kept them alive for hundreds of years. The bloodsworn watched Zoran Layin intently. He could see the same emotion written across the king's eyes that he could see in the faces of Zoran's warriors. Zoran was a warrior, not a politician. Without a word, the Mieran king motioned to one of his guardsmen. Torben looked from man to man as the guard placed a hand on the bloodsworn's shoulder and nodded towards the doors. Whatever decision that the Mierans made, foreigners would play no role in it. Torben led his companions out of the hall in the guard's wake. The Mierans stared as they watched the outlanders leave. All of them were fighting wars in their own minds. Torben risked a final glance back as the doors began to close. The last thing he saw was King Zoran's unrelenting gaze.

The guard was silent as he led them through the palace corridors. They were taken to a large room and ushered inside. The door closed. They were alone. For the first time he looked around the room. Like the rest of the palace, the room was bare of all bar necessities. The Mierans had no need of luxury or wealth, only practicality. There was a simple table, a few chairs and a fireplace that burned brightly.

"No books, no art, no decoration," Elise Delfeyre murmured as her eyes roamed the room. "As warm as winter."

"They prefer a simple life," Cleander replied with a shrug as he made for the fireplace.

One by one, the companions took the seats. Only Torben and Luana remained apart from the group. Torben closed his eyes and let out a breath. For many days, he had struggled to find a tale to tell and now that he had he felt only self-doubt. In that moment, Torben would have given anything to be landing on the Aureian coast as his people searched for the secret fleet. There was no thinking in battle, not for Torben. There was only instinct. No schemes, no plots or betrayals. Only steel and blood.

"You found the words." Luana's voice broke through his thoughts.

"Now we will see if they bear fruit," Torben replied.

"It will work," she told him. "Have a little faith."

Torben snorted in reply. Try as he might, he could not still the thoughts returning to his mind. "You are more than who you appear to be, aren't you?"

"What do you mean?" Luana asked with a frown.

"When you told me your story, you told me that you had cultivated your name." Torben was suddenly unable to neither take his eyes from her nor remove the suspicion from them. "You did not say how you had earned your name, and I wonder if you used your gift with words to build it rather than your talent with steel."

"Perhaps it was both."

"Perhaps it was. Or perhaps you told a simple story and let it grow grander with every telling. I have heard some stories from voyagers about you. I heard that you have taken ships without drawing a blade. How could that be possible unless those who captained those ships feared you far more than they feared their own masters? What if your name was based upon a lie? In which case, I am forced to consider that us being here may have been your idea entirely."

Luana smiled. "If that were true then I could well be a spider and you all flies in my web," she replied.

"Maybe we are," Torben said. "Maybe you are the greatest mind of our generation, but you hide it so that you can manipulate these stories from the shadows. But what I fear more strongly is that it was your words that convinced Erik to take this path. *Never underestimate the power of a good story or the strength of a song.* That is what you said to Erik. That was what you told him. It was you who convinced him to make war on Elara. It was you who spoke so often of the empire's plans for Miera. It was you convinced him that we would be next. It was you who supported his idea for us to be here in this moment. The song of the raven … that was you."

"Alright, you have my interest." Luana's eyes shone. "Say I was responsible for all of that. Say that it was me who through words made this all come to pass. What reason would you suggest guided my hand?"

"I do not know," Torben continued. "Perhaps one day soon I will know. Perhaps one day soon you will rule everything."

Luana raised her eyebrows. Her lips twitched into a smirk. Her expression glowed as amusement painted her face. "Well, as soon as you decide what it is," she said, "you let me know."

"You will be the first," Torben replied.

With an amused chuckle, Luana removed her tricorn and placed it on the table. She snatched up the plain silver jug and poured two cups of ale before she handed one to Torben. He took it gratefully. The cups clinked as the pair bumped them. Torben grinned and then took a long draught. The Mieran ale was everything he had heard it to be. Strong, bitter and it stung on the way down. Torben clapped Luana on the arm and then gestured towards the chairs. Together they joined their companions by the warm fire.

"That was some story, my friend," Calvillo said as they approached. "That Astrid sounds like a remarkable woman."

"She was."

"Was it true?" Tariq asked.

"Every word," Torben replied softly.

"You knew her well," Elise stated.

Torben gave the girl a sad look. "She was my jarl and my captain. I would have followed her to whatever end," he said. "When she was taken from us, there was nothing in this world that could fill the hole she left behind. All that remains is her legacy and her legacy will be peace."

Cleander met his eyes but said nothing. Pain was etched into the man's face, as deep as the lines he bore on his skin. He had lost something once too. Something that had meant as much to him as Astrid had meant to Torben. The bloodsworn took another drink from his cup.

"You know why I am here. You have heard my story," he said. "What are yours?"

Marshall was the first to speak.

"I grew up in the slums of Elara where I only lived if I fought for every scrap," the captain began. "I was good at it, and where I grew up, that got you noticed. A man by the name of Elain came to me one day. It was he who started to unite the gangs before Bhaltair rose to prominence. He used me as hired muscle. Before long, Elain welcomed me into his inner circle. As a test he took me with him one night and at the time I did not know why. A new family had come to the district, you see. When the man refused to pay the money he owed, Elain told me to break his arms. I refused and instead stood between them. Elain had no choice but to back off. The man I saved was Imriel Delfeyre." Marshall looked to Elise as he spoke her father's name. "It was he who found me a position as a mercenary aboard a trade ship. In time, I became a captain. In time, I returned to serve the family of the man who had taught me how to better myself."

He spoke with pride. He spoke with pain. The man who had helped forge him was dead, murdered. He had failed in his task. Elise knew he would not fail again.

"Tariq," Calvillo spoke up. "Strange name for a Berenithian."

Tariq chuckled. "The name I was born with comes deep from the mountains of my homeland. I doubt you could pronounce it and so Tariq I am," he replied. "When my parents were brought to Elara many years ago, it was not as travellers or freemen. It was as *slaves*. A man by the name of Aillard Viorica helped to change the laws of the League and in so doing set the slaves free. It was in Elara that I met Elise's family and joined their circus. After … after they were gone, I began fighting in the pits to win coin. Coin that was intended to set us both free."

"I saw you fight once," Cleander said. "Last year on midsummer's night. You were magnificent."

"Being good will get you killed," Tariq told him. "For us to survive, I had to be *great*."

"I know the name Aillard Viorica and I know it well," Luana said. "As you have probably guessed, Marquez is Medean. My father was a trader. Took me to the League as a child and ended up fighting by Aillard's side. Cost him his life and I ended up on a slave ship bound for the empire. Somehow the pirates received word of its course. Cillian Teague saved me. I stayed with them ever since."

Torben turned his attention to Calvillo. The Tariki pirate sat in silence listening as his companions talked. He held his wicked Dao sword with one hand and with the other ran a whetstone down the steel.

"What about you, Calvillo?" Torben asked. "Your people rarely come this far south."

A smirk played across Calvillo's lips as he worked the whetstone. "No dark deed or shadow of the past brought me here," he replied. "It was my own choice to leave Tarik. I came to the mainland for adventure … to explore the wide, wide world. I wandered the kingdoms for a time in the pursuit of knowledge. I found myself in Landonsport when Varsige Euceia tried to take control of the city. I was there when the Sacasians came to liberate the city. When Varsige sent men to kill all those whom he had imprisoned, I could not stand by. Dozens of slave ships were to be sent to Aureia."

"I was there that day," Luana added, smiling and gesturing towards her friend. "Saw him clear the deck of a galley like it was nothing."

"And so I stayed to help their cause," Calvillo concluded. "To help those whom the whole world had united against."

"Tell me, Calvillo," Elise said with a bemused smile. "Now that you have lived among us southerners for so long, do you feel better or worse?"

The Tariki chuckled. They all did.

"What of you?" Calvillo asked her. "How does one so young end up on the run with a mercenary and a pit fighter as her only companions?"

Elise's smile vanished in a heartbeat. She clenched her jaw, and it took everything to stop her hands from balling into fists. Pain washed across her face in an ocean of agony.

Tariq placed a hand on her arm. "You don't have to do this," he said softly.

"No … no, it's alright," Elise told him. "They all know what I was."

She relaxed her jaw and forced the sorrow back. Elise stared into Calvillo's eyes.

"How did one so young end up here? Her parents are murdered," Elise growled. "Her aunt and uncle are murdered. Her life is destroyed *twice* over. Yet she survives. I was from a poor family but a happy one. I had a roof over my head and clothes on my back. I had everything that anyone could have dreamt of: love, respect and family. As a child, I was a performer and an acrobat. As an adult, I was a noblewoman and thief. By day I would play the adopted daughter of a wealthy lord, while by night I would seek out those who had harmed my family. I took my own nightmares and cloaked myself in them. I became one. That is where the Nightingale came from: the fears of a girl who had lost everything. But my name became known. What I had done became known. Elara was not safe and so now I am here."

"I've heard the stories about the Nightingale," Luana said. "Was it hard living as that name for so long?"

"Yes … and no," Elise replied. "I was always Elise. I refused to let the Nightingale and my past change who I was. Elise Delfeyre. That is who I am."

"We've all come a long way, haven't we?" Tariq muttered.

"Slavery, murder, vengeance, secrets. Those have brought us together," Marshall replied as he brushed his thumb across his sun and moon amulet. "Yet here we all are, here at the same time, fighting for the same cause. No one can understand the fates or the gods' will."

"I would not even try to understand, my friend." Torben chuckled before taking another gulp of ale.

"What of you, Cleander?" Tariq asked.

All eyes went to the Annoran who had become a leader in the Elaran gangs. A man as skilled with a blade as any.

"I'm no one," Cleander muttered.

"That no one is pretty good with a blade," Marshall said. "I've seen you fight."

"All you need to know is that I am of the sword." Cleander gave him a dark look. "That is how I was born. That is how I was raised. Nothing more."

"I highly doubt that," Marshall countered.

"Let it go, Marshall," Elise cut in and rolled her eyes. "Let him keep his secrets. We do not know what the king will decide, and if we're done swapping our tales of grandeur, I would like to get some sleep."

Torben grinned. They all did.

"Grandeur, she says." Tariq laughed.

Luana downed her drink and rose to her feet. "We should all get some rest."

✦ ✦ ✦

Lord Zandir Barangir watched his king intently. Not long after the foreigners left the courtroom, Zoran dismissed all save Zandir and Lord Acrasia. As the door closed behind the last of those leaving, Zoran turned to the remaining lords.

"So the Accords have been broken," the king said. "The empire has come."

"The League has been emboldened by the western army," Acrasia cursed. "They would not dare test themselves against us if their allies were not so close."

"The slightest thing can cause a ripple," Zandir murmured. "Toss a pebble into one side of the ocean and you may well cause a flood on the other."

"And now we must act." The king gathered up his sword from beside the throne. "Lord Acrasia, take eight thousand riders and make for the mountain pass. If the enemy has not yet made the crossing, send men into the pass. Burn their outpost as a warning. Their betrayal will not be tolerated. Send riders along the south and gather as many men as can be found. If the League crosses those mountains, they will be met by a very unpleasant surprise. If the League crosses those mountains, wipe them out. I don't care how you do it, but wipe them out."

"It will be done." Lord Acrasia gave Zoran a bow before turning on his heel and marching from the hall.

The king waited until the doors closed behind Acrasia before he turned to Zandir.

"Did you see it in their eyes?" he asked.

Zandir nodded. "They have been impassioned," he replied. "It will not be long before the people cry out for justice."

"What did you make of that man Torben's story?"

"A little embellished maybe, but he was speaking the truth," Zandir said thoughtfully. "The west is marshalled. The full might of the empire is on its way. The League has turned, and we are surrounded. If Salvaar falls, if the Valkir fall, we will almost undoubtedly be next."

King Zoran turned towards the phoenix banner that hung behind his throne. The banner of Zavian. The banner of Miera.

"Once, a long time ago, we rose from the ashes and cast the Idrisians from our land," he said, sweeping his gaze over the blazing red songbird. "Zavian defeated them in such a way that they have not had the strength to rise against us for over five hundred years. Since that day, every threat that has come to Miera has been defeated. We pushed the League back once and we can do so again. Them we have fought before. Now the whole world stands against us. Can we stand against the strength of all Annora, Aureia, the provinces of Medea and the League? This war will test us. I have fought in battle many times and it is not death that I fear nor the swords of Aureia. It is seeing my people in cages, watching their land burn, hearing their screams. And so

I am resolved: this will not be our end. I choose life ... I choose *freedom* for my people."

"Then we will not lose," Zandir replied as he approached his friend. "For one man defending his home is more powerful than a dozen hired soldiers."

Zoran turned to his companion. "You once counselled me about the chance that we may one day need to make allies beyond our border. Part of me believes that this may be that day. The other part of me knows that the outside world is filled with betrayal. What do you believe?"

Zandir placed his hand upon the hilt of his sword. The worn leather comforted his calloused hand. Five long decades he had swung his blade. Five long decades of blood.

"Salvaar will fall and it will fall soon. In time, the Valkir will fall. Even if they defeat the empire this time, more will come. More legions. We will be all that remains of the free world. A last outpost. They will come for us, Zoran. It has already started. They will come time and time and time again. For every army we defeat, they will send two more. We are alone ... but that does not mean that we need to be."

"You once harboured a foreign girl, did you not?" Zoran began. "Kitara ... Yes, that was her name. Kitara."

Zandir stared at his king. It had not been so many months ago that she had fled. For a year he had housed and fed the girl. A girl who had unusual talent with steel. He could still remember the day he had found her crossing the border as clearly as if it were glass.

"I took her in, yes."

"And yet she did betray you."

"She did."

"I am told she had Salvaari blood. She turned her back on Miera and she turned her back on you. Do you truly believe that if I were to offer peace to Salvaar that they would not do the same? Do you truly believe that they would not raid across the border every year?

Do you truly believe that they would not kill our women and burn our homes and fields?"

"I know it may be hard to believe, but the woads have honour. They are loyal to both friend and tribe."

"And yet she betrayed you."

"She discovered her bloodline. She knew that in time our people would have turned on her. My name could only protect her for so long. She would have been killed and you know it. She betrayed me, yes, but it was the only way that she could survive."

"And so you would have me reach out to those people who year after year for centuries have made war with us?" Zoran questioned.

"Have we not done the same to them?" Zandir replied quietly.

"You are of the north. You spent decades killing the woads. You shed blood, sweat and tears in the Rift fighting to defend our land. How is a man of your past willing to make peace with an enemy we have been killing for generations?"

"Because I believe that things can still change."

"Say the woads are prepared to talk. Say that they are prepared to make a deal. If we defeat the enemy and all that we hope for comes true, what is to stop them from betraying us? What is to stop them from turning steel upon us as they so often do to each other?"

"Nothing."

"And so you would have me spit upon everything that we Mierans hold dear."

"I would have our people live."

Zoran turned back to the phoenix. "And so I am forced to choose. Will I be the king that betrayed Miera, or will I be the *last* king of Miera?"

✦ ✦ ✦

THIRTY-EIGHT

Salvaari encampment, Káli Lands, Forest of Salvaar

Darkness had crept back into the forest when at last the column of warriors and horses made camp. The order had been given that there were to be no fires. There was to be no song or music. Nor was there the blaring of horns. They would simply set up their tents and bedrolls, sleep and then rise with the sun. The westerners would not be alerted to their presence.

Kitara dismounted alongside the mercenaries. They had spent the day in the saddle alongside the people of Faolan, alongside Eivor and the rest of the Aedei. Only Aeryn remained on horseback. Only the moonseer.

"Going out again tonight?" Kitara asked her.

"It's my duty," Aeryn replied.

Kitara ran a hand across Aeryn's horse's flank and then gently placed it on the moonseer's leg. "Stay safe," she said.

Aeryn nodded before she clicked her tongue and urged her mount forward. She would not return until dawn. Kitara watched Aeryn leave and then her eyes were drawn to another sight. Another of the tribes had begun to set up camp alongside the Aedei. The Káli. Wreathed in black, they appeared as servants to the very spirit they held above all others: Tanris. Some were rubbing clear liquid into the steel of their weapons. Poison … it could have been nothing else. Kitara had heard stories during her time in Annora about the Káli. Some called them poison worshippers. They were not great warriors like the Icari, nor were they great riders like the Coventina. What they had in abundance was intelligence. They would do whatever it took to win. That is why they were so feared both within Salvaar and beyond its border. Kitara's hand rose to the necklace that she wore beside her mother's ring. A simple leather cord adorned with a single snake's tooth. It had been a gift from Morlag before he had been slain for Aureian amusement.

"What is it?" Bellec asked from her side.

Kitara took a moment to consider. "There is something that I need to do."

Bellec followed her gaze towards the black-painted warriors. "You have business with the Káli?"

"I must speak to Vaylin."

"Lead the way," Bellec told her.

Together, father and daughter made their way through the Káli camp. The tribesmen gave the pair no more than inquisitive glances. They could all see the blue woad on Kitara's face as well as Bellec's armour. The days of Káli and Aedei shedding each other's blood had come to an end and so now they paid them no heed.

They found Vaylin talking with Eirian. The chief of the Káli wore her long hair bound behind her. Eyes of piercing green flicked towards Kitara and Bellec as they made their approach.

"Chief," Eirian said in Salvaari before nodding to the newcomers. "Bellec and Kitara."

"Chief Vaylin." Kitara offered her a courteous nod.

"I remember you," Vaylin said in the common tongue as she looked to Kitara. "You were one of the chosen and then aided us in unshrouding that wanderer's, Kendrick's, lies."

"I was, yes."

"Also fought at Oryn," Bellec replied and gave a nod to Eirian.

Vaylin ran her eyes over the mercenary. "Is that so?" she said softly, walking towards them like a panther. Her lips curled into a smirk and the emerald of her eyes flashed. The black of her war paint only accentuated her ever-green gaze and lustrous lashes. It was brushed across her face and ran down her throat, beneath her clothes and onto her bare midriff. Her winding tattoos were as graceful as her figure and almost as mysterious. Like the rest of her people, Vaylin wore little enough clothing and that which she did was dark. A pair of silver arm rings in the shape of snakes adorned her wrist.

Kitara wasn't sure if it was the hunger in Vaylin's eyes or the crude knife at her back that she found most unsettling. The scent of wild berries grew as the chieftain approached.

"What is it that you wish of me this night?" Vaylin asked.

It was then that Kitara saw the necklace that hung from Vaylin's neck. A simple cord with a snake's tooth. The sister to Morlag's own; the one that Kitara now wore. Kitara reached up and pulled Morlag's necklace from her throat. She held it out to the Káli chief. Surprise flickered across Vaylin's face as she saw the snake's tooth. She reached out and took it from Kitara.

"How did you come by my brother's trinket?"

"Morlag gave it to me," Kitara replied.

"Where is he now?"

"He died."

"How?"

"Days after Kendrick's death, I was captured by his Medeans. They caged me with many others. Your people. Morlag was among them." Kitara swore angrily as she remembered. "They put us on a slave ship and sent us deep into the lands of the empire. We tried to escape many times. We were *so* close. They condemned those who survived to the arena. Your brother … the Aureians executed him for entertainment."

Vaylin's eyes blazed with raw anger. "And the others?" she hissed.

"All dead," Kitara told her sadly. "Some were killed when we rose against them, others in the arena, others murdered. We fought for everything, but none survived. Not even the girl. Not even Sereia."

"Then their souls will never reach the Plain," Eirian growled. "They will wander this world aimlessly for eternity. Unable to feel. Unable to find peace."

"No," Kitara replied. "I brought their arm rings back, as many as I could find. One of the Aureians … he wore them as souvenirs."

She remembered that day clear as glass. When Crastus Nilor had come for her. When he had *beaten* her with a club. When she had snapped his neck.

"He kept them as trophies?" Vaylin snarled.

"Until the day I snapped his neck," Kitara told her. "I took them from his corpse. When I returned to Salvaar, one of the Aedei helped me honour the dead. We buried them over a battlefield soaked in western blood. A place of victory."

Relief washed across Vaylin's face like water upon the shore. "Then they will at last know peace," she said softly.

"They will," Kitara agreed.

"I thank you," Vaylin said sincerely. "Thank you for bringing my people home."

They heard the commotion before a group of riders appeared. There were seven, five wreathed in black paint and two clad in western armour. Kitara's hand fell to her sword as she turned to face them. The riders slowed from a canter to a walk and then the man who led them held up a hand to stop the small column. He wore the dark clothes of a Káli warrior alongside a shirt of mail. Black markings painted much of his face and a thick strip of cloth covered his left eye. Shaggy brunette hair hung to the man's shoulders. A short beard covered his jaw. Kitara frowned as he dismounted. She saw him use a single leg to take his weight. She saw the brace wrapped tightly around the warrior's knee. The man took a crutch from beneath his saddle and began to hobble towards Vaylin. A silver arm ring hung at his left wrist, yet it was the war hammer at his belt that drew Kitara's gaze. She recognised the weapon and could see something familiar beneath the war paint and cloth. It was the Annoran prince. Lukas Raynor.

"One-Eye," Vaylin greeted him in Salvaari. "You return at last."

"My chief." Lukas gave her a nod before turning to the general. "Eirian."

"Your journey bore fruit," Vaylin observed.

"We killed many Annorans," he replied with a snort as he approached.

Kitara searched his face yet saw no emotion save for a hint of satisfaction. What had happened to make the prince she had known take comfort in killing his own people?

"Your strategy worked," Eirian said.

"As I knew it would," Lukas replied.

"He walks side by side with Tanris." One of Lukas' companions spoke up. "I have seen it. This great victory is but the first that he shall bring."

The woman wore the black of the Káli, but it was the greenness of her eyes that Kitara found most familiar. She was the woman who Lukas had saved in Oryn. The one they called a priestess. Maevin.

"Lukas?" Kitara's eyes widened as she swept them over the prince. She could barely recognise the man before her.

"Kitara?" Lukas said with surprise. "You're here?"

"I could say the same thing to you," she replied.

"You are no longer a slave, and I am no longer of Annora. How things have changed," Lukas said with a toothy grin, extending a hand.

Kitara took it. "It's good to see you alive," she told him.

"I heard tales about what had happened in our absence, yet I must admit that I did not fully believe them," Bellec said as he looked to One-Eye.

"I was banished same as you," Lukas replied. "And that is the end of it."

Bellec glanced at the two foreigners among Lukas' contingent as they made their way over. Annorans garbed in western armour. They wore black cloth and paint around mail and plate so that they would stand out on the field. Bellec could not stop a grin from twisting his lips as the two men pulled their helmets from their heads.

"My brothers," he called as Hadwin and Layan approached.

"Boss." Hadwin greeted him as them embraced.

The two broke off and Bellec hugged Layan in turn.

"It is good to have you back," Layan told him.

Lukas leaned on his crutch as he looked from the mercenaries to his chief.

"We passed the army of Annora and Medea on our ride north," Lukas said, switching back to the Salvaari tongue. "My moonseer is tracking them as we speak. The king's forces will have joined them by now."

"It is towards them that we now march," Eirian told him.

"By Henghis' order," Vaylin added. "We heralded victory in the north, but that army still outnumbers us like we are nothing. In order to kill a snake, you must cut off its head, and so we march on King Dayne. Piece by piece, we can pick our enemy apart. Piece by piece, we can win this war."

✦ ✦ ✦

Sakkar glanced up as he saw them in the distance. Coming towards the mercenary camp alongside Kitara and Bellec were the two sellswords that had been sent to warn the Salvaari, a Káli woman and Lukas. Sakkar's lips broke into a grin as he rose to his feet.

"Is that …?" Senya asked as she stood beside him.

"It is." Sakkar chuckled.

The mercenaries with the Larissans hurried over to greet their long-absent friends. Laughter, smiles and jokes filled the camp. Lukas' eye lit up as he saw Sakkar. The Larissan pushed his way through the growing crowd towards his friend. The pair laughed as they embraced. It had been a long time.

"You look well," Lukas said, stepping back.

"And you look like a fucking painting," Sakkar replied with a grin as he glanced at the war paint. "I thought that only Salvaari could be marked."

"He is one of us now," the woman said from his side.

"I remember you." Sakkar glanced at her. "You were in Oryn."

"This is Maevin," Lukas told him before looking towards his friend's wife. "And let me guess, you would be Senya."

"I am," she replied. "I have heard much about you."

"Oh, really?" Lukas said with raised eyebrows.

"The Black Eagle they're calling you now," Sakkar stated.

It was as much a question as a statement. What had happened in the months that they had been apart for a prince of Annora to become one with the Káli?

"Only my enemies," Lukas said. "Much has happened since we last met."

"Tell me, brother." Sakkar motioned for him to continue.

"We were betrayed." Maevin was the first to speak.

"By whom?" Sakkar asked.

Lukas placed both hands upon his crutch. "It was not so long after you left that the west attacked Oryn," he started. "My brother had come to find me and brought the boy Emilian Aloys with him. The war was over by the time that they arrived and yet they attacked the village. Men. Women … Even some of the children. They were ridden down like animals. When I arrived, only one remained. Only Maevin."

"The slaughter of innocents changed everything," Maevin growled. "The spirits wept, and the skies grew dark. So dark."

"In the bloody streets, I fought Emilian. That cost me my eye. That cost me my leg," Lukas continued solemnly. "When I was recovered, I went with Maevin and a company of Káli to avenge the bloodmoon. The cost would be Emilian's life. In the hall of Palen-Tor, I confronted my father. I told him that for the first time in my life I could see clearly. You see, Sakkar, Maevin and the Káli had opened my eyes to everything."

"The king and his lords used Lukas like a hound," Maevin hissed. "They caged him like a bird."

"I am an eagle," Lukas said. "I want to fly. I want to be free. I told them that. I challenged my father. In that hall, I slew Emilian Aloys. On that day, Father Bardhyl was killed. On that day, I severed my ties with Annora. After that, I was banished and the last of the chains that bound me were cast aside. I feel free, Sakkar. Free for perhaps the first time in my life."

Sakkar glanced at Senya. He could hardly believe what he was hearing. All the whispers and rumours that he had heard upon his arrival in Salvaar about his friend were true. He could see the pain in Senya's face. Pain for him.

"The story I have heard about Valham. Is it true?" Sakkar asked.

"The priests there betrayed us," Lukas said darkly. "We sought sanctuary and they in turn broke the trust that we had given them. What I did there was justice."

"Justice and vengeance are not the same thing," Sakkar countered.

"The holy men would have seen us all dead," Maevin growled. "We are not animals to be butchered at the whim of those who do not know what it is like to bleed. They held their trinkets close and prayed to their false *gods* for my people to be wiped out. They still prayed that night. They prayed on their knees for their salvation, and do you know what they heard in reply? *Nothing* save the chilling whispers of the wind."

Sakkar could barely meet his friend's eye. That was not the Lukas that he remembered. That was not the prince and brother that he remembered. Lukas clapped a hand on Sakkar's shoulder.

"Forget the past. What's done is done," he said. "We are reunited my friend. We should drink and celebrate that."

Sakkar managed a grin and gave Lukas a nod.

"Aye, that we should."

✦ ✦ ✦

THIRTY-NINE

Kilgareth, Valley of Odrysia

Lysandra's mind swam with words as she hastened through the labyrinth of stone corridors. More messages came each day. Letters from every corner of the world. Letters from every camp among the great army. Among the various camps within Salvaar, she had spies. It was these informants that kept her wise to even the darkest of secrets. Every message that came from the camps bore a second message, a secret message, written upon the back of the parchment in writing invisible to the eye. The arc'maija entered her study and slowly locked the door at her back. The hour was late, and she had heard the call. Her master's call. Lysandra made her way across the room to her chair. She took a breath after she sat down and closed her eyes. Lysandra let the air flow through her as she called upon her gift just as she had once been taught. When at last her eyes flickered open, her irises burned with crimson light. Her teeth had sharpened into fangs. The veins beneath her skin ran with black blood. The blood of the ruskalan had been with her family for generations. Once more, she closed her eyes. Her brow furrowed as Lysandra called her gift forth. She found it. Her eyes opened, and when they did, she was not sitting in her office. She had crossed the Veil and now walked in the other Plain. Dark trees arose all around her and great stones marked with old runes were conjured forth. The aura of magic was strong. Lysandra could feel the power radiating all around just as she always did. The blood of the ruskalan was the blood of Tanris. The blood of the Lord of the Veil. This mighty gift allowed her to transport her consciousness into the Plain with but a thought. She felt the presence behind her before she had the chance to see the man.

"I heard your call," Lysandra said in Salvaari as she turned.

Dark robes covered the shadowy figure. With a pair of pale hands, he pulled back his deep hood and revealed his face. Like her, he had eyes of blazing crimson. Like her, his teeth were as fangs and his hair was the colour of coal. That was where the resemblance ended. The man before her bore pale skin marked with the same runes that filled the Plain. His ears sharpened into points.

"Welcome, daughter of the blood," Harkan of the ruskalan called. "The shadows grow, and with each passing day the rope tightens around our enemy."

"My agent secreted within Duke Caspin's camp has driven a blade between even the most trusted of allies. In one stroke, they will have torn themselves apart before our army arrives."

"When the Salvaari arrive at King Dayne's walls, it will be over for Annora and her allies. Your agent, a loose end, will no longer need to be tied," Harkan replied. He drew closer and stared deep within her eyes. "Your blood may not be as pure as mine, but it is you whom I trust most of all to see this game to its end. We are bonded as much by the blood in our veins as the blood that we shed. I have felt confusion within you, Lysandra. I have felt it in my blood."

"The Annoran princess, Kassandra, she *knows* about the she-elf," Lysandra told him.

"What has the girl told you?" Harkan asked, his voice betraying no more surprise than his pale face showed.

"Nothing," Lysandra replied. "Yet she comes to me seeking answers. Some I have helped her find, others I have yet to tell her.

Yet one thing remains clear: the girl has a kind heart. I believe that if asked she would help free Naidra from her steel prison."

"If the girl knows of Naidra, then it will be because the she-elf called to her," Harkan explained.

"Why would she do such a thing?"

"If what I have heard about the princess is true, then she shows great promise. The elves, ever led by the heart, can sense the very nature of those around them. Naidra will have seen strength in the girl. She will have felt the goodness of her heart. A leader beloved by all. Someone in that position could be the very thing needed to free Naidra from her cage."

Lysandra lowered her head in reservation. "Then we must bide our time," she said. "Wait to act."

"Yes, good," Harkan replied. "We are here in this very moment because of patience. Patience has seen us grow strong enough to control every side in this war. Patience will free the she-elf. We must proceed with caution and only make our play when we can succeed with absolute certainty. Steel your nerve and strengthen your resolve, for we are in the endgame now. Freeing the she-elf and avenging our fallen blood … that is what this is all about."

"What of their holy leader?" Lysandra asked.

"He is nothing but a puppet," Harkan said with a savage grin. "A fool who speaks riddles and words of wisdom yet is anything but wise. He is a relic who does nothing – who *is* nothing. In time, this *cardinal* will be dealt with and held accountable for his sins: his own and those of his predecessors."

Lysandra nodded slowly. The thought of what had happened to the ruskalan a century ago made her blood boil. What Cardinal Octavan and his followers had done. They had all but wiped out the ruskalan and the elves. They had destroyed everything. No more.

"Then what is to be done?" Lysandra looked to her leader.

"You know what must be done," Harkan stated. "You will

continue to play the puppet master. Once again, you must control those lives around you. Send the birds. It is time."

"It will be done."

The arc'maija placed a fist over her heart and gave Harkan a short bow. If Harkan had given the order, then everything had proceeded as planned. She closed her eyes, and when they opened, she was once more within her study. The redness of her eyes shifted. Her teeth grew blunt. Once more she appeared *human*. Lysandra opened a drawer of her desk and pulled forth a pile of parchment. She wet her quill and began to write.

The aviary was empty save for the gentle echoes of pigeon song. No maija were present, for Lysandra had sent them to attend to various tasks. One by one, she gathered the birds. One by one, she pulled letters from her satchel and attached them to pigeon legs. One by one, she sent them from Kilgareth. Her dark gaze followed the last of the small messengers as they flew north.

✦ ✦ ✦

Kyler's feet slid back as his sword flicked up. The song of wood filled the small yard as Kyler's staunch deflected a thrust aimed at his eyes. He darted forward as he countered. Hugh Karter angled his wrists and sent Kyler's blade to the side. The two men circled. Every day since Kyler had left Kilgareth for Elara, he trained day and night with Sir Alarik. That had been months ago. His skills had grown with his confidence by the day. At the same time, Hugh had been taken under Sir Corvo's wing. The former lord with a talent for steel had only grown better. His sword appeared no less a part of his body than the hand that held it. Kyler raised his sword up into a high guard. Hugh mirrored him. Hugh moved first. He was fast. He was precise. He was deadly. The knights' armour barely slowed them as they engaged. Kyler attacked, changed angles and then attacked again. Each blow he threw, Hugh parried or allowed to pass him by a hair's breadth. Each counter that came back to Kyler gave him no time to react. He blocked some, while others touched his armour.

The pain inside Kyler's head grew without warning. Anger rose with it. Something clicked and then he attacked his friend with the ferocity of a wild bear. He *wanted* to fight Hugh. He *wanted* to hurt Hugh. Kyler's lips curled back into a wordless snarl. The confusion in Hugh's eyes only made him more wild. Hugh began to back away as he defended each attack.

"KYLER!" Hugh roared as he blocked blow after blow. "KYLER!"

Kyler couldn't hear him, couldn't see him. All he could feel was pain. Hugh changed angles once, twice. He feinted, deflected Kyler's blade to the side and then smashed his crossguard into the side of Kyler's head. As Kyler staggered back, Hugh moved again. His staunch cracked *hard* into Kyler's wrist and sent his friend's blade flying from his hand.

"KYLER!"

The two swift blows to his body and the sound of his name broke through the red mist. Kyler groaned in pain and raised a hand to his pounding head. He glanced up at Hugh who stood with his sword levelled.

"I'm sorry," Kyler said. "I'm sorry."

"What the hell was that?" Hugh growled.

"I don't know," Kyler replied with a grimace. "Since that day in the vault, all I have felt is pain."

Hugh placed his staunch down and gathered up a water skin. He took a draught before passing it to his friend. Kyle took it gratefully.

"Speak to the maija," Hugh told him. "If anyone knows what to do, it will be them."

Kyler could only nod. If he told Hugh the truth, then he would turn on him. They all would.

"The mark on your face," Hugh continued. "It grows day by day. What did they say about it?" He spoke of the rash that appeared as torn and warped skin.

"Some kind of rash," Kyler said with a shrug. "They said I'll live."

Hugh placed a hand on his friend's shoulder. "Tell them of the pain," he said. "Let them help you."

"Aye, I'll do that," Kyler lied before taking a drink.

Kyler's mind was absent as he made his way through the maze of tents. His hands were balled into fists so tight that his hands began to hurt. He had lost control *again*. Had he been sparring anyone other than Hugh, he might have seriously hurt them, just like he almost had that man in Loxford. He needed to find a way to keep his mind in check. He needed to find a way to stay in control before it was too late. He could only hope that the research that Lysandra was doing into his affliction would bear fruit. The pain and the torment that came with it ruined his already disturbed dreams. He barely slept anymore, and Kyler could feel the exhaustion beginning to whittle him down piece by piece. He kept his helmet on to help hide the growing mark upon his face. The silver- and blue-clad knights that filled the narrow pathways between the tents would only give him looks of pity to go along with their never-ending questions. A wave of pain hit Kyler and froze him to the spot. His hand clutched the hilt of his longsword tightly as he resisted the urge to reach for his pounding temple. The crowd passed on either side, oblivious to his agony. He fought back the pain and shook his head to clear it. He took a step forward and glanced up. He froze again. Through the crowd of faces, he saw her. Clothed in the garb of the maija with lustrous hair the colour of midnight and eyes like oceans of rich amber. Kyler stared, for his gaze was drawn to the specks of emerald shining in those brown pools. Every detail of her face he recognised, from the curl of her lips to the freckles upon her cheeks. Kyler could barely stop the name slipping from his lips.

"Elena."

She turned and began to walk through the crowd. Kyler set out after her as his heart was torn by a tide of emotions. Love, sorrow, happiness, grief. They propelled him forward. Each step he took was faster than the last as Elena moved further and further away. He caught sight of her and then she was lost. Through the crowd, he caught sight of her again. His legs moved faster and then he was running. Kyler forced his way through the throng of knights. He began to catch up. His heart raced. In his soul he knew that this was a lie and that she was dead. That did not stop him. The crowd thinned as he followed the twisting and turning paths between the tents. Kyler caught up. She was barely three feet away. He reached out towards Elena. Kyler could remember her lips curling into a smile. He could remember the softness of her skin and the tenderness of her touch. Instead of the soft cloth of the maija's garb, his fingers found nothing but empty air. At his touch, Elena vanished as if she were smoke. An illusion. A phantasm conjured by his affliction. Kyler stared down at his empty hands and fought back the tears that threatened. He would not fall apart. He refused to fall apart. Squaring his jaw, he took a long breath. He composed himself and stilled the war raging within.

Kyler made his way back to his tent. He unbuckled his sword belt and placed it to the side before falling to his knees. Kyler's hands flew to his sun and moon amulet. It was the only way to stop the trembling of his fingers.

"Be merciful to me, Silver Lady. Ghosts haunt my dreams in the deepest night and cheat my eyes come break of day. When I am afraid, I will trust in you. In you I trust. I will not be afraid. What can these visions do to me? Nothing. They conspire and lurk, eager to take my life. Yet you have delivered my soul from the Pale Horseman. My vows I will honour until at last you call me. Oaths I have sworn and pledges I have taken. In you I trust and in you I believe, knowing that I walk before you in the light."

✦ ✦ ✦

Sir Corvo Alaine was deep in conversation with his captains when one of the maija entered his tent. The man offered a short bow to the acting master and extended an open letter. "From Verena," he said.

Corvo frowned as he saw a flicker of fear cross the maija's eyes. He took the letter and slowly read every word. Corvo felt a fire awaken within his chest. He turned from the maija to his captains. To Sir Alarik and the other commanders.

"Verena is under attack. They call for reinforcements," he said.

"Attacked?" Alarik said with a furrowed brow. "By whom?"

Corvo met his friend's eyes. "Salvaar."

✦ ✦ ✦

Commander Velis Demir stared across the barren land of the Rift. The Salvaari were out there somewhere. Even from here he could feel them watching from the trees. Even from here he could feel their hatred. Velis could not blame them. He ran a gentle hand down his mount's neck as he examined every last inch of ground. His eyes were *always* searching for any kind of advantage that could help them in battle. He turned as a horse cantered up beside his own.

"Sir." Jasir gave him a nod. The Aureian captain held out a letter to his commander. "Word from Verena," Jasir told him as Velis took the parchment.

Velis read every word, and he read them carefully. With a growl, he scrunched up the note and let it fall to the ground. Velis turned towards his friend.

"Tell the men to break camp. We ride at once."

✦ ✦ ✦

King Dayne read the letter for a second time. He glanced up at Sir Garrik and Tristayn Martyn.

"They must have slipped past when we rode to meet my brother," Dayne murmured. "Thousands of Salvaari have spilled from their trees and now lay siege to Verena. All the tribes could be there … We do not know. General Tristayn, take five hundred riders and find the northern armies. I am sure that they will be on the move by now. Tell them that we shall meet at Cacera and from there march to Verena's aid."

"It will be done."

✦ ✦ ✦

FORTY

Aureian Coast, The Lupentine Sea

The twin ships sailed westward through the cold waters of the Lupentine. For days the vessels had cut their way through the sea until now at last land arose before them. Whether by fortune's grace or not, they were yet to come across an Aureian ship. Pirate and Valkir alike had seen not a single sign of life since they had left Nesoi Island. Perhaps it was because Jorun and the other captains had begun to raid along the coast. Perhaps it was because the empire had called for all of its warships to muster.

King Erik's eye was drawn to the Oridassey yet again. He could see the shadowy figure clad in a midnight blue coat upon the helm. Cillian Teague. A man who was both saviour and father to his people. A man once of the empire. Throughout his years, Erik had heard rumours about the southern expedition of the captain, yet even after meeting the man, he was unsure if he believed them. Cillian was a mystery; however, he was right. Jorun was unlikely to uncover more than whispers about the imperial fleet. This plan, despite its very real danger, could be the only way to save them.

The Oridassey led the Ravenheart into a cove ringed by steep cliffs. Trees grew high above. A place such as this would shield the ships from any unwanted eyes. They got as close as they could to the shore before disembarking in longboats.

Salty water splashed over Erik's legs as he vaulted over the side of his boat. As one the Valkir began to heave the small vessel ashore. The clear sea underfoot turned into wet sand that crunched with every step. The raiders were the first onto the beach though Teague and his people were not far behind.

"I tracked the coast as we approached," Erik called out as he walked towards Teague. "Valentia is but a few days to the north, while Nilorenn is the same to the south."

"South – that is our road," Teague replied.

"Nilorenn?"

"Yes."

"Manned guard towers, stone walls," Fargrim said with raised eyebrows. "Hundreds of soldiers."

"And that is precisely why they will not expect us," Teague replied. "There is always a way in, my friend."

"I begin to question his plan," Laerke Redleaf muttered.

"There is no other way," Erik told them before turning to the pirate captain. "I expect that you did not come all this way expecting two ships to take such a prize."

Teague snorted and gestured towards his people. Halitreia and the other pirates made their way over with large sacks slung across their shoulders. One by one, they dropped them onto the sand. Erik frowned as he heard the unmistakable sound of steel. He dropped to a knee and pried the sack open. His eyes widened and a smirk crossed his face as he saw the contents. He pulled a purple-crested helmet from the sack and held it out in the light. Glistening silver steel with a snarling griffin beneath the violet crest shone as the sun danced along it. The helmet of the Arkin Garter. Within the bags were bracers, greaves and cuirasses to match.

"Gifts from the Scaeva clan," Teague told Erik. "Ten suits. One for each member of a complement of the Arkin Garter."

Erik grinned and clapped a hand on Laerke's shoulder. "A way presents itself," he said.

"I will lead to Nilorenn and from there to Eonie," Teague

promised them. "Nightfall will be upon us in a couple of hours, and we must be ready to move by then."

"Would the guard at Nilorenn not be suspicious of us approaching from the north and without horses?" Erik asked.

"There is a farm not far from here," Teague replied as he pulled off his coat. "We can approach under the cover of darkness and find what we need there."

"And what of you?" Laerke asked. "We will be the Garter and can no doubt slip past the Aureians unnoticed? But you? One look at a pirate and they'd gut you for sport."

Cillian Teague gave the warrior a grin as he gathered up a new bag and pulled forth a brilliant purple cloak. "We all have our roles to play and mine shall be that of an imperial diplomat," Teague said. "If we make good time, and with a little luck, we can be back here in eight days."

"Then this act begins," Erik said before he glanced at his helmsman. "Fargrim. You have the Ravenheart. Take her out and hide her beyond the horizon. Return in eight nights. We will meet you here."

"Of course," the helmsman replied.

The pair clasped arms. Erik turned to his crew and began to name those other nine who would join him and Teague. The pirate captain changed into his Aureian attire and buckled on his deadly sidesword. He gave his command and then his people joined the Valkir leaving by longboat. By the time night fell, Erik and his people were clad in their new armour. Laerke, Nenrir and Mayrun were with him along with six of the Ravenheart's best. Erik pulled his violet cloak over his shoulders and slung his oval-shaped shield of the Garter across his back. He gave a final look out into the sea. The Ravenheart and the Oridassey had vanished. There was no turning back now.

They came across the farm when the moon reached its peak. Fields spread for miles in every direction; some grew wheat and barley, while others played host to cattle, sheep and horses. Towards the centre of the farm was a small, simple settlement. A thatched hall was surrounded by warehouses, granaries and a windmill. Further into the farm was a stable. That was their goal.

Erik's eyes scanned the farm from the fields to the settlement. He saw everything from the number of livestock to the size of the settlement. There would have been no more than twenty people lying asleep within the hall. Erik looked to Teague and then to his people. Nenrir, Laerke and two others gathered up their bows. This was a raid, and they all knew that not one of the workers could be allowed to leave this farm. Erik tore free a handful of grass, held it up and then let it fall. He watched as the wind blew it to the east. They had to make their approach downwind of the livestock or their presence may not go unnoticed. The company made their way down the paths towards the stables. Every footfall made Erik wince, every slight sound that they made chilled his blood. Whether by luck or not, the raiders made it to the stable unnoticed. They reached the large wooden doors. With the tenderness of a sculptor, Erik unlatched the lock and began to ease the door open. A squeak came from the hinge. Erik grimaced and flicked his gaze over towards the hall. Nothing. They were in. Without hesitation Erik walked through the doors and into the dark.

The smell of straw and horses hung thick in the air like a pungent cloud. Over a dozen stalls filled the stable and each played host to an Aureian horse. They were tall and muscular, built for sprints rather than distance. They were chargers. War horses. Erik turned to Laerke and gave him a nod. Laerke made his approach before the horses could grow skittish. If it was by talent, skill or luck, Erik did not know, but his friend had calmed the horses within moments. His touch was gentle, and his words hushed. Laerke gave his companions a knowing look before gesturing to one of the saddles that lined the stalls. Without a word, the raiders gathered up the equipment and approached separate cells. Nenrir returned to the entrance of the stable and nocked an arrow in his powerful bow. They could not risk discovery. Erik gently brushed a hand along a chestnut mare's long neck before he slowly placed the saddle over her back. He tightened the straps and kept his touch light as the bridle and reins followed. One by one, the companions finished preparing their horses. Erik began to lead his mount out from the stall. A hiss met his ears. It was quiet and lasted only a heartbeat, yet its meaning was clear. A warning. The king stared down the stable to see Nenrir beckoning him. Erik handed the reins of his horse to Mayrun before making his way towards the sentry. Nenrir gestured towards the closed entry. Erik placed his eye to the sliver of a crack in the shut doors and peered outside. A child, a boy, was approaching. Erik closed his eyes as a sigh slipped from his lips. Already he was at war with the decision. There was no mistake in which direction the child was walking. If he did nothing, they would be seen, and a warning would get out. If the boy's shout drew the farm workers, then they would have to fight. Erik knew that his people would win if it came to bloodshed, but what if even a single one of the Aureians escaped? There would be no Nilorenn, no Eonie. No future for his people.

"Wait here," he whispered to Nenrir.

He ignored the startled expression that contorted his friend's face. The boy drew closer. Erik eased his way through the doors and out into the boy's vision. The child froze.

"Don't be afraid," Erik told him softly.

The king took a few steps towards the boy and knelt upon the cold earth. Even in the darkness, he could see the fear in the child's face. He was no older than ten summers.

"My name is Erik of the Arkin Garter," Erik told him as he tapped the purple cloth bound around his arm. "I have important business to attend to on the empire's behalf."

He kept one hand behind his back as he spoke. His fingers

lingered tight upon the hilt of his knife. If the boy made to shout or scream, he would have no choice.

"What is your name, boy?" Erik asked.

"Varryn ... sir," came the quiet reply.

"Varryn? A strong name," Erik replied as he reached out and placed a hand on the boy's shoulder. The child stared at the king as he continued. "Why are you out here in the cold?"

"I couldn't sleep."

"I understand that," Erik said and gave him a smile. "Varryn, I need you to do something for me. This is a dream. Return to your bed. Close your eyes and go back to sleep. Do not wake anyone and do not speak of this moment. The empire's fate depends on it. Can you do that?"

His grip tightened on the hilt of his knife. All it would take would be a single cut. From this range Erik could not miss. It would be over in an instant. Erik's eyes never left Varryn's. He prayed that the boy would listen.

"I can do that," Varryn told him.

"Then go," Erik said and nodded towards the house.

The king tried to keep the tension from his voice as he released the boy's shoulder. If the boy shouted ... if he started to run ... The knife was partly out of its sheath when Varryn at last turned. Erik could not tear his gaze away as he watched the child walk back towards his home. His grip on the blade was the only thing that stopped his hand from trembling. Erik slowly rose to his feet and returned to the stable. He eased his way inside.

"Was that wise?" Nenrir asked. "If he wakes them then we will have to fight."

"Then so be it," Erik replied as he at last released his grip upon the knife.

Those were the last words that he spoke. Varryn did not wake anyone. They waited for a time before one by one the companions led their horses from the stable. They reached the edge of the farm before they at last mounted up and began their ride south.

They rode hard for a day and night. It wasn't the pace Teague set that forced them to such speeds – it was the fact that they all knew what was at stake. At dawn on the second day, the walls of Nilorenn arose before the company. Built against the sea and stretching for miles, the harbour city was one of Aureia's greatest maritime bases. Merchant vessels and warships were nestled tightly in the harbour. Purple banners bearing the silver griffin flew atop the walls and towers, while soldiers clad in steel manned them. The company circumnavigated the city so that they approached from the south, from the direction of the capital. They thundered through the fields surrounding Nilorenn, down the roads and past farms. The men working the fields and tilling the soil stopped and stared as the Arkin Garter rode through their midst. They slowed their horses to a canter and then a walk as they drew closer to the walls. The gates were already open to allow the steady stream of people, wagons and horses in and out of the city. Teague flicked his cloak across his left arm and squared his jaw. He appeared every part the Aureian aristocrat. Arrogant, proud and above everything around him. Before the gate guards had the chance to speak, it was Teague who broke the silence.

"Nestan Venan Havita," he said with authority. "Emissary of the silver court. Loyal servant to the future emperor Eladis, son of Darius."

"Lord Havita," the guard captain said as he bowed. "Welcome to Nilorenn."

Erik tried not to stare at the soldiers. As a Valkir raider, he was not accustomed to seeing them, especially not this close without steel in hand. As Arkin Garter, he would have seen hundreds of them every day. He had to act like it. He had to act as if they were beneath him. He did not even spare them a second glance.

"The court has instructed me to find Lord Lionidir Wylan," Teague continued. "I am told that he has retired to a coastal villa."

Without hesitation, the guard gave them directions to Lord Wylan's house. Erik was almost surprised by how easy it was. With Cillian Teague dressed the part and bearing a legitimate Aureian emissary's name, along with a complement of Arkin Garter, there was no reason for the soldiers to question them. Erik doubted that any of the men had even met Lord Havita.

They followed the streets into the upper district and then turned towards the sea. Lord Wylan's villa sat atop the cliffs overlooking the Lupentine. A stone wall wrapped around the house and the villa itself soared high into the sky. Red tiles covered its roof in the traditional Aureian style, while its walls were ivory white. More guards greeted them at the villa gates. Unlike the men at the walls of Nilorenn, these were not steel-clad Aureian soldiers. These were mercenaries. They were well trained and loyal to a fault. Lionidir Wylan was a *lord* and nothing more. A *retired lord*. There might have been five mercenaries in total protecting his estate. A few words with the mercenaries saw them within the villa walls. Their horses were taken by servants and then the guards led Teague, Erik and the rest of the Valkir inside the retired lord's house. Erik could barely hide his surprise when they were taken to the courtyard. He had seen many things in his life but never the inside of an Aureian villa. A crystal-clear pool sat within the centre of the room, surrounded by lavish furnishings and tapestries. Erik had time to examine it all before a pair of Aureian nobles walked down from the balcony. The man was dressed in fine silks. His hair was black yet greying and a slight smile flew across his lips. Magnificent rings adorned his fingers. His eyes were pale blue and shone coldly with intelligence. This could only have been Lord Wylan. The woman wore a long blue dress. Like her husband, her dark hair was streaked with grey. Unlike her husband, her eyes were as warm as summer.

"Lord Havita, please forgive my lateness," Lord Wylan began. "I was not aware I was to entertain."

"There is nothing to forgive, Lord Wylan," Teague replied.

The pair shook hands. Wylan glanced from Teague to his Valkir companions. His expression gave away nothing and nor did his eyes. What was going on in that head of his, Erik could only guess.

"I am told that you are here on court business," Wylan continued.

"Indeed, I am." Teague took a step towards the lord. "The matters are … delicate."

Wylan nodded as he understood. He turned to his wife who in turn clapped her hands to summon servants.

"These men have ridden a long way and are in need of refreshments," she said. "Bring wine."

Lord Wylan gestured for Teague to follow him. "This way," he said."

✦ ✦ ✦

Teague sat in the offered chair by a desk. Wylan poured him a cup of wine before sitting opposite. The lords raised their glasses.

"To the empire," Wylan said.

"The empire," Teague echoed.

He lifted the cup to his lips and then paused. Teague met Lord Wylan's eyes and lowered the cup to the table without taking so much as a sip. The smile on Wylan's face vanished.

"You know who I am," Teague said.

"Quite the opposite, I'm afraid," Wylan replied. "I do not know who you are; however, I know who you are not. You are not Lord Nestan Venan Havita. Just as I am sure that you have guessed that the wine was poisoned."

"Though I did not see you drug the wine," Teague countered.

"Then you know what I once was."

"You were a spy true enough," Teague told him. "And a good one at that."

"And you are not an assassin, else by now I would be dead," Wylan replied.

"No, I am not."

"You are not an assassin or emissary. Your companions are not of the Garter though they wear that armour. They are Valkir," Wylan said calmly. "If I were to guess, it would be that you are an Aureian from the Sacasian and they no more than raiders. Raiders who *killed* men of the Garter. That brings me to my next question. Why would a Sacasian and a band of Valkir raiders risk so much to enter my house? The house of a retired spy?"

"We need your help," Teague told him.

"Go on."

"We need a way into Eonie. *You* are that way."

"You seek information?"

"And you will help us get it," Teague said coldly.

Wylan leaned forward on the desk. "And why would I do that?"

Teague allowed a hint of satisfaction to cross his face. "A rare thing in an arranged marriage to find love, yet if what I am told is correct, then you, my lord, would be one of those rare cases," he said. "Right now, ten great warriors are within your walls. Warriors who have nothing to lose. You could order your men to attack. They will lose. You could raise the alarm. If you do, then your entire household will fall by the time soldiers arrive. Lord Wylan, you have spent much of your life taking risks for the empire. Is this a risk that you are willing to take?"

"You are that desperate to gain entry to Eonie?" Wylan's face was impassive, his tone flat.

"I am *very* desperate," Teague told him. "We leave today. Your wife will accompany us in case you have even the slightest thought of betrayal. If you do, there is not one man or woman in that room who will not kill her. Once we have what we need from Eonie, we will have no more need of you or Lady Esmeray. You will be free to go."

"Tell me: What is to stop you from killing us both when we leave Eonie?"

Teague snorted. "I could say honour. I could say respect. In truth … nothing. Nothing save my word. That is my offer, Lord Wylan. I suggest that you take it."

Thirteen riders left Nilorenn within the hour. They rode west towards Eonie and their prize. The grandest prize of all. The grandest risk of all. There was still time for Lord Wylan to betray them. Still time for him to see them all dead at the gates of Eonie. All that they could do now was pray and hope that his love for his family was greater than his love for the empire.

✦ ✦ ✦

FORTY-ONE

There were no bird cries nor were there the sounds of the wild. No trace of deer or wolf or bear. There was nothing. The silence gave Lukas pause as he led his band through the forest. His company of Káli had divided into smaller groups so that they could sweep the land undetected. Maevin was with him along with fifteen more of her kin. Sakkar and Senya rode with One-Eye as well. Lukas paid no heed to his companions as he listened to the gentle whispering of the wind. They had ridden west of the main Salvaari army to make sure that no ambush or attack was coming from the western forces at the river.

"It's quiet," Sakkar muttered as they rode.

"The stillness in the air speaks to me," Maevin replied. "Something draws near."

A single birdsong echoed through the trees.

"Aelida," Lukas said quietly as he peered towards the cry. "That was a warning."

Lukas clicked his tongue and urged his mount towards the moonseer's call. They rode through the woods until out of the shadow of a tree stepped Aelida. Her silver eyes shone with warning and in her hands was clasped her bow. She raised a single finger to her lips before nodding further into the forest. Lukas slid from his saddle and made his way towards his scout.

"We heard your call," he whispered in Salvaari. "What have you seen?"

"Soldiers. Scouts," she replied. "And in the wind, thousands more."

Lukas looked back to his companions as they followed him to the ground. Bows were gathered up and arrows pulled from quivers.

"The west is here?" Lukas asked Aelida.

"They move. To where, I do not know."

"Then these scouts will reveal the truth."

Aelida led them through the forest on foot. All of the party held their weapons tightly within their hands. They could not afford for screams or cries of distress to reach the army that Aelida was so sure marched nearby. The sound of hooves carried through the air. Lukas' gaze snapped towards the noise. A small hill arose before them and there was no doubt that the sound had come from beyond. The company began to spread out as they climbed the small peak. Arrows were nocked. The Salvaari slid silently from tree to tree. This is what the Salvaari were trained to do. What they were made to do. What they were born to do.

When they reached the top of the hill, Lukas hobbled to a tree as fast and quietly as he was able. Shoulder met bark and then he peered around its edge. Below, barely twenty feet away, rode two dozen Aureian scouts. They carried oval shields and long spears, while armour of chainmail and steel helmets covered their bodies in silver. Lukas glanced towards Aelida. A single arrow was nocked and two more were held within her fingers. She gave Lukas a nod. Lukas swept his gaze through the trees. Sakkar watched him expectantly. He could not see most of his own people for they had become like shadows. Lukas pursed his lips and let out a single birdlike whistle. The forest, once still and silent, awoke. Spears and steel-tipped arrows rained down on the Aureian scouts. Most fell to the first volley.

Aelida sprinted down the hill the moment her first arrow had left her bow. The small blade tore through an Aureian's throat and cast him from his saddle. Her second punctured the heart of another rider. A third challenger charged towards the lone moonseer. He was close enough that Aelida could see the colour of his eyes – ocean blue and churning with rage. Her third arrow found him as he raised his spear. The blue of his eyes faded as he fell from his saddle. The horse ran so close that it brushed the fur of her cloak. The Aureian landed at her feet, the arrow that claimed his life shattering as the force of the fall turned fall into roll. Aelida did not move save for forward. She knew that he would not have touched her. A fourth man with an arrow embedded in his side rose from the ground to meet her. In a heartbeat, Aelida cast aside her bow, tore free her axe and deflected the man's shortsword. She slid behind him, disarmed him with her axe, drove him to his knees and then placed steel against his throat.

"Aelida." Lukas halted her killing blow. "We need him alive."

The moonseer snarled and shoved the man face first into the ground. "These people can't fight," she growled with a vicious smile.

Lukas gazed around the killing field. Man and horse had been slain alike. They had caught the Aureians off-guard and unawares. In the chaos, none of the Káli had fallen. Blood flowed freely from wounded Salvaari, yet not one life had been lost. Lukas' eye turned to the Aureians. Three yet lived. Three from whom they could find answers.

"Gather the survivors," Lukas commanded in Salvaari.

Swiftly the Salvaari did as they were bid, and within moments the three men were kneeling before Lukas with their hands tightly bound behind them. One-Eye unbuckled his helmet and let his hair fall to his shoulders. He met the Aureians' gaze one by one. They could see his eye, they could see his brace and they could see his crutch. They knew that he was not Salvaari.

"You know who I am," Lukas stated.

None of the captives replied. He could see a sliver of fear emerge in their eyes. They knew.

"But what you do not know is what will happen if you do not talk," Lukas continued. "And so I will ask you now: Where is your army going?"

None spoke.

A dangerous smirk crossed One-Eye's lips. "Where?"

"I am a soldier of Aureia," one of the men growled back. "I will not bow to you."

Lukas turned to the man. His smile broadened and a chuckle slipped through his lips. "Yes, you will." He stared deep into the man's eyes. "Tie him to a tree."

Rodion and another of the Káli heaved the Aureian to his feet. Lukas did not look away from the man as his people tied the soldier to the trunk of a tree of yew. The rope bound the man's wrists before circling the wood. So tight it was that the Aureian could barely move.

"Aelida," Lukas called to the moonseer.

Without a word, Aelida stepped forward and nocked an arrow in her warbow.

"Where is your army going?" Lukas asked the Aureian.

The soldier squared his jaw. "I am a soldier of Aureia. I will not bow before you."

Aelida's bow sang. The bladed arrow sliced the Aureian's cheek and dug deep into the tree. Blood began to trickle from the shallow wound as the Aureian bared his teeth.

"Where is your army going?" Lukas repeated.

"I am a soldier of Aureia. I will not bow before you!"

"Again," Lukas growled.

Aelida's second arrow ripped through muscle and shattered bone as it sliced through the captive's arm. The Aureian cried out.

"I AM A SOLDIER OF AUREIA! I WILL NOT BOW BEFORE YOU!"

"Again."

The third arrow carved a path through his thigh.

"I AM A SOLDIER OF AUREIA! I WILL NOT BOW BEFORE YOU!"

His cry was little more than a pain-filled scream. The man's agony etched itself upon his face and finally broke the last of his emotionless façade. His will was close to shattering. All of this and more Lukas saw. One-Eye's smile broadened as he looked to Sakkar. The Larissan showed nothing.

"Again," Lukas commanded as he stared at the Aureian.

The Aureian screamed as Aelida's fourth arrow ripped through the softness of the man's stomach. Skin, flesh, bone and organ parted before steel as if they were no more than water. The man's head fell limp. Blood trickled from his lips. Step by step, Lukas made his way over to the tree. He handed his crutch to one of the Káli before he reached his captive. Lukas reached out and gathered a handful of the Aureian's hair, forcing his head up. He stared into the man's eyes. Lukas saw defeat. He saw pain and suffering. He saw absence of hope. The man was his.

"Tell me where your army is going and this can all be over," Lukas said.

The soldier's lips parted but he did not reply. With his second hand, Lukas grasped the arrow embedded in the soldier's stomach, forcing it up slightly. The man's breath grew ragged and gasps fled his lips.

"Tell me where," Lukas whispered as he leaned in close.

He heaved the arrow up. The man screamed.

"WHERE!"

"Verena …" the Aureian managed. "Verena … They call for reinforcement."

"Verena?" Lukas said with a furrowed brow.

"We all march … in victory or defeat … for our gods …"

"How many are you?"

"Every man …"

Lukas glanced back at his people. "This great western army is on the move. All of them. They will cross the river some place east of Cacera." Lukas turned to Aelida. "Ride to Vaylin. Stop for nothing."

Without hesitation, the moonseer leapt up into her saddle and galloped into the forest.

"What of the prisoners?" Sakkar asked.

"I may have use for them," Maevin said.

"Prepare them for travel," Lukas ordered.

One-Eye turned back to the man tied to the tree. The man still breathed yet his every breath was laboured. Lukas pulled forth his dagger and in a single stroke thrust it up under the prisoner's chin. A sigh left the man's mouth as life left his eyes. Here he would remain as a warning. Here he would remain as a feast for foxes and crows. Lukas tore the blade free and let the blood of Aureia stain the earth.

They made camp deep in the forest, miles from the dead Aureians. Slowly the other groups of Lukas' Káli warband began to gather. Soon they were all there, all two hundred of them. Scant dark clothes, black warpaint and spiralling tattoos. Many bore jewels embellished with the snake symbol of Tanris. The Káli believed themselves to be his chosen disciples. Aelida would reach Vaylin within a day, yet Lukas and his company would remain separate from the main army as a vanguard. One-Eye dismounted from his steed beside Sakkar and Senya.

"The man said that Verena calls for reinforcement," Senya murmured. "What meaning do you think he carried?"

"Either the city is under attack, or these men believe that it is under attack," Lukas replied. "No Salvaari is that far south, so if

Verena is under siege, it will be another force. Yet who would that force be, this army that has materialised from nothing? The west is united. The Mierans will not leave their own border. The Valkir remain at sea as they always do. Whether they are under attack or not, this grants us an opportunity to rid us of this army in one great battle."

"Do we have the warriors to defeat such an army?" Sakkar asked. "The Salvaari number thousands, yet the enemy outnumber us like we are nothing and this time they have King Dayne."

Lukas waved a hand nonchalantly. "My brother is just a man," he replied. "He is no god or divine being. He can be defeated. He *will* be defeated. Have faith. The spirits are with us."

Sakkar chuckled and shook his head. "It was not so long ago that you believed in neither god nor spirit," the Larissan said.

"I have changed," Lukas told him.

"And what of them?" Senya said and gestured towards a rider.

Lukas glanced towards Maevin who rode further into the camp with the Aureian prisoners tethered by long leads of rope to her saddle.

"What of them?" Lukas replied.

"What use does she have for the Aureians?" Sakkar asked.

Káli warriors untethered the prisoners from the horse and led them into the camp. Maevin made her way over to One-Eye and his companions.

"That is for Tanris to decide," Lukas said.

"If half the stories I have heard are true—"

"Aureia is the enemy," Lukas growled. "Have you forgotten that?"

"No."

"These *leeches* die tonight," Maevin told them.

"Then why are they still alive?" Senya asked her.

"They are to be sacrifices, and with their deaths, we shall gain victory," Maevin said.

Sakkar's eyes widened. "You are going to sacrifice these men like beasts?" he growled.

"Everyone is born to die," Lukas told him. "Everyone is born to be a sacrifice."

"They came to our land with an army. They came to our land not for the earth, the trees and water, but for *us*." Hatred flowed from Maevin's tongue as she spoke. "To them the Salvaari are nothing. They are worse than nothing. Every man, every woman and every child beneath these trees will be wiped out. For those men who enter Salvaar with steel, I have no mercy. I will greet them with nothing but death."

Sakkar turned to Lukas. "Are you happy about this?" he asked, venom lacing his tone. "Killing in battle is one thing, but this – this is *murder*."

"As they have done to so many of ours," Lukas said ferociously, teeth bared. He looked to Maevin. "Make them *squeal* like the pigs that they are."

✦ ✦ ✦

The moon began to rise over Salvaar. The Káli began to form a large crowd, for they had all heard Maevin's call. Sakkar stood away from the camp, his mind overflowing with thoughts. What had become of his friend, the man he had known for years? The prince that had been as his brother? He had always done what was right, yet now he had taken up human sacrifice. He had lost more than his eye and knee. He had lost his mind. Sakkar spared a glance towards the Káli encampment, awash with orange light. Chants in their mother tongue had begun. Sakkar saw the prisoners dragged through the crowd. Maevin stood alone in the centre beside wooden posts. The Aureians were tied roughly to them. They were spread-eagled. The Káli removed their gags. Sakkar looked away.

"I know what you're thinking." Senya placed a gentle hand on his arm.

"Lukas was a friend … a brother," Sakkar muttered. "We fought together, hunted together … Now I do not even recognise him."

Screams filled the forest.

"I do not know what to do," Sakkar admitted. "I am lost, adrift."

"You have a good heart. Search it and you shall find the answer," Senya told him. "To save a brother, what would you do?"

✦ ✦ ✦

"Time to die, Aureian," Maevin whispered to one of the bound men before she began her dark work.

It was slow and she was not gentle. The two men had been stripped of their shirts and now the priestess carved the silver blade of her knife through their flesh. Lukas watched as the blood of Aureians flowed. It ran in streams down the half-naked bodies of the prisoners. Crimson pools began to emerge upon the ground. Red tears streaked across Maevin's wrist and covered the hand that clutched her bloody knife. Dozens of wounds crisscrossed Aureian flesh. Chants, shouts and cheers rolled through the Káli warband. Elation covered their faces and fire filled their hearts. This same *joy* began to seep into Lukas' soul. Watching those men who despised everything that he had come to stand for die slice by slice awoke something new within the former prince. The earth awash with Aureian blood spoke to him. The cries of the tortured men were sweet lullabies to his ears. With each cut, the roar of the crowd grew.

The man was nearly upon Lukas before he heard the sound of Káli being roughly shoved aside. Lukas turned to see Sakkar push his way into the circle of the crowd. Maevin spun around only for the Larissan to shove her out of the way. Steel glinted in the moonlight as Sakkar drew a blade and drove it deep into an Aureian's heart.

Blood spilled down the tortured man's lips and then the light of life left his eyes. Shouts filled the clearing and Maevin charged at Sakkar, but it was too late. Once more the Larissan's blade tasted blood. Once more an Aureian died. Everything in the clearing grew still. The wind ceased to whisper. The Káli froze in shock. Lukas halted as he stared towards Sakkar. Then Maevin was on the Larissan, her knife at his neck. The priestess' lips were drawn back into a snarl as the blade drew blood. Sakkar met her stare.

"Go on, girl … Go on!" he growled.

Maevin tensed her arm. She made to strike.

"Stop!" Lukas' voice cut through the darkness.

He made his way towards the pair and did not look away. Maevin held her blade at Sakkar's throat. There was a slight trickle of blood where steel had pierced the Larissan's neck. Maevin grimaced, her face awash with warring emotion. She wanted to slide steel across flesh and kill the man before her. Lukas could feel the hatred flowing from her. Had it been anyone else, then Lukas would not have stepped between them.

Maevin shoved Sakkar angrily and then stepped back. "He interferes in things that he does not understand," she spat.

"I understand," Sakkar snarled back as he brushed a droplet of blood from his neck.

"Why do you do this, my brother?" Lukas asked. "We are united."

"Are we?" Sakkar countered. "The Lukas I know would not sacrifice even an enemy to appease some kind of god."

Lukas stared at his friend. He pointed to the Aureians. "These men—"

"Are *still* men." Sakkar cut him off. "Whatever their failings, do they truly deserve this torment before death? You have beaten them, yet that is not enough for you?"

"No, it is not," Lukas replied bitterly. "For what they have done and for what they were going to do. The westerners received no more than a taste of the suffering that so many beneath these trees have endured at their hand."

"You speak the words, but they are hers," Sakkar told him venomously. "You have allowed this *witch* to warp your mind and now you have become the very thing that you once hated."

Lukas ran a hand across the head of his hammer. "I warn you to choose your words with care," he said as his anger rose.

Sakkar strode towards Maevin, his bloody knife still in hand. Lukas' hammer cleared his belt and was between them. The wicked spike stopped Sakkar in his tracks. Surprise flashed across the Larissan's eyes as he looked from Maevin to Lukas. The pointed steel pressed into his chest. Sakkar snorted in disbelief before he stared at the priestess.

"Would that I could turn back the sun and end her madness in Oryn," Sakkar muttered.

"Then what is stopping you now?" she goaded him. "We could form the square. See this done."

"No," Lukas growled and shoved his way between them. His hammer did not leave Sakkar's chest as he spoke. "You will not threaten again. You will not question again. Do you understand?"

"You know I cannot do that."

"You were my brother," he replied. "Perhaps no longer. You meddle in matters beyond any of us."

"I don't think so," Sakkar countered as pain entered his voice for the first time.

Lukas pulled a small vial from his belt and extended it towards the Larissan. "The blade was poisoned."

Sakkar's eyes widened. He shook his head in disbelief before snatching the vial. He took a swig of the liquid before turning his rage-filled eyes on his friend. Sakkar pointed to Lukas as he spoke.

"You are not my brother. The man that I knew would have hated you for what you have become."

With that, Sakkar turned and began to push his way back through the crowd.

"Sakkar!" Lukas called after him. "You are banished from my side. Ride with the Salvaari if you must, but if you ever find yourself in my presence, if you ever speak out against the spirits again … I will kill you."

The words halted the Larissan for moment. He said nothing. He only walked away. Lukas glanced back at Maevin as she sheathed her blade. The priestess gestured towards the dead Aureians.

"Gather their blood," she commanded the Káli.

✦ ✦ ✦

Aelida leapt from her saddle as she reached the heart of the Salvaari camp. She had found her chief easily enough and now the others were gathering to hear the moonseer's words. Aelida told them everything: of the Aureian scouts and of what they had uncovered. She drew forth a knife and drew a curve in the ground.

"They march south this side of the river as to not get separated. This is Cacera," she explained as she marked a place west of the line. Aelida sliced her knife through the line marking the river. "And this is where they will cross. It is the *only* ford over which an entire army can pass that far south."

All eyes turned to Henghis as the king decided.

"This is a great risk," the leader began. "Against so many, if we take this fight, then victory is not certain. Even now we are outnumbered greatly. If we do not win, then we will all die. Our elders. Our children. Our culture. Salvaar will die." Henghis looked from face to face. "And yet everything that begins must come to an end. We all die. The innocent. The guilty. Nothing lasts forever. If this is to be our last song, then it shall be sung until the end of time. So I say gather steel. Gather axe and spear. Gather your courage, for we march. We march to victory or defeat. We march for Salvaar. We march for the spirits."

✦ ✦ ✦

FORTY-TWO

Káli Lands, Forest of Salvaar

The armies of Annora and of the houses Reyna and Caspin had marched come first light. The news that Verena was under attack weighed on Dayne's mind. How had so many thousands of the pagans slipped past them unnoticed and, better yet, why? The Salvaari knew the terrain of their homeland. They had every advantage beneath these trees, whereas on an open battlefield, it was the men of the west who stood above all others. Henghis would have known that. To leave the forest was a risk and if his people could not take Verena by the time that Dayne and his allies arrived, the Salvaari would be crushed. All of them.

The three armies stopped a few hours before sundown. Teams of soldiers armed with axes brought down sturdy trees to create marching camps while the rest of the warriors stood sentinel. Palisade walls grew from the ground and hundreds of torches were brought to life. The armies marched inside, the gates were closed and archers manned the walls. If an attack came, they were ready.

Dayne breathed in the cool northern air as he walked along the battlements. He greeted his men as he strode past them. He knew many by name and even the briefest of words could bring them comfort when the night drew near. He stooped when he reached Sir Garrik who stood sentinel. His eyes scanned the forest. Dayne said nothing as he stood beside his long-time mentor and friend.

Dayne placed one hand atop the palisade and the other upon his aching stomach. The pain never left these days. His armour and sword had begun to grow heavy, yet Dayne had spoken not a word of it. He would not. His people were at war and the king *needed* to appear as a pillar of strength.

"Have you heard from Caspin?" Garrik asked.

"Not a word," Dayne replied. "He will not see me. He will not see reason."

"Look." Garrik turned back to face the camp. The banners of the three armies flew, but they flew apart. "We are divided at a time where unity comes before all else."

"There is still time," Dayne told him. "We must be as one before the walls of Verena. Perhaps–"

"Your majesty!" a royal guardsman cried as he ran towards them. "Your majesty!"

Dayne's eyes flicked to the soldier who approached. "What is it?" he asked.

"Murder."

The guardsman led them to Dayne's own tent. Dozens of scarlet-clad guardsmen patrolled the area. Spears and shields were drawn and held at the ready. Tents were being searched and cries filled the air. They found the dead man at the back of Dayne's tent. He was one of the royal guardsmen. The king knelt by the dead man's side. It was Sir Edward, a man who had ridden with Garrik to Salvaar when they were trying to save Lukas. A man who had ridden at Kassandra's side.

"Light of the gods be with you, my brother," Dayne murmured as he closed Edward's unseeing eyes.

"This is a threat," Garrik growled. "A message. A guardsman is dead at your hearth. If the killer can reach so far into this camp, then even you are not safe, my king."

"They say that the killer wore a green cloak," said the guardsman who had fetched them. "They say that he wore the colours of Caspin."

Dayne bit back a sigh as he rose to his feet. He turned to Garrik.

"Gather the council," Dayne ordered. "This ends now."

They met in Dayne's tent. The lords Balderik and Asteryn were there along with Sir Garrik and the queen.

"I called you here today because there has been another death," King Dayne said. "I called you here today because I say *enough*. We must act."

"I will sound the call," Lord Asteryn told him. "If we attack now, we can crush them by first light. Let me kill Caspin for you."

"You want to go to war?" Sofia asked.

"They brought the war to us," Asteryn replied.

"And now you wish to give it to them?"

"There is no other way," Asteryn said.

"The men are ready," Garrik told Dayne. "If you wish it, I will see this done."

The king said nothing and instead unbuckled his sword and placed it on the small table between them. He brushed his hand across the finely carved eagle on the pommel.

"Many months ago, we became one family. Raynor and Caspin. One family, one goal, one common purpose," Dayne started. "Now this family is fractured and divided. We fight and kill each other. Did we not learn from the Gaedhela line? Did we not learn what happens when a family spills its own blood? When the great Chimera died, his sons tore their family apart and led Delios to ruin. An entire empire was wiped out like it was nothing. Will Raynor follow in those same footsteps? No. I refuse. Friends, there is only one way in which to end this. Only one way in which to stop this war among family. Tomorrow, as the sun rises, I will walk through the Caspin camp alone, unarmed and unarmoured as a show of friendship. I will seek out Santiago and then together we will make peace."

"My king, these people have no honour," Lord Balderik managed as he stared at Dayne. "They killed Lord Galan. They killed–"

"I am aware of that, Lord Balderik." Dayne's reply was calm.

"Alone?" Garrik said, anger contorting his face. "This will give Caspin the perfect opportunity to kill you. If you die–"

"Then I die trying to save this family," Dayne said.

"My husband is right." Sofia stepped to his side. There was worry in her voice, yet she did not shy away. "There is no other way."

"I swore an oath of honour!" Garrik snarled and thumped the Raynor insignia upon his chest. "Under the eagle! Those words have meaning."

"I am aware of that."

"My king, you will be slaughtered!" Garrik continued.

Dayne grimaced as he tasted a hint of blood in his mouth. The pain in his stomach flared.

"This is *not* a debate," Dayne told them. "In the morning, I will leave. In peace or death, I shall return."

"I cannot just stand by and watch you die," Garrik said.

"Then pray," Dayne told him.

The king sat alone by one of the campfires as the moon shone high above. Sleep would not find him this night. He sat and stared deep into the flames, one hand gently brushing the sun and moon amulet that hung from his throat. His faith protected him. It made him strong. Dayne was a king, and whether he died in the morning or in battle or from his sickness, he would die a king.

The sun rose all too soon.

In silence, Dayne returned to his tent. He unbuckled his sword and stripped free of his armour. He would not even wear his gambeson or cloak. Dayne wore only his boots, trousers and a fresh shirt. He placed his simple crown atop his head and allowed his silver amulet to hang free. He said not a word. There would be no goodbyes. He squeezed Sofia's hand as he left their tent. He gave Garrik a nod as he strode by. That was all there would be. If Dayne walked to his death, he would show no weakness.

He left the protection of the Annoran ring of steel and crossed towards the lines of Caspin tents and soldiers. They saw his face and they saw his crown. The green-clad soldiers stared at Dayne as he began to walk among them. He did not return the looks, nor did he speak to them. He kept his head fixed towards the heart of their camp, fixed towards the position in which Santiago's tent was risen. Word would reach the duke soon, if it hadn't already. Dayne's steps were slow and measured. His hands were loosely clasped at his stomach. The morning rays danced across the silver amulet at his throat. Soldiers rose around him and watched as he walked alone. Dayne saw it all. He heard it all. The viper banners that fluttered in the wind. The grind of a whetstone as it was drawn down the edge of a blade. Step by step, he drew closer to the heart of the camp. A shout came from behind. Dayne spun around and brought an arm up. The blade of a knife sliced along the back of his forearm. The soldier clad head to toe in Medean armour moved. Dayne's fingers latched around his attacker's knife arm. The soldier lashed out and slammed an armoured fist into the king's stomach and then his head. Dayne staggered back yet kept his grip. The assassin let the knife fall as they grappled, only to catch it with his free hand. The dagger drove towards the king.

Thud.

An arrow drove through the assassin's wrist and sent the knife flying from his hand. The assailant screamed and Dayne leapt towards the fallen knife. He snatched it up and whirled around just as his saviour arrived. The soldier tossed aside his bow, tore free his longsword and placed it upon the assassin's neck even as the assailant turned to face him. Blood ran from Dayne's lips as he stared at the assassin. Something about the scream had seemed *wrong*.

"What is the meaning of this?" Santiago's voice tore through the camp.

Medean soldiers drew steel and levelled weapons as they surrounded Dayne, the assassin and the saviour.

"You!" Santiago shouted at the man who had saved Dayne, the man who now held a sword to another Medean's neck. "You would turn on your own people?"

The soldier kept his sword levelled at the wounded assassin as he tore free his helmet. A very Annoran face emerged.

"I stand Annoran," the man said.

"This is Sir Destrian of my royal guard," Dayne told the duke. "I secreted him among your ranks in the night."

"You want to kill one of my men?" Santiago asked as he walked through his ring of soldiers.

"No, this isn't one of yours," Dayne replied as he gestured towards the assassin with the knife. "This assassin bearing your colours isn't who he appears to be. Duke Santiago, I give to you the one who set us against each other. The one who killed your brother, Aquale."

Santiago frowned as he looked towards the wounded soldier. "Soldier," he called. "Remove your helmet."

The assassin said nothing while he rose to his full height. He was not afraid of king or duke.

"Seize him!" Santiago bellowed.

Soldiers charged at the surrounded man. The first fell as the assassin's blade tore through his throat. The killer leapt back, blocked a sword and slammed a man to the side with his shoulder. The assassin moved across the ground like a dancer, as if the arrow lodged in his arm was *nothing*. Yet there were too many Caspin soldiers. The assassin struggled and fought, but the end was inevitable. The sword was torn from the assailant's grasp. Refusing to surrender, the assassin ripped the arrow from his arm and dropped its head towards his own throat. The blade nicked the assassin's neck as the first of Caspin's soldiers tackled him to the ground. Steel slid across flesh and blood flowed. The pommel of a sword was smashed into the assassin's head. His helmet rang like a bell as its owner was sent face first into the ground. The arrow was torn from the assassin's grasp and the man himself was pulled to his knees. A line of blood emerged along the right side of the assassin's neck. It was a shallow wound, barely more than a scratch. If Caspin's soldiers had acted but a heartbeat slower, the assassin would have stilled his own life.

Dayne wiped the blood from his split lip and glanced down at his wounded arm before he approached the assassin. Held tightly by two of Caspin's soldiers, there would be no escape for the man.

"I did not believe you to be responsible for the slaughter between our two peoples," Dayne told Santiago as he stood before the kneeling assassin. "And so I prepared."

The king crouched before the assassin and reached out. The would-be murderer did not resist as Dayne's hands went for the helmet straps. There was no point. The king pulled the helmet free. Deep brown eyes flecked with green greeted him. Aureian eyes. Eyes of great beauty and devoid of emotion. The gasps began even before Dayne pushed the assassin's coif back to reveal the roughly hewn, shoulder-length hair. The disguise of a full suit of armour had worked. With a full helmet and coif to hide the face, the assassin had remained hidden. *She* had remained hidden.

There, kneeling on the ground, was a woman.

Her hands were tightly bound.

"Sir Destrian," Dayne called to his knight. "Take her. She is to be watched by a company of my guard at all times. No one is leaving this camp today."

"Yes, my king." Destrian gave Dayne a short bow before he shoved the assassin towards the Annoran camp.

King Dayne ran a finger down the thin gash on his forearm as he turned to Santiago.

"I apologise for the deception, my lord duke," Dayne said. "Secrets do not exist in places such as these and this assassin's shadow was everywhere. I did not kill your brother. This fight between Raynor and Caspin was her doing and I would see us as one again."

Dayne extended a hand, holding fast in his heart to the truth. The Annoran king could not forget what Santiago had brought upon his family.

Santiago Caspin took Dayne's hand and clasped it tight. "As one," he said.

Dayne pushed back the tent flaps and entered into the gloom. Sir Destrian stood alongside Sir Garrik. Both men stared down at the bound assassin who knelt on the earth and was tied to a post. The armour of a Caspin soldier had been removed, but despite the lack of steel and lack of a weapon, she appeared as dangerous as she had when she had come for Dayne. Her face suggested a darkness within her that Dayne had never seen before.

"This is the one who killed Aquale?" Garrik asked.

"Perhaps Lord Galan too," Dayne replied as he looked at her face. "We may never know. All the others were killed in retaliation. She did her job, and she did it well. One more blow and this war would have been over. Annora and Medea would have torn each other apart."

Dayne raised a hand and revealed the assassin's dagger. He ran his eyes over the masterwork of steel.

"Leave us," he commanded.

"My king," Garrik said.

"My king," Destrian echoed.

Dayne waited until both the knights had left before he approached the assassin. He reached down and pulled the gag from her mouth.

"I would warn you not to scream because no one is coming to

save you," Dayne told her. "But you already knew that, didn't you? That is why you tried to take your own life."

The woman said nothing. Dayne ran a thumb across the surface of the knife as he stared down into her deep eyes.

"When I look into your eyes, I do not see truth or lies," Dayne said. "Perhaps you have told so many falsehoods that you can no longer tell the difference. I lie. I lied to be in this very position. The most recent was that I had no idea where the one who murdered my friend Darius was, yet I knew that you would have been in this camp the whole time."

Her empty glare never left him.

"And so I prepared," Dayne continued. "With the death of Edward, I knew that it was only a matter of time before your blade came for me, and what better way to start a war than to kill an unarmed king in his enemy's camp? To kill a king while disguised as one of his enemy's soldiers. That is what I would do were I in your shoes. If this dance that we have both played our part in has taught me anything, it is that you are most wise. This trap that I laid for you was only known by myself and Sir Destrian."

Still, she said nothing.

"I will offer you a simple deal, *assassin*," Dayne said slowly. "I know that you did not kill my father. I know that you killed my friend, but I need to hear you say it. Did you kill Darius? Tell truth and live. Refuse and die. You're only a puppet."

"Tell the truth and live?" The assassin scoffed. "I am your prisoner. No matter what I say or what truth I speak, you will kill me anyway."

"I will not ask you to reveal your paymaster, for I know that you will not," Dayne replied.

The assassin stared up at him. "I will assume then that this *deal* involves more than just my life," she said.

Dayne shrugged and gestured for her to continue.

"It was the death of your father, wasn't it?" she said at last. Her voice rang like any other Aureian yet there was a strength to it that Dayne had never heard before.

"Yes," Dayne replied with a nod.

"You know that it was Santiago Caspin who ordered his death, and so I will not hold my tongue on that," the woman said. "Darius' death would have sown unrest and disloyalty to Annora. This alliance that you have forged would have been broken with but a single swing of a knife."

"But Santiago–"

"Wants to be king," the assassin finished. "The death of Dorian merely added the question to which belonged the answer you sought. The murder counteracted Darius' death."

"As soon as I found proof that Caspin was responsible for my father's death, I knew that the two acts could not be related," Dayne told her. "I suspected that the killer would have remained in the camp to rectify the damage done by Caspin and yet I had no reason to believe. That is until you killed Aquale."

"And from there things escalated, as you well know," the assassin replied.

"It is clear to me that you are far wiser than you let on," Dayne said. "Your work shows as much. I am forced to wonder if you were a scholar in another life. That leads me to ponder how one so wise became a cutthroat. Your story is an interesting one, I am sure."

"Do you want to know something, King Dayne?" the assassin said. "If I were to tell you my name, you would have never heard of it. My family name – now that is written in the pages of history and will be until the end times. But that family is believed to have gone, a family that died out fifty years ago. The name that I was born with you would not have heard mentioned even once. Would you like to know why? Not only because I have not used it since I was a child but also because I am the best at what I do. You got lucky. Had you not gone to stand watch, it would have been you who had died and not your man Edward."

Dayne winced as pain surged though his stomach. The woman noticed.

"The sickness grows worse," she said. "I have watched it happen for many months."

"Then you will know by now that I, more likely than not, will not live to see another year pass," Dayne replied. "Win or lose, this will be my last war. Win or lose, this is how I will be remembered. That is the truth. I am not going to kill you for what you have done. You are only the messenger. What I would ask is that, if I survive this war, you in turn do something for me in exchange for your freedom."

"What do you desire?"

"That will come in time," Dayne told her. "For now, I would ask only one thing. If it is as forgotten as you say, then I would ask for your name. You know my truth. Now tell me yours."

For the first time a flicker of emotion crossed those dark eyes.

"Iris," she said. "Iris Deleonie."

✦ ✦ ✦

FORTY-THREE

Catuvantuli Lands, Forest of Salvaar

Dáire, chief of the Coventina, watched from the tree line as the great army of Aureian horsemen began to ride west. The sight of the invaders slipping away gave the chief no joy. Something was at work to make it so. They would not just break camp and leave. Dáire brushed his horse's neck before clicking his tongue and galloping back to the Salvaari camp.

Here in the eastlands, three tribes had remained separate from Henghis' coalition in the hopes of defeating the Aureian horsemen. The Belcar and Niavenn tribes stood shoulder to shoulder with the Coventina. While Dáire's people had been born to the horse, those of the two eastern tribes had spent their lives immersed in trading. In decades past, the twin tribes had forged a trade network with Tallis. In exchange for pelts, skins and carving, they had received something that no other tribe had ever used: armour. Though the days of trade had ended with the war, the people of the Belcar and Niavenn tribes wore that same steel through their garb. Many beneath the sacred trees of Salvaar considered them civilised. Some thought them *too* civilised, yet they were as Salvaari as the savage Sagailean.

Dáire dismounted before a large fire that burned before an even larger tent. Two women sat by the blaze and watched as he approached. One had hair as golden as the sun, the other had locks as dark as his. They were sisters. They were chiefs.

"They are leaving," Dáire told them. "For two days we have followed them, and they have not halted or turned back."

Morrigana, golden-haired chief of the Belcar, rose to her feet. "The invaders have taken no land and burned no villages," she said. "Yet they leave. Something has drawn them away."

"They march west," Eira said. "Towards their people. Towards *ours*. We should follow them. Keep to the shadows. If they make for the forest, if they make for our kin, we will ready be to greet them."

"I have sent a rider to warn Henghis," Dáire said. "Whatever has happened in the west must be great indeed to draw the silver riders from their task. Prepare your people to leave. We must ride."

✦ ✦ ✦

Henghis and the nine tribes marched as one and they marched with purpose. Nine tribes, nine colours of paint traversing Salvaari skin. They had fought as one when Annora had come, yet not like this and not in these numbers. The last time that they had been as united as they were now was a century before, when those of the old ways had been cast into the forest during the purge.

Kitara watched the great king as he led his people. There was no task that he asked of them that he would not do himself. He ate what they ate and drank what they drank. He stood beside them in battle and mourned those who fell.

The sun was all but gone when they at last stopped to make camp. Kitara glanced at Aeryn who rode at her side. The moonseer's eyes were fixed upon the east.

"Heading out again?" Kitara asked.

"The trees call to me," Aeryn replied. "This fight … it draws near. It is written in the stars. This is my duty."

"I know," Kitara said. "Stay safe."

"I will see you at dawn." Aeryn turned and gave Kitara a smile before she clicked her tongue and rode out into the forest.

"She's right," another voice called. "This fight … the time of great bloodshed is upon us."

Kitara glanced over her shoulder as Sakkar approached. Senya was with him and Sabra circled in the sky above. Lukas and his company of Káli had returned to the army during the day, and so far, Kitara had not spoken to him. He rode with his priestess and, for a reason beyond Kitara's understanding, Sakkar had left his friend's side.

"In victory or defeat, many thousands will die," Sakkar continued. "That is the truth."

"I know. I am ready to fight for my people. I am ready to fight for my homeland," Kitara said absently as her hand brushed against the sapphire ring that hung from her neck. Her mother's ring. Oriana's ring. "We are mere days away from battle so answer me this. What has happened between you and he?" Kitara nodded towards Lukas. "When you left, you were as brothers. Upon your return, you have kept far apart."

Sakkar exchanged a look with his wife.

"He's changed," Senya told her.

"The Lukas that I once knew is gone," Sakkar said. "I think he may have died that day in Oryn. The day that he met that *witch*."

"Tell me," Kitara said with a frown.

"He killed defenceless men," Senya replied with a growl. "Threatened my husband with death."

"What do you mean?" Kitara asked as surprise hit her. She had spent months with both men and knew them to be as family. She could not imagine Lukas threatening to *kill* Sakkar.

"The stories about what he did in Annora. The massacre at Valham," Sakkar started. "It's all true. Unarmed priests … and it did not stop there. We captured Aureian scouts days ago. He tortured a man to find out why the western army was on the march, and he took *joy* from it. The other two he gave to his witch to sacrifice to her dark spirits. And he revelled in their suffering. I tried to stop them, tried to reason with him, and he in turn banished me from his side under pain of death."

Kitara shook her head. The man she had known would never have cast Sakkar aside so easily. He would never have taken joy in the torture of the defenceless nor the slaughter of innocents.

"Then he is changed," Kitara said simply.

"It's that witch whispering in his ear."

"Perhaps," Kitara replied. "I have seen a lot of the world. I have seen people betray for no cause. I know what promises are worth. How many are loyal … How many stay loyal. Everyone is in this life for themselves."

"I do not believe that," Sakkar said.

"His mind is overthrown by Maevin," Senya added. "Surely you can see that."

Kitara looked at them both. They were hopeful and naïve to the ways of the world. "Or perhaps this is exactly who he was before but now has the freedom to follow his truth," she said.

"You say that you don't believe in loyalty, yet what about Aeryn?" Sakkar asked. "What about Bellec? What about all those who travelled hundreds of miles to save you? Does that mean nothing?"

Kitara ground her teeth and bit back a retort. She glanced towards the small band of mercenaries. Galadayne, the stoic second in command, who had abandoned his country for Bellec. All the Annorans in the company had lost everything in remaining loyal to their captain. Their brother. Jaimye still wore a bandage around his leg. He still limped from the wound he had taken in rescuing her. Bellec … Theron Malley. Her father. A man whose life had been destroyed twice over. His country was torn away from him. His wife torn away and his *daughter* torn away.

"Why do you think that they risked everything to rescue you in Aureia without hesitation?" Sakkar asked. "Why do you think

I did? Loyalty. Those men did not know you, but they were prepared to lay down their lives for you. For *you*. That is loyalty. To their captain perhaps, yet it is loyalty. We travelled together, fought together, shed blood together. Those bonds are not so easily severed. Loyalty. Honour. Brotherhood. I will not abandon my friend any more than I would abandon you."

Kitara was quiet for a moment. He was speaking the truth, and she knew it. Her hand rose once again to the sapphire ring. She thought of Aeryn and Bellec. She thought about what she would do if they walked down a darker path. At last, she nodded as she looked to Sakkar.

"And what are you going to do about it?" Kitara asked. "We are mere days away from the greatest battle in which we will ever fight and there is no certainty of victory. If it is true what you say and Lukas' mind is not his own, then it must remain so until after the battle is won."

"Why do you say that?" Senya asked.

"He walks in the dark," Kitara replied. "The time has now come for men such as he to do dark things. If we are to win this fight, then we will need One-Eye more than we need Lukas Raynor. That is the truth. The Salvaari follow him. They believe in him. Many think him to be some kind of saviour sent to protect them. To take that away on the eve of battle … I can think of nothing worse. So I beg you wait. Bide your time. Endure what you must. When the moment arises to make your move, then you must make it and not before. Do you understand?"

"Belief and symbols are power," Sakkar muttered. "Yes, I understand that. I will wait as long as I am able."

"When you decide what must be done, I will stand at your side," Kitara replied.

"What changed your mind?" Sakkar asked.

Kitara looked back towards the mercenaries. Towards her father.

"Loyalty," she said.

Kitara walked towards the mercenaries and made straight for Bellec. Her father glanced up as he saw her approached.

"We should talk," Kitara told him.

It was all that needed to be said before Bellec rose to his feet and followed her into the forest. They were some distance from the camp and alone when Kitara finally came to a halt. She gazed out through the trees towards the west. Not a word had been spoken between them. Not yet. Kitara just looked. She barely noticed all the greens and browns, barely felt the cool breeze upon her skin.

"What are we looking at?" Bellec asked.

"The west," she replied. "A few days through those trees. Can you see them?"

"They're there," Bellec murmured. "Waiting."

"In a few days, we will join with an army of unprecedented strength beyond these trees and meet with them in a battle of unprecedented importance. A battle that will decide the fate of Salvaar. A battle that, if we win it, will not defeat the west but will start something that could … and I cannot fight this fight without you."

"I am always with you," Bellec told her. "I have always been with you."

"Whether it be tomorrow or the next day, we ride to war at dawn," Kitara replied. "We ride not knowing if we will achieve victory. Even if we do win the fight, there is no telling if we may live to see the next dawn. This may be the only chance we have to speak, and I will not let words go unspoken again."

Bellec was quiet for a moment before he replied. "You know my truth. You know what I am, where I come from."

"I know that you came for me knowing that it could mean your life," Kitara said. "If I knew nothing else that would be enough … *Father*."

Bellec at last turned to his daughter as the word left her mouth. Kitara's eyes stayed fixed on the trees as she spoke. Her words were hard to say yet they needed to be said. Sakkar had been right. Bellec had never done wrong by her. Never. He had remained loyal.

"I have never trusted you and that is no secret," Kitara continued. "A man who I spent much of my life hating. A man who abandoned me. A sellsword who offers his allegiance to the highest bidder. That hatred ... that distrust kept me alive for so many years. Until I came to Salvaar, I had forgotten what trust was. You have never asked for anything yet have stayed by my side since that day in Miera. What I want to know, Father, is that when this is all said and done, when the war is over, will you leave, return to Medea and fight for coin until the day that you die? Will you return to your home in Annora, or will you stay here beneath these scared trees?"

Bellec took a breath. "Many years have passed since I first stood beneath these trees. I am an older man now ... and perhaps wiser. For forty years, I have swung a sword and now I feel in my bones that that time may be coming to an end. I will die in battle ... of that I am most certain, but it will be a battle of my choosing. When I search my heart, I do not know where my path will lead," Bellec told her honestly. "Where will you go? Who will you be?"

"Nowhere with cold and rain. Nowhere with kings or laws or taxes." Her lips twitched into a smile. "I would go wherever I wanted to go and do whatever I wanted to do."

Bellec chuckled. "You are my daughter," he said. "My home and my path are with you."

"We are family, you and I," Kitara said and held out her arm. "We will always be together."

Bellec stared into her eyes. "Always," he said as he took her arm.

Slowly, Bellec pulled her into his embrace.

Slowly, she returned it.

They returned to the mercenaries after a time. They supped and shared drink with the men. In no more than two days, they would meet the west in battle and who knew how many would live to see the third sunrise.

"Heard some of the Salvaari talking," Galadayne told Kitara and Bellec upon their return. "Said that a large force of mercenaries was seen shadowing the western army across the river. They will meet with Dayne's army at the crossing near Cacera."

"The last of the stragglers," Bellec muttered.

Galadayne gave a nod and passed him a wineskin.

"I wonder who has come," Jaimye said. "How many we have fought beside."

"How many we know," added Hadwin.

"They have come to take what we are here to protect," Layan replied. "That is all we need to know."

"At least O'Lacey and his men are in Tarik," Galadayne said. "Of all the men we are facing, I am glad he is not among them."

"What takes him to Tarik?" Kitara asked with a frown.

"Work," Bellec said. "The empress asked for his company personally. The last time I saw Malius O'Lacey, he was headed for the northern coast."

Hooves thundered through the camp. A small trail of dust was kicked up behind a single rider. The Salvaari wore the colours of none native to the nine tribes gathered.

"He's Coventina," Jaimye told them as he saw the man's garb and war paint.

"One of Dáire's men," Bellec said as he watched the rider. "Word has come from the east."

✦ ✦ ✦

"The Silver Riders will not be far behind me," the Coventina moonseer told the chieftains in Salvaari.

"How many are they?" Etain asked.

"As many as five thousand. Perhaps more. Dark men from the far west are with them."

Henghis, who stood at the edge of the gathered chiefs, turned to the moonseer. "Thank you, brother. You honour your tribe," he said before he extended an open hand to the Coventina. Without a word, the moonseer passed Henghis his spear. The Salvaari king drew a line in the earth with the silver blade. "The great army is upon us," he said.

A second line he drew to the side of the first.

"Mercenaries marshal in the west."

A third line followed.

"Silver Riders in the east. They will converge upon the crossing at Cacera all at once. An army so large that it will stretch from horizon to horizon," Henghis told the gathered chiefs. "Eira, Morrigana, Dáire and their people will sweep in from behind the Silver Riders. But not us. Our fight is with the army of King Dayne. We will strike them first and we will strike them hard beneath these sacred trees. We will push them to the river and throw them into its waters. We are outnumbered but not outmatched. Brothers … sisters … we have all lost at the hands of the invaders. The west will not stop. They will never stop. Not unless we break this army here. I will break it. By the spirits, I will break it."

✦ ✦ ✦

FORTY-FOUR

Road to Eonie, Aureian Empire

They rode hard for days after infiltrating Nilorenn. The sun had set when Erik at last let them make camp. As his companions sat around a roaring fire, the Valkir king walked up onto a small hillock. In the distance, he could see lights shining from a great city. Eonie. That was their destination. The messenger city that had long ago been a major player in the war with the Gaedhela bloodline. Erik stared across the plains towards the massive, walled city. If he squinted, he could make out the tower within its heart. An aviary sat at the very top and offices and libraries filled its middle. An unlimited amount of knowledge was held within those walls.

"Eonie," Lord Wylan said as he approached. "The city of knowledge."

Erik glanced at the former spy as he joined him upon the bluff. "Tomorrow, you will deliver us what we seek," Erik told him.

"And what is it that you seek exactly?" Lord Wylan asked. "We left Nilorenn days ago and yet thus far you have not spoken of it even once."

Erik pulled the helmet of the Arkin Garter from his head and placed it on the ground at his feet. "Months ago, after I took Vay'kis, one of your kinsmen arrived upon those shores," Erik stated as he gazed towards the walled city. "Valan Azure Aldrich was his name. An emissary of the silver court. He had come to recruit Earl Arndyr in a war against Miera. Upon discovering that Arndyr was dead, he offered this to me in his place. A great fleet is assembling in the south, he told me. A fleet so massive that it would erase Miera and its people from the histories. After the murder of my sister at the empire's hand, I am sure that you understand that there was but one choice. Valan did not understand this. Valan did not know that among the Valkir honour is everything. Valan and his men are dead. This fleet, if it hasn't left already, will leave its harbour soon. I need to know where it is so that I may fight it. So that I may defeat it."

"And you believe that Eonie will have the answers that you seek?"

"I have to believe that," Erik replied. "If this great fleet reaches my land, untold thousands of my people will die. If it reaches my land, we lose … and that is the end of it. There will be no Valkir. No children playing on the beaches or ships exploring the seas. There will be nothing."

"It is a known, is it not, that you cannot win this war," Lord Wylan said.

"I did not say that," Erik said. "My warriors are few, but they are strong, and as you will have guessed by now, we Valkir do not stand alone."

"Pirates and raiders standing side by side against the greatest empire the world has ever seen," Wylan mused. "That would be a grand tale to tell."

"I will let the poets decide that," Erik replied. "I am just a man trying to do what is best for my people."

"As you say, King Erik, as you say."

"Tomorrow, you will lead me through the gates of Eonie," Erik told the former spy. "You will use whatever leverage you still have and knowledge of this messenger city to locate information that will deliver me this fleet."

"And if I refuse?"

"Believe me when I tell you that I do not want war. I do not crave it. I want peace for myself and my people. Your empire started this, set me upon this fate," Erik said. "If you refuse to help me, then I will kill your family. You are Aureian and a spy. That gives me two good reasons not to trust you. As such, both you and your wife will remain with us until such a time as I find this fleet."

"And then?"

"Then you will be free to go."

They drifted into silence. Valkir and Aureian both stared towards the glowing lights of Eonie, towards their destiny.

"You are a good man, Erik," Lord Wylan said at last. "Whatever becomes of our people, both yours and mine, know that you have my respect."

Erik snorted. "The respect of a man who spent his entire life betraying men for coin."

"I did what I did for my people," Lord Wylan replied. "Just as you do now."

Erik turned to face his companion. "It is all a free man can do," he said.

They rode out in the morning. Cillian Teague and four of the Valkir remained with Lady Esmeray Wylan while the others rode in company with Erik and the spy. The sun glinted upon their armour of dazzling silver, while the violet of their plumes and cloaks only added to their majesty. They were soldiers of the empire's elite, some of the greatest warriors that the world had ever seen. Erik and his people held themselves as such.

The king rode beside Lord Wylan as they made their approach towards the citadel, a city made great during the fall of Delios. A city without which perhaps the Aureians would still be in chains. Farmland sprawled throughout the plains surrounding Eonie, enough to feed more than just the people within the city. Purple banners bearing the silver griffin flew atop the ramparts and soldiers in their magnificent armour stood sentinel. Erik spared Lord Wylan a glance as they neared the massive gates. He believed that he had judged the Aureian correctly. He believed that Lionidir Wylan would not betray him or his cause if only to spare his wife. What if the thing that bound the former spy to Esmeray was nothing? What if he sold them out to the guards at the first opportunity? Erik's hand stayed near his sword. He took comfort in knowing that even if Lord Wylan betrayed him, the Aureian's head would touch the ground well in advance of his body.

They rode through the gates of the outer wall without being stopped. The guards watched as they passed through their midst. Townspeople stopped and stared as the Arkin Garter rode among them. Erik kept his head straight, yet he saw everything. Hundreds of houses lay beyond the first layer of walls. Many were two or three floors, in the Aureian fashion. Red clay tiles covered the rooftops. Thousands of people filled the streets. The shouts from the market and sound of the blacksmith's hammer were well known to Erik but not to this scale. There might have been more people who called Eonie home than there were in the entirety of the Valkir Isles.

Through the winding streets they rode until they reached the great gatehouse that lay before the giant tower of Eonie. Soldiers of a different breed manned the walls and gate of the tower. Their armour was more plate than mail. Their cloaks were white and trimmed in violet; the plumes of their helms were the colour of snow. These men were more than just warriors; they were elite soldiers. Knights of the tower. Men who had dedicated their lives to the sword and to defending the knowledge held within their great city. Men who could not be bribed or bought.

"Hold there," one of the knights called as they reached the gate.

Lord Wylan held up his hand and the Valkir halted at his back. The knights watched the company warily. Though they wore the

remain safe from foreign attack, then that gold must be spent. It is here, in these logs, that those sums of coin are recorded, along with the men involved with construction, those who are to crew them. Captains, helmsmen, bosuns … it will all be written down within these pages. Now, the thing that we will be looking for is where the fleet was to be born."

Lord Wylan moved through the room towards one of the bookshelves. His eyes flickered across the titles until they came to a halt. He pulled a book from the case.

"It will be this section in which we will find what it is that you seek," he told Erik.

Candles were sparked to life upon the table and each of the four men gathered books. Erik had chosen the brothers because they had some knowledge of reading. They slowly made their way through the shelves and books. Numbers and names that appeared foreign to Erik began to tire his eyes, yet he read them nonetheless. He read every last letter and symbol. With so many upon the pages, it would be easy enough to miss what was important, and if they missed it, then his people would die. All of them. Erik unstrapped his helm and placed it upon the long table. Laerke made his way over to Erik.

"What if it is not here?" Laerke asked him quietly. "What if this way is not the way we should be proceeding?"

"It is the *only* way," Erik replied. "We do not have time to find another."

"And the Aureian. Are you sure we can trust him?"

"We have to."

Laerke sighed and nodded slowly. "I don't like it," he said.

"Nor do I," Erik agreed before making his way back over to the table and gathering up another book.

Day turned into night. More candles were brought in as the old ones waned. Wylan grimaced as he placed a book down upon the table.

"It's not here," he told the Valkir.

"What do you mean it's not here?" Nenrir asked.

"We have searched every book and scroll in this godsforsaken room that could hold the knowledge of the fleet," Lord Wylan replied. "It isn't here."

"It has to be," Erik growled.

"It's not."

"He is lying," Laerke snarled and took a step towards the Aureian.

"What would I have to gain?" Lord Wylan countered.

"Your people would be saved and mine lost." Laerke turned to Erik. "He is doing what he has lived his life doing. Deceiving. He is betraying us."

"At the cost of my family?" Lord Wylan said as he rose to his feet. "My beloved wife?"

"More lies," Laerke said.

"Laerke, let the Aureian explain." Erik cut him off and turned to Lord Wylan. "You say that the whereabouts of this fleet won't be found in this room. You have not said where they will be found."

"Speak while you still have a tongue to do so," Nenrir warned the Aureian.

"There is a chamber beneath this tower. Within it lies the most sacred of knowledge." Lord Wylan's voice was low. "Wisdom that if found in the wrong hands could destroy the empire."

"Why did you not speak of this before?" Erik asked.

"Because I did not believe that what you seek would be there."

"He's up to something," Laerke growled.

"No, there is something else," Erik said. "Something he's not told us."

Lord Wylan nodded. "Only two men in the empire have access to that vault," he said. "Only the emperor and his spymaster."

"You're a spy," Nenrir replied.

"Not anymore," Lord Wylan told him. "The only way to get to the vault will be with bloodshed. The guards down there will attack without warning. Such is the nature of what they protect."

Erik stared into the former spy's eyes. "If I get you in, can you locate this fleet?" he said.

"Or die trying."

"My king–" Laerke growled.

"Nenrir," Erik interrupted. "Ready the horses. We may need to leave quickly."

"And if you're discovered?"

"Then we'll be riding for our lives."

Lord Wylan led Laerke and Erik down through the tower and into its beating heart. The further they descended, the fewer people could be found. There were no scholars or maija, no spies or truth-seekers. There was just the quiet, broken only by the footfalls of three men.

Lord Wylan held up a hand as the light of torches came around the corner of the stairwell. Erik stepped past his companions and peered around the corner. They had reached a chamber that seemed more a shrine than a library. Instead of bookshelves lined with tomes and texts, the chamber walls were covered in carvings that depicted a great battle in a forest. Soldiers armed with swords, bows and spears covered the walls. However, most fiercely of all was a mighty griffin facing off against a snarling chimera. The carvings told a story of how the Aureians of old had stood against the might of Delios. A battle not far from these walls that had changed everything. At the centre of the room stood a carved statue of Azaria and within her hands rested an Aureian sword. A blade belonging to one who would forever be written in the pages of history. The man who had started the downfall of the Delion Empire had been from this city. The first man to earn the name Deleonie.

Four men stood in the room, soldiers garbed in white. Erik

turned back to his companions. Without a word, Lord Wylan led them around the corner. The three men made straight for the soldiers. Soldiers who were in this room because it was their job. They had done nothing but serve, yet now they had to die. Lord Wylan pulled a scroll from his belt and held it towards the guard captain. The soldier took the scroll as his companions watched the three men warily. The captain broke the seal and opened the parchment. Wylan's knife slide from his sleeve and before his victim could blink, the blade drove into the captain's throat.

There was no hesitation from the Valkir. Time seemed to slow as Erik's axe leapt into his hand and he sent it forth. It spun end over end. The soldiers cried, but it was too late. The axe buried itself in the neck of the first soldier. Erik tore his sword and shield free as he charged towards the three surviving men. He fought side by side with Laerke. They were shieldbrothers who had been in battle back to back times beyond count. They knew each other's moves before they made them.

The first soldier fell as Erik opened his neck. The second Lord Wylan took from behind with his own sword. Laerke felled the last when Erik deflected the guard's sword to the side. Then they were alone. The four guards lay around them, their blood watering the cold stone beneath. Erik turned to Lord Wylan, but he had already moved. Erik's gaze followed the Aureian to the back of the room. He watched as the spy's eyes swept across the stone carving of the griffin. Even a pagan warrior such as Erik was forced to admit that the artisan's work was beautiful. He watched as Lord Wylan reached forth and ran his hand across the carved stone. His fingers slid behind the griffin and pressed something. Something clicked. Metal grated. The wall turned like a door.

"Impossible," Laerke breathed as the stone opened.

Darkness lay within the chamber that appeared before their eyes. There was no light or flickering candlelight. Lord Wylan took a torch from one of the steel rings that lined the walls of the circular room. He glanced at Erik and led the way into the second room. The orange flame lit the darkness and made visible the carved brick walls.

"Guard the door," Erik ordered his friend.

Laerke nodded and flicked his gaze back towards whence they had come. With that, Erik followed Lord Wylan into the chamber. Erik's hand never strayed from the axe at his side. He knew that no warriors were within the room, yet he could not quiet the sense of dread seeping from his heart. It was as if the jaws of a wolf were closing in around him. The chamber unfurled before them. It was neither big nor small and was shrouded in shadow. Unlit torches hung from the chamber walls, torches that the spy took his own flame to. Slowly, torch by torch, the room was illuminated. Shelves of books and scrolls lined the walls, and a desk sat at the far end of the chamber.

"The heart of Eonie," Lord Wylan told Erik.

Once again, the two men began to sift through books, logs and scrolls in search of the message that would hold knowledge of the fleet. Despite the disquiet in his heart, Erik forced himself to read slowly. If the fear of discovery took control, he could miss the very thing he risked so much to find. Laerke Redleaf leapt into the chamber.

"Footfalls. Men in the tunnel," he said. "Aureia comes."

Erik exchanged a look with Lord Wylan before turning his full attention to the book in hand. The sound of the footsteps reached his ear. He continued to read. A shout came from the corridor outside. An Aureian shout. Laerke's cry rose to fight it.

"Here!" Lord Wylan cried.

Erik looked to the spy who swiftly shoved a logbook into his satchel. Whether it contained the secrets or was no more than a lie spoken by Lord Wylan, Erik was out of time. The clash of steel came from the chamber entrance. The king pulled forth his axe and leapt forth to help his friend. An Aureian lay dead upon the cold stone and two more were exchanging blows with Laerke. A fourth stood further behind. This must have been the guard change. Erik charged at the men engaged with his friend, but he was too slow. The fourth knight lunged forward and cut him off. They exchanged blow after blow. A sword glanced off Erik's armour as Erik barrelled into his enemy. His strength threw the man back into the wall behind him. Erik followed through and as he pinned the man back, he slid the blade of his axe across the Aureian's throat. The knight gurgled as blood cascaded from his ruined neck. It splashed across Erik and fell to the stone like a red waterfall. The king spun towards his friend as a scream echoed through the passage. An Aureian sword had slipped through a gap in Laerke's cuirass and drove into his stomach. As Laerke fell to a knee, Erik's axe caught the first of his attackers in the back. The last guard toppled over with Lord Wylan's blade embedded in his neck. Erik looked down at his friend and knew from the look in Laerke's eye that the wound was bad. He took his friend's arm and pulled him to his feet. Laerke groaned as his blood began to spill down his side.

"This is no place to die," Erik told his friend as he half lead and half dragged Laerke towards the stairs.

Lord Wylan went before them as they ascended into the citadel. They climbed higher and higher until at last they drew near the tunnel entrance. Erik looked to his friend and saw the whiteness of his face. Laerke could barely stand. His breathing was laboured. Blood was dripping from his lips.

"Wylan," Erik said through bared teeth. "Get to Nenrir. Bring the horses to the tower entrance or we all die here."

The spy vanished without a word and Erik could only pray that the man would not betray him now. He glanced at Laerke.

"We're going home, brother," Erik said. "We're going home."

A gasp came from the staircase entrance. Erik's eyes flicked up to see the face of a scholar. He could see the fear in the man's eyes as he saw two Valkir warriors drenched in blood emerging from the underworld. Erik could see the man's scream forming and without hesitation he launched his knife at the scholar. The man's cry was cut off as he fell to the ground. An echo of the shout rang in the stone staircase. It would have been heard. Erik grimaced. If they stayed here, then they both died in this godforsaken hole. He wrapped Laerke's arm around his shoulders once more and dragged him out into the light. Scholars, teachers and maija stared as the two blood-covered warriors entered their midst. Gasps turned into cries. Erik ignored them. He could see guards heading towards them through the throng of people. They were close to the gate. So close. Erik could see the sunlight shining clear through the doors. Shouts went up all around as knights drew steel. The scholars fled with screams upon their lips. The soldiers would be upon them before they reached the doors. With one arm Erik held his friend, with the other he grasped his axe. Shadows flickered at the tower entrance and then Valkir riders surged inside. They held back the storm of steel as Erik dragged Laerke into the courtyard. Knights came from every direction. The men on the wall began to take notice of the commotion. Lord Wylan appeared and tossed the reins of a riderless horse down to Erik.

"Come on," Erik muttered to Laerke as he took the reins.

The Valkir still within the tower charged out of the doors, and with that, the guards atop the walls levelled crossbows. Before they could shoot, bows sang. Valkir bows. Men fell from the walls. Men running for the gatehouse fell. *The portcullis.* They had to leave *now.* Suddenly, Laerke shoved Erik back towards the horse.

"GO!" Laerke bellowed as he struggled to stay standing.

There was no time for argument.

"GO!" Laerke cried once more as he ripped his sword free.

With a shout, Erik kicked his heels in and charged towards the gatehouse. Bolts flew down from the walls. Valkir died. Half their number made it through the gates. Screams and the clash of steel came from behind as Laerke made his stand. Erik could not spare his friend a final glance as they charged through the streets. They had to beat the alarm that any moment would be ringing. They had to get through the second gate before it closed. Townspeople screamed as the riders hurtled through their midst. Those too slow were knocked aside. The alarm bell began to toll. The gatehouse appeared before them. Soldiers turned their way. Men began to close the gates. Nenrir's first arrow stopped them as it tore life from one of the soldiers. The guards were smashed aside as the charging riders rode through them. Another of the Valkir fell … and then they were free. Of those who had entered Eonie, only six remained. Blood covered Erik's body. His own, his enemies … his friend's. The man who had stayed behind to help him deceive Earl Magnus was dead. The man who had been at his side since childhood. Laerke Redleaf had joined the halls of the fallen.

✦ ✦ ✦

FORTY-FIVE

Káli Lands, Forest of Salvaar

Scouts came and went through the evening. All brought the same message: the great western army was upon them. When the moon rose, they could see the orange glow of western campfires and torches. A walled camp was all that stopped the Salvaari from falling upon their unsuspecting foe. The Salvaari lit no fires and sung no songs. They would do *nothing* to give away their position.

Kitara had been in more fights than she could count. She had seen battle and war, yet this night sleep eluded her as if she were trying to catch mist with her bare hands. Try as she might, it slid through her fingers. This time was different. This fight was different. This time she had something to lose … and it terrified her.

The leather hilt of her sword comforted her fingers as she pulled the blade free of its sheath's embrace. The cool wind kissed her hair and caressed her skin as she began to slice the blade slowly through the air. The blue paint upon her face was a pact with the spirits. A symbol, one that she was committed to in her heart. This fight was for the fate of Salvaar, and she *was* Salvaari. Move by move, her body began to loosen. Her muscles flexed and relaxed as the sword became an extension of her arm. Kitara sang the swordsong with her steel as the first of dawn's rays began to emerge through the canopy. Soon word would spread. Soon they would ride into a battle where victory was far from certain. A battle in which all their futures would be decided.

Kitara turned at the sound of a horse arriving. Her heart skipped a beat as Aeryn slid from her saddle. She had come back. Kitara sheathed her sword as Aeryn crossed the ground between them. They were in each other's arms before a single word was spoken. Kitara held her tightly as if she feared that if she let go, Aeryn would disappear. She blocked everything out. She did not feel the wind nor the warm sun rays. All she could feel was Aeryn. Kitara ran her hand through Aeryn's hair and cupped her cheeks. The moonseer pressed her forehead into Kitara's.

"They have sent the call," Aeryn murmured. "We leave on Henghis' command. It will be soon, and I will be at your side."

The words comforted Kitara more than any others ever could. Aeryn would be at her shoulder for this fight.

"Together we face the west," Kitara said quietly. "To whatever end."

"To whatever end."

Kitara pulled Aeryn tight and placed a kiss upon her lips. Aeryn brushed her cheek as she returned it.

"I love you," Kitara told her fiercely as they pulled apart.

She had never said anything truer. It *was* her truth.

"As I love you," Aeryn replied. "Always."

✦ ✦ ✦

Maevin took Lukas' hand without a word and placed it upon her belly.

"You're …" Lukas trailed off.

"With child." Maevin nodded and the hint of a smile spread across her lips.

Lukas felt something in his heart stir. Joy. True joy. He grinned, stroked her cheek and then placed a kiss upon her lips. Lips that were painted as black as the rest of her body. This battle would require every advantage if they were to triumph, so the priestess had turned her body into the canvas of Tanris' own colour.

"I will win this war for you," Lukas told her. "For our child."

"I know," Maevin told him fervently. "I have seen it in my dreams: you bathed in the blood of the invaders."

"Today. It will be today."

"Then let us meet our destiny," the priestess replied.

A pair of druids entered the tent. They clasped waterskins tightly as they looked to the priestess and the Whisperer.

"It is time," one of them said to Maevin in their mother tongue.

Maevin took a step towards them. She closed her eyes and spread her arms wide. The druids made their move.

They left their tent together. Lukas had tied cloth around his head to cover his empty eye socket. He wore the black of the Káli beneath his armour of chainmail and plate. A dark sash ran around his body and black paint was drawn across his face and shield. His hammer was ever present at his side and a helmet was clutched in the hand that was not in command of his crutch. One-Eye he was called even by his friends. The Black Eagle he was known as to his enemies. He embodied those names well.

Maevin was clad in Káli pelts that left much of her skin exposed, skin now covered in ebony. Her dark hair was tied back and speckled with white grease. A snake amulet curled at her throat, and she clasped a vicious spear in her hand. A weapon that would soon be bathed in poison. Her green eyes burned with passion. It was not the paint nor the spear that made her the most ferocious. It was the blood. Blood taken from the Aurelian men that she had sacrificed ran through her hair, down her face and neck. It was dry upon her skin and stained her clothes. Maevin was a priestess to the Dark One. She played the part well.

All around them warriors were making their last preparations.

Blades were being sharpened and prayers uttered. Goodbyes were spoken. For some they would be final farewells. Chief Vaylin emerged as if from nothing and hastened towards the pair. Like Maevin she was bathed in black. Morlag's snake-tooth necklace hung at her throat. She would honour him this day.

"My chief." Maevin greeted her with a bow.

"My chief," Lukas echoed.

"The time of darkness has come. The time of Tanris," Vaylin told them. "The spirits are near. I can feel them. The people, some doubt. We chiefs are gathering to show strength and your words, priestess, may cause difference."

They followed Vaylin to the sacred ground upon which the nine chiefs stood. All were armed and armoured, covered in war paint and ready for battle. Thousands of Salvaari had gathered beneath the trees around the nine. Lukas' gaze swept the great crowd. The chiefs and their people stood in silence. The mercenaries watched alongside Bellec their leader. Lukas felt a ripple of unease move through the gathered crowd, could sense the war that many were battling within.

Many were nervous, while some doubted. Fear, strength and duty all came together. Some were fighting for the spirits. Some were fighting for family. For love. Some were fighting for their tribes, others for all of their people. All were fighting for Salvaar. Whatever they fought for, they would pay the price in blood.

All eyes turned towards Maevin as she entered the open circle around which they were all gathered. None spoke yet all felt a shiver as they looked to the priestess of Tanris. Her clothes were midnight black and covered in Aureian blood. Her bare midriff was painted as dark as her face. Her eyes blazed hungrily with emerald fire as she drove her spear into the earth. She walked before them as a demon. She walked before them as a Dark One.

"The Veil awaits us," Maevin began as her gaze swept the crowd. "Are we afraid of the west? No! Are we afraid of death? Not me!"

She thumped her chest with a fist. Her voice was strong and held an eerily musical tone. None could have looked away even if they had wanted to.

"Yorath, Brother of War," she called. "Give me rage and strength until the west bows before us. Sylvaine, Mother of Justice, give me life and steel my resolve until the west bows before us. And Tanris, Dark One, Lord of the Dead … grant me your eye, grant me your sight. Let me see the song of what is yet to come." Maevin's words grew louder with each passing word. She drew her wicked knife and held it to the palm of her hand. "Spirits … all seers, take my blood."

The priestess drew steel across skin. Her hand parted down the middle and blood began to flow. A tremble ran through her body. She dropped to her knees. The knife fell from her fingers as her bloody hand wrapped around her snake amulet. Maevin's lips curled into a twisted grin. Her teeth were made bare, and tears began to roll from her eyes. They caressed her cheeks and splashed upon the earth as she rose to her feet. A second shiver ran through the priestess' body.

"I see a river of blood," she said. "I see an ocean of fire. I see men drowning in their own blood. The spirits walk among us … they walk *with* us." Maevin's eyes stared into the crowd. They stared *through* the crowd. "I hear a whisper. I hear a song," she said with outstretched hands, her fingers curled as if the song flowed through them. "This day will be ours from now and for all time. Remember it. Remember it." Maevin's gaze swept the rows of warriors as she walked before them. "Salvaar is freedom, Salvaar is true, and we are Salvaar!"

A cry erupted from the lips of the Salvaari. Thousands of voices raised in unison. Lukas pounded a fist into his chest as he joined the cry. Slowly the chorus died down as Maevin approached the Káli chief.

"Chief Vaylin," she said. "You will drench the earth in western blood."

Something awoke in Vaylin's eyes as Maevin spoke to her. Passion, fury, belief ... they all swam within the chief's emerald gaze.

"Henghis, great king." Maevin turned to the ruler of Salvaar. "The Veil will sing your name until the end of time."

Henghis dipped his head in deference to her words.

Maevin's hair lashed through the air as once more she began to move. Her eyes went to Lukas as she approached. He was no chief or ruler, no king nor great warrior. They all stopped and stared.

"Whisperer, your words ring as true as they always have," Maevin told him as she looked deep into his eyes. "I see you standing upon a field of the dead. A field conjured by a whisper."

Lukas felt his blood chill as if a kind of icy fire coursed through his veins. He felt more awake, more alive, than he ever had. The priestess' smile was savage as she flitted away. All of the questions and all of the doubt that the Salvaari had once felt vanished like smoke.

"Today is a day that Salvaar will never forget," Maevin cried. "Today is a day that the whole world will remember!"

✦ ✦ ✦

The great line of western soldiers stretched out beneath the darkness of the trees. Dayne's gaze flicked to the canopy above. It was nearing midday, and the column was at last nearing the place at which they would leave this cursed forest and make for the crossing. Despite this, the king could not allow himself to lower his guard. The might of the Salvaari army was at Verena, but Dayne knew he'd be a fool to think that none remained. They would be out there somewhere. Were they watching now?

The song of horns echoed through the woods. Horses pawed the earth and snorted.

"The warning," Tristayn murmured. His gaze went to the east.

"It's a trap," Dayne called.

Flickers of silver and red broke the trees and the first of his scouts appeared.

"Salvaar is here!" the scout cried as he raced down the line.

Panic ran through the western column. They were spread out, their lines thin. They were not prepared for an attack. The clash of steel could be heard in the distance and war cries began to echo through the trees. They were coming.

"They're going to swamp us," Dayne said as he looked to his commanders. "We need to get out of the forest. Form up so we can break them."

"I will take them head on," Corvo Alaine told them.

"Lord Asteryn, take your riders north. Hold the flank," Dayne commanded. "Lord Balderik, you have the south. Do not get cut off. Do not let them get past. No matter what comes through those trees, you will hold the line. When you hear my horn, fall back and make for the flanks."

"Yes, my king," the high lords replied.

With that, Asteryn, Balderik and the grand master made for their lines and rallied their men.

"Tristayn, get word to Medea and General Ilaros," Dayne continued. "They follow us to the river. That is where we fight. Aureia will hold the centre. Medea the left flank. Annora the right. We will meet the Salvaari on our own terms. Go now!"

"King Dayne!" Tristayn called before he thumped a fist to his chest and galloped away shouting orders.

Horns sounded and commands rolled down the lines. Dayne watched as the men began to run from the forest, their captains trying to keep some kind of formation intact. The king froze. He turned to Sir Garrik as at last he realised.

"If the tribes are here, then they aren't in Verena," Dayne said. "This is a trap."

"But the message," Garrik countered.

"Think. We, all of us, are heading to the same place at the same time," Dayne replied. "Velis will have received the exact same message. Our lines are thin. There is no better time to attack than now. The men are weary, the morale low. If we are being attacked, it is because the Salvaari are here in *force*."

"If that is true, then all the tribes will be here."

"This is a risk, but this is our time, and I will risk everything," Dayne said. "Ride to Velis. Tell him to cross the river and double back only when he hears the sound of the Aureian horn."

"I will see it done," Garrik told him before turning his horse and kicking his heels in. "Yah!"

Dayne spared his friend a glance as the master at arms thundered south.

Sunlight assaulted Dayne's eyes as he broke free of the forest. Thousands upon thousands of soldiers fled across the open ground towards the river. Some had already reached its banks and began to form up with the ford at their back. Calvary formed up at the wings, while the infantry of the three nations began to create an unbreakable wall of steel and flesh. Rank upon rank of archers stood at the front of the army and prepared to unleash hell upon any Salvaari who emerged from the trees nearly two hundred paces from their position. Slowly, the western army grew in strength as more and more soldiers joined them. Supply wagons and carriages were taken to the crossing. Food, supplies, spare weapons. They were the least of Dayne's concern. He saw Sofia cross the river with her guard with the supply train. He watched her leave, saw her gaze back towards him. Another company of royal guard stood sentinel around a second wagon. This one held the assassin, Iris Deleonie. Dayne removed them from his concern as he turned back to the forest. He felt pain stir in his gut and the metallic taste of blood enter his mouth. He clenched his fist and spat it to the side. He would not be weak. Not here, not now. Every outcome, every plan and strategy flooded his mind.

"Sound the retreat," Dayne commanded his horn bearer. "Call the riders back."

Three long blasts sang through the wind. It would not be long before the western cavalry charged across the open ground towards them.

The cries and screams of dying men carried across the open ground from the trees. The song of steel. He knew that doubts and fears would be plaguing the minds of his men. Annoran, Medean, Aureian … all of them.

"Stand firm! Stand firm!" Dayne called down the line as he rode before it. His gaze went to one of the soldiers. "Willam. You slew fifty men at Bandujar. Will you do the same today?"

"Yes, my king!"

Dayne grinned as he continued his ride. Spears were beaten upon shields.

"Kaylun," Dayne called to another soldier. "Your father fought beside mine when they last came to Salvaar. He was a great warrior. A hero! Gave his life to save my father from the heathen. You honour him by being here today."

Weapons pounded shields. Fists pounded armour.

"And Robert Gabrielle. Champion of the bow. You won three tournaments in Palen-Tor. It was your arrow that took first blood in this war. Your name will be written into the pages of history!"

The army cheered.

"Sons of the west! Fight to see the next sunrise, for I promise you the dawn is coming!"

The roar was taken up by Annoran, Medean and Aureian alike. Weapons were thrust into the air. Shields were beaten and the melody carried across the open ground between the great army and the trees. Movement flickered beyond the tree line. Western riders materialised and surged back towards their ranks.

✦ ✦ ✦

FORTY-SIX

Káli Lands, Forest of Salvaar

Kyler took a blow on his shield as he swivelled in his saddle. He brought his arm around and thrust his spear through the Salvaari's heart. With a grunt, he tore it free and sent the dying man crashing to the ground. There was no time to pause, no time to think. Blood stained his armour and covered his spear. Sweat covered his body, yet he barely felt it. The only sound was that of battle. Salvaari riders swarmed the ranks of mounted knights. They screamed and cried out in their native tongue, foreign to Kyler's ears. He paid the shouts no heed. All that filled his mind was the enemy in front and his brothers at his side. He cut down another Salvaari who came at him with an axe and then threw his shield up in time to catch an arrow aimed at his face. He lashed out and launched his spear into the air. It caught the archer's chest and tossed him from his saddle with a scream. Kyler tore his sword free, kicked his heels in and forced his mount to rear. A Salvaari spear thrust missed him by a hair's breadth. Kyler brought his sword down and, with the momentum of his horse returning to all fours, smashed the blade through the spearman's head. With a shout, Alarik led a line of knights surging past Kyler and into the ranks of Salvaari. Kyler made to follow. He wasn't prepared for the pain. It rose from nothing and tore through his mind. It *burned*. Kyler grimaced and shook his head as he tried to clear it. He gnashed his teeth and cracked the crossguard of his sword into his helmet. It did not stop the pain, but it helped narrow his focus. The agony gripped him, but he resisted.

Horns sang in the distance. Annoran horns. Horns to signal the retreat. King Dayne was in position.

"FALL BACK!" Corvo's voice pierced the battlefield. "FALL BACK!"

The cry was taken up by knight captains as word spread across the line of western riders.

"TO THE RIVER!" Sir Alarik shouted above the clash of steel.

Kyler turned his mount and kicked his heels in. The line of riders thundered west beneath the trees.

✦ ✦ ✦

Lukas watched as the western soldiers galloped away.

"Reform the line!" he commanded. "Reform the line!"

He knew that if a scattered line of Salvaari pursued the westerners into the field they would be lambs to the slaughter. Salvaari horns rang through the trees. Horsemen rode to the wings while those on foot took the centre. Lukas' gaze did not leave the retreating westerners. Aelida, Rodion, Maevin and the rest of his warband rode with him. They would not leave his side. His grip tightened upon his spear as the last of the enemy slipped beyond the tree line. Lukas knew that by now they would have formed up with thousands of archers ready to unleash death upon the Salvaari. They would need to charge across the open ground and meet the enemy close enough for the sword.

Henghis levelled his sword forward and the line of Salvaari began to march slowly towards the end of the forest. No words were uttered for there were no more to give. They all knew why they were there.

Lukas stared out from the forest. He could picture where his brother sat atop his steed. Thousands of soldiers separated the brothers, yet it was as if they were the only two men there. Henghis raised his sword over his head and levelled it towards the enemy.

✦ ✦ ✦

King Dayne stared across the open field towards the trees. The last of the knights and Annoran cavalry that had held the enemy back sped back across the plain. They circled and formed up alongside the allied infantry. The king's eyes never left the forest. His visor remained up. He would see *everything*. Shadows flicked beyond the tree line and then the first of the Salvaari emerged. A great cry went up from the heathen ranks before they surged forward. Dayne raised his sword as the archers raised their longbows. He waited but a moment before he brought his sword down. The order was given, and a choir of bow song filled the air. Thousands of steel-tipped arrows speared into the sky. A second volley followed before the first came down. Sunlight glinted along tiny beads of steel before they came down in a great wave. They pierced shield, armour and flesh. Hundreds of Salvaari fell beneath the onslaught. Man and beast crashed to the ground as the Annoran rain did not relent. Dayne's eyes flicked across the ground as he calculated the distance. A final volley was sent skyward before the king's voice carried to the horn bearer.

"Call them back."

Two short blasts punctured the air. Gaps were opened in the lines of western footmen. Without hesitation, the archers began to pour back through their own ranks. Cavalry surged across the open field at the flanks. They lowered spears and lances mere heartbeats before coming together with their enemy in a great crash. Men were thrown from horses. Rider and mount alike screamed. The last of the archers began to run through the first ranks of infantry. The Aureians formed up without command. Shields were locked.

The first row crouched and braced themselves with their shields held before them. The second row placed their shields over the first and then a third rank followed. Spears drove through the gaps in the shield wall – not a moment too soon. The Salvaari reached the western ranks as the last of the wall rose. They threw themselves at the shields with savage cries upon their lips.

Dayne's eyes swept the battlefield as the Salvaari tried to swamp his great army. His men held. Their discipline held. Instead of soldiers and a battlefield, Dayne saw a board and game pieces. He saw moves being made and upon his own command countered them. He knew when to reinforce positions and when to push forward. Control at all times, even in battle. He was a master of war. This was his domain. He turned to General Tristayn who had long since reached his side.

"Pull the archers back across the river," he ordered. "Aim for the flanks."

"It will be done, my lord."

✦ ✦ ✦

Garrik saw the glint of sunlight upon armour as the cries went up. The shouts of alarm died when the Aureian scout riders recognised the red cloak of the Annoran guard. Two men met Garrik, and as the captain brought his horse to a halt, he could finally hear the sound of battle. It would have been over a mile away by now, but the song of steel carried far. A few short words spoken with authority was all it took for the Aureians to turn their horses about and lead Garrik towards the army of silver riders. The sea of silver and purple parted as he rode through their ranks until he reached their commander.

"General Velis." Garrik gave the Aureian a nod.

"Sir Garrik. What is it?"

Garrik gestured back towards whence he had come. "There is

a battle not far from here," he said. "The letter you received from Verena was a trap. They all were. Right now, King Dayne has engaged the enemy against the banks of the Arwan."

"Then we must help him," Velis replied without hesitation.

"No." Garrik stopped him before he pointed across the river towards a bluff that shielded the plains beyond from sight. "We must cross the river here. Wait for those who follow you to pass. Wait for the signal. Dayne's signal. Then we attack."

Without so much as a nod of agreement, Velis waved his spear over his head and thrust the tip southward across the river.

"We ride south!" he cried before he led his men into the waters of the Arwan.

✦ ✦ ✦

Kitara's sword tasted blood as she weaved among the chaos created by man and horse. The ranks of Medean riders had long since mixed with the Salvaari and their allies. An attack could come from anywhere at any time. Kitara kept her horse and her sword moving at all times. She cut down a man bearing Caspin colours as Aeryn felled the man at his side with an arrow. Bellec and his mercenaries carved a bloody path through the Medeans like they were nothing. They were cold, calculated masters of the kill. They wanted vengeance for Kompton and the rest of their brothers slain by western hands. They wanted vengeance against Annora that had so wrongfully banished them. Kitara's sword slid through a rider's throat and drove into the chest of a second. These people had come to take what she had grown to love. She swivelled and blocked a sword aimed to take her head. Sakkar's khopesh took the Medean from the side and sent him to the afterlife. A company of Káli riders led by One-Eye broke from the fight and upon his command fired a volley of poisoned arrows into the flank of the Medean lines. They circled and re-joined the fight. The ranks of

Salvaari had been all but halted against the western infantry, but slowly the children of the forest surrounded the invaders' army. Inch by inch, they pushed them back into the river.

✦ ✦ ✦

Dayne watched as the Salvaari began to surround his army. He had foreseen it. He had *enabled* it. Dayne allowed a glance back towards the river ford where the last of his archers had at last crossed. They lined the bank and readied their bows. With the Salvaari riders encircling his army, they had exposed their flanks to those men across the river. Dayne had to give no order for the attack to begin, for he had already given command. He watched as flights of arrows crossed over the river and speared into the sides of the Salvaari cavalry. Dozens fell beneath the storm of steel. Dayne looked to his horn bearer.

"Three blasts," he said and held up as many fingers.

A trio of chords echoed across the battlefield as Dayne's command was relayed. To the flanks of his army, riders began to move. To one side Annoran heavy cavalry charged forth; to the other were Knights of Kil'kara. They did not thunder towards the enemy. Instead, they made for the passages along the riverbank made bare by the storm of arrows. They surged around the Salvaari, circled and then charged into their flanks.

✦ ✦ ✦

Lukas had no time to think as he saw the Annoran cavalry surge along the riverbank, circle and charge towards his position.

"CUT THEM OFF!" he roared in Salvaari.

Dozens of Káli surged towards the Annorans trying to flank them. They vanished under the might of the western horsemen. Lukas turned his horse and readied his spear.

"TANRIS! TANRIS!" Vaylin's voice carved through the air like a blade. Her dark hair whipped through the wind like ebony fire as she led hundreds of her people towards the Annorans. She met them head on.

"TO THE CHIEF!" Lukas bellowed and kicked his heels in.

The warriors of his warband surged forth in his wake. They slammed into the Annorans like water upon rock, crashing and writhing as they fought to halt them. The Káli attacked like savages. They fought tooth and nail to the last. One by one, the warriors at Vaylin's side were picked off by the swords and spears of Annora. Lukas and his warriors fought hard but could only watch as their chief was surrounded by a ring of steel. Vaylin cut a man down with her spear, yet she was blind to a man at her back. Lukas launched his lance forth. It struck the Annoran in the back of the neck and sent him flailing to the ground. His body was broken by the churning hooves. Vaylin lost her weapon as an Annoran countered and tore it from her grasp. She pulled forth her dagger.

"TANRIS!" she screamed.

She did not see the sword come from behind. She only felt it as it drove through her back and tore through her heart. Blood poured from her lips as her attacker pulled his blade free.

"NO!" Lukas cried, watching the Káli chief fall.

Life left her body before it kissed the ground. She passed into the Veil and joined her brother in death. Cries of rage echoed above the ranks of Káli as they pushed into the enemy that had taken their chief, their beloved leader. They did not despair, yet tears ran freely down their cheeks. A great roar sung from the throats of Salvaari of every tribe rose high as hundreds of riders descended upon the Annoran position and charged to the aid of the Káli. Slowly, they began to push the outnumbered Annorans back.

✦ ✦ ✦

Dayne watched the flanks and saw that his cavalry had been halted. He had given the order for them to slowly begin to fall back and give the Salvaari the illusion that they were retreating. The centre held strong. Hundreds, if not thousands, of Salvaari lay dead before the shield wall. The archers across the river continued to shoot when given the chance. Dayne was winning this fight, but he did not want to merely win. He needed to crush this army here. He needed to destroy it. There was a traitor in his camp that had made this attack possible and to prevent another such trap he had to achieve total victory. He saw dust being kicked up to the east and this was the very reason why he had stopped his men from encircling the enemy. The three tribes that had stood against Velis were here.

✦ ✦ ✦

A sword glanced off Kitara's bracer. She countered with her own blade and tore through her attacker's neck. He fell with a scream and then vanished beneath the tide of horses. Through the chaos she could see that the Annoran cavalry was breaking. Slowly, the Salvaari were pushing them back. Some of the western riders began to splash in the river as the children of the forest fought for everything that they had. For every inch that they won, the Salvaari paid for it with their blood. With their lives. Men and women fell by the second to western blades and arrows.

Suddenly, the advance was stopped. The west dug their heels into the mud and the Salvaari were ground to a halt. The Annoran cavalry before Kitara cut their attackers down without mercy yet did not move to fill the gaps. They had decided to hold the Salvaari here. The discipline of the west was great. The shield wall of Aureia had defeated kings and ruined empires. It was turning back the Salvaari assault. A great thunder rose above the din of battle. The drumbeat of thousands of hooves. It came from behind, from the east. Kitara stared through the chaos and her eyes widened.

Cheers rang through the Salvaari ranks as the three eastern tribes arrived. The Coventina, Belcar and Niavenn had arrived. The swelling Salvaari numbers began to push the westerners back once again. Surrounded and against the river, Dayne's army began to be overwhelmed.

✦ ✦ ✦

Velis gazed across the land from his position behind the bluff. He had long since removed his helmet and now he waited and watched. He lay against the hill with no more than his eyes showing above the bluff. To his back both man and beast lay upon Mieran soil. He could hear the battle in the distance. He could see the dust and the smudge upon the horizon. Soldiers in formation encircled by a growing enemy. He heard the sound of hooves as the tribes he had fought in the east materialised from the forest. Lines of riders formed up before him and then charged west. They would have thought that Velis and his men had reached the battle. They would think that the Aureian cavalry was trapped against the river. Velis gripped his sword tightly as he watched the tribes ride by. He ran a hand over the triple-headed chimera ring, the band that had adorned the finger of Nykalous Gaedhela himself. A gift from Queen Reshada. The spirit of the greatest and last Delion hero rode with him. The spirit of the greatest conqueror that the world had ever seen. Velis' gaze stayed with the three tribes as they met the army against the river. He could not see flags or standards, yet he knew that the western army was holding. It reached his ear, caressed it like the wind.

The song of an Aureian horn. Dayne's signal. Velis turned back towards his people. To Garrik of Dayne's guard, to Jasir who had followed him to Irene and every battlefield since. To Chiher of

Larissa. Of the thousands of riders at his back, many had been by his side for as long as Jasir. They had gone to hell and back with him. He would not fail them today. Without a word, Velis strapped on his helmet. As one, the horsemen mounted their steeds and crossed the river once again.

✦ ✦ ✦

Aureian horns blared. Horses surged all around Lukas and he wove his way through the melee. He had long since lost his spear in the fight and now wielded his wicked hammer. The Káli around him fought like animals. They threw themselves at the western soldiers as if they were possessed. The death of their chief had turned them savage and with the arrival of their allies they had grown emboldened. They did not care if they died, only that they took as many westerners with them to the grave as they could. The Coventina horsemen surged all around the Káli as they raced to the fore of the fighting. The ferocious Salvaari tribe famed for their prowess atop horses hungrily engaged the enemy. The feathers woven into their hair and garments flew in the wind. White plumes were stained red as the Salvaari riders cut a swathe into the Annoran cavalry.

Lukas watched on as they led the Káli in the assault. Even with the fierce Coventina and the armoured Niavenn and Belcar, would they be enough? He stared through the battlefield. Dayne's banner was not with the Annoran horse. That meant he was still directing his men. That meant he was still in command. Through the chaos, he caught a glimpse of a red eagle atop a white field. It flew at the back of the western army. It flew from the position where the Aureian horns had sounded. Anticipation. That had been what Dayne had once tried to teach him. Lukas' mind went to work. The three tribes from the east were here now. They had been held in battle by silver horsemen for months. Aureian horsemen … and they had arrived *before* their enemy who had no doubt ridden first. His brow furrowed.

"What is it?" Rodion called from his side.

Lukas swivelled in his saddle as he searched the chaos. "EIRIAN!" he shouted as he saw the Káli commander. "EIRIAN!"

The general looked to One-Eye and galloped through the mass of Salvaari towards him. Lukas forced his way through the black-painted warriors as he fought to get to the leader.

"One-Eye?" Eirian called as he reached Lukas' side.

"This is a trick," Lukas snarled. "We need to turn back now."

"What do you mean?"

"The Aureian horsemen are not here," Lukas told him. "We're about to be surrounded."

Eirian's eyes widened as he understood. "KÁLI!" Eirian roared and thrust his spear to the east. "WITH ME!"

The black-painted riders turned and surged forward. Lukas locked eyes with Maevin as his horse spun around. His woman. His child.

"YAH!" Lukas cried as he kicked his heels in.

✦ ✦ ✦

Kitara heard Eirian's shout above the din of battle. She saw the Káli turn to the east. Above them, surging down towards the battle, was a line of silver. Aureia had come.

"FORWARD!" Bellec called as he twirled his blade towards the silver horsemen.

As one, the mercenaries turned and charged east with the Káli. With surprise lost, a great roar went up from the Aureian ranks. Thousands of imperial voices cried out the name of their great empire. Lances came down and the two sides collided. Man and horse screamed. Heavily armoured Aureian knights smashed through the Salvaari ranks like they were nothing. Káli fell all around and then the mercenaries crashed into the silver riders. Bellec cut a man from his saddle and a second charged past and angled straight for Kitara. She swivelled aside from the spear as it sped by her shoulder. She countered and thrust her sword deep into the Aureian's neck. He fell with a scream. Kitara tasted blood and sweat as silver riders and their Larissan allies swamped them. They had encircled the Salvaari. Dayne's great army to their fore. Annoran archers sent wave after wave of steel across the river into the flanks of Salvaari while the Aureians finished the noose from behind. Now they tightened it. Horns blew and commands were given. The shield wall advanced. A shout went up in a foreign tongue and a volley of Larissan arrows carved through the ranks of Káli. Black-painted warriors fell. Mercenaries fell. Kitara pulled her reins and forced her mount into a rear as a spear drove her way. It missed and a second Aureian charged into the side of her mount. The horse fell. Kitara fell. She rolled aside from the beast and leapt to her feet, moving like water. Her attackers fell in two moves. She looked to her horse, but it was long since gone.

Galadayne appeared at her side. His own mount had been felled by Larissan arrows. Other mercenaries joined them on foot. Aeryn put an arrow through an Aureian's throat, ducked a second man's sword and then a third's blade sliced across her arm. Kitara leapt to her aid, but she was too slow. Aeryn managed to get her bow up in time to deflect a second blow but not before a shield smashed into her head. She fell. Only the helmet given to her by Bellec saved her. Kitara's sword blocked the Aureian's blade aimed at her lover. She parried, slid inside the man's blow and drove steel up into his chin. He crashed to the ground as she wrenched the blade free. Kitara turned back to Aeryn, but she was already on her feet, axe in hand. Blood ran down the moonseer's arm. With Galadayne at her left shoulder and Aeryn at her right, Kitara fought the horde of Aureians head on. Lukas and his warband stood beside them. The

Káli chanted and screamed as they fought. An Aureian spear tore through one of the mercenaries' chests.

"LAYAN!" Lukas' cry was long and loud as he leapt at the Aureian.

One-Eye's hammer smashed through the western soldier's helmet and crushed the skull beneath. Blood cascaded like rain as Layan fell to his knees. Once of Annora. Once of the royal guard. He had followed Bellec for over two long decades. He had served Lukas for months while his comrades rode to save Kitara. He died side by side with both. More and more Aureians came at them, on foot and on horse. Larissans came with them. Men who served the queen. With great sorrow, Sakkar fought his kinsmen. Agony was in his cries as he killed them. Rodion of the Káli fell to Larissan arrows. Kitara cut down man after man. Blood covered her armour, that of her enemies and her own. The battle raged and ebbed like a tempest. The winds of battle separated allies. No longer could Kitara see Aeryn. No longer could she see Bellec. A shout went up in Ancient Aureian and then a wave of spears flew towards them. Those with shields raised them. Those without prayed. Kitara's eyes flew to the blood-soaked ground. They searched, and without hesitation she moved. Leaping forward, she threw herself to the ground. Her sword dropped as her fingers searched through the filth. They caught the rim of a shield and pulled it free of a body. Kitara heaved it up just as the spears descended all around. She had no room to move, no space in which to avoid them. Sunlight glinted upon silver. Steel rained. Men screamed. Dozens fell. Heavy spears slammed into her shield. Steel tips cut through the wood. One sliced her cheek and barely missed her face. The shield was smashed into her as the weight of the spears hit home. She fell to her back, casting the shield aside. An Aureian voice filled the air. The silver line advanced. Kitara's hands slid across the earth that had become a slurry of mud churned with bodies. Death was all around — she was familiar with it. She had grown up with it.

Kitara rolled back and reached for her sword. Only then did she realise that all those around her were gone. The mercenaries at her side were either dead or sprawled across the ground screaming. Further back were Aeryn, her father and the rest of the company. She met Bellec's eyes, and then Aeryn's. She saw them shout but could not make out the words. The roar of Aureia was deafening. Kitara was between both armies. Aureia charged. Kitara found her sword. Blood trickled down her cheek like a tear. It mingled with dirt and sweat before at last it dropped down onto the earth. Kitara rose to her feet. Her body ached. She took a breath as she raised her sword. Three mercenaries were with her. They were wounded and struggling to breathe, yet still they stood. Aureia closed in. A shout went up. A second line of Aureian spearmen emerged. As one, their arms came forward. As one, they sent a second volley into the sky. A tendril of horror seeped into Kitara's heart. This time there was no shield. This time there was no avoiding them. She angled her sword knowing that she could not stop the spears coming towards her. The mercenaries fell first. Their bodies were pummelled and sent crashing to the ground like boneless dolls. Shadows flickered. A horse screamed. A shield was thrust in front of her. The rider's horse crashed into Kitara as spears took its life. The rider's shield took the lance intended for Kitara. Bellec's shield. She caught a glimpse of his blue eyes as he saved her life. Bellec screamed. A spear tore into the back of his shoulder. The dying horse bellowed as it slammed into Kitara and sent her crashing to the ground. She gasped as air fled her lungs; its weight was crushing. Bellec's shield dropped from his nerveless fingers and splashed into the mud. The force of the spear sent him flying from the horse. Bellec's back hit the mud. His body twisted. The spear snapped as their momentum spun him.

✦ ✦ ✦

Pain erupted through Bellec's arm. It lay useless at his side, blood pouring from the wound. Beneath the crimson, his shoulder was all but destroyed. He gasped for air as it returned to his aching lungs. He gritted his teeth and forced his gaze to where Kitara lay. The dead horse was on top of her, crushing her to the ground. The back of her head was to him. She was still. Her chest did not rise and fall. Her arms were limp and unmoving. Hope fled Bellec's eyes. Blood trickled from his lips as he hung his head. Kitara was gone. She was dead. His will to fight vanished. He had failed her. The thudding footsteps of armoured Aureian boots drew closer. Bellec's eyes went to the line of soldiers as they approached. It was over. He struggled to breathe, and then he heard her cry. Bellec's eyes flew to Kitara. She tried to move, yet the beast upon her was dead and heavier than any boulder. He could hear the pain in her cry as he saw her move weakly. His gaze went back to the Aureians who had closed in half the distance. She was stuck. The Aureians would not spare her. They would not show mercy. Bellec snarled as he heaved himself to his feet. His fire still burned. He searched the ground for a weapon, yet his blade was gone. Bellec saw his daughter's sword. He took it up.

✦ ✦ ✦

Tears spilled down Kitara's cheek as she came to. Only then did she feel the pain. She was trapped. She was helpless. The weight of the horse pinned her legs and waist. Kitara roared as she pushed to no avail. Aureian war cries closed in. The sound of marching boots closed in. Kitara cried out, and then she heard her father's snarl. With a roar, he heaved himself upwards and turned to face the charging might of Aureia. His sword was gone, yet in its place was Kitara's. His right arm hung limp by his side. The steel tip of the spear had punched through one side, while the remnants of the shattered shaft protruded from the other. Blood poured down from the wound and dripped from his fingers. He stood alone as thousands of soldiers rushed towards them. Bellec did not look back as he raised Kitara's sword. Kitara screamed as she heaved against the horse. Her muscles burned. Her body screamed. Her hands scrabbled against the ground as she pulled. Her legs began to move. Her eyes never left her father's back. A sob shook her body as she fought to break free, tears spilling down her cheeks.

Bellec roared and in that moment he transformed. No longer was he Bellec. No longer was he a mercenary. He stood as Theron Malley. He stood as a father. Theron stood alone as the Aureians reached him. He moved like a man possessed. He felled one and took the life of a second. He made to raise his right arm, but it would not work. The Aureians surrounded him. The blows were fast and hard. His side, his back, his chest. They did not discriminate. Theron did not stop his roar. He fought. Blades sliced his arm. Kitara's sword fell. He bellowed as a blade sent him to his knees. Blood spilled from his ruined lips. Kitara screamed as she lost sight of her father.

✦ ✦ ✦

Dayne felt nothing as his plan bore fruit. He would allow nothing to cloud his mind, not even a hint of satisfaction at the knowledge that the battle was his. It was over only when it was over. His great army surrounded the Salvaari like they were nothing. Blow by blow, they were crushing them, but until the last sword was thrown down, until the last blood was shed, he would not allow himself to feel victorious. His hand stayed upon the eagle-shaped hilt of his sword as he surveyed the battle. Somewhere down there, somewhere in the fighting, was Lukas. He would be with the black-painted Káli. Was he still alive? As the song of steel continued, Dayne allowed his gaze to drift away from the battlefield. His eyes flicked to the east. Always anticipating. Always expecting a new threat. His gaze narrowed. A dark smudge appeared upon the horizon. Sunlight glinted upon steel. Armour. Spears.

"Tristayn," Dayne said and nodded towards the east. "There."

The general followed his king's gaze. "Moving fast," Tristayn muttered. "Horses. Thousands of them."

"Both sides of the river," Dayne murmured as he saw a second line in the Rift. "Miera." It had to be. "Pull the men back," Dayne commanded.

"But, my lord–"

"Do it now!" Dayne snarled.

Tristayn gave the command, and the song of horns echoed across the field. The king turned to another of his guard.

"The Medean sellswords across the river," Dayne said. "Tell them to form up against the attack. They must hold back Miera. They cannot fail me."

✦ ✦ ✦

Sir Garrik cut a Salvaari down and then spun in his saddle to fell a second. The sound of the horns reached his ears before the shouts arose from the western ranks. Screams and shouts to fall back across the river came from every side. Something had changed. There must be an attack coming. Garrik kicked his heels in as the Aureian lines began to break from the Salvaari. Through the breaks in the ranks, he caught sight of the shadow fast approaching. A great wave of cavalry. Tens of thousands of them. Mierans. He looked to the river and saw the western army surge into the waters. He could see the archers and Medean mercenaries forming up upon the opposing bank. Garrik turned back to the Mierans. They would not all be able to cross before the horsemen reached them. Garrik pushed his horse into a gallop as he rode around the edge of the great army. He made for open ground. The Aureian shield wall held the Salvaari at bay as their allies turned to flee. General Ilaros and his men would hold the line, but they would not be enough. When the Mierans reached them, they would break. Those not across the river would be slaughtered. He glanced from the Mieran lines to those of his countrymen. He could see Dayne commanding the retreat. His king. His liege lord. Garrik had sworn never to fail the Raynor line. He thought of his own family back in Annora. He would not fail them today. The master at arms exhaled slowly. He pulled a horn from his belt and gave a single long blast. The royal guard answered his call. Dozens became hundreds. Hundreds became a thousand. Garrik looked to Dayne staring at him over the ranks of soldiers. Garrik raised his sword in salute before turning to his men. Warriors he had known for years and decades. They made a line facing east. They all knew what they were about to do. Prayers were uttered. Garrik placed his sword over his heart.

"Under the eagle," he murmured.

He kicked his heels in. Horns sang. Cries echoed across the battlefield. The line of red-cloaked riders surged towards the Mierans.

✦ ✦ ✦

Torben of the Valkir followed Zandir Barangir as the Mieran lord led his column north. The phoenix banners of Miera soared high in the breeze above the greatest riders that the world had ever seen. Thirty thousand of them spread across both sides of the river. An unbreakable tide of horsemen. King Zoran's plan was to surround the enemy and break them. With Torben were Cleander and Luana Marquez alongside Tariq, Marshall and Elise. Torben watched as a force of Annoran cavalry broke from the retreating formations and charged straight towards the avalanche of Mierans. As they drew closer, Elise, Tariq and Marshall broke from the formation. She was no fighter. This was the time for war. This was the time of steel and blood. Torben levelled his spear. This was for Astrid.

"ANNORA!" The war cry echoed from the throats of a thousand men as they hurtled towards the Mierans.

The sides came together. Men fell. Horses fell.

✦ ✦ ✦

Kyler's blade was slick with the blood of Salvaari, of those who had tried to spill his own. He was on foot alongside hundreds of his fellow knights. They held a shield wall, and it was unbreakable. Alarik stood at his side. Together, mentor and student fought their way through the chaos. When the horns to retreat sounded, they worked in unison. When the Mieran riders smashed through the Annoran guardsmen and swamped the retreating army, it was the Order of Kil'kara that held firm. Alongside the Aureians, they would be the last to cross the river.

Kyler took blow after blow upon his shield as warriors swarmed all around them. His body was battered and bruised. He could feel blood hot upon his sweat-covered skin. His head ached as his disease threatened to tear him apart. Still, he fought. Salvaari or Mieran, they all fell to his sword. He took a blow to his shoulder and slew the man who dealt it. Slowly, the knights began to withdraw. The rear lines began to reach the river. The Salvaari threw themselves upon the shields with savage abandon. Knights began to fall. In the face of overwhelming numbers, with nothing but wet mud underfoot, the formation began to splinter. Warriors came at Kyler from every direction. They leapt at him. The fought and they clawed. He cut down one. He cut down two. A third fell to his sword. A blade slammed into his back and dropped him to a knee. Only his armour saved his life. Kyler turned, rose and thrust his sword through the body of the Salvaari warrior. The man screamed in Kyler's face. The knight drove his sword deeper and slammed his helmet into the man's head. The Salvaari fell back as Kyler's sword tore through his body. He was dead before he hit the ground. Kyler roared as he rose to his feet. Through the chaos his eyes were drawn. They locked with amber eyes. They saw the robes of a maija. She stared back at him through the battle before turning away. Elena. She walked through the ranks of Salvaari like a ghost. Everything slowed. He watched her walk away. She was a dream. Pain surged through his body. His head, his heart. Everything burned. Kyler screamed and fell to his knees. Vomit belched from his lips. It was dark, mixed with blood.

✦ ✦ ✦

Alarik watched Kyler fall to his knees. The cry that fled his lips was more akin to an animal than to man.

"Kyler!" Alarik called as he reached for his friend.

He touched the boy's shoulder. Fast as any man, Kyler rose and turned. His sword carved through the air. Alarik barely got his own blade up in time to stop the attack. Steel rang. He stared into Kyler's eyes and horror filled him. The boy's face was a mask of black veins. The wound to his face had grown, a great scab that spread around his eyes, eyes that now burned red. Crimson like the ruskalan. Kyler lashed out again. Alarik blocked one blow and then another. Kyler's sword angled towards another of the knights. The blade caught the man's shoulder and spun him around.

"TAKE HIM!" Alarik commanded.

Without hesitation, the battlemaster leapt upon his student. They all did. The knights dragged Kyler kicking and screaming to the ground. Alarik raised the pommel of his sword and brought it down hard on Kyler's head.

"GET ME A HORSE!" Alarik bellowed.

✦ ✦ ✦

Dayne looked on as the last of the Aureians and knights crossed the river under the cover of Annoran arrows. He directed soldiers to hold back and turn to those Mierans on his side of the river. The king moved his men like game pieces. He sent archers to the high ground to protect the men who swarmed all around them. He halted the attack. Slowly, the armies of Miera and Salvaar pulled back. They would not risk their numbers now that their enemy was free and held the river. The pagan riders of King Zoran had stolen Dayne's victory for now. For *now*. How the Mierans had come to be here was anyone's guess, but now the king knew that they stood as brothers with Salvaar. Knowledge was power. Dayne had not lost this fight. He would never lose this war. The passage to Verena was open and now he could find the traitor who had risked all to destroy him this day.

✦ ✦ ✦

Kitara pushed her way through the mercenaries. She cast her helmet aside. Her hand tightly held her aching stomach. Her eyes never left the place she had last seen her father. Aureian bodies lay all around. The sellswords gave way. Tears fell from eyes, their faces ashen. Kitara froze as she saw him. His body was covered in a thousand wounds. His eyes were unseeing. Pain filled her scream as her knees gave way. Kitara fell to her father's side as her cry echoed across the battlefield. He had given his life to save her. It was her fault that her father was dead. Once again, she was alone. Her heart broke. Her face contorted as she wept. Kitara shook as sobs wracked her body. A hand closed upon her shoulder. Kitara's unseeing gaze at last turned from Theron's body as Aeryn knelt at her side, cupped her cheek and stared into her eyes. The moonseer's arms wrapped around Kitara. Aeryn said nothing, she just held Kitara as her world fell apart.

✦ ✦ ✦

FORTY-SEVEN

Arwan River, Duchy of Caspin, Medea

Zandir Barangir slid from his saddle in the wake of King Zoran. The Mieran lords gathered together around their liege as he strode towards a party of waiting Salvaari. Word had been sent to the horsemen that the leader of the tribes wanted to meet. The Mierans suspected some kind of trap, as they would for any foreign invitation. A dozen Salvaari bearing different colours of war paint stood apart from their people. They were different in almost every way except one. They all stood proud. They all stood strong. They all stood fearless. The two armies watched with bated breath as their captains came together. The Mierans glanced warily at the Salvaari who watched them closely. Like Henghis, Zoran had been allowed to bring only a dozen of his people to the meeting. They wore their armour from helmets to greaves. Crimson cloaks trimmed in gold fluttered at their backs. They bore an assortment of spears, swords, knives, shields and war hammers. A magnificent phoenix was carved atop King Zoran's helm, while the red plume that crested his helm and hung down his back appeared as the songbird's fire. Crimson war paint shone in the firelight as one of the Salvaari stepped forward. He was no larger than average height and bore a mane of shaggy black hair. A sword hung from his side and an arm ring adorned his wrist. He was not a man built to rival the spirits that the Salvaari worshipped nor was he of any greater stature than a common Mieran. It was the look in his eyes and the power of his voice that revealed who he was before he spoke his name.

"I am Henghis of Salvaar," he said.

Zandir almost frowned. Much like the Mierans, the Salvaari leader seemed to take no pride in boasting his title. At last, King Zoran removed his helmet. He gazed at the Salvaari leader.

"Zoran of Miera," he replied, sweeping his gaze around the assembled tribal leaders. "I was expecting to be greeted by the twelve chieftains of Salvaar, yet two of your number do not bear the torcs of their clan."

"One fell in battle," Henghis replied. "The other was captured at Bandujar. The men you see here lead in their stead."

"I see," was all Zoran said.

A woman with flaming hair and green war paint stepped forth. She bore a sash wrapped around her body from shoulder to hip and a wicked axe hung from her side.

"And you, king?" she said as she nodded to one of the Mieran company. "They are not Mieran."

All eyes went to the pair of foreigners who stood with the Mierans. One was a grizzled warrior with the tattoo of a serpent wrapped around his arm. He wore armour that none of the Salvaari had seen before. A round shield hung from his back, a sword and axe sitting at his hip. The other was a woman who wore a tricorn atop her head and a duelling cape over her shoulder. A sidesword hung at her hip, while jewels shining every shade of green embellished her necklaces, rings and weapons.

"They traversed the oceans to be here," Zandir Barangir replied.

"Luana Marquez," the woman who wore black and green replied. "Captain of the Emeralis."

"Torben of the Valkir," the warrior said. "I came on behalf of King Erik. Far to the south, my people are besieged by our common enemy."

"*Our* enemy?" Henghis asked.

"The foreign emperor and his puppets have come to make slaves of us all," Luana said. "We are all here at a time when we could not be further apart. We who would be enemies united in common cause."

"Many days ago, the seafarers sailed to my land," Zoran told the crowd. "With them came tales of murder and treachery, love and loss. With them came a song. The Song of the Raven. The story of an innocent woman slaughtered for Aureian amusement. We are not friends. None of us here are friends. But we are here this day because our very survival depends upon it. To the south, the empire is marshalling a fleet that intends to sail to *my* coast. When it lands, the armies of the League will join it. The armies across the river will join it. My land will burn just as yours will. Towns and villages sundered. Crows feasting on the dead. The only thing that stands in the way of this fleet is a rabble of raiders, pirates and refugees. An unlikely alliance, yet it is the only thing giving the League pause. I have men at that border, but they will count for nothing if we cannot defeat the army at yours."

"We are all the same," Torben murmured.

All eyes went to the Valkir warrior as he spoke.

"To them," Torben said as he gestured towards the river, "we are all the same. There are those in the west who cannot tell Sacasian from Valkir or Mieran from Salvaari. We are all the same. Heathens. Barbarians. Pagans. Some of us are sailors, some of us riders of the plains, others are children of the forest. We are more different than we are alike save one thing. We are *free*. Truly free. That is worth fighting for. That is worth dying for. My great friend Astrid taught me that we are all free to choose our own path. Hers was to sail as far south as south goes. She was killed for that dream. She was killed for wanting peace. If we succeed, I would like to go there as well. I would like to honour my friend." Torben looked from Zoran to Henghis. It would all fall to them. "Ask yourselves this: What do you want?"

"Peace," Henghis said. "Freedom for myself and my people."

"My people have fought and bled for centuries," King Zoran said. "They have never known anything else. We are Mieran. We are *warriors*. I want what any Mieran craves. A beautiful death. If I find that while fighting for the salvation of my people, then there will be no greater glory."

"Never in history have our people been united," Luana added.

"And now the Sea-Father has chosen this day that our peoples should finally come together," Torben replied.

Zandir watched as Luana walked among the leaders of every nation. She gestured to Torben. "Whether the Valkir god is real or not, he brought us together," Luana said.

The Mierans said nothing. They held no belief in a god or higher power. They believed in only themselves and their actions. In days gone they might have laughed at the words of the Valkir or Salvaari – not today.

"Yes, we are not friends," Luana continued. "Yes, our hands are *stained* with each other's blood. But that can end today."

Silence wrapped the armies like a glove. At last, Henghis approached King Zoran.

"When the battle raged all around, when my people were surrounded by our enemy and all hope seemed lost, you came," Henghis told the Mieran king. "Even though we are enemies. Even though our people have killed each other for generations. Mieran and Salvaari. Yet still you rode. For this I thank you. There will be no more raids."

Henghis extended an arm. Zoran met his equal's eyes. He said nothing. He took the arm and clasped it tightly. The army around them roared. For the first time in their history, Miera had an ally.

"Close your eyes," Henghis started, his voice rising with every word. "Let your soul bear witness. The spirits are here. Can you see them?"

✦ ✦ ✦

Kitara barely noticed the battlefield as she stared at the flameless pyre. Her body ached from more cuts and bruises than she could count. An army of crows had already descended from the heavens and they now scoured the dead. Men and horses covered the ground for miles. Their blood mixed with the soil; they *became* the soil. Arrows littered the ground like grass. The Mierans walked the field and finished off any western survivors. Dead men could not return to Miera. Dead men could not take from Miera. Kitara felt nothing. A torch hung limply from her hand.

"Kitara," Galadayne called.

She turned as the old warrior's hand gripped her shoulder. He looked weary and there was a great sorrow hidden behind his eyes. Some of the mercenaries had been killed in the fighting. Many had been of the royal guard when they fought for Annora. Layan. Bellec. His brothers.

"It is time," Galadayne said quietly.

Kitara said nothing. She had no words. The mercenaries gathered all looked to her. Aeryn watched her with sad eyes. She had not left Kitara's side. Sakkar, Senya and Aeryn stood alongside Lukas the One-Eye and a number of his black-painted Salvaari. In their midst was the pyre of wood and earth. Atop it lay Theron Malley and Layan. Both were clad in their amour. Both held swords over their chests. Their eyes were closed and unseeing. All watched on sorrowfully. Some shed tears while others showed little emotion in their faces. They had all lost friends and brothers this day.

Kitara gripped her torch tight. Tears streaked her cheeks as she slowly moved towards the pyre. She had barely known Layan, but he had been kind. Theron had been her father. He *was* her father despite the mistrust and anger she had greeted him with. Despite the pain and rage, he had accepted her. He had fought for her trust and respect. He had fought for her love. Now it was too late for her to tell him that he had them. Words would forever go unsaid. He had died so that she may live. He had taken a spear meant for her without hesitation. He had fought against an army alone to give her time. The future together yet to be lived had been stolen. Snuffed out in an instant. Kitara bit back a sob as she thrust the torch into the pyre and set it alight. Fire crackled and burned. The torch fell from her fingers as she began to cry. A hand found its way into her own. Aeryn's hand. The moonseer gripped hers tight.

"Rest easy," Aeryn said quietly. "Drift deeper and deeper. The sirens are calling your name."

The moonseer had only heard the words once but knew that they had meaning. Kitara held her hand tightly as her tears fell freely.

The cool waters of the river lapped at the bank. Kitara knelt at the edge of the water, staring deep into her reflection, her mother's ring in the palm of her hand. She barely recognised the woman who looked back. The only movement that disturbed the calm waters was that of the tears that splashed down one by one. Her misty eyes saw little, yet the image was clear in her mind. That of her father. Kitara did not realise she had company until a footstep sounded close behind. She had been blind. With a grimace, Kitara stuffed the ring back into her shirt and splashed water across her face in a fool's attempt to clear the tears. She rose to her feet and turned to see Aeryn approaching.

"I thought that the moonseer had been sent out." Kitara's voice was hollow and cracked.

"They have," Aeryn replied simply. "I do not ride with them. Some things are more important."

Kitara's lip trembled as Aeryn spoke. She could see nothing but love in the moonseer's eyes.

"He was a great man," Aeryn continued.

Together they sat beside the river and looked out across its waters. Aeryn placed a gentle hand over Kitara's.

"When I was a girl, I often dreamt about my father," Kitara started. "Perhaps he was a knight or a lord, maybe even a farmer tilling the fields. The only thing I knew was that he had abandoned my mother for dead and left me to a life of nothing. I hated him for that. I used to dream about how I would meet him … about how I would kill him. This man whom I had never met yet despised with my whole heart. I did not know how to trust or how to love. I knew only how to survive. When I met the one who abandoned me to the world of men before I was born … it made my blood boil. I pushed him away. I let him glimpse my hatred. He was no family of mine. Yet this man I despised and distrusted risked his life time and time and time again for me. He saved me from slavery. He saved my life in battle. He gave me love. He gave me trust. He gave me time. He was patient even though I had done nothing but curse his name. I … I learnt to trust him. I learnt to love him. I loved him and I never told him." Kitara took a shuddering breath.

"He knew," Aeryn told her as she reached out a hand. The back of her fingers caressed Kitara's cheek. "The words may not have been spoken, but he knew."

Kitara took Aeryn's hand and held it against her cheek. Aeryn squeezed it and placed it against Kitara's heart.

"Kitara, he will always be with you."

Kitara stared at Aeryn. Kindness and compassion filled her silver eyes, yet she could see the sadness beyond. Sorrow for Bellec. Sorrow for her.

"My lady," Galadayne's voice came from behind.

They both turned to see the Annoran warrior approach. His face was ashen, and his eyes held great pain. The pain aged him more than his fifty years ever had. Kitara and Aeryn rose to meet him.

"He would have wanted you to have this," Galadayne said as he held out a fist.

Kitara extended a hand. The mercenary placed a golden ring in her palm. It was plain and bore no more embellishment than a tiny sapphire.

"Your father's wedding band," Galadayne explained. "It belongs to you now."

Kitara ran her eyes over the band before she placed it upon her right index finger. "Thank you," she told Galadayne gratefully.

Galadayne nodded slowly. "Bellec … Theron was my closest friend in the world," he told her sadly. "From the age of sixteen, he was my brother. Theron was the strongest man I ever knew. He had pain, he had fears, but he was unwilling to let them dictate him. He was proud of you, of the woman you became. You meant the world to him. You *were* his world. Know that you are one of us," Galadayne continued. "You are family and will always be held as such."

Kitara stepped towards the old warrior and held out a hand. Galadayne took it, and she pulled him into an embrace.

"You are a good man, Galadayne," she said into his shoulder. "But one more loyal … there is none."

Galadayne tightened his arms around her. They stood like that for a moment before they at last broke apart. The old warrior dropped to a knee before her. He met her eyes.

"I pledge my sword and my life to you, Kitara Malley," Galadayne vowed, his voice as strong as any steel. "In the name of the gods, and my great friend Theron, if by my life or death I can protect you, I swear I will."

He did not look away from her as he spoke. Kitara knew that the rest of the company would do the same. The mercenaries, they would look to her now. She knew not of their families back in Annora nor did she know if they even had them. She knew that they were loyal, brave and fearless. She knew that they were good men. They had lost their captain in this war that was far from over and would need someone to lead them. She could not fail them, for her father. She could not fail her father.

✦ ✦ ✦

Elise Delfeyre watched as her kukri danced around her hand. Flamelight danced along the steel blade as the fire that they sat around burned bright. She had not worn the garb of the Nightingale in a long time, but the kukri, like her other knives, was always close at hand. She took comfort from the blade as it moved. Beside her was Tariq, while Marshall tended to the blaze. Footsteps crunched on the cold earth as Cleander made his presence known.

"Torben is at the table of King Zoran and Henghis," Cleander explained as he sat by the flame. "They are discussing strategies … what is to come next."

"And what is to come next?" Tariq asked.

"They talk of peace," Cleander replied. "They've had enough. The Valkir and Salvaari, at least."

"War is all the Mierans know," Marshall said. "There is only one thing that they understand. Steel."

"And horses," Elise added.

"And horses," Marshall agreed with a chuckle.

"If the Mierans *really* want this alliance, then *his lordship* Zoran had best get used to the notion of *not* swinging his sword at everyone that arrives at his border," Elise continued. "Though he doesn't strike me as a peace lover, so the gods only know how long this truce will last."

"You've given it some thought," Cleander said simply.

Elise raised her eyebrows and gave him a sarcastic smirk. "I have a keen mind for politics, *sweetheart*," she replied.

They all laughed. Elise sheathed the blade and turned to the fire. Tariq wrapped an arm around her shoulders and Elise leaned back into her friend.

"Where are the others?" Cleander asked.

"Luana said that she had business with an old friend," Elise told

Cleander. "She and her companion are gone, doing whatever it is that pirates do."

"Why? What have you heard?" Tariq asked Cleander.

"The army will cross the river tomorrow," Cleander told them.

"Salvaar and Miera united," Marshall muttered. "Never in my wildest dreams would I have believed it possible for such hated foes to become as one."

"It may not last," Cleander replied. "All things change with time; however, this alliance will last long enough. They follow the same course."

"For now," Elise said.

"For now," Cleander agreed.

"And what of us?" Tariq asked. "We have made it this far and you have not led us astray."

Cleander nodded and glanced up from the fire towards the Berenithian. "We follow the army south until we reach the valley," he said. "From there, we ride west. We cross Medea and Annora. In little over a month's time, we will reach Valentia."

"How do you propose we cross the Valley of Odrysia when it is swarming with western soldiers?" Tariq asked. "Filled with men who have called it home for a century."

"I know the valley," Cleander replied. "I know its secrets. Its ways and its hideaways."

Tariq gazed at the warrior warily. "You know a lot for a common cutthroat," he said.

Cleander said nothing.

"Tariq," Elise warned as she caught the wary tone in her friend's voice.

"No." Tariq shook his head. "If we are to travel together, if we are to follow this man, then tonight I want the truth. How did an Annoran with more knowledge than any scholar become one with the gangs? How does he become so cold?"

Shadows danced across Cleander's face as he looked through his companion. "When a man has everything taken from him," he said. "When a man has nothing left to live for except to claim vengeance upon those who had so wronged him. That is how I came to join Bhaltair in his fight."

"Then it was the magister who wronged you?" Tariq asked.

"Ghosts and shadows of the past do not serve us. Where I come from does not matter. All that matters is that I am here now. In this moment." Cleander rose to his feet. "Get some rest. We have a long road ahead of us."

✦ ✦ ✦

FORTY-EIGHT

City of Verena, Valley of Odrysia

Sir Alarik Sindra gripped the reins of the horse he led. The western army had walked for some miles to create a distance between the pagan force and their own. King Dayne's riders held the rear and kept a watch on the river. The Salvaari and their new allies held the land north of the Arwan. There would have been no crossing it without taking heavy losses. No doubt Dayne was trying to draw the enemy across. Mutterings of Miera were on everyone's tongues. Where had the horsemen come from? Why had they come? It was no secret that the warriors of Salvaari and the riders of Miera slaughtered each other in their hundreds every year. Raiding parties crossed the Rift from both sides. Now something had changed. Now Miera had ridden out and become the saviour of Salvaar. The west had been close, so close, to achieving their goal. Whether the men in the great army fought for their gods or their lords or for the sake of the Medeans butchered each year by Salvaari warbands, it mattered not to Alarik. What mattered was that they were here now. United as one.

The battlemaster barely acknowledged the weariness that he felt. For well over a year now, he had been in the saddle or in battle, ever since he had ridden out in pursuit of Durandail's Spear. His armour was drenched in the blood of his enemies. His boots were caked with mud. To the veteran warrior, those were nothing. He glanced back at the horse, at the man tied to its back. Kyler. His eyes had burned red, and he had attacked his brothers. It was the work of the ruskalan, of Elena. Alarik was certain of it. Even now while unconscious, the boy's eyes still glowed crimson. Whatever was in him was still there. The boy who had changed in the battle was not Kyler Landrey. For the first time in a long time, Alarik felt something. Worry. All around him, a tent city began to emerge. Alarik turned to the knights who walked with him.

"Take Kyler," Alarik commanded. "Strip him of his armour and tie him to a post. Bind him tight. Whatever turned him, whatever demon is trapped inside his head, it's still there."

"Sir," the knights chorused before one took the reins and began to lead the horse further into the camp.

Alarik rolled his shoulders and unstrapped his helmet. He pulled it from his head and pushed back his coif. His armour would need cleaning before the day was done. *He* would need cleaning.

"Sir Alarik."

The knight looked to see a royal guardsman approaching.

"King Dayne has summoned his council," the guard told him. "He awaits you."

Alarik gave the man a nod. "I'm on my way."

The lords and commanders of Annora, Medea, the Order and the legions gathered in the heart of the camp. Dayne stood with his hands loosely clasped before his stomach, as he often did. He had not cleaned his face of dirt and blood. Crimson coated his armour. He wanted to show his soldiers that, like them, he had fought. He was not above them. Alarik felt his respect grow for the young king as he saw the image. A king who fought beside his men. A rare sight.

"Sons of the west," Dayne began. "This is our time. The east has rallied against us. Miera has come. Do we fear the horsemen and their ways? No. If you cut them, they will bleed. This is just another test in which we will succeed. Commander Velis and his riders are watching them in the north. We may still have the advantage of numbers, but only a fool would try to attack his enemy across a river. We will wait for them to cross."

"We could fall back to Verena and the other cities," one of the lords suggested. "The pagans have no catapults or rams. We would slaughter them as they tried to climb the walls."

"Yes, we could," Dayne replied. "However, that would allow them to freely navigate the valley and the lands that surround it. How many would die while we hole up in our castles?"

"To fight the Mierans in open combat is *insanity*," another captain cried.

"I did not say that we would fight them," Dayne countered. "I said that we would defeat them."

"What of our supplies?" General Ilaros asked. "We had to abandon them at the river and have had no chance to replenish. Riders have been sent to Verena, but if they are cut off, we do not have the food for a prolonged fight."

"Neither Salvaari nor Mieran will stand idle," Dayne said. "They will see us falling back across the river as a victory. They will press their supposed advantage, and they will press it soon."

"An army of the greatest warriors alive stands a few miles that way." The captain pointed north as he spoke. "An army that has not known defeat since *before* Zavian."

Dayne moved through the crowd and stared at the man with his cold blue eyes.

"They have never fought me," the Annoran replied, sweeping his gaze around the gathered lords and knights. "Were they not stopped at the gates of Elara? My own guard halted them at the river. You saw that with your own eyes. I will make a pact with you. I give my solemn word that I will defeat them. Stand with me. Stand with me one last time."

One by one, the captains and the lords of the western armies pledged their support. They all knew King Dayne. They knew what he was capable of. He had won them the day in Bandujar. He had almost annihilated the Salvaari yesterday and had managed to pull back tens of thousands of men with few losses when Miera had come. If anyone could defeat the pagans it was him.

Alarik's hand twitched upon his cane as he walked through the tent city. The battlemaster found his way to a tent no larger or grander than any other, yet one with a pair of knights standing guard. The men greeted Alarik as he walked by, pushed back the tent flap and entered. Kyler Landrey sat with his back against the post to which he was chained. He wore only his shirt, trousers and boots.

Alarik knelt before Kyler. His eyes never left the boy's crimson gaze. Whatever burned within him was still there. The wound upon his face could only have been caused by the sickness within. He looked more dead than alive. Alarik showed none of the sadness that he felt. He had learned to hide his heart a long time ago.

"What is inside that head of yours?" Alarik murmured as he stared at his pupil.

Kyler gazed back at his mentor with empty eyes. Light flickered into the tent as the flap was opened once more. Alarik glanced over his shoulder as Hugh Karter walked inside.

"How is he?" the Annoran knight asked.

"I don't know," Alarik replied as he rose to his feet. "Whatever ails him … it's still there."

Hugh glanced down at his friend. "What does your heart tell you?" he asked.

"This is the working of the ruskalan," Alarik replied. "Some dark remnant of the spell that Elena cast on him in the Vault. Whatever it is, it's killing him, and it has been for a long time. The maija say that only Lysandra may have an answer. She is the key."

"Then we had best get him back to Kilgareth," Hugh said.

Alarik grunted in reply and led his former student from the tent. Hugh's horse was waiting for him. The young knight turned to Alarik.

"I am leaving on patrol with Sir William Peyene," he said as he strapped on his helmet. "When I return, we can talk about Kyler. Watch over him."

"Always," Alarik told him. "Light of the gods be with you."

Hugh swung himself up into his saddle before he replied, "And with you, my brother."

With that, Hugh Karter kicked his heels in and was gone. Alarik watched him leave. The boy had come a long way since he had first arrived at Kilgareth so long ago.

"By the gods," an Aureian voice called out.

Alarik turned as a horseman approached. He recognised the voice long before he saw the man. Clad in the garb of an Aureian knight, from the griffin embellished helm to the longsword at his hip, was a man he held as a brother. The horseman pulled off his helmet and gracefully dropped to the ground.

"Velis." Alarik greeted his friend.

The Aureians embraced.

"It's been a long time, my old friend," Velis told him as he stepped back.

Alarik looked his friend up and down. It had been many years since the battlemaster had last seen Velis Demir. Not long after the Silver Horseman had earned his renown, Alarik had made for Kilgareth and his future with the Order and hadn't seen him since.

"You look well."

"The armour of a knight suits you," Velis told him.

"I am battlemaster now," Alarik replied.

"A title well earned, my brother."

"Come," Alarik said as he gestured into the camp. "Share a drink with me."

The veterans of Irene found themselves a jug filled with Aureian wine, a pair of cups and stools to go with them. They took refuge in Alarik's tent.

"The last thing I heard before I took the road north was that you had been offered command of the emperor's legion," Alarik said at last. "Yet I see that you did not take it."

Velis drank. "No, I did not," he replied. "I am a horseman, I told him, not a general. Instead, I was granted command over the riders who had followed me that day in Irene. I was sent to Larissa as an emissary."

"An emissary?" Alarik replied with a chuckle. "I can't imagine you in the robes of a diplomat."

"In truth, I never wore them," Velis said with a grin.

"Nor should you, my friend."

"Nor should you."

Both men laughed. That was when Alarik noticed the golden ring upon his comrade's index finger. A long jewel that covered most of his finger. One that bore the shape of a chimera.

"The ring of Nykalous Gaedhela," Velis told him as he noticed Alarik's gaze. "A gift."

"A gift?" Alarik replied with a frown. Who would willingly hand over such a jewel?

"From the queen," Velis said.

"Queen Reshada gave you the symbol of her family?" Alarik asked in disbelief.

Velis nodded slowly as if in thought. "We are bonded, she and I," he replied.

Alarik raised his eyebrows. "A common soldier and a queen. You're mad."

"And I relish this madness." Velis smirked. The horseman drifted into silence for a moment before he spoke again. "I heard the men talking about your protegee."

"Kyler," Alarik told him.

"Kyler," Velis repeated. "They say that some kind of devil has possessed him. They say that his eyes burned crimson and that he turned upon his brothers."

"I do not know what has become of him, but his mind has been overthrown," Alarik told his friend.

"How?"

"The ruskalan."

"The ruskalan?" Velis scoffed incredulously.

"They are not as dead as we once supposed," Alarik said. "I have seen one with my own eyes. At least a half-blood."

"A great enemy approaches," Velis murmured. "Monsters hunt us in the night. Be careful, my friend. Who knows what lies beyond the dawn."

Alarik brushed his medallion. The sacred symbol of his gods. "Have a little faith."

✦ ✦ ✦

Dayne watched from his position atop a small hillock. His eyes were drawn to the north. The moon shone high above, yet he would not be getting any sleep this night. His mind never stopped working. It was his gift. It was his curse. The king glanced behind him as footsteps approached.

"My king," the man called in greeting.

"Tristayn," Dayne replied.

The Annoran general made his way to Dayne's side and joined him looking across the open field towards the river.

"Hundreds of our riders patrol the horizon. If there is an attack coming, we will know," Tristayn said.

"It's not Salvaar or Miera that keep me from sleep," Dayne replied. "There is a traitor in our camp. One who did all in their power to destroy us yesterday."

"You're certain of it?"

Dayne nodded. "I have spoken to the heads of each army. Each group that was spread apart got the same letter. *Verena is under attack. They call for reinforcements.* The fastest way to the city was at the ford through which we crossed. The writer of these letters knew this. They knew that we would gather at the crossing and then press towards Verena. Salvaar was lying in wait with Miera not far behind them. Perhaps I am mistaken and that was not the great Salvaari army. Perhaps a larger force waits to greet us at Verena, but if it does not …" Dayne trailed off for a moment. "We have been betrayed from within. Betrayed at a time when there are some within our alliance who would gladly take the lives of their brothers."

"Caspin."

"My fight with him is not over. Not yet," Dayne replied.

"What of this traitor?" Tristayn asked. "Who do you think it could be?"

"I have suspicions," Dayne admitted. "It will not be the maija who signed the letter for that would be too obvious. Whoever this trickster is, they wear the garb of the Order. In time, the truth will reveal itself. It always does."

"This traitor robbed Garrik of his life," Tristayn muttered. "We will avenge his passing."

"The wrath that I shall inflict upon the betrayer knows no bounds," Dayne replied coldly. "Garrik was of Laeoflaed. He fought beside my father in Salvaar. He saved my brother and I as children. He opened the gates for my father and allowed him to defeat the tyrant Balinor, his own king. Garrik taught me the sword. He taught me honour. He protected my brother and my sister in Salvaar. He lived and died for my family. He *was* my family. He will be avenged."

Hooves thundered towards the two men. A rider hurtled across the plain and up onto the hill. A man bearing Annoran armour. A scout.

"My king!" he cried as he raced towards them. The scout leapt from his saddle. His eyes were wide and his breathing ragged.

"What is it?" Dayne asked.

"The heathens," he said. "They're coming."

Horns sounded through the western camp. Tents were pulled down while soldiers gathered their arms and armour. Slowly, the army began to form up. The first hint of sunlight began to emerge over the horizon. Dayne could see no movement yet. No sign of their enemy, though it was coming. The leaders of his great army began to assemble. They would follow his lead. He would win them this fight.

Dayne and Tristayn thundered towards the commanders atop their mighty steeds. They reached the generals. Dayne opened his mouth to speak. A shiver ran through his body. No words left his mouth as he coughed. Only blood did. Fire raged through him; he felt nothing but pain. The king fell from his horse. He struggled to his hands and knees as he coughed up blood. He could barely hear. He could barely see. Tristayn dropped to his side. He appeared as a shadow and his words were foreign to Dayne's ears. His vision wavered as the men around him began to shout. Darkness took him.

✦ ✦ ✦

Tristayn's roars for a physician were answered. They took the unconscious king and on the general's command made for the wagon train.

"We have to stand and fight!" Tristayn called as he turned to the other commanders.

"We don't have the numbers, and our leader has fallen," Santiago Caspin yelled. "If we don't fall back now, then we may not live to see another dawn."

"The king–"

"Isn't here!" Santiago countered.

"We can hold them at the cities," Corvo cut in. "We divide between Verena, Kilgareth and Odrysia. They cannot surround us all. We can use the tunnels."

"My lords, we have to fight them here," Tristayn bellowed. "The king knew that!"

"We have no choice," Corvo countered. "Without Dayne, this army is divided."

Tristayn bared his teeth in frustration. He knew that the grand master was right. Horns sang. The cries to fall back had already begun.

✦ ✦ ✦

FORTY-NINE

Aureian Coast, The Lupentine Sea

The Ravenheart sliced through the gentle waves of the Lupentine. The crew of pirates and Valkir hurried about the deck and scurried through the rigging to keep her true to her purpose. Erik, Cillian Teague, Lord Wylan, Nenrir and a number of their companions gathered in the captain's cabin. The ride from Eonie had been hard. They could not afford to be captured by any who rode in pursuit and so they had travelled fast through night and day until they reached the coast. There had been no time to read the manuscript that the former spy had stowed in his satchel. There had been no time to grieve for the dead. Laerke was gone. His loss weighed heavily on the Valkir. His brother had barely said a word. He was gone and they had to see to the living. Valkir and pirate alike watched as Lord Wylan took the book from his satchel and flicked through the pages.

"It's all here," the Aureian told those gathered. "Written in the old tongue of my land. Few enough speak this language. Fewer still can read it. Many would kill for these secrets. Many would die for them."

"Some have," Nenrir growled.

Erik turned to Nenrir and placed a hand upon his shoulder. "My heart breaks for your loss," Erik told him. "You know that. He was my friend. My shieldbrother. He was your blood. We will mourn for him. But first we must learn the knowledge held within those pages," Erik said as he pointed to the book. "We can avenge his death. We can honour him with blood."

"Then let us honour him," Nenrir muttered. "What do the words say, Aureian?"

Lord Wylan nodded and flicked his eyes to the page. "There is a lake a day's ride south of Aureia. A lake so massive that it can harbour many ships. That is where this fleet was made. It will sail at the summer solstice."

"The summer solstice?" Cillian Teague said. "That is little over two weeks from today. I know the lake. There is no river or canal that can connect it to the sea."

"There is now," Lord Wylan replied. "An army of craftsmen and slaves will have joined lake to ocean by now."

"They created a river?" Erik said incredulously. "That is madness."

"Madness that worked," the Aureian replied. "Were it not for the loose tongue of the emissary Valan and the book now in my possession, you would have not heard so much as a rumour about this fleet. Nor would I have. Nor the world. The empire was taking no chances with an undertaking of this magnitude. Many of your nations have spies. Within a month at the most, this fleet would have been common knowledge and yet it is not. The fleet was to serve as a deadly surprise to whichever shore it arrived at first, be it Miera or some place in the Sacasian. How many nations could it have struck before its existence became known? The river, the secrecy, as mad as it is, worked."

"We have been given a chance. One last chance to save our people," Erik said. "We do not have much time. We have none to return to Nesoi and gather our armada. Teague, send your birds. Call our people here. We will need every man, every woman, everyone who can hold a blade, and even then it may not be enough. Make no mistake, this will be the greatest battle that any of us have ever fought in. We will make the place in which we meet this fleet famous. We will meet them not far from the Aureian coast, as close to the mouth of this river of theirs as we can get."

Teague stepped forward. "My people have ways of fighting upon the sea that the Aureians will never forget," he said.

"Good," Erik replied. "We will need every trick that you can conjure. Go now; send the birds. Our people must sail within two days."

Silence wrapped around the ship as Teague and his crew made ready the pigeons. Valkir and pirate alike stopped and stared. Those in the rigging looked down while the rest gathered on deck. All watched as three birds were sent skyward with messages tied to their small legs. There were many predators throughout the Lupentine. Only one bird had to make the crossing, yet it *had* to make it. In a matter of days, the combined fleet of Valkir, pirates and Elaran refugees would make their stand. Erik said a silent prayer as he watched the birds fly. His hand clasped the raven amulet at his throat. The end of the road was near.

Erik closed the door behind him as he entered his cabin alone. He closed his eyes and unstrapped his cuirass. He pried the steel armour off as it stuck to his sweat-soaked gambeson. Placing the cuirass aside, he removed the padded gambeson and undershirt. He tossed them onto his desk. Erik could not stop his gaze from shifting to the steel cuirass. Dried blood still stained the silver. Laerke's blood. The blood of his friend. His brother. The man who had stayed behind in Agartha as a prisoner to help Erik bring down Magnus from within. Erik ran a thumb over the blood-stained steel. Laerke had not been supposed to die. With a shout, Erik snatched up the cuirass and hurled it into the ground. He slammed his fist down into the table and bared his teeth. His whole body was tense. He felt fingers upon his back. He felt them caress his muscles as they traced the raven tattoo. Erik had not heard the doors to the cabin open or close. He had not heard her approach, nor had he seen her face, yet he knew her touch. Erik turned to see the vision standing before him. Blonde hair cascaded down her back and shoulders like a golden waterfall. Eyes of shining copper danced as the sunlight kissed them through the windows. Halitreia.

"In this sea, I am torn," Erik told her. "Part of me wants to win this war, liberate my people with peace and then sail away from it all. The other part of me wants to sunder their coast, lay waste to their cities and burn every trace of Aureia from this world."

"What is it that you want, my king?" she asked.

"I just want to go home," Erik replied.

"To Agartha?"

"No," he said. "To the sea. To sail across the ocean without concern. To feel the salt spray upon my face and the cool breeze through my hair. That is my home."

"It is so close that you could almost reach out and take it," Halitreia said softly.

"I feel the weight of this crown I bear," Erik told her. "I did not long for it nor ask for it. It was given to me, and I had no choice but to take it. What do I want? A future for my people. A future not plagued by violence. A future not darkened by the shadow of death. Once this battle is won, I will lay down my crown."

Halitreia's hand traced the scar that severed the snake tattoo of the bloodsworn. Her fingers ignited a fire within him as they slid down his arm and slowly weaved through his own.

"I was born and raised in the slums of Elara where we lived only if we fought for every breath. I learned never to let anything go, no matter how hard they fought you to take it. You hold on to what is yours. I was bound for the empire upon a slave ship," Halitreia told him. "It was Teague who saved me from that fate. It was he who took me in. I have never known freedom. True freedom. Not until now. Do you know something? Now that I have a choice, I will do whatever I want to do" – she slowly directed Erik's hand through the air and her eyes flicked up to his – "and kill anyone who tries to stop me."

Halitreia stepped closer. He could smell the salt spray in her hair and could almost see the gentle waves in her eyes. She placed a hand on his chest. A steady hand. Weathered and strong from a lifetime at sea.

"Don't ask yourself what a king should do, or what a jarl should do," Halitreia murmured. "Ask yourself what your heart desires. Only you can decide that. Only you can follow that path."

Golden hair brushed his chest and sent shivers through his body. He tasted the sea in her lips. Her body, as wild and strong as an ocean storm, melted into his.

The cool sea breeze washed across Erik's face as he left the captain's cabin. He took a long breath in through his nose and savoured the smell. It caressed his skin and lightly brushed the fresh shirt and trousers that he wore. Once again, he was clad in the clothing of a Valkir. Waves splashed against the Ravenheart and Oridassey as they sailed north. *North.* A frown flicked across Erik's brow as he realised the direction in which the ship was sailing. To the south lay the river from which the dreaded Aureian fleet would sail. To the east lay Nesoi and the army of Valkir, pirates and refugees that was beginning to assemble. To the north there was nothing but the Aureian coast. Sail far enough and you might reach Annora. He had given no such orders.

"Fargrim," Erik called as he turned to the helm. "Where do we sail?"

"North, my king," Fargrim called back. "Along the Aureian coast."

"By whose order?"

Fargrim gestured to the prow in reply. Standing there, garbed in midnight blue, was Cillian Teague. The pirate captain had not returned to his own ship. Erik strode across the deck of the Ravenheart and made his way to Teague's side.

"I see that you did not return to the Oridassey," Erik stated as he joined the pirate in looking out across the sea.

"I thought it best to remain," Teague replied. "We need to talk about this fight to come."

"Nesoi and our allies lie to the east. This river from which the Aureian fleet will sail is to the south," Erik started. "Why in the Sea-Father's name do we sail north?"

"This armada that we have created, you and I, will soon be sailing towards a foe that with luck will only outnumber it four to one," Teague told him. "To conjure a fleet so swiftly, the empire will have been forced to pull men from the legions to man it. Soldiers who have never sailed. They will not be used to the sway of the waves and the sickness that comes with them. It will be crewed with inexperienced sailors while we have spent a lifetime at sea. Even then with all of our tricks, with all of our strategies, we will need the gods. I am Aureian. I was born with these people. Raised by them. Fought with them. Sailed with them. I know how they fight. I know how they think. I know their greatest weakness and we will win by bringing our full might down upon it."

"And what is this weakness?" Erik asked.

A whistle came from high in the crow's nest. All eyes went to the man atop the nest. "Sail north-east!" the sentry cried.

Teague pulled a spyglass from his belt and turned it to the sea. A smirk crossed his lips as he handed it to Erik.

"Aureian merchant," the pirate said. "The reason for which we sailed north. The trade routes between the empire and her colonies are still open. We need that ship."

Erik watched the merchant vessel through the spyglass. Triple-masted, fat and laden with cargo of unknown wealth. Erik handed the glass back and turned towards the deck.

"Up for a little hunting?" he called.

The Valkir cheered.

In a few hours, the Ravenheart and Oridassey had caught their prey. When the merchant had seen the two ships angling towards her, she had tried to run. Designed to carry heavy cargo and not for speed, the chase had been lost before it had even begun. Teague directed the Oridassey in such a way that it had stolen the merchant's wind. The Ravenheart reached her first. Arrows were nocked in Valkir bows. The order to unleash hell upon the Aureians was about to leave Erik's mouth when the white flag was risen. The merchant vessel was not putting up a fight, not when two warships were breathing down its throat. The Aureian captain had made it all too easy. Erik felt his small respect for the man vanish like smoke. Bows were kept at the ready as hooks were sent across to join the two ships together. Gangplanks followed. The Oridassey began to do the same from the opposite side. Erik clambered up onto one of the makeshift walkways and strode across. The Aureian crew stared at him as he dropped down onto the deck. During the chase, he had put his armour on and was clad head to toe in steel and leather. His red shield marked with the black raven was strapped to his left arm and he clasped his axe firmly in his right hand. He could see the fear in the Aureians' eyes. He could see it in their pale faces. The rest of the Valkir poured across from the Ravenheart. The Aureians were forced down onto the lower deck. Most were sailors, some were hired soldiers. Erik directed warriors to sweep the hold for any hidden threats.

"Which one of you is the captain?" Erik called down into the lower deck.

All eyes went to a man more finely garbed than the others.

"I am," a strong voice called.

"Your name?" Erik asked.

"Milan Driseige," the captain replied. "Of the Corvina."

Erik allowed a dangerous smirk to cross his lips as he met the man's eyes. "Erik Farrin of the Ravenheart," he told the Aureian crew.

Word of his name had travelled. They would have heard about Vay'kis, about what he had down to Jormund Scaeva and his men. What else had they heard?

"I would like to thank you for the early surrender of your ship," Erik said. "Most are not so wise."

Milan shoulders dropped in defeat. The crew heard the hint of mockery in Erik's tone. They knew that he called them cowards.

"You do not know why we are here," Cillian Teague called out. "But what you cannot do is spread the tale of us being so near to Aureian soil. Word cannot reach Aureian ears that Sacasian and Valkir sail together."

"You are Aureian," Milian Driseige challenged Teague.

Teague leaned close to the captain. "My name is Cillian Teague," he growled.

Milan's breath caught in his throat. Teague's sword opened his chest.

✦ ✦ ✦

The sound of hammers on steel sang upon Nesoi island. The sound of training warriors had become common. Many who would sail against Aureia had never been in battle before. They needed every man strong enough to swing a sword.

A thousand smells assaulted Bhaltair's nose as he made his way through a steam- and smoke-filled warehouse. He wore his mask up over his mouth and nose, yet nothing could stop the stench. Artisans, craftsmen and apothecaries all worked together to create tools that the gangs had used for years with recipes brought all the way from Tarik. Vials of yellow liquid covered one of the tables, while another was laden with small, silver cannisters. These instruments had become some of the greatest weapons that the gangs had possessed. His friend Cleander had made good use of them hundreds of times in the past. Would they serve the gangs now?

"Bhaltair!" a cry echoed through the warehouse.

The gang leader turned to see o ne of his men hurrying towards him. Bhaltair closed his eyes for a moment. He knew what news the man brought.

"The day has come," Bhaltair said as the man reached him.

"They have found the fleet. We must sail by first light."

"Then it begins."

Word spread around Nesoi. The night came and went all too soon. Tearful farewells were spoken. Loved ones were held close. Win or lose, many would not be coming back. They all knew it.

Bhaltair armoured himself in chainmail and his black cloth garb. The cool wind swept through his dark cloak. Silently, he led his men towards the harbour, towards their ships and their destiny. Priamos Stentor joined him. The Elaran lord said not a word. It was to them that their people would look in the battle to come. Harald and the Valkir earls made ready. Garrett Laven prepared the Sacasians. Horns sounded all around as the warriors boarded their ships. Bhaltair paid no heed to the tears of the families they were leaving behind. As the last of the horns echoed and the ships began to sail, Bhaltair caught sight of Mellisanthi on the beach. She stood with all those who would remain on Nesoi. If he died, it would be she who led them. Bhaltair allowed a short nod of respect before he turned to the west. He did not look back. They were not going that way.

✦ ✦ ✦

FIFTY

Kilgareth, Valley of Odrysia

Dayne awoke to the warmth of the sun upon his face. His eyes slowly flickered open. He lay in a white bed. One of many that filled the room. Each of them played host to someone wounded by the war. Maija flittered around the room. They tended to the patients and talked to them in soft tones. Dayne was in the Kilgareth infirmary. A wave of pain washed over him as he pushed himself to his elbows. He bit it back with a grimace and swung his legs free from the covers.

"My king," called one of the maija as she approached. "You should be resting."

"How long was I asleep?"

"Four days."

Four days.

"What of the battle?" Dayne asked. "Were we victorious?"

"There was no battle," the maija replied.

Dayne stared at her. It took all his will not to show the irritation within. His command had been that they *needed* to face the pagans in open combat.

"What do you mean?" he asked.

"The army fell back to await a more favourable moment," she told him. "It has split in three. The legions hold Verena. Medea and your people hold Kilgareth. Sir William Peyene and a company of knights have reinforced the militia in Odrysia."

Dayne ran a hand across his brow. This was precisely the outcome he had wished to avoid. He rose to his feet and bit back the pain that burned within his stomach. Dayne felt weak. He knew that his face was pale and gaunt.

"My king—"

"I have rested for four days and now I wake to find that we have no time." Dayne cut her off. "Summon the generals."

They came together as fast as they were able. The Annoran high lords, the Medean dukes and the three members of the Circle who remained in Kilgareth. Lysandra, Alarik and their commander, Corvo Alaine.

"Friends," Dayne said as his eyes swept those assembled. "Brothers and sisters. We now find ourselves surrounded. For too long, I have been asleep. Now I am awoken."

"We thought it best to fall back so that when the pagans enter the valley, we can surround them on all sides," Santiago Caspin told him.

"I do not care that we have pulled back to these walls," Dayne replied. "You acted on what you thought was right. Now we must act again and to do that we need information. Tell me about our enemy. Tell me about our supplies."

"The heathen entered the valley two days ago," General Tristayn said. "They have surrounded our brothers in Verena. It will not be long before they march on us. On Odrysia."

Corvo Alaine stepped forward. "Verena, like Kilgareth, was built as a fortress before it became a city," he said. "There are cisterns beneath the city that supply water from the mountains. There are caves, a network of tunnels that links the city to Kilgareth."

"It is a three-day journey through the tunnels," Alarik added. "Yet if Verena is breached, if *we* are breached, we have options. The passages also lead deep into the mountains. We can escape if need be."

"These tunnels," Dayne said. "Are their entrances not beneath Kilgareth but near to its walls?"

"Some," Corvo told him. "Kilgareth was designed to hold out against a siege indefinitely."

"We have food to last us almost six months," Lysandra said. "If needed, we can send hunters into the tunnels to track game in the mountains. We can last."

"What of Odrysia?" Dayne asked. "The city has walls, but it is no fortress."

"Near eight thousand people call Odrysia home," Corvo told him. "Two thousand soldiers man the walls while Sir William and a thousand of our knights stand with them. They have food, and the river supplies fresh water."

"There are no tunnels?" Dayne asked.

"No." Corvo shook his head. "The gates are the only way in and out of the city."

Dayne thought for a moment. The information passed on by the commanders turned over and over in his head.

"Neither Salvaari nor Mieran use siege engines," he said. "They are brave enough to attempt an attack without them; however, they are not stupid. They will know that we have divided our forces between the three cities. They will know that their army is greater than any one of our armies. They know that Odrysia is not a fortress like Kilgareth or Verena. Odrysia is weak. When they bring their full might down upon us, it will be Odrysia that they attack first. They will try to divide us, kill us one by one. We must be ready. Grand master, your men know this valley better than anyone. When the war comes to us and Odrysia is under siege, your riders must lead the way. If we can surround the enemy between Kilgareth and Odrysia, I have no doubt in my mind that we can defeat them."

Cool air caressed Dayne's cheek as he walked out onto the ramparts of the Citadel. All of Kilgareth lay beneath him. Orange torches lit up the darkness of night while the brilliant silver moon shone above. From up here, the city seemed peaceful. Dayne rubbed his burning stomach. He was being tested. His resolve was being tested. His faith was being tested. Dayne would lose neither. Pain was irrelevant and there was much work to be done. This war was far from over.

"Welcome back, King Dayne," Cardinal Aleksander's voice came from behind.

Dayne turned as his spiritual leader approached. "Your holiness," he greeted the man.

"It pleases me to see you from your bed at last." The cardinal joined Dayne at the railing. "Your strength returns."

Dayne stared down from the balcony, over the fortress and plains beyond the walls. Instead of stone and grass, he saw a gaming board. Instead of soldiers along the walls, he saw pieces. How could he manoeuvre it all to his advantage? The king's fingers brushed the amulet at his throat. It comforted him even as the pain within threatened to return him to his bed.

"Sometimes the god of war revives you," Dayne said, "and says that there is more to be done. The blood, the pain: they count for nothing. Whatever becomes of me, I will not let this sickness destroy everything that I have built. Everything that my family has built. My father once told me that everything he did was for our family. The Raynor line has been forged by tragedy. It was my father's wish that it never saw such pain again. I will honour his memory by doing all in my power to make it so. Those men beyond the horizon, be they Salvaari or Mieran, stand in the way. But nothing, no man, no sickness, will stop me from achieving this end."

"Fate is fickle, and the gods can change it in an instant," the cardinal said. "Soon the Pale Horseman will descend from the heavens to cast fire upon the earth. Where this fire blazes, who it consumes, only he knows. Azaria gives us all life, but the horseman can take it away just as easily. He stands with us, Dayne. A harbinger, a sentinel, a judge: he comes in many forms. You have shown yourself worthy a thousand times over. He is with you, Dayne, all the gods are. Never doubt that."

"I do not doubt, your holiness," Dayne replied. "I only pray that once more I can prove myself worthy."

"It is for that very reason that I know you will."

Dayne said nothing. He believed as fiercely and as strongly as he always had. Ever since he had been a boy, his faith had helped forge him into the man he was.

"Beautiful night," a woman's voice came from behind.

Sofia's voice.

"My lady," the cardinal greeted her.

"Cardinal Aleksander," she replied and offered a short bow. "Pardon me, but I would ask for a moment with my husband."

"Of course," the cardinal told her. "A peaceful night. The last that we may have for many days. I bid you goodnight."

"Goodnight, your holiness."

Dayne gave the cardinal a nod and then the high priest was gone. Dayne's lips twitched into a smile as Sofia approached.

"So, it's the words of the cardinal that keep you from our bed," she said.

"It would take more than the words of an old man to keep me from you," Dayne replied.

Sofia took his arm and joined him in looking down across the city. The moon shone silver above them, and the stars twinkled like diamonds.

"Then what is it, my love?" Sofia asked as she squeezed his arm. "You've come back after days of no one knowing whether you would return, yet I do not believe it is this sickness that troubles you."

Dayne glanced at his wife. Her beauty was matched only by her intellect.

"Before I fell, we were prepared to stand against the heathen. I wanted to fight them in the field away from our town and cities," Dayne said. "I awoke to a world in which our army is split in three ways. A world in which, though we are surrounded by high walls, people have been put in the greatest of danger. There are many thousands in this city that have never known the weight of a sword. There are many more in Odrysia and Verena. Children, elders, women. They must be made safe."

"You will make them safe," Sofia told him. "You will save us all."

"I swear to you that I will," Dayne promised her. "For you. For our child."

✦ ✦ ✦

Lysandra glanced up as Kassandra Raynor entered her study. They had spent a great deal of time together over the last weeks. They had talked about the past in ways that would have had them mocked, if not arrested. Despite her age, the princess was brave and had a sharp mind. Both things Lysandra admired. It was almost a pity to use her so. She gestured for Kassandra to join her by the fire. Soon enough the princess was sat beside the arc'maija. Lysandra stared into the flames as she spoke.

"You know about her, don't you?" she stated.

"My lady?"

Lysandra looked into Kassie's eyes. "Naidra," she said. "The she-elf."

Kassandra froze. Her eyes widened for a moment before she composed herself.

"We've talked in this room, you and I," Lysandra started. "We've talked about the past. We've talked about the elves and the ruskalan. We've talked about balance. We've talked about wonders so impossible that they cannot be real. We've talked and now perhaps we've been given a chance to do something about that which we've only talked about behind closed doors. Beneath this Citadel, in the maze of stone, an elf is held in chains. The *last* elf. You know this. You have seen it. The truth is in your eyes. I am committed to freeing Naidra from her bonds. I asked you here today not just to talk, but to join me. I will need your help to see this through."

"How can I help?" Kassandra asked her.

"There is a drug used to lace all of her food, all of her drink," Lysandra explained. "It keeps her weak. It keeps her in shackles. So important is this drug that only the cardinal and his guard know of its existence. It is the guard captain who administers it to food and water. I am too well known to the cardinal's guard to be able to get close, but he does not know your face. Kassandra, I did not want to ask this of you, but you are the only one who can put an end to a century of horrors for Naidra."

"If this drug is as potent as you say, then we must destroy it," Kassie replied.

Lysandra shook her head. "No, we cannot destroy it," she said. "If we did, then they would know that there are those seeking to liberate Naidra. I know the drug that they use. I know how it is made. I know what can be added to it to remove its abilities."

Lysandra held up a small vial of dark liquid.

"A concoction made from cintilla," Lysandra explained as she handed the vial to Kassandra. "An exceedingly rare plant that only grows in the heart of Salvaar. Its properties negate many poisons including that which controls Naidra. Administer this to the captain's brew … even a few drops … and its power will vanish like smoke."

"No one deserves to endure entire lifetimes of cruelty," Kassandra murmured. "I will do what you ask."

"What you do here, know that it will not be forgotten," Lysandra told her sincerely.

Naidra was the key to everything. She was what this war was all about. Lysandra was close now … so close to achieving her goal.

"I have read that an elf's true name carries meaning," Kassandra said. "Naidra. What does it mean?"

"It means Snowflame."

The dawn sun had risen when Lysandra was at last able to visit the Salvaari prisoners. The Knights of Kil'kara let her into the cell and locked the door behind. Cailean looked to the arc'maija as she approached him and his wounded friend, Scada. Thanks to Lysandra's efforts, the Salvaari who had been badly wounded at Bandujar was at last beginning to regain his strength.

"Help is nearly here," Lysandra whispered in Salvaari. "Henghis' army has breached the valley. They will be at these walls in a matter of days. You and your people must be ready for the attack that is coming. I will free you. I will free all of you, but you must be ready to fight."

"Just say the word," Cailean replied. "We all hunger for blood and the death of our enemies."

"Good," Lysandra told him. "There are two hundred of you trapped within these walls. You are all warriors. Enough to make a difference."

"When the time comes, we will be ready."

"There is another," Lysandra told him. "She of Sylvaine's tears is shackled deep in the mountain. We will get her out. Above all else, she must get out."

Lysandra saw flames ignite in the eyes of those few who had heard. They knew of what she spoke. They all knew about the elves, about how they had come to be.

Cailean placed a fist over his heart. "If by my life or death I can protect her, I will," he vowed.

✦ ✦ ✦

The trees of Salvaar were so tall and thick that little of the morning light could break through the canopy. Mist and shadow spread through the undergrowth and shrouded all from sight. Harkan of the ruskalan stared out from the trees. His crimson gaze washed across the open plain and the river beyond. For the first time in a century, he could see Medea. He could see Miera and the mountains surrounding the Valley of Odrysia. Five others stood with him, men and women both. All bore the same features. Pale skin and angular bones. Dagger-like ears pierced the air. Dark hair hung down their backs and black runes covered their faces. Like Harkan the Firstborn, they were ruskalan. The last of their kind. The last pureblood ruskalan.

"Within a matter of days, the three cities will be under siege," Harkan told his brethren. "The revenge we seek will be ours in time."

"We have seen empires rise and fall; we have seen entire dynasties sundered," one of the women said as she stared across the plain. "We have manipulated kings and controlled events to reach this moment. The tribes to the north and the seafarers to the south. The phoenix to the east and the griffin to the west. They all bow to our will. Now they at last come together."

Wind blew across the open plains and washed across the Firstborn's face. Harkan closed his eyes and took a long breath of air.

"For a hundred years, we have waited and prepared, enshrouded in the darkness," Harkan said as he stared across the land he had once called home. "Soon those who did this to us will know what it is like to fear."

"This path upon which Naidra set us shall end with her liberation from heretic hands," one of the ruskalan said. "She will at last be free after a century of torment. She started this war. She has the power to end it and slay all those who made her suffer."

"The chained, the exiled and the damned will lay claim to what they are owed," the woman spoke again. "These are the last days of the Order. The last days of those who destroyed our people. Salvaar, Miera, Medea, Annora, even the empire … all are here to witness what we do to those who harm us."

"But what fate will present itself when they entangle?" Harkan murmured. "Who shall lead us into the light? Henghis, Zoran, the Whisperer … together they will destroy those who serve the sun and moon. The eyes of Tanris walks among them."

"In my dreams I see fire."

"It is as the Dark One has foretold," Harkan replied. "The revenge will be upon us on the day that the eyes of Tanris slays the cursed blood. Soon the day of reckoning will be upon our enemy. Soon the purge will be answered. When Kilgareth falls, the river will run with the blood of heretics. They took everything from us. Now we will take everything from them."

✦ ✦ ✦

FIFTY-ONE

City of Odrysia, Valley of Odrysia

Bells echoed throughout Odrysia. The barracks were filled with thousands. Any who were strong enough to fight had been called to arms. Knights handed out chainmail, gambeson, spear and shield to the men who flooded the barracks. Those who took up bows hurried to the city walls. As many women, children and elders as could be found were sent to the castle for protection. The militia was made ready. Mercenaries employed by merchant lords were called upon by the governor.

Hugh Karter ran up the stairs that led to the wall beside the eastern gate. William Peyene was a few steps in front. They reached the battlements and stared across the plains. Mieran scouts had been seen earlier in the day and all within the walls knew that it was only a matter of time before the army appeared. Hugh's left hand rested atop the pommel of his sword. He was calm and composed. Fighting was in his blood. The sword was all that he had ever known. Whatever enemy came over the horizon, he was prepared.

"Whatever happens in the days to come," William said as they gazed towards the north, "stand by my side. I am Warden and you apprentice to one of the greatest warriors this world has ever seen. We will show the people of this city strength at a time when fear is about to set in. These people do not know battle. They do not know fire and war. They will need us, Hugh. They will need us."

"I understand," Hugh replied.

Silhouettes flickered in the distance. Riders appeared in the north. A great line of men and horses. Tens of thousands of them. Miera and Salvaar had come. Knight, militia and mercenary alike watched the pagan army descend into the valley. Hugh swept his gaze down the ranks of soldiers that manned the walls. The eyes of knight and mercenary alike were devoid of emotion. They had all fought before. They had all tasted blood. The militia had not. It was plastered across their faces as they saw the horde arrive in their valley.

"There is not going to be a battle today," William murmured.

"Sir?" Hugh asked as he glanced at the Warden.

"See their formation." William gestured towards their enemy. "They are not going to attack. These pagans – they have a strategy."

"Sirs," an Aureian voiced called out.

The two knights turned as one of the militia made his way towards them. He removed his helmet and revealed a weathered face. He might have been fifty, but his eyes showed the strength and pride of a man half his age.

"Those warriors out there," the Aureian said. "They do not intend to advance."

"I thought as much," Sir William said as he looked the man up and down. His eyes locked on the shortsword at his side. "You served in the legions?"

"Gaius Aureilian," the man told them. "I served under the griffin for more than twenty years."

"Aureilian?" Hugh said with a frown. "You had family in the Order?"

"A son. Torin," Gaius replied. "He gave his life fighting to recover the Spear."

"Yes, I remember. A good man and a better knight," William

told him. "Gaius, we will need good men to win this fight. You say that you served in the legions and no doubt survived many hells. Take the militia. Command them. Lead them. You know this city better than I. You know where to construct barricades, where to funnel the enemy if they breach the walls."

"I do," Gaius replied simply.

"Then go," William told him. "See it done."

Gaius planted his fist over his heart. "Yes, sir," he cried.

Within moments, the Aureian's voice was echoing from atop the walls. Odrysian men hurried this way and that to do his bidding.

"Hugh," William said as he looked to his companion. "Come with me. We must speak to the governor."

The two knights left the battlements and mounted their horses in the street below before they rode towards the heart of the city. Only soldiers and steel filled the outer roads, for all others had found sanctuary in the citadel. The governor's guard stood sentinel along the castle walls. The gates were opened, and the two knights rode inside. Thousands of people filled the keep and the warehouses, barracks, stables and courtyards that surrounded it. Hugh did not let his eyes wander into the crowd. He knew what he would see. Some stood and talked in small groups. Some sat with ashen faces, while others shed tears. Hugh could almost taste the fear in the air. He prayed that panic would not set in. He ignored it all. Instead, his eyes stayed locked to the castle itself. The two men would show strength to all those who watched in a time when it was greatly needed.

They reached the castle courtyard and dismounted. Soldiers came to take their horses, and they made their way towards the keep. Something bounced into Hugh's foot. The knight glanced down in surprise and saw a small ball. His lips twitched into a smile as he glanced around and saw a young girl to whom the ball belonged. Hugh took a knee and gathered up the ball.

"Is this yours?" Hugh called to the child.

The girl nodded. She was frightened.

"Here," Hugh said and held the ball out.

Tentatively, the girl approached and took it from his hand. She might have been eight or ten. It did not matter. No child deserved to see such times. No child deserved to know this fear.

"What's your name?" Hugh asked.

"Lucia," she said quietly.

"Lucia," Hugh repeated before he took his helmet off. "My name is Hugh." He gave the girl a smile and met her eyes. "Are you brave?" he asked. "You look brave. I wonder, can you do something for me?"

Lucia slowly nodded.

Hugh clasped his sun and moon amulet and lifted it up. "Can you protect this for me?" Hugh asked her. "Keep it safe, and then return it when we stand within the temple of Kilgareth?"

Again, Lucia nodded.

"Do you promise?"

"I promise."

Hugh gave her another smile before pulling his medallion from his neck and placing it around the girl's. "There," he said. He gave her shoulder a squeeze and stroked her cheek before he rose back to his feet.

"I will see you in Kilgareth," Hugh told her.

The knights made their way into the castle and then through to the governor's court. The room was packed with nobles, merchants and aristocrats. All turned as the heavily armoured knights strode into their midst. All conversation ended and silence reigned, the eyes of the crowd locking on Hugh and William. The knights ignored them and instead looked to the governor who sat on a chair raised upon a small dais.

"Governor Lorenz," William started. "I am Sir William Peyene, Warden of the Order of Kil'kara. This is Sir Hugh Karter,

and then take your soul? When I saw what she did to those men in the tunnels of Elara, I began to fear for what she could do to you or any other. Now those fears have been realised. If I had killed her then, would you still be this way? If I had killed her in the Vault? I do not know. You are a fighter, Kyler. Get up and fight."

Kyler's eyes flashed dangerously. With a roar, he leapt at Alarik. Only the chains held back the fingers that reached for him. Only the chains stopped Kyler from leaping onto the battlemaster. Alarik did not even flinch. He stared into Kyler's eyes. He searched them. There had to be some trace of the boy he had trained there. Some trace of the man he had become.

"I had such hopes for you, Pisspot," Alarik told him. "I will find a cure."

With that, he left. Alarik did not know whether Kyler could hear his words let alone understand them. The boy he once knew might be gone and it was to that end Alarik was preparing himself. Even an old veteran such as the battlemaster felt sadness in his heart when he thought of the boy. He had said it a thousand times before: the boy had potential. Stone echoed as he climbed back up the staircases and returned to the keep.

"Sir Alarik," a knight called out as he saw Alarik enter the Citadel.

The battlemaster turned towards the voice. "Sir Mortimier," Alarik greeted the man.

"The grand master awaits you in the courtroom."

Alarik nodded his thanks to the knight who had watched over Kilgareth in the absence of the battlemaster, Sir William, and Sir Corvo. He made for the courtroom as fast as he could. When he arrived, he found Corvo Alaine alone.

"Grand master," Alarik called and gave a short bow.

"How are the men?" Corvo asked as he approached.

"Our brothers are ready," Alarik told him. "As for the others …
shitting themselves."

Corvo snorted. "And your pupil?" he asked.

"He yet lives," Alarik replied. "Though for how long, I do not know. The ruskalan have overthrown his mind. I can only hope that Lysandra has found a cure."

"If only they had been destroyed when our Order had the chance," Corvo muttered.

"Elena is dead," Alarik said. "But my heart tells me that we have not heard the last of the ruskalan. They are out there somewhere in the dark. Laughing as they manipulate innocent lives however they see fit. Just as they once did. I wonder, are they more involved than we suppose?"

"Once, a long time ago, they nearly saw the world to ruin. I will not allow that to happen," Corvo replied. "I have seen the creature that the cardinal keeps. I have seen the she-elf, Alarik, with my own two eyes. A relic from the ancient world. She lives and breathes like you and me. They call her the last elf and perhaps that is true. If the ruskalan are out there, they will be coming for her. We both know that."

"Then we will be ready for them," Alarik said seriously. "No man can break us. No beast can break us. We are the sword of the gods. If those demons come, if they crawl out from the shadows as all evil things do, I will greet them with *nothing* but steel."

"When this battle is won, our Order will once again hunt in the darkness," Corvo said after a moment. "If the ruskalan are indeed returned, then we must stand against them before it is too late. You've read about them same as I."

"A nation in flames. Innocents dead. Those trying to save it all murdered at peace talks," Alarik growled. "I have read enough. When the time comes, I will venture into the darkness myself and find them before history can repeat itself."

"This time we will be the hunters and they the prey. The Order of Kil'kara must be ready."

"It will be," Alarik vowed.

"Alarik, I must ask something of you," Corvo said.

"What is it, brother?"

"When we fought upon the banks of the Arwan, it was the whispers of a traitor that sent us there," Corvo continued. "The words of one drew us towards Verena. Towards a place we would all be together. Towards a place where all could have been lost in one battle. These messages were sent using birds, and while they directed us to Verena, I do not believe that it is Verena in which they were born. One thing is clear to me: the traitor is of the Order. Only one of us could have sent so many of our birds. I believe this traitor is within these walls. With the swords of our enemy at our front, we cannot afford to have the knife of a traitor at our back. I need you to help me find the one who tried to send us to our deaths. They must be found before this battle starts. The traitor must be dealt with. You are the only person that I can trust."

"I will not let you down," Alarik told him.

"You never have."

✦ ✦ ✦

FIFTY-TWO

Valley of Odrysia

Thousands of torches and fires were sparked to life in the Salvaari camp as night fell. Darkness blanketed the valley as the sun slid behind the horizon. The taste of strawberries filled Lukas' mouth as he swallowed Maevin's brew. The pain wasn't what it once was, yet the cold wind always seemed to find a way into his ruined knee. Lukas' warband of Káli were camped all around him. They had followed him onto the plains of Bandujar and every battle since. There was a loyalty among the Salvaari that he had never experienced before. The tribes were more than just tribes; they were families. Lukas glanced at Maevin as she absently moved her hand through the campfire. The flames kissed her skin but left no burn or wound. He saw the concentration in her eyes. He had seen it before.

"What do the spirits tell you?" Lukas asked.

"They came to me last night," Maevin told him. "They showed me a great battle at the walls of the Citadel. I saw a familiar place covered in shadows. Demons hunt in the darkness, hidden as they wait to pounce on fear. I saw eagles, black and red, fighting over a courtyard of stone. I saw a river filled with the dead, yet there was no blood. I saw the death of a king … and with him, his kingdom. Chaos is unfolding, chaos to consume the world. The Dark One is coming to lay claim to what he is owed. He is here already. Can you feel his presence?"

Lukas stared into the fire. "I can," he replied. "In the dark and among the shadows."

The sound of hooves drew their gaze as a rider approached. A dark-haired Káli with silver eyes dismounted and made her way towards the pair. Aelida.

"Lord," she called as she reached them. "Eirian has commanded his moonseer to watch the valley between here and Verena. He wishes us to leave this night."

Lukas nodded slowly. "With the death of Vaylin, does Eirian bear the mantle of chief?" he asked.

"No," Maevin told him. "Eirian leads in her stead just as Eilith leads for Cailean."

"In war, surrounded by our enemies, we do not have the time to decide upon who should take the mantle of chief," Aelida added. "Eirian is a great warrior who commands a large following among our people. When Vaylin fell there was but one choice."

"When the war is over, there will be a choosing," Maevin said. "The people will gather and decide who will take Vaylin's place as chief."

"And who will they choose?" Lukas asked.

"The future is not yet written," Maevin replied. "In Salvaar, your blood does not make you a leader. The one chosen will be one believed to be most important for the future of our people, be they warrior, war chief or druid."

"One must prove themself worthy," Lukas said as he rose to his feet. "Aelida, you will not ride north. Your path will take you west beyond Odrysia. Watch the river. Kill any sentinel that you see. We will meet you at first light."

"Yes, lord." Aelida's lips curled savagely. Her family had been slaughtered by a Medean raid a long time ago. Every drop of blood that she shed was to honour their memory. Lukas extended an arm. Aelida took it and they pressed their heads together.

"Be a shadow." Lukas gazed into her silver eyes.

"And may the spirits watch over you whenever I cannot," Aelida replied.

The moonseer swung her leg up over her horse and with a click of her tongue rode into the west. Lukas watched her leave. His eye stayed with her even when Aelida was enveloped in darkness.

"You defy Eirian," Maevin said, moving to his side.

"I told you once that I would compose a ballad that would reach the stars," Lukas said, staring into the night. "That story is only just beginning. Rouse the warriors. Gather all those who know poison. We must follow Aelida with haste. Odrysia will fall."

Lukas led his warband through the night. They marched along the foothills north of the valley so that they could remain within the trees. It was not long before they found the first Odrysian body. The wounds belonged to arrows yet of the shafts there was no sight. The hunter would not waste good steel. Aelida had been here. One body became several as the Káli continued on their way. The song of a bird echoed through the trees. Lukas froze. They all did. A figured materialised from the blackness. It was the moonseer.

"The path to the river is open," Aelida said.

She joined them for the rest of the journey. The sound of running water reached Lukas' ears long before he saw the river. It lay just beyond the cover of the trees. It was wide and the silver moonlight sparkled upon water as it gently lapped at the banks. Lukas' gaze followed the stream downriver until it came to rest on the glowing lights of Odrysia. Maevin moved to Lukas' side. He knelt by the river and ran a hand through the cool water.

"By your order," Maevin said.

"See it done," Lukas replied. "Their impregnable walls shall become their greatest enemy."

The Káli set to work. Many of the westerners had long since called them poison worshippers. The stories of how the Káli had applied poison to their weapons in battle used to strike fear into the hearts of Annoran children. Lukas had seen them do it with his own eyes. The Káli were wise to the inner workings of plant and rock. They created remedies as often as they created that which could kill. It was not a remedy that had made them famous. It was not a remedy that they prepared in this moment. Plants that the Káli had brought all the way from sacred Salvaar to lace weapons with their deadly properties were crushed. Every trace of nectar that could be squeezed from them was.

Maevin pulled a small vial from her belt and held it out. "The antidote," she said.

Lukas uncorked the stopper and drank the foul-tasting brew. The Káli began to bring across long pieces of bark laden with crushed plants. Plants that had been brought from Salvaar. Plants from which poison was created to lace Káli weapons. Aelida extended a piece of bark towards Lukas. One-Eye gathered up a small handful of the sticky plants. He held it over the river.

"For Vaylin," Lukas murmured.

He squeezed hard and watched as nectar flowed between his fingers and dripped down into the river. Lukas released the plants and let them fall into the water. One by one, the Káli followed suit. The poison began to flow downriver towards Odrysia. Towards their enemy.

Lukas' hair streamed in the wind as he galloped back through the trees towards the Salvaari encampment. Most of his warband had remained at the river. Seven of his Káli rode with him, with Aelida leading the way. They made their way through the camp towards its heart. Towards Eirian. They found the Káli general gathered with three of the other chiefs. Henghis, Etain and Balor were with him. The four leaders glanced up as the riders approached. Aelida dismounted first. Lukas, Maevin and the others were not far behind.

"My chiefs, my king." Aelida bowed as she spoke.

"You should have been in the north, moonseer," Eirian told her.

"There was a task first to be done," Aelida replied and gestured towards Lukas.

One-Eye approached slowly. "A curious thing, is it not, to hold the power of life or death within your hand," Lukas said and held aloft a cutting of the crushed plant.

"Vaelloma," Eirian murmured as he recognised the plant. "The serpent's kiss. One-Eye, what did you do?"

"To Tanris, I have given the holy city." Lukas dropped the plant. "I have destroyed Odrysia from within. The river, once their salvation, now their greatest enemy. Poison flows through its water as it will soon flow through their veins."

"The deaths of those in Odrysia will make our ancestors weep tears of joy," Maevin said with a malicious grin as she stopped to Lukas' side. "Their screams shall lull them to sleep."

Eirian's eyes ignited as he turned to his fell chiefs. "The poison when laced upon steel kills within moments because of its potency when mixed with blood," he explained. "When watered down, when drank … it creates chaos, calamity and death. It becomes a sickness that can spread through the air. Those affected can take days to die, yet they spread it like a plague."

"The healers of Kilgareth could put a stop to it," Lukas added. "But there are too few within Odrysia to make a difference."

"If they escaped to the Citadel, they would be saved?" Henghis asked.

"I believe it so," Lukas replied.

"Then we cannot let that happen," the Salvaari king said. "Odrysia must be surrounded."

"One-Eye shows us the way." Etain of the Icari spoke up. "I am of the mountains. Blood and battle are all I have ever known. My heart is a warrior's heart. It beats with the same fire that ignites my tribe. The people of Odrysia will die, yet we could take this chance to create an even more favourable outcome."

"You wish to negotiate?" Eirian asked.

"Hundreds of our people are trapped within that fortress," Etain replied.

They all knew people that had been captured at Bandujar. They all knew people held captive by the Order of Kil'kara. Cailean was among them – the man who had set Lukas upon this path. A friend he had fought beside many times.

"We could force a surrender," Henghis said. "Make them forfeit these lands and give back that which they have taken."

Etain turned to Lukas. "Your brother, would he be willing to talk?" she asked.

"Talk, yes," Lukas replied. "We have thousands of people at the tip of a knife. Will he surrender? That is another question entirely. He has never fought in a battle he did not win. He has never tasted the shame of defeat. There will be a strategy inside of that head of his, I am sure."

"If they surrender, what would stop us from engaging them on the plains?" Maevin asked. "They will have nothing to hide behind, no walls to cower behind. They will be slow … They would not suspect an attack."

"Honour," Etain told her. "Honour would stop an attack."

"Honour?" Aelida questioned. "These people know nothing of honour. How many of your people have they killed without cause? How many of your family? I lost a father, a mother and two brothers to their raids. Do you truly believe that if our places were changed that they would not do the same to us."

"Perhaps they would, perhaps they would not," Etain replied. "Do not mistake honour for weakness. If the order comes, then I will fight them and I will kill them. I will do so proudly. This decision rests with Henghis alone."

"It's settled then," Henghis said. "Our people shall create a wall of steel between Odrysia and Kilgareth. When this poison begins to take its toll, we shall negotiate with these people."

"My king," Lukas called. "Whoever is sent to ask to negotiate will be in great danger. I will ride to the gates of Kilgareth so long as I have a seat at the negotiations."

Henghis gave him a nod.

Days passed and the poison at last began to take its toll. Lukas watched from the plains of Odrysia. The city had grown quieter. The waters of the river flowed and with every passing moment death spread behind those walls.

"The people speak your name," Maevin said. "Your story begins to grow. Palen-Tor, Valham, Bandujar, the night that was pierced. Now, Odrysia."

"My story has only just begun," Lukas replied.

"You know your path, you know where it will lead, and I will be by your side," Maevin told him. "In my dreams, we are always together."

"Always," Lukas said fiercely.

Shadows moved above Odrysia. Lukas' gaze flicked to them. They flew through the sky. Some went east, others north.

"Birds," Lukas said. "They call for help and there will be none."

"Then it begins."

Odrysia was sending word to Kilgareth and Verena. The poison had begun to take root in the city. Lukas gathered up the reins of his horse and turned back to Maevin. He kissed her deeply and swung up into his saddle. Maevin handed him a spear adorned with a large white flag. Lukas kicked his heels in and made for Kilgareth. He rode alone. He rode with purpose. He crossed the river at the bridge and began his ascent up the mountain. The woodland on either side of the paved road thinned and then vanished as he rose. He reached the causeway and looked at the towering fortress as he approached. Massive doors the colour of bronze were tightly shut. Massive stone towers stood either side of the gatehouse and pierced the sky. Banners of Annora, Medea and the Order flew atop the walls. Silver-clad soldiers stood with them. Lukas had never seen Kilgareth before, nor a fortress of this size. He was from Palen-Tor, a great city in its own right. He knew that no matter its grandeur, a castle *always* had a weakness. None of the soldiers atop the walls said anything as he approached. They respected the white flag and did not attack. Lukas brought his mount to a halt before the gates. He looked up at the gatehouse.

"DAYNE!" he bellowed.

Time stretched as Lukas waited. Word had been sent for his brother and it was only a matter of time. He kept his gaze fixed upon the gatehouse. From the distance, the men atop the walls would not have seen him as Annoran. If they had been mere inches away, perhaps they would not have either. Over a year had passed since he had ridden out from Palen-Tor and many things had changed.

The doors of Kilgareth slowly eased open. A single rider clad in silver armour emerged. Unlike Lukas who wore black, the rider wore a surcoat and cloak of brilliant ruby. Unlike the ebony-skinned horse Lukas rode, the rider's was the colour of ivory. Lukas wore a rugged piece of cloth around his face and over his empty eye socket. The rider wore a thin crown. A war hammer was at Lukas' hip, whereas a sword with the hilt sharped like an eagle sat at the rider's. For the first time in months, the two brothers faced each other.

"Lukas," the king called.

"Dayne," One-Eye replied.

"You wish to speak?"

"By now, word will have reached your ears about Odrysia," Lukas told him. "You will know of their suffering. What you cannot know is that it was my doing."

"You poisoned them?" Dayne asked. His voice was clam and measured as it always was. Lukas would see nothing that his brother was feeling in his face or eyes. No one ever could.

Lukas gave him a nod. "Odrysia will fall in a matter of days," Lukas continued.

"What is it that you want, brother?" Dayne said. "Or did you merely come here to gloat?"

"When the sun reaches its peak, you and five others will meet with us at the river at the foot of the mountain," Lukas said.

"You wish to negotiate?"

"Do not be late." Lukas turned his horse to leave.

"Lukas," Dayne called after him. "Why do you choose them?"

"They are my people."

The noonday sun burned in the sky when the two sides met. They met upon the western bank of the river across the stone bridge. Here Lukas had driven the spear wielding the white flag into the soil. It fluttered gently in the breeze. With Lukas were Henghis, Etain, Eirian and the Mierans, King Zoran and Silas Barangir. They had chosen not to bring either pirate or Valkir, for the west did not know of their allegiance. They would give Dayne and his allies no reason to suspect that a pagan fleet was assembling in the south. Lukas watched the western delegation closely as they dismounted and approached. Those he had never met he recognised because of their symbols. With Dayne were Santiago Caspin, Alejandro Aloys, Tristayn Martyn, Corvo Alaine and a knight bearing the white colours of the cardinal. They all stood with their hands gently resting atop their weapons. They were under the white banner of truce yet neither side trusted the other.

Henghis glanced from face to face. "You are wise not to bring the cardinal this day," he said. "We would not want to stain his white cloak with blood."

The soldier of the cardinal's guard glared at the Salvaari king. "You would kill a high priest under the banner of peace?" he growled.

"I would not be killing a *man*," Henghis replied.

"You," Lukas called to the soldier. "I don't know you."

"I am Farris Quinnal of His Holiness' Cardinal Aleksander's guard. Challenge me if you wish, but do not insult my lord." The soldier flexed his hand on his sword. "Do not put yourself to the test."

There was danger in his eyes. Like most in the west, he was a son of the gods. To have earned a place in the cardinal's guard meant not only was he good with a sword but almost fanatical in faith. Farris, like the rest of the guard, would be a mighty opponent.

"And what are you then? They call you One-Eye, they call you the Black Eagle, yet I know that those names are something other than the truth," Alejandro snarled at Lukas. "You betrayed your own blood, betrayed your own family. You are a cripple. A murderer. A traitor. For what you did to my son, I swear that one day I will kill you."

"You can try," Lukas countered as his lips twitched into a smirk.

"We did not come here to exchange insults." Dayne stepped between the two sides. "King Henghis, King Zoran, why did you wish to meet?"

"I had hoped that an Aureian voice would have been among you," Zoran growled. "A man who I could look in the eye and ask why we were to be next. But that is not so. Those cowards who hide behind their griffin banners are trapped within Verena. Surrounded. I am here to lay waste to an invasion before it arrives in my land. I am here because of you."

The king of Miera spat between the opposing sides. His eyes burned with the fires of war. He was not a politician. By blood and bone, he was a warrior.

"Your spiritual leader commanded you be here," Henghis said. "He commanded that you march on my land, kill my people. And why? Because his *gods* told him to."

"The gods set us upon this path," Alejandro Aloys shot back.

"To avenge the massacres that your people inflict upon ours. Every year Salvaari attack. Every year they kill our people. Medea is here to answer that."

"Odrysia is about to fall," Henghis said. "Every man, woman and child in that city will die if you do not hear my words now."

"Then speak them," Corvo Alaine said, "if you must."

Lukas folded his arms as he looked to the grand master. He knew of his reputation as Sword of Kil'kara long before he took Amaris' position. It was said that Corvo was one of the finest swordsmen that the Order had ever known. It was said that no man could stand against him and live.

"Your people are dying. Thousands of them. Warriors and those yet untarnished by blood and battle," Henghis said. "Only the healers in Kilgareth can save them."

"You took many prisoners upon the northern fields," Etain growled. "Among them is Cailean of the Aedei. Do they yet live?"

"I give you my word that they do," Dayne replied.

"Your word?" Etain scoffed before she spat to the side. "Your words are nothing."

"If my words mean nothing, then why come to negotiate?" Dayne asked. "Unless, of course, this is not a negotiation, and instead you came not to speak but to demand. Go on then, make your demands."

"Leave your cities," Henghis said. "Leave their high walls and towers. Free those you have caged in steel and stone. Swear that you will never return to this valley. Swear that you will never again bring war to us. Swear it on your gods. Surrender to me. Only then can we have peace."

"Save your people, brother," Lukas said. "Bring them home."

"Peace?" Dayne replied with a frown. "You come here this day speaking as if you truly want peace, yet we both know that is anything but the truth. Much has come to pass in the last year. Our father died and we both became kings of sorts. We are brothers and now we fight each other. I have hope that one day this vicious cycle will come to an end."

"I agree." Lukas shrugged. "That is why I came here to negotiate. We can put down our swords and live to fight another day. What do you say?"

Dayne met his brother's eye and shook his head. "I have to reject your offer of peace. You ask me to leave the valley," Dayne replied. "You ask me to put down my sword to save thousands of lives, yet in doing so I would also be betraying thousands more. The valley is not my home. It belongs to the people of Odrysia, to the people of Verena and Kilgareth. You would ask me to turn my back on them as they are cast from their homeland? You don't really want peace, do you? I have seen what Salvaari do to those who surrender. If we were to leave these walls absent weapons, I believe that we would be dead before we reached the valley mouth."

"You have no choice," King Zoran said. "Leave the valley or watch the people of Odrysia die. You have two days. On the third, there will be no more offer, no more negotiating, no more talks of peace."

"Speak to your gods," Silas Barangir added. "Speak to your cardinal, if you must. If you do not send word, if you let Odrysia fall, then death will find you long before your sickness takes its toll."

"You know *nothing* of the gods," Corvo Alaine growled. "You know nothing of the divine purpose of their will. This land is theirs, the people here their children. And you would take both? As their holy warrior, as their first sword, I will not let that happen."

"Then Odrysia, this great city, will become a tomb," Eirian told him.

✦ ✦ ✦

FIFTY-THREE

Hugh Karter pulled his grey cloth mask over his mouth and nose as he walked into the town square. A vast tent had been created in the square, one crafted with hundreds of smaller tents. It had become an infirmary for the sick. The few maija that had accompanied the knights worked closely with the city healers to tend to the sick. The plaguelike illness had struck days ago, and it had struck the city hard. It did not discriminate. Man, woman, child and elder all suffered. Those weaker had already begun to die, while many of the strong had been forced to their knees. When it first hit the city, they thought it some kind of plague, yet the maija were saying that they now believed it to be of poisonous origin. Hundreds had died. Most suffered from coughing, and all had pale skin and weary eyes. Whatever it was, the sickness was strangling the city into submission. Hugh wound his way through the city of makeshift beds until he came to the one he had spent many hours beside – that of the girl, Lucia. Her breathing was ragged and often broken by coughs. Her tiny hands were wrapped around the medallion that he had given her only days ago. One of the maija tended to the girl.

"How is she?" Hugh asked as he knelt at her side.

"She sleeps," the maija replied. "She finds comfort in her dreams though I do not know for how long. We do not have the supplies nor the knowledge in this city to stop this infection."

"What is it?" Hugh asked. "Some kind of fever? Contagion?"

"No," the maija told him. "I have never seen its like before, yet I believe it to be poison."

"Why do you say that?"

"This girl is from the lower district," the maija said. "The man two beds down from the palace. Even in the keep there would have been little interaction between those of low and high birth. The only thing in common that they share is water."

"The river," Hugh murmured.

The maija nodded. "Unless we get the supplies sorely needed, I fear for this city."

"They will come," Hugh told him. "They have to come."

Bells sang through the city. The alarm. Hugh shared a glance with the maija before looking to Lucia. She was a child. Too young for this hell. Hugh strapped his helmet on and ran from the hospital. He made it to the city walls in time to see the pagan army move. Slowly, step by step, the warriors of Salvaar and Miera surrounded the city of Odrysia. No attack came. None was needed.

✦ ✦ ✦

Dayne stared up at the cold, stone faces of Durandail and Azaria. He held his amulet tightly. Night had fallen and he had so little time to make his impossible choice. Watch on as the people of Odrysia suffered and the city fell or stand aside and let the army camped outside the city walls through the gates? Either action would condemn the people he was sworn to protect.

"You come for salvation?" a Medean voice called from behind.

The king glanced back to see Alejandro Aloys and another man, a Medean knight, approach. Dayne knew him as the captain of the Aloys house guard. Berwin Isandro was his name.

"It is easy to turn to the gods for salvation," Dayne replied. "But this decision falls to myself alone. I come seeking counsel."

"It is a heavy burden that you now carry," Alejandro said.

"I did not ask to be king," Dayne replied. "It happened because of an assassin's blade. I did not ask to lead this great army, but once again, I had no choice. Here I stand as both king and commander of many thousands. I cannot condemn those who call this valley home by surrendering it and nor can I idly stand by and watch Odrysia burn. The funeral pyres have already been lit. I have spent a great deal of time thinking and praying, Duke Aloys. The counsel that I seek belongs to a third path. A harder path. One that will likely lead to our doom. I am resolved. When the moon reaches its peak, I will decide."

"This path that may see us to our end, how does it begin?"

"At dawn, I lead our army out onto the plains of Odrysia," Dayne replied. "At dawn, we meet them in open combat. We meet them without the aid of the legions in Verena, without Velis and his riders."

Slowly, Duke Aloys nodded. "If you lead us, I will follow you," he said. "We will all follow you."

"You say that knowing that if we lose, if the heathen achieve victory, then it would not just be our end but the end of Annora. The end of Medea."

"There is not a man within these walls who would not stand with you," Alejandro replied. "Whatever path you take, we are with you."

"Your loyalty will not be forgotten," Dayne promised him.

"Aloys and Raynor. Our families were forged by tragedy and united by sacrifice," Alejandro said after a moment. "You will have been told perhaps that a long time ago I was supposed to be wed to your father's sister, Lady Iona. Balinor took that future from me the night that he cut her throat. That started a war that ended with the tyrant's blood being shed. Your own sister was betrothed to my son, but once again it was not to be. Now, much like Santiago Caspin, I am the last of my house. I am the last Aloys." The duke let his gaze wander to the statues of the gods. "I am old, Dayne. I feel it more with each passing day. The burden of command is one that I never wished for, yet seeing my house crumble into dust is even worse. The lands that have been protected by my family for a hundred years … I fear for them, Dayne. I fear for the people that for so long we have watched over. Already I see them in my own court, in the eyes of the other dukes. Their kingdoms. They are all around, circling like vultures. Ambition, pride, greed. They corrupt all men."

"A thing well known to me," Dayne replied. "What is it that you want, my lord?"

"When the war is over and we return home, I plan to retire to the coast," Alejandro said. "To live out the rest of my days in peace. No man should bury his entire family."

"And your lands, your people? What will become of them without an Aloys standing sentinel?"

Alejandro pulled a scroll from his belt and held it towards the captain of his guard.

"This is a written proclamation of my last command as duke," Alejandro explained. "Sir Berwin has served my nation for many years. His voice is one well respected upon the council. When I am gone, it will be he who oversees this last command. After this battle, I will renounce my lands in your name. In time, you will become King of Annora and the lands of Caspin and Aloys. No man has ever been lord of lands both sides of the Eretrian. Your kingdom will be great. I understand that greed is not your ambition. I understand that wealth is not your master. In you I can see a man who can unite them. It is you whom I believe is most important for the future of our peoples."

Dayne hid the surprise that he felt, and he hid it well.

"You would choose a foreign ruler over your own lords?" Dayne said. "I am not of your land. I am not even Medean."

"I do not trust those who could take my place as duke."

"Yet you trust me?"

"I do." Alejandro's voice rang clear. "In these dark times, it is a thing to be a man of honour. I believe you are. The mere fact that you are in this moment deciding upon the best outcome for people not your own shows what kind of king you are."

"It is no secret that I may not live to see another year."

"Then I pray that whomever you choose to succeed you shares your heart."

The moon was nearly at its peak when Dayne reached the aviary. Aside from a single maija, he was alone. The king went to work with quill and ink and soon was tethering a small scroll to the leg of a pigeon. Dayne watched the small bird fly from the tower towards Odrysia. He had made his choice.

✦ ✦ ✦

Hugh's mask did little to stop the stench of the funeral pyres. The smell had become inescapable. He found himself in the hospital once more just in time to see Lucia breathe her last breath. It was laboured and riddled with agony. Her eyes grew wide and then she was gone. The grief of her parents echoed around Odrysia. In this city, pain had become a melody. The cries of the dying were mingled with the screams of the grieving. It was inescapable. The few healers and maija in Odrysia were trying, but there were too few and they lacked the medical supplies to combat the poison. When Hugh looked them in the eye, he could see the lack of hope. With each step he took towards the barracks, his anger and his sorrow grew. He reached his room and shut the door behind him. It was the room of an officer. Maps, scrolls and books filled the chamber and covered the small desk. Hugh pulled his mask down and placed his hands on the edge of the table. He saw Lucia's face. He had made her a promise days ago. Now she was dead. They all were if a miracle did not come to pass. A roar left Hugh's lips as he hurled almost everything from the table. The sound of a cup ringing on the ground had not yet ceased before Hugh's fist slammed into the desk's surface. He fought to compose his breath. He closed his eyes for a moment before he reached for the only thing he had not sent to the ground: a small wooden box. Hugh pushed the small lid up and stared down at the pair of plain rings held within.

"You fear for what is yet to come," Sir William said from behind.

Hugh did not turn to face the Warden. He had not even heard the man enter.

"Children are dying," Hugh hissed. "Parents grieve before they join them in death. Funeral pyres burn day and night and there is nothing I can do."

"There is *always* something we can do," William replied. "Word has arrived from Kilgareth."

Hugh turned to see William extend a piece of parchment. "Word from the king?" Hugh asked.

William nodded. There was something in the Warden's eyes that gave Hugh concern.

"What is it?" Hugh took the paper. "You do not have the look of a man who may yet lead this city to salvation."

"The king wants to attack at dawn," William told Hugh as the younger man read the parchment. "He wishes to face the enemy in combat and defeat them before all within this city perish. If we are to fight, it will be without the aid of the legions in Verena. They are too far away to arrive in time. We would be outnumbered. We would have to win, and we would have to win quickly or the people of Odrysia die anyway. Even if we win, there will be many thousands of wounded that will take the maija away from healing those poisoned. If we lose, then all three cities shall fall."

"What if the battle was to be a distraction?" Hugh asked. "What if it was to merely buy time for the people of Odrysia to flee to Kilgareth?"

"That would never work else King Dayne would have commanded it," William replied. "The population of Odrysia is too vast. Some would make the crossing true enough, but if our army broke … Even if it didn't, the pagans are such in number that they could fall upon the people at any moment. With what the heathen demand, this choice has been removed from our hands."

"So we fight for our very salvation," Hugh murmured as his eyes wandered back to the rings.

"Those are no mere trinkets, are they?" William flicked his gaze to the jewels.

"Memories from a lifetime ago," Hugh replied. "Before this. Before the Order."

"Tell me."

"The Karter family is small yet one of great prominence in Laeoflaed," Hugh started. "It was expected that one day my family would rise to become high lords. My father was even more ambitious. He had his eyes on the throne. He wanted me to marry the daughter of High Lord Balderik and in so doing position our family to take his place one day. I fell in love with a peasant girl. Her name was Mara. She was as radiant as the sun and as fierce as a winter storm. We were married in secret and planned to flee Laeoflaed … to start a new life. My father found out and, in his rage, had her killed. He commanded that I submit. That I obey his will and marry Balderik's daughter. I refused. I joined the Order and gave up all claim to my family lands. He will be the last Karter to hold land and title. The last Karter to hold sway over others and condemn innocent people to death."

"I am sorry for your loss." William placed a hand on Hugh's shoulder.

"It has been many years, yet I can still see her face," Hugh said quietly. "I will do all in my power to not let any others know of my pain. I would sacrifice my own life to see the people of this city happy again."

"As would I," William said. "Perhaps there is another path, another road that we may take. One that would not condemn many thousands to death at pagan hands. We need supplies, we need maija – perhaps hundreds of them. Both are within Kilgareth barely a mile from these walls."

Hugh met the Warden's eyes. "You are thinking about creating a diversion," Hugh muttered. "One that would draw the enemy away from Kilgareth, away from our eastern gate. You know what this diversion would be, same as I."

"If we do this, are you with me?" William asked.

"To the death," Hugh replied and extended an arm.

William took it. "Then send the birds," he commanded. "Meet me at the western gate."

"Sir," Hugh replied.

Every knight met Sir William at the western gate moments before the sun was due to rise. There were two thousand of them. They had voted unanimously. The birds had arrived at Kilgareth. Hugh created a fist around the pair of rings that hung from a cord at his neck. He closed his eyes and uttered a silent prayer. The people of Odrysia watched from the streets and houses all around. Many wept.

"Knights, brothers in arms," Sir Hugh called from the head of the column. "Today we honour every oath that we have ever sworn. Today we bring the wrath of the gods down upon those heathens who spread darkness across the land."

"The sun rises," one of the knights said as the first of its rays began to cross the horizon in the east.

"Durandail's sun," Sir William called.

Hugh glanced from the Warden he rode beside to his brothers

before him. He looked from face to face. They all knew why they were here.

"I swear this sacred oath that I shall render unconditional obedience to the gods," Hugh began.

As one, the Knights of Kil'kara joined him. They all knew the words; the oath was branded within them.

"I will set aside the deeds of darkness and put on the armour of light. I shall honour the man and honour my faith. I shall give all glory to the gods, and whenever they deem it, as a loyal servant, I will surrender my life for this oath."

The gates of Odrysia opened. Hugh and William led them onto the plains. They spread out and a great line was formed. A tide of silver and blue surged west as the sun arose at their backs. Hugh's shield weighed nothing. His spear was as a feather. His armour shone as it caught the sun.

"AREUT TALC CUUN'ECT!" Sir William roared.

"AREUT TALC CUUN'ECT!" the knights echoed.

The roar was long and loud, sung from the lips of two thousand. A dark line of Salvaari began to appear before the charging knights, a shadow on the plain. A single warband spread out before the main Salvaari army. Horns sounded. Arrows began to cascade down upon the knights. All fell as wicked steel bit home. Man. Horse. Volley after volley. A storm of steel. Hugh could see the black-painted enemy clearly. A cry came from his side and then Sir William crashed to the earth as a trio of arrows tore him from his saddle. The knights slammed into the Salvaari line. Hugh's spear found a home in a Salvaari chest. His horse smashed aside two more. He lost his spear in another. Knights and Salvaari fell all around. Riders were dragged from horses and butchered upon the ground. Those who survived stood against thousands. The riders pulled free of the warband. They surged towards the main heathen army. Arrows and spears followed them. Half had already fallen.

"KIL'KARA!" Hugh roared.

The cry was taken up by all those still with him. He drew his sword. Arrows flew from the armies in front and behind. Every Salvaari and Mieran in the valley began to descend upon the knights. More men fell to the arrows of their enemy. A shaft sprouted from Hugh's left shoulder. He barely felt it. The knights crashed into the Salvaari. Hugh brought his sword down. Blood flowed.

✦ ✦ ✦

Gaius Aureilian watched from the walls of Odrysia as the Knights of Kil'kara were swamped. A dark tide engulfed the silver and blue. Not a single knight would survive. Thousands of townspeople flocked to the walls as their saviours were cut down. They shed tears. The diversion had worked. The entire pagan army had hastened to stop the attack and had left the plains between Kilgareth and Odrysia open. Hundreds of maija had made the crossing on horseback and even now the eastern gates were closing at their backs. Dayne had answered William's final words. The people were saved. The knights had given their lives to give them a future.

✦ ✦ ✦

FIFTY-FOUR

When the last of the merchant crew of sailors and warriors had been put to the sword, the Valkir and Sacasians went to work. The first thing to be thrown overboard were the bodies.

Erik followed Cillian Teague into the hold. It was filled with silks and furs, jewels and all manner of oddments. The value of such a holding would have been vast and in another time would have fed them for months, if not an entire year.

"See it to the water," Teague commanded as his eyes washed over the fortune. "All of it."

The chests and crates were taken up onto deck and hurled into the depths of the Lupentine. Erik watched them sink piece by piece. To see such a fortune wasted would in normal times have awoken anger in both Valkir and pirate alike, yet they all knew that whatever Teague was planning was of vital importance. Instead of leaving the hold of the merchant ship empty, Teague's crew brought barrels across from the Oridassey and filled it to the brim.

The pirate captain approached as Erik watched them work. The crew worked slowly and were careful to not allow even a single chip to damage one of the barrels.

"What is in the barrels?" Erik asked Teague.

"When the emperor branded us pirates, he did not seek to make us thieves or murderers. He sought to make us beasts," Teague replied. "From the lands of the empire to the shores of the League and beyond, we were hunted. It's been thirty years to the day since I left Aureia. Thirty years that everyone around us has wanted us dead. With the might of the empire to the west, the League to the north and Idrisir to the east, we had little choice but to adapt. How else could a few fledgling colonies of slaves, refugees and privateers survive against such foes? We learnt to fight back in our own way. Tricks, deception, a clear strategy. That is how we survived. I served Aureia for many years. I know how they fight and how they live. Because of that, I know how to kill them."

"Then when this fleet at last comes, we will kill them," Erik replied. "All of them."

"We may have to," Teague said. "And even then, it may not be enough. This is a battle in which we cannot *just* win. We will have to sow such fear into our enemy that they will never turn steel upon us again. Whatever it takes."

"Whatever it takes," Erik echoed.

"As for what is in the barrels," Teague continued. "A little trick I learnt long ago."

"Tell me something," Erik asked. "I have heard the stories a hundred times, each different from the last. The tales of the south, the whispers of the sirens. Is it true what they say?"

A smirk crossed Teague's lips. The pirate captain clapped a hand on Erik's shoulder and walked towards the deck. "Every word," Teague told him.

The last of the barrels were placed in the merchant ship's hold and then pirate and Valkir alike returned to their own vessels. Teague left a skeleton crew behind to sail the Corvina, and the three ships turned to the south. They carved through the waters of the Lupentine, heading towards their destination, towards their fate. What that fate was, what destiny awaited them when they reached the river, Erik did not know. Only the Sea-Father held that kind of wisdom. Only his god.

Mayrun stood at the prow of the Ravenheart, her eyes fixed upon the south. Erik made his way over to her. Though they had rarely sailed together, she had been a friend from childhood – one of the few that remained. Mayrun glanced at him before her eyes were once again taken by the south sea.

"The first time I sailed upon a raiding ship was when we took Lumis some months ago," Mayrun told her friend. "I had never raided before, never sailed somewhere with the intention of blood or spoils, yet here I stand again, and it is sometimes hard to remember my life as a tanner of pelts. I will admit that I never really understood the strange pull that the sea held over so many. The salt spray and the endless plains of sapphire that stretch from horizon to horizon. At last, I understand it. At last, I am captivated like so many of our people across the centuries. Lief, Astrid, Hélla, Laerke, Raol. They all lost their minds to the ocean's beauty. One day, when I see them again, I will tell them that they were right."

"Each time we step onto the deck of a ship, we know that it may be for the last time," Erik replied with equal weight to his words. "Whether by the sword or the sea, for it is harsh, we know that we likely sail to our doom. It is in that moment between life and death that a man is most alive. Where we sail now, what we do, even if we achieve victory, we will likely not live to see the next dawn. But if we win, then our people will be safe. Our fathers and mothers, our children, they will have a place to call their own. That is what this war is about, more than anything. I once fought for vengeance … I am not so sure that is true anymore."

"Then what is true?" Mayrun asked.

"My sword. My axe. My shield. My family … my scâldir, those with us and those in the afterlife."

"And those in distant lands."

A fleeting smile crossed Erik's lips. "Torben will be enjoying the hospitality of Miera," he said. "We can only hope that his words carried meaning, or all this will have been for nothing."

The three ships sailed south for a number of days. They stayed far from the coast so that none of the Aureian harbours and ports would even catch a glimpse of them. If the information had been correct, then the great fleet would, more likely than not, have already left the lake and in this moment be sailing in the channel towards the Lupentine. The secret of the Valkir and Sacasian armada only had to be kept for a little while longer. They furled their sails a few miles offshore. From their vantage point, they would not be seen by the most keen-eyed sailors.

It began with a cry sung from the lips of the lookout high above in the rigging. All eyes of those aboard the three ships went to the east. They flocked to the railings and stared across the open ocean as the dark shadows began to emerge upon the horizon. There were dozens of them, for all had come. Garett Laven and his pirates. Bhaltair and Primos Stentor led the soldiers and gangs of Elara. All of the jarls and earls of the Valkir had come. This was no mere gathering of ships; it was a true army. One that could stand against the might of Aureia.

✦ ✦ ✦

Kitara found herself by the Odrysian River. She had pulled her armour from her back to clean it of blood and filth. Every ring of mail had to be tended to. Every inch of hardened plate on her bracers and greaves. After scrubbing the steel to perfection, she looked to her gambeson and then to herself. The markings of battle covered her face and clothing. Dried sweat, blood and dust. As Kitara cleaned her skin, she felt the sting of small cuts and the ache of fresh bruises.

"Kitara," a strong Medean voice called out. "It's been a long time."

Kitara froze. She would know that voice anywhere. The voice of one who had been her closest confidant for nearly two decades.

The voice of one who had been friend, sister and mother all in one. It chilled her to the bone. Slowly, Kitara turned from the river and her eyes widened in disbelief. Standing before her was a pirate captain who bore a green sash around her waist. The Jade Queen. Luana Marquez. Anger, blinding rage and sorrow grew mightier than a tempest. Images flickered in her mind. Everything from Barboza to the cages, to slavery, Annora, Miera and Aureia. The beatings. The torment. The suffering. So much agony. So much *pain*. Kitara rushed to Luana; pressed a knife to her throat. Her eyes were wet. Her teeth were bared. Her face was lit with fury. One move would end the Jade Queen's life. It could all be over with a single stroke.

Luana just stared into Kitara's eyes. "I'm sorry," she said.

"You're sorry?" Kitara managed.

One hand gripped the knife, the other held Luana tightly so she could not escape. Her knuckles were white and her body tense.

"You ruined my life and now you will answer to me!" Kitara snarled.

Luana did not look away from her eyes. Kitara's grip tightened. With a shout, she took hold of Luana's chainmail and threw the pirate behind her. Luana crashed to the ground. Dust sprayed around her. Kitara shivered. The knife fell from her fingers. She did not look back at the fallen pirate.

"You deserve death!" Kitara shouted.

Luana gazed up towards her with sorrow in her eyes. "I heard you were gone," she said.

"Gone?" Kitara seethed. "They fucking sold me as a *slave*!"

"They did what they were required to do," Luana countered. "Barboza—"

"Barboza tried to rape me," Kitara shot back, turning to face the pirate at last. "He held me down bathed in my own blood and gave me this." She gestured to the scar across her face. "You were my captain. My sister. My friend. *You* were supposed to protect me."

Luana's face paled as the words greeted her ears. "I did not know."

"You were not there that day, yet you have avoided the past," Kitara growled. "Would you like to see what they did to me?"

She turned her back on Luana and lifted her shirt. Kitara revealed the canvas of scars to Luana. Some were from blades and arrows, and there were the unmistakable markings of a whip. The markings of daggers used upon a defenceless girl bound by chains.

"Not the face, they said," Kitara told Luana bitterly. "There is a market for ruined beauty. There are none for puzzles."

Luana rose to a knee as she stared up at Kitara. "I failed," she said. "I failed to protect you. I loved you, Kitara. I still love you."

The warring emotions inside Kitara lashed at her as she glared down at the woman who had once taken her in. "You abandoned me!" she snarled. "Seven years *alone*. Seven years of being treated with nothing but mockery and scorn." Kitara's hand fingered the hilt of her sword. She did not remember picking it up from the ground.

"Are you going to kill me?" Luana asked.

Kitara glanced from the blade to the pirate captain. "I should," she replied venomously. "Spirits only know you deserve it."

Luana slowly rose to her feet. She tentatively took a step towards Kitara. "You have the right to do so," Luana said. "Spill my blood. Take your revenge."

Kitara breathed heavily through bared teeth. "There is *no* honour in vengeance," she growled.

"Then let me make amends." Luana took another step closer to Kitara.

Kitara stepped back as the pirate approached. She did not know whether or not she would draw her sword. The dangerous glare did not stop Luana as she drew closer. Steel leapt into Kitara's hand. She thought of her father. She thought of words that had gone unsaid, of his deeds that had earned him her love. Luana took another step. She did not look away from Kitara's eyes. The sword came up. Luana stepped closer. She slowly raised a hand and pushed the blade aside. Kitara couldn't will herself to move as the pirate stepped closer. Luana embraced her. Tears streaked down Kitara's cheeks. She tried to resist but instead her blade lowered and then fell from her fingers. Luana held her tight. Slowly, Kitara returned the embrace.

Kitara watched the flames of the fire burn as a thousand thoughts mulled over in her mind. She held her mother's ring tightly in her hand. She sat with Aeryn beneath the dark sky. The flames of a fire warmed her skin. The moonseer crafted arrows absently.

"Do you recall when we first met that I wore a sash of emerald?" Kitara said quietly.

"I do," Aeryn replied, looking up from her task. "I remember that day like it was yesterday."

"You will also no doubt have noticed that Luana Marquez and the Tariki she travels with wear the same," Kitara continued. "This is because once, a long time ago, I served aboard the Emeralis. They are from another time. Another life."

"You have told me about Luana," Aeryn said. "You said that she betrayed you, that they all did. All from that place you once called home."

"Lamrei," Kitara murmured before she turned to her love. "When I washed up on those shores and had no one, it was Luana who took me in. She gave me a home, a family. Calvillo, my mentor, taught me the sword, but Luana was more than a teacher. She was a friend. A sister. For eighteen years, I served beneath her sails, and I served with pride. She was a queen of the sea. One day she was taken ill. Calvillo never left her side. Word reached our shores of an Aureian merchant laden with a cargo so rich that it could give the raiders the means to create a true kingdom. It was heavily guarded, a prize stronger than any faced before. Captain Raeleigh Barboza, one of the founders of the colonies, was to lead the attack. While

Calvillo remained to watch over Luana, I, being a Tariki-trained sword, was chosen to be a part of the fleet, chosen to serve beneath Barboza. We sailed north and found the merchant ship not far from Elara. The fight was swift and bloody, and we won the day. The stories that we had been told about the cargo were true; an unimaginable amount of wealth was stored within its hold. More gold and silver than you could possibly imagine.

"That night, as we celebrated taking such a grand prize, Barboza tried to rape me. That night he scarred my face. That night I killed him. All those among the fleet could not believe that a man of such stature would do such a thing and so they turned on me. Many I had known for years. Some had been among Luana's crew ... and they cast me aside like I was nothing. They said that even Luana would be ashamed to know me. They beat me, cut me, humiliated me and then sold me for half a coin. I escaped that hell, but it was within those cages that I was forced to create a mask. The mask of a Kitara who could make sense of the darkness. A part of me feared the woman that I was about to create. A woman who, after all the horror that she had been condemned to, had only one thing to keep her warm. Hate. I hated the Sacasians. I hated Calvillo. I hated Luana. I hated my father," Kitara said as she remembered. "It consumed me, this hatred towards the world. In the darkness I did things to survive ... terrible things. The anger that burned deep inside kept me alive so that one day I could kill all those who had done this to me. I thought myself abandoned and betrayed by all who had been supposed to protect me, but that wasn't true. You taught me that again, and again, and again.

"Luana ... she spoke to me by the river. She had not heard why I killed Barboza, for his crew had spread what they believed to be true. Luana explained this to me. She did not ask for forgiveness, only for the chance to make amends. This hate – I think it's finally time I can let it go. Who I will be without it, what I will be without it, I do not know. But I think it's time I find out."

"Who you are is Kitara, daughter of Bellec," Aeryn told her after a moment.

"Daughter of Oriana," Kitara replied as she brushed her mother's ring before she turned her eyes to her father's band, "and daughter of Theron Malley."

✦ ✦ ✦

Torben arose before the sun as he always did. Decades of fighting and training had forged him into a man of great discipline. Near him were the four from Elara. Marshall tended to his horse while Elise and Tariq talked in hushed tones. The girl absentmindedly twirled a knife through her fingers. Cleander sat a little by himself as he always did. He held a pipe to his lips, and his wary eyes kept flicking towards Kilgareth. The man had a dark past, that much was certain to Torben. He *was* a dark man. Torben ran a whetstone down across the edge of his axe. The steel sang and the fresh morning rays glinted against its surface. Torben's eyes drifted south for a moment.

"Thinking about home?" Luana Marquez asked as she approached.

Torben looked at the captain before turning his attention back to his axe. "It's out there, many hundreds of miles away," Torben replied.

"You have never travelled this far from ship or sea, nor have you spent such a time away from them, have you?"

"No Valkir ever has," Torben said. "My people sail to war, and I am not with them."

"What we do here is more important than what you could accomplish were you with them," Luana told him.

"I know," Torben replied with a grunt. "And that is why I stay."

"Your story, it gripped the Mierans by the ears," Calvillo of Tarik said. "It reached into their hearts. They speak it every day, and each time it grows grander. These men of horse and steel have come to believe your words with their very souls. I have heard it spoken among the Salvaari now."

"I merely spoke my truth," Torben said.

"And sometimes that is enough," Calvillo said. "I would like to take the song back to Tarik one day. Our storytellers and poets would bask in its magnificence."

"One day, perhaps, I will come with you," Torben suggested. "Travel to the far north. See the snowbound lands."

"You would have a tale or two to tell when you came back," Calvillo replied.

"It is a beautiful place, Tarik." Galadayne's voice reached them as the mercenary and his comrades approached.

The three sailors turned as the newcomers arrived. A strange band of Annorans and Medeans, joined by a pair of Larissan desert dwellers, Aeryn the Salvaari archer and the blonde-haired daughter of Bellec. Like Torben's company, these people were different. These differences had drawn them together when surrounded by thousands of Mierans and Salvaari alike.

"You have been to Tarik?" Calvillo asked.

"Once, a long time ago," Galadayne replied.

"What took you that far north?" Luana asked.

"Work," the mercenary Jaimye said simply.

"Mind if we join you?" Kitara asked.

Torben shrugged. "Come sit by our fire," he said.

"Here," Tariq called and tossed a wineskin to the mercenaries.

One by one, the sellswords made themselves at home around the campfire.

"Quite the merry gathering," Elise Delfeyre said with a snort.

"We ride with two armies yet have none of our own," Galadayne said. "We are all here for our own reasons – fate has brought us together. We are not of Miera or Salvaar. We are outsiders. Seems only fitting that we few foreigners should stand together."

"As you say," Marshall said as he made his way over.

Kitara sat by the fire and pulled a dagger from her belt. It was short and plain, a weapon that had been forged in the savage lands of Irene. She held it by the blade as she drew a second knife and began to add notches to its wooden hilt.

"That blade, I have never seen one of its like before," Elise said.

"It comes from Irene to the far west," Kitara explained as she added a final notch. She held the dagger out to the Elaran girl. "It is tradition for the people of Irene to notch the hilt of their blade. A mark for a kill."

"There are so many." Elise examined the blade.

"I have seen enough bloodshed to last two lifetimes," Kitara told her simply.

Elise looked into her eyes, and Kitara could see a shadow that plagued the Elaran girl. It was clear that she was no warrior or soldier, yet Elise knew death like an old friend. She was haunted by it.

"As have I," Elise said as she handed the knife back. "A beautiful blade."

Kitara ran her fingers across the notched wood before she sheathed the blade. These marks were the sum of those lives she had taken since she had left Miera little over a year before. Names she knew and names she would never know. Once, they would have given her nightmares, but no longer. She was not ashamed of her past, nor did she regret what she had done. She was at peace.

"Here," Elise said after a moment.

She pulled a longer dagger from her belt. It had a wide blade that curved downwards and lacked a crossguard. Its length stretched from the tip of her fingers to her elbow.

"This is a kukri," Elise said as she extended the weapon to Kitara. "Made by the Delions. Only the nobility was awarded the privilege of carrying such blades."

Kitara took it. She felt the weight and the balance. It was a weapon designed more for slashing than stabbing. Its weight made it feel almost like a small axe. Kitara gave it a spin and felt it flow effortlessly through the air.

"This is a fine weapon," she said. "I have never been so far west as to see the ruins of their empire,"

"Nor have I," Elise replied. "This blade has been in my family for generations, ever since the fall."

Kitara handed the kukri back. "One day you will have to go there," she said. "See the place that your ancestor took this blade."

Aeryn felt a smile grace her lips as she watched Kitara talk with the Elaran girl. She looked to Luana who stood at her side. "She told me who you are and what you did," Aeryn said to Luana.

"I only did what was right," Luana replied.

"You helped to forge her into who she is," Aeryn said. "You kept her alive when no one else would. There are no words for what that means but know that you have my gratitude."

"What I did you would have done were you able to be there. My only regret is not saving her from Barboza and his crew. She is safe now, with you, with them." Luana nodded to the mercenaries. "Her family. Think no more of it."

Kitara rose to her feet and looked to Calvillo. "Tariki," Kitara called as she gestured down towards the plain.

"You want to fight?" Calvillo called back.

"It's been a long time."

The mercenaries cheered as Calvillo rose to his feet. Kitara handed her sword belt to Aeryn. The Tariki gathered a pair of training swords from his saddle and made his way down to the field with Kitara.

"First to three?" Kitara suggested.

Calvillo nodded and passed her one of the wooden training blades. "Show me if you have learnt all that I have to teach," he said.

All eyes turned towards the pair. They exchanged a short bow in the Tariki fashion.

"A dozen crowns says the Tariki lands the first blow," Marshall called.

"I'll take those odds," Galadayne replied.

As Kitara and Calvillo strode back five paces, Galadayne made his way over to Marshall. Cheers of support for each combatant were cried as the pair bowed once more. Many of the onlookers began to place bets, most in coin. The cries died down as Kitara and Calvillo raised their blades. Their stances were almost identical, for Calvillo had trained her. Their eyes locked. When they moved, they moved fast. Torben had once heard tarkaras described as the swordsong. A ballad of steel. It was more than a dance or a fight – it was a song. It was as beautiful as it was deadly. Calvillo landed first. His blade glanced into the chainmail of Kitara's stomach. Both fighters stepped back.

Galadayne handed a coin purse to Marshall.

"Twenty on Calvillo," Marshall said.

Galadayne nodded his agreement.

Again, the combatants came together. This time the fight was longer. The swords rang as they came together. The wind whistled as they missed by a hair's breadth. Calvillo's blade clipped Kitara's side. The crowd laughed as Galadayne handed coins to Marshall once again.

"Thirty on Cal–"

"Kitara wins three blows to two," Galadayne interrupted. "I'll wager everything."

"Done," Marshall agreed with a laugh.

None of them saw Kitara's smirk as she locked blades with Calvillo again. This time she flowed more freely than water. Within moments, her blade found Calvillo's shoulder. Galadayne grinned. Wood sang as the pair fought. Again, her blade found a home as it sliced into the Tariki's thigh. All sound stopped. There were no hushed voices. There was no whispering of the wind. Kitara had learnt how to fight like a Tariki blademaster from Calvillo. She had learnt to fight like cut-throat and vagabond from Luana. She had trained in the slums of Annora and the sand circles of Miera. Her iron had been hardened in the arenas of Aureia. There was nothing in the world that she feared, no man who gave her pause. Calvillo was her first mentor. It was he who had given her the sword that she now possessed. Yet he had only been taught to fight like his people. That was his weakness. Kitara had made the read as they exchanged blows. Her blade knocked Calvillo's to the side, and before he could adjust, her boot drove into his stomach. Kitara continued her spin. Calvillo raised his sword. Kitara changed angle and drove forward. Her bracer deflected Calvillo's thrust as the edge of her sword glanced off his cheek. Those watching cheered as Kitara danced backwards and twirled her blade. She bowed to her former mentor, and he returned it.

Galadayne clapped a hand on Marshall's back. "Game well played," Galadayne said and held out a hand.

Marshall grimaced and handed over the sum of what was owed. Galadayne gave the guard a wink as he took the bulging purse. Kitara and Calvillo re-joined the companions. Shoulders and backs were thumped. Aeryn gave Kitara a grin as she returned her sword.

"Riders," Sakkar's voice called over the din.

A small company of heavily armed Mierans cantered towards them. They rode in tight formation as only masters of the horse could. The foreign contingent rose to meet them. The lead Mieran unstrapped his helmet and let his long hair fall free. Six gold rings adorned his ear and his young face was weathered and scarred from fighting. It was the face of a northerner.

"Silas?" Kitara called as she recognised Zandir Barangir's son.

The last she had seen of him had been in the ruins of Israfil when she had freed Lukas, Cailean and Sakkar from captivity. Silas ignored her as his eyes swept across the group of foreigners.

"We are at war and here I find you playing?" Silas said distastefully.

"You are welcome to test yourself, Mieran," Galadayne replied.

"Games are for children, not warriors," Silas told him. "The kings are gathering to plan our attack. They request the presence of Torben and the seafarer Luana. You must come with me."

Silas turned his baleful gaze to Kitara. His anger burned bright. Kitara met his stare and raised her eyebrows at her former companion. Silas snorted and spat to the side. It was a challenge. A show of disrespect. Kitara's hand fell to her sword. She knew what the Mierans were like.

"She fights shoulder to shoulder with you. Have some respect," Aeryn growled as she stepped to Kitara's side.

"Respect?" Silas snarled. "I will *never* respect a traitor."

"Yet you condemn someone for not bearing the title of Mieran?" Kitara shot back. "I could have killed you that day in Israfil. I didn't."

"The only reason you live is because for now we are allies," Silas told her darkly. "But if you wish to correct that mistake, then I will gladly form the square. Steel instead of your wooden toys. Blood instead of merely landing a blow."

"Are you man or beast that you would seek the blood of an ally?" Aeryn growled, approaching the riders. She nodded over her shoulder at Kitara as she spoke. "Her blood. She who has done more in this war than you. She who has won more glory. She who has won more honour than you ever will."

"Mind your place, Salvaari," Silas shot back. "I have no argument with you, but if you question my honour again, if you take one more step, it will be the last step you ever take."

Aeryn took that step. Silas' sword leapt into his hand. Steel sang as the Mierans and those who stood opposite followed suit. Silas' horse turned and the Mieran captain levelled his sword at Aeryn. Its tip fell to the moonseer's neck. She did not flinch. Her gaze did not waver. She glared up at him. She dared him without uttering a single word. Bows and spears came up.

"Easy there, friend," Galadayne called as he approached.

Silas' eyes went to the mercenary. "You are the one they call Galadayne?" he asked.

"I am."

Silas snorted. "I know your name and I know it well. You earned King Zoran's mark fighting against your own people many years ago at Carn-Dair," Silas said contemptuously. "You lost it when you killed Azian and saved Kitara's life fleeing Miera." The Mieran nodded at Kitara as he spoke.

Azian had been the broken-nosed Mieran who Kitara had met in Chausac with Sakkar and Prince Lukas. She had killed him barely a day later while Bellec and his mercenaries had slain Azian's men.

"We are here as friends, as family and most importantly as allies," Galadayne replied. "We are fighting on the same side and all you want to do is put one of us in the ground. Go. There will be enough bloodshed in the days to come."

Silas glowered and turned his gaze to Kitara for a moment before he at last sheathed his blade. He gave the foreigners a contemptuous look. "Betrayers, traitors, Elarans and men who kill for coin," Silas spat. "You are not warriors. You are not soldiers. You are nothing."

With that, Silas whistled and kicked his heels in to the sides of his horse. The Mierans surged back towards whence they had come. Kitara watched them go. She spat and then shook her head. Mierans.

✦ ✦ ✦

FIFTY-FIVE

Kilgareth, Valley of Odrysia

Kassandra Raynor bit her lip as she stared down at the vial given to her by Lysandra. If what the arc'maija had said was true, then the concoction created from the cintilla plant would save the she-elf Naidra. Kassandra was about to take a very real risk – if she was caught, she would not be merely thrown behind bars. She would be killed regardless of her title. If that came to pass, then only the gods knew what would happen in the wake of her death. In his rage and anger, what would her brother the king do? She pushed it from her mind as a knock came from the door. Kassie shoved the vial inside the satchel that rested upon her table.

"Come in," Kassie called, turning to the door.

The door opened and in walked her maid, Marian Martyn. Marian frowned as she closed the door. No doubt she had seen the look in Kassie's eyes.

"You sent for me," the maid stated.

"I need your help," Kassie told her.

"Anything, my lady." Marian approached Kassie.

"I need your clothes this night," the princess said.

"My clothes?" Marian questioned and her frown deepened. "Kassandra, what is it?"

"Please be my friend now and do not ask questions," Kassie begged.

Marian gave her a smile and nodded. The pair had been friends for many years. They had grown up together after all.

"As you wish," Marian said.

It did not take long and soon Kassandra was dressed in the clothes of a servant girl. Instead of fine silks that shone in the light, she wore faded browns and greys. Her rings, necklaces and other jewels were placed upon the table and a dark scarf was run through her hair. No longer was she a princess of Annora. She was a lowborn peasant girl who served the aristocracy. Kassie gathered up her satchel and slung it over her shoulder.

"I will be back soon," Kassie told her friend. "Wait here until I return."

"Yes, my lady."

Kassie took Marian's hands and then pulled her into an embrace. She held her tight. "Thank you," she said. "There are no words for your friendship."

"Just promise that you will come back safely."

"I promise."

With that, Kassandra was gone. The door closed at her back and she strode out into the stone corridors of Kilgareth. She saw everything as she walked through the Citadel. From the knights in their shining armour to the aristocrats in their fine silks and the servants in their rags. She kept her eyes low yet walked with purpose. Dressed as she was, none gave her a second glance as she drew closer to the heart of Kilgareth. If a servant was here, then her lord and master would have sent her with reason. She knew that the prison in which Naidra was caged was deep underground. She had seen it herself. However, while a few guards might not be missed, if many were to venture to the tunnels below, it would be noticed. Kassie doubted that the cardinal would be foolish enough to station a large number of his men underground to guard the elf and keep her poisoned. Instead of making for the hidden entrance, Kassie made for the cardinal's quarters. White-clad knights bearing the sun and moon insignia of their gods strode through the corridors. The cardinal's guard. These were dangerous men, men whose blood flowed with their faith. The disguise allowed her to pass through their ranks almost unnoticed. Lysandra had said that the captain of the guard laced Naidra's food and drink each day. To remove any suspicion or evidence that a secret prisoner was kept, the food would be the same that the guards themselves ate. It would be prepared in the kitchens same as any other meal. Only then would it be tainted with poison.

Kassie blended in with the other servants as she made her way to the kitchens. The rooms were hot and filled with the stench of food, steam and sweat. The cooks wound their way around the kitchens as they prepared food for the guards' dinner. Kassie kept her head low, making her way through their midst. A huge pot of soup was simmering over an open flame. Kassie glanced around, watching a cook tell one of the servants to run to the knights and notify them that the food was prepared. A bell was rung, and a pair of cooks made for the huge pot of soup. Kassie ducked inside a cupboard and closed the wooden door behind her. She put her eye to the crack and waited. From her position, she could see where the cooks took the pot. She could see the knights come and go with their bowls. One by one, the cooks began to ration out the meal to the soldiers. So intent was she upon the soldiers that she barely noticed another of the guard slip into the kitchens from the back. Farris Quinnal. The captain of Cardinal Aleksander's guard. This was it.

He gathered up a wooden tray and placed a small bowl and a cup upon it. Kassie had but a few moments to administer the cintilla or her one chance would fade. She crept out of the cupboard and made her way over to one of the kitchen benches. Her eyes were fast and her hands faster still. She gathered up the closest vegetables she could see and began to chop them with a knife left on the bench. Kassie's eyes wandered to Farris. The captain filled the cup with water and then pulled a flask from his belt. It was the poison ... it had to be. Farris placed the flask on the bench beside his tray and took the small bowl over to a second simmering pot. Kassie was quick. She stepped behind the guard, crossed to his bench and reached for the flask. She popped the cork with one hand and took up the cintilla with her other. Two drops were all she had the time to administer before she heard the captain place soup in the bowl. Kassie jammed the cork back into the flask and placed it on the bench. Nerves set in as she heard the footsteps approach. She composed her face and walked with purpose back to her bench.

"Girl."

Kassandra froze as Farris said the words. She slowly turned to face the guard. She offered a bow. "My lord," Kassie said.

"I don't know you," Farris said with a frown as he approached.

"The cooks, they asked—"

"Do not lie," Farris interrupted. "I know every one of the cardinal's staff. I have never seen you before and there are others upon whom they would call to help in the kitchens before an unknown Annoran servant. So I will ask you again: Who are you?"

Kassie kept her eyes downcast. She allowed a slight stammer to enter her voice. "My name is Aileen," she said. "My father is dead. I needed food and I ..."

Kassandra trailed off. She thought of her father. She thought of the memories that she had shared with him and those that they would never see. She remembered the night that he had been murdered. There had been much feasting and laughing. The final meal before the men rode to war. A tear trickled down her cheek.

"This war has taken a lot from us," Farris said softly. "Know that it will be over soon. Peace will be restored. The gods will make everything right in the world. Your father ... he lives in memory," Farris placed a pair of fingers to his brow. The guard looked away for a moment and took up a loaf of bread. He held it out to

Kassandra. "Our food is your food," Farris said. "We are, all of us, in this together."

"Thank you," Kassie replied gratefully as she took the bread.

"May the light of the gods watch over you always."

Kassie gave the guard another bow and made for the kitchen entrance. Her heart raced. She wiped the tear from her cheek, glancing back in time to see Farris drip poison from his flask into Naidra's food and water. She could only pray that the cintilla did its work.

✦ ✦ ✦

Lysandra glanced up as Kassandra entered her office. She was not dressed in the gown of a princess but rather the rags of a servant. Kassandra tossed her the vial of cintilla. Lysandra caught it.

"A few drops, that was what you said," the princess stated.

Lysandra nodded. "That is all it would take," the arc'maija replied.

"Then it is done."

"You have played your part well," Lysandra told her. "Naidra will be free. I cannot thank you enough."

"There are many who would have done the same."

"But only you did," Lysandra replied. "You have a big heart, and it is a good heart. I pray that it never darkens."

Kassandra gave her a smile. "I must go before I am missed," Kassie said. "I will speak to you later."

Lysandra returned the smile and watched Kassandra leave. The smile faded as the door shut behind the princess. She had acted out of the kindness in her heart yet did not know what she had just done. She did not know who Naidra was, nor what had condemned the elf to live out all the ages of the world behind bars. The princess would find out soon enough.

Lysandra bolted the door. She made her way over to her desk

and glanced down at the vial of cintilla. She took a long breath and closed her eyes. Lysandra called upon her gift, and it answered. Her blood ran black. Her teeth sharpened into fangs. When her eyes at last opened, they burned as crimson fire, and she found herself kneeling in a black forest. Dark stones marked with runes grew all around. Lysandra could feel the magic radiate through the trees. She felt stronger than ever before. Lysandra slowly rose to her feet. This was the Veil, and she was not alone. This time it was not Harkan who greeted her. This time it was another. A woman with hair the colour of winter snow and eyes bluer than the most brilliant of sapphires yet webbed with cracks of white. A woman with black tattoos that crept across the right side of her head. Her ears were pointed and her skin pale.

"Naidra," Lysandra greeted the she-elf in the old tongue.

The elf stared at her. She stared *through* her. "A half-blooded daughter of the ruskalan," Naidra replied. "I have felt your presence for many months, yet never have you attempted to speak."

"There were things that needed to be done," Lysandra replied. "Harkan himself gave me this command."

"Harkan yet lives?"

"With deadly purpose," Lysandra replied. "He seeks vengeance for what the west did to our people and yours. We share your pain."

"What do you know of my pain?" Naidra growled through bared teeth. "Do not attempt to place our losses on equal footing. You were not there one hundred years ago. I was. Your people were not slaughtered until only one remained. You may have ruskalan blood, but ruskalan do not feel everything that every one of their people feel. We elves do. Every joy, every tear, every pain. When the purge came to my people, I felt it all even from a cage in Aureia. Every scream, every hurt, every drop of blood and every heartbreak. I felt it all. The ruskalan and the elves once stood side by side. Your presence here tells me that you knew of my existence the whole time. You knew what the emperor condemned me to, and you did *nothing*."

"We had no choice," Lysandra replied. "After the purge, only six of Tanris' children remained. They had to gather their strength. They could not throw their lives away attempting the impossible. This is a plan long in the making. Know that those who did this to you are about to fall. That is why I am here. The empire is weak. The Order is weak. Medea and Annora are weak. You know this; you will have felt it. It was Harkan who made it so. The poison with which they have tainted you is destroyed. Your strength will return and all those who did this to you will suffer."

"If I was a common elf, they would suffer," Naidra snarled and curled a hand into a fist. "I am not merely the last of my ruined kind. I am autieyar. The strength of Sylvaine flows through my veins. The strength of the Veil. No, they will not *suffer*. I will kill them all."

"They will fall," Lysandra said. "In time. Your strength will return in a matter of hours, yet I would ask you wait but a handful of days. You must wait or else this battle may yet be lost and the revenge you seek will die along with you."

Naidra drew close to Lysandra. The elf circled her, and a malicious grin contorted Naidra's lips. Lysandra had been around the ruskalan her whole life. She had spent years living among the enemy. She had never known the kind of fear that the end instilled in her heart. She knew what Naidra had done. She knew what she was capable of, and it terrified her.

"I have spent many lifetimes in a cage," Naidra said, circling like a vulture. "Though I was trapped behind bars when they came for my people, I could see everything. I could *feel* everything. Such is my curse. My sister … I do not even remember what she looked like. What I do remember of the darkness, I remember each night. I remember each waking moment. The faces of those slaughtered. The screams of my people. The cries for mercy. The searing agony of flesh burning in flame. The passing of friends for the purpose of sport. Every cut and blow. All of the fear and all of the pain. Every heart ripped from chest … I feel it even now. Elf-kind and ruskalan, our lives are our own. We have lived at the whims of the outside world for too long. That time is done. It is done. Soon they will see."

✦ ✦ ✦

Sir Alarik Sindra wound his way through the passages of Kilgareth. The time had come to speak to Lysandra about Kyler. He could only hope that despite the ruskalan in the boy's veins, she would be willing to help.

"Sir Alarik," a knight called as he approached.

"Sir Mortimier," Alarik greeted him.

Mortimier held out a small scroll. It had come from the aviary. "Someone sent a bird for you," the knight said.

Alarik nodded his thanks and broke the seal. He frowned as he saw who had sent the message. Arntair. The merchant from Elara whom he had worked with twice in the past. With each word that the battlemaster read, his frown deepened. The words spoke of a fleet of Valkir and Sacasian raiders. It spoke of why the Mierans had joined the Salvaari in this war. Surely, word such as this should have arrived before. Surely, Lysandra would have known. It was to her that all messages went. It was to her whom their network of intelligence wrote. She had to have known … but then why had none within the Order been told? They could have foreseen the Mieran attack, and this war would have already been over. Realisation hit him like a hammer. There was a traitor within these walls. If what Arntair had written was true, then that traitor had been Lysandra the whole time.

Alarik pursed his lips and stashed the letter in a pouch before he made for the arc'maija's office. The thoughts plagued his mind every step that he took. It took all of his experience to keep them from showing in his face. He knocked on Lysandra's door and then entered. The arc'maija sat at her desk.

"Alarik," Lysandra said with a smile as she gestured to the chair opposite. "Join me."

"Thank you, my lady," Alarik replied as he shut the door and made his way to join her at the table.

"Wine?" Lysandra asked as the battlemaster sat.

Alarik nodded. The arc'maija poured two glasses and passed one to her companion.

"What can I do to help?" she asked.

"It's about Kyler," Alarik replied after he had taken a sip of wine.

"I thought as much."

"I believe that his blood has been cursed by that of the ruskalan," Alarik said. "You saw what Elena's blood did to him after the Vault. He suffered a mortal wound, but whatever she did saved him. Her blood still courses through his veins … I think it might be killing him. Help me save him."

Lysandra looked him in the eye. "I promise you that I will do all that I can to help," she said.

"The boy has seen too much, has suffered too much, just to die like that," Alarik muttered. "Each day his suffering grows."

"You care for the boy, don't you?"

"Aye," Alarik admitted. "I do."

"Funny then that you would put him in harm's way by murdering Amaris."

Alarik froze. Of everything that he had expected when he had come here, that had been a thought far removed. If Lysandra knew, that meant only one thing.

"He told you, didn't he?" Alarik said quietly.

"He did."

So Kyler had done his duty after all. That meant his own time was short. Alarik had no choice but to play all of his cards.

"I see," Alarik replied before pulling Arntair's letter from his pouch and placing it on the desk. "Word has reached my ears from the Elaran merchant Arntair. Word of an alliance of Valkir and Sacasian raiders. Word of a song that brought Salvaar and Miera together. Word of things that you would have known yet did not speak of. Words that someone in your position would have been sent many months ago. Word that if known could have won us this war a long time ago. I did wonder how the enemy always knew how to divide us and, when the time was right, bring us together. The battle in the forest and the battle at the river. Just as I have often wondered how Wa'rith knew of our search for the artefacts, how he was always one step ahead. When we learnt of his identity, it all became clear. Only one other was with us that day. Only one other knew of the artefacts. Only one other could have told him our secrets. Now I hear that it was a maija's hand that sent us towards Verena and death. You are the traitor. Aren't you?"

If she was surprised, Lysandra did not show it. Instead she gave a deadly smile.

"Yes. That was all my doing," Lysandra admitted, for there was no use denying it any longer. "When the Silver Tower fell, I told you that I remained to help with the wounded and, while that is true, I also pulled Markus from that river. It was I who nursed him back to health. It was I who found him a place in Elara."

"But why?" Alarik asked. "You betrayed everyone you knew, sided with our worst enemies ... and for what?"

"For what?" Lysandra hissed through bared teeth.

For a fleeting moment, her eyes flashed red. Alarik felt it in that moment: fear that he had not felt since the forests in Irene. The ruskalan were back. Elena was just the first, but this was different. Lysandra had wormed her way into the Circle. She had wormed her way into knowing every last secret that the Order had.

"One hundred years ago, your people sundered mine," Lysandra snarled. "You slaughtered us in our hundreds. Barely a handful survived your cruelty, and the elves endured even worse at your hands. There is a debt in blood, and I am here to claim it."

"A debt in blood?" Alarik replied. "You started this war, just as you started it a hundred years ago. You plunged Medea into darkness and tore the heart from Aureia long *before* my ancestors stood against you. Seeking revenge for that which you began is the act of a monster."

"*You* purged us from our land and drove us to the brink of extinction, and yet you brand us *monsters*?" Lysandra countered. "It is honour that started this war. Honour is the reason I am here."

Alarik did not look away from her. "Tell me something, Lysandra, if that is even your name. You speak of honour, you speak as if your people are the heroes of this tale, when we both know that that is something other than the truth. Do not forget that neither the empire nor the Order wanted war. Do not forget that it was your people and the elves who sent agents to the south again and again and again. Despite everything, despite the will of his council, the emperor refused war. He wanted peace. He wanted to live in harmony. Do not forget that it was you who slaughtered a peace delegation. Do not forget that it was you who gave the empire no choice. Do not forget that it was you who united the houses. And do not forget what happened last time you stood against the empire."

"You are in no position to make threats," Lysandra replied. "Not when it was the words of a ruskalan that saw all of your armies here. It was not the cardinal nor the Spear that started this war. It was us. Everything that has happened in the last century happened because we allowed it to. After your murder of Amaris was revealed, you were only allowed to live because I knew that you alone would be able to protect Kyler once he turned. Now he is returned …"

Alarik rose from his chair. His hand went for his sword. A cough broke free of his lips. He stumbled. He felt weak. His eyes went to the wine cup he had drunk from. *Poison.* Lysandra rose before him.

Her eyes turned red. Her blood ran black, and her teeth sharpened into fangs.

"Markus Harvarder doesn't bear the black blood, nor does he know of my plans," she told him. "He is but a pawn in this game in the dark. A tool. A sword. Many of our agents are just like him. When you killed Amaris, I was forced to adapt. You see, Alarik, he was one of us. He bore the ruskalan blood. This war is about reclaiming our artefacts. It is about reclaiming our relics, our history and our homeland. More so, it is about avenging the dead. I was not there, but in my blood I remember. The screams of my people burning ... all that death. You will fall ... like all the others."

Alarik forced himself away from the table and managed to draw his sword. He staggered as pain tore through his body. His vision grew blurry. He could not speak. He could not breathe. Alarik lunged with all the strength that he still possessed. It was feeble and weak. Lysandra stepped to the side as his blade sped past. Steel glinted in the light as her dagger came up and drove deep into Alarik's throat. The battlemaster fell as his red blood spilled. Lysandra stared down at him as he died. The ringing of bells came from fortress. Bells that meant only one thing: they were under attack.

"I am going destroy Kilgareth and whatever remains of your Order."

✦ ✦ ✦

FIFTY-SIX

Kilgareth, Valley of Odrysia

Bells rang through the great fortress. Their song echoed from the vast stone walls to the dark corridors within. Knight captains, generals and noble lords shouted commands as their soldiers ran to position. Armour was tightened and spears gathered from the barracks as tens of thousands of warriors made ready.

Dayne blocked out the grotesque feeling in his stomach left along with the burning pain it caused. His mind was stronger than any stone or steel. He would not bend or break. Dayne placed his hands upon the walls of Kilgareth as he stared down from his vantage point. The might of Salvaar and Miera was assembled before him. Warriors and horses swarmed across the plains and up the slopes of the mountain that led to the fortress. Without the fear of being struck from behind by the soldiers of Odrysia, the heathen army had grown emboldened. They had spent days preparing for their assault upon Kilgareth. Now they came up the mountain with ladders, crude catapults and wooden mantlets, movable wooden walls created to protect archers. All were forged from the forests of Odrysia itself. The defenders were to be attacked by the very land they now protected.

Dayne's countrymen armed with longbows crafted with wood from the bosom of Annora itself lined the walls. Knights of Kil'kara held their wicked crossbows close as the enemy began to make their approach up the mountainside. The catapults unleashed huge stones against the walls and buildings within Kilgareth long before the rain of arrows began. Dayne knew that the storm of rock and stone was to instil fear within the defenders more than it was to bring down walls. The heathen believed that if the buildings were crushed and splintered, those who protected them would panic. This was something other than the truth. It enraged them. It kept them true to their purpose even as they unleashed hell upon their enemy. A barrage of arrows and bolts spewed forth from the walls as the heathen archers marched within range. The defenders used the merlons along the high walls to shield them while they reloaded bow and crossbow. Many of the attackers hid behind their wooden mantlets, returning fire. Some were not so lucky and were cut down by Annoran arrows. Dayne saw all. He watched and commanded as the battle raged. Those defenders caught by arrows were hurried from the wall. The wounded were taken to the infirmary and makeshift field hospital closer to the walls. The dead were burned. A haze of smoke covered Kilgareth, masking the noonday sun above. A roar came from the heathen army and horns sounded through the valley. Man and horse surged towards the fortress walls. They had ladders and, more fiercely, a huge ram covered in a wooden house and thick pelts that they pushed towards the causeway. The enemy surged forward as the siege equipment was brought to bear.

"Prepare to defend the walls!" Dayne cried from his station.

Warriors and knights armed with sword, spear, hammer and axe made for the stairs and towers that led up onto the ramparts. The king's hand rested on the pommel of his sword as he watched the enemy charge. They would fall upon the walls like water upon rock. Heavy arrows tore through the approaching horde. Shields and mantlets could not protect them all. They fell in droves under the fire of the legendary Annoran archers. The Salvaari, akin to the Mierans, were as brave as they were fearless. They were not scared of death any more than they were scared of the men atop the stone walls. The storm of steel did not stop them. The ladders reached the walls first and within moments warriors were swarming up them.

"My king, is it time?" Tristayn asked from Dayne's side.

"No," Dayne replied, eyes locked on the approaching ram. It was more than halfway down the causeway that led to the thick gates.

"SWORDS!" Sir Corvo's voice rang along the battlements.

Steel sang as the Knights of Kil'kara leapt forward and drew their mighty blades. The enemy clambered up onto the walls.

"KIL'KARA!"

The war cry echoed through Kilgareth as its greatest defenders attacked all who reached the top of the ladders. The Salvaari and Mierans lashed out all around, leaping onto the stone. Blood flowed, and soldiers fell. The defenders held fast. Corvo led the defence. After the death of Amaris, he had become master of the Citadel, but he had first been the Order's finest warrior. He had been its Sword. He cut through the attackers like a knife carving a cake. His longsword wept and tears of blood covered the fortress' walls.

"My king?" Tristayn asked yet again.

"No," Dayne told him.

Archers upon the gatehouse rained arrows down upon the encroaching ram. The housing protected most of those warriors heaving the machine forward, yet some found their way through and speared those within. Archers further along the wall swung to face it and unleashed their arrows upon the exposed sides. They fell in droves to Annoran bows and knight crossbows. The torrent of steel slowed as more ladders arose and more soldiers poured over the walls. The painted Salvaari howled vicious war cries and chanted while they fought. The ever-stoic Mierans barely made a sound as they killed and as they died. The ram reached the gate.

"King Dayne?" Tristayn said, a hint of desperation edging into his voice.

"We hold."

A thunderous crash echoed through the fortress: the ram began its work. The song of steel rang along the walls. The melody of bows joined it even as the beat of the ram rose ever louder. Dark smoke from a dozen fires enveloped the fortress in a black mist. Screams filled the air in a grotesque chorus. Blood watered stone, earth, steel and wood. Through this, Dayne found calm. Through this, he found peace. The high king of Annora turned to his general.

"Now," he said.

Tristayn looked to the horn bearer who stood with them and nodded. The unspoken command was all the man needed to raise the instrument to his lips. A single long note rang across the battlefield. It carried in the wind and whispered through the corridors of the Citadel. It was heard by another horn bearer, one who stood at the entrance to the tunnels that led deep into the mountains. He raised his horn, and a second note rang true. Through the stone tunnels and rock caverns beneath Kilgareth it sounded. It spoke to the men deep within the bowels of the earth. One thousand heavily armoured Knights of Kil'kara mounted atop their warhorses. The old and wizened Sir Mortimier led them. He raised his spear.

"Areut talc cuun'ect," Mortimier cried.

The battle prayer was chorused by the one thousand as they held their amulets. When the last of the sacred words left their lips, they swung their shields from their backs and strapped them to their arms. Sir Mortimier kicked his heels in.

King Dayne's eyes swept the battle. He was calm and composed as he always was. To fear battle was a choice. To fear death was a choice. It was a choice that to Dayne held only one option, and he had no fear in his heart. He had played this battle in his mind a thousand times. He knew all of the pieces and he knew the board as well as he knew his own name. The Salvaari and their Mieran allies were eager to take the city and kill every man and woman within its holy walls. They had pressed their attack. The alliance of Annora, Medea and the Order was trapped within the city. The warriors inside Odrysia numbered few and they were little more than a militia. The heathen had no fear of an attack in the flank and so had pushed forward.

"To the gate," Dayne commanded as he strode down from the inner wall.

What little remained of the royal guard was joined by heavily armoured Annoran knights as they marched through the streets. They reached the courtyard before the gatehouse. Every man held a shield. Every man held a long spear. Dayne grimaced as pain rolled through his body. He spat to the side. He spat blood. Dayne ignored Tristayn's worried expression as he wiped his mouth with his leather-gloved hand. The king pushed down his visor and took up the spear his general offered. Turning to his men and beating the lance upon his shield, he roared a vicious war cry that was taken up by his knights. Horns blared from the mountains that surrounded Kilgareth. Stone and earth fell as hidden postern gates were heaved open. Sir Mortimier and his knights surged forward from the tunnels to either side of the attackers. The holy army drove deep into the sides of the heathen horde with battle prayers upon their lips. Massive horses crushed warriors beneath while their riders cut men down with sword and spear. The crash of the ram stopped as the Salvaari and Mierans at the gate turned to face the enemy that had appeared from the mountains.

Dayne rolled his shoulders back, beat his spear upon his shield, and levelled it at the gates. Annorans milled all around him. The guards at the gate took hold of the locking bar and pulled it free. They tossed it to the side and heaved the gates open.

"ANNORA!" Tristayn roared.

"ANNORA!" the cry echoed from the throats of his comrades.

The knights formed a solid shield wall and began to move. Dayne held his position until a number of the ranks had passed and then joined them. They marched under the red eagle banners that soared above. The Annorans jogged out from the gates and swamped the ram. They spread out as they looked to the battle unfurling before them. The charge of the knights had broken the enemy army in two. The smaller force stood between Kilgareth and Kil'kara steel. The larger spilled down the mountainside. A last volley of arrows speared down from the walls and into heathen backs before Dayne and his people surged forward and crashed into their rear. Mieran and Salvaari alike fell beneath their spears.

"FIGHT FOR YOUR KING!" Tristayn bellowed. "FIGHT FOR YOUR GODS!"

The Annorans roared. Dayne counted under his breath. They had won the ram, yet his army beyond the walls was massively outnumbered. The shock of the knights' charge and the Annoran shield wall would only last so long. The echoing thunder of falling rock came from the far sides of Kilgareth as the Order sealed the tunnels from which the knights had ridden.

"TURN THE RAM!" Dayne yelled above the din.

The king pushed his way back through the ranks of his men and led a small company towards the siege engine. He swung his shield onto his back and drove his spear into the ground before he pushed his visor up. Together with fifteen of his warriors he took hold of the battle ram and started to push it back from the gate.

"HEAVE!" he cried. "HEAVE!"

The king counted the steps, and on his command, the Annorans began to turn it. Dayne's muscles burned as his men chanted his words over and over. Slowly, it moved. Inch by inch, the ram swivelled.

"IT'LL MAKE A NICE WALL!" one of the Annorans called as they at last heaved it into place.

Dayne took a short breath and stepped backward. "Cut rope

and sever chain," he commanded, turning back to the battle. The tide was about to turn. Dayne turned to his horn bearer. "Sound the retreat," he said.

A long blast rang out across the mountainside. The shouts of commanders rose above the chaos of battle. Dayne pushed his visor down, snatched up his spear and unslung his shield.

"SHIELDS ON ME!" he roared.

The horn bearer blew again. The Annoran shield wall began to fall back step by step. Four solid lines formed a semi-circle around the ram that joined back to the walls of Kilgareth. The rest fell back inside the fortress. This time, Dayne stood near the front of the formation. The men who had smashed everything within the ram joined him. Sir Mortimier and his knights broke off from the battle and charged back towards the gates.

"OPEN!" bellowed the king.

Gaps opened in the shield wall as the Annorans obeyed without question. The knights flooded back through them as only masters of the horse could. Arrows and bolts rained down from the walls, over the heads of the defenders and into the ranks of the invaders. They would not stop the pursuing heathen army, but they would slow it.

"STEADY," Dayne called as he saw the enemy charge forward. "STEADY!"

The last of the horses reached the gates and galloped inside. The shield wall joined once more.

"BACK!" Dayne roared.

On command, the shield wall started to fall back. The retreated slowly, one step at a time. Tristayn chanted to keep them in step. The line thinned as men reached the fortress walls. A great war cry rose up as the heathen charged into their formation. The ram slowed the approach and only a few screaming Salvaari reached the lines. They were cut down in moments. More Annorans slipped inside. Dayne's spear drove forward and tore into a Salvaari chest. The enemy surged forward into the dwindling number of defenders. They saw an open gate and that emboldened them against arrow and thrown spear. Dayne glanced over his shoulder. They were mere steps away from the gated courtyard.

"SPEARS!" he bellowed.

As one, the Annoran line stepped back and launched their lances forward. Their attackers fell like flies, giving the defenders space. They turned and sprinted back inside the walls. Knights were ready at the gate. Dayne turned as they began to close. He took up his eagle sword. A tremble ran through his body. He focused on the eagle pommel. He focused on his lineage, biting back the overwhelming pain that arose within him. A Salvaari leapt at the ever-closing gap in the gate with a vicious howl upon his lips. Dayne's sword rose to meet him. Steel tore through flesh as the eagle blade claimed its victim. Dayne threw his weight into the gate as the heathen reached it. The Annoran army charged forward. They planted their shields into the backs of those to their front. Those at the front heaved on the gates. The heathen pushed back. Dayne snarled and he drove forward with his failing strength. A trickle of blood rolled from his lips. Little more than the shield pushed into his back kept him standing. Inch by inch, the gate closed. Dayne lost sight of the screaming enemy and then the doors shuddered shut. The knights were already holding the locking bar ready. They heaved it up and drove it into place. Roars of triumph echoed through Kilgareth. Dayne knew that the enemy would be pulling back now that the gates were closed. He started to walk back through the lines of his men. The sickness grew stronger. He stumbled and fell, his hands and knees catching him as he crashed to the ground. His sword had not stopped ringing on stone when he started to cough up blood.

"PHYSICIAN!" Tristayn shouted.

Dayne barely heard him. The last of the coughs began to die in his chest. With a grimace, he curled a hand into a fist and punched the ground. He took a deep breath to quiet his mind. Rising to his feet, Dayne's fingers found his sword. He shrugged off the hands reaching to aid him. He could see the pity in their eyes.

"I'm fine," Dayne muttered to his men as he saw a maija approach.

"Lord king," the healer called.

Dayne remembered the maija. Her name was Kaira. He gave her a nod before he turned to Tristayn.

"Make sure the tunnels are fully sealed," Dayne said. "I doubt they will attack again this day."

"By your order."

With that, Dayne looked to Kaira and followed her from the square.

Dayne pulled his shirt back on as he sat upon his bed. His ever-constant companion, pain, lingered even hours after the attack. It would never fade; of that he was most certain.

"Take this, if you need," Kaira said as she handed him a small vial. "It will help with the pain."

"And then?"

"In truth, I do not know," she replied.

Dayne stared at the vial for a moment before he held it out to the maija. "Thank you, but I cannot take this," Dayne told her. "I am dying. Give it to someone with a life ahead of them."

"Do not despair. There may yet be a cure."

"You are a good woman, Kaira," Dayne said, "but we both know that I do not have much time. Until the day the Pale Horseman comes for me, until the day he greets me as a friend, I will control my own destiny. My mind is my own and I would keep it as such until my last day."

"I understand." Kaira took the vial back.

The doors to the room opened. Riona and Kassandra walked in.

"Thank you, Kiara, you may go," Dayne told the maija.

"For all the lives you have saved in the defence of this valley … no thanks will ever be enough," she said. "Light of the gods be with you, my king."

Dayne stood to his feet and reached for his red gambeson. He pulled the thick long-sleeve shirt on.

"How are you?" Riona asked.

"Alive," Dayne replied, buckling the straps of the gambeson.

"You push yourself too hard," she told him.

"If there is another way to live, I do not know it," Dayne said.

Riona stared at her stepson. "When you saved Odrysia, you knew that the only way to make certain that its people lived was to use the knights within as a distraction. You knew that only they could hold the heathen at bay long enough for the maija to make the crossing," Riona said. "Yet you would not command those men to sacrifice themselves even though you knew that it would lead to the most favourable outcome."

"All life is sacred," Dayne said simply. "It should not be thrown away so easily. Had there been another way, I would have found it."

"Still you did not sacrifice them. They chose their own fate as all free men should," she said. "You are a good man, Dayne. The people can see it."

Dayne looked her in the eye. "You may not be queen anymore, but you are family," he told her. "You will *always* have a place in Palen-Tor."

She smiled softly at his words.

"Now, please, I need a moment with my sister," he said.

"Yes, my king," Riona replied and with a short bow she left the room.

"You're trembling," Kassie said once her mother had gone.

Dayne looked down at his hand and saw that she was right. "This sickness takes its toll," Dayne replied. "Please, my armour."

Kassie's eyes widened. "Are you sure?" she said. "What happened in the courtyard … You're not strong enough."

"I am strong enough for this," he told her. "Please, Kassie. My armour."

Kassandra hesitated for a moment before she reached for the chainmail. She knew that he was not strong enough to put it on himself. She knew that he may not be strong enough to wear it. Slowly, she helped him into it.

"I am aware that I have been distant and perhaps cold at times," Dayne admitted. "Know that it was not my intent to ever cause you hurt."

Kassie froze and stared into his eyes as she finished pulling her brother's surcoat over his head.

"Dayne–"

"It needs to be said," the king told his sister as she strapped his bracers to his arms. "You are my sister, and I love you with all my heart."

After the bracers came the polished steel greaves. Kassie gathered up Dayne's sword and held it out to him. The king took it.

"You were born on the darkest day of winter. Your blood is like ice, though it does not freeze. It burns like fire. There is a blizzard inside you, a blizzard that can shape this world. Maybe not today, maybe not tomorrow, but soon there will come a time when you are responsible for our people," Dayne said. "A wise leader knows to use his head but to always listen to his heart. Whatever happens in the coming days, my dearest sister, it is you whom I believe is the most important to the future of our people. Never doubt yourself. Never look back, for you are not going that way. The past is gone. The future is yet to be written. It is in your hands." Dayne took her hands into his own. "Craft it. Tender it. Know that I am and have always been proud to call you my sister." He pulled her into a tight hug. He held her. In many ways, this could be his farewell. They both knew it.

"I love you, brother," Kassie said.

"I love you, my dearest sister," he replied and kissed her brow.

There was a knock at the door. Dayne stepped back. No longer was he Dayne, no longer was he a brother. He was a king.

"Enter," he commanded.

General Tristan Martyn entered the chamber. "You sent for me, my king," the general stated.

Dayne gathered up a sealed letter from his desk and handed it to his former mentor. "Take this. Ride to Verena. Hand it to General Ilaros of Aureia alone. Use the tunnels," Dayne commanded. "Tell no one."

"It will be done."

✦ ✦ ✦

FIFTY-SEVEN

Salvaari encampment, Valley of Odrysia

Cleander stared out from the tree line as night fell. His gaze was fixed upon Kilgareth, the very place he had once called home. Memories flooded his mind from a time long gone. When the Salvaari and Mierans had attacked the fortress, he had watched them cut at its walls. He had not fought, nor had the Elarans he watched over. Cleander's hand rose to the amulet that hung at his throat, the last relic that remained from his time in the Order.

"What vexes you?" Elise said as she walked to his side.

"I am going to stay," Cleander replied without so much as giving her a glance.

"What do you mean?"

"I am not going to Valentia," he told her. "My fate is tied to this place. It always has been. When our army attacks, I will join it."

"No," Elise said. "No, you cannot leave."

"I am not," Cleander said as he at last turned to her. "But you must. Take your friends. Lead them to Valentia. You will all be safe there."

"Not without you."

"Elise, you must do this," Cleander told her.

Elise shook her head. "I do not understand," she said. "Why are you staying? What is it about this place that has taken your mind? You once told me that your name is Markus Harvarder. You are a great warrior. You bear that amulet. In my heart, I know the answer, but I must ask it of you. You were once a knight, weren't you?"

Cleander sighed and slowly nodded. "It is true," he admitted. "I once bore steel for the Order of Kil'kara. I once devoted my life to serving the Twins."

"And now you wish to turn that same steel upon them?" Elise said. "What happened that a man as loyal as you broke every vow he once swore?"

"There are things in this world that go beyond understanding," Cleander said. "Things that go beyond loyalty and brotherhood. You would not understand. Something happened a long time ago that must be corrected."

Elise placed a hand on his arm. "You say that I would not understand," she said, looking up at him. "Then help me to understand."

The memories surged to the surface as if he was waking from a dream. He had not even told Mellisanthi, his closest friend, those memories that lay in the dark. "No," he told her.

Elise ground her teeth. "It strikes me that though we have travelled together for hundreds of miles, though we have stood side by side as the world burned around us, though you know my story and all of its demons, I do not know anything about you," she said. "Who are you?"

"It doesn't matter."

"So everything we have been through counts for nothing?" she shot back. "I know that look in your eyes, Markus. We are much alike, you and I, even if you deny it. Aye, I have not shed blood, yet I understand your heart. For two years, I hunted those men who took my home and murdered my parents. That pursuit cost me my dearest friend and what remained of my family. What I see in your eyes once haunted my own. When my parents were murdered, when my friend, my aunt, my uncle were murdered … I saw the world through your eyes. The rage, the vengeance … and it just wants to see the world burn. We are much the same, you and I. Whether you admit it or not, you know that."

She was right. Cleander knew it. He had blood on his hands, and she did not, but their paths were alike in more ways than they differed.

"Alright," Cleander said after a moment. "This battle into which I am about to walk may be my last. I have fought the Order before, but this is different. I suppose that if I am to die in the days to come, then someone should at last know my story."

"Then speak it," Elise said. "You will find no judgement here."

"It is true," Cleander said. "I was once a knight. I served the Annoran crown long before I rode east to join my brothers in Kilgareth. When I first arrived, I was young, naïve. I had no cause, no purpose. The Order gave me one. In time, I was apprenticed to one of the greatest warriors that the Order had ever seen. Edwin Vuliir was his name. There were two of us whom he was to train. We became closer than brothers, Corvo Alaine and I. When Edwin fell in battle, everything changed. His position as Sword of Kil'kara had to be filled. Rumours and dreams descended upon the Citadel. Whispers about a relic forged by the gods had appeared far to the west, buried deep beneath Azaria's rose."

"A relic of the gods?" Elise raised her eyebrows.

"I do not lie. Four of us rode out. Lysandra, who had heard of the relic, the battlemaster Alarik, Corvo and myself. When we reached the tower and travelled into the tunnels and caverns beneath, we found it. A staff bursting with power. When it was taken, the cavern collapsed, and the tower fell. Untold hundreds of people died …" Cleander trailed off as he remembered it all. "I saw them when we walked out of the cavern. Broken bodies crushed beneath an avalanche of earth and stone. One of the most holy and scared sites of our faith lay in ruins all around. The very air we breathed was filled with dust and blood and screams. The people cried out for mercy but there was none. The staff that I held within my grasp had enacted this dark fate upon all those innocent people. I cast it into the ravine. Alarik and Corvo, my brothers, said that this calamity could not have been caused by the staff. They could not believe that it could have been capable of such slaughter. They were wrong.

"When confronted, I knew that they would search for the staff. I knew that they would continue the search for other relics so that they could make sense of it all. I could not convince them otherwise. I broke my oath so that I may save thousands. I fought my brothers atop the broken ruins of the tower. I knew that if they defeated me, they would find the staff … and if they found the staff, they would find more relics. More artefacts. How many more would die for their zeal?

"I walked off the cliff that they had cornered me against. I fell down the mountainside and into the river below. The waters kept me alive, but I was badly hurt. I stumbled across the staff. The next thing I remember is waking up to Lysandra. She tendered to me, whereas Corvo and Alarik believed that I was dead. She kept me alive, while they believed the staff lost. She told me that she believed that the relics were not of the gods and that they should remain hidden from the hands of men.

"When I regained my strength, I made for Elara and took a new name. I became Cleander. I joined the gangs so that I may disappear into the shadows. Lysandra fed me information over the years. Any rumour and whisper and tale or song of a relic, she sent word to me. I fought the Order for five years to stop them claiming that which they sought. Dozens of those who were once my brothers were slain at my hand. I had no choice. I had no choice."

Cleander knew that Elise could see the pain in his eyes. She could see the sorrow in the clenching of his fist around his sword and the stiffness of his jaw.

"Then why now?" Elise asked. "Why do you choose to step out from the shadows now?"

"The most important thing that every man should know is what he would die for," Cleander replied sadly. "I will gladly give my life so that no more innocents are killed by those artefacts. There are few who know how to listen for the whispers that speak of the relics. Evalio Delrovira is dead. Bavarian is dead. Matias was slain by my own hand. Lysandra has no desire to find them. That leaves only two. Alarik Sindra … and Corvo Alaine. I must secrete myself beyond those walls. I must find them, and I must stop their hunt for these things that they do not understand. I will kill every man who defends them if I must."

Elise shook her head with a snort. "Killing," she muttered. "If killing is your only talent, then I say you are cursed."

"What would you have me do?" Cleander countered. "Let them live so that they may lay waste to this world with their zealous greed?"

"No!" Elise snapped. "I would have *you* live!"

"If you live a life knowing that you could have done more but chose not to, then that is a life not worth living," Cleander said, gesturing down towards the camp. "If the army attacks the fortress, they will die. All of them. They will not get in. That is why I must help them. I must show them the way."

"No, you are helping them for your own selfish reasons," Elise told him bitterly.

"So says the woman who spent years fighting in the darkness against oppression so that she may have her chance at revenge," Cleander said.

"How dare you!"

"You and I are not the polite people from stories and poems," Cleander continued. "You could not spend a life in luxury pontificating with nobles any more than I could. Yes, perhaps you do know my heart, but I also know yours. Elise Delfeyre, the

Nightingale – that is who you are. You may hide it behind words, you may have hidden it so well that you can barely see it, but I can. I have illuminated it. You cannot look me in the eye and tell me that you took no enjoyment when you masqueraded as the Nightingale."

"I did not–"

"Yes, you did," Cleander interrupted. "You know it to be true. I know that you are trying to hide it. I know that you are not trying to hide from your past or run from it; you are trying to destroy it. Yet who you want to be doesn't always win."

Elise's hand slowly fell to her kukri. There was a war in her eyes that only Cleander could see. She drew the steel and watched as the silver moonlight caressed its edge.

"This blade has been with my family for over one hundred and sixty years," Elise murmured. "It was taken from Alekos Gaedhela himself by my ancestor. The first Delfeyre. The man who liberated his city from Delion tyranny by killing the Chimera's son. We are separated by time, yet there are days when I feel most strongly connected to him. Liberty or death … Those words forged my family. They burn within me even now. You are right. You are right about me. I did take joy from what I did. Taking from those men who wrought so much pain upon those beneath them … it gave life meaning. It helped me to make sense of the world. And now …"

"Now you're a soldier without a cause."

Elise nodded and sheathed her blade. She reached for her satchel and opened the flap. "Perhaps I have found one," she said. "Perhaps I am the Nightingale." She pulled forth a mask of finely embellished silver. Her mother's circus mask. "This belonged to my mother," Elise explained. "She died fighting for the liberty of my people just as you now do. I will come with you."

✦ ✦ ✦

"So, I will ask each of you again." Henghis' voice echoed through the clearing. "How do we take such a fortress from our enemy? We have tested their defences, and they have shown their strength. They cannot use the mountain paths again for they are sealed, and that gives us an advantage."

Lukas the One-Eye flicked his gaze around the gathered leaders. Salvaari chieftains stood alongside Mieran lords. Kitara, Galadayne and a number of the sellswords were with them. The sight would have given any believer of the Twins pause.

"I have something to say." Lukas spoke up.

"Speak then, Whisperer," Henghis bid him.

Lukas hobbled into the centre of the group. He was not cowed by them. He did not fear them.

"If we truly believe that we saw the full strength of the west when we tried their defences, then we are fools, all of us," he said. "Dayne would not give away so much. He is a great warrior and an even mightier commander. We all know this. We cannot outsmart him in the field. He has thought of every attack we might make before we have even made it. If we are to win this war, then there is only one name with which we need concern ourselves. The name of a man who is not lord or king, knight or warrior. That is their cardinal, Aleksander."

"How do you mean?" King Zoran asked. "Why should we fear a holy man?"

"I did not say that we should fear him, King Zoran," Lukas replied. "We lost near a thousand men yesterday. Even if we breach their walls, then they can simply slip back to their Citadel and hold out indefinitely. If they reach their keep, then we cannot win. We do not have the numbers to overcome both their army and its leader. We must do something unexpected. Something bold. If we capture their holy leader, then we can force a surrender."

"Why would they so easily surrender?" Chief Etain asked.

"Because every man and woman inside those walls has faith,"

Lukas said. "There is not a soul inside Kilgareth who would not give their life for the cardinal. They would put down their steel as soon as we got near to him. If he fell to us, then so too would their resolve."

"Say that you are right," Henghis started. "Say that they would give up if we captured their holy leader. How would we take him? No doubt he will be hidden within their innermost sanctum."

"We would need to divide," Lukas replied. "While our army attacks the main gate, a smaller group would infiltrate the southern gate."

"How?" Zoran asked. "The diversion would indeed draw their forces to the main gate, but how would our people slip over the wall and past their sentries unnoticed?"

"Leave that to me," a woman's voice called out.

All eyes turned as a pair of the Elaran contingent approached. The Annoran warrior, Cleander, alongside the younger woman, Elise. Lukas knew little enough about either of them.

"What would you know about it?" one of the Mierans called.

"You watch your tongue, sweetheart," Elise replied. "I spent years fighting in the shadows against the magister of my city. You are in the company of the Nightingale."

"I have heard that story," Lukas told her. His spoke with part disbelief and part admiration. "I heard that you led the attack upon the palace. Is that true?"

"It is," she told all assembled before turning to her companion. "This is Cleander. He was once a knight of Annora … and after that, he served with the Order of Kil'kara."

Weapons rang as Salvaari and Mieran alike drew steel. Cries of 'Traitor!' filled the air.

"Kill him," Balor of the Sagailean cried, striding towards Cleander with an axe in hand.

"No!" Kitara said and stepped between them. "He is here with us in this moment. He knew the risk in telling us what he once was. I bear no love for the Order, yet he would not be fool enough to admit it here knowing what it meant."

"You wish to attack the walls," Cleander said loudly. "Yet if you do that, you will die – all of you. I can you show another path."

"What path might that be?" Etain asked.

"Those tunnels from which you were attacked are not the only ones," Cleander explained. "There is a labyrinth that stretches underground for miles all the way to Verena itself. All the way into the mountains. You cannot starve them out. You cannot defeat them in battle. What One-Eye says is true. The only way to win this fight is to take Aleksander. I can show you how to navigate those tunnels."

"If what he says is true," Morrigana of the Belcar tribe started, "then could he not free those of our people trapped within the stone fortress?"

"Hundreds of my people are caged within the Citadel," Henghis said as he looked to Cleander. "If you lead us in and free those trapped, then we could take the fortress from within."

"That is if he is not lying," Zoran growled.

"I am not," Cleander countered.

"He speaks the truth. Do you not see it in his eyes, hear it in his words?" Luana Marquez told them all. "This is a man who dreams of vengeance. For that is true, is it not? The Order wronged you?"

Cleander gave a single nod.

"I trust the man," Luana said. "We have no other choice. There is no other way."

"I do not trust him," Zoran muttered.

"Nor me," Balor echoed.

"To prove his words, I will follow him with my own men," Kitara said. "If he lies, then we lose a company of sellswords, and with my last breath, I will take his life. If he speaks true, we may yet herald victory."

"You would risk your life in trusting a man none of us know, a man who did not fight this day, and who has revealed himself to have been of the Order against which we fight?" Henghis said.

"Lukas is right," Galadayne replied. "I have fought with and against those we now face. I know how strong their defences are. We cannot defeat them with strength of arm, not while they sit behind those walls. This may be our only chance."

"And you would risk all?" Lukas asked him.

"Aye, I would," Galadayne replied before he turned to Cleander. "I will follow you. Make no mistake that if you betray us, then I will kill you."

Cleander held out a hand. Galadayne took it.

"Together then," Cleander said, "we find our fate."

"The prisoners will be freed," Kitara declared. "We will forge an army behind their walls."

"And the cardinal will be captured," Cleander swore.

Lukas took a step towards Elise. "We will still need a diversion," he said.

Elise nodded and glanced at King Zoran. "If I can get the gate open, can you take the fortress?" she asked.

"Or die trying," Zoran vowed.

✦ ✦ ✦

"Kitara and her people plan to enter the labyrinth," Sakkar told his wife as they sat by the fire.

"And you fear what will happen in that maze of stone?"

"I do," Sakkar admitted. "We do not know if that man Cleander is angel or devil. He could be leading all those who follow him to their deaths."

"And he could be leading them to victory."

"Aye," Sakkar replied. "He could be."

Senya brushed her husband's cheek softly. "And what of your friend?" she asked. "What of Lukas?"

"I fear for him," Sakkar whispered. "It is true that he has become a great leader, yet with that witch looking on, his soul has blackened."

"You have decided," Senya said. "I can see that look in your eyes."

"The time for words is done," Sakkar replied. "I know what I must do."

"Whatever path you follow, I am with you. Now until the end of time."

Sakkar kissed her deeply. Her cheek was soft to his touch, her eyes as beautiful as they had always been. "That knowledge gives me hope, my dearest love," Sakkar told her. "We are to wait for a cloud-covered night, and then we attack."

That night the moon shone brightly, and all thoughts of fighting were far removed. Soldiers laughed and joked; lovers shared tender moments. When the sun rose, Sakkar found Elise. She sat alone and her blue gaze washed across the unveiled blades of half a dozen knives. From what Sakkar had been told, the Nightingale had great skill with blades. Beside her, Cleander mixed some kind of brew in a small wooden bowl. Sabra cried high above and then with a flapping of wings, descended to land on her master's outstretched arm.

Elise glanced up as the Larissan approached.

"You will need me as well," Sakkar Alsahra told Elise. "I am good with the bow."

"So be it."

✦ ✦ ✦

FIFTY-EIGHT

Kilgareth, Valley of Odrysia

"The attack was merely to test our defences," Sir Corvo said to those who stood with him in the chambers of the Circle. "Their defeat was merely a delay. They are not beaten yet."

The congregation was formed of leading members of the Order. With the death of Sir William Peyene upon the plains of Odrysia, Sir Mortimier had assumed his role. Two other veteran knights joined them. An Aureian named Ryseige led those of the Order who had marched from his homeland, while Sir Aderas was the southern Sword of Kil'kara.

"They wait outside our city, laughing as they bombard our walls and the township beyond," Mortimier said. "All those who cannot fight have been brought to the Citadel where they will be safe. Teams patrol the city to put out any flames caused by their assault."

"They ignore Odrysia as they know that there is no danger from such a small number of militia," Corvo added. "Their fight is with us, not the people of the valley."

"Now they come for us, and our leaders are dying like flies," Ryseige said. "In only a few months, we have lost many great knights." He looked to Mortimier. "Your predecessor, the Warden, Sir William Peyene. Grand Master Bavarian whose mantle I now bear. Now it seems that even from behind these walls Sir Alarik has gone missing."

"And they are not alone, Master Ryseige," Corvo added. "For we cannot forget those who fell not so long before this war began. Sir Matias Valenquez, and the grand masters Amaris Delodrysia and Evalio Delrovira. These cannot all be mere coincidences. We know that the ruskalan stalk us in the dark. Watching us … waiting to strike. They wish us to believe that we are in the end times, yet we are not. When we win this war, we will usher in a golden age of liberty. Of freedom. Of faith."

"In times like these, we must look to our oath and to our flag." Sir Aderas gestured towards the banner of the Order that hung along the chamber wall. The white sun embraced by a crescent moon atop a sky of midnight blue. Aderas stared at the sacred image as he continued. "Our flag does not fly because of a gentle breeze or billowing storm that moves it. It flies with the breath of each knight, of each maija, of every member of this Order who has given their life to defend it."

"That is true, Sir Aderas," Mortimer said. "And that wind cast from the breaths of our brothers who now walk in immortality grants us strength over all those who would see this Order fall."

The door to the Circle chamber opened and Lysandra walked in. Her robe was stained with dirt and blood, just as the garb of the knights was. While they had fought on the battlefield, she had tended to the wounded. There was deep sorrow in her eyes.

"My lady," Master Ryseige greeted her.

She gave the southern master a nod before she approached Corvo.

"What is it, my lady?" Corvo asked. "There is a darkness in your eyes."

Lysandra held out her right hand and opened her fist. There, lying in the palm of her hand, was a ring bearing the symbol of their order.

"The battlemaster's ring," Corvo breathed as he took the jewel. "Alarik is dead."

"He is," Lysandra said simply.

"How?" Mortimier asked, a note of sorrow gripping his voice. "He was not seen upon the field of battle."

"He died by my hand," Lysandra said.

"You killed him?" Corvo asked. The biting rage that had once gripped him as Sword sparked a flame in his breast.

"Not without cause," Lysandra told them. "You must believe that."

"Tell us what happened," Master Ryseige replied.

"Alarik was my friend, my brother," Lysandra started. "You all know this. You must believe that. He was my brother until the day I found out that he killed Amaris."

Surprise echoed through the small chamber. Eyes widened. Faces paled.

"How did you come by this?" Mortimier asked.

"When I examined Amaris' body, I knew that it was no mere sickness that had claimed his life. It was poison," Lysandra said. "And so I tasked the boy Kyler with uncovering the truth when he and Alarik rode for Elara. It was on this journey that, when confronted, Alarik admitted his crime. Upon their return, the boy told me of his master's sin, though it broke his heart to do so. I believe that Alarik found out about Kyler's betrayal and in that moment decided to turn him."

"What do you mean?" Corvo asked.

"Alarik bore ruskalan blood," Lysandra lied.

"That cannot be," Corvo muttered.

"And yet it is so. I discovered as much when I confronted him before the battle. I'll admit I had my suspicions, which is why I secreted a concoction into his wine that would slow him in case I was right. That poison saved my life. Alarik tried to attack me. I had no choice but to kill him."

"Why do you only come forward now?" Ryseige asked.

"To learn that a friend, a brother, a mentor to so many within these walls had betrayed them and been killed for that betrayal while going into battle … I can think of nothing worse," Lysandra replied. "To learn that he was ruskalan, can you imagine what that would do to the men? One who was trusted above all others wished to see them dead and our order fall. Suspicion and fear would creep out of the darkness. Brother would turn on brother."

"Alarik was the traitor," Mortimier breathed. "The one we've been looking for."

"He was," Lysandra said sadly. "I am looking into Kyler's affliction. I believe that there may be a remedy to cure what both Elena and Alarik did to him. When he is healed, Kyler will tell you what he knows, for it was he who first discovered his mentor's treachery."

"We cannot tell the Order," Corvo said thoughtfully. "Not yet at least. We cannot have their attention divided with the enemy at our gates. There being a traitor hurts the Order but knowing that the betrayal came from Alarik would only make that betrayal worse. I thank the gods that you uncovered the truth before this battle was over or we may have been undone. We must be patient. The heathen must be dealt with and then we must track down the ruskalan ourselves."

✦ ✦ ✦

Lukas found Cleander with the Elaran girl Elise. The former knight handed the girl a vial that was no bigger than a finger. Lukas watched Cleander place a hand on Elise's shoulder and murmur something to her. Cleander took her hand and curled it into a fist around the vial as he spoke. The girl nodded and secreted the vial in her satchel. Elise glanced towards Lukas and then was gone, swallowed by the forest.

"What is it that you want, Lukas Raynor?" Cleander called.

"You know the secrets of Kilgareth better than anyone," Lukas replied as he approached the former knight. He placed his hands atop his crutch as he looked Cleander in the eye. "Tell me about its streets and walls."

"To what end?"

"Victory," Lukas told him. "When we breach those walls, King Zoran will lead the way, and I will lead my warband in behind him. I do not wish to attack directly. Anticipation. Possibility. These are the downfalls of many men. I try to see what lies ahead, rather than what is before my eyes. Tell me about any weakness in the city that we could use to gain advantage."

"This is not just about victory, is it?" Cleander asked. "I can see the ember smouldering in your eye."

"I will not deny that I am an ambitious man," Lukas replied. "You can see that, but do not be so blind as to believe that this fight may go as perfectly as we have planned. What if you fail and the cardinal escapes? We would be trapped inside those walls with an enemy stronger than us, an enemy that knows that city better than us, an enemy that would *never* surrender. To win this battle, we may need another strategy. That is why I am here. I have a strategy, but I need the knowledge inside your head to make it happen."

Cleander ran his eyes over the crippled outlaw prince before him. He felt no pity, only curiosity. How had a man banished from his own country and position survived a crippled knee and the loss of an eye? How had he not only survived but thrived amongst the Salvaari? Lukas could see the questions in Cleander's gaze.

"Alright," Cleander said. "I will help you."

The sun began to set, and flames blazed to life in the Salvaari camp. They were all prepared for whatever the night would bring. If a cloudy sky arose, then battle would rise with it. They all knew that.

Lukas stared up at the heavens as the sun began to fall behind the thick clouds that were already forming. In his heart he knew that his destiny would be revealed this night. In victory or defeat.

His gaze turned to Maevin who sat at his side. They were alone save the blaze of the fire and the whispering of the wind. He looked into her emerald gaze. Her eyes burned with evergreen flame as they caught the light of the fire. Beautiful, fierce, honest and as passionate as she had always been.

"When I was a girl," Maevin started, "whenever I was afraid, my mother would run her fingers through my hair." Maevin moved her fingers through the air slowly as she spoke, as if she was reliving the memory. "And she would sing. Not of great victories or noble deeds, but of home. Of trees evergreen and rivers as clear as the summer sky. When she died, I cried for an entire day and then never cried again. I was alone ... I have been alone for a long time, but I have not been afraid. Not until now. I am not alone anymore but now I am afraid. I am afraid."

Lukas stared at Maevin. He could see tears in her eyes and hear the tremble in her voice. He reached out a hand and pushed a strand of dark hair away from her cheek.

"What do you fear?" he asked softly.

Lukas could see how the words left unsaid tormented her. He could see it in the tenseness of her jaw. He could see it in the way she bit her lip as if to stop them from falling from her tongue. At last, she looked up into his eye.

"I am afraid of the words in here," Maevin said as she took his hand and placed it over her heart.

Lukas froze as she gazed at him. His heart raced as he stared deep into those burning emerald eyes. Spirits, she was beautiful. Lukas ran his hand through her hair and pressed his head into hers. He closed his eye.

"Say it," he murmured.

She said nothing though the words were in her eyes.

"Say it," Lukas said again.

"I love you."

Maevin's words ignited a fire in his chest.

"I love you," he told her as he echoed the words burning in his soul.

Maevin nuzzled Lukas and then kissed him deeply. Her lips sang the words that they had last spoken.

✦ ✦ ✦

Kitara stared up at the heavens as darkness began to blanket the earth. Her back was pressed into a thick oak as she looked skyward. Dense clouds covered the moon. The only light came from the fires and torches that the Salvaari had brought to life. The camp had grown quiet, for all knew what this meant. Only one voice could be heard. A man's voice rose in song. The Salvaari words echoed beneath the trees and across the plains. Kitara held Aeryn tight in her arms where they sat.

"Tanris paints the world in blackness," Aeryn said quietly. "He shows us the way."

"And so he does," Kitara replied.

Aeryn turned and planted a kiss upon Kitara's lips before they rose to their feet. The mercenary company arose all around them. No words had been spoken, no orders given, yet the sky said more than any order could. Kitara strapped on her sword belt and gathered up her helmet. Aeryn slung her quiver across her back and tested the draw of her bow. Galadayne and the men prepared. Weapons were sheathed and prayers muttered. The Salvaari song haunted the wind as three Aedei warriors approached on horseback. Aeryn's father, Eivor, led them. He dropped from his saddle and strode towards them. He clasped arms with his daughter and pressed his head into hers. They rode into battle yet not together. Aeryn's path would take her deep into the mountains. Her father's road led to the walls. They might never see each other again and both knew it. They exchanged quiet words. Eivor clasped Kitara's arm and then nodded to Galadayne before he mounted his horse and set off to join his people. It was then that Cleander arrived.

"Are you ready?" he asked.

Kitara nodded. "This ends tonight," she told him.

A figure emerged from the blackness. Hands went to swords and gasps fled lips before the shadow lowered its hood and pulled free its scarf and mask. A woman's deep blue eyes appeared. She did not come as Elise Delfeyre. She came as the Nightingale. A rope was wrapped around her from shoulder to hip.

"Did it work?" Cleander asked.

Elise nodded. The former knight pulled one of the silver canisters from his belt and handed it to the girl.

"You may need this," Cleander told her.

"Thank you," Elise replied sincerely.

"I will see you in Kilgareth."

Elise took her friend's arm. She met his eyes and then pulled him into an embrace. The Salvaari song rang true as the mercenaries led by Cleander mounted their horses and made for the east. Elise was joined by Sakkar and a company of Salvaari archers, warriors chosen by Henghis himself. They all bore silver eyes. The last notes of the Salvaari song faded.

✦ ✦ ✦

Káli warriors garbed in dark clothing and faces awash with black surrounded their leader. Two hundred of the tribe's finest had been joined by many of their brethren as Lukas the One-Eye strode through their midst. Aelida and Maevin were by his side. Eirian, who led in Vaylin's stead, watched as Lukas jammed his crutch into the earth.

"You know who I am," he began in their tongue. "I was Lukas Raynor, son of Dorian. I was Lukas Raynor, Prince of Annora. I was not born of Salvaar. I was not born beneath those sacred trees.

You did not know me then, but you know me now. I am Lukas the One-Eye. The ring that I bear upon my wrist" – Lukas held his arm to the heavens – "belonged to Vaylin. She gave it to me because she believed that I could help her people, but I have come to understand an altogether new truth. I *am* Salvaari. I can feel the forest in my blood. I can hear the spirits in the breath of the wind and the thunder in the skies. You know me. I am the Whisperer. I am the Black Eagle. I have given my life to the Káli. You know me!"

With each word the passion in his voice grew. With each word he took those watching by the heart.

"This night we lay claim to what we are owed!" Lukas cried. "This night we show them that the gift of freedom is ours by right! If this is to be our fate, then so be it, but first we will drench the spirits in western blood! Are we afraid of death? NO!"

The Káli cried and shouted as he spoke. They roared and pounded fist upon chest.

"I would be glad to die knowing that Tanris awaits!" Lukas bellowed as he walked among his people. "The western plague has spread across the world and now it encroaches upon our home. They thought that we would be meekly swept aside, yet they forgot that we are Káli! They forgot that we *long* for the Veil! Come with my and take this city! Come with me and conquer our enemy! Come with me and reach for the Veil!"

Salvaari roars echoed through the forest.

✦ ✦ ✦

FIFTY-NINE

Aureian Coast, The Lupentine Sea

All eyes stared out across the open sea as the Aglaeca, captained by Garrett Laven, led the army of raiders, pirates and refugees towards the Oridassey and the Ravenheart. While those around him cheered and cried out as their allies and friends numbering thousands approached, Cillian Teague watched in silence. The enemy that they were to face in the days to come was a mighty opponent. All of the planning, all of the strategy … it may not be enough, and he knew it, for he had once served with the same men he was about to kill. The Aglaeca ran alongside the Oridassey. Ropes were thrown between the two pirate vessels and planks were heaved over the railings to create walkways. Garrett Laven and a pair of his raiders crossed onto Teague's ship. The two captains embraced. They weren't merely dressed in the garb of seafaring brigands; now the unmistakable silver glint of chainmail adorned their bodies. Now they wore armour beneath their coats and sashes.

"It's good to have you back," Garrett told Teague.

"How many are you?" Teague asked, leading his friend into the captain's cabin.

"Some thousands. All of our warriors, all those of the Valkir and Elaran refugees … more," Garrett said as he shut the door behind them. "Everyone knows how vital this fight is. They all know what it means and so they have come. They may not be trained with sword or axe, but they can still fight. Why should they not have a say in their future?"

"We decide our fate," Teague told him. "Not the league, not the empire … not even the gods themselves."

A smirk crossed Garrett's lips. "A belief that I did not always share," he said.

"A thing well known to me," Teague replied.

"Yet you have proven it so time and time again. A thousand times you should have fallen and a thousand times you should have taken our world with you. You are a difficult man to kill."

"I have survived storms, great navies, a magister, an emperor," Teague said, "and the sirens' song. Everyone has a purpose. I refuse to die until mine is complete."

"And what is that purpose?" Garrett asked. "You have often spoken of this sirens' song. Among our people, it has grown into myth and legend, yet none know the truth, do they?"

"Only one," Teague told him.

"Marquez?"

Teague gave his friend a nod.

"I see," Garrett said simply.

"The empire and I … we have vexed each other for many years, and both suffered great loss at the other's hands," Teague told him. "When I abandoned the silver crown and the idea to create a haven where everyone was equal was forged, I became an oath breaker. Building that nation deep in the Sacasian has been my greatest love, yet it is not what tore me from the empire. I remember thirty years ago as if it were yesterday. I remember the cave and the sirens within. I remember their song. I remember their beauty and the kiss that she with the dark hair granted me. Yet it is not the music nor the taste of her lips that has drawn my mind. It is the words uttered in the shadows. Words that set me upon this path. They told me that I would stand against the empire in victory or defeat. They told me that if I failed, then the world would fall. Whether true or not, those words are the reason I am here in this moment. Perhaps I will live to see this new world that they spoke of, or perhaps I will die in battle. I do not care, but I will fight."

"Then we fight," Garrett said, "and whether the sirens' words were magic or not, they brought us together. That has to count for something."

"Together then we at last see this journey to its end."

"It was always fated to be so," Garrett replied.

Teague held out a hand and his friend took it.

"Go now," Teague said. "Our strategy is in motion. There is nothing else to be done but wait. See to your crew. It has been an honour to fight by your side."

"The honour was mine."

✦ ✦ ✦

Erik stood at the prow of the Ravenheart as the first of the sun's rays emerged over the horizon. His eyes were fixed to where he knew the merchant ship to be lying in wait. When the imperial fleet was spotted in the channel, a signal would be given, and Erik would be ready. He held the raven amulet in his hand as he stared across the sea. His thumb brushed across the perfectly carved wood. The medallion was crafted by his mother and had passed from her to his father to Astrid and then to him. One by one, he had seen each member of his family die. One by one, he had seen his friends and companions taken.

"What is on your mind?" Jorun Bloodaxe asked as he moved to his friend's side.

Erik glanced at the captain of the Harpy. "Memories," Erik replied, looking at the raven amulet. "Those who survived and those who did not. My mother died to a plague. My father, Raol, and Hélla were killed by Magnus' schemes. Astrid and Laerke fell to the will of the empire. I would not see their passing go unremembered. I am here to honour their memory."

"Then today we make famous these waters in the Lupentine," Jorun replied. "Today we fight, so that no other can know that pain."

"Astrid wanted the freedom to choose," Erik said. "She believed that every man, every woman had the right to live without the fear of war or death. She believed that everyone had the right to live in peace. She believed that everyone had the right to follow their heart. This ship was her ship. Her heart. She planned to sail south, further than even Cillian Teague sailed. She wanted to see what was out there in those uncharted waters. She wanted to be the first one to see it all. That was her dream."

"And after this, when all is said and done, what will you do?" Jorun asked. "Who will you be?"

"I'm not sure," Erik replied honestly. "But one day I will sail south. One day I will fulfil Astrid's dream."

"You would have a grand tale to tell."

"Aye." Erik chuckled. "That I would. You will have to come with me."

"I will," Jorun said and clapped his friend on the shoulder.

For a moment they both stared out across the waves.

"The imperial fleet will be nearing," Jorun said quietly. "I had best get back to my ship."

"Farewell, my brother." Erik extended his arm.

Jorun took it and held tightly.

"I will see you again," Erik said. "In this life or the next."

"May it be in victory," Jorun replied.

Then he was gone. The Ravenheart and the Harpy parted as the ropes were withdrawn and planks returned. Erik made his way below the deck and to the brig. Lord Lionidir Wylan and his wife sat within the confines of a small cell. The spy stood as Erik approached.

"King Erik," Lord Wylan greeted him.

"If your words are true, then within a day, perhaps within hours, we will meet your people in open battle," Erik told them. "You will remain here until this battle is over. In victory or loss, know that you will be safe. If we defeat your people, you will be freed, yet no mention of your name will ever be uttered by any who calls themselves Valkir. You will be forgotten to history and be able to return home without fear of persecution or death. If your people triumph over us, then they will find you as prisoners taken captive when you rode to the aid of a fellow Aureian nobleman. When questioned, you will tell your liberators that this fleet was the beginnings of an invasion, that we barbarians sought to take your land and cities while the silver army tangled with the pagans in the north. You were to be kept as hostages."

Lord Wylan watched Erik curiously. "In Aureia, the tale spread that you were no more than a warrior who murdered a jarl, took his city and slaughtered an unarmed delegation," Lord Wylan said. "I see now that you are far more than a common warrior. It has become abundantly clear to me that your people are not so very different from my own."

"We are all the same, are we not?" Erik replied. "Flesh, blood and bone. Nothing more. We all seek to make our way against the will of kings, the will of politicians and the will of gods. Fate has made our people enemies, but perhaps it will not always be so. I may never speak with you again, Lord Wylan, so I thank you for what you have done."

"Farewell, Erik," Wylan said. "Though I pray for my people's victory, I hope that you live to fight another day."

"Lord. Lady." Erik nodded to the Aureians in turn before he made his way back above.

Erik glanced across the deck of his ship. His people, his crew, his friends were quiet. Some made ready their weapons. Some prayed to their god. Others talked in hushed tones to their companions or lovers. All felt the weight of the battle to come. They knew in their hearts that many would not live to see nightfall.

"My lord," a woman's voice called out.

Erik turned to see her approach. Her features matched her Elaran voice. Her blonde hair had been braided to keep it from her eyes in battle. She wore a shirt of chainmail alongside bracers and greaves of steel. A sidesword hung at her left hip and a long knife adorned her right. The blue sash belonging to Cillian Teague's crew was wrapped tightly around her waist. Even without the rings that adorned her ears and fingers, that would have been enough to tell that she was one of the pirates.

"You stayed," Erik stated as Halitreia approached.

"I did," she replied, joining him. "Which ship I sail with, which crew I sail with … which captain I sail with: that is my choice. I choose you."

"Halitreia, why did you come?"

"For the same reason you did," she replied. "We are fighters, you and I. When I was born, I was abandoned as Elaran slum filth. I was sold as a slave. When I was rescued from that hell, I made a home in Ephelion. Yet once again they came for me. My home burned; my people slaughtered on the beaches. Once, I had neither the strength nor the means to stand against those who came for me. I do now. I am sick of running and I am tired of hiding."

"And as you once said, now that you have a choice, you will kill anyone who tries to take it from you."

"Or die in the attempt," Halitreia said. "It is all a free woman can do."

"Whatever happens this day, it happens because we choose it," Erik told her.

His fingers found the raven amulet at his throat. The symbol of his family. He pulled it free and lowered the medallion around Halitreia's neck.

"Hold the raven," Erik told her. "Hold it steady."

Her eyes did not leave his as he took her hand and placed it over his chest.

"Know that you have my heart," Erik said as he stared into those amber eyes.

He kissed her on the lips, pressed his head to hers and then was gone. There were words that needed to be spoken and preparations that were needed to be made. His gaze swept the deck as he crossed it. Fargrim rested by the wheel at the helm and Mayrun stood by his side, for they were as close as family. Nenrir sat upon the steps that led to the helm. He sharpened arrows and one by one placed them in his quiver. Erik didn't say a word as he crossed the deck towards his cabin. He was resolved that he would give his life so that they could live to see another day. He had led them here, and whether they rose in victory or became one with the sea, that was on him.

Nenrir rose to his feet and strode in front of his friend and king. He took the king's arm and placed his forehead against Erik's. He said no words, for there were none to say. His meaning was clear in his eyes. Nenrir intended to die today. He wished to join his brother in the golden halls of the Sea-Father.

Erik clapped his friend on the shoulder as he stepped past and reached for the cabin door. It closed at his back, and he approached his desk. The carved figure of the Sea-Father stood atop the wood. Erik knelt before the idol and closed his eyes.

"Sea-Father. Lord of Skûra. Lord of Ocean and Sea. Hear me now, for I am in such need of your mercy. Not for myself, but for my people. Deliver them from the trial ahead and I will repay this debt with whatever sacrifice you desire. If you decide that that sacrifice is my life, given so that my people may live, then I will gladly make that pact." Erik reached out and touched the idol as he spoke. "They say that the Farrin line is descended from your own mighty blood. They say that your strength guides my hand. Accept this covenant, great lord, and I will shower you in a sea of Aureian blood. That is my oath."

Erik's eyes opened and for a moment he thought he could see a tear spill down the face of the carving. The king took a deep breath as he rose to his feet. He placed his crown upon the table and took up his shield. Erik ran a hand across the raven symbol. He pictured his mother. He pictured his father. He pictured Astrid. All had been taken so cruelly from this world. All had been stronger than the greatest of dragons.

"May the spirits of my ancestors envelop me," Erik murmured as he slung the shield across his shoulders.

He could feel his family with him as he took up his helmet and walked out onto the deck. The cool wind caressed his cheeks and ran through his hair. It carried the taste of the sea to his lips. The warmth of the dawn rays brushed against his skin. Fire danced along armour and sword as the light shone upon them. All eyes went to Erik as he walked among them. He did not walk like a common man, a sailor or a warrior. He did not walk like a bloodsworn or a jarl. He walked like a king. His shoulders were steady and his stride firm. His people watched in awe as the man they'd known as Astrid's younger brother stepped forward into his position as king.

Erik's gaze swept from face to face. From Mayrun to Nenrir to Fargrim. Dozens of Valkir that he had known since childhood were with him now. Halitreia had not returned to the Oridassey and instead stood among them. His friends, his family, his scâldir. They were as good as blood.

"Brothers and sisters," Erik started as he looked around. "Sons and daughters, fathers, mothers, lovers and friends. Soon the head of that fleet will give command, and they will enter the Lupentine. Where we are now in this moment there is no walking away from. There is no running from. The shadow of Aureia is vast. It spreads from west to east, from south to north. Now it is cast upon us. The legions of Aureia come to place their heel upon our throats. They think us savages. They think us barbarians. Let us teach them that that is not so. Let us teach them that all who draw breath are of equal worth. This day we shall seek our destiny together. This day we will face them whatever the cost. We have all lived and lost at the hands of tyrants for too long. I would not have it so. Today there will be vengeance for the death of Astrid Farrin. Today there will be vengeance for all those who were taken from our arms."

Erik beat a fist against his chest as he thought of his sister. He could feel the tears threaten his eyes, yet he did not care. For so long he had carried the weight of her passing upon his shoulders and been unable to do so much as grieve. Burdened with command, he had forged his own path, yet now, finally, that weight could be unleashed upon his enemy.

"For Astrid!" Erik cried.

"For Laerke!" called Nenrir.

"For Hvitsred and Hélla!" shouted Fargrim.

"Lief!" called another.

One by one, names were cried out. Some of the Valkir openly wept as they remembered their friends and family taken so cruelly.

"Raol!" called Mayrun.

"Fabian!" chorused Halitreia.

"Osval!"

"Astrid!" the shout went up once more.

"Astrid!" echoed Nenrir.

"Astrid!" The name rang across the deck as the entire crew chanted her name.

The cry was taken up by hundreds and thousands as it sounded across every ship, sung from every throat. Her name became a battle cry. This moment was hers alone. Her song. Most had not known her, yet they all knew how much she had meant to the future of their people. They had heard it in story and poem, in song and legend. For a fleeting moment, Astrid Farrin was alive again.

"ASTRID!" Erik bellowed as he joined in the chant. His eyes went to the east.

"SAILS!" the shout came down from the crow's nest.

Erik's hands shot to his spyglass, and he held it to his eye. The sails of the captured merchant ship had unfurled.

"The signal," Erik muttered.

The silver fleet had been spotted in the channel. Aureia had come. The merchant vessel began to move southward as its skeleton crew went to work.

✦ ✦ ✦

SIXTY

Kilgareth, Valley of Odrysia

Dayne Raynor stared at the flag of Annora that hung in his chamber. The banner of his father. The banner of his family. The red eagle was as much his emblem as it was Annora's. The night was old, yet the king had not yet slept. How could he when so much hung in the balance? Thick clouds shrouded the moon from sight and darkness had long since engulfed the land. Torches burned brightly atop the walls. Dozens stood sentinel while thousands awaited the call to arms. Men slept in their beds or talked amongst each other. Those soldiers of Kilgareth stayed close to their families within the Citadel. All of their lives stood on the edge of a knife. All of them looked to their commander. All of them looked to Dayne. The song of bells began. Their ringing echoed across the walls and battlements, to the keep and tunnels below, to the fields and plains below the mountain fortress. The attack had come at last.

Dayne turned to see Sofia approach. She carried his sword in her hands. The eagle-shaped crossguard screamed a silent cry. Taking the sword from Sofia, Dayne placed a kiss upon her lips and held her tight. Perhaps for the last time. All too soon the king relinquished his hold. He stared into her eyes and did not look away as he backed towards the doors. Sofia's fingers slid through his own, and then he was gone. Dayne buried the emotion welling within his chest. It would not serve him now. He buckled his sword to his waist and strode into the fortress.

✦ ✦ ✦

Tariq awoke to the ringing of bells. His eyes flickered open, and pain lanced through his head. He gasped and held his brow as he pushed himself up onto his elbows. His cup lay in the dirt beside where he had fallen. There was a grunt as Marshall awoke beside him. What had happened? One moment they had been sharing a drink with Elise and then the next they had awoken in the dirt. Tariq shook his head as he tried to clear it.

"The army has moved on," Marshall said, rising to his feet.

Tariq followed his companion's gaze. A great army of torches had ascended the mountain to Kilgareth. Catapults were firing over the walls and the Mierans alongside the Salvaar were about to attack.

"What happened?" Tariq muttered as he reached down and took up his cup.

"Here," Marshall called.

Tariq turned to see the guard holding a letter. He watched as horror blanketed Marshall's face.

"No, no, it cannot be," Marshall muttered. "She poisoned us."

Tariq took the letter from his friend's hand and began to read.

Tariq, Marshall, my dearest friends,

The people in this army are fighting for no glory nor crowns for they will win neither. They are fighting so that they may one day be free. Though they march with purpose, they march to their deaths, and I cannot allow that. They are gathering all of their strength for one final attack, and I may not ever have another chance. I cannot allow any more people to suffer how I have suffered. They cannot do this alone. I must help them. I knew that you would try to stop me out of love, and so I prepared. When you awake, I can only hope you remember me well and forgive my betrayal. If Miera and Salvaar are to be free, then they must win this battle, even if it means my death. Go to Valentia. Live a new life as you both deserve. I will see you in the heavens.

Elise.

Tariq looked up from the letter. His face was pale, and he could feel moisture in his eyes. The battle was miles away. Elise Delfeyre, the girl who was as good as his daughter, had left knowing that she could die today.

"We go to Kilgareth," Tariq growled.

Marshall said not a word yet made for their horses without hesitation.

✦ ✦ ✦

Shouts and screams filled the air as the attack began. Catapults bombarded Kilgareth while thousands of warriors charged towards the walls. Shields were raised overhead as the rain of arrows and bolts poured down. Ladders were heaved up against the walls and soon the fighting spread along the battlements. Captains shouted orders and the song of steel carried in the wind. The fires of torches illuminated the main gate. Blood flowed as soldiers fell, both the attackers in the plains and the defenders on the walls. All of this and more Elise Delfeyre pushed from her mind as she and a small team of black-garbed warriors circumnavigated the battlefield and approached the southern gate. Once more she wore the dark clothes of the Nightingale. Once more she wore the mask, though this time it was different. This time she wore her mother's circus mask.

The cloudy night covered them as they made their approach. The fight at the main gate was a full assault and had drawn most of the defenders away. The team moved in silence and no steel was drawn. Any stray moonlight that crept through the clouds would find nothing to illuminate. They reached the tall walls. Shadows flickered as the sentries patrolled the walkway above. There were two of them. Elise gripped the rope that was wrapped around her body from shoulder to hip for a moment before she ran her hands along the stone wall. She felt the chips and breaks in the stonework. She searched for handholds or anything that would help her climb. The fortress was a century old, and time had begun to take its toll. For an experienced climber like her, there were many options and paths to take. Elise glanced at Sakkar and then one of the Salvaar and gave a single nod. They pulled arrows from their quivers and nocked them in their war bows. The sounds of the battle were so loud that Elise could barely hear her heartbeat. As the noise echoed around them, Sakkar and the Salvaari archer stepped back and aimed their bows up. Step by step, they moved further from the wall. The guards atop the structure were not prepared. Bows sang and steel-tipped arrows were driven deep into their bodies. The battle covered the sounds of their lifeless corpses crashing to the walkway. Elise waited for a nod from Sakkar before she left the cover of the case of the wall. Her eyes washed over the rock and she began her run. Accelerating as she sprinted at the wall, she kicked off the ground and took a trio of steps up the stonework. Her hands went up and her fingers slid against the wall. The handholds would have been impossible to find for a normal person, yet she was far from a common woman. She was the Nightingale. Her fingers found homes in cracks and crevices. She began her ascent, flying up the wall like a wraith. Every inch she climbed, she listened past the sounds of battle and directed her hearing towards the gatehouse further down the wall. That was her target. It would have soldiers within, though she did not know how many. She reached the top of the wall and peered between the merlons … Nothing. No shadows flickered; no warriors watched on. No shouts lit the air; the dead had not been found, nor the song of bows heard. She heaved herself up between the merlons and onto the walkway. Torches burned all around. A pair of fallen knights lay upon the stone with unseeing eyes. Elise's eyes went to the gatehouse. Light flickered within – that meant soldiers. Elise unslung the rope from her shoulder and bound it tightly around a merlon. She tossed it over the edge and down to her companions below. She could do nothing but watch and wait as they made the climb. She kept low and hidden in the shadows as her eyes searched the fortress. Four knights stood at the base of the gatehouse, and she caught sight of two more within. There were more inside, that much was certain. Sakkar joined her on the wall, and then the first of the Salvaari. One by one, they joined her. One by one, they readied their bows. They began to move towards the gatehouse.

The knights in the courtyard saw them first. The cry of alarm left a soldier's lips as an arrow entered his throat. Shouts echoed around them. Elise had no time to think as Knights of Kil'kara ran towards the stairs leading to the walk and materialised from the gatehouse. Torchlight flickered along the steel of their armour and the blades of their swords. The archers opened fire. Arrows arced through the air. Knights fell. The song of a horn echoed from the street and was quickly silenced. Only one knight made it to the top of the stairs and onto the wall. His sword narrowly missed a Salvaari and then Sakkar shot him from barely two paces. The arrow ripped through his face and tore into the brain beyond. The knight fell with a scream. The last of the gatehouse guards died mere feet from the attackers. His shield was covered in arrows, yet the Salvaari had been without mercy. Shafts were embedded in his legs, and as he had fallen, more had riddled his body. The Salvaari led the way into the gatehouse. They fanned out to keep a watch on the streets and courtyard below, as well as the walls that ran to either side.

Elise and Sakkar ran to the portcullis wheel while a pair of their companions ran down the stairs and to the gate below. They had to get the locking bar free. Elise glanced at Sakkar and then as one they began to turn the wheel. One thought plagued Elise's mind as she worked. The horn that had been blown. It would not be long before more defenders arrived.

✦ ✦ ✦

Lysandra had left the infirmary as soon as the battle had begun. Few knights and western soldiers remained in the Citadel, no more than guards of the Order and those who had been wounded in the fighting. She wound her way through the fortress that she knew so well she could have navigated blindfolded and before long reached one of the dungeons. Only a single cell was occupied, with a pair of knights standing guard. Lysandra knew them both by name.

"My lady–" one of the knights began.

Those were the last words that would leave his lips. The eyes of both men had met Lysandra's that now burned brighter than the reddest ruby. Fangs lined her maw as she called upon the power of her people. In silence she commanded the knights and in silence they acted. Hands pulled forth steel. The first drove a dagger up under the arm of the second and plunged it deep into his heart. The second thrust his own knife into the first's throat. They both collapsed at Lysandra's feet as she approached the cell. With her eyes still flaming with crimson light, she gathered up a key from one of the dead men and pushed it into the lock. It turned, and with a click, the door opened. Lysandra stared down at the cell's sole occupant.

"Kyler." She called his name.

The knight stared back. He looked more dead than alive, yet his empty eyes were as red as hers. His face was scarred and withered. Little of the Kyler Landrey remained in the creature that looked back. Though he wore the blue gambeson of a knight, he was no more than a broken soul. The blood sickness had taken its toll, as Lysandra had known it would. She freed him of his chain bindings.

"Follow," Lysandra commanded.

Kyler obeyed without a word or question. He gathered up a sword belt and shield from one of the dead knights. They were men who had once been his brothers, now he no longer knew them. Their blood pooled on the cold stone floor, yet Kyler did not see. His mind was gone, his spirit broken. This was the final stage of the blood sickness before death. Elena had not known what she was doing – the very act of trying to turn a mortal had long ago been forbidden. Without proper skill and training, this was the result. Twisted and grotesque.

Lysandra led the way through the castle and her eyes shifted back to copper. They made their way deep into the bowels of the earth. The grand network of tunnels and caverns stretched all around them, yet Lysandra never wavered in her path. One hundred years of planning had led to this moment, and she would not fail now. The stone floor evened out and then they arrived. The heart of the mountain. Four of the cardinal's guard stood sentinel before the cage that lay beyond. Lysandra and Kyler approached.

"The cardinal sent me to see to your prisoner," she told the guards.

That brought them a few moments.

"None pass," the guard growled back as he reached for his sword.

Kyler's thrown knife caught one of the white-clad soldiers in the throat. Lysandra's eyes turned red and froze the guard who had spoken for but a moment. Her dagger drove up under his jaw. As he fell, the last of the cardinal's men attacked. Kyler's blade flew into his hand as he engaged one of the men with sword and shield.

✦ ✦ ✦

Naidra heard the voices echo along the stone and rock around her. She heard the cries and the clash of steel. This was her time. The poison had long since worn off, yet she had waited. No longer. She was autieyar. She knew power that few among the elves had ever been blessed with. A gift from Sylvaine herself. She felt the power coursing through her veins as she called upon it for the first time in a century. It strengthened her weary body. The blue of her eyes shone. She grimaced and her hands curled like talons. The shackles shattered and rang as the pieces of steel hit the cold floor. She rose to her feet and approached the cage door. Naidra could remember the pain of using her gift, but it was a good pain. She could see a red-eyed knight fighting a pair of the cardinal's guard. She could see Lysandra behind him. Naidra could almost taste her freedom. A freedom that for so long had been denied to her. Calling upon her gift, she shattered the lock to the cage. One of the guards turned at the sound.

"NO!" The shout left his lips as he saw the elf before him.

Few of the living knew of the elves, and fewer still knew what they were capable of. It was said that while the ruskalan were great thinkers, the elves were creatures of action. They were born fighters. The cardinal's guard knew that. He thrust his sword at her, yet Naidra was prepared. She slid to the side, stepped forward and used the man's momentum to tear the blade from his fingers. She turned the sword and drove it deep into his neck. Naidra met his eyes as blood spewed from his lips. The soldier fell before her. He was dead before he hit the ground. The last guard fell to the red-eyed knight's sword. Naidra could feel the gaze of Lysandra and her companion upon her. She closed her eyes and spread her arms. She took a deep breath, the first free breath she had taken in a hundred years. Despite the musky air of the tunnels far beneath the open skies, the air was the purest thing she had tasted in a long time. She felt life in her again. When at last Naidra's eyes opened, she looked down at the fallen guards and then at her liberators. The half-blooded ruskalan and a knight who had been half turned. Lysandra fell to a knee in deference and the knight did the same.

"Take me to the cardinal," Naidra said.

Lysandra dipped her head. The elf followed the arc'maija through tunnels and up stairs. With each passing moment, she felt stronger. The air grew fresher and the corridors warmer. Clad in little more than rags, Naidra felt it all. She extended her mind as they walked. As autieyar she could command otherworldly forces and bend elements to her will, yet as an elf she could feel the emotions of all around her. Thousands of feelings and senses came from all around. Naidra allowed it all in for a moment before she cut the gift off. Before long, they reached the Citadel and from there Lysandra led them though secret tunnels and passages that only the Circle knew existed. They had to keep far from the eyes of those maija and knights still within the keep itself. At last, they reached a door and Lysandra pushed it open. The three companions walked out into the temple of Kilgareth.

Naidra's eyes swept the hall. She took in the statues of the Order's false gods. She took in the Spear of Yorath held by the carved deities. She could feel the power of the silver lance as it radiated. The cardinal and six guards stood facing the gods, while another two stood at the entrance. None were looking towards Naidra. She led Lysandra and the turned knight into the centre of the temple. The sun and moon symbol was carved into the stone beneath their feet. Naidra felt her emotions stir as she stared into the cardinal's back. A hundred years of torment and torture. She could still hear the screams of her people dying one by one. She could feel the flames of their lives being extinguished. Naidra was the last elf because of another cardinal. Anger, rage, sorrow, pain, fear … they ripped through Naidra's soul like a blade.

"Heretic," she growled.

Cardinal Aleksander and his guards turned. Naidra saw confusion turn into pure fear as they saw her free. Steel sang as the guards drew their weapons and surrounded her. Swords and spears were levelled. Eight soldiers. One holy man.

"Surrender to me and you will be spared," Aleksander bid her.

"You took *everything* from me," Naidra snarled.

Her body shook with the force of her anger. Her hands curled and her eyes ignited. Aleksander's face paled as she took him in.

"KILL HER!" Aleksander shouted.

A great scream left Naidra's lips as she unleashed all of the pain trapped within her. The guards had barely taken a step when the power of the autieyar gripped them. Their armour cracked and dented before it was contorted beneath Naidra's strength. Their suits caved in and crushed the men they had once protected. Their screams lasted only moments. Dull thuds sounded as the eight bodies hit the ground. Blood ran like a river from the ruined bodies. The stone symbol of the twins was painted red. A trail of white blood ran from Naidra's nose. The magic had a cost. She stepped through the carnage towards the cardinal, staring at her in horror. Her burning blue gaze never left his eyes as she took up a sword and drove it deep into his heart. The holy man cried out. Naidra savoured his scream. She could taste his fear. She watched as the light left his eyes and he joined his guards in death. Naidra let the Aureian sword fall from her fingers. Her breathing was ragged, and trembles ran through her body. For a century, she had dreamt of this moment.

The red-eyed knight slammed the doors of the temple closed as an alarm was risen. The screams had been heard. The knight gathered up a spear from the dead guard and jammed it through the rings on the doors. Shouts came from the far side as something heavy slammed into the entrance. Knights were coming. Many of them. They did not have long. Lysandra strode past the elf and made for the silver lance. The Order had believed it to be the Spear of Durandail, the false god, but it was not. The weapon was the Spear of Yorath, the spirit of the sun. Lysandra took the weapon in her hands and turned back to her companions.

"Harkan awaits," she told them.

Naidra gave her a nod and the pair made for the hidden passage.

Lysandra glanced back towards Kyler. Her eyes shone red as she met his gaze. Kyler bowed and turned towards the temple doors. He held his sword tightly as Lysandra closed the passage door behind her and Naidra. They left the fallen knight to his fate.

✦ ✦ ✦

SIXTY-ONE

Kilgareth, Valley of Odrysia

Kitara kept her hand tight upon the hilt of her sword as she ventured into the mountains. Cleander led the mercenaries for hours on foot. Horses would have been faster, but they made too much sound. The chasms and valleys that ran through the mountains created a natural maze. The trees and woodland that covered them only made it harder still. Even in the darkest night, Cleander never lost his way. He had walked these hidden paths many times. The only light that they saw in the darkness came from Kilgareth miles away. The attack had begun.

Cleander held up a hand to stop the company and pulled a vial from his pouch. He pulled the stopper out and drank it all. Within moments, the yellow brew began to take effect. His vision became clearer, and he could see almost as if it was day.

"Wait for my return," Cleander said softly.

Then he was gone. Kitara exchanged a look with Aeryn as they waited. The moonseer focused her gaze on where Cleander had vanished. She had been raised as a hunter, tracker and scout. If Cleander betrayed them, or another threat arose, she would be the first to know. An arrow was already nocked in her powerful bow.

It did not take long for Cleander to return. Without a word, he gestured for the company to follow him. Only bows were to be held in hand. No steel was to be drawn for it could reflect light.

Cleander led them to a slit in the earth. He crouched and dropped through the small opening. Aeryn went first, and then Galadayne. The company followed Cleander inside. Kitara stared at the sight that awaited them. The darkness of the mountain clouded her vision, and she could see little within, but a vast passage opened up before them. It wound deep into the heart of the mountains. Cleander had told them that the tunnels stretched for miles and only those who knew them could ever find their way out. A pair of armoured bodies lay on the ground. Their blood soaked into the earth and their unseeing eyes were drawn to the heavens. They were why Cleander had left. Cleander nocked an arrow in his bow and then the company began to make their way into the mountain. The air grew thicker and more stale by the step. Noises came from the deep. Bats and other creatures called the cave system home. Those without bows clamped their hands down on their sheathed weapons. They knew nothing of this place. They did not know of its dangers. They did not know whether it held traps. They stayed close together and kept their eyes moving as they wound through the labyrinth of earth and stone. For hours and hours, they followed their guide and prayed he led them well. Here in the blackness, all they could have was faith. The passages were a secret greatly protected, so few knights stood guard and few men needed to die.

The air began to grow cleaner as the passages led upwards. They found their way through corridors and caverns, great chambers and even a tomb. Kitara could see characters written around the chambers that held stone coffins, yet it was in a language unknown to her. Perhaps it was Old Aureian. The passages turned into stairs, and they climbed. At last, a faint orange glow emerged far in the distance. Step by step, they closed in. All eyes focused on the light. Kitara prepared herself. She relaxed her breathing and loosened her grip on her sword. This was it. The end of the line.

Cleander stopped at the corner of a turn and gestured for Aeryn to follow. The moonseer readied her bow as together they peered around the bend. A great cavern walled in stone brick opened up before them. Torches lit the walls, while passages ran in many directions. Some went up to what appeared to be a second level. Knights stood at the centre, while others with crossbows stood at the elevated level. This had to be the final room before ascending into Kilgareth. The vast staircase at the far end had to be the way out.

At a nod from Cleander, the company armed themselves. The comforting weight of Tariki steel relaxed Kitara's hand. Cleander stepped around the corner with Aeryn on his heels. Bows sang. The mercenaries charged. Kitara rounded the bend to see knights fall beneath Aeryn and Cleander's arrows. Those who didn't fall drew steel. Knights descended from the second level and shouts echoed through the tunnels. Lights flickered down passages. More would be coming. Cleander tossed his bow aside and pulled forth his sword as he joined the fray. Kitara fought side by side with Aeryn. Those that the arrows didn't kill were slowed. Kitara had space to move. She created angles as she attacked. Her sword was a part of her body. She moved on instinct. The first knight fell as her blade found a home in his neck. Aeryn killed another as he tried to come at Kitara's back. They fought as one. They fought as if they shared the same mind. As Kitara killed a man on the right, Aeryn felled another on the left. Kitara exchanged three blows with a knight. She sliced his leg, opened his arm and then took his head. More knights began to descend upon them. Galadayne shouted commands and his men obeyed without question. One by one, the knights fell to their blades, though not without reply. Two mercenaries were cut down by swords, while a third was taken by the bolt of a crossbow. Still, they fought. A pair of knights surged towards Aeryn. She brought her bow up in time to deflect a thrust as she leapt backwards. She slammed into the cavern wall. Kitara lunged forward and knocked aside the first attacker's sword. He brought his shield around in an arc aimed at her head. Kitara ducked and slammed the pommel of her sword into the knight's jaw. Something cracked and the man stepped back with a shriek. Kitara's knife leapt into her hand and then was thrust deep into the man's throat. The second attacker barrelled into Kitara. He drove her up into the cavern wall. Only her helmet kept her conscious. Her head rang and she barely managed to get her sword up in the way of the blow aimed to skewer her. The knight's face was inches from her own. She could see the hatred in his eyes. She could taste the stench of his breath. Suddenly, he fell with a scream. One of Aeryn's arrows sprouted from his side. The moonseer's bow connected heavily with his head and he crashed to the ground. Kitara grimaced as a bolt of pain lanced through her head. She bit it back and made herself as stone. Without word or hesitation, Kitara and Aeryn waded into the knights and started killing without mercy. The song of steel ended as the last of the defenders fell. A bloody gash had been opened on Kitara's arm in the melee. She exchanged a look with Aeryn. Cleander's voice broke the silence.

"We have to go," Cleander said. "We cannot stay here."

Kitara crouched at Galadayne's side as he knelt next to his fallen companions. Four had died in the fight, and many more had been wounded. She placed a hand on the old warrior's shoulder as he closed the eyes of his friend.

Half a dozen tunnels branched out in every direction, yet all eyes were drawn to the great staircase. They all knew what lay beyond. Kitara nodded, and as one the company began to ascend. Torchlight flickered down the corridor as they came to a small room at the end of the staircase. Four knights stood within. They were not expecting to see a band of mercenaries covered in dirt and blood emerge from the heart of the mountain. Kitara led the way as cries of alarm filled the room. Aeryn's first arrow caught one in the throat. He started to fall. Kitara skipped past the dying man. Her sword deflected a knight's blade. She stepped in close and drove her knife into his neck. Blood flowed. Kitara spun as a sword thrust at her face. She parried and countered with her knife. The knight turned his shoulder, and the dagger whipped by his face. Kitara deflected his next blow, and Cleander felled him from behind. The last knight collapsed as Jaime's hammer took his life. The company did not stop. They could not stop.

"I can get you to the dungeon," Cleander called out. "But where the cardinal is, I do not know."

"Go with him," Kitara told Galadayne. "We will handle the rest."

The old warrior nodded before he called the names of half the remaining mercenaries. The company split in two. Galadayne would lead one group with Cleander, Kitara the other. The sellswords and Cleander made their way down the hallway, and then they were gone.

"What about the holy man?" Aeryn asked. "If we do not find him, then everyone dies. I could try to navigate these halls, but they are unknown to me. It could be our only chance."

"Wait," Kitara said.

She glanced at Aeryn … then she remembered. She remembered the words that Aeryn had once spoken to her by the river in Salvaar.

"Remember the sea," Kitara said in Salvaari.

"You were born for this," Aeryn replied in the same tongue, realising.

The company looked to Kitara.

"I have something to say," she told them as she strode into the centre of the room.

"You have a plan?" one of the mercenaries asked.

"I have far more," Kitara replied.

She unbuckled her helmet. She let it fall to the ground, forgotten as her golden, braided hair cascaded down her back. She crouched and placed a hand upon the cold stone. She closed her eyes and sought out the power that lay within. The gift that had come from her mother. She felt the flame inside. Kitara tendered it until it burned. Once, it had caused her great pain, yet now she felt its warmth. She opened her eyes, and they blazed with violet light. Cries and gasps filled the chamber as surprise ran through the ranks of mercenaries. Kitara expanded her senses. Her mind traversed the tunnels. The stone talked to her. She could feel the presence of every soul within the fortress.

"The temple," she said. "It has to be." She rose to her feet and turned back to Aeryn.

"Then that is where we begin," the moonseer said.

"We go that way," Kitara replied, gesturing down the passage.

Kitara could almost hear the questions in the faces of the mercenaries as they stared at her. Aeryn said nothing, though a thin smirk crossed her lips. Kitara turned and led them from the room.

✦ ✦ ✦

Sir Mortimier's head whipped towards the temple as he heard a woman's scream followed by the bloodcurdling cries of soldiers. The sound echoed through the stone corridor. It was the song of nightmare. Another pain-filled shout came from the temple. That of an old man.

"The cardinal," said one of the knights at his side.

Mortimier drew his sword. "WITH ME!" he cried as he charged towards the temple entrance.

The doors slammed shut in his face and the metallic rasp of something being pushed through the locking bars greeted him. Mortimier threw his weight into the doors. They shuddered but remained closed.

"YOUR HOLINESS!" Mortimier shouted as one by one the four knights battered at the thick doors.

Something splintered on the far side. Mortimier led his men again and again. There was a mighty crack, and the doors boomed open. The wispy smoke of newly extinguished candles wafted through the temple. Bodies lay strewn across the bloodstained floor. Mortimier's skin crawled as he saw the ruined corpses of the cardinal's guard. Their armour had been crushed. It had broken the men within.

"What kind of hell is this?" one of the knights muttered.

Mortimier's eyes went to the white-clad body at the centre of the slaughter. The man was awash with blood though his body had not been destroyed as his companion's had. Mortimier strode across the temple floor and knelt beside the cardinal's body. He reached out a hand and closed Aleksander's unseeing eyes.

"Be at peace," Mortimier murmured.

The knights began to fan out. One walked up onto the dais and stared towards the stone statues of his gods. Something was missing.

"The spear is gone, and the cardinal is dead," Mortimier said. "Who could have done this?"

Lysandra had told him that Alarik had been the traitor but now he began to rethink her words. Perhaps more had infiltrated the Order, or perhaps the fallen battlemaster had remained loyal.

"They have vanished like ghosts," one of the knights muttered as he walked around the chamber.

Mortimier rose to his feet. A shout rang through the temple as the knight who had spoken fell. His blood watered the temple floor, and then steel sang as it hit stone. A shadow stepped out from behind a pillar. A shadow bearing the blue gambeson of the Order of Kil'kara. Though he appeared more dead than alive, Mortimier recognised Kyler Landrey. His eyes were red, and his face twisted and grotesque. A shield was strapped to his left arm with a bloody sword clasped in his right hand.

"Kyler?" Mortimier called the Medean's name.

Somehow, the boy had been liberated from his cell days after Alarik had been killed. Had Kyler Landrey killed the cardinal and slaughtered his guard? Whatever the case, Mortimier was sure that the battlemaster had been loyal. Had Lysandra deceived them? He raised his shield and nodded towards Kyler.

"Take him," Mortimier commanded.

The three remaining knights levelled steel and started to close in on their enemy. Kyler had once been their brother, yet now he had killed one of them. He was a traitor. Brother or no, a traitor deserved to die.

Kyler dashed through the temple and used the pillars to create distance and isolate the furthest knight. Kyler engaged the knight and pushed him back across the temple towards the statues. He fought more like a beast than a man. His blows were fast, and he did not stop moving, putting himself in harm's way to attack. Steel sang as Kyler exchanged a flurry of blows before he ducked back, once again using the pillars to stop himself from being cornered and surrounded. The knights came from different angles as they tried to cut him off. Kyler kept moving. He used the knights' strategy against them as he went for the man furthest from his companions. Sword met shield. The knight's blade sliced Kyler's cheek, yet the Medean had taken the blow to get in close. His shield came up and met the knight's jaw with a crunch. The knight staggered backwards, and Kyler's sword sliced his leg open. The knight dropped his sword as he staggered back. Kyler pressed his advantage, but the knight was ready. He slid to the side, took hold of Kyler's shield and spun, tearing the shield from Kyler's grasp and sending it flying across the temple floor. Kyler rained down blows without mercy. Mortimier and the third knight charged Kyler. Mortimier's sword was blocked by Kyler's, but the veteran knight drove forward with his shield and barrelled into him. Kyler braced and drove his weight into Mortimier's shield. His boots slid across the stone floor. Kyler stepped to the side, the third knight slamming into him. Kyler fell, rolling as a blade barely missed his face, and gathered up one of the cardinal's guard's swords. Kyler rose to a knee, blocked the blow aimed at his head with the guardsman's sword, and thrust his own blade forward. Mortimier deflected the blow. Kyler leapt to his feet. The two uninjured knights worked in unison. They pushed him back through the centre of the temple to the stairs leading up onto the dais. The guardsman's sword was beaten from his hand as he was backed up the steps. Before steel had finished ringing upon the stone floor, Kyler lunged. Mortimier was faster. He had served as a warrior for longer than Kyler had been alive. He began to turn, bringing his shield in close and pinning Kyler's sword to his armoured side. His spin tore the weapon free of Kyler's grasp. Mortimier stepped forward as his momentum brought him around. His blade came up. The thin light that came from the stained-glass windows danced along his sword before it was thrust deep into Kyler's body. Kyler cried out as the mortal blow was dealt. His shout echoed through the temple.

Mortimier met the boy's eyes. The monster in Kyler's red gaze faded, and Mortimier could see the man within. He tore his blade free. Tears of blood sprayed the air and splashed down onto cold stone. Kyler fell backwards as strength left his body. He crashed down onto the steps mere feet away from the idols of the gods he had once served.

✦ ✦ ✦

The wheel in the gatehouse clicked and locked into place. The portcullis was fully raised. There was a burst of flame as Sakkar ignited some oil-soaked cloth around an arrow. Elise Delfeyre ran out onto the walls and looked down at the Salvaari below. They pulled the locking bar out of its place and tossed it to the side. Within moments, the doors to Kilgareth were opening.

Sakkar stepped past Elise and aimed his war bow skyward. The bow sang and the blazing arrow shot towards the heavens. That was the signal. The shaft wavered in the sky before arcing back down to the earth. Within moments, horns blew and horsemen began to race along the mountain towards the southern gate.

Elise could see defenders moving through the streets and along the walls. The alarm had been raised and they were coming. She brushed the hilt of her kukri as her companions lined the walls and the courtyard below. Arrows were nocked and bows made ready. The first defenders came one by one from the streets. Cries were upon their lips and steel in their grasp. The archers began to shoot without hesitation. None could make it within twenty paces of the gatehouse and live. The trickle of defenders became a stream. They started getting closer as they banded together and raised shields. Still, they fell, yet it was only a matter of time. Elise knew that. She glanced back towards the pagan army. They were closing in. Horns blew from the streets of Kilgareth, and a flood of knights appeared. The Salvaari began to fall. Crossbow bolts sent them crashing down from the walls. Those further in the courtyard tried to rally to hold back the storm yet quickly were butchered by an onslaught of sword, spear and arrow. Elise leapt back inside the gatehouse as bolts ripped through the air all around her. Horror gripped her as she realised that the knights would reach the gates before the pagan army did. Screams came from below as more Salvaari fell to the storm of arrows. It was over. They would not breach the walls. The west would triumph and there was no going back. Elise's hand fell to the silver shell that Cleander had given her. Elise realised what she had to do. For the free nations beyond western rule. For the thousands of Salvaari and Mierans who were fighting for their freedom. For Tariq and Marshall who would surely die when the western cavalry swept the countryside.

"I'm sorry, Tariq," Elise said.

The knights began to approach the gatehouse through the courtyard. Sakkar and the few remaining defenders were barely holding the walls against the men who charged along them. Elise leapt through the rear opening of the gatehouse and dropped into the courtyard below. She stood alone as the tide of knights came towards her. Elise gripped the silver shell tightly as she raised it over her head. The first bolt shattered her left thigh. She fell to a knee as she brought the shell down. Her roar was long and loud. It held no pain. No fear. She tore her kukri free as bolts slammed into her stomach and chest. Her blood cascaded through the air as she fell back. Dark smoke filled the courtyard, conjured from the silver shell. The last thing she saw was the defenders halted in their tracks, afraid to enter the smoke. The last things she heard were the screams of the knights as the smoke pushed them back and the roar of Mieran riders as they galloped through the open gates. The last thing she felt was the softness of a nightingale feather as it slipped through her fingers.

✦ ✦ ✦

SIXTY-TWO

The Lupentine Sea

Erik closed his eyes as he painted the white ochre across his face. Everything that had happened, everything that he had done since the death of his sister, had led to this moment. He took comfort knowing that whatever happened to his people, it happened because they made it so. Erik's mind took him back to his last conversation with Cillian Teague, one that they had soon after they had captured the merchant ship. Now going into battle, he remembered.

✦ ✦ ✦

"You never told me their greatest weakness," Erik stated as he leaned upon the rails beside Teague.

The words had been spoken before they had taken this prize, and Teague had been interrupted before he could complete them.

"The greatest weakness of Aureia is its greatest strength," Teague told him. "Discipline … a curious thing. The very trait that enabled them to carve out their mighty empire is the same that could serve as their downfall. It is both sword and shield. When they attack, discipline breaks even their greatest enemy. When assaulted, outnumbered, outmatched, it is discipline that holds the line and turns back fear. They believe themselves unbeatable, yet that is not so. For what would happen if that discipline were to fail? What would happen if their world began to crumble around them? Those men beyond the horizon that sail towards us do not know chaos."

✦ ✦ ✦

Serian Katan, commodore of the Aureian fleet, stared eastward from his position atop the helm of his flagship. Finely decorated steel armour covered his weathered body from head to toe. The long cloak that billowed at his back was as purple as the crest upon his helmet and the sash at his waist. His strong grip tightened around the sword at his hip as his keen eyes flicked to the merchant vessel that navigated along the coast. Serian had served Emperor Darius and his father before him for many years. At twelve, he had been taken aboard a trading shop as a cabin boy. Within three years, he had found himself in the imperial navy and then had spent three long decades climbing through the ranks. The position at the head of this newly founded dread fleet had been hard earned, not given.

Serian's ship was the first to enter the waters of the Lupentine, and then Aureian vessels began to leave the river mouth one by one. They were massive warships, each bearing no fewer than three masts. Sailors crewed their decks and helm, while the men of the legions lounged below and above. Now they could rest, for in little over a week they would be fighting upon the beaches of the Valkir Isles. The heathen who called those islands home had slaughtered a peaceful imperial delegation and that could not go unpunished, nor could the threat of war that their new king, Erik, had spoken. In the months since, there had been reports of dozens of raids upon Aureian lands and villages. Hundreds had died.

Now, Serian Katan served as the empire's wrath. Again, Serian's eyes drifted to the merchant ship that steadily moved southward down the coast. The ship was just far enough south that he could barely see any movement upon the ship's deck. Serian pulled free his spyglass and peered through it towards the merchant. He scanned the ship from helm to deck and could see no movement save one man. The helmsman. Serian frowned. The man wore no shirt nor boots. His trousers were his only garment, while his hair was longer than any Aureian. The sailor stepped away from the helm and now Serian could see that rope tied the wheel so that the ship could not alter course. Serian watched as the man strode to the edge of the merchant ship and dove overboard. Serian followed the dive until the man was swallowed by the sea. Only then did his eyes catch sunlight dancing upon a dark liquid that slowly poured from the back of the ship.

"COMMODORE!" a shout came from the crow's nest.

Serian glanced towards the lookout and followed the man's pointed arm eastward. Dozens of white sails began to emerge. They must have stayed hidden beyond the horizon with their sails down and then moved when it was too late for the imperial fleet to turn back. Serian watched the new fleet though his spyglass. He could recognise the make of the ships and their sails. Valkir. Lamrei. Elara. His eyes returned to the merchant vessel as he saw a small flame spark to life. Serian shouted orders as he realised the trap that his fleet had sailed straight into.

✦ ✦ ✦

Erik watched from the helm of the Ravenheart as the imperial fleet began to splinter at the river mouth. The armada of Valkir, Elaran refugees and pirate vessels surged westward. Five ships that Cillian Teague had sent ahead of them travelled towards the imperial navy from the north. They were far in advance of those ships that Erik led, yet it was not to the five that the king looked. It was to the captured merchant vessel. He saw the dark spot of a Valkir man leap overboard and then vanish into the Lupentine. Moments later, the first flicker of flame emerged. There was a roar, and then fire engulfed the merchant ship. The blaze did not stop there. The dark trail that the ship had spread through the ocean ignited, and suddenly the line that stretched near four hundred paces turned into flame. It burned almost as tall as the great warships as it split the ocean, a burning scar upon the sea. Shouts and screams carried across the ocean as Aureian soldiers and sailors began to panic. The fires stopped their eastward advance, and instead they were now forced to hug the coast to the north and south. Erik strapped on his helmet. Valkir warriors covered the deck of the Ravenheart. Cheers roared from their lips as they watched the fires burn. Only Erik remained silent as they made their approach. His eyes never left the five ships that sped towards the imperial fleet from the north.

✦ ✦ ✦

Serian's commands echoed across the water as he shouted above the roar of the flames. Bells rang as his words were spread through the fleet. In this moment, he had to keep discipline amongst the men. Many of the sailors were fresh recruits, while few among the soldiers had ever set foot upon a ship before. If order fell and chaos ensued, then this fleet could be undone.

"ARCHERS!" Serian cried as the five northern ships closed in.

Soldiers armed with deadly crossbows lined the sides of the ships and raised their weapons. The ships crafted in the pirate-infested waters of the Gulf of Lamrei did not turn or run. They came head on. Serian shouted his command and steel-tipped bolts arced across the water. It was only after the first volley landed, only when wood was chipped and splintered, that Serian could see that there were few sailors upon the five ships.

"BREAK!" Serian bellowed as he realised what was happening. "BREAK THE LINE!"

Shouts carried across the waters as men aboard the pirate vessels gave command. The pirate sailors leapt overboard and heaved themselves into the longboats that they had lowered. Small explosions began to rock the ships. Almost as one, the line of fire began to ignite. Fire blossomed to life. It ignited in the holds and spread through the interior before snaking its way up onto the deck. Flames sprang upwards into the rigging and sails.

✦ ✦ ✦

Erik watched with a steely cold gaze as the battle began to unfurl before him. They had caught the Aureians by surprise. They did not expect an attack, for who of those who knew of their existence would dare challenge them? Who would be so bold? The lone merchant ship that sailed beyond the river mouth had given them no qualms nor even a second thought until it had been too late. Panic spread through the Aureian ranks as the fireships descended upon them. Shouts and screams carried across the waves. The Aureian vessels began to move, yet there was nowhere to run. Some managed to angle away from the incoming attack, and then the fireships were amongst the fleet. They crashed into Aureian vessels one by one. Embers cascaded across the ships. Flames ignited their rigging. Fire spread and a burning wave seemed to engulf the ocean. Smoke filled the air. The sky turned black. Men screamed as the flames consumed them.

Erik unslung his shield and pulled free his axe as the Ravenheart rounded the wall of flame and surged towards the broken ranks of Aureian ships. Steel rang as Erik slammed the flat of his axe into his shield. Everything that he had done since he had held Astrid's body in his arms had led to this moment. All of the pain and all of the tears. To get a chance at liberty had come at a heavy price – one of blood – and it had been paid. Now, that payment bore its fruit.

Despite the wall of fire and the burning ships, the Aureians still outnumbered the allied fleet. Arrows sped forward from the allied fleet, while heavy bolts were returned from the Aureian lines. Loud shouts and wicked war cries chorused with the roar of burning ships. The Valkir locked their shields and raised them high as a rain of bolts descended. Fire and steel. That was the hell that awaited Erik and his people … and how they *welcomed* it.

Erik braced as Fargrim's voice carried across the ship. The Ravenheart crashed into one of the Aureian vessels. Imperial shouts filled the air. Hooks were thrown to tether the vessels while gangplanks were extended. Erik waited for neither. He heaved himself up onto the rails and leapt across. His war cry shook the heavens as he landed amongst his enemies. There were those who said that the Farrin bloodline was descended from the Sea-Father himself. Erik did not know whether that was true or not, yet he would find out. His axe spilled blood as he moved among the imperial soldiers. His shield repelled blows from sword and spear. Valkir swarmed across the imperial deck and cut down the defenders in droves.

✦ ✦ ✦

"We break apart their formation and instil such fear in them that their discipline will begin to crack and crumble," Cillian Teague told Erik. "They do not know chaos, but we know its name. We know its face. We can turn this battlefield into their hell. A place where their discipline holds no value. They will be broken, shattered, lost. It is in this moment that we bring down our full strength upon them."

✦ ✦ ✦

Bhaltair glanced at the faces of his men beneath the deck of his ship. Even from below they could hear the shouts and screams, the roars of the fire and the clash of steel that echoed across the water. For many long years, he had fought for justice and liberty. For years he had lived like an animal because he believed that all had the right to live free. He had always been prepared to give his life for that goal. The gangmen downed the contents of the vials that they each held. They pulled their cloth masks up over their mouths and noses. A bell began to ring. The signal.

"Liberty or death!" Bhaltair cried.

"Liberty or death!" the men answered.

Bhaltair led the way up onto the deck of his ship. The heavily armoured soldiers who served Priamos Stentor and manned the deck moved aside as the gangmen emerged from the hold. Grapples were thrown, and Bhaltair and his people went to work. Silver cannisters were cast across onto the imperial deck. Dozens of small explosions went off, and smoke erupted everywhere. Bhaltair made no sound as he leapt across the gap between the ships. The enemy soldiers cried out in fear as their vision was taken and they doubled over in coughing fits as foul smoke filled their lungs. Bhaltair's sword flew into his hand. The liquid in the vials had done its work. He could see through the smoke as clear as day. The screams of the Aureians created a hellish choir as the gangmen went to work. There was no resistance. There was no mercy. Bhaltair and his men were demons from the underworld.

✦ ✦ ✦

Cillian Teague roared as his sword cut through the throat of an Aureian. The pirates swarmed the imperial vessel. Smoke and ash filled the air. Blazing red flames scorched the heavens. The alliance tore into the scattered Aureian ships. Teague could see the fear in the eyes of the men that he killed. He could see it in the confusion as the pirates leapt amongst them. He could see it when the cries for the Aureians to rally were drowned out. None had been ready for the attack. Their formation was in ruins, and their discipline was wavering. Screams overcame the roared commands of officers. One by one, the Aureian ships were swept aside. One by one, they fell. Vessels became entangled. Where only two or three had been bound by hooks and planks, now many joined until they became floating islands. The dozens of men fighting aboard became hundreds. The vast imperial armada began to move. More ships spilled from the river mouth. Some broke through the lines of attackers and started to surround them. Some of the flames began to die. Teague's cheek was opened by an Aureian sword. Pirates and Valkir alike began to fall. The imperial flagship drove though the chaos and slammed into the Ravenheart.

✦ ✦ ✦

The world shook beneath Erik's feet as the massive Aureian vessel crashed into the Ravenheart's side. Men and women crashed to the ground. Erik managed to keep his footing. Erik's axe tasted blood as he cut down two soldiers scrambling to their feet. His crew fought against those of three ships and were not prepared for the soldiers of the imperial flagship that now spilled onto their deck. The men that came from the flagship came in a shield wall. Their armour was fine and their blades sharp. These were the commodore's guard. The surrounded Valkir began to fall.

"WITH ME!" Erik roared defiantly as he leapt at the newcomers.

✦ ✦ ✦

"Nothing lasts forever," Cillian Teague said to Erik as they stared out across the open waters of the Lupentine. "Trees, animals, empires, even the gods. The griffin comes now, and the world will burn. It will burn everything, *everything*. But we cannot fear it, for everything that begins must come to an end. When the fighting comes, chaos will only grant us a moment in which to act. We could sink half their fleet and still be gravely outnumbered. They will know that and through the chaos will rush to defeat us. We will need more than chaos to win this fight. Far more. We must know in our hearts what we are fighting for, and what we are willing to sacrifice."

✦ ✦ ✦

Thunder rolled through the clouds, and then the heavens opened. Rain torrented down. It rang upon steel and splashed upon wood. Blood covered Erik's armour and blade as he wove through the Aureians. His own blood. That of his enemies. He could barely tell the difference. He saw his friends die, those he had known since childhood. He could do nothing as Aureian steel claimed their lives.

Shouts went up from the Aureian flagship. Erik's eyes flicked towards the words that could only have been commands. The commodore and six of his guard stood atop the helm while archers prepared their wicked crossbows. The man who led the fleet, the commodore, was the thing that held this mighty armada together. He may have had more experience on the sea than any of the thousands of men at his command. Crossbows sang and bolts arced towards the Valkir.

"SHIELDS!" Erik bellowed.

Some reacted in time, others were too slow. Those unable to raise their shields were thrown to the ground beneath the weight of the heavy bolts. Cries and screams filled the air. The wood of Erik's shield cracked and splintered. Suddenly, two of the crossbowmen fell backwards as arrows tore into their hearts. Nenrir, brother to the fallen Laerke Redleaf, rained death upon them.

"SPEARS!" Erik cried.

A wave of lances was hurled by the Valkir. Aureians fell in droves and a gap opened between the two forces.

"BACK! BACK!" cried Erik as he gestured across the island of ships.

Without hesitation, the Valkir began to swarm towards the rails of the Ravenheart. They leapt across the watery abyss and onto the deck of the next ship. Dozens made it away. Many lay behind on the blood-soaked wood of the Ravenheart. Their friends, their family, their scâldir. A storm of arrows kept the Aureians at bay as Nenrir and the other bowmen unleashed hell. It would not last for long. Erik's arm snaked out as one of his crew made to pass.

"Fargrim!" the king growled as he snatched his friend's shoulder. "What's left of this crew is yours to command now. Go!"

Fargrim stared into Erik's eyes. He saw that there was no argument to be had or compromise made. The helmsman clapped his friend on the arm and gave him a single solemn nod before he followed the crew. Fargrim hadn't made it across before Erik's axe began to sever the ropes that tied the ships together.

"GO NOW!" Erik cried to Fargrim.

Few of the crew could hear his words above the roar of the rain, the screams of the fire and the song of steel.

"WITH ME!" Fargrim bellowed. "STAY TOGETHER!"

The helmsmen led his people across the deck and leapt from one ship to another. They smote down those few Aureians who stood against them as they made their way across the battlefield of flame and storm. Dozens left; only one looked back. Only he who knew of the king's fate. Only Fargrim.

The rain of Valkir arrows died and the Aureians could now emerge from behind their shields. They could not stop the ships from drifting way, but they could kill the one who remained. The Aureian commodore's voice rang true. His finger thrust towards the Valkir king. Soldiers roared and surged forward. Three arrived in unison. The first fell to the king's axe. Erik weaved amongst them. The deck of the ship was slick with rain. Blood flowed as Erik took the second man's life. The third fell to an arrow. A fourth and fifth fell as the unseen bowmen sent them to the afterlife. Erik spun around as the bowman emerged from the darkness.

"NENRIR!" Erik cried out his friend's name as he cut down an Aureian soldier.

Soldiers charged the archer. Without hesitation, the king ran to Nenrir's side. They fought in unison as they made their way across the deck. They did not stop moving. They did not stop killing. The lifeless bodies littered the deck. Nenrir's bow sang again and again. Warriors fell. Soldiers who raced down from the helm to stop him fell. Then his last arrow was gone. Nenrir tore free his sword and barely deflected a soldier's blow. Erik lunged forward and buried his axe in the skull of the man who attacked his friend. They fought side by side as soldier and sailor alike came at them. The commodore's guard began to descend upon them. Bolts slammed into Erik's shield as he raised it to defend both men. Nenrir cried out as one of the steel-tipped shafts drove deep into his shoulder. He fell backwards into the main mast and nearly crashed to the ground. Pain filled his every breath. The commodore's guards reached the deck. Erik cast his shield aside as the dozen bolts that had struck it made it unwieldly. He pulled forth his sword as his eyes washed over the cracked raven image atop his fallen shield.

"Erik, go," Nenrir managed through bared teeth.

Erik glanced down at his friend as Nenrir rose to his feet once more. Nenrir angled his sword towards the left staircase that led up onto the helm. Nenrir gave Erik a nod. There was no pain in his eyes. There was no fear.

"This is my time," Nenrir growled as the guards drew near. "Now go."

Before Erik could reply, before he could so much as move, Nenrir leapt in front of him and charged towards the guards.

"FOR LAERKE AND FOR THE KING!" Nenrir cried as he lashed out with his blade.

There was nothing Erik could do as the guards swarmed his

friend. All he could do was honour his sacrifice. Erik ignored the screams as Aureian steel found its way into Nenrir's body over and over again. The king's hands turned white around the handles of sword and axe as he made for the bowels of the Ravenheart. He cut down one guard, cut down two. He took the stairs three at a time as he descended. A bolt slammed into his side. It tore through his armour and dug into the flesh beyond. Erik roared as he vanished into the darkness. The soldiers pursued him into the black labyrinth. Erik heaved barrels and crates aside to create barriers between him and the men who came after him. He slammed doors shut as the cries drew closer. His heart raced. Sweat, the water of rain and blood covered his body. The king descended another level. The bolt in his side slowed him. He killed the first man to catch him. Sword and axe moved in unison as he felled a second. Erik's axe found its way through a guardsman's defence and slammed down into the man's chest. Erik threw himself backwards as a sword angled at his neck. His back slammed heavily into the ship's railing as the sword sliced through his arm. A guardsman's spear barely missed his leg as he moved again. Erik killed them with sword and axe. Another attacked when Erik turned to retreat. The king heard the man's movement upon the wood. He spun back. His arm came up. The steel sword met his bracer and drove down onto his helmet. Erik's head rang and blood flowed where the blade sliced a shallow cut in his neck. Erik's axe fell from his fingers and the soldier's hilt smashed into the side of his head. Erik tasted blood. A wild slash opened his assailant's throat. Footfalls sounded upon the stairs. Erik staggered backwards as his blood splashed on the wood below. The pain from his wounds started to set in. He was cold, colder than he had ever been. Erik took a long shuddering breath through gritted teeth. Blood dripped from his mouth. It pooled down his neck and arm. His clothing was soaked from more than just water where the bolt had made its home. He was the last Farrin. Erik could feel them as his fingers found the handle of his axe. His family. His ancestors.

Astrid's will. Leif's power. His mother's love. Erik felt strength fill his weary body, his bloody, battered and bruised body. Wrapping his hand tightly around his sword hilt, he heaved himself forward. Shouts came from behind as he was heard. Erik staggered into the hold and slammed the door at his back. He pushed the lock home just as something heavy smashed into the other side. The king's eyes left the door as he peered around the hold. It was filled to the brim with casks and barrels. He placed his sword to the side and then swung his axe into one of them. Thick, dark liquid flowed.

✦ ✦ ✦

"GET US UNDER WAY!" Fargrim's voice carried through the wind as he reached the helm of a Valkir ship. It was not a vessel that he had sailed, yet it was Valkir, and Valkir were sailors to the bone.

The crew swarmed into the rigging. They severed roped and pulled away gangplanks. Some fought Aureians trying to board them, while others unleashed arrows in every direction. The silver fleet was vast. Death was sown all around them as the Aureians began to take control of the battle. The Oridassey was besieged from all sides. The Elaran refugees were being cut down.

"FARGRIM!" Mayrun shouted above the storm. "Where is Erik? We cannot find him!"

Fargrim said not a word and instead let his eyes drift towards the Ravenheart now far away. Hundreds of Aureian soldiers swarmed its deck. Many more commanded the vessels all around it. The commodore's flagship sat tethered to the Ravenheart.

"We cannot leave him to die!" Halitreia shouted. "We have to go back!"

✦ ✦ ✦

The door shuddered and splintered. Erik cast aside his axe. He bore down as his shuddering hand gripped a flintstone. He pulled forth his knife. He had made this choice a long time ago. This was for his people.

"Your will, my strength." Erik murmured the words that he had once shared with Astrid.

He sparked the stone.

The door caved in. Soldiers cried out. Sparks flicked from the stone and kissed the liquid. Sparks became fire. There was a great roar. The explosion shook the heavens. The Ravenheart vanished beneath a pillar of fire. The commodore and his ship were obliterated. The closest vessels were torn apart. Men screamed like animals as those not devoured by fire were wreathed in flame. The world turned into hell.

✦ ✦ ✦

SIXTY-THREE

Kilgareth, Valley of Odrysia

The thunder of hooves shook the heavens as the Mieran riders surged into Kilgareth. They flooded the courtyard and the streets. Fighting erupted all around as the defenders began to be pushed back. Sakkar's khopesh spilled blood as the razor-edged blade tore through the neck of a Medean soldier. Sakkar sprang forward along the wall, ducked a spear and buried his khopesh into the chest of a second warrior. The man fell from the wall with a cry. Sakkar stared out across the battlefield. His body was covered in the blood of his enemies. His left hand clutched his recurve bow, while a small shield was buckled to his arm. His right carried his bloody sword. High above, he could see the faint outline of Sabra circling. Sakkar saw the smoke in the courtyard begin to dissipate. He leapt down the steps and ran to the foot of the gatehouse. She lay there upon the ground. Her eyes were open yet unseeing. Her kukri lay inches from her nerveless fingers. The feather of a nightingale lay in the palm of her left hand. Elise Delfeyre was dead. Her sacrifice had brought enough time for the Mierans to breach the gates. Sakkar slung his bow across his shoulder, clipped his khopesh to his belt and pulled Elise's body up into his arms from the courtyard. He would not leave her to be crushed. He carried her into the gatehouse stairwell and leaned her gently against the wall. One by one, the last of the Salvaari who had taken the gate joined him. Three remained. They said nothing as they placed their fists over their hearts. Sakkar tightened Elise's right hand around the hilt of her kukri and her left around the feather. Then he closed her blue eyes.

"The eternal garden awaits you, Elise Delfeyre," Sakkar said softly. "May you at last know peace."

Slowly, Sakkar backed away from her body and left the gatehouse tower. He saw a warband of mounted Káli charge through the gates behind Lukas the One-Eye. The former prince gave command, and his black-painted warriors turned to the east away from the battle. Sakkar unslung his bow and gave chase.

✦ ✦ ✦

Lukas galloped through the gates of Kilgareth with two hundred Káli at his back. The fighting had spilled deep into the city as the Mierans ahead rode through the streets. The clash of steel echoed around the holy city. In one hundred years, the walls of Kilgareth had never been breached. That ended today. He was supposed to follow the Mierans down the centre as they fought to reach the Citadel walls, yet that was not Lukas' path.

"WITH ME!" he roared over the din.

He steered his horse to the east and kicked his heels in. The Káli warband raced behind him as they left the war-torn streets. The further they rode, the quieter everything became. The soldiers and knights that had manned the outer walls and lower districts had withdrawn to hold the Citadel and its perimeter. Lukas kept repeating the words Cleander had told him in his head. He had memorised the paths to take. He called a halt to his warband and then as one they dismounted. He led the way with Aelida and seven other archers at his side. Glancing at his crutch, he threw it aside – the clack of wood upon cobblestone could give them away. With a grimace, he marched on. Maevin's brew minimised the pain, yet there was a dull ache that flared with every step. The priestess was but a little way behind him, covered head to toe in black paint. Her spear was deadly and her faith even more so.

Lukas unslung his shield from his shoulder and strapped it tightly to his hand. He pulled forth his hammer, while Aelida nocked an arrow and held two more in her hand. Her silver eyes glinted beneath the dawn sun as it rose over them. They kept to the shadows of houses as they wound their way through the roads and streets. The fighting grew louder as they neared the Citadel. They rounded the corner straight into a band of Annoran soldiers. The westerners had no time to react. Aelida and the Salvaari archers opened fire. The Annorans fell before they could so much as shout. More came around the corner. Aelida's arrows left her bow with lighting speed. In little over a second, she had killed three. The Salvaari advanced. Their bows were raised and their eyes watchful. Kilgareth had been built by Aureian craftsmen long ago. It was vast and strong, with thick gates and thicker walls. Not with fifty thousand men could you have taken it in a frontal assault. Yet Aureian castles and cities had but one weakness. The sewers below.

The entrance was exactly where Cleander had promised. Lukas' hammer saw to the lock, and then he led the Káli down into the darkness. The stench was nearly enough to make Lukas retch. Filthy water splashed over his boots and trousers. He heaved himself up onto the small stone walkway that ran alongside the muck and gestured down into the blackness. Aelida led the way. Her silver eyes pierced the darkness like it was nothing. They said not a word as they marched through the sewers. The fighting raged above; it echoed through the stones and rang all around them. Shouts, screams and the clash of steel assaulted them. Lukas let the din wash over him as he walked.

Finally, the sounds of battle began to grow quieter. Instead, all he could hear were shouted orders and hurrying feet above. They were getting close. The company took another turn and at last they came to the bars of a drain entrance. Rays of light illuminated the darkness around them. The entrance was large, nearly the height of a man. Lukas slowly made his way over to it. He peered around the stone wall and through the steel bars. The inner courtyard of Kilgareth was before them. Out of the corner of his eye, Lukas could even see the gatehouse of the Citadel. Knights of the Order and soldiers of Annora ran though the courtyard, though they were few and far between. Most within the Citadel manned the wall and gatehouse. The rest of the western army was in the streets fighting against the hordes of Salvaar and Miera. Atop the wall, Lukas could hear Dayne's voice. His brother's voice. The king was here. The leader of this great army. Lukas turned back to Maevin and gave her a simple nod. She stepped past him and pulled a vial from a pouch. She was more than a common Káli – she was a priestess of Tanris, a servant of the spirit of death. It was her order that had given the Káli power over poison. It was her order that knew plant and mineral as well as they knew their own names. Maevin poured the contents of the vial along the top and bottom of the steel bars. She stepped back into the darkness as the poison went to work. The liquid barely even hissed as it ate the metal. Lukas' eye swept from the drain entrance to the Káli at his back. Those not yet armed lowered their hands to their weapons. Some had been with him when he had travelled to Palen-Tor over a year ago. Others had followed Aelida and joined him after Bandujar. Maevin had been with him from the start, before he even knew who he was. Soon she would be the mother of his child. They were all Káli. They all wore the black and many bore poisoned weapons. They were ready to die in the attempt to take that gate. Now Maevin nodded.

"Tanris, I come to you," Lukas murmured in Salvaari.

He took hold of one of the bars. Maevin gripped another. As one they pulled, and the steel came free. The poison had done its work. The foul liquid remained thick, and the bars did not so much as grate as they were pulled aside. Lukas placed his bar against the wall of the sewer and then pulled his hammer free. He squared his jaw and stepped out into the light.

They weren't seen immediately, for who could have expected so many Káli to appear from underground? They were quiet as they emerged from the blackness. Over a dozen had left the tunnel before the first eyes turned towards them. Káli war cries lit the air as the first shouts of alarm began. The Salvaari charged the courtyard and swarmed into the scattered defenders. Horns sang as those at the gate cried out for help. The blood of western soldiers painted the ground that they had been sworn to defend. Salvaari archers rained arrows down upon the gatehouse guards. Men fell. Annoran, Medean, those of the Order. The tide of steel did not discriminate.

"TO THE GATE!" Lukas bellowed as his warband milled all around.

A Salvaari shield wall was formed at the gate as the defenders in the city answered their brothers' call and charged. The Káli within the courtyard formed a circle to hold those within the keep at bay, for they were coming. They took the gatehouse before the men who held it could react. Two hundred Káli swamped the surrounding yard and walls. They held firm as western soldiers came from the keep, the city and the walls all around. They had but to keep the gate up and they could win. Lukas' hammer tasted blood again and again as he fought beside his warband. Maevin never left his side, while Aelida held the wall. Her archers used their vantage to keep Annoran bowmen and the wicked crossbows of the order at bay. Through the chaos, Lukas saw a small band of scarlet-clad knights surge into the ranks of the Káli. Annoran royal guardsmen. Their leader wore a blood-red surcoat over his armour. The red eagle outlined in white flew upon his chest. His steel helmet had its visor down, obscuring the man who wielded it. Lukas knew the armour as he knew the eagle-hilted sword that the warrior carried. It was

Dayne. His brother. With a roar, Lukas hefted his hammer and led his people towards the King of Annora.

✦ ✦ ✦

Cleander led Galadayne, Jaimye and the other mercenaries through the keep. They had been slow and wary as they navigated the empty corridors around the entrance to the underground labyrinth. The sound of horns echoed through the stones around them. Galadayne frowned and glanced at Jaimye before he peered around a corner and into a large hall. Knights who had stood sentinel thundered towards the alarm.

"What is it?" Jaimye asked.

"I'm not sure," Galadayne replied as he watched the knights leave. "Something has drawn them away."

"We go now then. The gods have given us a chance and we cannot waste it."

Galadayne gripped his sword as he ran through the now empty hall. The knights were leaving, yet this was their castle. Who knew what could lie in wait behind the next corner. They ran down passages and staircases, through rooms and vast chambers. They saw few enough people, though the sounds of fighting came from beyond the keep doors. Someone had breached the second gate. The mercenaries turned into a corridor and ran into a band of knights. Shouts of surprise left the lips of men on both sides. Jaimye's arrow felled the first knight, and Galadayne's sword the second, and the third crashed down as Cleander took his head. The fight lasted moments. Blood painted the walls and stone floor. Shouts came from down the corridor. Their fight had been heard.

"We have to keep moving," Cleander said, running towards a staircase that descended into the heart of the keep.

The mercenaries said nothing as he led the way down the torchlit staircase. A pair of knights stood guard at the bottom of the steps. They cried out as they saw the mercenaries sprinting towards them from above. One ran to the steel-barred door. He heaved and started to close the heavy door. Jaimye's arrow sliced through his throat. The second man was too slow to get the gate closed. Before the first knight had hit the ground, Galadayne's shoulder smashed into the door and sent it flying open. He fell and barely managed to toss himself to the side as the last knight's sword sliced towards him. The blade bit into his shoulder before Jaimye and the other men swarmed the guard. As Galadayne rose, the knight fell to the swords of his enemies. Galadayne grunted as he gripped his wounded shoulder. He could feel the sticky blood beneath his shirt. He gritted his teeth and then forced the pain back. It could wait. Instead, he turned his eyes to the cells that ran all around. Salvaari of every tribe stared through the bars. Jaimye dropped his bow and snatched the dungeon key from the belt of a slain knight. He pushed it home into the lock of a cell door as a man approached from the other side. Jaimye recognised the long hair and beard as well as he knew the man who bore them. He turned the key and flung the door open.

"Do my eyes deceive me?" the Salvaari man asked. "When last we met, you rode for the empire."

"And have since returned, Chief Cailean," Jaimye greeted the Aedei. He tossed the keys to another of the mercenaries.

"See the rest of these people free," Galadayne said. "Too long have they lived in darkness."

He took Cailean's arm and felt his powerful grip. One by one, the Salvaari left the cells in which they had been long imprisoned. Their clothes were tattered and covered in filth. Their bodies were weaker after months in confinement, yet their eyes burned.

"We could leave now, take the tunnels that we used to gain entrance to his keep," Cleander told the prisoners. "Above, Salvaar and Miera besiege the Citadel's walls. Above, the fate of the east is being decided. Do we let them stand alone?"

Cailean stepped forth. His gaze swept the faces of his people. Rage, anger and, above all, hope, filled their eyes. He took up a spear from one of the fallen knights and turned his eyes to the steel-bladed tip.

"No, we do not," Cailean growled. "We are warriors of Salvaar, and warriors of Salvaar do not flee from a fight."

✦ ✦ ✦

Kitara's gift led them to hidden tunnels that few within the Order would have known existed. They made their way through narrow corridors barely wide enough for a single person to walk. Eventually, Kitara did not need to call upon her gift, for the way became clear. They stopped in their path and Kitara ran her hands across the stone wall. A small crack in the mortar was all she needed to find. She reached inside with a finger and pressed something beyond. A secret door was opened. The four companions raised their weapons as they walked out into the light. Kitara's eye widened. She had expected to see a cardinal. She had expected to be fighting for her life against his guard. A hundred possibilities she had expected, yet not the very real vision before them. Fallen knights in crushed armour lay strewn around the body of the fallen cardinal.

"NO!" Aeryn shouted as she saw Aleksander's body.

They had needed him. Capturing him had been their plan, their quest. Aeryn's pain echoed around the temple. This war on her people would have been over with a word from the cardinal.

"He's dead," one of the mercenaries confirmed as he checked the cardinal for breath. "Gods' help us."

"We needed him," Aeryn cried. "Without him to end this war, what will become of my people?"

"There is only one path now," Kitara said. "We have to fight. We have to win this battle. We have to break the Order here."

Aeryn met her eyes and gave a single nod. If the blue painted upon her face had no meaning, then it was clear in her gaze. She was prepared to die to save her people. A grunt came from the stairs. Kitara turned to the knight fallen atop them. He could not move, for his wound was mortal, yet he was alive. Kitara approached him.

✦ ✦ ✦

The cold of the temple began to grow dark as Kyler watched. Shadows kept forth. They filled the hall. Only bodies lay before Kyler. Bodies slain by the elf and those he too had killed. He had been in a nightmare and now had started to wake to an altogether new hell. He knew what he had done while under the ruskalan's spell. Tears rolled down his cheeks.

Someday, I'll be a knight.

Kyler heard the words that he had once said as a boy. He had been, and then he had betrayed his oath. He had killed his brothers. The knowledge tore at his soul. Out of the darkness, he saw a woman approach up the stairs. She wore a dress of flowing silk that belonged to a Medean summer. It was as white as winter snow yet as filled with life as spring. He saw her face. Those deep brown eyes stared into his heart as a smile graced her lips. Elena emerged from the darkness and began to walk up the stairs. The shadows fell away as she climbed. Light appeared behind her, as did tall trees and rolling green fields. Adrestia. Kyler knew those lands well. He reached out a hand as Elena approached. The woman he loved.

✦ ✦ ✦

Kitara watched the fallen knight curiously as he stared at her face while she approached. His eyes were red, and his face covered in blisters, scars and warped skin. He extended a hand towards her with the last of his strength. She knew from his look that the knight saw something else. He did not see the woman covered in blood, dust, sweat and earth approaching. He did not see the sword in her hand. Kitara could barely keep the sadness from her eyes as she crouched before a man she did not know. Whatever had happened to him was terrible, and despite them being enemies, she could not help but feel sorrow for one afflicted by such torment. Kitara placed her sword to the side as she stared into those faded red eyes.

✦ ✦ ✦

Kyler could only watch as Elena crouched before him. He felt his heart soar … and then he remembered. He remembered watching her die. He remembered holding her in his arms. He remembered her blood that had painted the tunnels red. Tears spilled from his eyes as he realised that this was just another vision caused by the ruskalan blood. He blinked and the world changed. The greenery vanished and once again he was in the temple. Once again, he felt the excruciating pain of his wounds. Once again, he saw the darkness. It was not Elena crouched before him; it was another woman. Beneath the filth, he could see her golden hair. Her face was bruised and covered in blood and dirt. A long scar crossed over one of her green eyes. The blue woad of Salvaar was painted across her skin, yet there was no malice in her gaze. Pain rolled through Kyler. He could feel the ruskalan blood destroying him. With the last of his strength, his fingers reached for the dagger at his side. He barely managed to pull it from its sheath.

✦ ✦ ✦

Kitara watched as the knight's hand weakly fell away from the knife he had tried to pull free. His broken lips moved.

"Free me … please."

Kitara's eyes did not leave the knight's as she reached for the knife. She gripped his hand and took the blade from his fingers.

She placed the tip of the dagger against the side of his neck. A single thrust was all it took. The knight lived for mere heartbeats. The crimson in his gaze faded to brown. The torn and matted skin seemed to vanish like smoke, revealing the Medean behind it. Kitara saw relief in his eyes as the pain ended.

✦ ✦ ✦

SIXTY-FOUR

The circle of outnumbered Káli around the gatehouse began to shrink as the western soldiers descended upon them from every direction. Men fell – Salvaari, Medean, Annoran and those of the order. Tanris walked among them as thousands sought to pass the Veil. The Mieran and Salvaari army had not yet broken through, yet as the westerners pulled back to make safe the inner gate, they took the city step by bloody step. A great roar came from the steps of the Citadel and a tide of Salvaari poured forth from its doors. Their war paint had long since faded, but their garb gave them away. Warriors from all twelve tribes materialised from the keep. Wearing no armour and poorly armed, they attacked the western soldiers fearlessly. Galadayne and a number of his sellswords were with them. The mercenary had done it. The Knights of Kil'kara formed a shield wall to protect their back as they fought for the courtyard. They were surrounded, yet not outnumbered or outmatched. This was their city, and they would die to defend it. Nearly four hundred Salvaari set upon them, yet they did not so much as take a step backwards. Dayne Raynor and his guard cut a path through the Káli as they made for the gatehouse.

"DAYNE!" Lukas bellowed as he saw his brother through the chaos.

The Annoran king's head turned as he heard Lukas' call. The eagle sword drew blood as Dayne cut down a black-painted Káli. Lukas' hammer smashed in a man's ribs, and his reverse swing crushed the soldier's skull. An opening appeared between the king and the outlaw prince. Lukas roared and levelled his bloody hammer at his brother as a challenge. Dayne gave a solitary nod in reply. His fingers adjusted upon the eagle sword and then the brothers moved towards one another.

Lukas kept his shield up and his hammer down. He moved fast. He moved recklessly. The shield hid his hammer until it came around towards Dayne. Dayne stepped back to avoid the first blow, slid to the side to avoid the second and lunged. Steel grated along Lukas' shield as he deflected the blow. Dayne's shield came up and battered into Lukas'. His sword followed. Lukas' hammer knocked the blade off line, and instead of driving into his neck, it glanced off his armoured shoulder. They began to circle. Lukas beat his hammer upon his shield and growled. He paid no heed to the crowd around them that had slowly stopped fighting as the Eagle of Annora stood against the Black Eagle of the Káli.

Maevin began to chant in Salvaari. The sound of battle came from the other side of the gatehouse as the Káli fought to hold their enemy at bay, but the courtyard was still. The desert hawk Sabra circled high above. Lukas gripped his hammer tight and attacked. He rained down blows, to which Dayne always had an answer. He was a master of the sword, a master of war. The king's blade glanced off Lukas' helmet as his shield took his brother's hammer. Lukas caught a flash of Dayne's eyes through the king's visor as they fought mere inches away. Lukas drove the edge of his shield into Dayne's stomach even as the king battered the eagle pommel of his sword into the side of Lukas' head. Sunlight glinted upon steel as Lukas pushed forward. Dayne landed three blows upon his brother. He opened shallow wounds one by one. Each one only strengthened Lukas' resolve. He fought to close the distance. Every step he took, every move he made, was to inch closer to his brother. He took blow after blow to get in close. Lukas used hammer and shield as he attacked in a flurry. Dayne deflected, blocked and avoided the blows one by one. Lukas' hammer battered Dayne's shield aside, and then the edge of his own found Dayne's stomach once more. The blow was hard and without mercy. The chainmail stopped the steel edge of the shield from opening a wound, yet it still caused damage below. Lukas saw Dayne stagger. He pressed his advantage. Dayne blocked again and again but eventually Lukas' hammer slid through his weakened defence and was thrust into his belly. Dayne roared and brought his crossguard up and around. The heavy steel smashed into Lukas' helm and drove him back. His helmet rang and pain blossomed. A flowing cut nicked the skin of Lukas' neck.

The damage had been done. Dayne stumbled and coughed. The king tore his helmet free and cast it aside as blood began to spill from his lips. The illness was taking its toll. That had been Lukas' plan. Lukas advanced. Dayne had grown weaker in the years since Lukas had left Palen-Tor. The once legendary swordsman had become a pale shadow of his former self. Dayne barely managed to get his shield up as Lukas lashed out. He smashed Dayne's shield again and again. The wood cracked and splintered, pieces falling away. The king could not stop coughing as he fought for his life. He spat blood to the side. Another blow smashed what little remained of his shield. Dayne cast the last of it aside with a grunt and gripped his sword with both hands. He was the King of Annora and would not fall so easily. He moved quickly as he fought. He kept range between them and prepared. Lukas cut him off and stepped in. He lashed out. Dayne moved fast. The king slid to the side, stepped in close and caught Lukas' hammer under his arm. Lukas raised his shield for a blow that never came. Instead of countering, Dayne slammed his sword hard into Lukas' forearm. Hammer was torn from grasp. Before it had finished ringing on the stones, Lukas charged. He barrelled into Dayne, locked the king's body in his powerful grip and tangled Dayne's legs with his own. They fell. Lukas took him down. The eagle sword flew from Dayne's fingers. The king snarled as the wind was driven out of him. He caught Lukas' shield and wrenched it to the side. Lukas let the shield be torn from his grasp as he brought his fist down hard.

✦ ✦ ✦

Kitara made for the temple entrance with Aeryn and the final two mercenaries. They had to join the fight and try to make a difference. She reached the door and was about to turn down the corridor when Aeryn's hand latched onto her arm and the moonseer heaved her backwards. Something whistled through the air and then a pair of bolts slammed into the wooden doors behind where Kitara had been. Aeryn had saved her life. Shouts of alarm lit the air as the Salvaari and their allies were spotted in the heart of the Citadel. Aeryn swivelled around Kitara and sent arrows back down the hallway in reply.

"BACK!" Kitara cried as she leapt at one of the doors.

With a grunt, she heaved it shut as footsteps sounded upon stone. Aeryn sent another arrow down the hallway before she leapt back through the gap as the second door closed. There was a cry of pain from the corridor. The mercenaries leapt at the doors and pressed their shoulders into wood as the knights reached the far side. Aeryn joined them as they pushed back. A gap appeared as the doors began to open. Boots slid back on stone. Kitara ran back to the bodies and snatched up a long spear from one of the fallen guards. She jammed it through the rings on the door. Aeryn stepped back and sent an arrow through the small gap. A knight screamed and fell.

"The tunnels," Kitara cried. "Quickly!"

The four companions sprinted back through the temple as the knights rammed the doors again and again. They reached the tunnel entrance. Aeryn led the way. Suddenly she froze. Her silver eyes followed the passage around.

"What is it?" Kitara asked.

"They're in the tunnels," Aeryn murmured.

Kitara glanced back at the temple doors as the knights continued their assault. The spear would not hold for long. The tunnels were their only way out. Aeryn's bow sang as footsteps rang on the stones in the corridor. The thud of crossbows answered. Heavy bolts chipped stone and ricocheted in the tunnel. Shouts came from the hallway. The companions stood back from the entrance as the knights drew closer. Kitara held her sword high and drew her knife. Aeryn stood at Kitara's back with her bow raised. An arrow was nocked and drawn as two more hung from her fingers. The mercenaries prepared sword, shield and hammer. Shadows flickered, and the first of the knights surged forth from the tunnel. Kitara deflected his spear thrust with her weapons and held it at bay with her knife. Her sword danced forward and glanced off his raised shield. A sellsword hammer smashed the knight's side while Aeryn's arrow killed the second man to leave the tunnel. Then they were swamped. Knights poured forth. Kitara killed one, killed two and then a third opened her cheek with his blade. A mercenary knocked his sword aside, and Kitara's drove up through his jaw. There was a cry as Aeryn was sent crashing down. A knight landed on top of her. He drew a knife and thrust it down. Aeryn moved her head, and the blade sang as it hit stone. The knife came down again. Aeryn crossed her arms and blocked his wrist as her drove the blade towards her throat. She wrapped her hands around his wrist, but he was too strong. Aeryn snarled through bared teeth. The knife descended.

✦ ✦ ✦

Sakkar sprinted through the sewers in the wake of Lukas. The fighting in the streets above had grown fierce. Warriors died in their thousands as they fought for the city. The sounds of battle assaulted his ears as he reached the end of the tunnel. The sunlight danced upon the armour of thousands. Hundreds of Salvaari stood against far more western soldiers. Lukas' warband of Káli was surrounded at the gatehouse, while a second company fought for the Citadel steps with Galadayne. The prisoners had been liberated. An Annoran turned as he saw Sakkar emerge from the sewer. Before he could shout, Sakkar put an arrow through his neck. He ran towards the wall stairs as western soldiers saw him. His khopesh tasted blood as he sprinted up the steps and onto the wall. His bow sang again and again. His shield turned away sword, spear and axe. The walkways were thin and only two could approach him at a time. Through the battle, he saw Lukas fighting a man clad in the crimson of Annora. A circle had been opened, though the battle raged around them. Sakkar recognised the sword and armour and felt horror enter his breast. It was Dayne. Lukas was fighting his brother.

Sakkar turned as a man charged him. He cut the Annoran down in two moves and shot the man behind with his powerful war bow. Sakkar's eyes searched the wall. He could not get to Aelida and her warriors atop the gatehouse. Too many westerners were between them. Sakkar leapt back as a hammer smashed the ground next to his feet. The Annoran charged up the final steps only for Sakkar's boot to send him flying from the wall. Sakkar ran. He cut down one, cut down two. He reached a tower and slew the man who guarded it. Soldiers shouted and roared as they charged after him. Sakkar fled into the tower and started to ascend. He took the steps four at a time. He killed again as a man followed him up the stairs. Sakkar reached the top of the tower and ran out onto the small balcony. He slammed the door down and forced the locking bar across just as something smashed into it. Sakkar looked all around but he was trapped.

The only way in or out was the tower door. He reached up and ran a hand through the arrows in his quiver. He still had ten. Not enough. Sabra cried high above and Sakkar watched her soar through the heavens for a moment. His eyes turned to the duel between brothers. He could see Maevin at the edge of the crowd urging Lukas on. He could hear the crowd shout and cheer as their champions fought. He could see those not at the edge of the ring fighting for their lives. More bangs came from below as the men in the tower sought to claim his life.

"Amkut guide me," Sakkar murmured, pulling an arrow from his quiver.

He stared down across the battle and then let fly.

✦ ✦ ✦

The tunnel opened up, and for the first time in a century, Naidra walked out into the light. Lysandra emerged behind her and held the Spear of Yorath close. Naidra ran her hand through the long grass that no longer seemed real. She closed her eyes and look a long breath of air. The wind caressed her cheek and brushed through her snowy hair. She did not hear them approach though she could sense their presence. Naidra's sapphire gaze opened and flicked towards the six ruskalan that had appeared in the forest around them. All but one kept to the shadows. He walked towards the elf and the half-blooded ruskalan without a word. This was Harkan, the one who had planned this war. He held out a hand and Lysandra extended the Spear towards him. Harkan took it. His eyes blazed for a heartbeat as he felt its power. That blaze spread through the eyes of the other ruskalan and to their half-blooded kin. To Lysandra and Luana Marquez. To Silas Barangir and the others secreted amongst western ranks. Those who had manipulated people, nations and events to lead to this moment. The blaze lasted a moment and then went out.

✦ ✦ ✦

Kitara's boot cracked into the head of the soldier atop Aeryn. She leapt upon him as he fell back, her sword descending and taking his head. Kitara swivelled as a thrust came her way. It grazed her upper arm as she moved. Her crossguard smashed into the knight's helmet and drove him back. Kitara kept moving. She opened both of his thighs and buried her sword in his throat. The temple was open ground. She had room to breathe, room to move. Here she was untouchable. Here there was no song but tarkaras. One of the mercenaries screamed as the last knight cut through his defence and drove his longsword through his heart. The mercenary fell. Aeryn leapt at the knight from behind. She wrapped his legs and brought him down. Her axe found his neck three times. The knight's blood drenched her in red. She rose to her feet with a groan. Blood ran down a cut on her arm, yet she offered no complaint. She gave Kitara a nod as the doors rang again. The spear began to splinter. The final mercenary stood with them at the top of the dais. His shield was battered and scarred, while his hammer was more red than silver. He knelt beside his fallen friend and closed his unseeing eyes.

There was no way out. The spear shattered and the doors flew open. Knights of Kil'kara poured in, cutting off the entry to the hidden tunnel. The man who led them wore a silver chestplate. He was more than a normal knight. He was one of the Circle. He was the Sword of Kil'kara. Corvo Alaine. The knights surged forward.

Aeryn's bow sang. Kitara moved as the swordsong took her. She slid aside from a thrust, feinted, changed angle and dispatched the first knight with her sword. A second fell to her dagger. Corvo reached her. Instead of a shield, he held his sword with both hands. Kitara moved first. She had held a sword before she could walk. She was born with one in her grasp. Corvo read her feint and deflected her blow like it was nothing. Like *she* was nothing.

Steel sang as they came together. Corvo knew tarkaras too. He avoided her attacks by a hair's breadth. Sword slid against sword. Corvo twisted his blade and tore Kitara's dagger from her grasp. It rang as it bounced upon the stone floor. Pain exploded as his fist connected with her cheek. She rolled with the blow, but blood spilled forth. His gauntlet opened her lips. Kitara bellowed as she drove forward. Corvo parried her blow, stepped in close and hammered the pommel of his sword into her stomach. Kitara gasped as air fled her lungs. She lashed out. Corvo avoided the blow. His blade nicked the side of her face. Kitara blocked once, twice. She thrust her blade forward. Corvo twisted to avoid the blow. His fingers wrapped around her wrist and then he drove his own blade forward. Kitara ducked the blow aimed at her face. It sliced across the side of her neck. Kitara screamed. The pommel glanced off her head. She staggered backwards. Horror ran through her flowing blood. Corvo knocked her sword aside and smashed his crossguard into her face. Her blood watered the air as she fell backward. Her sword flew from her fingers as the blow spun her. She crashed to the ground as air fled her lungs. She could taste her blood. The world grew dark. Her eyes closed.

✦ ✦ ✦

Lukas' fist smashed down into his brother's face. Dayne fought back. He blocked blows and tried to throw his own from beneath Lukas, yet the illness had taken its toll. His breathing was laboured, and blood still trickled from his lips. With each punch, Dayne's strength faded. He could barely raise his arms to stop the onslaught. Lukas roared as he lashed out. He did not see Dayne's face. He saw the faces of those who had mocked and ridiculed him in Palen-Tor. He saw the faces of those men who had come to take the things he had come to love. Dayne blocked a punch, extended his arm and grabbed the back of Lukas' neck. He pulled Lukas' head down until their foreheads met. There was no anger in Dayne's eyes, no rage or pain. The ice cold that so often lay behind his eyes and took emotion from his face was gone.

"I love you, brother," Dayne told him.

Lukas bellowed and broke free of his brother's grasp as the words hit him. He raised his fist and brought it down again and again. Shouts, screams and the clash of steel echoed around the courtyard. Warriors fell on both sides. The guilty, the innocent. It did not matter. Death came to them all. The song of a horn reached the Citadel, a horn blown from the plains beyond Kilgareth. An Aureian horn.

✦ ✦ ✦

Tristayn Martyn rode beside the Aureian commanders, Ilaros and Velis, as Kilgareth rose before them. Thousands of armoured cavalry were at their back. Velis' army, the Larissans sent by Queen Reshada, the mounted contingent from Ilaros' legion and all those knights who had been garrisoned at Verena to the north. There were over ten thousand of them. When Dayne sent Tristayn through the tunnels from Kilgareth to Verena, this had been his plan. A small garrison of Aureian soldiers had remained to stand against the heathens that had encircled them, while every man who could ride had made their way through the tunnels until they in turn surrounded their enemy. With the horde of Miera and Salvaar trapped within the walls of Kilgareth, it would be a massacre. General Velis raised his spear over his head. Aureian horns blared across the plains. There was a great roar, and then the riders charged.

✦ ✦ ✦

Lukas bellowed as he fought his brother, as the battle raged all around. His teeth were made bare as emotion I fuelled his blows. Rage. Fury. He had heard Dayne's words, and they echoed in his mind. Memories started to break through the dark veil. His childhood memories. Lukas roared and brought his fist down as he fought against the visions. Tears fell freely as he pulled forth his dagger. Dayne met his gaze, and the king lowered his hands that had been raised to block the dagger's fall.

"You're my brother," Dayne murmured through bloody lips. "I will not fight you."

Lukas snarled as he raised the dagger high. The words cut him more than any blade ever could. Dayne had to die. He gripped the knife tight and started to bring it down.

"LUKAS!"

The voice rose above the chaos of battle. It cut through the clash of steel and screams. A woman's voice. Kassie's voice. Lukas' eye flicked up and he saw her push through the ranks of Annoran royal guard. She wore chainmail and carried a sword bearing the eagle crossguard. Lukas' sword. Only then did he hear the Aureian horns.

✦ ✦ ✦

Kitara's body burned. Blood trickled from her wounds. It stained the stone atop which she lay. Her head pounded. She could not move. She could not open her eyes. The sound of fighting began to fade into whisper. Footsteps echoed behind her. Darkness seeped in. She lost track of thought as the world dimmed.

"Well, here we are." A voice broke the silence.

Bellec's voice.

Kitara's lips twitched into a sad smile and her eyes flickered open as she heard her father speak.

"I wish I could say that I could help you, but I can't," Bellec told her. "Truth is, you've always been strong enough."

Kitara did not move, though her eyes remained open. Her father's words reached into her heart. Beneath the pain, beneath the sorrow, her will was still there.

"Aeryn, Galadayne, the Salvaari … they all need you. What do you say? Two times down, three times up."

Kitara let out a breath. She could see her will. She reached for it. Kitara grimaced as she fought against the pain. Her hands slid across the cold stone. Her fingers wrapped around the rough leather of her sword's hilt. Her eyes closed. She exhaled, and she pushed against the stone. Droplets of blood splashed against the floor as she heaved herself up. For a moment, she saw Bellec as she slowly rose to her full height. He sat upon the stairs of the dais. Kitara turned to face her enemy. Her sword felt heavy. Her hands tightened around the hilt as she raised it. Her eyes went to the warrior who approached. Corvo Alaine. He knew tarkaras. He knew far more. He lunged. Kitara blocked. Her feet moved. Her body twisted. Angles changed. Corvo parried and countered. His sword slid along her armour. Kitara knocked it aside with her blade, spun and drove her elbow hard into Corvo's head. Chainmail grated against steel plate. Corvo stumbled. Kitara swung back. Her sword glanced off Corvo's helm as he turned his head. The knight kept moving forward. He landed blows again and again and again. Blood began to roll freely from Kitara's lips. His knee drove into her stomach, and she was thrown into a cold stone wall. Steel parted air as Corvo's sword sliced towards her neck.

Then it stopped. Steel rang. Cleander knocked Corvo's blade aside. He was fast. Strong. A master of the sword just as the man who had been his brother was. Blow after blow rained down as the two men fought. Cleander's sword opened Corvo's thigh. Tears of blood fell as steel kissed Cleander's cheek. Corvo parried and thrust in a single motion. Steel danced off steel. Corvo's blade angled towards Cleander's chest.

Two times down, three times up.

Kitara snarled and then lunged. Her blow sent Corvo's sword to the side. He was fast, stepping back from her follow through. Side by side she fought with Cleander. Side by side against the Sword of Kil'kara. Blood began to flow drop by drop. As Cleander attacked, Kitara thrust her blade forward. Corvo anticipated the move. He twisted aside and brought his sword around. Steel kissed Kitara's bracer and pinned her sword arm tight to Corvo's side. The knight started to turn. His sword started to come up. It would take her head. Kitara allowed the momentum of her lunge to spin her. She roared. A second dagger flew into her hand as she brought it around backhanded. She thrust it up for all she was worth. There was a scream. Kitara's dagger drove up beneath his right armpit. Steel bit into flesh and tore through the underside of Corvo's shoulder. His arm froze and his sword fell from his nerveless fingers. Kitara's roar echoed through the temple as she tore her knife free. She staggered away from the knight, barely able to keep on her feet.

Corvo stared at her as his sword arm fell limp to his side. Blood ran down his useless limb. Kitara met his eyes. She could see the anger, the rage. His fire still burned. The last of the knights in the temple fell to Aeryn's arrows and the mercenary's blade. There was a thud, and a gasp fled Corvo's lips. Steel sang as his body hit the stone floor. Corvo Alaine took a final breath, and then lay still.

Cleander pulled his sword free from his once brother, his eyes wet with tears and his face a mask of pain. Footfalls sounded behind the former knight as warriors of the Order materialised behind him. There were dozens of them. Kitara bared her teeth and gripped her sword tightly. Cleander stepped to her side and turned to face the oncoming tide. The mercenary joined him. Kitara's gaze moved to Aeryn. The one who had saved her so long ago. The one whom she loved. Aeryn met her eyes. Unspoken words passed between them. The cardinal's death had taken their victory when they had been so close, yet at least here in this temple where they would die, they would die together. Kitara gripped her sword. Aeryn raised her bow. The knights came to meet them.

✦ ✦ ✦

"LUKAS!"

Kassandra's shout tore Lukas from his dream. He saw her standing in the midst of a battle that she could not escape. A battle that he had brought to her. Memories flooded his mind. Their rides beyond the wall of Palen-Tor. Sneaking through the castle corridors as they navigated the guards. The sword lessons. Their laughs. She was his closest friend. Tears ran down Lukas' cheeks as his hand tightened upon his knife. His eye went to Dayne. Everything that he had and everything that he had lost he remembered. His father's love that he had spurned. Dayne's brotherhood. His friendship and lessons. They had fought together, bled together, laughed together. All around him, Káli and Annorans slaughtered each other. Aelida and her people held the gate, while the battle in the streets beyond was drawing near. Soon the Salvaari and Mierans would break through. The song the Aureian horns sang washed across the battlefield again and again. Murmurs of Aureia left the lips of both attacker and defender alike. Lukas realised what it meant. They had been deceived. Dayne had not been idle. He never had been. The armies of Verena were here. The pagans were trapped within a foreign city assaulted from two sides. Salvaar would die here. Everyone to hold the title of Mieran or Salvaari within Kilgareth would be dead before nightfall, yet they would not be alone. In payment for their lives, the Salvaari and Mierans would turn the holy city into a tomb. Kilgareth would run awash with blood. Thousands would die at pagan hands. All within the Citadel and city streets below. The Order of Kil'kara would be no more. Dayne would die. The Annorans and Medeans would be slaughtered, and not just the warriors. The maija, the servants, the women would die. Kassandra would die. His sister would die if this attack wasn't stopped. Lukas trembled as he stared down at Dayne. He roared and brought the knife down. The tip halted at his brother's throat. What was he doing? What had he *done*? The roar turned into a cry as he cast the knife aside. He snarled through bared teeth as he rose to his feet. Lukas looked to his sister and made his choice.

"STOP!" he shouted.

Lukas pushed his way into the battle without a care for his own life and pulled people apart.

"STAND DOWN!"

He repeated the command in Salvaari and the common tongue over and over. Dayne heaved himself to his feet and bellowed the order to his own people. Slowly, the clash of steel in the courtyard began to fade. Bows and swords were lowered. Captains on both sides echoed the calls and forced the warriors apart.

"LISTEN TO ME!" Lukas bellowed as all eyes turned towards him. His arm gestured out beyond the gates towards the line of charging horsemen as he spoke. "Those horns sing that Aureia has come. The legions of Verena are here. For those of you who call this city home, you will believe these horns to be your saviour, but they are *not*. You will believe when this day is done you can return to your home and families, yet this is not so! You will believe that the silver riders will descend upon Kilgareth and cleanse it of my people, and perhaps they will. Yet know this: Salvaar and Miera are here within these walls united with one purpose. If the flame burning for that cause is snuffed out by the horns of Aureia, do you believe that we will simply accept the shame of defeat? No. Those horns tell that the empire is at these gates. They will kill every Salvaari and Mieran within these walls. None will survive. Before our lives are done, all those within this Citadel will fall long before we join them in death. Your kings, your dukes, your beloved Order and it will not stop there. Your families are within those walls. That is no threat; it is the truth. You all know that! Here, for the first time, we are many; you are few. If we do not stop fighting, then we die today, my brothers. Do you want to fall, knowing that your families will soon be greeted by death, or do you want to go home to them?"

Lukas turned his gaze to his brother who watched him with curious eyes.

"Choose war, if you wish," Lukas told him. "Now you know the truth. This is your chance to see it. Do not be convinced otherwise."

Lukas' eye followed Dayne's gaze as the Annoran king looked to the banner of his people. A brilliant red eagle trimmed in white atop a sky of crimson. Their family's symbol. Nothing would ever change that. Dayne turned back to Lukas. His face was bloody and his skin pale. The sickness had taken its toll. Lukas could see that only his brother's will kept him standing.

"Only I can call off Aureia," Dayne said. "Only I can give the command for my people to lay down their weapons. But I cannot give that command unless we make a pact. This battle ends now. Your people will not give up the ground they have taken by leaving this fortress, and so we make peace. Tonight, we bury the dead. Tomorrow, we negotiate and end this war. We have a chance to end the cycle of blood. It falls on your nod."

Lukas held up his knife, the very blade that he had attempted to use to take his brother's life. Salvaari steel. He cast it aside. Cold stone rang as the dagger bounced upon it, and then all was silent. Dayne gathered up his fallen sword. He gave Lukas a nod and sheathed the blade.

"Put down your weapons," the king called to his people.

It started with the Káli and Annorans and quickly spread through the ranks. Despite the hateful glares that passed between the groups, both sides put aside their blades and spears.

✦ ✦ ✦

Kitara's grip tightened upon her sword as the knights advanced towards the three on the dais. A wave of silver, blue and white came towards them with blade and shield held high. There would be no escape for her, for Aeryn, Cleander or for the mercenary who stood at their side. Horns sang in the distance. The sound echoed through the Citadel and down into the temple. Confusion ran through the ranks of knights for but a moment before the holy warriors who stared at the three so darkly sheathed their swords. Kitara frowned. Was this some kind of trap?

"What has happened?" Kitara called. "What does that mean?"

"The battle is over," Cleander murmured.

Kitara stared at their enemy as they backed away. She could barely believe Cleander up until the moment that the knights left the temple. Only then did she lower her sword. Only then did she look away from the men who had stood against her. Blood covered her just as it did Aeryn, but she did not care. She placed a hand on the moonseer's cheek and pressed her head into Aeryn's.

✦ ✦ ✦

Stones sang beneath the hooves of racing horses. Tariq saw everything as he and Marshall raced across the long causeway. Soldiers from both sides watched each other suspiciously as they tended to the wounded and fallen. The battle was over. That did not give Tariq comfort. He had read Elise's words and knew what she had intended to do.

The two men reached the main gate and were directed south by Salvaari warriors. The city smelt of death as they rode down the long streets. Thousands had died in the attack. While the Aureian riders controlled the plains, it was the Salvaari and Mierans who patrolled the outer city. A deal must have been made. Once again, Tariq found no comfort in the uneasy peace. Instead, he felt fear claw its way into his blood. The two men reached the southern gate and were directed towards the gatehouse. Tariq leapt from his mount and let the reins fall absently. All thoughts of the horse, the soldiers and the blood-stained roads were swept from his mind as he ran into the gatehouse. He cried out as he saw Elise leaned against the far wall. Aureian bolts were driven into her body. Tariq knew that she was dead long before he reached her. His heart broke as he dropped to his knees before Elise's body.

✦ ✦ ✦

Lukas' eye swept the courtyard as he made his way through the crowd. Word had been sent to Henghis and the chieftains, and they were now on their way. Through the throng he saw a familiar face appear, a Salvaari face. His clothes were ragged and his mane of hair a mess. It was Cailean. The long-imprisoned Aedei chief approached, and the pair embraced.

"Perhaps your woman was right," Cailean said as he met his friend's gaze. "Perhaps you were sent by the spirits to save us."

"Lord," Aelida called from behind. "Lord."

Lukas turned to the Káli moonseer. She was not alone. Four of her people carried a body upon a shield. The wind brushed through the dead woman's hair as the Káli placed the shield before their leader. Her once evergreen eyes were closed, and her life-filled breath was no more. Lukas stared down at Maevin's body as he fought back the boiling emotions beneath. Rage, pain, loss, heartbreak. He felt something snap and for a moment all he saw was fire. All he wanted was to watch the world burn. He knelt beside the woman he loved and brushed a stray lock from her pale face as he did everything in his power to remain in control. Aelida dropped to a knee beside her leader and extended an arrow. Blood covered its steel tip. It was not Annoran, nor was it Medean or a bolt belonging to the Order. It was Larissan, and only one Larissan had fought in Kilgareth. Lukas took the arrow and stared through the crowd. His eye locked upon the man to whom the arrow belonged, the man who had killed Maevin. Sakkar Alsahra.

✦ ✦ ✦

SIXTY-FIVE

Coast of Aureia, The Lupentine Sea

Flames kissed the heavens. Debris flew through the wind. Men were thrown from their feet. Waves were sent forth from the explosion. The ships not taken by the fire were shaken and their crews knocked aside. The roar of the blast was deafening. Fargrim's head rang to the choir of a thousand bells as he staggered to his feet. Only charred remains floated where the Ravenheart had once sat. Three Aureian ships had been completely destroyed, while a dozen more burned hot. Fargrim could barely hear his own groan as he raised a hand to his head.

"ERIK!"

Halitreia's scream at last brought back sound. The Valkir crowded the rails, their faces awash with ash, dust, blood and tears. The king was gone. The king was dead. In a single blow, he had taken hundreds of the enemy with him. Soldier and sailor alike fled from burning ships and straight into the arms of the Valkir and their allies. There was no fighting, for there was something new in the Aureian gazes. It was not fear; it was defeat. They were leaderless, their morale broken, and they had lost over half their great armada. It started with the ringing of a sword upon the wooden deck of an Aureian ship. Blade, spear and shield joined it as one by one the soldiers of the silver army threw down their weapons.

"They're surrendering," Mayrun said quietly in disbelief.

✦ ✦ ✦

Cailean of the Aedei made his way through the streets of Kilgareth with those of his people who had escaped captivity. Scada walked at his side. The man's once-infected wound had been fully healed by Lysandra and now no more remained but a thin scar. Cailean's eyes scanned the streets as he walked. He took in the faces of all he saw. Salvaari of every tribe. Warriors of Miera. Not so long ago, the two nations ever being united would have seemed like a fairy tale, yet now it was so. Months spent in a cell had taken their toll. Cailean was not as strong as he once had been. His hair and beard were wild and untamed. The sword taken from a dead Knight of Kil'kara felt strange to his hand. He found his people soon enough. Their faces and bodies were awash with blue woad paint. The Aedei cheered as they took in their once-lost chieftain. Eilith, who had led the tribe in Cailean's absence, embraced his chief.

"This belongs to you, my chief," Eilith said in Salvaari as he held out his sheathed sword.

The blade of the Aedei leaders that had been held by Malakai and Cyneric before Cailean. Cailean tossed aside the blade that belonged to the Order and grasped the Aedei blade. It fit his hand as if it had been made for him. The Aedei cheered once more as he tore the sword free. Light danced upon the steel as he held it up to the sun. Cailean ran his eyes along the blade and then he returned it to its sheath.

Within moments, the Aedei were not alone. A congregation of green-painted Icari moved amongst them. The hardened mountain warriors made way for their chieftain as she strode to the fore. Her shield was slung across her back and her sword rested at her side. The green lines upon her face were broken only by streaks of blood. Etain. His betrothed. A path was made between the two chiefs as the Icari approached. Cailean's gaze did not leave her face. He had not seen her in almost a year, not since he had been taken captive at Bandujar. His heart ached as they came together. No words were spoken as they pressed their heads together, for there were none that needed to be said. Cailean could see the love in her eyes though she would not speak it amidst such a crowd. Etain stepped backwards and nodded towards the castle Citadel that soared into the sky.

"King Henghis wishes us to join him tomorrow when we meet with the western leaders," she told him. "Perhaps words will make a difference, perhaps they will not, but all of the tribes will have a say in our future."

"Tomorrow then," Cailean replied, looking towards the keep within which he had long been imprisoned. "It will be the day."

Orders were passed along as night fell. King Zoran of Miera and his people took refuge in the lower city where they could keep watch on the plains teeming with Aureian tents. Makeshift walls formed a line between Kilgareth and the Aureian encampment. The Salvaari positioned themselves from the lower city to the inner gatehouse. If the westerners broke the peace, then the eastern warriors could hold the gate and swarm the Citadel. Warriors of Medea, Annora and the Order took refuge within the Citadel itself. Soldiers from every side watched the others with great suspicion. When at last the darkness of night arrived, it was broken by the bright flames of hundreds of funeral pyres. There was no celebration or drinking, for who knew when the fighting could start anew. Despite the peace, they were still enemies.

✦ ✦ ✦

Cleander quickly made his way through the passages of Kilgareth. He had not set foot in the great Citadel for many years, yet he knew every stone, every statue and every room as if he had built it all. Corvo Alaine was dead at his hand. Amaris was dead. Alarik was dead. Bavarian and Evalio were dead. It would be centuries before the Order so much as heard a whisper of the ancient relics, let alone found one. But his time in Kilgareth was not over. Not yet. Cleander came to the end of the corridor, reached for the door handle, turned it and then pushed the door open. He walked inside.

"Markus Harvarder," a woman's voice greeted him.

"My lady." Cleander offered a short bow as he looked to Lysandra who sat behind her desk.

"Welcome back," Lysandra said as she gestured to the seat opposite.

The former knight did not take it. "I saw you fleeing the Citadel," Cleander stated, watching her carefully. "You were not alone. I saw her. I saw the Spear."

"Then you know the truth."

"I know that you used me," Cleander replied.

"We used one another," Lysandra shot back. "You wished to keep the relics from the Order and so I fed information. You wanted to prevent another disaster and save innocent lives and so I aided you in your endeavour ... and in return you made safe the relics for me to collect. You played your part in this war same as I when you destroyed Elara from within."

"That was your doing too, wasn't it?" Cleander asked as he at last realised.

"It was."

"And you played the role of the puppet master, manipulating the lives of those around you as you see fit," Cleander told her fiercely. "Tell me, Lysandra, who are you? What are you? I know the tale of the elves just as I know that one was at your side last night."

"You have many questions."

"I begin to question everything," Cleander snarled. "Everything I fought for was a lie. A LIE!"

"And what is the truth then?" Lysandra asked him.

"If you used me to bring Elara to its knees, then you had

something to do with this war. You are a traitor like me. You're hiding behind a different name like me. You once saved my life and for that I will keep your secret, but know this: our partnership, if it was ever a partnership, is over."

Lysandra rose to her feet. "Then I have no more need of you," she said.

Cleander opened his palm to reveal one of his smoke bombs. He shook his head to warn her.

"I wish you good fortune in the days to come," Cleander said before he left the room.

✦ ✦ ✦

Night fell and the blazes of funeral fires lit up Kilgareth and the plains beyond. Many hundreds had died on both sides. Prayers and farewells were spoken in many different tongues. Many watched as the Nightingale of Elara was sent to the heavens. Without her sacrifice, the Salvaari and Mierans could not have breached the wall. Kitara stood with Galadayne as he said words for his brothers who had been killed within the Citadel and the labyrinth below. Lukas watched the fires take Maevin as rage boiled within his heart. Aelida placed a hand upon her leader's shoulder. The priestess had granted Lukas a new life, she had been his greatest love, and now she was gone. Lukas watched the pyre until nothing remained but ash. He watched until the sun rose. Aelida never left his side. Only when the horns sounded did he at last move.

The delegation of tribal chiefs and Mieran leaders rode through the empty streets and up into the Citadel. White flags blew in the breeze. Lukas knew that his brother would respect the truce, but even so he watched the enemy warily. Knights of Kil'kara, Annoran royal guard and the private guard of Medean dukes watched them ride into the Citadel courtyard. Under Dayne's watchful eye, all were stripped of their weapons. No man or woman from either side was allowed armed within the sacred passages of Kilgareth while under the flag of truce. The foreign company was led deep into the fortress and taken into Kilgareth's main hall. Once, as a younger man, the castle and its grandeur would have given Lukas a sense of awe and amazement. Now he felt nothing.

Dayne Raynor stepped forward. Instead of the armour and garb of a warrior, he wore the robes of a king. Cuts and bruising covered his face, yet he stood tall.

"Friends, brothers and sisters," Dayne started. "Two long years ago, the horns of war sang and led us to this moment. Thousands have died, your people and mine. Their blood waters the ground from Medea to Salvaar and Odrysia. We remember those brave souls who gave their lives, and now we must honour them."

"You speak well, King Dayne," Henghis of Salvaar said. "Yet this fight did not begin two years ago at the steps of Rovira, as you say. It began a century ago in the councils and courtrooms of Medea. The world has changed and yet nothing has changed. We few that you would brand pagans are still divided by ancient wars and feuds, while your people and allies have grown strong."

"Alone we are weak." Luana Marquez spoke up. "Together we are strong. We all know this now. We have all come to the understanding that unless all of us are safe, none of us are. Is that not so?"

"Aye, it is," Henghis replied before he nodded to Torben. "Valkir?"

"Aye," Torben said in agreement.

"And you, King Zoran?" Henghis continued.

The Mieran king snorted. "Miera is never weak, but we will stand beside you," Zoran said. "We shed blood together. That bond cannot so easily be broken."

Lukas stepped forward. His crutch clacked upon the cold stone.

"This alliance is strong," Lukas told the western lords. "Stronger even than yours. I know your history and I know it well. I know that within a matter of years, Larissa shall be just another piece of the empire. The western plains belong to you just as the eastern wind is ours. You all talk about this war between us and you, yet it was never started by Medea or Salvaar or Annora. No, the one thing this fight has in common with our ancestors is who started it. A century ago, it was Duran Cormac and Cardinal Octavan. In this moment, it was Aleksander and Bavarian. The Order along with the highest office of your faith started this war, not king, not emperor, not soldier."

A knight of the Order stepped forward. "You would blame this fight on my Order?" he questioned. "That is not what history remembers. It was the ruskalan and their dark magic who brought chaos, calamity and death upon us all."

"Now the ruskalan are dead," Luana Marquez replied. "Only greed remains."

"You," Henghis said as he looked to the older knight. "I do not know you."

"I am Mortimier," he replied. "When the grand master fell in battle, it was I who took command. For now, I lead in his stead. This is my home, and I grow weary of silver-lined words. We are all warriors here and should talk as men, not politicians. King Henghis, speak your terms, let your will be known and we will try to come to some kind of agreement."

All eyes went to the Salvaari leader as he stepped into the centre of the room. His words were as powerful as his presence.

"There will be no more raids or attacks across the border against my people and those of Miera and the Valkir," Henghis said. "No more will our people suffer at your hands."

"I take it that you will do us the honour of not crossing the borders with ill intent yourself," Dayne questioned.

"Of course," Henghis replied. "My word is steel. Do you agree?"

"Done," Dayne said. "Aloys?"

"I agree." Duke Alejandro Aloys added his assent.

With the support of both Annora and one of the bordering duchies, it would have been foolish for the other four houses to resist the decision. One by one, they followed suit.

"And I," Santiago Caspin said.

"Aye." Bailon spoke up.

"Aye," added Reyna.

"Aye," chorused Salazar.

Velis of Auriea stepped forward. "With the deaths of my beloved emperor and his holiness, Cardinal Aleksander, I stand as the voice of the empire," Velis said. "I will take your terms to the Silver Throne and do all within my power to make them so."

Torben snorted and gave the horseman a dark glare. "I do not trust the word of the empire," Torben growled. "My people have suffered much under the yoke of yours, horseman. Treachery, war, assassination. They do not go unforgotten. When Vallan Azure Aldrich came to speak of friendship, he instead turned his words into those of war."

"Do not mistake me for a politician," Velis retorted. "I do not hide behind words."

"No, but you—"

"The empire once broke its word." Lukas cut Torben off. "We have the word of Velis. That is good enough."

The Valkir warrior glared at One-Eye. "Be it on your head," Torben muttered. "We will soon see how much his word is worth."

"We have agreed that there will be no more raids, no more fighting," Henghis started, and this time he addressed Dayne directly. "You called us friends, yet this is not so. We are not friends. We have never been friends. We will never be friends. This peace is not about friendship. It is about the survival of my people and your own. If I were to accept what we have discussed and leave now, I would be dead before nightfall, either by a deception of yours or to the blades of my people. We have breached your mighty fortress and to abandon such an advantage would be a grave mistake. So, I have one last demand."

Growls and mutters of discontent came from the western lords.

"You go too far, Henghis," Santiago Caspin told him. "You are surrounded, outnumbered and outmatched."

Henghis spread his arms wide and give the duke a savage look. "If that is so, then unleash your dogs," he growled. "See what happens to those of your people trapped within this Citadel."

"And the fate that will await your own," Caspin retorted.

"Enough," Dayne called as he held an arm towards Caspin to silence him. "Let the king speak. What is your demand?"

"Your holy Order must leave these lands," Henghis declared. "Kilgareth must empty; no longer will it be a fortress to man. For what they have done to my people, they must leave and never return. That is the demand of Salvaar. Only then can we have peace."

The stunned silence was followed by shouts and jeers. Lukas watched the chaos unfurl. A smirk tugged at his lips. Henghis had presented them with an impossible choice. Dayne watched the Salvaari king thoughtfully. He raised his hands and silence once again descended, such was his power.

"Once again you ask this of me," Dayne said. "You offer me a choice where turning left will mean the destruction of all within these walls and where going right will mean taking the homes of many thousands."

"It is the only choice," Henghis replied.

"If I may." Sir Mortimier spoke up.

All eyes went to the old knight as he took the centre of the room.

"Lords of the east, hear me now." Mortimier addressed Salvaari, Mieran, Valkir and pirate alike. "This valley plays host to more than just the Order, but to thousands of those yet untarnished by blood and death. The people of Odrysia. The families of those within my Order. Mothers and fathers, sons and daughters, husbands and wives. These people have never raised an arm against you. Would you condemn them for the crime of living in this valley? I made a promise, a sacred vow to defend those who cannot defend themselves. If I must be a shield and stand between you and them, then I will. The Order will."

"Then you die," King Zoran told him.

"If that is my fate."

"Then it seems that this peace is over," Zoran continued. "We will uphold this truce until break of day."

Henghis turned. The chieftains followed.

"Wait!" Dayne called out. "Wait. Perhaps we can compromise."

Henghis looked back. "I doubt your words will make difference," he said.

"All that I ask is that you hear them," Dayne told the Salvaari.

"Then speak, King Dayne," Henghis replied. "Let us judge their worth."

Dayne gave the Salvaari king a nod in thanks before he swept his gaze around the room.

"Your quarrel is with the Order of Kil'kara and for that there can be no argument," Dayne started, clasping his hands. "It is not with the people of Odrysia who, until you entered this valley, gave you no grievance. This is their home. They have lives and families here. If it is agreeable to you, I would ask that you let them stay."

Henghis watched Dayne thoughtfully. "My fight is not with them. If they wish to stay, then so be it," Henghis said.

"King Henghis." Sir Mortimier addressed him. "Many of the Order have families within Odrysia."

"There will be no Order in Odrysia," Henghis said. "Not anymore."

"You cannot kill the Order," Mortimier replied. "We are united by our creed, not our walls and cities. If it is the will of the council, then we will leave this valley. To protect innocent life. That is the Order of Kil'kara's law. Whatever we may wish, the good of the people is paramount. What I would ask is that those of the Order who wish to remain with their families can live out their days here in peace. They will stay in Odrysia if they must and will swear never to take up arms again."

"And what would stop them driving their steel into our backs?" King Zoran asked.

"An oath, a vow to the gods that those who remain here leave the Order and swear never to hunt you again," Mortimier said.

"Again, it comes down to words," Henghis said in disdain. "Who would ensure that such a promise is kept? Who would stop them from rising against us?"

"I will," Mortimier said. "I will stay and make such that this pact is kept. I swore an oath when I joined the Order to protect these people and I will. What do you say, King Henghis? The bloodshed can end upon your word alone."

"You would leave the valley?" Duke Reyna asked. "Where is the justice in that?"

"There is no justice," King Dayne said as he extended a hand towards Henghis. "Not in this world."

Henghis looked from Mortimier to Dayne. "That is something we agree upon."

Henghis clasped Dayne's arm. The deal was struck.

✦ ✦ ✦

Word spread fast. The armies began to break camp, while those of the Order began to make preparations to leave. Sir Mortimier oversaw it all. King Zoran and his riders would remain until the Order had left the valley. From then it would be up to Mortimier to make sure that those who remained never picked up a sword again.

Lukas made his way through the Citadel alone. His crutch echoed upon the cold stone. No weapon hung at his hip, for the truce was still in place. No blood was to be shed or those responsible would be severely punished.

"Lukas." Sakkar's voice broke the silence.

Lukas stopped in his tracks and turned as the Larissan approached.

"I am glad to see you alive," Sakkar said.

"Are you?" Lukas replied as he turned his dark glare upon the man he had once called brother. "If bloodshed were not forbidden, I would kill you now."

Lukas could see a hint of sadness in his old friend's eyes. One-Eye clenched his jaw. It took all of his strength not to strangle the man.

"I hope that one day you understand why I did what I did," Sakkar replied.

"You took her from me," Lukas snarled. Rage, pain and anger gave venom to his words as he spoke them. "You took my child. For what you have done here, you will spend the rest of your life looking over your shoulder and you will see nothing. One day, on the day that you stop looking, I will be there. On that day, I will kill you. That is my oath."

He saw a flicker of fear move across Sakkar's face. Lukas let the man stare through his eyes into his soul. The arrow that had killed Maevin had awoken the beast deep inside of him and now Sakkar knew that. Lukas pushed past the Larissan and continued on his way.

"Go home, Sakkar. You are not welcome in the east."

He arrived at the doors to Dayne's study. A pair of royal guard stood outside. They saw Lukas approach and opened the doors for their former prince. Lukas did not give them a second glance as he passed them. No longer would they know him as Lukas Raynor. Now they would fear him as the Black Eagle. They knew his name and what he had done.

Dayne and Kassandra were already sat around a thick desk of

fine oak. The doors closed at Lukas' back as he joined his siblings at the table. Dayne's face was battered and bruised, yet his eyes were chilled like winter ice. They showed the intellect of his mind. His face was as expressionless as stone. Kassandra's face was untarnished and revealed her heart. She wore her emotions on her sleeve as she always did. Despite everything, there was deep love in her eyes when she looked at Lukas. Then came the Black Eagle. A rugged eyepatch covered his empty eye socket. His hair was long, and a beard covered his jaw. Black Káli war paint was smeared across his face. A scholar king, a graceful princess and a savage from the east. The three sat in silence for a moment before Dayne at last spoke.

"There are things that have gone unsaid, things that must be discussed before we at last leave this city," Dayne told them. "No doubt you will have your own suspicions about my illness, but the truth is that I will not live to see another year."

"That cannot be!" Lukas said in disbelief.

"And yet it is so," Dayne replied. "This is my time. Before he died, Father told me that everything he did, every drop of blood that he shed, was for family. He believed not in legacy or wealth. He believed in family, and everything he did was to make it strong. Every choice he made was for us so that another tragedy would never occur. Here, now, at the end of my days, I will do the same. We all know what can happen when a king dies and leaves behind no heir of age. Perhaps the peace will be held, but perhaps it will not. The lords of Annora, no matter their words, all have kingdoms behind their own eyes, and so I have given command."

King Dayne held aloft a sealed scroll. He held it out to Kassie.

"My child is next in line to the throne as is the law; however, there will need to be a regent to not only protect Annora, but to help guide and teach the child as well," Dayne said. "For this great task, I have chosen you, my dearest sister. May you rule well."

"Why me?" Kassie asked as she took the parchment. "I am no

commander or scholar. As a lady, they want me to follow, not to lead."

"You have never been a follower," Dayne replied. "You are the Lady of Annora. The people, the soldiers, they all love you. Annoran, Medean. You will need both, for you will rule the seats of power in the duchies of both Caspin and Aloys."

"How do you mean?" Kassandra questioned.

"A few days ago, Duke Alejandro gave his final command," Dayne said. "When this war is over, his lands pass to Annora. As of this moment that command is being sent back to his homeland. Before the next full moon, Annora will grow beyond the Eretrian River."

"And what of Caspin?" Lukas asked. "He and his people left hours ago."

"It was Santiago who gave the order for our father to be killed," Dayne said.

"What?" Kassie breathed.

Lukas' eye widened.

"Greed corrupts," Dayne continued. "Over a year ago, I discovered the truth, but I could not act. That time is over. The duke has been dealt with."

✦ ✦ ✦

Santiago Caspin galloped through the forest. Trees hurtled by on either side. He held his spear close. Caspin riders fanned out. Ever since boyhood, the duke had been an avid hunter. Now, the green-clad horsemen pursued a magnificent stag within one of the valleys many forests. Shouts and the thunder of galloping hooves were the only sounds that the duke could hear. They echoed through the woodland. Santiago ducked under a low branch as mount and rider surged forward. A shadow flickered and a second branch swung around from nowhere. It smashed the charging duke in the face. Blood erupted as his nose shattered. Bone was driven back. He fell from his horse and crashed into the undergrowth. The stallion charged by and vanished into the forest. The woods grew silent. Caspin's gaze flickered. The blow had driven the bone of his nose into his brain. He had but moments to live. Blood spilled from his ruined face and lips. A figure wearing a dull, hooded cloak appeared. A branch was clasped in the shadow's hand; the one that had struck him from his horse. Caspin's eyes flicked up to the second branch, the one that he had ducked. This would appear as an accident to any who found his body. His tried to speak but words would not leave his bloody lips.

"It will never be you," Iris Deleonie told him as she crouched at his side. "You will never be king."

Fear entered the duke's eyes. This was Dayne's revenge. The king had known all along who had killed Dorian Raynor. Santiago should have killed him long ago. The assassin pulled a white swan's feather from her pouch and stained it with the dying duke's blood. She turned her attention to the branch above and scraped bark from its length. A wineskin filled with blood was splashed upon the wood. A hunting accident, nothing more. Iris held tight the branch that had dealt the mortal blow as the last light faded from Santiago's eyes. She vanished into the forest like smoke.

✦ ✦ ✦

Dayne clasped his hands upon the desk as, in the forests of Odrysia, the deadly game he played with Santiago at last came to its end.

"You killed him?" Kassandra asked.

"The Caspin line has ended. I could not kill Santiago until the war was done, for his death would have torn this alliance apart," the king explained. "It will appear as an accident, and the crown of Caspin shall pass to me."

"Plans within plans," Lukas muttered.

"Santiago Caspin was a threat to our family," Dayne replied. "He wanted to spread unrest and disloyalty to Annora. No more. That in turn brings me to you, my brother."

Lukas said nothing and instead watched Dayne closely. He held his face still, though his gaze sparkled with curiosity. The king gathered up a sword from beside his chair and placed it upon the empty desk. The sheath was as plain as the steel beneath, though the handle was carved in the shape of an eagle. Lukas had not seen his sword since he had driven it into the earth at Valham.

"When I am gone, Annora will need you, Lukas," Dayne said seriously.

"I am an outlaw," Lukas replied.

"You are my brother first, and whatever your sins, you are of great importance to the future of Annora," Dayne continued. "You can see through the lies of the courtroom; you can see through the schemes of pampered aristocrats and arrogant lords. You know the game and this war has taught you well. I believe that you understand that the passing time between kings is more dangerous than any battlefield. Annora will need you, Lukas. Kassandra will need you. Sofia and my child will need you."

"There is nothing that I would not do for my family, you know that," Lukas said. "But I am banished. To return would mean my death."

"You are an outlaw, yes," Dayne said. "But not forever. The men saw us fighting. After what happened at Palen-Tor and Valham … This war … You cannot be pardoned until after I am gone. You understand this. My last command as king will be to absolve you of all crimes and pardon you of all sins. You will be free to return home."

Lukas stared at his brother. He had not expected to be freed. Though he was now Salvaari, he could not deny the part of himself that was still Annoran. He made to speak but could see that words were still upon his brother's tongue. The king turned to Kassandra.

"No doubt this pardon will create some ill will within the courtroom and that is why this will be my last command and not your first," Dayne continued. "The burden of this decision and its consequences will rest with me alone."

"Despite what Raynor has done for Annora, if I were to pardon my brother, we would be cast aside," Kassandra said softly as she realised.

"Or worse," Dayne told her. "Your position will be precarious until my child comes of age. Put your faith in Tristayn and Landon if you must but trust only family."

"I will not fail you," Kassandra swore.

"I know." Dayne gave her a slight smile. His eyes went to Lukas, and his hand brushed the eagle sword on the desk as he spoke his next words. "You may not be prince anymore, but you are a Raynor. This sword was made for you on the day that you were born. Whether you fight for Salvaar or Annora, you bear the eagle's blood. Take it. It is yours."

Lukas' gaze did not leave his brother's as he reached out and wrapped his hand around the blade's hilt. It fit his fingers perfectly. It was made for him. He took the sword.

"I will protect my sister and watch over your child," Lukas vowed. "I swear it."

"Then once again our family is united," Kassandra said. "Whatever the fates have in store for us, I will not fail you or Annora. The bond between family is the sword that defends our kingdom."

"You grow wiser every day, my dear sister," Dayne told her before his eyes and words turned to Lukas. "Now, you have convinced the whole world with your words. Those spoken in the courtyard of the Citadel. Those that ended this war. Everyone outside of these walls believes their truth, yet I know they are anything but. I understand you, Lukas. I understand the Káli and their beliefs, which you now share. I know that you and they would have happily given your lives so that your enemy was defeated. But it is not so. I understand that the battle is not over because of those many thousands who will be spared. This battle is over because of a man's love for his sister."

"What difference does it make?" Lukas asked.

"If you do not understand that, then a world of difference," Dayne replied sadly. It was the first time that Lukas could recall emotion entering his brother's voice. "I can only hope that one day you find the answer."

✦ ✦ ✦

SIXTY-SIX

Kilgareth, Valley of Odrysia

There was no celebration that night. No great feasts, no songs sang and no dancing in the streets. The fight was over, and though the men of Medea had left for their homeland, those who remained were far from friends. There was a divide between the two camps that would take a long time to repair. Though the war had lasted barely two years, they had been foes for far longer. The people of Kilgareth and the members of the Order were sullen. They had one night to choose whether to leave and honour their vows, or to stay and spend the rest of their lives in their home with their families. Kilgareth was to empty. Those who remained in the valley would find housing within Odrysia. For one hundred years, Kilgareth had been the stronghold of faith in the north. No more would the great city be a fortress to godly men, or any other. Hammers sang as the massive wooden doors were stripped from their moorings.

Tariq and Marshall worked in silence as they saddled their horses to leave at daybreak. The night was late, and they were alone in the stables. Tariq ran a gentle hand across the neck of his horse. Pain, rage, sorrow … His mind was clouded.

"I thought you'd be here." Cleander's voice broke the silence.

Tariq froze as the words sparked anger. He said nothing and did not turn to face the man.

"My heart is broken for your loss," Cleander told them as he approached.

"Heart?" Tariq spat. "You have no heart. You did not care for her. You care for nothing but yourself and your own desires."

"I suggest you leave," Marshall said, approaching Cleander from behind. "There is no place for you here." The guardsman's hand rested upon the hilt of his sword.

"No," Cleander replied. "I grieve for Elise. I cared for Elise."

Tariq snarled as he lashed out. His fist balled and then connected with Cleander's face. The Annoran staggered backwards as blood spilled from his split lip.

"YOU GRIEVE?" Tariq shouted. "YOU LED HER TO HER DEATH!"

Steel rang as Marshall drew his sword and placed it upon the side of Cleander's neck. "You overstep, Cleander," Marshall growled.

Cleander wiped blood from his lip as he stared at the Berenithian. Tariq heard the despair laced through Cleander's voice as he spoke, but he did not care.

"I wanted to give her the peace and freedom that she so rightfully deserved," Cleander murmured.

"Peace? On the very night that she was about to ride south to claim it, you took it from her," Marshall told him. "And freedom? She's free now. She's dead."

Tariq reached into his pouch and pulled forth the letter that Elise had written. He shoved it into Cleander's chest.

"You may hide your intentions behind silver words, perhaps they are even the truth." Tariq glared at the Annoran. "But those same words killed her more than any arrow."

Cleander was silent as he read Elise's letter. Her last words.

"I'm sorry," Cleander said as he finished reading. "I didn't mean for this to happen."

"Yes, you did," Tariq countered. "Perhaps not her death, but you led her into war with your words. I have never trusted you and that is no secret, but she did. She trusted you and you got her killed. It has not yet been two years since you came into her life, but I was there from the beginning. Everything that you have heard, I witnessed. Her parents, they were my closest friends in the world. I was there when Imriel Delfeyre was murdered. I saw Catinya Delfeyre breathe her last breath. I knew Raphael and Claudia Delfeyre. I fought at their side when the magister's soldiers came. I tried to save them, but there was nothing I could do. I loved Elise like my own and you killed her. You only knew her as the Nightingale. I knew her as far more. The only reason you can stand within my presence and live is because she had some affection for you. Press me again and I may just forget that. Go now. Leave."

Cleander met his eyes. He could see that there was no argument to be made. Instead, he took a small bag from his satchel and extended it towards Tariq. The Berenithian snorted, but after a moment snatched the offered bag. He undid the fastening and revealed the medallion within. A large ornate silver circle imbued with the image of a griffin.

"The mark of Valentia," Cleander explained. "The coin Elise stole from the nobility will be enough for you to live out your days in wealth, but the mark will give you the peace you so deserve. It will never be enough, but know that I am sorry."

Tariq stared into Cleander's back as the Annoran left the stables. He exchanged a look with Marshall before he tucked the mark safely in his saddlebags and then mounted his horse. The moon was still high when the Elaran riders rode out the city gates. There was no fight here. All they could do now was honour Elise's last wish. All they could do now was find peace.

✦ ✦ ✦

Kitara drank in the morning rays of sunlight as they caressed her cheek. She knelt by the Odrysian river and splashed the cool water across her face. The blood, the dust and the blue war paint were all washed away. All that remained were cuts and bruises – they too would fade with time. Kitara pulled her mother's ring from behind her shirt. The sapphire blazed in the morning sun. She ran her thumb across the jewel. After a moment, she pulled it from its cord and placed it around the ring finger of her right hand. It sat next to her father's wedding band.

"They will always be with you," Aeryn comforted, standing quietly by her side.

"I know," Kitara replied as she looked up at Aeryn. "In the temple, I saw him."

"Your father?" Aeryn gave an inquisitive look.

"For the briefest of moments," Kitara said. "He looked at peace and I think now I finally understand why. For so long, my father blamed himself for what happened all those years ago. He blamed himself for Oriana's death, for losing me."

"And then he found you."

"And then he found me," Kitara echoed. "I am glad that he was able to find some measure of peace before he passed."

"I admired him," Aeryn told her. "He suffered much. He lost his home and his family. Enough to make any man fall, yet he did not give up. He had the heart of a lion."

Kitara smiled, recognising the truth in Aeryn's words. "I miss him," she said. "I miss them both, yet I take comfort in the fact that, wherever my parents are, they are together now."

"They are proud of you, of what you've done, of who you have become … all of it," Aeryn gave her a smile. Her eyes were tender and filled with love as she watched Kitara. "I am too."

Her words warmed Kitara as much as the sight of her always did. Aeryn reached down. The back of her fingers gently brushed Kitara's cheek before she extended a hand. Kitara's lips twitched as she took the hand and allowed herself to be pulled to her feet. The touch was brief, but it sent sparks across her skin. It was like they were connected, two sides of the same coin. Kitara squeezed Aeryn's hand as she looked into her silver eyes. Sunlight kissed the freckles around the moonseer's nose. The happiness in her sparkling gaze was reflected in the curling of her lips. She had never been more beautiful.

"I love you," Kitara murmured in Salvaari.

Aeryn did not look away. She stroked Kitara's cheek and then kissed her tenderly on the lips.

"I love you," Aeryn replied in the same.

With entwined fingers, they slowly made their way back up onto the fields that surrounded the river. The great sea of tents had all but vanished. A line of horses and warriors snaked northward into the valley. They vanished into the horizon towards Salvaar. The children of the forest were leaving. Few remained, though they too were ready to leave. Galadayne and the other surviving sellswords were gathered. Sakkar and Senya were there too, while the Aedei tribesmen prepared to travel all around them. Sabra flew high in the cloudless sky.

Jaimye raised a hand in greeting as the pair approached. Aeryn grinned and clapped a hand on Kitara's shoulder. At last, they were to return home. At last, the fighting was done. The mercenaries began to mount up. From their first fight against the Catuvantuli two years ago to the battle beneath Kilgareth, many of their number had fallen. Each loss was keenly felt by those who remained. They had all been there from the beginning. Galadayne joined the pair as they headed towards Sakkar and Senya. Hooves thudded upon the earth as a small contingent of Aedei riders approached. Cailean dropped from his saddle and made straight for Sakkar.

"I cannot believe that you are leaving us," Cailean called.

"My heart aches for a home that I have been too long absent," Sakkar replied.

"I understand. When next we meet, we will share drink and you can share your tales of that sea of sand you call home," Cailean said.

"The gods themselves could not stop that, big man." Sakkar grinned as the pair embraced.

"You are my brother," the chief replied. "You will always have a place at my table." Cailean clapped a hand upon his friend's shoulder as he stepped back. He turned to Senya and pulled her into a bear hug. "Keep an eye on him," Cailean told her. "His mouth often gets him into trouble."

Senya laughed as she hugged the Salvaari back. "Both eyes," she replied with a grin.

"I wish you would stay," Galadayne told the Larissans. "You will always have a place with us."

"Even if I wanted to stay, I could not come with you," Sakkar replied. "One day he would come for me … Perhaps he will hunt me still to Larissa and beyond."

"Or perhaps he will one day awaken from the nightmare that his witch created," Kitara said. "I know that what you did pains you, but you had no choice. He has become a monster that she created. Without her, there is hope."

"There is always hope," Senya added as she took her husband's hand.

Sakkar glanced at his wife. "Always," he said.

Kitara took a step towards the pair. She gave Sakkar a nod. He had been a loyal friend from the start despite mistrust between them. They had come a long road since they first met in Miera. He had known her for but a blink of time yet had travelled for months and risked his life to save her.

"You came for me when I was a slave," Kitara told him. "I will never forget that."

"Goodbye, my friend," Sakkar replied, pulling her into a hug. "I know that you will find the peace you deserve."

Kitara glanced at Aeryn. "I have found it," she replied honestly.

"May the spirits be with you, desert man," Aeryn said with a grin as she embraced Sakkar in turn.

"And with you, Salvaari."

The sun was at its peak when Sakkar and Senya mounted up and turned their horses westward. Sabra circled above them, and her cries echoed across the plain. Kitara watched them leave. For months they had shared food and drink. They had fought side by side. It was a bond not so easily broken.

Galadayne Eralys stepped to her side as her gaze followed the two riders. "You ride for Salvaar?" he asked.

"It is my place," Kitara told him simply.

"Alright, well, that sounds good enough to me," Galadayne replied with a smirk.

Kitara glanced at the old warrior and saw the gleam in his eye. He was serious.

"Not Annora?"

"Annora will always have a place in my heart, but it has not been my home for over half my life," Galadayne told her. "No, my place is not there. My place … *our place*," he said as he gestured at the rest of the mercenaries, "is with you."

Kitara paused as the words reached her ears. She had suspected as much yet they had never spoken of it. This was loyalty, the kind she had only known after she chose to side with three stray foreigners barely two years before.

"Your lives are your own," Kitara said as her gaze drifted back to the west.

"They are, and the men have chosen," Galadayne replied. "You're a Malley. You're our captain now."

The old warrior clapped her on the shoulder and together they made for their horses. The company mounted up as one.

"We ride north," Kitara called as a grin spread across her lips. "Salvaar awaits."

✦ ✦ ✦

Káli riders filled the Citadel courtyard. Opposite them stood the

Annoran royal guard. The silver armour of the westerners shone in the sunlight and their red flag fluttered in the wind. The Káli still wore their dark paint. It mingled with the black tattoos that spiralled around their scantily clad bodies. They looked like demons, while the Annorans appeared as scarlet angels.

King Dayne stood before the bottom step alongside Kassandra, Sofia and Riona. All of this Lukas saw as he made his way before them. His crutch clacked upon the stone ground. Like his brother, One-Eye wore his eagle sword at his hip. Aelida walked at his back. Her silver eyes were cold and untrusting and her hand sat gently atop the axe at her belt. She could see everything. She could *feel* everything. Aelida was Lukas' eyes and ears. Lukas' gaze flicked from one face to another as he approached his family, for that was what they were. Whether he liked it or not, they were kin. Riona was the second mother he had always hated. Sofia, the sister he never knew, yet had sacrificed her Caspin heritage for her new family. No doubt she knew her father was dead by now. By her side was Dayne. His eyes cold as ice and sparkling with wisdom. Despite knowing that he was soon to die, the king carried himself with great pride. Kassandra stood at his right arm. In the last two years, she had seen battle and blood. She was near eighteen now and a woman in her own right. She was beloved by her people. With the death of Dayne fast approaching, the four were about to enter a most dangerous game. When word of the severity of the king's health began to spread, the kingdoms hidden behind the eyes of every noble would grow. The halls and corridors of power would become as blood-soaked as the fields of Odrysia. Without Dayne and with the arrival of his child, this could be their greatest test.

Lukas came to a halt before Riona. He reached out and took her hand. "We have not always seen eye to eye, but I want you to know that the ill will I once bore you as a child is gone," Lukas told her.

Surprise showed on her face for an instant. "I have only ever wanted what is best for you," Riona said.

"I know," Lukas replied before he kissed her hand. "Watch over my sister."

The former queen gave him a solemn nod before Lukas moved on. Sofia was next. She wore the open, flowing clothing of her country, yet she was as Annoran as any of them. It was she who approached him first, stepping forward from the Raynor line. Her deep brown eyes bored into Lukas' gaze. There was no enmity or hate.

"I wish you safe travels, my brother," Sofia told him. She took his hand and pulled him close. Sofia kissed his cheek. "I can see it in you," she murmured. "We all can. You are a Raynor."

Lukas remembered those words from the forest shortly after he had captured her many months before. He nearly scoffed before realising the weight of her words. She had done much for his family despite what it had done to her own. There was blood on her hands that would never wash off.

"As are you," Lukas told her sincerely before he stepped away.

He had barely taken a step when Kassie flew into his arms. She hugged him tight. Lukas' eye closed and he wrapped his arms around his sister. He had stopped the war for her alone. He had ended the fighting so that she may live.

"I'm going to miss you," Kassie murmured as she squeezed him tighter.

"We will always be together," Lukas replied. He pulled his arm ring from his wrist and handed it to her. "Take my ring. If you ever need me, send this to Salvaar and I will come."

Kassie wrapped her fingers around the silver band. Lukas felt fear flow through his heart as he looked at his sister. When Dayne died, she would become a target. Those who did not try to kill her would try to use her and he would be a world away.

"Protect the family," Lukas told her.

She was strong, brave and had a good heart. If anyone could stand against the forces that were about to emerge from the shadows, it was her. He placed a kiss upon her brow. Lukas stroked her cheek before he moved to meet his brother. The pair looked at each other curiously. One clad in black, the other in red and silver. One crippled, one sick. One Annoran, one Salvaari. One fire, one ice. Days ago, Lukas had nearly killed him. They could not be further apart.

"Whatever has passed between us, know that you are my brother and will always stand as such," Dayne said.

"Brother, friend, mentor: you have been all three," Lukas replied. "I will never forget. I will not forsake my vow."

"I know," Dayne replied as he extended an arm.

Lukas took it. The king's grip was tight. It held more meaning than the small emotion shown upon his face.

"We will never meet again," Dayne said simply.

Lukas nodded. There were no words to be spoken. None were needed to be said. Dayne could see everything clearly. Lukas gave his brother a final look as he pulled himself up onto his horse. Dayne was right: it would be the last time they ever met. Lukas watched his family for but a moment before he spurred his mount forward. With Aelida at his side, Lukas led the Káli home.

✦ ✦ ✦

SIXTY-SEVEN

People flooded the harbour as the fleet of Valkir, Elaran refugees and pirates returned. Their return could mean only one thing. Victory. Horns blared from the town. The sound echoed across the waves as the ships drew closer. The people sang and cheered as their saviours came home. Only when the ships began to dock did the people realise that the Ravenheart was not among them. Only then did they realise what had been lost. The Oridassey was the first to make port, though its captain was not the first to disembark. Tears spilled down Fargrim's cheeks as he walked down the gangplank onto the docks. A pillow was clasped in his hands, while atop it sat a crown. Erik's crown. Mayrun walked behind the helmsman along with Halitreia and the rest of their crew. Erik's scâldir. Erik's family. The horns stopped blowing. The cheers and song drifted into silence as Fargrim walked forward. They all wept for the loss of their brother, their captain, their king. The man who had given his life to deliver them into something better. Thousands gathered around. Mellisanthi, Bhaltair and the Elarans. Cillian Teague, Garrett Laven and their pirates. Every earl and every jarl, every farmer and warrior. Sadness was shown in the faces of even those not Valkir.

"The king has come home," Fargrim cried. "Returned to the deep, into water where all great heroes sleep. Beneath the waves and ocean song. Let it be known, the king is dead. LONG LIVE THE KING!"

"LONG LIVE THE KING!" The cry echoed from thousands of throats.

Steel was thrust high towards the heavens. Tears fell like rain. The crown was placed atop the stone dais in the town square upon a flag bearing the raven symbol. Candles burned around it on the stone. The people came and went. They said their goodbyes and mourned the passing of their friend. Gifts were left for the fallen king. Like his sister before him, Erik was a hero.

✦ ✦ ✦

Weeks passed. The Valkir from the other isles returned home to their families. There was to be no new king or sole ruler of their people. The earls would once again govern. Life returned to the Valkir Isles. A single ship emerged upon the northern horizon. A ship with green sails. The Emeralis had returned. Word spread like wildfire. It was not long before the doors of the great hall boomed open and in walked the crew bearing green sashes about their waists. Luana Marquez walked at their head, while the Tariki Calvillo and Torben of the Valkir strode at her side. Harald Vrandyr, the steward of Vay'kis, greeted them, along with Mellisanthi, Bhaltair, Garret Laven, Priamos Stentor, Cillian Teague and Fargrim. The helmsman grinned as he approached the newcomers. It widened as he pulled Torben into tight embrace.

"Torben, my brother," he greeted his friend. "It is good to have you back."

"It is good to see you, my friend," Torben replied. "I have been away from the sea for too long."

The hall was filled with laughter and cheers as friends were reunited. It had been almost a year since the Emeralis had sailed for Miera. Almost a year since their worlds had changed.

"The war in the north," Teague said as he gestured to the new arrivals. "We have heard nothing save whispers."

"Your words," Priamos Stentor called to Torben. "Did they carry meaning?"

The old bloodsworn nodded. He looked from face to face. "The song of the raven was said and heard," Torben replied, scanning the room. "Those men once our hated enemies became our allies. King Zoran and warriors rode north to the aid of Salvaar."

"To what end?" Mellisanthi asked.

Luana stepped into the centre of the hall. "Kilgareth has fallen," she told them all. "No longer shall it cast a shadow across the land. This war was long and bloody, yet let it be known beyond doubt that the west was defeated!"

Torben made his way to her side. "And from the chaos of war an alliance was born," he said. "One stronger than any oath. One between the forests of Salvaar, the plains of Miera and the seas of the Valkir. Every man and every woman born free is as one united in the knowledge that if one of our peoples is attacked, we all are."

Cheers rang around the long hall as the pair spoke. The impossible had been achieved. Torben could see the elation in the eyes of his people, his friends. Yet there was something else held behind their gazes. Something more. Something darker.

"Tell me of home," Torben implored. "The streets are filled with far more than the faces of the people of Lumis."

Harald Vrandyr took the floor. "The time of the earls of Vay'kis is done," he said. "This isle has become home to more than just my people; it is now home to all those in search of a better life. Those who fled Elara, those who took up with the Sacasians. No, this safe haven is now governed by Lord Stentor, Bhaltair, Cillian Teague, Mellisanthi and myself. It was Erik's dream to achieve victory, and we did … at great cost."

Torben stared at Harald, and then his eyes went to Fargrim. Why was the helmsman here to greet him when Erik was not?

Why was the Ravenheart not at port? The cold claws of dread sank into the old warrior's heart.

"Where is Erik?" Torben asked as at last he realised. "Where is my brother?"

The sun rose high above Lumis as Torben walked through its streets. He found a horse and galloped from the city as he had been directed. For the first time in his life, he felt the biting cold. It wasn't that of the cold wind and icy breath of the sea. It was great sorrow. The Farrin line had been destroyed. It had been broken by tragedy. None of his friends who had borne the name had lived to die a natural death. Whether by the plague, by murder or by battle, they had all been claimed by the Sea-Father. Mountains and forests rose around Torben. He could see the river and heard the crash of a waterfall. Torben stared across the lake that opened up before his eyes. He remembered this place like it had been yesterday. The Tears of Freydis. Torben could almost see Astrid sitting on the beach. The waterfall marked the beating heart of Vay'kis, the centre of this island that Erik had turned into a haven of peace.

Torben dismounted by the lake and tethered his horse to a tree before he crossed to the falls. The water splashed across his face as he passed behind the downpour. He sparked a torch to life and strode into the cave behind the falls. The firelight danced across the smooth stone. Carvings adorned the walls all around. They showed everything from the birth of the raven amulet to the murder of Lief, from Astrid toppling Magnus to Erik's sacrifice. The story of the Farrin line. The story that he had been a part of. A great carved stone slab adorned the centre of the cavern, while an empty coffin sat atop it. The wood was embellished with raven images. Erik's crown sat atop the coffin. It was a hero's tomb. It was as beautiful as it was heartbreaking.

"Goodbye, my old friend," Torben said quietly as he stared at the coffin. He placed a hand over his heart. "The world will never forget you. Generations may pass, our bones will fade to dust, but the world will never forget. You are the man I always knew you would become."

Time passed as he stood in the shrine. He had no more words, but he had memories. He had known Erik since the day he was born, just as he had known Astrid. Their father had been his closest friend, and he had failed to protect them both.

"This was his choice," a voice said from behind. "Do not let grief give way to guilt."

Torben turned as the woman approached. Golden hair and copper eyes greeted him. Around her neck hung the raven amulet.

"You're Halitreia, aren't you?" Torben asked.

The woman nodded as she walked to his side. "I questioned myself after his death," Halitreia told him. "In part I blamed myself. What could I have done to prevent this? If I could have given my life in place of his own, I would have. For some days I despaired, and then at last I understood."

"Understood what?"

"Look around you, Torben," she replied. "The people are happy. The streets are filled. They are safe. No longer do they live in the shadow of death. That is all Erik wanted. If he had known that this would be the outcome of his death, he would have chosen to sacrifice himself time and time again. That knowledge means more to me than anything. He would not have wanted us to give in to grief and despair. You see, Torben, we are free now. That is what Erik's soul craved above all else."

Halitreia's eyes shone bright as she spoke. There was something in her words that went beyond their meaning.

"You knew his heart, didn't you?" Torben asked.

"And he knew mine," she replied simply.

The old warrior watched her for a moment. There was love in her voice but something else as well. Halitreia met his eyes and slowly lowered a hand to her belly. Torben stared at her.

"Erik is the father, isn't he?"

A smile graced Halitreia's lips as she nodded. The Farrin line was not over. Not yet. There would be another to bear the mark of the raven. Torben chuckled and gently placed a hand on Halitreia's shoulder. Inwardly, he knew a vow had been sworn. He would give his life for this woman he barely knew and the child that grew inside her.

"Then the world has just grown brighter," Torben said. "Together we can ensure that the legacy of Erik and Astrid remains intact."

✦ ✦ ✦

Sunlight pierced the canopy of evergreen trees as the small company rode through Salvaar. It had taken time to reach the great forest, and when the great army finally did, it splintered. Catuvantuli returned to their lands, Káli to their own. Each tribe went their own way. As the days wore on, the Aedei began to disperse as they made for their own towns and villages. Soon few remained with Kitara, only those who called Faolan home and the mercenaries who rode with them. Cries and cheers filled the air as the village came into sight. Happiness covered the faces of the Aedei who raced into the village. Those women, children and old folks not already outside emerged from their dwellings. A girl with dark hair cried out and charged towards the riders. A grin lit up Aeryn's face like the sun as she leapt from her horse just as the girl reached her. She threw herself into the moonseer's waiting arms and then was spun around. Aeryn laughed as she held her tight. Kitara chuckled and slid from her saddle. Seeing the happiness radiate from Aeryn filled her with joy.

"Kitara, this is—"

"Vanya," Kitara finished as she grinned at Aeryn's sister.

In turn she embraced the young girl. In turn she felt the same happiness that Aeryn did. Eivor joined them on the ground and hugged his youngest daughter tight. Only then did the woman racing behind Vanya arrive. Corre. Aeryn's mother. She embraced her husband and kissed his lips

It was not long before the music started. Fire burned bright. Song and dance filled the village. The people revelled in celebration. They embraced Galadayne and the sellswords as their own. They shared drink and played games. Musicians gathered in the town square. Laughter echoed through the forest as the night descended. The old watched on happily as the young danced. They spun in circles and clapped as they moved through the town. Kitara leaned against the post of a shed as she watched the party grow. Her face ached from the grin that had not faded and the laughter that had not stopped since she had arrived. So, this was peace.

"Laughter, music, song, life has returned to Faolan," Aeryn said, smiling as she approached.

Kitara raised an eyebrow as she saw that the moonseer walked with both arms behind her back.

"This place, it's like nowhere I have ever seen before," Kitara told her honestly. "I have never seen so much happiness."

"I have never seen you so happy," Aeryn countered with a grin.

Kitara stared into those beautiful silver eyes as she stroked Aeryn's chin. "Because of you," she replied.

"I have something for you," Aeryn told her as she at last pulled her arms from behind her back.

Kitara's eyes went to the closed palms Aeryn presented her with. Leather cord hung between her fingers. At last, Aeryn opened her fists and revealed the necklaces that lay within. They were twins. Both bore carved sapphires that shone in the firelight. Small, silver tendrils wrapped the gemstones and bound them to the cords.

"This is a life stone," Aeryn told her quietly. "It is yours, if you wish. If you take it, it means we are bonded."

Kitara's eyes widened. Her lip trembled as she realized the meaning of the gift. It was no different than the rings passed between her parents. Without thinking, she kissed Aeryn deeply and pulled her into a hug as her heart melted. Tears of joy rolled down her cheeks, tears that Aeryn all too readily brushed away before helping her put on the necklace. When the second life stone hung at Aeryn's throat, they re-joined the party. Kitara was pulled into the circle of dancing. A laugh left her lips as she at last knew true happiness.

✦ ✦ ✦

Harkan of the ruskalan stared into the blackness of the deep forest as what remained of his people gathered around. They were not alone. The she-elf was with them. Naidra held the Spear of Yorath close. The blade had been in western hands for too long. Now it had returned home. Harkan watched as the elf placed a hand upon the trunk of a tree. He could see the pain crawling across her skin as she closed her eyes. A hundred years stolen from her.

"A century has passed since I last breathed this air," Naidra said quietly.

"You are free now," Harkan told her. "The forest has awaited your return."

"And what will happen now that my cage is gone?" Naidra wondered. "Do you know that I cannot even remember what my sister looked like. I cannot remember her voice or her face. All I know is darkness. On the day of my capture, I swore war eternal upon those who caged me like an animal and slaughtered my people. It is not over. It will never be over."

Harkan took a measured step towards her. Beneath the strength of the visage that she wore, he could see what lay within. He could see the monster awaiting to be unleashed. She had grown patient in her servitude. She had learned to hide her breaks and mask her pain, yet Harkan saw right through her.

"I cannot let you leave this forest," he told her.

Naidra stared at him. Her sapphire eyes blazed with light. Harkan could feel magic rippling all around them. It was invisible to the eye, yet he had been born in it. It whispered to him. It called his name.

"You cannot stand against me," Naidra snarled. Her lips curled viciously. There was a dark joy that burned in her gaze as she reached for the ancient power within. The ruskalan watched her from every side. Some were as old as her, others far older. All knew what she was capable of.

"You hold no power over us, autieyar," Harkan told her as his eyes lit up like crimson fire. "There is much you must learn about this world in which you have awoken. Everything has changed. The laws and rules of men have changed. The wolf of black and white is out there. It sleeps as it did a century ago."

Naidra's sapphire gaze shifted from ruskalan to ruskalan. Their hands balled into fists as they felt the magic grow around them. They watched her with wary eyes. Elves and ruskalan … they were not so very different. Black and white. Red and blue. Tears and blood. One ruled by the mind, the other by the heart. One the children of death, the other the children of life. Autieyar were feared by both. She could see a flicker of it hidden behind the eyes of all of them. She could feel it. The monster within Naidra stirred. A century ago, she could not have controlled it. A century ago, she would not have wanted to. Now she could. The flames within her eyes faded as she locked her gaze with Harkan's.

"Teach me."

✦ ✦ ✦

The Sacred Grove of Salvaar was all but empty. The druids were gone. The shaman was not here. Cailean felt the ancient wind upon his face as he strode through the small clearing towards the sacred tree. It was here that the fighting had begun. It was here that oaths had been sworn. Mere steps away, Cyneric had challenged Henghis. Cailean remembered his brother – he remembered them both. Cyneric and Malakai. Both chiefs. Both warriors. He reached the tree and stared up into its canopy. The spirits were here. He could almost feel them. His gaze lowered to the axe dug into the trunk of the great tree. Cyneric's axe. He had buried it here before his people had marched to war. Here it had remained through two wars. One amongst the children of Salvaar, the other against the west. They had lasted years. Now the wars were over. Cailean extended a hand. His fingers brushed the worn handle of the axe. He remembered his brothers, and then he pulled it free.

✦ ✦ ✦

Milton Keynes UK
Ingram Content Group UK Ltd.
UKHW021941201124
451474UK00014B/1146

9 780645 184228